Cover Illustration by Diana Corredin
Book design by Jen Hsieh

http://www.tishabender.com

First Edition: August 2018

**3 9547 00441 1265**

*To That House*

*Time flows away like the water in the river.*

CONFUCIUS

# PROLOGUE

*IT'S A BELIEF COMMONLY ACCEPTED* though infrequently acknowledged, that every happy story ends in grief. But this might not necessarily be so if Time is circular. So we will neither be happy nor sad all the time, however much we might want to prolong the former and curtail the latter. She knew this now, of course. Now, on September 11th, 2031. She hadn't known it when it had mattered the most.

The day was crisp, bright and clear skied, much as it had been that day thirty years ago in New York City. She imagined that they probably still acknowledged that anniversary in America. Here in England it was not much talked about any more, relegated, as it was, to dusty old history text books where nothing ever feels particularly real and always quite far away and happening to entirely different people.

She stepped across the hall towards the living room, glancing, as she did so, at the reflected face of the grandfather clock in the large gilt-edged mirror, telling her that it was ten minutes before nine when she knew it was really ten past three. She entered the living room with its forest green walls and freshly contrasting white window frames, doors and ceiling. She and her husband had mutually decided that the deep color of the walls made such a nice backdrop for the photos and pictures that hung on them. Thinking of photos, and also perhaps because it was September 11th, she was suddenly eager to look through her dark maroon photograph album. It must have been more than a decade since she had last looked at it.

She lifted the album from the bookshelf, slipped on her reading glasses and started turning the pages. She wanted to first find her three favorite photos; the one when she and her cousin, both children at that time, were playing with a toy boat at Whitestone Pond by Hampstead Heath; the one where she and Lance, fresh faced and eager, were delightfully roaming through the countryside, though they'd never been able to determine if they were in the Catskills, or in the Lake District; and the one of Karinna, who was such a sweet little girl, playing in the garden at 'Fern View.'

All cameras, she thought, record special lost moments in time. Lost because the photographer and the event had been together, and are now no longer so, separated by the passage of time. It is the genius of a camera that can take care of that by making those moments eternally present. And then, when each new event of significance takes place, these are also dutifully photographed and recorded, and so it goes on. New events, new photos. On and on chronologically.

Just not *her* camera.

David had always assumed that her photos weren't arranged chronologically in her maroon album due to her lack of fastening them onto the pages as soon as each film had been developed. And she chose never to explain the truth of the situation to him, even though she was entirely open to him about everything else. The fact that there was nothing conventional about her camera was something that only she and Lance had known, and it preserved her memory of him to keep it that way.

Depite the lack of chronological arrangement and the length of time since she'd last looked at them, she still remembered, even now, how to quickly find her three favorite photos. Must be because of how she'd obsessively looked at these three for years and years. She looked at each of them caressingly, rubbing her fingers over their edges, wanting the physical contact, yet not wanting to smudge them. Then she took off her reading glasses, and carefully placing the album on the table beside her, still open to that lovely scene of when she and Lance were romping through a verdant field with a steep wooded slope behind them, she stood up and went to the cupboard to fetch her old camera.

Just as with her maroon photo album, so too with her old camera, which she'd also not looked at for years. She ran her fingers over its soft brown leather case, inhaling its musty, almost animal-like smell. She picked it up and was newly amazed by its bulkiness and weight. How had she managed to carry it around when she had gone on holiday?

She slung the strap around her neck, and clicked open the camera case, which felt stiff, almost hesitant. She looked at the camera's buttons and dials, and popped off the lens cap, a gasp catching again in her throat caused by the memory of how the center of the lens had acquired a crack zigzagging viciously across it. Estimating how much light there was in the corner of the room, she turned the ring on the lens to the correct F stop. Next she stared with fondness at its viewfinder with its familiar and indelible smudge. Putting her eye up close to it, she looked through, reminded now of how that smudge created a halo of light that always slightly distorted the object she was viewing; in this case, a vase of apricot colored roses. She twirled the ring on the lens to make them come into sharper focus. She snapped down the shutter and took the photo. Advancing the dial, she took a photo of the bookshelf. And another of the sofa. She snapped many times.

But really she knew there was no film in the camera. It was pretty well impossible to find film for Single Lens Reflex cameras these days. Even when she'd used this camera extensively, way back in her twenties and thirties, it had been somewhat of a relic then and film was scarce. Had there really been film in the camera now, though, who knows what photos would have emerged? Certainly this camera always surprised her. It had its own agenda; this freaky, fantastic, photo-taking apparatus. It occupied a different dimension of Time. It had terrified, fascinated, intrigued, and rescued her; she had tried to shake it off, but always it was there. She became reconciled to it, even grateful for it, and that fond gratefulness remained. It linked her to the swirls and whirlwinds of Time itself.

# PART ONE

# ONE

*HE WAS A PORTLY, BLUSTERY MAN,* with a vivid, ruddy complexion and a bristly moustache. And she detested him. She told him diplomatically yet definitively, that she needed to be on her own for a while. She mentioned this at the breakfast table, watching his spoon dip into the deep red bowl of milk and floating Cheerios; watching it emerge at an angle so that some of the contents slipped off onto the table top; watching how it dipped again for a second try, and was abandoned, irrelevant, no longer desired.

She'd pushed her chair back from the table then, unable to watch any more, and heard herself say, "Look Howard; I'm going to be going away for a few days. I'm leaving Friday morning."

She hadn't known what she would say until she heard herself speak. She was almost as surprised as he seemed to be at her own words.

All he said though was, "What've you done with your hair?"

"I cut it last night." She had in fact felt so depressed the previous evening that she'd taken out the scissors and savagely and severely cropped her hair shorter than she'd ever worn it. She'd accidently snipped her finger too, and narrowly missed cutting her ear. She'd wondered whether this had been how Van Gogh had damaged his ear, and whether he'd felt quite as depressed as she did.

"It looks as though you had an altercation with a lawnmower," he sniped.

She self-consciously ran her fingers through her hair, feeling its unaccustomed spikiness. But, not wanting him to gauge her embarrassment about her appearance, nor wanting him to distract her from what she needed to say, which was a common tactic of his, she continued, "After all, it's summer time, and I want to have a brief summer holiday."

"Honestly, Flo. 'Summer holiday!' Might I remind you that this is the year 2000, and you're no longer a school girl!"

"What difference does that make? I'd just like a little break, that's all."

"Where will you go?"

Never mind. Never mind. She'd find a place. It didn't matter where, really. She was struck by her brilliance! To go away! To leave all this. Suddenly she felt uplifted.

On her way to work she passed Adolph's Assortments, an intriguing shop of ancient collectibles. The window was full, as it always was, with old dolls; their round, blue plastic eyes and perfect line of stiff brown eyelashes, gazing without expression from their porcelain pink faces, grubby and smudged now from years of abandonment. Scattered around the dolls were tarnished gold pens, pocket watches, and a Singer sewing machine. There was a three-legged table, too, which might be glorious with a bit of sanding and varnishing. And on the table was a camera, a bulky, Single Lens Reflex, in a brown leather case with a long strap. And there were piles and piles of old magazines, with pictures of people who just don't look like that anymore, and in the corner, stacks of yellowing paperback books with pages curling at the corners.

She walked on. She'd miss her train. She couldn't stop thinking of his bowl of Cheerios.

He phoned her during the morning and asked if she really meant it. Yes, she meant it. Meant what? Who knows? At least a trip. A break. Some distance. Then they'd see.

She was excited about the idea of a trip, and when Elizabeth Carlisle, her boss, wasn't looking, she did an Internet search of places to stay in the Lake District. And later, when Elizabeth was in a meeting, she made a phone call and reserved a room in a nice looking, small guesthouse called Landsdowne's. Simple as that. Then she remembered the camera in Adolph's Assortments' window. She badly wanted it. Why hadn't she bought it when she saw it? Maybe she'd have time on her lunch break to run back there. Of course not. Leave early? No. Besides which, she'd have to ask for some days off, rather at the last minute, for her trip. Her trip. That sounded nice.

When Elizabeth had gone for lunch, she picked up the phone.

"Mr. Adolph?" Could that really be his name?

"No, this is Tom. Can I help you?"

"Please. I noticed a camera in your window as I was passing this morning. Is it still available?"

"Let me go and check."

He took an unusually long time. She'd have to ring off if this was an express-lunch day for Elizabeth.

"Yep. Still there. You mean the Nikon, don't you?"

"I think so."

"Yes, well it's there all right. It's a bit dusty. But it works well. Takes lovely pictures, it does."

"Good! How much does it cost?"

"Cost? Oh, now I can't say exactly. Mr. Adolph's out to lunch and he'd know. Shall I get him to phone you when he returns, miss?"

"No; that's OK. It won't be necessary. What time do you close tonight?"

"Tonight!" Tom laughed, followed by a hacking cough. "We clear off early today seeing as it's Tuesday. Shut by 3.00 this afternoon."

"3.00? I can't be there by then. Listen, can you please put it on one side for me, and I'll be back in the morning."

"Certainly, miss. Your name?"

"Florence Hamilton."

"Right you are then, Mrs. Hamilton. We open at 9.30."

"Actually, it's Ms. Hamilton."

"What?"

"I said Ms, not Mrs."

"Right you are then, Ms. Hamilton," he said, unnaturally drawing out the 'z' sound on the word Ms.

And that's how Florence agreed upon the purchase of the camera, sight practically unseen, and price undetermined. She knew nothing about how to use it.

"It's not your Point-and-Click," Howard retorted when she brought it home. He did a lot of work with Web pages, so generally spoke in brief technical jargon. "Speaking of which, why didn't you buy one of those disposable cameras? Would've been much easier to use."

"I wanted this one." She sounded like a petulant six year old, even to herself.

"Nothing like lugging around a heavy camera to spoil a trip." He turned the camera around and peered at it, and then rummaged inside its case. "Oh look," he said. "It's got a light meter. It needs fresh batteries, if it works at all, and a battery charger. But I suggest you use it, as otherwise you're going to have to be good at estimating the light on your own, and knowing which F stop to use."

He continued inspecting the camera. "Flo!" he said, almost triumphantly. "Heaven knows why you bought this old camera. Look; there's a smudge on the viewfinder. Give me a hanky, will you, and I'll wipe it off."

She handed him one and he blew on the viewfinder and wiped methodically. "Actually, it's not a smudge, but a scratch. Won't come off. Quite ridiculous, if you ask me, that you bought this piece of rubbish. You won't even be able to see what you are photographing. Take it back to the shop; you'll still have time."

"No; I want to keep this camera. I like it. I'm sure it will work well. The man in the shop said-"

"Oh yes! The man in the shop! Trust the man! Well, it's your money and your holiday. But believe me; you don't know a thing about cameras, and this one won't make it any easier."

--------

Florence left later on Friday morning than she'd intended as packing seemed to take her ages. Howard took her to Euston Station, and this little act of kindness surprised her. She'd expected some shouting, but all he said was "It's a little disheartening," which actually made her feel worse than if he'd raised his voice. He didn't come into the station, as he didn't want to park the car. She gave him a quick kiss, which landed on his ear as he unexpectedly turned his head at that moment. Then she dashed into the station, and finding her train to be a bit delayed, she popped into Smith's to buy a novel, choosing one she didn't know but which had quite favorable reviews on the back cover.

The train eventually pulled out of the station, groaning through several tunnels, and then through the suburban ring of identical brownish grey houses clinging on in obedient, exasperated rows around the edges of the city. When Florence next looked out of the window, after reading the novel for some time, she saw rather nice countryside. She sat and stared at it, trying to ignore the superimposed faint hovering reflection of her new and fairly disastrous haircut in the glass.

The journey seemed quite quick, and having arrived at Penrith, she found a taxi to take her to Landsdowne's Guest House. She noticed how crisp and cold and fresh the air was, and she felt excited, like a little girl going away on her holidays. She soon arrived at the guesthouse, which was a high, grey Edwardian building, with lots of pretty flowers outside. She was amicably greeted by Mrs. Landsdowne, who was a woman of enormous girth, and a kindly smile, and was shown to her room. It was a plain but very well scrubbed room, with lovely views of Bassenthwaite Lake in the distance, with some mountains surrounding it. Since it was dinnertime, confirmed by the mouth-watering smell of a hearty meat dish, Florence was eager to go downstairs. She thought for a moment about what Howard would have for dinner, assuring herself that he'd be fine as there was stuff in the freezer, but then she remembered that she'd forgotten to go shopping, so there was nothing particularly nice or even substantial - some frozen peas, clustered together in icy chunks because they'd been there for ages, and a few frozen pizzas. Is this what their relationship now amounted to?

Feeling self-conscious about her haircut, and conspicuous because of being alone, Florence entered the dining room. There were only four tables. The one in the corner was empty so she sat down quickly, not wanting to draw attention to herself. She brought along her novel, and had just started reading when Mrs. Landsdowne came to take her order. She highly recommended the roast beef and Yorkshire pudding, saying her husband does all the cooking and won a prize once for this dish. She also advised her to order a sherry trifle now, as they're very popular and sure to go fast.

As Florence ate, she glanced up from her book now and then to look at the other diners. There were two women at a table by the mahogany sideboard, and it seemed that the older of the two did most of the talking in a commanding and sometimes scolding voice. The other seemed to visibly diminish and humbly fiddle with her fingers, and when her food arrived she ate it quietly and carefully. On the table next to them was a studious looking man, with a tiny and extremely ancient woman, her face a veritable spider's web of wrinkles. The third table was occupied by a group of German or Austrian tourists. They were really noisy, flourishing their maps and speaking rapidly.

Looking out of the large dining room window, Florence realized that it faced a different direction than her bedroom window. Through the drizzle she saw an impressive mountain in silhouette, of a deeper grey than the grey skies surrounding it, which she assumed, according to what she'd read of the tourist information, was probably Skiddaw, the fourth highest mountain in the Lake District. She hoped that the weather might clear up by tomorrow, so that she could do some hiking.

As soon as dinner was over, Florence went back upstairs to her room. But she was almost immediately surprised by a knock on the door. It was Mrs. Landsdowne asking if she'd like coffee and truffles, which are served every night in the lounge. So she went straight back down and had just sat down on a comfortable armchair by the unlit fireplace when the ancient woman from the dining room shuffled past her to the stairs, assisted slowly by her male companion. She thought it only proper to say "Good night!" but, assuming a woman so advanced in years might be a little deaf, barked it out rather too loudly causing the man to turn from the first stair and smile at her in a quiet, yet sweet manner.

Florence took two truffles, wriggled between the soft cushions of the armchair and returned to her book. After having felt conspicuously uncomfortable in the dining room, she now started feeling glad she'd come. Perhaps it was the truffles, which were gorgeous! She was just getting absorbed in her novel when the two women she'd noticed at dinner came and sat down next to her.

"Mind if we join you?" the older one said. She had no eyebrows, but instead had painted in two flat, brown lines in the space that the eyebrows should have occupied, which made her look rather like a clown. "I'm Rose! And this is Allison."

Florence told them she was pleased to meet them, though really she wanted to read a bit more, as she had just reached an exciting scene. The one who was called Rose, outspokenly said, "We thought you were a boy when you first entered the dining room, didn't we Allison!" which made Florence's hand shoot up to her hair. But recovering herself quickly, she laughed and said, "This is the latest look from London."

"Very becoming," Rose replied, with a quizzical expression on her face. "So, are you here on your own?"

Florence replied that she was, to which Rose replied, "Well, you'll get some peace and quiet, which is a very good thing. Yes, a very good thing. Of course, it's hard to have quiet with those noisy Austrians around. I was just saying to Allison, why can't they put on their hiking boots and hike over the Alps instead! I mean, it's not like they don't have perfectly decent mountains over there too, is it!"

This seemed to make Allison uncomfortable, as she wrapped her cardigan more tightly around her narrow frame.

"Well, it's true," Rose continued. "Joining the European Union! A load of twaddle, if you ask me! Oh, but don't think for a minute that I don't like foreigners! Oh no; not me. I lived for quite some time in India when I was growing up!"

Florence thought that sounded quite exciting, so she asked her about it.

"Well, my father had a job on one of those tea plantations," she replied. "That was the life! We had plenty of servants, naturally, and they really loved us. They were always most solicitous. Grand old souls, they were! And of course one met the most marvelous ex-patriots there, as well.

Why, only the other night Cecil phoned (he's been back here for years now, as have I) and invited me to a very jolly sounding dinner."

Florence smiled, which encouraged Rose to tell more.

"Oh yes, dear. He said he'd be dressed in his full regalia, and he advised me to wear a long dress. 'Oh, but I haven't bought a long dress with me,' I told him. 'But I do have my nightdress which reaches my ankles. Will that do?'"

A moment later, Rose noticed a Scrabble board over on the shelf, and asked Florence if she'd like to play it with them. Allison turned out to be quite a skilled player, but Rose made sprawling words which never had much numerical value, and which, despite their length, never seemed to land on double or triple score squares. As she played, she interspersed oral calculations of possible letter combinations, ("G-E-M-E; that's a word, isn't it?") with comments about the other guests. "Allison and I always stay here for a month and a half in the summer. Have been doing so for years. It's good for my condition, you see. We've seen all sorts here. Of course, there are the regulars such as us. And then the ever-changing array of over-ambitious, noisy tourists, wanting to scale every peak. They come from all over, but mostly from Germany and America. Now, in contrast, though, take dear old Mrs. Ramsey, and her rather peculiar son, Dr. Ramsey. They're regulars. Come every summer. She really is quite a poppet, but I hardly ever hear a peep out of that man, despite the fact that we see him every time we're here. He's reputed to be quite brilliant, though I wouldn't know of such things, and of course he is definitely a gentleman and shows us much civility, but beyond that he has nothing to say for himself."

Florence asked Rose if she was referring to the ancient woman and the gentleman she'd seen in the dining room.

"Well, my dear; yes, of course I am," Rose said, popping a chocolate truffle between her fleshy, painted lips. "They say he's glued to his mother. Always has been. Never struck out on his own. It makes you wonder. She can't last for ever, and then what will he do? Ah! H-A-N-D! That's a good word!"

From Rose's word, Florence made the intersecting word 'Q-U-A-Y,' which luckily landed on a triple letter score.

"You're good!" Rose declared. "Or should we call it beginner's luck?"

The game soon ended, and Rose declared that it was time for bed, and she and Allison left the lounge, first advising Florence that she shouldn't come down any later than 8.00 am, otherwise she might find a shortage of food, especially of drop scones, which apparently are the house special.

Florence, too, returned to her room, but despite the heavy meal and her exhaustion from the journey, she couldn't sleep. She assumed her room must be next door to the Austrians', as she kept hearing rhythmic creaking of bedsprings, deep satisfied grunts of *"Ja, ja, mein schatz! Ach so!"* footsteps padding down the corridor, doors being opened and shut, and even a high, thin, tinkly sound as of breaking glass. So she switched on the light, and read more of the novel, looking forward to more truffles the next day and hoping Rose would not have eaten them all up.

Consequently, Florence woke late the next morning. Her first thought was of how strange it felt not waking up with Howard beside her, tugging in his customary fashion at the duvet, but it also felt like a great relief. She experienced a momentary pang of guilt for her wayward feelings, but it didn't last long as she had to hurry to breakfast, and in any case, she'd wanted to get away from Howard as he'd been so ghastly recently. Despite rushing, she nearly missed breakfast, but as she was spreading butter on the rounds of dry toast that Mrs. Landsdowne brought her, she saw the Austrians by the reception desk, ready to check out. After they'd left, there was a heavy silence, and it seemed that her knife and fork made an exaggerated sound as they scraped against her plate. Occasionally, though, she heard the various trills of bird song, and the distant barking of a dog. She promised herself that she would rise earlier the next day.

The picture window offered a better view now than the previous evening, of the glorious garden in front of the guesthouse, framed by flowerbeds filled with an abundant variety of flowers, and the mountain beyond. Also, through the trees, she could just make out the edges of the lake, and she decided that today she would walk along its shores. She went up to her room to fetch her light jacket and camera, and then thanking Mrs. Landsdowne for such a good breakfast – the woman was now on her knees vigorously scrubbing the wooden floor of the reception area - she stepped outside.

She walked that day much further than she'd anticipated. The

9

lakeshore path rose and fell, and occasionally she even made some detours to explore little wooded inclines to gain a better view of the lake. She took many photos with great satisfaction, especially of the lake which looked glinting and shimmering. By afternoon the light drizzle that had been falling, gave way to bright sunshine, and Florence used the camera even more. But she realized that Howard was actually right; it was strange looking through a viewfinder which was scratched as badly as a grazed knee. It made everything in the left section of the frame appear ringed in a golden light, and it also made focusing a bit haphazard.

By about 3.30 pm, having only eaten a chocolate bar since breakfast, she decided it was time to return to Landsdowne's. She felt hungry, and hoped that there might be some of those delicious truffles still lying in their blue and white porcelain bowls in the living room. As she approached the guesthouse, she noticed Mrs. Landsdowne weeding around the deep crimson roses, accompanied by a black Labrador who ran towards her, vigorously wagging his tail. Florence decided to take another photo, but the film would not advance, neither would the shutter click. This surprised her, but also made her feel extremely frustrated. She wished she'd asked Howard more questions about how to use this camera. Maybe he was right that it was a piece of rubbish, and if that were the case, she felt furious that she wouldn't be able to take more photos of her holiday.

She walked inside, hoping that she might see Rose and Allison. Maybe one of them knew more about cameras than she did. But they were not there, and so she glided to the window seat, her face turned to the view of the countryside she'd just explored, and to Mrs. Landsdowne who now seemed to be planting a row of leafy green vegetables. Really that woman had unstoppable energy!

She turned back to the room, and was surprised to see Dr. Ramsey, seated near the bookshelves, bent over a sheath of papers, under the light of a green-shaded lamp. She hadn't noticed him there before. She looked back down at her camera, and started fiddling with it, peering into the lens and looking for clues, but of course there were none to be found. She tried again to advance the film. Nothing. It was quite jammed.

"Do you want some help with that?" It was Dr. Ramsey, standing over her, holding the bundle of papers, the pen in his mouth.

"Oh, don't worry! I wouldn't want to disturb you. You seem to be pretty busy."

"That's OK. I've just about completed what I was working on." Seeing him up close confirmed her impression that he looked studious and intelligent. His eyes, behind light framed glasses, were luminous with engagement. "What seems to be the problem?"

"It's just a little jammed. That's all."

"Mind if I have a look? It would be a shame if you couldn't take any photos while you're here on your holiday," he remarked, mirroring her thoughts.

She handed him the camera, and he sat down beside her on the window seat, spreading out his papers, but still chewing on the pen. "I'm Lance Ramsey, by the way," he said, taking the pen out of his mouth, and reaching over for her hand to shake. He had a slightly Northern lilt, and so when he said his first name, he pronounced it as if it rhymed with 'rants'. But her early impressions of him suggested that he was far removed from being a ranting type of person.

"Lance," she repeated, her London accent broadening and flattening the vowel. "I like it. It's a fairly unusual name. I'm Florence. Florence Hamilton."

"Pleased to meet you, Florence!" he said, smiling at her. Then, bending over her camera and examining it closely, he said, "Your camera's a real beauty! An old SLR Nikon! I haven't seen one like this for years. These Single Lens Reflex cameras are a marvel of engineering; such elegant design and so durable. You must be a very ambitious photographer to have a camera like this!"

"Not really. Actually I rather impulsively bought this camera second-hand from a dusty old shop, without knowing anything about it."

He laughed. She didn't expect that.

He twisted the lens in and out and twirled a few dials, and then looking up, he said, "Actually, Florence, I believe it isn't jammed, but it might just possibly have reached the end of the film. Would you like me to unwind it for you? After all, you'd have to do that, whether the film was jammed or completed."

"But it's only at 27, so there should be nine more exposures to take," Florence said, feeling confused.

"Actually, I think you might find that this was a film of 24, and, depending on how you loaded it, you might well have eeked out a few extras. That's what I'm imagining to be the case. So, what do you say; shall I unwind it?"

"Well then, yes please."

He did so, and then carefully opened up the back of the camera. "Ah! As I thought," he said, lifting out the film, and smilingly handing it to her. "It's a film of 24 possible photos, so no damage done! I hope the shop in which you bought this didn't charge you for a film of 36!"

"I hope not, too! But I never knew I'd take so many pictures on my first day here!"

"Did you bring more rolls of film with you?"

"No, I didn't," she replied, only much later remembering that of course she had brought several rolls.

"And are you here without a car?"

"Yes, I came by train to Penrith, and took a taxi from there."

"Well, if you'd like, I could drive you into Bassenthwaite now to pick up some film. It's the closest village to here. And in fact, while you're doing that, you could have this one developed. Believe it or not, even in Bassenthwaite there are modern conveniences such as one hour film development!"

"Oh, but I couldn't ask you to do that!"

"It's perfectly fine with me. I was heading that way myself while Mother has her nap. I have to go to the Post Office and send off this paper I'd been working on," he said, nodding to the sheaves of scattered pages. "I've proof read it so many times it hardly makes sense to me any more."

"Well, I--"

He gave her a jolly smile, and said, "Come on! If we leave now, we'll be back in time for dinner. Mrs. Landsdowne doesn't tolerate tardiness at her table."

"Oh dear; then I probably insulted her a bit at breakfast."

"Slept late, did you?"

"Rather."

He chuckled. A little later they were in a cramped, narrow, and dimly lit shop that sold sweets, and also functioned as a Post Office. Lance coaxed the series of papers into a neat pile, and slid them into a large envelope, which he addressed to the University of East Anglia.

"I teach there," he explained. "In the Anthropology department." And turning to a nearly toothless woman behind the counter, he said, "Good day, Mrs. Pratchett! Here's an important letter I need to send off today. I should've actually sent it yesterday, so please do all you can to hurry it along!"

She laughed, showing her pink gums. "Right you are, love. And here's a letter for you from the Missus," she said, handing him a bulky white envelope. "I hope she's well."

"Oh yes; I'm sure she's quite well, thank you."

"It's been quite a while since we've seen her around these parts. Remember me to her, won't you, and tell her to come back quickly, as we've been missing her. Such a fine lady."

Nodding briefly, he took the white envelope and stuffing it in the pocket inside his jacket, turned back to Florence, saying, "I think you can purchase some film here, if you'd like. Isn't that so, Mrs. Pratchett?"

"Yes, dear. Over there against that wall is where our films are. And we develop film here, too, if you would like."

"Yes, if you could please develop this film, it would be great," Florence said, handing her the film.

"Thanks, dear," Mrs. Pratchett said. "Your film will be ready for you in an hour."

"C'mon," Lance said to her, after she'd paid for a new roll of film. "I'll buy you a cup of tea while your film's developing."

"Thank you!"

They walked down the village high street, Florence liking the way he walked so jauntily, and pushed open the door of a little teashop with a steamy plate-glass window. They sat across from each other at a small table covered by a red and white checked tablecloth, which rocked back and forth depending on whose elbow was on it. They ate squelchy, stodgy sweet buns, which felt good after such a long hike. Florence felt her cheeks turn rosy.

"So, you're Florence," he said.

"Yes, my parents originally intended calling me Caroline, but I was apparently such a big baby that the maternity nurse talked them out of it, saying Caroline was not a fat person's name."

He chuckled. "Well, you're certainly not fat now," he said.

She appreciated his kindness, but thought to herself how she better slow down on the truffles tonight, assuming Mrs. Landsdowne put out more. "What about your name?" she asked. "Is there a story behind it, too?"

"As a matter of fact, there is. Mother had apparently read *Mort D'Arthur* so many times when pregnant with me – it was a type of obsession, driven I'm sure by the hormonal changes - that she fell in love with Sir Lancelot."

"Quite the nobleman!"

"To be sure."

"Parents must have so much fun naming their innocent babies," Florence said, taking a sip of warm tea. "I have a friend, Greg, whose full name's Gregor Ian Chant!" at which point she started singing accordingly. Lance exploded with a little bubble of laughter, and then, as if reminding himself to behave well, ducked his head and cut off a neat slice of his sticky bun.

"You said you teach anthropology. How interesting!"

"Yes, that's right. And you? What do you do?"

"I write for a magazine, which is positioned somewhere between popular and scholarly."

"Nice. What's it called?"

She told him.

"Yes, I've heard of it, but have never read it. What sort of topics do you write about?"

"It depends. Recently mostly about topical urban issues, though it can be broader than that."

She enjoyed their conversation. There were none of the usual platitudes, or conventional dull questions as to why she had come here, but spoke instead about a range of subjects in a light-hearted way. She found it incredibly easy talking to Lance; he was amusing, stimulating, intelligent and fast paced. She particularly liked his bright, luminous, engaging eyes, and how they crinkled into an expression of genuine mirth when something amused him. Playfully, they poked fun at the other guests at Landsdowne's.

"What do you know about Rose and Allison?" she asked.

"Know about them? Actually very little. Only that Rose is, what one might call, a 'woman of independent means.' And Allison is her paid companion. And has been for years. At least as long as we've all been coming to Landsdowne's, which amounts to more summers than I care to remember."

"Oh really? And what is Rose's 'condition'? She mentioned it last night, and said coming here for a holiday was good for her health."

"Nothing more, I suspect, than a stiffening of the joints, impeding her quest to gain the maximum amount of gossip in the least amount of time!"

Florence laughed, and took another bite from her bun.

"And what about Mr. Landsdowne? I've not seen him. Does he even exist?"

"One tends to 'feel' Mr. Landsdowne's presence more than see it, through the banging of the pots in the kitchen, and the often delectable dishes that are served. Though I should warn you. They're not all good. Take extra caution over his steak-and-kidney pie. I might even go as far as to warn you to stay away from it all together!"

Their conversation continued in this delightful manner, and then it was time to pick up Florence's developed film, return to Landsdowne's, and change for dinner. As she did so, Florence realized that she'd completely changed her impression from last night when she'd thought Lance looked studious in a solemn way. Now she thought that even though he seemed clearly intelligent, he was not at all solemn, but engaging, good humored, and fun.

And now Florence suddenly saw that she really liked Lance. She definitely felt a rapport developing between them, a real connection and familiarity, as if they'd always known each other. How odd. How could that be? But then she remembered how the woman in the Post Office said to him, "Here's a letter from the Missus" and that statement inexplicably upset her. So Rose, who'd said Lance was stuck to his mother like glue and had never struck out on his own, was quite inaccurate and certainly misleading. Florence found herself wondering how old Lance was, but then remonstrated herself as there was no point in thinking about him if he was married. Rose had said he was in his mid-thirties, but she clearly wasn't a particularly accurate source of information.

Once back in the dining room that evening, Florence sat at her corner table, looking through the photos she'd taken that day, being careful not to spill any of her food on them. Though some of the photos were nice, she realized that imposing a frame around a tiny square of landscape never could do justice to the actual majesty of the entire whole.

She looked around the dining room as she ate, noticing some newcomers; a man wearing a felt cap who kept a pipe in his mouth between every course, and his wife with an immense bouffant hairdo. She saw that they each ordered a different main course, ate at exactly the same speed, and then when they were each half way through, they silently picked up their plates, exchanged them with each other, and quietly resumed eating the other half. It seemed such brilliant choreography.

This time Lance and his mother finished their meal while Florence was still eating. He gave her only a tiny nod of acknowledgement as he steered his mother past her table. She felt it odd that he didn't talk to her or introduce her to his mother, but taking her cue from him, she reciprocated with a brief nod to them. And in fact this was just as well, as she had her mouth full at the time with treacle pudding.

After dinner she went to the lounge, and gobbled up lots of truffles, glancing guiltily around to make sure no one had seen her. A short time later, Rose and Allison came and sat down beside her.

"Enjoyed your meal, dear?" Rose asked. "Mr. Landsdowne always boils the Brussel-sprouts a little too long, don't you think?"

"I thought it was delicious. But I was quite hungry. I'd been on a long hike today."

"Really, dear? Where did you go?"

"I walked to the lake, and then along its shoreline for a bit."

"Goodness! It sounds as if you must have covered a lot of ground today. Even walking to the lake and then turning around and coming straight back is enough for me!"

"Yes, I walked quite far, but it was terrific!"

"No wonder you keep so trim! Anyway, dear, how about a game of Scrabble again? Would you like that?"

"Yes, of course. That would be nice."

"Allison; go and fetch the board!"

Soon they were settled, their letter tiles distributed.

"Might I also participate in this game?" It was Lance, who had quietly slipped back into the lounge.

"Why, Dr. Ramsey! Naturally, we'd be delighted!" Rose exclaimed.

"I'll go and get my other glasses and be back in a moment!" he said, turning and heading towards the stairs.

"Really, my dear, that's most unusual!" Rose commented in a bubbly manner, as soon as he'd left the room. "Dr. Ramsey talking to us! And asking if he can join in our Scrabble game! Isn't that unusual, Allison? In all our times being here, he has never once returned to the lounge after dinner, let alone talked to us at his own instigation!"

Allison nodded, coughing and tugging at her cardigan.

"Oh, pull yourself together!" Rose told her. "No need to act so afraid. I imagine that Dr. Ramsey wants to talk to me about some of the elite in society, who we both have the privilege to know."

Dr. Ramsey stepped back into the lounge, and took a seat on the sofa next to Rose, causing her to be all flustery with excitement. She at once declared, "My dear Dr. Ramsey! I assume your sweet mother is all tucked in for the night."

"Yes, yes. She is already sleeping comfortably, thank you."

"You and she must have been so amazed by that incident of Lady Rhiannon Gunter-Groves and that fine horse of hers. Goodness gracious me; what a remarkable event! What *did* you think?"

"I'm afraid, Rose, that you know more about it than do I. I hardly know the woman, and certainly never heard any stories about her horse. Shall we play?"

"Yes, yes. Allison; do redistribute the letter tiles now that Dr. Ramsey has joined us! And look sharp about it, as I suspect he is tired and wants to soon retire to bed."

Quickly the four of them settled into the game. Rose continued to make her rambling, loopy words, while Allison was frequently stuck. Dr.

Ramsey played thoughtfully and quietly, laying down splendid sequences of letters in modest haste. Florence was absorbed in the more stimulating challenge than the one that had presented itself the previous evening, when she felt her leg nudged under the table. She shuffled in her seat, adjusting her position, at the same time as laying down the letters F-I-L-M. It wasn't particularly good, but was the best she could do and it was on her mind. Almost instantaneously, Dr. Ramsey made the word M-E-E-T, using her M. Rose rocked back and forth a while, her mind seemingly consumed for the moment with complicated letter permutations, and then made only the word C-A-T.

Allison, hugging her cardigan, went to a different area of the board, making a word as insignificant as herself, but which opened up new possibilities for Florence. Again it was Dr. Ramsey's turn, and he did so with great economy, laying down only one letter M to intersect with the E of his previous word M-E-E-T. Florence felt her knee nudged once more, and looking up, she saw Dr. Ramsey briefly looking at her intensely and meaningfully. She wasn't sure if his Scrabble words were meant for her, and faced the next round with great amusement. And then, when it was next his turn, he lay down the letters L-A-T-E-R. Allison surprised them all and clearly terrified herself, by following with a word which used up all her letter tiles, and coincidentally landed on a triple score area which won her the game, although of course Rose took a long time noisily adding up the score.

"Let's have another game!" Rose said, and so they did; a lengthy, elaborate game in which Dr. Ramsey made no further attempts at communicating with Florence through his Scrabble letters. Rose seemed content to prolong their evening well beyond the hours of the previous night, and might in fact have continued still longer, when Lance said he was afraid he must be taking his leave of them as his mother woke so early.

"Thank you, ladies!" he said, rising from his seat. "I wish you a good evening." He shook hands with each of them, surprising Florence as he grasped her hand, by surreptitiously slipping a tiny square of intricately folded paper into it. She felt intrigued and excited, but then caught sight of her reflection in the mirror on the opposite wall and thought she'd better control herself before Rose or Allison noticed her flushed cheeks. She sank into her seat again, and helped clear away the letter tiles.

A little while later, the Scrabble board neatly back on the shelf, Rose made her way upstairs, with Allison trailing after her, and Florence followed them both, showing extreme calm to the point of slowness of movement, prolonging the deliciousness of anticipation of what Lance's note would say. Once in her room, she uncurled her fingers from around the tiny square of paper, and read the words *"Window Seat, 11.00,"* written in a neat, squarish print, in a bold Royal blue ink. It made her feel a happy shouting inside her head, accompanied by a bright light and a merry sound of a tambourine.

She looked at her watch. It was 11.11, which was her favorite time, as it's the only time on a 12 hour digital clock when all the digits are the same. So she stealthily went back downstairs, surprised that in the few minutes she had been in her room, the lights on the staircase and downstairs had now been turned off. She groped onto the banister as she descended, careful not to trip, but worrying that as she was late Lance might have already left. Entering the lounge, she noticed the sole source of illumination was from the mushroom shaped green-shaded lamp, spilling only a soft downward pool of light, which did little to illuminate much more of the room. But there, to her relief, was Lance, sitting beside it as he'd done earlier that afternoon.

"Good! I'm glad you came!" he said, rising from his seat to greet her, and smiling broadly. "All the main lights are out, I'm afraid. Must be on a time switch, except this little one. It seems they go to bed early in these Northern parts. But if this lack of light doesn't bother you-"

"No, not at all. It's fine!"

"Good! Then let's talk a while. You're fun to talk to."

"Thanks. So are you!" she replied, finding her way to the window seat, which was slightly illuminated by a watery shaft of light slanting through the window from a lamp on the grounds outside.

"I've been thinking, Florence," he began. "If I may, I'd like to take you to explore some of the countryside, beyond where you can reach on foot. Do you have any plans for tomorrow afternoon?"

"None whatsoever. That would be nice. I'd like that," Florence said excitedly.

"Terrific! I'll pick you up, then, by the stone wall at the edge of the garden, at 1.30. As you remember, I have a green Fiat."

"Thanks!"

"I come to this area so frequently that I know it very well, and I always enjoy showing people around, whenever I have time."

His words about always enjoying showing people around this area made her feel a little less special. But she tossed this thought aside because she was so excited by his invitation. And she realized she'd never before thought so much about someone she knew so little about. Indeed she hadn't stopped thinking about him since they'd sat together on the window seat and he'd helped her with her camera.

Because her favorite time of 11.11 was still on her mind, she said, "Speaking of Time, which we weren't actually doing, but I just picked up on you mentioning '*whenever you have time*' - isn't it fascinating how Time means different things to each of us. I don't know how it's impacting you, since you seem to have been busy with your work, but for me, I feel as if I've been here for ages, yet it's only been slightly more than twenty four hours!"

"Yes, Time for me *had* seemed to be rushing past over the last few weeks, as I'd been working against a deadline. Such a relief to have posted it off today!"

She smiled at him, but because she thought he might not notice since the room was so very dark, she murmured, "That's good."

"Yes. I imagine that with your line of work, you must be used to the same sort of thing; deadlines and all that."

"Definitely!"

"But now, in contrast, the feeling you describe of having been here for ages is probably because you're in a new place, and you're cramming so much new information into every moment, concentrating on all the details."

"Yes, that's very true," Florence replied, thinking of all she'd done since parting from Howard, so very long ago it seemed, at Euston Station. She became aware, as she spoke, of the ticking of the clock, which she remembered as being on the mantelpiece, even though the clock itself had merged into the shadows. But she was growing accustomed to sitting together in the room like that, Lance's facial expression oblique in the dimness of the room. It made her focus even more keenly on what he was saying.

"I've actually heard this described by a writer called de Botton as having a 'traveling mindset,'" he continued, "how we're much more observant when we travel than when we're in our usual place where our behavior is habitual, and as he says, 'therefore blind.' I've used his work in some of my classes."

"'A traveling mindset.' I like that. It sounds very appropriate."

"Yes! And what's fascinating is that it proves there's nothing absolute about Time. It's all relative, depending on the subjective experience. For you, Time is slowed down; for me it's recently been sped up."

"That's what I've often thought, too," Florence said, feeling exhilarated to be discussing Time, a subject that had long fascinated her. And it seemed that the topic excited Lance too, as she felt slight rhythmic vibrations through the floor and noticed in the dimness that one of his legs had started jogging up and down. She dug into her bag and pulled out a tiny black leather covered notebook and a pen. "I've always been intrigued by the concept of Time. I must write these terrific thoughts down," she said, angling the notebook to catch the shaft of light from the window. But it was an erratic, intermittent source of light, obliterated at times when the wind blew a branch from a heavily foliaged tree across it. Even so, she started hurrying to jot down what he'd said about the traveling mindset.

But suddenly she lost her grip on her notebook and heard it drop to the floor. She exclaimed in surprise and shock at what seemed like such a loud noise in the hush of the night. She knelt down to try to find it, and brushed against something soft but firm, which she realized was Lance's shoulder. He was squatting on the floor beside her, and as he handed the book back to her, she smelt a liquorice aroma of fresh fennel root about him.

"Thanks," she said, her face close to his. She saw the light reflect off his glasses and his teeth as he smiled up at her. Then he was swallowed up again in the darkness and she saw him reemerge at his seat under the green shaded light.

"We can't have you lose your notebook," he said simply.

She laughed, stimulated still further by the close physical proximity of him, and wishing he might have joined her on the window seat, just as he had earlier that afternoon when he'd helped with her camera, rather than going back to his former seat.

"So many people feel determined by the constant, regular ticking of the clock," she said, continuing her thought from before she'd dropped her notebook. "But I think Time's an artificial construct."

"You don't seem the type to be determined by the regular ticking of any clock. You strike me as a free spirit."

"Absolutely!" she agreed. "That's why I came away. I wanted to bend Time, create more options, escape the routine."

He could have asked what her routine was. She was glad he didn't. Instead, he said, "Yes! Bending Time. I like that! By the way, you're right that time is an artificial construct. It's just a model – a paradigm, really – that we superimpose on reality, in order to try to understand it. So, in effect, we're trying to comprehend the model rather than reality itself."

"Yes, as you said, there's nothing absolute about Time. It's based on our subjective experience of it. But, on the other hand, though, don't you think that physicists might argue that Time isn't subjective? That it's real and objective, as measured by the Earth's rotation around the Sun, captured by sundials and clocks, and reflected in the cycles of nature such as a new plant shooting up, blossoming, reaching full bloom, and then wilting again?"

"Florence, that's true. But is it possible to argue that we *perceive* this happening, as it's filtered through our *subjective* minds, which have been trained to conform to viewing things within that accepted paradigm of reality?"

"Yes, I like that interpretation."

"And consider how not all countries use the same calendar as we do. That's what made our global celebrations last New Year's Eve, for the start of this new millennium, even more fascinating as across the world we agreed to adopt the same time measurement just for that occasion.

But there are some primitive populations who normally measure Time by certain periodic customs and rituals." Lance was now leaning forward as he spoke, with his elbows on his knees, so his face was no longer illuminated. "Take for example-"

They talked on and on, ideas about Time from one of them sparking a glowing shower of new ideas about Time from the other. Their exchange of thoughts zigzagged around the room in dizzying and inspiring bursts of intellectual stimulation, their voices animated, and their faces glowing with excitement. And all this while, Florence was excitedly jotting down notes and diagrams as fast as she could in the flickering shaft of light coming through the window.

They were almost in a timeless state themselves, until Lance, a finger of his hand posed against his lips, said softly, "Florence, listen! Do you hear that? I think that was the lark calling. It must be nearly dawn. The dawn chorus."

Florence sat quietly and listened. At first she heard nothing. Then she noticed a sweet high trill of a bird, and an answering bird song. "My God! Is it that late?" And it was then that she realized that she was shivering with exhaustion.

"Indeed it is. Look out the window. There's the first crack of light. I think we'd better go straight to bed!" It was true; even the lounge in which they sat seemed a little lighter now.

"Oh dear; you'd said you wanted an early night because of your mother," she said, remembering that this was what he'd told Rose in what hardly seemed to be the same night.

"That's all right, Florence. I'm afraid I'd told a bit of a fib, as an exit strategy from any more Scrabble games. You see, I wanted to spend some time with you alone, and I didn't know how late you stay up."

"Oh," she laughed, gathering up her notebook and putting it in her bag.

"And I must admit that when you hadn't come down by ten past eleven, I was beginning to think you wouldn't come. I'm so glad you did, though. I've loved every minute of our conversation."

"Me, too, Lance! This has been amazing," she said, thinking what a phenomenal conversation it had been, and how Lance was extraordinary and exhilarating, and how she could've carried on talking, on and on, and didn't want to stop.

"So, until tomorrow afternoon, then!"

And so saying, he switched off the green shaded light, held the lounge door open for her, and together they climbed the staircase which had gradually changed from its former monochrome, the red of the carpet on each stair now faintly reemerging, and a few of the gold anchors on them glinting with reflected light filtering gently through the landing window.

--------

Feeling replete from a heavy lunch of a generous slice of meatloaf stuffed with a hard-boiled egg, a sweet carrot-raisin salad, and some crusty bread with a thick spread of golden butter, Florence walked down to the stone wall, where she saw Lance's green car just pulling up. He wound down his window, calling happily, "Hello Florence! Jump in!"

"How did you sleep?" he asked as she sat down beside him, his intelligent eyes shining, she assumed, with the shared and secret delight of their conversation the night before.

"Amazingly!" she replied. "But the odd thing is that when I woke up, I couldn't remember a thing about what we'd said about Time. And we'd felt then that we'd understood it so well!"

"Neither could I!" he exclaimed. "It was like a dream, which receded further and further the more I tried to capture it. How peculiar that neither of us remember! What about the notes you took, Florence? Do you have those on you?" he asked eagerly.

"Yes!" she said, picking up her bag and pulling out the little black notebook. "Admittedly it was quite dark in the room, but I've written in the dark before, and on moving trains and buses. My job has often necessitated that. But this is quite different. I've looked at these notes and they are completely indecipherable. It all looks like hieroglyphics. I can't make out a thing I wrote!"

"Could I have a look?" he asked. She handed him the notebook, and he frowned at it, shaking his head. "It's as if we discovered things we're not meant to know," he said. "That we reached an understanding about Time that was not meant to be unlocked."

"I thought that, too!" she said. "We had such inspirational clarity on it last night, and now it's all obscure. It's incredible."

"I can't understand this at all," he said, starting up the ignition. "Something very profound happened last night. I'm sure of it. But come; let's go for a drive. Perhaps we'll remember things as we go along.

# TWO

*PUTTING HIS FOOT ON THE ACCELERATOR,* Lance pulled away from the wall and turned right out of the driveway. "I was thinking of showing you St. Bega's church, which is a lovely little old stone church built in the thirteenth century. Would you like to see it? It's not too far from here, quite close to the lakeshore."

"I'd love to."

The narrow, twisting road with hedgerows either side, eventually descended and widened slightly. He stopped the car, and suggested that they have a walk.

"Actually, we're not nearly there yet, but I wanted to show you this area rather than just drive past it, as I think there's something exceptional about it."

"Oh? What?"

"You'll see!"

They climbed over a style. Crossing into the next field involved stepping through a wide, muddy patch and then along the edge of a little stream. The footpath started to climb a little. Florence stopped frequently to take photos.

"Are you enjoying this?" he asked.

"It's marvelous!"

"It gets even better soon. It's funny; very few people know anything about this area, even those who come every summer. Come now! I've had a thought. There's a little house around here that I'd love to show you."

"Around here? But it seems so isolated. I wouldn't have imagined that anyone would live around here."

"That's what's so intriguing. The house I'm referring to is just through that patch of trees. I discovered it quite a while ago, and I've been to it loads of times since, but I don't think anyone else knows it exists. And certainly I've never told anyone, as there's something very strange about it."

"What? What's so strange?"

"Well, each time it seems that someone is about to move in, they then appear to abandon the idea at the last minute. Let's go and look at it now!"

She enjoyed his boyish sense of adventure. And she also felt how nice it was that he was taking her to see that house now, especially if he hadn't told anyone else about it. It made her feel very special.

They scrambled through the trees, and along a tiny lane, which twisted and then revealed the house Lance was talking about. It was a square, stone house, bordered by a neatly trimmed hedge.

"I think it's still empty now," Lance whispered, even though if it were indeed empty, whispering would have been entirely unnecessary. "Let's go and peep through some of the windows."

"Are you sure? I don't think we should."

"Come on! I'm sure it's fine! And if we see anyone, we'll just say we're lost and looking for directions back to Landsdowne's."

Reassured, Florence nodded happily. He pushed open the garden gate and motioned for her to go through. They walked along the short garden path which led straight to the front door, above which was the name 'Fern View.' The lawn had been recently mowed, and there were some rose bushes and honeysuckle growing in the beds.

"Look!" said Lance, who had now walked around to the side of the house and was peering through a window there. "Come over here and look at this kitchen, Florence! You can tell it's been recently remodeled. Look at the new appliances, and the fridge still has the tag on the door."

Florence still felt a little uncomfortable about looking into a house to which she hadn't been invited. But joining him at the window and seeing the kitchen, she caught his sense of adventure. "You're right!" she exclaimed, "And look at the oven! It's clearly brand new and has never been used. How odd! This is a gorgeous place. I wonder why no one has moved in. Maybe they are just about to in a few weeks."

"No, I don't think so. I heard that the latest estate transaction fell through. And it was empty the last time I looked, too, which was some time ago. It wasn't fitted with all those modern appliances then, though. But come on! Let's come around to the back of the house," he said, pulling at her arm, which increased her feeling of excitement. It was lovely being with Lance. He made everything so intriguing, which thrilled and stimulated her. She was especially drawn to the shine in his eyes.

At the rear of the house was a more recent extension with windows too high to reach, but on the other side of this extension there was a lower window looking into a living room that appeared beautifully furnished – plump sofas with rose patterned pillows, freshly painted walls, and gleaming wood floors and sideboards – and again it looked perfectly untouched. It ran from the front to the back of the house, as they could see its opposite window facing the front garden. They returned to the front door and peered through the window on its other side, and now looked upon a dining room with a shining, dark wooden table, and wood beams on the ceiling.

"It's lovely here!" Florence remarked. "So beautifully renovated. Why on earth is this house uninhabited?"

"It's almost as if people found out something ominous about the place just as they were about to move in. Something so strange that it scared them away. I know this has happened several times."

"How remarkable! I wonder what it can be."

"I don't know. But if it keeps happening, it must be something pretty horrendous!"

They both chuckled.

"I'm going to take some photos of this house," Florence remarked. "It's so lovely. Why don't you stand over there by the front door, Lance, just under where it says 'Fern View,' so I can get you in, too!"

They each took several photos from different angles, confident now, that they could walk around as much as they wanted without fearing that they were trespassing. And eventually they left to continue their walk, across the garden at the back of the cottage to a stream. They took off their shoes, and tried to leap from one boulder to another. Lance fell in, splashing his glasses, and wetting his trousers up to the knees, which made them both giggle. Then they each sat on a boulder, feet dangling in the crystal water, contemplating the sparkles and beams of sunlight scampering on the water's surface, all thoughts of driving any further now abandoned.

After dinner that night back at Landsdowne's, 'Dr. Ramsey' again joined Florence, Rose, and Allison in a game of Scrabble. The short sleep of the previous night was catching up with Florence, so after the end of the first game, she decided to take her leave and go to bed. She mounted the stairs, looking out of the window at the turn of the staircase to the black night beyond. She stopped off in the bathroom, and then as she approached her bedroom door, a figure stepped out in front of her.

"Oh, Dr. Ramsey!" she exclaimed, still using the name by which he was called by Rose. "You quite startled me!"

"Sorry, Florence! I didn't mean to. Let's go for a drink! The pubs are still open for another hour or so."

A surge of energy bolted through Florence, causing her to forget how tired she'd been.

"That's a nice idea," she said excitedly.

They drove to a lovely, old tavern, with sloping, uneven floors covered with sawdust, and wood-beamed ceilings, and sat down comfortably at a small table.

"I'm delighted you curtailed that Scrabble game tonight," he chuckled. "It might have gone on interminably!"

She smiled. "I am, too," she said.

"How about one more drink before closing? And then let's go for a bit of a drive! I love these country lanes at nighttime. The effect of the headlights shining against the hedgerows makes it feel like driving through a twisting tunnel."

Back on the road, they were speeding along exactly as if in a tunnel, and Florence marveled at how well Lance seemed to know his way around.

"Hey, Florence! I've just had an idea! Let's go back to Fern View! Let's see that house at nighttime! It's not that far from here, as you know, and I think it would be fascinating to see it before returning to Landsdowne's."

"OK," Florence agreed, unsure as to why he suggested it, but feeling willing.

"Actually, we could park here, and walk up the lane to it."

They left the car, and stumbled up the dark lane, their footsteps making an exaggerated crunching sound on the stones beneath their feet. They opened the garden gate, and softly entered the garden. They stared at the dark, empty house, its windows like closed eyelids. All was completely still and tranquil.

"Look!" exclaimed Lance suddenly. "Stand over here!"

Florence stood close to him and looked towards the house. Out of the lower window by the front door, the window of the dining room, a glow of light emanated. It did not light up the whole window, but was one isolated luminescence, leaving the rest of the window black.

"Do you see it?" he asked animatedly.

"What is it?" Florence asked, somehow loving that strange light and feeling attracted to it.

"I don't know!" Lance answered, his voice quick and urgent. He glanced up at the sky. "There's no moon tonight, so it's not a reflection of moonlight."

"And it's not coming from within the room, as we know the house is empty. And in any case, if someone *had* switched on the light inside this room, it would light up the whole window, and not just be this solitary glow," Florence remarked, still entranced by the white pouring of light.

"And it's not reflected from anywhere outside, either. Besides there being no moon, there aren't any other sources of light anywhere close to here. Not even the car headlights, as I'm pretty sure I turned them off, and in any case, the car is parked all the way down the lane."

"That's true," Florence replied, still gazing at the glow, feeling somehow peaceful and enraptured.

"Let's get out of here!" Lance said sounding very alarmed. Florence was surprised; she was content to keep staring at the light, and contemplating the possibilities of what it could be.

"No, not yet. Let's stay a bit longer. Perhaps it's caused by-"

"Florence! I mean it! We must leave. Come on!" And grabbing her hand, he started pulling her. She gave a backward glance to the window, and then together they started to run. Perhaps it was the suddenness and panic of the run, but now Florence felt afraid, too. They ran until they reached the car, and Lance, fumbling with the lock, opened the passenger door and then his own, and they both jumped into the car, panting heavily. He drove off rapidly. "Now we know why no one has moved in there," he said. "A ghost! Some sort of spirit!"

"But there must be some rational explanation," Florence said, once they were back at Landsdowne's, her temporary fear averted. She was now thinking back to how she had loved that light. Was almost drawn to it. This time Lance sat next to her on the window seat, after switching on the mushroom shaped green-shaded lamp. His long, thin leg clothed in dark denim, was jiggling up and down.

"No. None at all," he answered, still breathing quite heavily. "We went through all the possibilities."

"You're right that it was no ordinary sort of light. It was just a small white glow."

"Yes, in the lower corner of the window."

"Could it be the effect of the drinks?"

"No. We had very little. Certainly not enough to create illusions or hallucinations. Anyway, we both saw it, so it must have been there." He stood up and sighed, taking her hand momentarily in his. "It's late. We should both go to bed. Sleep well tonight, my dear."

She smiled.

Turning off the green-shaded light, he added, "I won't go back there again. Ever. That's done it for me! But might I see you after lunch tomorrow, when Mother takes her nap?"

"That would be lovely. Perhaps we could return to the village, as I used up this roll of film, and would like to develop it. And buy more film, of course!"

"Good! Let's do it! I'll meet you by the stone wall at 3.00."

# THREE

*"GOD! I CAN'T BELIEVE THIS!"* Florence said, putting her teacup down in its saucer.

"What?"

"I mean, I'm not going mad or anything, am I? We did take lots of photos of the countryside yesterday, didn't we?"

"Florence, what are you talking about?"

He looked across the table at the untidy pile of photos that Florence had just had developed and had been looking at while waiting for their scones to arrive. Then he looked up at her face. It was very red and glittering with perspiration.

"I can't...I don't...Can we please leave? I need some fresh air."

"Of course," he said, reaching into his pocket for his wallet and putting a generous bill on the table. "Come on, let me help you."

He scooped up the photos and swept them back into the envelope, called to the waitress to cancel their order of scones, and then gently wrapping his arm around Florence's shoulder, he helped her out of the tearoom. She gulped the air deeply.

"Would you like to sit down on that park bench?" he asked solicitously, indicating a secluded bench a little back from the street, which backed on to some rhododendron bushes.

She nodded and he guided her over to it.

"You're not unwell, are you?" he asked.

She shook her head. "It's the photos. I mean, it's - it's inexplicable."

"What is?"

"Please look at them. You were with me when I took most of them. I thought at first maybe they gave me someone else's film."

He started to look at them. "How extraordinary!" he said. "That's you, isn't it – in a wedding dress! Are you sure these are the pictures you picked up today?"

"Yes, absolutely! But I'm not married. Never have been," she said hoarsely, turning away from him.

"But this is definitely *you* in the wedding dress. And who is that man?"

Florence turned back to him straight away as she thought she detected a note of anxiety, perhaps even jealousy, in his voice.

"That's Howard. We've been living together for a while." Seeing Lance's features appear to darken and indicate that he was visibly taken aback, she rushed on to say, "But we have some, um, well, let's put it this way – we have some problems in our relationship. That's why I decided to come to the Lake District on my own. To get away. Think things over." Unknowingly, she chewed on a fingernail, biting it so low that it hurt.

"You're not married to him?" he asked suspiciously, his leg starting to jog up and down.

"No!"

"But then, what are these pictures?" he asked, sounding incredulous.

"I don't know! I'm so frightened." She didn't know if he believed her doubts about Howard. Had she felt better she would have protested the truth of her statement more, but now she simply did not have the energy.

"Please try not to be," he said, surprising and then reassuring her with the gentleness of his tone of voice. And it was then that she realized that he now appeared to be focusing more on the peculiarity of the photos, than on questions about Howard. "But this is indeed very strange. Look," he said shuffling through more photos, "Some pictures *are* of places we saw. Look! Here is a picture of the stream we walked along! And there's one of me getting into my car in the drive at Landsdowne's. And see that meadow with the yellow flowers? That was the meadow near the house, Fern View, that I took you to yesterday. Let's see how the house came out. What? More wedding pictures! And none whatsoever of that house! It's extraordinary! There must be some rational explanation."

"Lance," she said, looking at him intensely. "It seems that we've been saying there must be a rational explanation about something ever since we met each other."

"It's true," he agreed. "First that profound conversation in which we thought we cracked the interpretation of Time only to forget it all again by morning; then the strange glow of light from the window of that house last night; and now this!"

"Yes!"

"Somehow I wonder if it's all connected. No, don't panic. I don't know how. I don't yet even know what I mean by this. But one thing is for certain. You must take some more photos!"

"No! I couldn't possibly. I'm very afraid. I wish I never bought this camera! I should've just bought a disposable one as Howard suggested."

"I'd like to examine your camera, if I may. Perhaps it will offer some clue. And do please continue to use it. Either it will provide a perfectly nice record of your trip here, or-"

"Or it will provide some terrifying pictures of something quite different!"

"Florence, I know what I'm about to say sounds absurd, but do you think it's plausible that this camera is somehow recording pictures of the future? I can't see how, but I'd like to speculate that this is what it might be doing."

"But that makes absolutely no sense logically. How can the camera take pictures of an event that hasn't yet happened?" Florence said, starting to gather up the photos and put them firmly away into her bag.

"I don't know. It's marvelously intriguing. Let's probe this a bit more deeply. Let's not ignore where these wedding pictures appear to be taken. Did you recognize the place?"

"No! I mean, I don't know. It looks as though it might be in the courtyard of my synagogue. But no! That's impossible. It can't be!" she replied, feeling the heat of a rising panic.

"Please excuse me for being too personal, Florence, and you don't have to answer this if you don't want to, but *do* you expect that you might marry Howard some day?" He was looking at her pointedly. His hands, which had felt so warm and comforting when he was guiding her to the bench, were now far away from her, tucked into his pockets.

"I don't know! I haven't a clue. Actually, I doubt it, given how I've recently been feeling. But look, I want to show you something!" she said, again pulling out the photos from her bag. She rifled anxiously through them, accidentally dropping two on the ground, which Lance picked up. "Yes, here it is!" she continued, having found one of the wedding pictures. "Look at that! Look at my face. It's absolutely stricken with terrible anguish and misery!"

He took the photo and examined it. At the first superficial glance, there appeared a bride in floating white chiffon, alongside a stocky man in a top hat. But when he looked more closely at the bride's face, he saw indeed an expression of despair, and that the hand that clasped the bouquet of flowers gripped them as tensely as if it was a vice, her other hand hanging limply at her side rather than around the man who was to become her husband.

"You're right," he said. "In the short time I've known you, I've seen you animated, delighted, even passionate. I'm afraid all of those emotions seem to be lacking in this picture."

"But Lance, what if you're right? What if this camera is somehow glimpsing my future? The fact that it can do this, if true, is terrifying enough, but on top of it, if this is what my future holds, this is appalling. No, I won't take another picture with this damn camera! I don't want to know any more!"

"Come, come. Calm yourself! Let's not speak of it for now. And let's not tell anyone else about this just yet. We first need to understand it ourselves. Agreed?"

"Yes, agreed," Florence said, trying to look braver than she in fact felt, while at the same time liking the idea of sharing a secret with Lance.

That evening she sat at a table with Rose and Allison, and found to her own surprise, that her appetite was restored and this replenished her will. She noticed that Lance was seated with his mother at a different table than their habitual one, his body turned three quarters away from her, and his leg, disappearing into the folds of the white tablecloth, was a source of excited fascination to her, though she did not know why. She briskly returned any questions that Rose asked.

"My dear Florence," Rose stated imperiously. "You should have a boat ride on Derwentwater before you leave. You are leaving the day after tomorrow, aren't you? Allison and I took that boat trip today. The views are simply outstanding."

Florence dabbed at her lips with her serviette. "It does sound lovely, Rose. Thanks for telling me about it. I'll try to fit it in before I go."

"Perhaps you could ask dear Dr. Ramsey to take you out there in his car. Not only would it provide you with a means of getting there, but if you ask me, I think you'd be doing him a favor! The poor man seems to be quite at loose ends while his mother has her nap. And besides, I simply hate to see a young woman such as yourself on her own."

"Please don't concern yourself about me," Florence said. "I'm perfectly happy to spend some time alone. That's why I chose to come away."

"It's not natural, dear," said Rose. "In fact I will make a point of asking Dr. Ramsey directly after dinner. It's not much to ask. The lake's not far away by car, and he could take you there, and be back to pick you up when the tour is over."

"Oh, please don't trouble yourself."

"Nonsense, dear! It won't be any trouble."

To Florence's embarrassment, as soon as Rose had scraped up the last spoonful of her bread-and-butter pudding with custard, she bustled over to Lance's table, where he and his mother were eating in calm silence.

"Dr. Ramsey!" she said loudly.

He carefully laid down his spoon, pushed his chair back, and stood up to shake her hand. "Good evening, Rose," he said with much civility, so that if her sudden arrival annoyed him, he certainly gave no indication.

"Forgive me for interrupting your meal! I have an important favor to ask of you. Our friend, Florence, will be leaving the day after tomorrow, so I wondered if you could drive her down to Derwentwater tomorrow in time for the 3.30 boat. And then you'd just need to pop back there at 5.30 when the boat returns. I thought she really should do this boat ride before she leaves."

"I'd be charmed," he said.

"What a perfect gentleman! Thank you! And now I will leave you to your pudding. It's good, isn't it! I think Mr. Lansdowne's cooking improves every year, wouldn't you agree? Well, I do hope we'll see you for Scrabble in half an hour or so."

"Of course. As soon as I've got mother settled."

He resumed eating his dinner, never once looking up at Florence, who felt herself blushing uncomfortably.

And she blushed frequently, too, during the game of Scrabble, and unaccountably played very badly, which he mischievously pointed out to her once Rose and Allison had retired to bed. (Rose was so very exhausted after all that fresh air on the boat, that, much as she wanted a second round, she simply had to resist.)

"Now Florence," he said. "Would you be so kind as to show me your camera?"

She went up to her room to retrieve it. Then, seated side-by-side on the window seat, he examined it. As it was empty of film, he opened it up and looked inside, several times advancing an imaginary film.

"Do you know, Florence, why this camera is called a Single Lens Reflex?"

"No," she said.

"It's because the Single Lens Reflex cameras use an internal mirror and what's called a roof pentaprism at the top inside part of the camera. Light coming through the lens is reflected upwards by the mirror, onto the pentaprism, which is located by the viewfinder, and so you can see the image when you look through it. That's why it's called a 'reflex' camera, as it uses the mirror's reflection to allow you, or any photographer, to see exactly where the lens is pointing. When you take a photo, the shutter is released and the internal mirror flips up briefly, allowing the light from the image to shine directly on the film, and then the mirror returns to its natural position after exposure."

"How interesting. What a clever mechanism."

"Yes. And your Nikon was quite special, as it was amongst the first of the Single Lens Reflex cameras to have a so-called 'mirror lens.' It was designed to fold the light, allowing for the lens to be more compact so you don't have to lug around quite such a huge, heavy lens if you wanted to use a telephoto lens. Although admittedly your camera is still quite heavy."

"Yes, it is."

"Look closely inside, Florence! I'm going to take an imaginary photo, and you'll see the shutter slide open and shut. I'll make it do it as slowly as possible so you can see what's happening. I'll do that by opening the aperture all the way, as if I were taking a photo of a very dark place. This way, by keeping the shutter open for a longer time it lets in as much light as possible, but if we were taking a real photo, your camera would obviously have to be kept completely still to stay focused on the object it's filming. That's why some people use a tripod to keep the camera steady."

Just as Florence was peering inside the camera, though, the lounge, which had been brightly lit, was plunged into darkness as the time switch turned off all the lights, except for the solitary mushroom-shaped green-shaded lamp. They were both quite startled.

"I'll have to show you another day!" Lance laughed. "And I'll study your camera again by natural daylight, if I may, to see if we can find any clues as to how it can take photos from another Time. God, even saying that sounds so amazing!" He closed up the back of the camera, and put it back in its case.

In the sudden dimness, Florence was reminded of how she and Lance had sat in this darkened room a few nights ago, and the same feelings flooded over her as the ones she'd experienced when they'd talked about the meaning of Time. The lack of clarity, the pursuit of understanding, the shared intimacy with Lance.

"Maybe that house had a time switch too, just as this one does, and that accounted for the strange light in the dining room window," Florence suggested.

"No, I don't think that's the answer. Remember how we agreed that this was no ordinary light, as it didn't light up the whole window."

"True," Florence agreed. "And how odd that not a single one of the photos that we took of that house came out." Just speaking about the photos again made Florence feel shuddery, but she thought it should be easy to conceal it in the darkness.

"Yes, there's so much more to be understood."

Florence thought, despite the dimness of the room, that she detected that Lance seemed to be frowning, and wondered whether he was freshly afraid once more about that odd light from the house. But instead he went on to say, "It's a shame you're leaving the day after tomorrow. I hadn't known. I know I've already said this, and should not repeat it again for fear of upsetting you, but I think it might be extraordinarily fascinating if you do find that you can bring yourself to continue using this camera. Then perhaps you could write and tell me about the pictures it's taken."

"I'm still not sure that I dare. Perhaps I should return it to the second-hand shop where I purchased it."

"What? And never know? That would be a shame."

Florence was thoughtful for a while. Eventually she said, "I can't use this camera without you! I couldn't go through what just happened alone!"

"Well, how's this for an idea? You could use up the new roll of film tomorrow and have the photos developed before evening. We could spend the whole day together! Forget Rose's plans for that boat ride. It would be full of tourists, anyway. Let's meet straight after breakfast, and then I'll take you to the most photogenic places I know! If you'll permit me, *I'll* take some pictures again with your camera, too!"

Florence could now make out that Lance's eyes shone eagerly. He unexpectedly touched her hand and then moved his hand up to lightly brush her cheek. She lent against him, and they hugged.

"It's extraordinary," he said. "We'd been talking about Time, but what I haven't mentioned is that it seems that I've known you for three years, not three days!"

"I feel the same way!" Florence said, feeling the warmth of his breath against her neck. "It seems so long, yet how fast approaches the time of my departure!"

They were both silent.

"I'm going to extend my stay here!" Florence said suddenly, pulling back and looking at Lance with laughing eyes, her outstretched arms grasping him at his elbows. "I'm going to stay for a few more days, at least until next Saturday. You're right that there are profound things happening, and you and I need to understand them! Besides, I still have some unused holiday, and what's more, it's a slow time at work. I'll tell Mrs. Landsdowne in the morning. I only hope she has room for me!"

"That's marvelous! And I'm sure she'll be able to squeeze you in. There's a room in the attic that's unused, if it comes to that."

"I hope so, now I've made my decision to stay!"

"But Florence, forgive me for mentioning it, but what about Howard?"

"I'll phone him in the morning. It shouldn't be a problem."

They kissed then, though she didn't enjoy it as much as she expected.

"One of the other profound things which I don't think we've mentioned-" Lance started to say, twirling some of Florence's hair through his fingers.

"But your wife-" Florence interrupted him. This, she realized, was what troubled her when they kissed.

"What are you talking about? I haven't got a wife!" he snapped, sounding very different from his usual self, and dropping his hand from her hair.

Florence, habitually scared by anger in another, felt startled and afraid. She tried hard to pick out his facial features in the dimness, but couldn't. The faint light, intermittently coming through the window from the outside lantern, was partially obscured as a leafy branch swayed backwards and forwards over it because of the breeze outside. "Oh. Maybe I misheard," she stammered, "but the woman in the Post Office, Mrs. Pratchett – I thought she handed you a letter from your wife, and she asked after her, and hoped she'd be coming here shortly."

"Oh that!" he said laughing. "Ms. Ramsey is not my wife, but my sister! I'm not sure why, but I never got round to correcting Mrs. Pratchett's erroneous assumptions."

"Your sister?"

"Yes, Juliet and I share a house, and have done for years. The arrangement suits us both quite well. And we take it in turns to come out here at different times of the year to be with Mother."

"I see," Florence said, still feeling a little jittery from when he'd spoken so sharply. But then a calm wave of relief swept over her with the realization that Lance wasn't married, and this mingled with happy swirls of greyness from the room itself.

Lance held both of her hands. "But then there's Howard. And while you're in the undecided stage about him, perhaps it's best for us not to embark on anything more amorous between ourselves, as it might only complicate matters and make you more confused."

"No, Lance. I-" she started to plead, feeling so drawn to Lance.

"Come, come, my sweet Florence. Let's be patient with this, as with all our other discoveries. But I'm so pleased that you intend to stay here longer. That extra time will be so worthwhile!"

He kissed her lightly on the lips, and then hugged her against himself. She yielded completely to his embrace, now feeling so entirely happy, and she hugged him back enthusiastically. His kiss felt so lovely, and hugging each other felt beautiful, warm and comforting to her. She was enthralled by his attentive kindness, his radiant intelligence, and his pursuit of understanding and knowledge. Being with him, she realized she didn't feel scared any more. Instead she thought that she and Lance were now involved in something incredible, and was so pleased that they were pursuing it together.

"You're a brave woman, Florence, and an extraordinary one!" he remarked. "Don't worry about those photos today. It's undoubtedly complex and startling, but it's also phenomenally exciting and important. I feel that we're on the brink of some discovery of exceptional proportion. I'm going to repeat myself and say that I'm so delighted that you came to such a sensible decision to stay. Let's meet early tomorrow morning, straight after breakfast! Is 9.30 good for you? Good! Then let it be then!"

And arm in arm, they left the darkened downstairs rooms, clambered up the staircase, hugged each other on the landing, and went into their own bedrooms.

# FOUR

*FLORENCE SLEPT DEEPLY,* but towards morning she had a very disturbing dream, which woke her in a panic. She dreamed that she was floating in water, which felt cool and silky. She then climbed out onto the riverbank and looked for her clothes, which she found heaped under a large rhododendron bush. As she slid her arms through the sleeves, she realized she was putting on a wedding dress! Suddenly she heard a noise, and looking up, she saw Howard's mother staring at her. Not only was Howard's mother staring, but she'd also started slowly running her long fingers down her wrinkled face, from her forehead to the bottom of her sagging cheeks and jawbone, and onto her sinewy neck. Florence realized with horror that the long, varnished finger nails of her new mother-in-law weren't finger nails, but were instead sharp claws, which left deep red lacerations diagonally down the mask of her chalk white face.

Florence opened her eyes with a start, and then closed them again, willing herself to go back to sleep and try to change the ending of that dream so that Howard's mother would not inflict such pain on herself. But it was useless; Florence was wide awake, and even though it was only just after 6.00, she threw off the blankets, dressed and went downstairs. In the hall, she practically collided with Mrs. Landsdowne, who was carrying an armful of serviettes which she was about to fold into fancy shapes. She was clearly amazed to see Florence at this hour.

"My word, dear! You're up early!" she said. "You quite startled me. Everything all right, is it?"

"Mrs. Landsdowne," Florence said, trying to recapture the excitement of the conversation with Lance from the previous evening. "It's so lovely here, so I was wondering if could extend my stay until Saturday. Would that be possible?"

"And you got up early to ask me that, did you? How nice. Now let me see." And so saying, she made a big business of putting down the serviettes, pulling up her glasses from where they dangled on a chain on her ample bosom, hooking them behind her ears, and licking her plump forefinger to turn over the pages of her appointment book.

"Well, yes dear; you're lucky, especially as this is high season. You can stay on, but you'll have to switch rooms on Thursday. I have another nice room, which I can show you after breakfast. Speaking of which, it's not quite breakfast time yet, but are you hungry? Maybe I can fetch you a little something from the kitchen now. Mr. Landsdowne could probably find something. I'll just go and check."

Eating a portion of yesterday's quiche, which must have been hurriedly microwaved as it was not evenly warmed through, and washing it down with a sturdy cup of tea, Florence started to feel better. She was excited about being able to extend her stay, and what was more, the awful dream seemed more remote, lost in the tangle of sheets of those grey early morning hours.

As she was finishing her breakfast, the man with the pipe and his wife with the bouffant hairstyle, not a hair out of place from the previous night, came down to breakfast. Florence greeted them quickly, heard them place their breakfast order of different dishes which they would no doubt share, and then, neither feeling like talking nor of inhaling more of the smoke from the pipe, she stepped outside to have a short walk.

After a little while, deeming it by now not too early to phone her boss, Elizabeth Carlisle, she sat on the stone wall and took out her mobile phone, and dialed her number. Her boss answered on the seventh ring, just as Florence was thinking that perhaps it was too early after all. After exchanging pleasantries, Florence asked for an extended leave from work.

"Well, Florence," Elizabeth answered, clearly playing for time, and Florence could almost visualize her rolling her pencil along the edge of her desk as she had seen her do so many times before, a habit she seemed unaware of doing while she was thinking her way through some challenge. "Let me see. Now, we are quite busy," (which Florence knew was not the case) "but perhaps I can make an argument for you being out of the office if we find a story for you to work on there. Remind me where exactly it is that you are."

"In the Lake District."

"Ah yes; the Lake District! Well now, that's perfect. I'd like you to do a short piece on the local bird population. That would fit in very nicely with the theme of the next issue."

Florence agreed, trying to sound as enthusiastic as she could, while thinking how Elizabeth Carlisle never could resist taking full advantage of any new opportunity. Why couldn't she be allowed to just have a slightly longer holiday?

The bigger challenge, though, was phoning Howard. Florence had to jump down from the wall, and take several turns around the garden before she felt that she could cope with speaking with him. He, unlike Elizabeth Carlisle, answered on the first ring.

"Flo! I've been missing you!"

Florence felt guilty because she clearly had not been missing him at all. There was a moment of awkward silence, and then Howard continued, "But I'll pick you up at Euston station tomorrow evening!"

"Hold on, Howard," Florence said quickly, feeling flustered. "I've got some news for you. I just found out that Elizabeth Carlisle wants me to do some research on the local birds here, so I will need to extend my stay till Saturday. It'll only be a few more days."

"Now wait a minute! You don't know the first thing about birds."

Of course that was true. But Howard was always telling her that she was ignorant about everything, which annoyed her. Still, perhaps this time he did have a right to be angry. "Well, that's why I need to be here to find out about them," she said weakly.

"I know!" he said triumphantly. "I'll come up and join you the day after tomorrow, and then we'll go back together."

This took Florence completely off guard. She definitely didn't want him here.

"Oh, that's kind, Howard. But you absolutely shouldn't waste your time coming here. It's really rather a shabby guest house, and you wouldn't like it at all."

"Look, you're fussier than I am. If it's good enough for you, it's good enough for me."

"But Howard, I'll be preoccupied with this bird research, so I wouldn't be much company."

"Listen here, Flo," he said, shouting now. "I've been bloody generous in allowing you to go away. I've even fucking well re-papered our bedroom – shit! That was meant to have been a surprise – and all you're doing is rebuffing me!"

Oh no! This was going all wrong. Florence tried to apologize. "Howard, how kind of you to have done that!" she said, trying to sound delighted while secretly thinking, though, that he should have waited for her so they could pick out the pattern of the wallpaper together.

"Look, Flo. You caught me at work. I can't talk properly now. I'll drive up there tomorrow evening! See ya!"

"Wait, Howard!" she cried anxiously. "I'll phone you again this evening, after work." But he'd already rung off.

Florence took many more walks around the garden to try to establish her equilibrium. She didn't want Lance to see her upset. Then she quickly went up to her room and perched herself on the edge of the bed to read a short passage from the novel, but it did not hold her attention. So, rather briskly, she took her camera and returned to the stone wall. She was a few minutes early, which was unusual as Lance was generally there before her. This time, though, she would surprise him.

But her wait for Lance seemed to stretch on and on. She thought it must be much later than 9.30 now, but she refused to look at her watch as she didn't want to appear to Lance to be impatient or cross. But she couldn't help wondering where he was. And then she glanced at her watch without meaning to, and saw that it was well after 10.00 am. And she realized with a sickening thud that clearly he wasn't coming.

Was it because of knowing about Howard, she wondered, remembering how he'd said that they should not rush into anything between themselves because of him. And then she thought of that terrifying photograph of her marrying Howard. However horrifying it was to her, it must feel more than off-putting to Lance, even though she'd told him marriage between her and Howard was extremely unlikely.

But then her mood of utmost sadness inexplicably gave way to that of anger, and she asked herself how well did she know Lance, this bright yet perplexing man, this man who seemed so quietly studious, yet could become surprisingly animated and even boyish. This gentleman of supreme manners who was now treating her in such a rude and inconsiderate manner.

But her mood swung back again to that of despair because now she wondered whether Lance was really married after all. Was that why he'd kept their growing friendship secret from his mother and the other guests at Landsdowne's? Could this account for his almost curt response when she asked him about his wife? He'd used a tone so out of character with the way he usually spoke. Rose said he was peculiar and she'd ignored it, but maybe Rose was right. Even though she and Lance both felt they'd been friends for ages, the reality was that they had not. It was a mere few days. How could he invite her to spend the whole day together today, only to not show up now? How could she be so foolish? She might have now jeopardized her job and her already damaged relationship with Howard. She should have left everything alone and returned home the following day, as originally planned. She could still do this. In fact she probably would.

As Florence was experiencing these black thoughts, she noticed that Mrs. Landsdowne had just come out into the garden. She was wearing an immense pair of turquoise gardening gloves and was carrying a heavy looking, rusted garden shears, with which she immediately busied herself dead-heading the roses. She hadn't noticed Florence, which made her glad as she didn't want her wondering why she was lurking aimlessly around the flowerbeds, and what's more, she now had no interest in seeing the room she'd previously asked to move into on Thursday. She envied this woman, who seemed so contented, always occupying herself with practical matters.

Florence slipped away before she could be seen. She'd go for a walk now. Anywhere. Just to get away. She deeply regretted not having the boat ride that Rose had suggested. She took a path she had not walked along before, and was surprised that it soon became quite a steep ascent. There were fields of sheep on either side, and some sheep looked placidly at her through their liquid eyes. She continued to trudge up the path, the backs of her legs aching and her breath quickening. The sun shone down on her relentlessly and there was little shade. The air was surprisingly muggy.

She thought she might as well try to spot some birds, to gain some initial impressions before doing research from primary sources or local experts, but all was still and quiet. She remembered that first night talking to Lance about Time, and how they had talked so long that the birds had started energetically chirping their chorus to the newly approaching dawn, and how, amongst the birdsong, he picked out the sound of the lark. That thought saddened her now.

Ahead of her in the distance, in a quiet valley, lay a cluster of trees, and thinking that she would probably be able to find some birds there, she walked on towards them, the camera heavy over her shoulder and weighing her down. Still she walked, switching the camera to the other shoulder.

She expected that going downhill towards the trees would be easier, but that was not so. Finally entering the wooded area, sweating quite profusely, she had a thought that she could not rid herself of. *She needed to discard the camera.* Besides being much too heavy, it was dangerous and frightening. No, she could not do this! Yes, she could! What would it matter what Lance thought? She'd be leaving in the morning, anyway. Of that, she'd made up her mind. And if, by some remote possibility, she did decide to stay, then she could buy a disposable camera just as Howard had initially suggested. No! This camera was precious and unique; she couldn't discard it. Yes, she could.

She found herself wandering off the path, into an area of ferns and bracken. In the midst of this bright greenery was a rocky boulder, and she placed the camera down on it, wrapping the strap carefully around the camera case. Without a backward glance, she climbed back to the path, a stinging nettle hurting her ankle and a fly buzzing persistently around her head.

She continued to walk, expecting it to feel easier now she was not burdened down by the weight of the camera, but it did not. Instead she had a terrible feeling as of the ferns wrapping themselves around her chest, inhibiting her breathing. The path was going uphill again, and she could hardly make it to the summit. But she challenged herself to continue, convinced that once she reached the top, she'd feel better. But she did not. Her path now twisted downhill towards a smallish lake, and she followed it, loosening the buttons around the neck of the shirt she wore. Once on the lakeshore, she wished she had the camera with her, so that she could fling it into the water. She would have delighted in watching it sink to the deep floor of the lakebed.

She stood on a promontory above the lake and started to cry. And then it was as if she could see herself, standing there neither propped up nor supported by anything or anyone. A single silhouetted figure, despairing in her solitude, her confusion, her abandonment. Why had Lance let her down? Why had he done this, especially as he had seemed so excited by her presence, urging her on, showing her secrets he alone had cherished, conversing with her in such an original and intense way? Why had he not introduced her to his mother if he indeed liked her as much as his outward behavior to her implied? And why were events so strange? Normality grew bewildering, terrifying: that house, the photographs, that exciting yet completely obliterated conversation about Time.

Somewhere in the back of her mind, she registered that there were plenty of waterfowl on the lake; ducks, geese, a white gull, possibly a heron; and in the woods she heard the constant tweeting and chirping of birds and even the hammering of a woodpecker, but this hardly mattered now. It no longer interested her.

And now she was hugely afraid to be out here by this lake, all alone. The countryside, so luscious and exquisite when viewed with Lance, was now a hostile place. She turned away from the water and started to run. She must get back to Landsdowne's. She must return to the dependability of

Mrs. Landsdowne's gardening and scrubbed floors; to Rose and Allison's laborious games of Scrabble.

She could run no longer, though continued to walk as quickly as she could. Her ankle was itching and a series of small red dots indicated where the stinging nettle had made its mark, and she had scratches on her arms and legs. She rounded a bend, expecting to see the meadow of wild flowers and then Landsdowne's beyond, but what she saw was more glinting water of the lake. Or maybe it was another lake. Her agitation grew, mounting to panic. Should she retrace her steps, or keep going forward in the direction she thought it was?

She looked back. The path she had just taken now seemed too steep to climb back up, and too overgrown. It appeared dark, sunless. She stumbled on, aware now of her parched throat, the sweat making her hair stick to her forehead. Rivulets of perspiration coursed down her neck, and she kept tugging at the strangle-hold of her shirt, despite the fact that she had undone the top buttons. Swarms of gnats blurred her vision, whined in her ears, bit her burning skin. She thought she heard a sound behind her, as of a light shuffle of a shoe, but turning, she saw nothing. She was uncertain as to whether this fact increased her mounting consternation or was instead a relief.

She needed a drink badly, and she needed to rest. Her watch told her it was now 1.30 pm. But still she walked on. She felt a momentary spasm of hopefulness when she thought she saw a house through the trees, but as she walked towards it, the shifting perspective indicated that no house was there; it was just the shape and density of more trees.

She'd call Mrs. Landsdowne, that's what she'd do. She thought she remembered the number. She'd ask her to send out a rescue party, despite her embarrassment. But how could she explain where she was? Never mind; she'd describe the surrounding scenery; the size and shape of the lake, how it was steeply hilly and wooded. And Mrs. Landsdowne would recognize it and come and get her. It couldn't be too far by car. She thought all this while she was reaching for her phone. But when she took it out, she saw it had no signal. She kept swiveling it in different directions. She even walked back up a hill. But no. Nothing. It was clearly too remote and isolated and mountainous.

Feeling utterly defeated, she sat on a mossy carpet at the base of a tree, wishing she were at least near a stream so as to splash her heated face and scoop up handfuls of cool water to drink. She told herself she must have a short rest, but would get up soon and keep walking. Surely there must be a road somewhere close by, and she'd be able to find a car and hitch a lift. Perhaps it would be some kindly woman who knows Mrs. Landsdowne and sees her in church every Sunday. On the other hand, though, hitch hiking could be dangerous. She might be kidnapped and shipped off to China, spending the rest of her days stooped over in paddy fields. She was so thirsty. And terribly tired.

The dappled sunlight through the leaves overhead played with images behind her closing eyelids, and she touched the edges of sleep. There was a river and she needed to cross it, as Landsdowne's was just on the other side, but it was swift and deep flowing, and she knew she could not leap over it. So she followed it along its banks, trying to keep Landsdowne's in sight, but after she'd rounded a curve of the stream, she could no longer see the guesthouse. She did, however, see a low, hump-backed bridge, and though she had a feeling of hardly being able to move, she advanced towards it. But, just as she was about to cross it, a beautiful, shining stallion of chestnut color, noisily galloped over it towards her, foam splaying from its liquorice lips. Its movement – large, powerful, yet graceful – made her hastily retreat from the bridge and completely prevented her from crossing the stream.

She regained full consciousness, even thirstier now than before, fragments of that odd dream of the horse and the hump-backed bridge coiling in wispy bursts through her mind. She looked at her watch. It was already 7.15 pm! Had she slept that long? They would be sitting down for dinner now at Landsdowne's. Rose and Allison would wonder where she was, imagining perhaps that she took the later boat ride. Lance would not care, and would be calmly conversing with his mother. Mrs. Landsdowne would be annoyed that her husband's carefully prepared meal was going to get dried out, that it was going to go to waste. And the man with the pipe and his wife with the bouffant hairdo would be steadily chomping through their food, ready when half eaten, to exchange plates with their usual precision.

She groaned, and raised herself up on one arm. Just that small movement made her aware that her back felt very stiff. She forced herself to stand, to start walking. Keep walking. She was feeling distinctly chilly now. A bitterly cold wind had sprung up. She looked at her watch again. It was 5.42 pm. Which was it? 7.15 or 5.42? Time! Lance's face. That house. She forced herself to think of ordinary things; the smell of Mr. Landsdowne's cooking, Rose's opinionated remarks. Oh, how she needed to celebrate the mundane. But even the ordinary seemed extraordinary.

It hurt to swallow. She must find water, even if it was from the lake. She would turn back and find that lake. She felt pleased that she'd made a decision, as it gave her a direction. She walked steadily now, surprising herself at her heavy resignation and lack of panic. But mist was pouring into the valley, and in the approaching gloom, she tripped over a protruding tree root and fell, banging her face on some stones. She pushed herself upright, breathing fast, heart pounding, noticing that one of her finger nails was ripped off almost completely and the heals of her hands were badly grazed. She uncertainly explored her face with her hands, and felt the wetness of blood. Despite this revulsion at the thought of her injuries, she felt no physical pain.

Some way off, she heard a dog barking angrily, snarling. She was afraid. She listened again, but the barking stopped. There was nothing. She glanced at her watch. 10.15 pm! Now there was complete silence. But no, there wasn't silence. She realized that for some time she had been hearing a very faint series of electronic beeps. Utterly incongruous in this wooded setting. She listened more closely, straining her ears. There it was again; faint but distinctly there. She tried moving towards it, though she found it hard to locate sound. But why try? What relevance did it have, anyway? Still she tried. And then she caught sight of something like a dark smudge in the denser gloom beyond the path. It was her camera! And the beeping, she realized, was indicating to her that the batteries of the light meter were getting flat!

It was incredible. She couldn't believe that she found her camera in this virtual wilderness of open space. And not since she was a young child, finding after a long and seemingly fruitless search for her panda bear, limp and floppy from a depletion of its stuffing because of being hugged so much, had she felt so happy to be reunited with an inanimate object.

Clearly this camera was not meant to have been abandoned, as it must contain some deep significance. And not only that. Also it laid out to her the way back to the guesthouse, as she remembered where she had cast it off. It was not so very far away.

The weight of the camera around her neck nearly brought her to her knees, but she trudged on in the direction she thought it was, even though the mist swirled mercilessly and obscured her vision, and the light was dim – a sort of woolly white and grey. She again felt frightened that she had strayed from the true direction. She imagined a column written about her in next day's local newspaper; "Young woman, thought to be from London, found dead close to Lake -. Authorities say..."

After a while, her tread changed, no longer a stony path but something softer and bouncy, which she could only assume was grass. She made out vague lights in the distance, and then was certain, to her supreme relief, that this must be Landsdowne's ahead as its high Edwardian shape seemed to flutteringly float towards her out of the fog. Now she knew she was in the meadow of wild flowers in front of the house.

The front door, when she reached it, was inexplicably locked – either that, or she didn't have the strength to push it as it felt so heavy - and so she banged on it several times. It was opened by someone she did not recognize, and an American voice called out, "There's a young guy – no, excuse me, it's a lady at the door! And Jesus; she looks real hurt!" For a moment, Florence was confused as to whether this was Landsdowne's after all, but then Rose's inquisitive face appeared behind the American, accompanied by a shriek. Other people now gathered around the front door, and then she felt a gentle arm around her waist, and saw that it was Allison guiding her in.

Images flashed through her mind: Rose is sitting on a high-backed chair in the hall, covering her eyes and emitting shrill little cries; the door to the dining room is open a chink and as she passes it she sees Lance half rising from the table at which he sits with his mother, the serviette dropping from his lap and his face full of alarm. And now a turn in the stairs; the polished rich brown banister. A babble of excited American voices behind her. Red carpeted stairs, some with gold anchors. Someone inserting a key into a keyhole. Her room. The light is switched on and the window shut.

The white candlewick bedspread pulled down. Her head against the soft pillow. A shiny silver bowl. A pale green flannel dipped in and out of the bowl. A smell of Dettol. Dabbing at her face. It hurts. Dabbing again. She opens her eyes to ask Allison to stop. It's not Allison, but Mrs. Landsdowne. She shuts her eyes, only to open them again as a plastic cup is put to her lips. Desperate thirst just remembered. Trying to swallow. It hurts. Liquid dribbles down her chin. She tries to apologize but thinks quite possibly it comes out only as a groan. Wants the cup again. Must drink more. But no one offers it to her. Can't quite get the energy to speak. Opens her eyes. The light seems to have changed. Sunlight streams through the window. Someone is talking. She can't remember where she is. Oh yes, Landsdowne's guesthouse. She slowly turns her head towards the speaker. Not Mrs. Landsdowne, but a new face she has not seen before. Checking her pulse against a stopwatch. A straw inserted between her lips and she sucks. Too hard to keep her eyes open. A woman in a black tailored suit and stiletto heels, crawling on the ceiling, her red lips smiling beckoningly. A bee flying in through the open window, stinging her face. Can't move her arm to brush it off as her pulse rate still being measured.

Someone is calling her name, and with an effort she opens her eyes. Howard. He's sitting by the light so it's hard to see his face. Footsteps in the corridor and American voices. Howard not there. A giant stopwatch. 7.52. Tick tock. Tick tock. Loudly. A man with a grey moustache walking the length of the underground tube platform. His steps. Tick tock. The station clock reading 11.14. No train. No train. No train! Voices on the escalator, crowding on to the platform. American voices. Rush hour. White steam. Someone putting a coin in the vending machine. It clatters hollowly. A bar of chocolate thuds to the window and is plucked out by a hand wearing a thick turquoise gardening glove. The train clatters into the station, with an explosion of hot, dry air and dust. Lance gets off the train and walks towards her. He holds up the stopwatch. 11.47. The train departs and the platform clears of people. It was the wrong train. She stands alone on the deserted platform. Tick tock. Tick tock. Howard is speaking. She opens her eyes. It's daylight, but heavy rain is falling.

"You're looking bloody awful, Flo," he said. "And you've been sleeping for ages. Can't you stay awake now! I've driven all this way to see you,

you know, and if you ask me, you're bloody lucky that I have." She tries to nod her head. It hurts. Dark. Light. The camera clicking violently as a photograph is snapped. A burst of light from the flash. Someone forcing each of her eyes open and peering into them with a blinding spotlight. A man with a gray mustache. The same man as was walking along the station platform.

"Hello! I'm Dr. Briggs. So glad you're awake." But she wasn't awake. Let me sleep more, she thinks. "You've been mostly asleep for the last two days. Best thing for you!"

She's amazed. Two days!

"The body knows what to do," he continued cheerily. "And the body is remarkably resilient. It looks as though you went through a lot. Lost out there, were you?"

"Yes," she whispered.

"Had no map on you? Now that's a serious mistake. Of course, you never should have ventured out alone, without telling anyone where you were going." His tone was much more serious now. "And it seems you had no provisions either. No drink. No raisins, or other high-energy foods. You're lucky to have found your way back."

"Yes," she repeated.

"You're to stay in bed and drink plenty of fluids. Understand?"

She tried to nod, but he didn't seem to notice or care

"I'm going to bring your fiancé into the room, so you can both hear what I'm going to say."

Her fiancé? Yes, she vaguely remembered that Howard was here. But why was he telling everyone they were engaged? A click of the door, and he joined them in the room.

"She has a serious case of an illness with symptoms which manifest themselves very much like the flu," Dr. Briggs was telling him. "And if you ask me, it's lucky that that's all she has."

"What about the cuts and bruises she has?" Howard asked.

"They don't impress me. Nothing serious there. Just keep applying the Dettol, or some antiseptic ointment to the cuts until they're less inflamed, and Witch Hazel to the bruises. And that finger nail will grow back in time."

Florence lay there, eyes flicking open and shut, feeling as though they were talking about someone else.

"She was, however, seriously dehydrated and she still has an elevated fever. It's going to take a while, I'm afraid, until she's herself again. She's going to need a lot of rest. Does she work?"

"Yes, she writes for a magazine."

"And I suppose that keeps her out and about a bit, does it?"

"Yes, I like what I do," Florence managed to mumble.

"Well, you're not going to be going back to work for at least ten days. Maybe more. In my experience, this type of flu-like illness can be cyclic, and just as you feel you've recovered, you could feel under the weather again. You can't ignore this. Plenty of rest is what you'll need."

"I understand, Dr. Briggs. I'll take her home, and she'll be able to rest there. I'll look after her. I'll take time off work. I'm an expert chef, and I'm very competent at all other household chores."

This was Howard, who never took time off work. Never cooked. Expected his meals prepared for him, and his house clean and tidy for him. So was this a brave statement, or was it merely brazen? Florence turned her hot face to the beige wall, examining the pattern made by a long, jagged crack in the plaster.

"Very good. I must insist, though, that my patient stays here for another three to four days. I think she's too weak to travel now, and I want to keep her under observation. I want to make sure there are no complications, you understand."

"Certainly, doctor. In that case, I'll go home and get some work done, so as to free up some time when she returns. I'll be back in three days."

Dr. Briggs had left the room, and Florence realized Howard was saying this to her alone. "Thanks," she said, the heavy, dozy feeling again overwhelming her. "It was kind of you to come."

"Glad you think so. But we'd arranged that I'd come when you phoned to say you were extending your trip. Or don't you remember?"

"Oh yes, that's true," she said weakly, her protestations about his coming having been redundant.

"Yes; but given the fact that you've been asleep for the whole bloody time I've been here, I could have saved myself the trouble. True I've befriended some of the old biddies downstairs in the lounge area. Very nice ladies, especially Rose. But hardly worth the long drive."

"I'm sorry, Howard."

"Well honestly, Flo, let's face it; you *were* idiotic to have gone wandering off without telling anyone and without taking a map. Whatever were you thinking?"

"Yes, it was silly of me. I didn't mean to go so far."

"Really rather selfish, wasn't it! After all, I came all the way here for nothing, and you worried a lot of people, and have created a great deal of extra work for everyone."

She felt herself grow burningly hot, and she tried to heave her body into a new position. "You're right," she mumbled. "And I'm terribly sorry. I'll make my own way home as soon as the doctor releases me, if you prefer."

"What, and make yourself even more ill? That's rubbish. I'll be back in three days. So, see you then, Flo. I won't kiss you now, as I don't want to catch anything."

Feeling troubled by this conversation, Florence drifted in and out of sleep, but must have eventually drifted off into a deeper, more healing slumber. She awoke later to a tray of breakfast food, and felt more alert. Allison was pouring out some tea for her, and offering her buttered toast.

"Would you care for some marmalade on it?" Allison asked.

"Yes, please," Florence replied, thinking how delicious that sounded. "Thanks. You're so good to me."

"Think nothing of it! You had us all quite scared when you didn't come in for dinner that night. And then when you did come, and you looked so terribly wounded and unwell - well, I can tell you; Rose went quite hysterical. It was well into the night before she would calm down."

"I'm sorry."

"And Mrs. Landsdowne was quite out of her depth with a noisy crowd of Americans – thank goodness they've left now - who kept asking if the 'veggies' were organic, if the milk was fat free, and if the pudding was made with saccharine and instant cake mix," Allison recalled, rolling her eyes. "I get the feeling that Mr. Landsdowne had never been so insulted in his life! Well! After all, we know what delicious food he makes."

Florence chuckled.

"So there we were that night, with those Americans taking up all the room in the dining room, it seemed, and Rose and I squeezed into one corner, and Dr. and Mrs. Ramsey in another corner, when a very odd thing happened," Allison said, pulling out a pink lacy handkerchief from her sleeve.

"What?" Florence asked, more alert now at the mention of Lance's name.

"Dr. Ramsey stood up and came over to our table, and said in a worried sounding voice, 'Has Florence left? I was going to take her to the boat ride today, but couldn't find her anywhere.' Well, as you can imagine, that was when Rose and I grew really concerned, because up until then, we thought you'd be down to the dining room at any moment, and told him so."

Florence gasped, but luckily the sound of her gasp was masked by Allison who made an elaborate business of blowing her nose into the handkerchief.

"Yes," Allison continued, slowly poking the pink handkerchief back up her sleeve again. "Dr. Ramsey then asked me if I would be so good as to go up to your room when I'd finished dinner, and see if you were there. And of course, that was what I was going to do. But then, just as I was having the spotted dick – which is my very favorite of all Mr. Landsdowne's desserts, you know - we heard the ring of the doorbell, and given the commotion in the hall, Rose and I ran to see what was happening. Poor you! What a sight you were."

Florence rolled over to face the wall, hardly believing that Lance would have been concerned as to where she was.

"Oh, and that reminds me," Allison continued. "Later that evening Dr. Ramsey asked me to give you a letter he'd written to you. I kept forgetting about it, and you were asleep anyway," Allison said, digging slowly through her handbag. "Yes, here it is. He's such a polite man. I think he wrote to wish you better."

Florence turned back immediately, looking at Allison expectantly. Allison handed over a gray envelope with Florence's name written in Lance's easily recognizable royal blue squarish script. She wanted to open it immediately, but of course had to wait until Allison left the room. Her buttered toast with marmalade no longer interested her, and Allison, who had always been so quiet before, seemed not to want to stop talking, which made Florence long for her former timidity. When Florence could stand waiting no longer, she declared herself a little sleepy, to which Allison, meek and apologetic once more, said she did look a little flushed and she hoped she had not overstayed her welcome or tired her.

As Allison opened the door to leave the room, a sudden cross draft from the open window caused Lance's letter to flutter off the bed where it was perched, and glide to the floor. Florence tried to lean out of bed to reach it, but this made her exceedingly dizzy. She leant back against her pillows, almost crying out with a frustration that was heightened by the fact that Allison had not given her this letter before now.

With an effort, she pushed the blankets off her, and rose from the bed. She felt peculiarly light headed and disorientated, and feared she might faint. Stooping down to pick up the letter made her feel even worse, and the top of her back between her shoulders ached horribly. She gratefully slumped back on the bed, sweating profusely.

She had to wait for the room to stop sliding sideways as if she were on a ship, before she could focus on tearing open the envelope. But her impatience to read it made her heart race, and she forced herself to slit the envelope and take out Lance's letter. It covered several pages. Sweat poured down between her breasts and from underneath her arms. It also beaded her forehead and then dripped down into her eyes, and she had to blink several times to stop the stinging and focus on his words. And this is what she read:

*Florence,*

*Many times this evening I started composing a letter to you, and ridiculously found myself unequal to the task. I simply don't know how to express what is in my mind. When I saw you pass the dining room door, it was a confirmation of everything I dreaded. But wait, I'm ahead of myself. When you were not in the dining room for dinner, and instead a group of Americans were tormenting me with their loudness, I felt mortified. I thought perhaps you had decided to leave after all – in fact one day early - with no contact address and no way for me to get in touch with you again. But even that eventuality, I thought, would not be as bad as the other more shocking possibility, that you were lost or hurt.*

*But wait, I must reach yet further back. This morning I was to meet you by the garden wall at 9.30. But then, while having breakfast, I received a reminder from my sister, Juliet, that I had to take my mother to her doctor's appointment some distance away in Cockermouth. Frankly, I had become so absorbed with you that this had completely slipped my mind. But once remembered, Mother and I had to hurry through breakfast and leave immediately. Naturally I hoped I would find you before we left, but I could not see you anywhere. But I did ask Mrs. Landsdowne to meet you outside by the stone wall, at the appointed time and explain the situation. And I told her, too, to tell you that I could meet you instead this afternoon and take you to the boat ride. I thought it was 'safe' to tell her this, since dear old Rose had made such a public announcement of this in the dining room last night.*

*But when we returned from the doctor and I asked Mrs. Landsdowne if she had delivered the message to you – and I was so looking forward to spending the afternoon with you – she said she had not seen you, and how she had even stayed outside longer, clipping the roses, in the hopes that you would appear. (She did, apparently, cut a nice bunch of roses to bring inside and put in a vase on the hall table, but when she showed them to me, all I could see were the thorns.) I complimented her speedily on the roses, and dashed outside in the hope you might be there, but how could you be? It was already close to 2.15 by then.*

*And now I hear from Dr. Briggs, who is a good chap and has attended to my mother on occasion, that you are very ill. I am sitting on the window seat alone, thinking of the quiet, lovely lady who was fiddling with her camera, not wanting to disturb me, yet in need of some assistance. And I'm thinking, too, of the extraordinary friendship that blossomed between us from that moment onwards, and how we'd often share this window seat and talk! What a very great deal we always have to talk about!*

*So now our mutual friend and source of intrigue, Time itself, feels to me, ironically enough, somewhat of an enemy. Its insistence on precision is unrelenting, as when I made an error in scheduling this morning. Furthermore, I realize, that one of the things that I believe we didn't mention when we spoke of Time (funny that I only remember what we did not say about Time, and not what we did say) is that for it to be meaningful, there must be knowledge and awareness. But I have neither now, in terms of how you are. All I have is the horror of the image of you passing the dining room door, so terribly hurt and unwell. Beyond that, nothing. And this is appallingly burdensome. Of course there is, too, the added fact that Time is hastening forward towards the point of your departure, if you are indeed still here...Oh yes, Time no longer feels such a friend to me.*

*Please Florence, give me some sign as to how you are, or if I might visit you, even though common decorum dictates that it would be improper for me to enter your room if you are in bed. Please let me know what I might do. But if you don't wish to see me, or if we run out of time, then I must accept my punishment, and thank you for what was a startlingly unexpected and exceptionally brief interlude of inspirational friendship. I'm truly so sorry, Florence, for not being at the stone wall this morning, and for all the atrocious things that I can only guess happened to you as a consequence.*

*Always (said deliberately, with great consideration of the implications of Time) – your friend, Lance*

So, he had written – and such a lovely letter too. How good it felt to understand now why Lance had not met her that morning by the stone wall. What a silly fool she'd been to walk off so impulsively, so distrustfully, and cause so much trouble. What a shame, too, that she'd deliberately avoided Mrs. Landsdowne, whose message she did not then know, but had she heard it, everything would have worked out so differently. She must tell him this. He might be thinking that since she hadn't responded all this time, that she was exceptionally angry with him. In fact, he must have seen Howard, and so might have now expected to be shut out completely, especially if Howard was telling everyone that they were engaged.

But then an even worse thought struck her forcibly. What if Lance was no longer here? What if his visit with his mother was over? She must ask someone. But there was no phone in the room, and she had already proved herself incapable of getting out of bed. She tried to call out, hoping someone would hear her, but no one did. She grew increasingly agitated, at the same time being aware that this was not good in terms of her recovery. Suddenly she profoundly hated Allison for not waking her and giving her the letter all this time. But no, that was ridiculous. And in any case, Howard was here.

But even though she could not hate Allison, panic ripped through her at the thought that perhaps Lance had left the guesthouse. He'd asked in his letter for a sign from her, but she'd given him nothing! And now it might never be possible to explain. How she wanted to talk to him, to tell him she didn't blame him at all! And what's more, she wanted to tell him about the incredible incident with the camera; how it had, in a way, rescued her. She saw it now on her dressing table, inexplicably out of its case and with its lens cap off, staring at her as if through a blind eye. She wanted to replace the lens cap. She wanted to recharge the batteries. She wanted to use the camera again, extensively and without limit. And she wanted Lance.

After much agitated tossing and getting entangled with the bed linen, she slipped into a fitful doze. She was shuffling in slippered feet down the corridor, trying to call out. And then Mrs. Landsdowne was in front of her, which startled her so much that she stumbled backwards, knocking over a vase of roses. She saw her camera lens pointing right at her, not blindly now, but accusingly. And behind the camera was Lance. There was a loud snap and a blinding flash as he took the photograph.

She whimpered, and woke to realize that her door had just banged shut and the overhead light switched on. Mrs. Landsdowne stood surveying her, and then said, "You've eaten practically nothing for several days. And the doctor said it's important that you have a lot of liquids. So Mr. Landsdowne made some of his special oxtail soup. I remember you liking it the first day you arrived. Here, we put it in a cup for you as it's easier to drink it that way."

"Thank you, Mrs. Landsdowne. That was very kind of both of you. Was it Dr. Ramsey who recommended liquids?" she asked, pretending to be naïve but thinking it was a good way of finding out if Lance was still here.

"Oh no, dear! It was Dr. Briggs, the one that's treating you," Mrs. Landsdowne replied as she set the cup of soup beside Florence on the bedside table.

"Oh, I see. But the other doctor, Dr. Ramsey; is he still here?"

"Well now, as I understand it, he's not a medical doctor but one of those clever types at the university."

"Oh. But is he still here?"

Mrs. Landsdowne eyed her shrewdly, and then putting the empty tray sideways under her arm said, "Well now, dear; I can't be giving out information about the other guests. You do understand, I'm sure. Not unless they send you a message, or give me permission." And with that she started heading towards the door. "Now have your soup while it's still nice and warm."

"Wait, please, Mrs. Landsdowne!" Florence cried. "I did in fact receive a note from Lance – I mean, Dr. Ramsey. Allison just gave it to me. Look! Here it is!" she said, pulling it out from where she had placed it under her pillow. Seeing Mrs. Landsdowne's surprise, she added, "He was kind enough to write to wish me better."

"Well, that's very nice, I'm sure," Mrs. Landsdowne said, shifting the tray to her hip.

"So is he still here? I know that he wrote two days ago, so I'd just like to write back to thank him, and to apologize for not being there when he was kindly going to take me to the boat ride."

"Oh, I'm sure you don't need to apologize, dear. I'm sure he understands."

"So he *is* still here?"

"Well now, dear; I didn't exactly say those words. I just said I'm sure he would understand. So no need to trouble yourself with writing anything."

"Yes, but I would like to all the same."

"Well, it's nice to see young people being so polite with each other these days," Mrs. Landsdowne sighed, handing Florence, at her request, some Guest House stationery and a pen from off the bureau. Florence scribbled a quick note, her writing seeming very jerky and uncertain, even to herself, telling him she had only just read his letter and would be delighted if he could come up to visit her. Then she settled back against the pillows, sipping the soup, which tasted very good indeed.

# FIVE

*SHE WAS PROPPED UP IN BED*, smiling, and drinking some cool orange juice, golden sunshine pouring in through the window. The previous evening had initially been filled with amazing excitement that Lance would be up to see her at any moment, but this gradually gave way to a terrible anxiety as the evening stretched on without him coming. During what seemed to be a long and agonized night, she was pierced with the thought that she'd never see him again; that Mrs. Landsdowne wouldn't give him her note, or that he'd left the Guest House, or that he had no interest in seeing her because of Howard being there. But now it was a beautiful morning, and Lance was standing shyly at the door, smiling and holding a bunch of wild flowers that he must have just picked, as they still shimmered with droplets of dew.

"We're more night-time friends than morning friends," he said. "But when Mrs. Landsdowne gave me your note with breakfast just now, I couldn't wait until tonight!"

Oh! So he'd only just received her note, and then come straight away. She could have spared herself all that anxiety during the long night hours.

She said simply, "Thank you, Lance! It's so nice to see you. And what lovely flowers! How kind."

He smiled again, and walking over to the sink and taking a glass, he said, "I'll pop them into this glass, if I may," and ran some water into it.

"I would've responded to your kind letter sooner, only I've apparently been asleep," she said.

"I'm so sorry you're ill," he said, seating himself in the armchair across the room from her bed. "How are you feeling now?"

"Actually, I'm starting to feel much better, thanks. But your mother; how is she?"

"My mother? She's fine, thank you. Why do you ask?"

"I wondered, as you said you had to take her very suddenly to the doctor."

"Oh that! No, that was just a routine checkup. That's why it had slipped my mind when I'd asked you if we could meet that morning. Luckily, Juliet apprised me of my obligations by an early morning phone call."

"Who's Juliet?" she asked, pretending once again to be naïve.

"Juliet's my sister. We share the responsibility of looking after our mother, although obviously she does a better job of it than I do."

There! She had her confirmation. Lance was not married, and she should not have doubted him about this, or about anything else, for that matter.

"I wouldn't say that! It seems that you're a wonderfully attentive son," she said.

"Thanks." He smiled, and then continued by saying, "So, it seems you took yourself for quite a walk!"

"Yes; it was foolish of me to have wandered off like that, though I never expected to get lost. I hadn't intended going so far, only I was looking for birds."

"Looking for birds? Are you an ornithologist in addition to all your other qualifications?"

"Not at all. Actually, my boss, Elizabeth Carlisle, asked me to do a story on them, when I phoned her to request extending my stay here."

"I see! As a matter of fact, that should make quite an interesting story, as there are many species of birds around here. Do you happen to know about how the osprey come to this region to nest every spring and stay until autumn, when they then migrate to Africa?"

"No; I didn't know that."

"Well, that's all I know about them, but I thought I'd mention it," he said with a short laugh.

"I appreciate it. Actually, I'm afraid I probably wouldn't recognize an osprey if I saw one. But thanks for the information. I'll be sure to cite you in my article."

At the thought of all the work that would be entailed in writing the article, her head started to hurt intensely, and she momentarily closed her eyes with an involuntary moan.

"Are you all right?" he asked.

"Yes, sorry; I'm fine again now."

"But the conversation is tiring you. I should leave."

"No! Don't go yet. I'm enjoying talking with you."

He smiled gently. "What a shame it was that I couldn't find you that morning, to tell you about the change in plans. I thought perhaps you were sleeping late. I went and stood outside this very door, poised ready to knock, but I thought better of it. I wish I hadn't been so hesitant."

"No, actually, you wouldn't have found me. I woke unusually early that morning, and was downstairs soon after 6.00!"

"Goodness! That is early! Mrs. Landsdowne must've found you entirely perplexing, what with being the last in the dining room for breakfast one morning, skipping it entirely another morning, and then being such an early riser that day. Was breakfast ready at such an early hour?"

"Well, Mr. and Mrs. Landsdowne were very kind to me, and warmed up some quiche from the day before. And after it I walked around outside for a bit, and then phoned both Elizabeth Carlisle and Howard, to tell them I was staying here longer than originally planned."

"And now you're staying longer, not for fun reasons, but because you're ill. Florence, I'm so sorry about all that happened. You must have been terrified being lost like that. Thank God you made it back here!"

It was then that she told him about the camera; how she had indeed been terrified and had no idea which way would lead back to Landsdowne's.

But then how, in the midst of her despair, she'd heard some faint beeps and discovered it was her camera.

"That's amazing! What a story!" Lance said. "You mean you'd literally discarded it without any attention as to where that was! And then you found it again. It could've been anywhere out there! Even finding a needle in a haystack seems more likely than that, given the vastness of the countryside."

"Yes, it was incredible. And I felt so grateful. I think I probably kissed it!"

"Florence, we've thought this before, but I feel it even more now. There is something very special about your camera. It's unfathomable, but there it is. It saved you! It brought you back here! Thank God."

"Yes, it did."

"Actually, I'd like to use your camera right now, if I may, to take your picture. If you don't mind me saying, you're looking very pretty."

She did not mind. It was better than being told she looked "bloody awful" as Howard had said, even if she knew that, with her unwashed hair, scratches and scabs on her face, and fever flushed complexion, Howard's description was probably the more accurate of the two.

"Thank you."

"How much longer will you be staying here now, Florence?"

"Actually, Howard is returning the day after tomorrow to bring me back home."

Lance spontaneously clapped his hands over his eyes. She was astonished by his uncensored display of emotion.

"He wanted to take me back with him when he left," she continued, "But Dr. Briggs advised against it, and thought I should stay a little longer."

"I'm glad he said that."

"Me, too!"

"Well," Lance said, recovering himself, and rising from the chair. "I think I'll take your photo now." He pointed the camera at her, and snapped. It reminded her of her dream, when the snap of the camera had sounded accusing. Seeing nothing temporarily because of the blinding light of the flash, she turned to face the familiar long crack in the plaster of the beige wall, and stared at it until she could once again see it quite clearly.

"Lance, I don't want to go. I hadn't wanted to leave before, and now I want it even less," she whispered into her pillow.

He approached the bed, and she turned to him. They hugged each other firmly. Then he pulled up the little round stool from the dressing table and placed it alongside the bed, and held her hand.

"But I can't stay here any longer," she continued. "Everyone's been so kind to me, but I have to leave."

"I know," he murmured.

"Lance, you shouldn't be so close, really. I don't want you to catch anything."

"It's OK," he said. "I'll be fine."

They sat quietly for a few moments. Then Lance remarked, "I saw Howard, you know. Overheard his conversation with the inquisitive Rose. He seems like a good man."

But Howard's a sociopath, Florence thought. She could well imagine how he could so smoothly put on an act to charm everyone staying at Landsdowne's. Should she tell Lance what he was really like? But would this make her seem nasty and unappreciative in Lance's eyes? On the other hand, maybe Lance could see Howard's true nature for himself. After all, he was so perceptive and intelligent. And there again, maybe Lance was taken in by Howard, too, and found him a decent fellow. Perhaps he said Howard was a good man to comfort her about returning. It was generous of him, but it would not do. "I'm too confused, Lance, to comment on that," she said.

"And yet that photo – the one of you as his bride-"

"Don't! I don't want to be afraid of the camera again!"

"You can't be afraid. It saved your life."

"Look, Lance. This might be madness, but I assume you're going out today. So can you please take the camera with you, and use up the film?"

"Of course I'll be glad to use up the film. But what I can't agree to is going out today. We have so little time left together. I'll devote this film to pictures of you, and if you become tired of that, I'll take pictures from your window. You have a lovely view."

"And I'll take some photos of you, too!"

"If you wish."

"Yes, yes! Assuming it comes out, I want to look at your picture every day, Lance. We will stay in touch, won't we?"

"Just being out of touch over these last days caused me to experience such misery. Of course we'll be in touch. And now," he said, jumping up, "I'll take more pictures! And if you need a little snooze later today, I'll go to the village then to develop this film. Tell you what, I'll pop into the teashop while I'm there, and bring us back some buns!"

They took pictures of each other, and as they did so, they started to laugh. Florence completely forgot the stiffness in her back, or the general ache of her limbs. They made funny faces at the camera, and in one picture, Lance balanced the camera on the bureau and set the time release, running to the bed so that they could have a photo of themselves together.

She wished it was not happening, but she was growing sleepy. She tried to fight it off, but Lance knew. He rose softly, and taking one of her hands, brushed it with his lips, and then headed quietly to the door. She closed her eyes, warm and happy, and slept deeply and without dreaming.

When she awoke later he was just reentering the room. She felt as though she had been asleep a long time. He approached the bed, bringing with him the scent of the cold, fresh air of outdoors. He was carrying a white paper bag, from which he offered her a bun. It tasted divine.

"I also picked up the photos," he said.

"How did they come out?"

"I haven't looked at them yet. I wanted us to look together."

He took a thick green and white envelope out from his jacket pocket, and pulled it open. She was just biting into the bun when he called out, "Oh!" She looked at him directly.

"What is it?"

"It's happening again. Maybe you shouldn't see these pictures, Florence," he said, quickly scanning them. "I don't know what else we'll find in here. Let's wait until you have your strength back. Actually, let's just chuck the whole lot away. "

"Why? What are they? Please show me!"

"Florence, when we started out on this strange adventure, you were well and strong. I felt then that whatever this was about, and however frightening it might be, we were on to something extraordinary and could research this together. But now I've changed my mind. You'd wanted to stop taking pictures with this strange camera, yet I had urged you on. It turns out, though, that your instincts were correct. Let's forget this whole thing."

"What are you talking about? Let me see the pictures, Lance!"

"No, I'd rather not."

"Come on, Lance!" Florence said, growing hot and agitated.

"I wish to God I'd looked at them first. How foolish of me."

"It wouldn't have made any difference. I would've known something was odd if you hadn't shown them to me. And you couldn't have lied to me about them. One of the things I like so much about you is your integrity. Now please show them to me!"

"Very well."

He looked at each picture solemnly and then handed one at a time to her. There, amongst some fairly decent pictures of each of them in her room, and a lovely one of the view outside her window with the meadow with the wild flowers beyond, was a picture of Lance, on a stage shaking hands with a large man wearing a Royal blue blazer with gold buttons. He was beaming. Another showed him boarding a plane. There was also a photo of Big Ben, its clock face obscured by the hurried flight of a pigeon. And another photo showed Florence seated on a sofa reading a book.

"Hey, Florence!" Lance exclaimed, taking that picture back from her. "Do you recognize where this is! That looks like the sofa in that house! 'Fern View.' Remember when we peeped through the windows? I could swear it's there. I recognize the fireplace!"

"Oh, I sincerely doubt that. Peering through the windows was trespassing enough for me! I doubt I'd go inside. But what do you make of this one of you on the stage? It looks as though you might be winning an award!"

"Florence, I don't know. But I'm feeling that we have no right to dabble in things we don't understand."

"But Lance, this is so exciting!" she replied, secretly harboring such relief that there were no more photos of her as Howard's bride. "Maybe these pictures are out of order. Maybe this picture of you boarding a flight comes first, and is because you won the Nobel Prize, and you're on your way to Sweden for the award! And then next is the photo of the man shaking your hand, presenting you with your prize!"

"You flatter me! But I sincerely doubt that's ever in my future. Look Florence, it's true that we're both fascinated with trying to understand the meaning of Time, but this-"

"But don't you see, Lance, that this is phenomenal. Everything is. The way we met and immediately started talking about Time, as if Time had placed us together for years before we had consciously met. It's something very special between us." She sat higher up in bed.

"Yes, undoubtedly," he said. Then he rose and walked to the window. "But," he continued, "I'm now thinking that this strange camera use should be stopped at once."

"No, Lance! We've only got a day left. Please take this camera and use it tomorrow. I discovered that I have one more film. It's in the top bureau drawer. Go out with the camera somewhere, and use up that film!"

He looked at her pleading face for a while. Then sighing he said, "All right! Against my better judgment, though!"

The following day, Florence's last full day at Landsdowne's, appeared to be bright and mild, so she, immensely tired of being confined to her room staring at the crack in the plaster, or trying to read that novel which now could not hold her attention, put on a warm jumper and made her way downstairs. She felt a little unsteady, but she didn't want that to stop her. She'd made up her mind to sit on the verandah for a while.

She was so delighted to be outdoors, rocking backwards and forwards on a nice white wicker rocking chair, and breathing in the sweet, fresh air. As she looked out into the sunny meadow she saw Lance striding across it, and in at the gate of the stone wall, a bunch of wild flowers in his hand, and her camera slung over his shoulder.

As he walked up the path to the Guest House, he saw her sitting there and broke into a trot, and then leaped up the steps to the verandah, two at a time, the camera banging against his hip. "Hello! I didn't expect to see you sitting here! You must be feeling so much better. That's terrific," he said.

"I am! It's lovely outside."

"Here, these are for you, Fleur," he said, handing her the pink, white and light purple flowers.

"Thank you! They're so gorgeous. Actually, what did you just call me?"

"I called you 'Fleur.' The flowers. Your name. I just combined them. It seems to suit you. I can call you that, can't I?"

She nodded, her nose in the flowers, breathing in their fragrance. "It's a beautiful name, Lance," she said, looking at him over the tops of the petals. "No one has ever called me that before."

He smiled down on her. "I went for a short walk and used up the film, though now I wish I had some left to take of you holding those flowers!"

"Thanks for doing that, Lance. I know you hadn't wanted to take more photos with my camera."

"Actually this morning I found that I agree with you about continuing to use this odd camera. Who knows what we'll find? It's too intriguing to set aside. Hey Fleur, if you're feeling up to it, let's go out! We can have lunch in the nice pub we'd gone to that evening before we'd returned to see that house, Fern View. And also we can get the film developed. What do you say? Are you well enough to venture out?"

She nodded. "Yes, I'd love to do that," she said.

"That's terrific! Well, I'll just nip inside and put these flowers in water. And I'll inform Mrs. Landsdowne that you won't be needing any lunch here today."

"Thanks! And tell her I'll be down for dinner tonight, too, rather than eating it in my room!"

"You will, Fleur?" He looked pleased, and then in an instant was inside the house, the front door clicking behind him.

'Fleur.' The name, though she immediately loved it, felt strange to her, and would take getting used to. He called her that many times on their drive to the village, as if he could sense that saying it frequently would help her to feel used to it more quickly.

Being in the little green Fiat together felt exhilarating. Lance shifted into fifth gear and they sped along the country roads. They had the windows down, and the warm wind playfully whipped through the spikiness of her hair. She looked hard at the green hills, and shimmering bodies of water, knowing this was for the last time. She had been painfully lost out there, full of panic and helplessness, and the landscape had seemed like a hostile place. Now, in the serenity of Lance's company, that episode seemed so far removed from her.

"How are you feeling?" he called to her, over the roar of the wind.

"Marvelous!" she replied.

He smiled, and placed a hand on her thigh.

Soon he pulled up to a parking space in the high street of Portinscale, and ran in to the Post Office to take the film to be developed. Florence reclined in her seat, letting the warm sunshine wash over her. She felt so radiantly happy. Then Lance was back in the car, and they drove the short distance to the pub. Once inside, they each ordered a Ploughman's lunch, and it had never tasted so delicious before. The slab of golden cheese was nutty and bold, and the French bread crusty with a soft, white chewy center.

After lunch they drove through the countryside, for a final scenic tour, and then picked up the developed film on their way back to Landsdowne's. Florence was feeling quite tired by then, so she rested in her room before dinner.

Entering the dining room later, to the sound of the dinner gong, Florence thought things looked subtly different, as if she'd been away for a long time, rather than just a matter of days. It could be that she was feeling slightly feverish again. The tables seemed to be in a slightly changed position, the tablecloths of a different color, and Rose, who waved emphatically, motioning her to join them, also appeared not as she was before.

"Well, my dear; how lovely to see you back down here again! Feeling quite better, are we?"

"Yes, thank you, Rose! I am so much better now, thank you."

"That's nice. We were all so worried about you, weren't we, Allison!"

Allison nodded, and then carefully spooned some tomato soup into her mouth.

"It seems that I've been upstairs for such a long time. It's good to come down and join you, again. You both look very well."

"Oh yes, my dear. I spent the day at the hairdresser in some very remote town, miles from here. Do you remember that man who was here, who kept smoking that ghastly pipe? Well, I so admired his wife's hairdo, so I asked her where she had it done, and immediately made an appointment for myself at the same place. Do you like it?" she asked, her fingers scrunching the precise place where her hair was swept back from her temple in a stiffly lacquered wave.

"Very much," Florence said, and was then distracted by Lance entering the dining room with his mother on his arm. He nodded quickly, saying good evening to them, and inquiring stiffly if Florence was feeling better now, to which she quietly said she was.

"I say, Florence," Rose continued loudly and certainly within earshot of Lance as he guided his mother across the dining room to their table, "That young fiancé of yours is such a nice fellow. Howard, is that his name?"

Oh yes! Florence had forgotten about Howard's ludicrous claims to the guests at Landsdowne's about their imminent marriage. She was aware of a twang of tension in Lance's retreating back as he and his mother slowly approached their table. She was about to tell Rose that there was some misunderstanding as she and Howard were not engaged, but just then the waitress arrived with her tomato soup, and in any case, Rose would make such a big and noisy display of shock and further inquiries, that Florence just did not have the energy to correct her. But she made an urgent point to herself that she must tell Lance explicitly that Howard was quite mistaken if he thought she'd agreed to marry him. That's why those photos of her marrying Howard were such a horrible shock. Lance *must* believe her!

Seeing Rose eying her keenly and expecting an answer, Florence wiped her lips with her serviette, and said, "Actually, you'll be seeing him again tomorrow, as he'll be coming to pick me up." It was all she could manage.

"What a kind man! And he clearly dotes on you. But oh dear; we'll miss you! We've all grown quite fond of you here. And what with you having spent the last couple of days alone upstairs…"

Florence did not have the appetite for dinner that she had had for the Ploughman's Lunch, but Rose kept suggesting that she try to eat a little more. And then, when dinner was over, Rose insisted on a final game of Scrabble, "for old time's sake." They sat in the lounge, and Allison started distributing the letter tiles as before. And also, as before, Lance came over to them after having taken his mother to her room.

"You're looking jolly nice tonight, Rose," he said cheerily.

"Why, Dr. Ramsey! You're too kind! Do you like my new hairstyle?" she said, her hand again going up to her hair.

"It's most becoming," he said. "I see you're playing Scrabble again. Might I join you?"

"Yes, yes; of course. I'd be only too delighted, Dr. Ramsey! We haven't seen much of you the last few days. I expect your work has been keeping you frantically busy."

"Yes, frantically!" he echoed.

He sat next to Rose on the sofa, and the game began. Rose continued to clutter the board with one point letters; Allison played cautiously, hugging the tiles to her narrow chest; and Lance seemed contentedly absorbed in thoughts of his own. When it was Allison's turn, she put down the letters T-I-M-E. Florence and Lance exchanged glances. She urgently wanted to tell him that she and Howard were not engaged, but clearly there was no way of telling him now, and in any case he seemed strangely in such good spirits. Maybe he hadn't heard Rose's remark after all. Then swiftly, Lance, whose turn it was, spilled a sequence of letters on the board, and using the 'I' from Allison's word and spanning across another to use the 'U', made the new word I-N-T-R-I-G-U-E. Now it was Florence's turn. Her letters, in combination with some on the board, seemed to arrange themselves in her mind, and she made the word D-E-T-E-R-M-I-N-E-D. Rose, in another section of the board, made A-P-P-L-E. Allison drew in a sharp breath and said she would pass. Lance thought for a moment, and then made the word R-A-N-D-O-M.

Rose, oblivious to all but her tiles, made H-O-T, and then admonished Allison for taking so long. That poor woman hurriedly made the word T-A-P, to intersect with Rose's word. Lance leaned forward, and with a look of puzzlement, created the word W-H-I-C-H, to intersect with 'Intrigue'. He looked up quickly at Florence. Frowning, she made the word I-N-T-E-R-V-A-L. The game accelerated and spun around again to Lance's turn, which was all that mattered, and he made F-L-O-W, landing on a triple letter score. Florence, who only had a few remaining letter tiles, placed them down to make H-O-W. The others attempted to use up all their letters, the scores were calculated, and the game was over.

Lance rose. "Ladies, I must be retiring now," he said. "I thank you for a good game." He shook hands with Rose and Allison in turn. Then he came up to Florence, and grasping her hand, he said in a formal tone, "It's been a pleasure meeting you. I wish you a good trip back tomorrow, and a complete and speedy recuperation."

And then he was gone. No note in a tiny folded square exchanged hands. Nothing.

"Would you like another game, dear?" Rose asked her.

"No, I don't think so, thanks. I'm feeling a little tired."

"Yes, yes; you don't want to overdo it. You're starting to look a little wan. And you'll be having a tiring day tomorrow, what with all that traveling back to London. What time is Howard coming?"

"About 2.00, I believe."

"Would you like Allison to help you pack in the morning? You must have so much to do, and you must be so excited! How nice to be going home to your fiancé!"

"Oh, no thank you. I don't think that would be necessary. I didn't bring many things. And now, if you'll excuse me, I think I'll be going upstairs."

Florence felt extremely weary, and she almost had to pull herself up the stairs by the banisters. The night had turned abruptly chilly, and her room was particularly so, as her windows stood open as a testament to the day's former sunshine. She slipped into bed, grateful to be lying down, but the sheets felt cold and slightly damp. She shivered, and wished she'd put on socks, but lacked the energy to get out of bed and find a pair. A persistent worry tugged at her mind. Would she see Lance in the morning? There would hardly be much time, as she'd be preparing to leave, and Howard would be on his way. She and Lance had not even exchanged phone numbers. Maybe, having heard that remark of Rose's about Howard being her fiancé, he'd decided to make a clean break. Maybe that's why he spoke to her so formally just now at the end of their Scrabble game, and gave her no nice note to unfold. She felt almost sick with worry.

She pulled out her novel and, peeping out from underneath the bedclothes, the minimum of her body exposed to the frigid room, she tried to read, but it did not engage her. She flicked over the pages, not really concentrating. And then a new thought struck her. The newly developed film! They had not yet looked at it. She couldn't look at it now, since even though it was her camera, Lance was the one who had taken the pictures. Why, this would be tantamount to prying! But she knew of course that there was another reason for not looking at the photos. And now she wanted even more to find a way to see Lance in the morning.

She tried to shift her focus back to her novel, and with supreme effort was gradually becoming more absorbed in it, although still feeling freezing, when she heard a soft knocking on the door. Lance! She felt an immediate glow of warmth rush throughout her body.

"I knew the window seat was out of the question, so I took the liberty of coming up here to say goodbye to you, as there probably won't be a chance in the morning," he said.

"Thank you for coming up! I'm so glad. I was worrying about whether I'd see you before I leave. And I don't even know your address or phone number!"

"Here's my card," he said. "Do you have a card, too?"

"Not on me. But I'll write it down." She reached over to her bedside table for paper and a pen, and wrote the information. He approached the bed, placed his hand gently on the back of her bent neck, and kissed it. It felt divine. All paranoid thoughts were washed from her.

"Meeting you has been extraordinary," he said.

"Yes," she said, looking up at him with a smile, and grasping his hand. "Going back to our own lives won't be the same now."

"That's it! Hey Fleur, that's just reminded me of something we'd talked about when we had that conversation about Time!" he said excitedly, squeezing her hand tightly. "This is phenomenal! Maybe we'll gradually recall more and more!"

"What is it? What've you remembered?" she asked, picking up on his excitement.

He pulled the little round stool up close to the bed, and sitting down and reaching again for her hand he said, "It was the idea of how there might be parallel axes of Time."

"Oh Lance, yes! I *do* remember! And that's just made me remember something as well! Do you recall how I'd said that Time could possibly be thought of as the interval between two events, just as Space is the distance between two locations!"

"Yes, Fleur! We are really onto something now! Your idea of Time being the interval between two events connects very nicely with what I just said. Because, if Time is actually an interval between two events, let's call them 'A' and 'B,' then we could draw a line, or mathematically speaking an *axis*, between them, and there'd be a little one-dimensional point, 'T,' which is Time, which travels along that axis between these events. And the only way we'd know how fast 'T' itself travels is if we introduce another graph to time *its* progress. And then another graph to measure the Time it takes for the Time to travel along the axis, and so on, as an infinite regress, all parallel to each other. And that's how there could be an infinity of parallel axes of Time!"

"Yes!" she exclaimed, feeling thrilled. "It's funny, but the way you describe this reminds me of pictures of Cornflakes boxes on Cornflakes boxes on Cornflakes boxes, until they're too small to see, but still existent. So, what you're suggesting is that there are an infinite number of Times!"

"Precisely! And I strongly believe that any of us can slip between these axes of Time, although most people are unaware of this. But Fleur, I'd like to think that you and I have created – or maybe more accurately, 'discovered' - a Time axis exclusively for us, along which we can always travel together, whatever else we might be doing with the rest of our lives. When you just spoke about us returning to our own lives, you reminded me of this idea of the parallel axes of Time. So, we can indeed return to our own usual routines, but we can still be together, as well."

"I love that thought," she said, feeling comforted despite their imminent separation.

"Fleur, I've just realized something else!" he replied, leaping up from the stool. "You actually made the word '*interval*' in the Scrabble game just now, right after Allison made the word '*time*'!"

"So I did! How funny. It was as if the letters just formed themselves on the board. I wasn't even aware that I'd been thinking of this!"

"This is fascinating!" Lance said, sitting again on the little stool, his leg jiggling up and down. "You know, it's made me realize that there were other words you and I made, just now playing Scrabble, that I think we'd also talked about in our conversation about Time."

"Really? Such as what?" Florence asked, sitting up higher in bed, burning with excitement and with all previous thoughts of how cold she'd felt completely vanished.

"Yes, well; you'd made the word 'determined' and I'd made the word 'random.' And, if I'm remembering rightly, we'd also spoken that night about the intrigue of whether events in Time are determined or random."

"Oh, this is phenomenal! You'd even made the word 'intrigue' on the Scrabble board just now."

"So I had!"

"It's almost like Spirit Writing, Lance. The things we'd talked about in that forgotten conversation are coming through to us when we play Scrabble! I didn't know quite how I'd made these words; they both just seemed to flow onto the board!"

"Yes, that was true for me, too, Fleur! It's fascinating! We should play more Scrabble and see what else we remember!"

"But I do know something, Lance, and that is that I would like us to determine when we next see each other, rather than leaving it random and open, and hoping we'll find each other on another Time axis. After all, it took long enough for us to meet this time! So, can we do that? Can we arrange a next time to meet?" She could hardly stand the thought of not seeing him.

"Absolutely, Fleur. We should definitely set a time."

"Whatever date we set, though, will seem so long. I know that proves the subjectivity of Time that we were just talking about, and that makes me excited, but it doesn't help me now in terms of knowing how hard it'll be for me to wait until the next time I see you."

"Yes, it will be arduous for me, too. But we'll make it soon. And now," he said, standing up abruptly and moving the stool back to its correct position by the dressing table, "I must go and let you have some sleep." He kissed her briskly on the forehead and paced rapidly to the door. But, with his hand on the doorknob, he spun around, his face pained. He rushed back to the bed, and flung himself on Florence.

"Forgive me, Fleur! I can't do it! I'm unable to go. Can I stay here with you tonight?"

"Yes!" she gasped.

"I told myself I shouldn't come to your room after the Scrabble game tonight. But the thought of possibly not seeing you in the morning prevented me from attending to anything else. I had to come! So I told myself I'd be brief. God help me; I can't even be that. Fleur, if I stay, please don't think I'm taking advantage of you."

"I won't, Lance. I want you with me. Nothing could make me happier."

"Thank you for that, my sweet," he said, looking into her eyes and caressing her cheek with the palm of his hand.

He went over to the armchair, took his shoes off and placed them neatly side-by-side, putting a sock in each one, and then slid out of his trousers and pulled his jumper over his head. He returned to the bed, and slipped between the sheets that she had pulled back for him. He lay on his back, and looking up at the ceiling he let out a deep sigh. Then he took his glasses off, put them on the bedside table, and turned back to her, putting his arm around her shoulder. He commented on how pretty she looked in her lacy Victorian nightdress, but he did not try to take it off. He showed restraint and complete respect for her. They kissed tenderly, softly, and Florence felt so comfortable and contented because of his gentle affection, and she responded in kind. They fell asleep still holding on to each other.

When the sun first poured shafts of pale golden light through the chink in the curtains, Florence was vaguely aware that Lance had quietly risen and was pulling up his trousers. They kissed in a lingering fashion, and then with shoes and socks in his hand, Lance tiptoed to the door and was gone. Florence, when she awoke fully a few hours later, basked in the glow she still felt from having been intertwined with Lance throughout the night.

But then things moved quickly; her breakfast hurriedly eaten, her bags packed, a brief visit from Dr. Briggs who found her remarkably improved. Howard arrived earlier than expected – fortunately she was ready – lunch was consumed, transactions were settled, money exchanged, hands shaken, and then Florence and Howard left. A small crowd, consisting of Mrs. Landsdowne, Dr. Briggs (who'd stayed for an early lunch), Rose, Allison, and the little maid who had so diligently cleaned her room, had gathered by the front door to wave goodbye. Walking towards Howard's car, Florence turned and looked back towards the Guest House. She thought she saw Lance standing at an upper window, but the sun was in her eyes, so she could not be sure.

It was only after she climbed into Howard's car and he started to drive away, that she realized, with a spike of panic, how she and Lance had forgotten to look at the most recently developed film. And with even greater panic she realized she'd forgotten to reassure him (and herself) that the portly man next to her in the car, who was swearing at a sheep as it was slowly crossing the road, was not her fiancé.

# SIX

*FLORENCE HAD NOW RETURNED TO WORK,* and was busy with a story about travel patterns of London commuters. Even though she was fully engaged with this, she loved the concept of the Time axis exclusively for her and Lance, on which she could devote herself entirely to him, and they did this, with an abundant exchange of phone calls on her mobile phone or at work. They also e-mailed each other frequently, commenting on how this asynchronous form of communication stretched Time, made it more elastic, and therefore should expand their understanding of Time itself.

But she knew there was one thing she avoided and that was looking at the most recently developed batch of photographs. To Howard she'd said nothing about the strange pictures when he'd asked to see the photos of her trip the day after he'd brought her home. She'd been lying in bed, feeling more fatigued and achy than she had for the last few days at Landsdowne's, staring at the newly papered mustard colored walls, chasing the pattern of the sideways diamonds around the room, up to the window, inwards to the concave recessed area, and out again, not at all liking his choice of wall paper, and wishing instead he had waited so they could pick out the wallpaper together, yet at the same time feeling guilty for not feeling more grateful to him. She replied – how interesting that the word 'replied' contained the root word 'lied' – that the camera was too big and heavy to use, so he'd been quite correct that she would've been better off with one of those small disposable cameras instead. He was all too pleased to say, "I told you so!" He liked saying that, and said it often.

"If that camera's impossible to use," he continued, "take it back to the shop! I'm sure they'll take it back. They only have junk in there anyway."

"Oh no; I think I'll keep it. I like the way old-fashioned cameras look. And besides, I might use it one day."

"Flo, you're such a clutterer! See how I made everything neat and tidy while you were away, and it's already getting messed up. You didn't even wash up the saucepan and bowl from when you had that chicken soup earlier. Everything gets untidy straight away when you're around."

She thought he'd told Dr. Briggs that he'd make the food and generally run the household when she first returned, but she had no energy to criticize him. Earlier that day, when she'd started feeling thirsty and lacking in energy and Howard had left for work, she'd gone to the kitchen, seen that there was nothing much to be had, and so had heaved herself out of the flat, and down the street to the nearest corner shop where she bought some tins of soup which she lugged wearily home. But now, instead of reminding him of how he'd said he would stay home and help, she whispered, "I'll get up soon and clear everything away."

"Quite right! And you should unpack your clothes properly, too. I don't want everything lying around in our newly decorated bedroom, especially since I worked so hard making it look nice. Tell me, don't you think I did a great job with the wallpapering!"

He'd mentioned his wallpapering skills too many times to count. "Yes, you really did very well," she said as she had done so many times before.

"Yes, it wasn't easy, let me tell you. See how I matched up the pattern of the diamonds so well in that corner. That was the hardest part of all. But I did it really nicely."

"Yes, you did."

He went to fetch himself a beer from the larder and sat drinking it in front of the television, where he soon fell asleep, and his ragged, uneven snores, in combination with the blare of the program he'd left on, prevented her from having a proper rest. After a while she thought that she might as well get up and make the dinner.

While she stood drably stirring a white sauce to pour over a slightly discolored cauliflower that she'd found at the back of the fridge, half-heartedly trying to smooth out the lumps while propping herself up with the elbow of her other arm against the wall, she thought about how she and Howard had first met. Surely what had started off as an obligation, and then as a neurotic fear, no longer needed to have such a hold on her, did it? It had started when her friend, Bess (who was now an actress, and married and living in Northern Australia), had asked her to accompany her to a party, for moral support, as there was a certain guy there, John something, now long forgotten, who she'd had her eye on. Florence had intended visiting her parents that weekend, but Bess's entreaties were so emphatic that she told her parents that she would visit them the following weekend instead. This unexpectedly produced naggingly persistent emotional blackmail on the part of her mother, and fury from her father in her mother's defense, as they'd invited over their long-time friends, Sadie and Wesley, with their recently divorced son, Howard, and apparently they'd all been so looking forward to seeing Florence.

Florence had been torn in that emotional way that her mother had perfected inflicting on her, and acutely unhappy and fearful as a result of her father's temper. She had no interest in seeing these people; Sadie was always making annoyingly inappropriate observations, such as that she had a hole in her stockings, and Wesley always drank too much and then brought his face too close to hers so that she could smell his stale breath. She had not met Howard since they were small children, as he'd been away at boarding school, university, and then worked overseas for a while, before getting married. But, given his parents, how interesting could he be?

Even though she'd clearly wanted to go with Bess to the party, she had done the opposite. She had returned home to a house in chaos; her mother cleaning the kitchen floor and preparing mountains of food, and her father obligingly being sent on little errands, to buy the wine or plump up the pillows. Neither took the least bit of interest in her being there, and she wondered why she had come.

The guests had arrived early, which flustered her mother still further as she had not finished preparing the potatoes. But it had worked out in its manner, and Florence had to admit that Howard, though tending to be on the large size, sitting squarely in the armchair and filling it almost completely, seemed reasonably affable and did have very nice shiny dark hair. However, after chewing many handfuls of peanuts with an open mouth, he'd started talking endlessly about computer programming, something none of them could understand, and whether he was naturally talkative, or wanted to do this to deflect any possible mention of his recent divorce, was unclear.

When they'd moved into the dining room for dinner, Sadie had insisted that Florence sat next to him, and well, she couldn't refuse, could she! As she passed him those just-cooked-in-time potatoes, she accidentally bumped the hot dish against his wine glass, sending an abundant splash of red wine against his elegant, pale green silk shirt. She'd been apologetic, he'd been slightly perturbed, her mother had seemed agitated, but Sadie had looked strangely elated. There followed much fussing and sponging with Club Soda, and then the meal had continued, with Howard sitting there wearing a pale green shirt with a wet and much spread out pink stain across his ample stomach.

Everyone had stayed the night, and the following morning, during brunch, Howard had asked if there was anything else she wanted to spill on him. The orange juice would do, but perhaps she'd be better off with the tomato juice as the color was more vivid. Florence, unsure how to interpret the sarcasm, had laughed. This seemed to have encouraged him, as he'd then immediately suggested that they take a stroll in the village, and as they walked, he'd clamped a heavy arm around her.

"It seems we live close to each other in London," he'd said, which had startled her.

"How do you know where I live?" she'd asked.

"There's a lot I know about you," he'd replied. "And I think, by the way, that you should go out with me, in repayment for my favorite shirt."

"Please allow me to pay the dry cleaning expenses!"

"I wouldn't hear of it. But I do think we should go out. You amuse me. You're merry and bubbly. You laugh at my jokes. It's what I need to cheer myself up."

She'd been flattered at that. It had felt nice to be complimented on her personality. And, after all, he probably did need cheering up after what had seemed, according to her parents, to have been a long and complicated divorce. She'd still felt uncertain as to how much she liked him, but it seemed too early to tell. She did, though, find him moderately attractive and she'd especially liked his hair.

He'd interrupted her thoughts by suddenly saying, "So how old is your son now? Must be about two, yes?"

"What? I haven't got a son." Maybe he did not know as much about her as he thought, and was confusing her with someone else.

"Oh, was it a daughter, then?"

"No, I don't have any children."

"That's odd. I'm sure Carmelita had told me-"

At the mention of the name Carmelita, a name Florence had not heard for so long, she'd stopped in her tracks, completely stunned.

"Ah, I see we're getting somewhere," Howard had said. "Allow me to explain myself. Carmelita is my ex-wife's second cousin's wife. Remote connection, but there it is. There are only about six degrees of separation between people. One person knows someone, who knows someone else, who knows...Did you hear of that?"

Florence nodded blankly, still taking in the mention of Carmelita.

"And I remember her telling me about three years ago," Howard continued, "how you were going out with a friend of hers, the hot-blooded Renard."

"Oh my God!"

"Small world, isn't it! Yes, I remember it was you, because at the time she mentioned it, I recognized your name as being the daughter of friends of my parents. I'm not mistaken, am I? You did go out with Renard, didn't you?"

"Yes, briefly."

"Well, not so briefly that he didn't have enough time to impregnate you. Isn't that right?"

Florence was appalled. This had been an ugly phase in her life that she had not thought about for some time.

"It was date-rape," she'd said. "And I stopped seeing him immediately after that."

"But he knew you were pregnant. That whole gang knew. Carmelita was so excited about that. So what happened to the *bambino*?"

"I had an abortion," Florence had burst out, recalling the sordid incident and instinctively holding her stomach.

"I see! And what did dear Mama and Papa say about that?"

"Oh, they must never know! I didn't tell them. That would shock them too much."

As soon as she'd said that, she instantly regretted it. She had given him power over her; power to spill her horrible secret to his parents and thus to hers. She'd tried to backpedal, to change the way the story had unfolded, but it was too late. She'd been shocked by his knowledge of her past and completely caught off guard.

"Don't worry. Your little secret is safe with me. And since my divorce I have nothing more to do with Carmelita or any other relatives of my ex-wife. In fact, I don't have anything to do with my ex-wife, either."

His statement, delivered from a face that exhibited narrowed eyes and a little sour and cynical smile, had increased her feeling of vulnerability. And that was how it had started. A stain on a shirt which no longer fit him, leading to the revelation of a secret, long covered over and not thought about. Florence often wondered miserably what would've happened had she gone to that party with Bess, instead of trying to please her parents. She knew, though, that they were delighted by her relationship with the son of their good friends, and that they hoped for an eventual union between the families.

And at the start of her relationship with Howard Florence enjoyed trying to make him feel happier, as the nurturing trait was strong in her, and she wanted to do all she could to help him. And she enjoyed the thrill she always heard in her mother's voice when she phoned, more frequently now, to see how she was. But, as time wore on, she came to increasingly realize that Howard's moodiness and gloom went deeper than being caused by his divorce, and were more likely characteristics of his personality. So rather than her being able to elevate him and cheer him up, he was dragging her down. This was especially caused by his misplaced anger which often accompanied his mood swings, and which frightened her.

She'd tried to comfort herself in the thought that he was fairly attractive and successful in his career, and that she might grow to like him more if they were together long enough and she'd become accustomed to his ways. Indeed, on a few unpredictable occasions he did something nice – said a gentler word or took her to a good restaurant – but these intermittent gems just served to make it much harder to break up with him than if he'd been relentlessly awful to her all the time, as they heightened her expectations and left her imploring for more. But in reality, when he behaved in an ugly way, she saw the ugliness reflected in the way he looked, so he no longer was attractive to her. And it was at these times that she knew that she wanted to leave him, but felt trapped because always, in some corner, she felt that panicked vulnerability that he might speak of her abortion. What's more, if he could scare her when she was trying to please him, how much more terrifying might he become if she ended their relationship? It was bloody brave, when she thought about it, that she had dared go away by herself to the Lake District.

These memories, combined with how Howard had been behaving since her return, made her feel in desperate need of speaking to her best friend, Anna. So she rapidly and carelessly cut off bits of mold from a piece of hard cheddar cheese, added the rest of it to the white sauce, poured it hastily over the cauliflower even before the cheese had blended in, put it in the oven, and dialed Anna's number. Anna was training to be a rabbi, and was married to David, a nice wavy haired man, who was an accountant.

Anna, in her characteristic way, sounded delighted to hear from her, and this fact alone made Florence start to feel better.

"Did you have a wonderful time in the Lake District?" she asked. "I think it's so gorgeous there."

"Yes, it was terrific," Florence replied, glad to be thinking back to how much she'd enjoyed it. She told Anna a little about the places she'd seen, but then, starting to again experience that awful feeling of fatigue and trembling, she plopped herself down on a chair and admitted that she'd been foolish while there by walking alone and getting lost and then becoming ill. Anna was concerned and asked if she felt better now.

Florence, about to answer, hastily drew in a breath as Howard, awake from his nap, walked into the kitchen and fired at her a series of questions: who was she speaking with, when would dinner be ready, and what were they having? Florence hurriedly told Anna she had to go, but before ringing off Anna quickly offered to come over the following day.

Anna visited Florence frequently during the time she was recuperating, always with a cheery manner, and a nice, specially selected variety of foods, aimed at raising Florence's spirits and her strength. Florence loved those visits, and was so grateful to her friend. She talked to her a lot about her holiday in the Lake District – the funny, eccentric people in the guesthouse, the delicious food, and the lovely scenery, and also about her interest in the meaning of Time, which she said keenly increased while she was there. But for some reason, not properly understood even to herself, she did not tell Anna about having met Lance.

One day, as Anna was unwrapping some pots of humus and baba ghanoush in the kitchen, she surprised Florence by starting to talk about Time herself.

"You know, Florence," she said, spooning the humus into a little bowl, "All your talk about Time has started me thinking. And I realize that if we're to believe in what we're told in *Genesis*, then we could say that until Eve ate the apple, there was a Timeless world. A world without change. But that was lost when Adam and Eve ate from the Tree of Knowledge."

"You mean, because they were expelled from the Garden?"

"Yes! But it shows how Time is tied up with the idea of knowledge, because once they were thrown from the Garden of Eden, they could no longer access the Tree of Knowledge, and what's more, they had now experienced a change rather than endless bliss in the Garden."

"Yes! Yes!" Florence said excitedly. "Time is related to knowledge, and a recognition of change!" It reminded her of the note Lance had written to her when she'd been ill, saying '*for Time to be meaningful, there must be knowledge and awareness,*' and how he'd gone on to lament that he'd felt so bad as he had no knowledge of how ill she was.

"But in fact there are two versions of the story of *Genesis*" Anna continued. "In the first version, the earth and everything that lives on it was created in six days, and on the seventh day, God rested. But what is really strange is that although on each day, new things were created, it was not until the *fourth* day that God created the sun and the moon, and their orbits provided measurements for Time. So Time, as we traditionally understand it, did not start until the fourth day, so what were the units of Time measuring the three days which came before it?"

"Wow, Anna! That's quite profound!" Florence replied. "Maybe we can speculate that there truly are different versions of Time; the one that predated Time, if you see what I mean, and then the more conventional one."

"Very possibly," Anna said, spreading some humus on a cracker and handing it to Florence. "And getting back to the *second* version of Genesis – that of Adam and Eve being exiled from the Garden – that meant they also no longer had access to the Tree of Life. So Time is related to mortality, as then they were condemned to die, and had to procreate, so as to continue their species, if not themselves."

"Anna, this is brilliant! So not only is Time related to knowledge of change, but also to urgency, as we all know we're going to die. So it's absolutely natural that we'd invent a measure of Time, to see how long we've got in this conscious state, in this place that we know about, which we call our life." Florence bit down on the cracker, savoring its taste, and making sure to accurately recall all that Anna was telling her so as to tell Lance about these phenomenal new insights on Time.

"Yes; even if we take a scientific view, rather than the religious one, and investigate the process of evolution, we see this fundamental urgency, this race against death for all species, as measured by their innate desire to survive," Anna concluded, pouring herself some tea.

"So if there was immortality, as in the blissful state of innocence in the Garden of Eden before Eve ate the apple, there would be no need to measure Time!"

"Supposedly not! After all, if species didn't have to worry about their survival, there'd be no reason to time their existence, as they would last for ever."

# SEVEN

*AND NOW, SEVERAL WEEKS AFTER* returning home from Landsdowne's Guest House and completely recovered, Florence was on her way home from work one day when she started experiencing a nagging, insistent feeling that she must look at the last batch of photographs. But she was afraid to do so, as she feared seeing what they might show. She realized that she was close to the store, Adolph's Assortments, where she'd purchased her camera, and thinking about what Lance had said about how they needed to try to understand more about her camera, she decided spontaneously to go into the shop and ask about it.

As she pushed open the door, she inhaled the dry smell of old papers that she recalled from when she'd come to buy the camera. At first it seemed no one was in the shop, but then a grizzled, wizened old man shuffled forward from the back and positioned himself behind the counter, and asked her if she needed any help.

"Good afternoon," she said cheerily. "I'd like to ask you about a camera I bought from you several months ago. I don't actually have it with me at the moment-"

"All sales are final!" he retorted. "You can't bring anything back. That's the policy!"

"Oh no! I wouldn't dream of returning it. I love that camera. I just wanted to ask you some questions about it."

"Well now, see here, miss. We're an antiques shop. If you've got questions about your camera, you'd best go to a camera shop. There's a nice one on the High Street."

"Oh no; it's nothing like that. I was the one who purchased the Nikon you had. I think the man who helped me was Tom. Is he here now?"

"No; Tom's not here today, seeing as it's Wednesday. I'm Adolph, and I know more about the goings on in this shop than anyone else. Now let's see; I do recall that Nikon. Quite a beauty, it was."

"Yes! Now, I was just wondering if you have any records of where it came from before you had it. And its age. That sort of thing."

"And your name is?" Adolph asked, leaning his elbow on the counter and squinting at her.

"Hamilton. Florence Hamilton."

"Well, give me a few minutes, Mrs. Hamilton," he said, pulling open several drawers behind the counter, and placing on the shelf many piles of invoices. "What was the approximate date of purchase?"

She told him. He leafed through the piles rapidly, with nicotine stained thumb and forefinger, and to her great relief, he was quite fast at finding the information.

"Yes. It was the Nikon 'F' Model, manufactured in 1961. That'll be all, will it?"

"Do you know where it came from?"

"Well, I can't tell you the supplier. That's against our policy, because we don't want our customers bothering those folks what supply us here in the shop. Or buying from them directly, and not purchasing from us. But what I can tell you is that it was purchased from up North."

"That's so interesting! I understand that you can't provide names, but could you tell me approximately where it came from in the North?"

"You are an inquisitive one; that you are! What would you be needing to know that for?"

"Oh, just out of interest. This camera fascinates me in all sorts of unexpected ways. But if you can't tell me more than that, that's fine. You've already been very helpful," Florence said, preparing to leave.

"Well, I can tell you that it was from Yorkshire. But don't you go telling anyone I told you."

"Thanks!" she said, and rushed home. Howard was not yet back, so she took out her mobile phone and called Lance. But her excitement about talking to him was tinged, as it always was, with the fear that Howard might suddenly arrive and discover them in conversation. It was imperative that Howard must continue to know nothing about him.

"Fleur!" Lance sounded so pleased to speak with her. "I have some rather nice news. I've been informed that I'm to win an award for the paper I wrote at Landsdowne's Guest House. Do you remember I'd just finished it when we met, and you were with me at the Post Office when I sent it off. You must have been my lucky charm!"

"I do remember, Lance. That's marvelous. Congratulations! I'm so pleased for you. I'd love to read it. Can you send me a copy?"

"Absolutely. I'd be honored, especially since you're such a talented writer. I'd be most interested in hearing what you think about it. Oh, and Fleur, there's to be a small award ceremony at the end of October, here at the university. Would you like to attend?"

"Most certainly! I'd love to be there." It might be difficult, of course, to conceal this trip from Howard, but she would have to find a way to do it. A quick journey up and back in a day. Any fear of discovery was certainly outweighed by her impassioned desire to see Lance again.

"That's so kind! It probably won't be much, though. A handshake and a luncheon following. That sort of thing."

"Tell me the date, and I'll mark it down. I can't wait!"

"Fleur! The handshake! I've just remembered. One of the photos! It showed-"

"Oh my God, yes! I do remember. How incredible!"

"Fleur, the most recent photos…what do they show? You hadn't told me."

"Lance, just before we speak about the photos, there's something exciting I wanted to tell you. I just found out a little more about my camera!

I went into the shop where I bought it, and they said it was made in 1961 and they'd received it from someone in Yorkshire."

"Yorkshire! So it could've been very close to the Lake District. But it's really old – about forty years, in fact – so it might have changed hands many times, and been moved around a lot."

"Yes, and it seems to have stored up lots of secrets."

"I agree! But it's up to us to decipher them! So what about that most recent batch of photos? What did they show?"

"I don't know. I still haven't looked at them."

"Do look through them, Fleur. I mean, if this award is anything to go by, perhaps we should take seriously the fact that the photos from your camera really might be telling us something about the future! We might make extraordinary discoveries about Time!"

She hesitated.

"Are you free next Wednesday?" he asked suddenly. "My faculty meeting was canceled. I could come into London and meet you for lunch. We could look at the photos together then, as I know you're not keen on looking at them by yourself. And also I could bring you a copy of my paper then, too."

And so it was arranged. Seeing Lance even sooner than she'd originally thought. She could hardly contain her excitement. But it was dangerous, too. What if Howard saw them? But really the chances of that were so remote. London is a huge metropolis, after all.

The evening before Lance's visit was exceptionally mild, and Florence decided to walk home from work. She stopped in a café on the way back and, seated at the counter, was absent-mindedly stirring her coffee when suddenly she flung the teaspoon in the saucer, opened her bag, took out the green and white envelope of photos that she'd been carrying around with her so long but assiduously avoiding, and slit open the envelope with a knife on the table. She pulled out the pictures, aware of the knocking of her heart.

It was going to be fine. The first several pictures were of the gardens and meadow around Landsdowne's Guest House. She felt herself relaxing. Even felt a bit of disappointment. An ordinary camera with ordinary photos after all. The next photo, though, caused her to sharply inhale. It was of a stop watch, the type used in a sports event, but the glass cover had fallen off and lay in shards next to it, and the hand, rather than lying flat against the watch face, was stretching perpendicularly upwards, the tip looking like a clenched fist with one tiny finger pointing. When Florence looked even more closely at the finger, she saw the nail was jagged and partially ripped off. She instinctively glanced at her own fingernail, which was slowly growing back.

Florence looked around the café in search of something to normalize her feelings, and settled on the sugar bowl with its crusted mounds of coffee stained granules. Then, breathing rather rapidly, she turned to the next photo. It showed a young girl, playing in a sun filled garden. She did not know who this was, or where it was taken, but it was pleasant, and made her feel contented.

The next was of that house, Fern View, that she and Lance had spied on; the one with the strange glow of light in the downstairs window when they'd returned at night. The photo showed the house was lived in by a couple who had their arms around each other, and were waving merrily from the front door. Since the picture was taken into the sun (breaking one of Howard's categorical imperatives of taking good photographs), the couple was in silhouette and she could not see who they were, but she presumed they were quite elderly as the man seemed to be leaning on a walking stick, and the steps to the front door were replaced by a ramp which twisted first one way and then the other. The outside of the house looked well cared for, as flowers grew in the window boxes, the lawn looked freshly mowed, and the trees seemed to nod their approval to the bright sunshine.

An expansive woman with a plastic headscarf came and sat down next to Florence at the counter.

"Looking at pictures from your 'olidays, are you?" she asked.

"Yes, that's right," Florence replied, trying to move over a bit, to regain some elbow-room.

"Where d'you go, then?"

"The Lake District."

"Oooh; it's meant to be lovely there! Had a nice time, did you?"

"Yes, very; thank you."

"Wouldn't mind going there meself, I wouldn't, but my Bob - he is a one - he insists on Margate every bleeding time!"

Florence gave a polite weak little laugh, and then returned to her photos. There was one of the guesthouse itself.

"Very nice, isn't it," the woman said, "'aving all those memories. What did we do before the age of photography, I ask meself?"

"Yes, that's right," Florence said, trying to angle the photos away from the woman, so that she'd stop looking at them. She decided to shuffle through the rest quickly.

But one picture arrested her rapid viewing, and made her stare at it in horror. It was grainy and black and white, but it unmistakably showed a scene of complete chaos and destruction. People were running down a crowded urban street, looking terrified, a dense white cloud billowing behind them, and there were ambulances, fire engines and police cars parked haphazardly.

The next photo, also black and white, zoomed in more closely, and there she saw Lance on a stretcher, a dark inky substance staining both legs of his light colored trousers, one of his legs hanging over the edge of the stretcher, grotesquely bent and twisted. What was happening? How badly was he hurt? Would someone please help him! Where was this? Feeling sick, she rushed on to the next photo, expecting a sequence, anticipating answers, but the remaining photos were again serene views of the Lake District.

Badly shaken, Florence stuffed the photos back in the green and white envelope, put it in her handbag, put down a tip by the side of her saucer, and nodding quickly to the woman next to her who called out rather indignantly, "Tata, love," rushed out of the café.

Two things were clear to her; she would remove those two horrific photos before showing this batch of photographs to Lance the next day, and would certainly never speak of them so as to protect him from needless fear of being hurt; and second, even though she would not return the camera to the shop, she would never use it again.

But as she walked on she kept hearing Lance's happy pronouncement; "*...these pictures really might be telling us something about the future.*" If that was so, what was this horrible scene of terror and injury? Would Lance survive it? She wished she had not seen those two photos, wished Lance had not taken this last film, wished she had not asked him to do so, wished she had never bought this camera. How dangerous it was to dabble in the future.

But maybe it was better to know, as a warning to change it and prevent it from happening. In this case, though, it might imply that this never really would become a future event. She did not know. Could not tell. Did not like it.

--------

"Fleur!" Lance said warmly, rising from the table as she entered the restaurant the following day at 12.30. "I'm so pleased to see you! You're looking very well!"

She hugged him ardently, feeling his goodness revitalizing her after her restless night's sleep. They released each other, looked deeply into each other's eyes, and hugged again. It reassured her of his solidity, his firm grip on life. Nothing bad could happen to him.

"It's truly wonderful to see you," she said. "I'm so glad you could come into London today. It feels like such a long time since I was at Landsdowne's."

"Seven weeks."

"Was it?" she laughed. "It feels much longer."

"Yes, you left on August 17th. So it was exactly seven weeks yesterday. Do you remember that we said there is such a difference between subjective and objective measures of Time?"

"Yes, I do. That's so true," she said. "Objectively speaking, seven weeks doesn't sound that long, but *to me* it's felt like ages and ages since I last saw you."

"For me, too."

"Yes, this is a true demonstration of how subjective Time is, depending on what the events are - which in this case is seeing each other - and how we interpret both the events and the interval between them."

"Quite right, Fleur," he smiled, clearly delighted to be back to discussing their favorite subject of Time again. "It's as if it's the relative pull and magnetism of the events themselves which determines how fast time will flow."

"But it's funny," she said, accepting the menu which a waiter was handing to her. "We say Time is subjective, but we once equated the measurement of Time with the way we measure distance in Space, and Space isn't subjective."

"Oh yes, it is," he said, his eyes gleaming. "There is a little known study on 'cognitive maps,' which is all about how people perceive, record and then access information from their minds when navigating through places, and the distortions are astounding. There might be whole gaps where certain features exist which they don't record, or they might over-exaggerate certain things such as the locations of restaurants if they're feeling hungry. And speaking of which, perhaps we should order first, and then continue. The waiter keeps looking at us. God, it's always so good talking to you!"

"Yes, we just so simply pick up where we left off, almost, in that sense, as if no Time has passed at all!"

They placed their order, and then Lance said, "Your friend, Anna, sounds fascinating. The way she interpreted *Genesis*, by pointing out that some form of Time existed before Time started formally being measured on the 'fourth day' by the sun and the moon, is key. I think it's perhaps within this other form of Time that all our answers are to be found!"

"Yes, Anna's great. And what do you think this other form of Time actually is?"

"I've no idea. But clearly Time *was* measured, in order to be able to define the three days leading up to the fourth day."

"Yes, we really should explore this further, somehow."

"Indeed we must!"

Their food arrived, and they started eating. After a little while, Lance looked up and said, "Do you know, after you left Landsdowne's, Rose insisted that we continue the nightly Scrabble games, but it was never the same without you."

"No one to have conversations with through the letter tiles!"

"That's right! Do you remember that last game of Scrabble we played, when we kept coming up with words to do with Time? Rose and Allison didn't have a clue what we were doing!"

Florence laughed. "Actually, I received a nice letter from Rose the other day," she told him.

"Yes, she liked you a lot. She often spoke of you. She and Allison left Landsdowne's a few days before my mother and I left last month."

"Is your mother well?"

"Yes, thank you. She's always a bit sad when Juliet or I have to go back home, but she adjusts in time." He twirled the spaghetti around on his fork, and then looking back up at her, he said, "Oh, and Fleur, back on the subject of Time, there's something I must tell you. On consideration, I realize it was precipitous of me to jump to conclusions that the person who will give me my award will be the same person as the man we saw shaking my hand in the photograph. I became overexcited and unscientific. Why, it might actually be a woman who gives out the awards!"

"Well, when I come to the ceremony, I'll bring the photo with me, so we can make comparisons."

"Yes. Please do that. But at this stage it was clearly irrational of me to have said categorically that these photos predict the future. I was saying what I wanted to be the case, using inductive reasoning in the most inaccurate way. I think it's important that we remain open-minded, and collect as much information as possible. So, did you bring the last developed film with you? If you're not uncomfortable, we can look at the photos now."

"Yes, I have them with me. As a matter of fact, I already saw them. I looked at them yesterday evening," she said, taking them from her bag and handing them to him.

"But Fleur, I can tell this frightens you. I'm sorry. Would you prefer it if I don't look at them?"

"No, it doesn't frighten me anymore."

"Your expression changed as soon as you passed me this envelope. That calmness and serenity, which is so much part of your sweet face, has gone. It happens every time, but this time is the most remarkable."

"No, it's nothing. Why don't you look at the pictures?"

"Are you sure?"

"Of course."

She pushed her plate aside, and sat back and watched him as he scanned through the pictures. Periodically, he glanced up at her to check her reaction. "Hmm," he said, and "That's a nice one," as he looked at photos of the gardens and meadow around Landsdowne's. Then he said, "That's odd!" and she saw he was looking at the one of the stopwatch with the broken glass and extended hand. Then he turned to the picture of that house.

"Ah! So it's inhabited after all, or will be, I assume. I wonder who these people are."

"Brave souls!" Florence remarked, "If indeed the place is haunted."

"It's remarkable to have this photo. Remember that when we'd taken pictures of the house on a previous roll of film, they never came out!"

Florence nodded, crumbling a piece of her crusty French bread.

"That's a sweet one! I wonder who this child is," he said, looking at the little girl playing in a garden.

"Yes, and where it's taken."

"Is this the end already? How strange! It seems that some photos are missing."

"Really?" How could Lance be so perceptive?

"I'm going to count them. I know this was a film of fewer exposures, but still this seems low, as I definitely used up the whole film."

Florence sat back and watched, willing herself to keep calm

"As I thought. Twenty two. Two are missing. Very odd. Even when, in the past, not all the pictures we took came out, that was only because they were substituted by other views, so there was never any overall depletion in total number."

"Perhaps they were under or overexposed, and so not worth developing," she suggested.

"One way to tell. We'll look at the negatives."

Oh no; she hadn't thought of that! Luckily, though, the light was insufficient in the restaurant for Lance to be able to determine any details on the negatives.

"We'll have to leave it until we go outside," he said, and she nodded. "Oh, and before I forget, here's a copy of my paper that you said you were interested in reading."

Very strangely, though, as they stepped out of the restaurant when they'd finished their meal, a sudden hailstorm, completely unpredicted and a total surprise for this time of year, had whipped up and was raging around them. Visibility was obscured as the stinging hail pounded them, zipping down diagonally from a gray-white sky. People hurried along, hands pressed into their pockets, their faces down-turned. Sounds were muffled, in that peculiar way sometimes created by storms.

"Perhaps you should come to my office," Florence suggested, shouting over the sound of the wind. "I don't think you should travel in weather like this."

"I'll be all right, Fleur. I'll take the bus to the train station. But what about you? You shouldn't stay out in this hail!"

"I'll be fine. I'll wait with you until your bus arrives."

They huddled into the doorway of a shop, peering out from time to time at the headlights of approaching vehicles, trying to tell when the bus was arriving.

"Fleur," Lance said, pulling her to him affectionately. "It's been so lovely being with you. I'm really looking forward to your visit to the university. It's only just over a fortnight away!" Then he again peeped out from the doorway, and yelled, "Look, Fleur! It's my bus!" He kissed her quickly and ran out into the hailstorm, his vague, shadowy silhouette seeming to merge with the gray shape of the bus. Watching him, her eyelashes felt heavy, and with a fist made purple and pink from the cold, brushed away the ice crystals that had formed on them.

She returned to her office, but found it impossible to work because she was terrified that Lance would be horribly injured in the dangerous travel conditions brought about by this freak weather. This must be what that photo was showing. Why didn't she insist that he stay longer in London until the weather cleared? She felt a rising surge of panic, but she tried to force herself to be calm by telling herself that she'd phone him later that afternoon, when if all went well he should be back. But when she did phone there was no answer from either his office or his house. She then tried his mobile phone, but it was switched off. She told herself to complete a section of work before phoning again, then another. It was now 5.45 and still no answer. She did not know what to do. Call the police? Listen to the news on the radio?

"Are you still here?" It was her boss, Elizabeth Carlisle, glancing around the door. "I thought you might have wanted to leave early given this peculiar weather."

"I'll be leaving shortly," Florence replied. "It's going well at the moment, so I want to keep working while I feel inspired."

"Good for you, Florence! Lock up when you leave, won't you. I'm on my way now."

Florence continued trying to phone Lance, and in her despair at still not getting through to him and the fact that it was now close to 7.00 and she really must go home, she did what she knew might not be particularly prudent; she left him a voice message asking him to call her at home. She tried to justify this to herself by saying the battery power was low on her mobile phone, and also that it might not be accurately working in this bad weather. Having given this message, and with horrific scenes in her mind about bus accidents or train derailments, she left the office. After all, it seemed that if Lance were involved in an accident, it might be deserved punishment to them both for having so furtively seen each other.

Once on the bus, after a wait made to feel longer not only because of the unusual cold (the hail had now abated, but had turned to a steady drizzle) but also because of her gnawing worries, she sat down behind a man who was a persistent head scratcher. With black rimmed fingernails he kept digging into his scalp, so that little flakes of dandruff periodically drifted into her lap. She wanted to move, but no other seats were available, and she had no energy to stand.

As she opened the door to her flat, Howard called out, "Flo, is that you? There's someone on the phone for you. Didn't catch his name, but he's tried a few times."

She took the phone from him anxiously. "Thanks," she said, and then in to the receiver she breathlessly said, "Hello?"

"Fleur! I received your messages. So kind of you to be concerned, but my journey back was totally uneventful, despite the weather in London."

She felt her body grow limp as all the tension melted out of it. "I'm so glad," she said. And then, still remembering fragments of her worry, she added. "But it seemed to have taken an immensely long time."

"No, there were very few delays. I stopped off at the library before returning home. It's not hailing or even raining here. Maybe the storm will blow this way later tonight."

"Oh," she exhaled, so immensely grateful. But now she felt stupid for having let her worries grow so disproportionately. She mustn't let Lance know about those two photos and how they'd terrified her, and furthermore, she mustn't let Howard know about Lance. She had been careless.

"I'm looking forward to your visit up here soon!"

Howard walked back into the room, having gone before to the kitchen to fetch himself a beer.

"Me too! Bye, then," she said hurriedly, and put the phone down.

"Who was that?" Howard asked.

"Oh, just a new assistant at work."

Howard raised an eyebrow. "His voice sounded familiar," he said.

"Probably just one of those voices," she said, feeling afraid.

"Yes, probably so," he said in a tone that sounded sinister.

Howard straightened some pillows on the sofa.

"So what did he want that was so important, that couldn't wait until tomorrow?"

"Oh, nothing much. Actually, he doesn't work every day, so he won't be in tomorrow."

"I see."

"And he had to leave early today because of the weather, so he was checking in with me to see what he needed to do."

"Right."

Howard drew the curtains against the blustery night outside, and switched on a lamp. Then, with only half his face illuminated and one eye glowing, he asked, "And why didn't you leave early, too? I was getting worried about you. Almost half of London left their jobs early today because of the weather. I certainly did. Why didn't you?"

"Sorry I made you worried, but I had something to finish up. I hadn't realized how bad the weather was."

"I see."

He walked to the other end of the room and switched on another lamp.

"How could you not have realized? You have a window in your office!" he said, his voice rising from its former quietly menacing tone, and slamming down the beer bottle on the table so hard that she thought it might shatter.

Florence felt her heart beat more quickly, and she knew she was on the edge of one of those fear-spiked panics that Howard's anger sometimes made her spiral towards. "Yes, I do. But I was so focused on what I was doing. I didn't notice the weather," she said slowly, very carefully trying to camouflage her emotions.

"It started at lunchtime. Didn't you go out for lunch today? I thought you normally went out for lunch."

"No, today I ordered in as I had this deadline, so I ate at my desk," she said, despairing that her web of lies was increasing in depth and complexity.

"I see. And what is it that you are working on so frantically?"

"I'm doing a story on environmental concerns in different neighborhoods of London."

"You don't know a thing about environmental concerns."

Here he was, doing this again, this telling her that she did not know, that she was an ignoramus, that she was a fraud. What right did she have to publish in a well-read magazine when she was surely so incompetent? She felt small, lacking in confidence. She would surely make a mess of things. After all, how could she get away with it?

"I've found what I think are good sources, and I've been interviewing some neighborhood activists," she said, trying to justify what she did to him, but feeling her skills and expertise unraveling under his poor judgment of her. It could have been a relief to her that they'd left the topic of the phone call she'd just received from Lance, but it was not, as it in fact replaced one uncomfortable feeling with another.

"Neighborhood activists? Neighborhood activists?" he repeated sarcastically. "You wouldn't even know a neighborhood activist if you stared at one in the face!" He sat down on the sofa. "Come and sit next to me," he ordered.

She moved away from the little table with the phone on it, and sat down beside him on the sofa.

"Closer!" he demanded.

She moved closer. He laid a thick hand on her thigh.

"You're all wet!" he remarked. "Go and change your clothes!"

Relieved at last, she stood up and walked quickly out of the room. As she stood in the bedroom with very few clothes on, preparing to have a shower, Howard came steamily into the room, pushed her onto the bed, and forcefully and aggressively had sexual intercourse with her.

The next morning they sat together at the kitchen table, eating Cheerios and toast. The weather was calmer, with a few blue patches between the clouds.

"Why did you tell me it was your assistant on the phone yesterday evening?" Howard asked, pushing back a thick wedge of his black hair.

"Because it was," she replied, crinkling her brow.

"Really? So why did he call himself Lance? That's a fairly unusual name, you know. If I'm not mistaken, wasn't that the name of that 'mamma's boy' in the Lake District?"

Florence rose from the table, went over to the red kettle, and stood at the sink refilling it with water. He'd told her yesterday evening that he hadn't caught the name of the caller.

"Why did you ask me who it was when you knew all along?"

"I asked you a question first, Flo! Don't answer it with another question! I refuse to be distracted that way."

"I'm sorry, Howard," she said, putting the kettle back on the stove and turning to him. "I didn't mean to appear dishonest."

"Appear dishonest?" he said mockingly. "You *were* dishonest!"

"Yes, I was. I'm sorry. I thought you might get the wrong idea if I told you it was Lance on the phone, so I stupidly pretended he was someone else."

"Wrong idea? Whatever do you mean?"

"I thought perhaps…well, you know."

"Actually, I don't know. But what I do know is that because of your stupid behavior and attempts at obfuscation, you've made me more suspicious than if you *had* told me who he was and why he'd phoned, from the start!"

Florence sat down at the table, and sighed. "I don't know why I behaved as I did. I think I'd been freaked out by that strange storm yesterday. So uncharacteristic, especially for this time of the year."

"Hmmm," Howard said into his bowl of Cheerios, looking unconvinced.

"But you've nothing to be suspicious about, Howard. Lance was just someone staying at Landsdowne's Guest House, and we were cordial towards each other, that's all."

"Nothing more?"

"No; nothing more. He didn't much notice me. As you'd said many times to me then, I looked bloody awful because of that very short haircut I gave myself."

"Yes, that haircut made you look like a fucking Martian."

"Well, there you are. And later I became ill and was scratched and bruised all over, and according to you, I looked even worse."

"True. But you were in bed then, so I presume he didn't see anything of you," Howard said, taking a large slug of tea. But then he banged his mug down and said, "Or did he?"

"No, of course not!" Florence said, carefully carving her toast into fingers so that he wouldn't see her face as she softly recounted in her mind that glorious last night when Lance, unable to leave her room, had stayed with her.

"Yes, well I suppose he seemed like a decent chap when I met him. You do remember that I met him, don't you!"

"I hadn't known. But now you mention it, it does seem likely that you would've seen him in the dining room when you drove up the first time to see me."

"Right. Pretty peculiar, though, how he was so overly attentive to his mother! If you ask me, he should put an old hag like that into a Home, and get on with his own life."

"Howard! How could you say something like that? She's his mother!"

"Well, she clearly contributes nothing to society."

"That's up to them to decide. But the point is, he *was* tied to looking after her all the time. So you see, we were nothing other than polite acquaintances. He was the sort of person you say 'good morning' to when you come down to breakfast, and you say 'good evening' to at dinner time." That was true. But what about the rest? Was the sin of omission as bad as telling an outright lie? "It was one of those hotel relationships," she rushed on to say, cramming the toast fingers into her mouth. "The formalities punctuate the day and make it more pleasant. Primarily, if I was with anyone, it was with Rose and Allison."

"Yes, I remember them. Rose was quite charming."

"So you see, there's nothing of any significance about Lance."

"So you've told me. We'll leave it there. Odd how you behaved about his phone call, though. And incidentally, why did he phone you, out of the blue like that?"

"What makes anyone think of someone else when they do? I don't know. I think he phoned because he'd heard about the storm in London on the radio and wanted to see how I fared during it. Oh, and now I remember! He actually phoned to ask if I was fully recovered from having been ill in the Lake District."

Howard swallowed the last of his tea noisily. "You'd better remember that it was me who looked after you when you came home from that rotten trip completely unwell. I don't know – most people go on holiday to rest and recuperate. You - you go and get ill! But it was me who nursed you back to health again! And don't you forget it!"

"I won't forget it, Howard! Thank you!" she said. She patted his shoulder, cleared the bowls, plates and mugs off the table, and prepared to leave for work.

Later that day, seated in her office, she pulled out Lance's paper and started to read it. She did not expect to understand much, and thought the writing would be dry and stuffy, as much academic writing was. But his writing style was pleasant and airy and very accessible, and even sounded similar to the way he spoke. Also, the content of the paper was fascinating and very topical and relevant, and she was completely immersed in it and extremely impressed.

The two weeks went by; dull days of mist and drizzle, the nights elongating backwards to capture part of the late afternoon. Florence was working hard, and Howard, who was also working hard, was possessive of her in a grabbing, somewhat callous way, each evening and throughout the weekends. He was frequently moody, and quibbled over insignificant things. His trousers were tight, which was most likely due to his insatiable appetite, yet he blamed Florence for not washing them carefully and causing them to shrink. They were late arriving at his parents' house one Sunday for lunch, and he humiliated Florence in front of them, by saying it was her fault as she refused to wake up on time when the real cause was that he wanted to watch a program on television before they left. And, during the time spent with his parents, he interrupted her every time she started to speak, as if her opinion was too insignificant to matter. It wasn't just around his parents that he did this, but whenever they were with other people he spoke over her, or belittled and demeaned her. Florence found that she frequently cheered herself up by secretly glancing at a photo she'd taken of Lance. In the photo he was seated in her bedroom at Landsdowne's Guest House by the splay of wild flowers that he'd picked for her, and he seemed to be looking directly at her wherever she positioned the photo, smiling his beautiful smile.

On the day of Lance's award ceremony, Florence and Howard left their flat at the same time, and walked to the tube station, Howard walking his customary five paces in front of her, however fast she walked. They each took separate tube lines to work, so Howard knew nothing of it when Florence later switched to a different line that would take her to Liverpool Street Station.

Once on the train to Norwich, East Anglia, she thought about Howard's general grumpiness and decided that she didn't need to put up with it, didn't need to continue sharing a flat with him despite her fear of the consequences. She'd tell Lance that she was going to move to a place of her own, away from Howard! How she looked forward to seeing Lance, this man with whom she had spent only a handful of days! He had such an exciting, inspirational presence.

She arrived at the university in plenty of time, and consulting campus maps as well as strolling students, found her way to his office. He was dressed in a suit and a maroon tie, and looked very lovely and very important. He looked up from the computer when he heard her step pause at his open office door, and standing up, gave her his radiant smile and a warm hug.

"So this is where you work!"

"Yes. How good of you to come! Your journey was quite straight forward, I hope."

"Yes, it was."

"Please sit down and make yourself comfortable."

She looked over at the only chair across from his desk, but it had a large box on it, which was filled with books and papers.

"Um; where would you like me to sit? There's a box on this chair."

"So there is! Let me take it!" he said, springing around to the other side of the desk, removing the box and putting it down in a corner of the room. "There!" and he gestured with his arms for her to sit. "I think," he continued, "that we have time for some coffee before we go over to the auditorium. Would you like some after your long journey? I should warn you, it's not very good, but it'll warm you up."

"Thanks. I'd love some."

He walked down the corridor to a coffee percolator, and poured coffee into two sturdy paper mugs.

"Sugar? Milk?" he called.

Standing in the doorway of his office watching him, she shook her head. "Neither thanks."

He walked rapidly back to her, the mugs evidently hot to hold as he put them down quickly on his desk, and wriggled and blew on his fingers. "Thank you so much for coming today!" he said.

"I wouldn't dream of missing it!" she replied. "I have that photo with me, by the way, so we can make comparisons."

"Excellent!" he said, sitting now and indicating for her to do the same. He sipped his coffee. "Ah, I don't know why I drink this stuff."

"It *is* pretty ghastly!" Florence agreed.

"Well, it looks as if I'm not going to have to put up with it much longer, at least for a while."

"Really?"

"Yes, Fleur. I've had an invitation to go to New York University – NYU as they call it - as a Visiting Scholar for a year!"

Florence felt her face turn red and her heart rate speed up. "Have you? When do you go?"

"January."

"Oh."

"I won't be away *that* long, relatively speaking. Some scholars go for up to five years. I will go just for one calendar year – which actually is a bit unusual as it's usually the academic year, but that's what they have invited me for."

Florence could find nothing to say. She twirled a paper clip around and around on his desk. "How long have you known about this?" she asked eventually, not looking up.

"Not long. A few days. I wanted to tell you to your face. Look, let's talk about this later. We must be going over to the auditorium in a moment."

"So it's all rot then, isn't it; this traveling on our own Time axis, just the two of us."

"No, it's not. Don't say that," he replied, a wrinkle she had not remembered seeing before pleating the skin between his eyebrows on his fresh, open face.

"But it clearly is. We can't just make it happen. It's nothing we can construct."

"I think we can. And we are."

"I feel that I've just been pushed off," she said, rising.

"No, Fleur! No!" he said, rising too. "This is quite complex, and we need to devote some time to talk about this properly, only not now or we'll be late."

"You go. I must go to the ladies' room. Just tell me how to find the auditorium."

"I'll wait for you. Just be quick."

"Go without me!"

"No! I wouldn't dream of doing that! I want you there. You've come all this way! Fleur, I can't believe we're arguing. Please don't be upset about my trip to NYU. We can be in touch with each other all the time as we are now, by phone and e-mail. And you can come over to visit! Would you do that? I'd really like you to. And I'll be returning for a break in the summer, to see Mother. We could spend so much time together then."

"I'm going to the ladies' room. I think I saw it by the lift," she said, aware of how nasty she was being, ashamed at her behavior, but unable to shake off this mood. Why, she hadn't even congratulated him on his great achievement.

"Yes, that's right," he replied. "I'll meet you by the lift when you're ready."

She walked off quickly, her eyes smarting. She did not need to pee. When she entered the ladies' room she looked with disgust at her face in the mirror. The face that stared back at her looked crumpled and haggard. She splashed cold water on it. And then, without even a glance at it, she took the photo of the handshake out of her bag, and dropped it into the waste paper basket. She walked out, and followed the corridor to the lift, where Lance was pacing around in small circles.

"Great!" he said, "Now I hope you won't mind if we run a bit across campus."

"That's fine," she said.

When they left the faculty building, he took her hand and ran swiftly, pulling her along beside him, checking with her every few moments to see if she was alright, and assuring her that there was not much further to go. They arrived at a sleek, gray building, and entered the lobby, in which a few latecomers were darting about.

"Hopefully you'll still find a good seat," he panted. "I need to go backstage. I'll meet you here in the lobby when it's over." He kissed her lightly on the forehead, and dashed towards a heavy set of double doors.

Without him she was no longer angry, but just terribly sad. With her breathing returning to a normal rate, she entered the auditorium and found a seat next to a woman who was reading the Bible. Although she was near the back, the seat in front of her was occupied by a small child with a tussle of very blond hair, so she had a nice, clear view of the stage. Moments later three men walked formally across the stage, one taking his place in front of the microphone. There was a sudden hush from the audience, and he immediately started talking in a nicotine-ravaged voice. Glancing at the program of the woman next to her, she gathered this was the Vice Chancellor. He talked at length about the distinguished scholarship at this university, the prestige attached to the awards themselves, and the pride he felt to be amongst intellectuals of such exceptional caliber. He went on to say that he would read out the names of all those to be honored today, and his esteemed colleague, a Dr. Erikkson from a chilly sounding place in Northern Sweden, would present the awards.

At the mention of his name, Dr. Erikkson stood up and bowed, and it was then that Florence noticed that he was wearing a blazer of Royal blue with gold buttons. Wasn't this the color worn by the man shaking Lance's hand in the photograph? She couldn't be certain, but thought it might be. She wished she had not so impulsively discarded that picture. She'd have to return to that ladies' room and retrieve it from the bin.

And now the first distinguished professor was walking across the stage. It was a woman with tight raven black curls, and spiky stiletto heels. Florence marveled at her composure. She would never have been able to wear shoes like that for fear of tripping on stage. She tried to imagine what it would be like to be a student in this professor's class. Next was a heavily bearded man, who, as soon as he came to the center of the stage, was met with a roar of approval from members of the audience in several rows near the front. Many people stood to take photos and cameras flashed.

Then two things happened at once. Lance entered the stage, and the little girl in front of Florence dropped her carton of orange juice with an explosive pop, which immediately spilled and spread out like a puddle of urine beneath Florence's own feet. The girl's mother rose sharply from several seats away, and climbing over her other equally blond children, stood in front of the offending child, fussing and reprimanding in a guttural tongue that might well have been Swedish, with the result that Florence could not see Lance receiving his award. By the time the scene immediately in front of her had cleared, with much mopping of the floor with wads of tissues, and stifled sobs from the little girl, not only Lance, but the four remaining professors, had all now left the stage.

When she picked out Lance later in the crowded lobby, his eyes were glowing with excitement, and he was bending this way and that to thank the people who were enthusiastically congratulating him. He caught sight of her, and smiled even more broadly.

"Ready for the luncheon?" he asked her.

"Definitely! Well done, Lance! You're certainly very brilliant! Your paper was incredibly impressive, as I'd said in my e-mail. You absolutely deserved that award!" She sounded too gushing, even to herself.

"Come, come," he said modestly. "Let's go. It's being held on the third floor, in a very splendid dining hall. Shall we go up the stairs? The lift is very crowded."

"Certainly."

As they were climbing the stairs, Lance stopped and took hold of Florence's elbow excitedly. "Thanks so much for being here, Fleur! So tell me; was he the one? Was Dr. Erikkson the man in the photo?"

"I'm not sure."

"Well, let's look at the picture quickly. You said you brought it with you."

"Lance, I need to go back to the ladies' room."

"OK; there's one upstairs by the Faculty Club."

"No; I'd like to go back to your building and use the ladies' room there."

"But Fleur, there's no time for that now. I would imagine that one ladies' room is very much like another."

"But I need to go to that one, Lance."

He dropped hold of her elbow and looked at her. "Why? Did you leave something behind there?"

"I might have done. I'd like to go there now and see."

"What was it?"

"I'd rather not say."

Lance's eyes no longer looked illuminated by their bright glow, and again she saw that crease in his skin between his eyebrows. "Fleur, the luncheon is scheduled to begin immediately. As I understand it, it's a sit-down meal with everyone being served at the same time, so we can't arrive late."

"But-"

"Please listen to me," he said gently reaching for her hand. "If this is about my appointment at NYU, I'm more sorry than I can say about how I've upset you. It might help you to know that I expressed interest in the possibility of going over there before I met you. And as I thought I didn't stand much chance of being accepted, it promptly went right out of my mind."

A rowdy crowd of young students came running up the stairs, preventing any continuation of their conversation.

"So, shall we go to the luncheon?" he asked her after the crowd had pushed past, to which she quietly demurred.

The meal was served at a very long table in an exquisitely beautiful paneled room, with large floor to ceiling windows overlooking a spacious green field below. As soon as she walked in, Florence was surprised to see the little blond girl, her gaggle of blond brothers and sisters (all with blue and white checked serviettes tied neatly under their chins), and the woman who had scolded them about the spillage of the orange juice in the auditorium, sitting next to Dr. Erikkson. So they must be his family! Florence and Lance swiftly sat down in the only remaining seats.

"Hello there! You must be Lance's sister!" a man to the right of Florence said to her.

"Oh no!" she exclaimed. "I'm his – we're just – " What?

"Fleur and I are close friends," Lance jumped in, rescuing her.

"Pleased to meet you!" the man said cheerily shaking hands with Florence. "This is my wife, Nanette, and I'm Percy!" They talked about some fairly mundane topics, and then Florence noticed that Lance now seemed deeply involved in an animated conversation with Dr. Erikkson. What an impressive academic he was! No wonder he won awards and was invited as a visiting scholar to exciting internationally renowned universities. His intelligence, energy and engagement were, after all, what first attracted her to him.

She plunged her spoon into her bowl of chilled vichyssoise and watched him in admiration. She was only half listening to his actual words, but then was startled to hear her name mentioned. Dr. Erikkson turned to her, and graciously asked, "So what specifically are you discovering in this study of yours on the concept of Time?"

"Oh," she said, patting her lips with her serviette and glancing quickly at Lance, who smilingly nodded at her. She thought back rapidly to the most recent conversation she and Lance had had in the London restaurant on the day of the bizarre hail storm. "Our discoveries are uncertain, and we need to be cautious," she began. "But Lance and I are trying to ascertain to what degree Time is an artificial construct that is entirely subjective."

"Most interesting. And with what university are you affiliated?"

"I'm not. I'm a writer and researcher." She told him the name of the magazine she worked for. "Lance and I embarked upon this question quite by chance."

"That's often the way the best discoveries are made," he said. "Now, tell me by what means you are testing your hypothesis."

Florence felt a little trapped by the intense beam of his concentration on her. "We are still in the early phases, so are theorizing first."

"But, by your very words, Time is subjective. So your so-called 'early stage' might indeed be ancient by other people's subjective outlook!"

She was not sure if he was mocking them, but Lance took this idea very seriously.

"Excellent point, Dr. Erikkson!" he exclaimed. "That may indeed be a possibility. Fleur and I have also considered that there might be an infinite number of parallel axes of Time, so it's conceivable that some advancement on this project could already have been made on a different axis, even, might I add, by us."

Dr. Erikkson took out a spotlessly white handkerchief, and examined it for a long while before saying, "Dr. Ramsey, I am a man who is fortunate to have a country house far to the North of the mainland of Northern Norway, in the little town of Longyearbyen, which is in the archipelago of Svalbard, located within the Arctic Circle. Because of its extremely northerly location, it is subjected to six months of darkness and six months in which the sun does not set. If you were to visit me there now, you would detect that we are within the six months in which there is no sun apparent, and the only faint light is the moonlight (when the moon is sufficiently full) reflected off the snow. My point in telling you this is to ask you to examine how you can question the steady progress of Time, when we see it displayed so exquisitely – exquisitely and explicitly - year after year after year. We measure Time by the tilt of the Earth on its axis, and its orbit around the sun. Even my little children know this. I have two older sons, and then there are the triplets. And they all know this. They ask to go to Longyearbyen each year when it is dark."

"Yes, but-" Lance began.

"There simply is no 'yes, but' dear man," Dr. Erikkson said, mopping the corners of his eyes and then stuffing the handkerchief back in his breast pocket. "I wish you both luck with your project, and when you reach conclusions which, without any doubt, contradict what I am telling you, I will be all too eager to hear about them. Until then, Dr. Ramsey, I would advise you to stick with Globalization, for that indeed did merit an award; not this subjective poking into objective reality."

Florence, appalled, was about to speak, but Dr. Erikkson scraped back his chair, rose to his feet, and holding his wine glass high and striking it with his fork, proposed a toast to all those worthy professors gathered around the table at this delicious luncheon.

The rest of the meal was consumed rapidly, one course succeeding the last by a fast exchange of plates. Dr. Erikkson, his chair now angled in the direction of the Vice Chancellor, spent the remainder of the meal speaking with him. Lance shrugged slightly in answer to Florence's questioning expression, and then introduced her to Stella Brightly, the professor with the stiletto heels, who apparently taught sociology.

After it was over, Florence and Lance walked back to his office.

"How could he have been so scathing?" she asked.

"Who? Oh, you mean Dr. Erikkson. I wouldn't worry. That's what a lot of academic debate is like. It's actually helpful to hear some opposing views, as it tells us to avoid complacency and it keeps us thinking. I found it quite stimulating, actually."

"But he was so condescending! I think he was immediately put off by the fact that I'm not an academician. I didn't think he was debating at all. He just gave us an opinionated criticism on the little we told him, and then literally turned his back on us and wouldn't let us speak."

"True, but I'd prefer to think that he's given us things to think about, challenges that we'll hear from others. Also, he's ironically made this more of a project for us both to continue, rather than just being some exciting ideas that we've spoken about a few times. Fleur, I'd like to continue investigating this with you in a more methodical, systematic sort of way."

"Me too!"

"That's better!" he said, taking her hand. "I was starting to fear that we were spinning apart."

"No! No!" she said emphatically. "I'm sorry. I behaved abysmally this morning."

"It's OK, Fleur. Think nothing of it."

She couldn't understand it. So, Lance was slow to anger. Why, even her father, who was generally an easy-going man, to this day would fly into a sudden rage if she contradicted her mother, and Howard, well, Howard, was angry more often than not. So she had developed a strong association between men and anger. And she had to face it; anger terrified her. Possibly Lance never grew angry at all. She was stunned. What's more, his calm attitude made her feel even more ashamed than she had before about how horribly she had spoken to him; how she had nearly caused him to miss his ceremony; how she would have made him late for the luncheon if he had not been firm and level-headed. But not angry. No, not at all angry.

"I hope I didn't ruin your day."

"To the contrary! It was marvelous having you here."

They had reached his building, and went up to his office. She sat, as she had before, on the chair facing his desk. "Lance," she began slowly, "You said just now how you wanted us to be more methodical in our investigations of Time."

"Yes, that's right. I think we should."

"And I believe you'd said, when we saw each other in London a few weeks ago, how you felt you were being unscientific and irrational when you'd initially claimed that the photos from my camera predict the future." Here she paused briefly, thinking not only of those horrific photos of Lance injured on a stretcher, but also those showing her to be marrying Howard, but however much she did not like what she was about to say, she felt obliged to continue: "But I wonder if it makes any sense to link what you said about the parallel axes of Time, even though that snob Dr. Erikkson was unimpressed with the idea, to what my camera might be doing."

"What do you mean, Fleur?" Lance said, looking interested.

"Well, and this is pure conjecture, but-"

"Go on! All that we're saying is conjectural at this stage."

"Well, I wonder if my camera is somehow occupying different axes of Time when it records those photos."

"What a fascinating thought, Fleur!" Lance said. "Yes, I think the idea of parallel Time axes could explain why some people feel that they can look into the future, or have prophetic dreams, and might even account for reincarnation, if people have indeed been on a different axis of Time. And so maybe you're right! Perhaps your camera does record moments from different Time axes!"

"Yes," she replied. "And if anyone can switch onto a different Time axis, and retain the *memory* of that experience, which comes back to us as thinking we can see into the future, or that we've been reincarnated, then perhaps my camera, by analogy to memories, is recording photos."

"Yes, Fleur! Yes! That's a nice process of deduction. But how can we record any of this scientifically and methodically? Who else would understand? I'm still not sure we completely understand any of this ourselves."

"But we're getting closer all the time."

"I agree. I believe we are." But saying this, Lance pulled off his glasses and rubbed his eyes. "What a confounded nuisance not remembering that conversation we first had about Time! We knew all the answers then! It was all crystal clear. How could we both have forgotten?"

"We're remembering bits slowly. Just look at how much we've remembered!"

"You're right, Fleur!" Lance said, putting his glasses back on and smiling at her.

Thinking about being methodical and the necessity of providing evidence, Florence remembered the photo of the handshake, and excused herself and went to the ladies' room. There were three or four women in there standing by the sinks, washing their hands or tidying their hair. She went into a stall and waited for them to leave. When they'd gone, she emerged from the stall and quickly started to sift through the paper towels in the bin. The door swung open, and someone else walked in, so she had to pretend to be busy at the sink. But even as she resumed looking, she knew it was hopeless. The photo was no longer there. The morning's rubbish had most likely been emptied. How could she explain this to Lance?

She scrubbed her hands and wrists, and returned to his office.

"Did you find whatever it was that you had misplaced?" he asked her.

So he'd remembered! "No, it was no longer there."

"That's a shame. If you would like to tell me what it was, I can check in the Lost Property Office tomorrow, and see if I can find it for you."

"Thanks, but don't worry about it. It's really not so important after all."

They discussed train timetables, and it made her sad.

"Before you leave, Fleur, let's look at that photo! Let's see if we can start compiling evidence to refute Erikkson!"

She opened her bag and pretended to look, and faked shock at not finding it. He was a clever man. Only his good manners and his calm demeanor must have been preventing him from accusing her of leaving that photo in the ladies' room.

"How odd!" she said. "I don't understand this. It's just like forgetting our conversation about Time! Maybe we're not meant to know!"

"It's possible, but ultimately very disappointing. Anyway, as far as you remember, did this ceremony look to you like the photo? *I'm* not sure, as I had a different perspective on the stage."

It was then that she told him about Dr. Erikkson's daughter in the seat in front of her spilling her drink, and how she consequently did not see the moment of him getting the award itself.

"You didn't?" He looked disconcerted. "Maybe you're right. Maybe we are not meant to know about the future, by its very definition." He again took off his glasses. That gesture of removing his glasses was reminiscent to her of her last night at Landsdowne's, when he had shyly come to lie in the bed beside her. She went over to him, put her arms around his neck and kissed him.

"As an overall impression," she said, "I would hazard a guess that the photo was genuinely – and inexplicably - of the event itself. I remember the man in the photo wearing Royal blue as did Dr. Erikkson, and he did shake your hand, didn't he?"

"Yes, so it seems likely. But we need a better, more scientifically rigorous approach. The logical thing would have been to have taken a picture with an ordinary, conventional camera today at the ceremony, and compare the two photos, assuming this lost one turns up again."

"Yes! That would've been irrefutable."

"Right! Next time, then. We should look again at all the photos taken with your camera, and see if there is another likely event that we are heading towards."

"God! Is that the time? I really must hurry to catch my train!"

He went to the railway station with her. On the platform she said, "You know, Lance; it really is a terrific honor that you've been invited to NYU as a Visiting Scholar. They'll be lucky to have you."

"Thank you!" The rest of his words were lost by the clatter and rattle of the approaching train. He folded her into his arms and they kissed warmly.

After dinner that night, Florence waited until Howard went into the bathroom, and then surreptitiously took out the two haunting photos that she'd hidden away; one of the chaotic street scene, and the other of Lance on a stretcher. Despite what she'd said to Lance about linking her camera's photos with parallel Time axes, she now ardently hoped Dr. Erikkson was right in being so disdainful of their hypotheses. As she looked and looked at the photo of Lance, willing it to never happen, she had a sudden realization that gave her a profound shock. The picture was taken in an American city! She was certain from the look of the police cars and fire engines!

She was so agitated that she could scarcely breathe. She did not even hear Howard returning from the bathroom, and only just managed to tuck the photos behind a cushion in time. What could she do? It would be impossible to tell Lance not to go to New York, as he would think she was continuing her infantile behavior in his office that morning, and then he might really lose patience and become angry. All she could think to do would be to visit him in New York, as he'd suggested, and if she'd studied the photo really hard and knew what that street looked like, maybe she'd find it when she was there, and make up some reason why he must never go to that area. It seemed so highly implausible, but it was the best she could come up with.

Florence returned for one more visit to the university, and met Lance's colleague, Ned, who occupied the office next to his, as well as again seeing Stella Brightly, the woman with the stiletto heels. And Lance traveled down to London a few times, and they met for lunch. Sometimes Florence would take the rest of the afternoon off, and they would stroll around the crowded city streets, or escape into the cool interior of the Tate or National Gallery. But all along Florence knew that the date of Lance's departure was drawing nearer and nearer.

# EIGHT

*FLORENCE WANTED TO GO TO* Heathrow Airport to see Lance
off. They decided to meet at the airport, since they were coming from
different directions. Florence arrived at the Virgin Atlantic check-in
counter before him. She was feeling numb; a result of her psychological
immune system setting to work to suppress and combat her sadness about
his relocation to such a far away place. And she expected that this numbing
feeling, in combination with that peculiar juxtaposition of the tedium of
waiting in long queues along with the dread that it was getting closer and
closer to the time that he would go through the restricted area without
her, would lead them to not know what to talk about, would drive them to
platitudes. She watched a large Indian family with trolleys and trolleys of
suitcases wheel up to the counter; and a young woman who she was certain
must be American, as English people just don't become suntanned like
that, and don't wear T-shirts with such loud messages across their chest,
and don't have so many gleaming white teeth.

The crowd around the check-in desk swelled. But where was Lance?
He was now half an hour late. She called his mobile phone, but there was

no answer. She tried again, becoming more concerned. If he had been more punctual, he would have beat this crowd and would more likely have been given a better seat on the plane. The crowd swelled still further, the line serpentining around the ropes. People with impossibly huge bags shuffled forwards, sliding their bags with their feet. Young children were restless, some crying, and ruffled; sleep-deprived adults were picking them up. Another weight, along with the shoulder bag, backpack, carrier bags.

Florence looked at the clock. Lance was still not here and it was an hour and ten minutes past the time they said they would meet, and the recommended time for check-in. What could have happened? She fruitlessly tried phoning him again. Maybe he was not going to New York after all! That would be terrific! Maybe he had a last minute change of heart, and had e-mailed her about this, and she would see his message when she returned home.

Then, over the PA she heard, "We are now boarding Virgin Atlantic flight 001 to Newark Airport. All passengers please report to Gate 57 and have your boarding passes ready."

The crowd at the check-in counter had noticeably dwindled, and some of the neatly dressed, shapely Virgin Atlantic staff in their red uniforms were now closing down their stations. Perhaps there was some mistake. Could this be the wrong day? Perhaps she was waiting for Lance at the wrong part of the airport. She rushed forward and asked one of the women behind the desk if a Lance Ramsey had already checked in. The woman eyed her impatiently, and then typed a lot of things into her computer before looking up and saying that this passenger was soon to be labeled a 'No Show'.

Florence did not know what to do. She heard other boarding announcements for his flight, and tried phoning him again. No answer. Time? Telepathy? None of it was functioning correctly between them. And then she heard, "This is the last call for Virgin Atlantic, Flight 001 to Newark..." and she knew that was that.

She turned away from the check-in area, and that was when she was peripherally aware of someone swiftly running towards her. It was Lance!

"Fleur! Lovely to see you! Quick! I need to check my things in and then I'll explain-"

He dashed to the counter and begged the one remaining check-in attendant to check him in. She showed reluctance, but in a disgruntled manner, picked up the phone to call the gate. She then nodded and started working incredibly fast. Lance turned to Fleur and twinkled. Then, on being told he had to get to Gate 57 immediately, and Heathrow being as large as it was this meant it was a long way, he hugged her quickly and tightly.

"So sorry to have brought you here for nothing. I have to run! I'll phone you as soon as I get settled!"

So saying, he pressed a tiny square of folded paper into her hand, and darted off into the crowd. He did not turn to wave.

Florence traveled back on the almost empty train. She waited until she was past Hounslow before reading his note. She had not let go of it all that time, so her hand felt clammy and her fingers a little stiff as they unfurled around it.

*Fleur, you're probably at the airport now, and I am on the train, willing it to move. We've been sitting at this red signal, waiting for a Thameslink train to pass. None of the other passengers seems agitated. Only I. Ah, that's better. We're on the move again.* (Here there was a jerk in his handwriting, probably corresponding to when the train lurched forward.) *Oh, but what a snail's pace. It's tempting to jump out and run along the railway line! NO! We've stopped again. I suspect a mechanical failure. All the lights have dimmed.*

*But Fleur, my purpose in writing is not to tell you about this terrible train ride, but to tell you the things that I might not have time to tell you as a result of this terrible train ride. How clichéd it sounds to tell you that I will miss you, but it's true. Sometimes I wonder if I should be going to New York. But we can't 'turn the clock back.' Or can we? Perhaps the Future can influence the Past.*

*I think that is what is happening to you and me, though I don't know why I think this. We'll have to talk about this.*

*Ah! The train is picking up speed. They're making announcements, Fleur. I think we're getting close. How clearly a train ride illustrates the concepts of the interrelatedness of Time and Distance, as we hurl along this straight axis of the railway line towards the final destination which has a 'must arrive' Time strongly associated with it. A little eight year old boy once said to me that "Time goes by as quickly as scenery." What a profound little chap, and how well his words are illustrated on this train ride.*

*Perhaps I will arrive in time, after all, to see you. And to make my flight. And if I don't find you, I'll post this from America!*

*With great affection and tenderness,*

*Lance*

*P.S. Train stopped before pulling all the way along the platform. Can you believe it? I wish I could have phoned you, but I stopped my mobile phone account yesterday, as it won't work in US. Good! Moving forward again. Definitely good, only there's so much more I want to tell you. No time! Must get off this train and RUN!*

Florence read the note twice, and then folded it several times back into its characteristic tiny square, and put it in her bag. It made her feel better. And then a random thought popped into her mind, unexpected and uncalled for, and that was that one of her photos from last summer showed Lance boarding a plane!

--------

Lance e-mailed frequently with detailed information about his impressions of everything in New York.

> *Names,* (he once wrote), *are so different over here. Can you believe that the Dean of my division of the university is simply called Bob! I don't need to tell you that over in an English university, the Dean would have a stuffy, pompous name, such as Dr. Sebastian Higginsbottom who is our Dean at East Anglia. Student names are different, too. I expected all-American names such as Mary-Lou, but haven't come across any. Instead there are Marissa and Seth, and a girl called Robin! And then a whole slew of names such as Taylor, Trenton, Cameron and Paisley, which sound more like surnames to me but aren't. I have to make a particular effort to remember, when looking through the class roster, the gender of these students.*

And another time he wrote:

> *Manhattan is truly amazing. The people are so confident and vibrant — what a change from the self-deprecating manner we adopt in England! The energy here is almost palpable. Women mostly dress in black, which makes them look strikingly elegant, and the men dress very casually. Everyone is informal and friendly. People throng the streets at all times, even late into the night, and the subway runs all night, as opposed to the London tube. Greenwich Village, where I live close to NYU, is fabulously attractive, with a mixture of busy commercial avenues and gorgeous tree-lined streets with beautiful brownstones.* (Beautiful what?) *And then, not far away, just a little further downtown towards the Southern tip of the island, is the Wall Street area. I love it there! There are tiny, narrow streets, with old grey churches, and also the imposing Grecian New York Stock Exchange, juxtaposed against the tallest,*

*sleekest, gleaming skyscrapers which soar upwards. I can't wait to take you to the top of the World Trade Center. In fact, I can't wait to show you around. I'm so glad you've decided to come in April! The views from the top of skyscrapers are unbeatable. You'll love it here, I know.*

And another:

*Look for me tomorrow and you will find me a fat man!* (Oh no, would Lance become portly like Howard?) *The food here is phenomenal! As an example, I went for lunch with Marissa, and she suggested we get sandwiches. Sandwiches? I fully expected the equivalent to the English sandwich – two thin triangles of bread, curling up at one corner, with a scrap of wilted lettuce, a slice of squashy tomato, and a thin square of ham. But no! American sandwiches are so immense, that I feel we need jaws like snakes to be able to get our mouths around them. They are crammed with half a pound of meat, and assorted crisp fresh vegetables. I heard the woman on the next table order a salad, and when it arrived it would have been considered adequate to feed a family of six in England! And the ingredients looked so imaginative, fresh and wholesome. You would love it! Just walking past food shops in Greenwich Village – and there are many – it's amazing to see that everything looks as if it is straight out of the Garden of Eden! And here temptation is not a sin. In fact, the society thrives on it, and makes hedonism seem like a pretty excellent idea! Apples are huge, perfectly round, crisply green and unblemished. Tomatoes are deeply red and none are squashy or moldy. Oh, and the desserts!* Here the e-mail trailed off, as if he were about to depart to find himself a meal.

A few days later, Lance wrote:

*Americans adore English accents and think the speaker so intelligent! What's more, you'd think we speak the same language, but we don't. Some words are understood differently. And then, there are some things we say in England that they haven't heard over here, and that causes such merriment. For example, the other day Marissa had been showing me around midtown – the Rockefeller Center is very smart and you'd like it (now, here's an example of a word understood differently…we of course understand 'smart' to mean 'well turned out', but in the US 'smart' means 'intelligent') – and after having walked half the day, and skated on the open-air rink the other half, I told her I was 'knackered'. That word was met with peels of laughter. By the way, Marissa is my TA, which stands for 'Teaching Assistant'. She's actually working on her Ph.D., but helps me out in my class by taking attendance, doing the grading (they don't say 'marking') and other helpful things.*

Florence read of Lance's enthusiasm, and frankly it made her sad. What if he loved it so much there that he decided to stay? This thought changed from being a nagging worry, like a stone caught in one's shoe, to an obsessive fear. And who was Marissa who he mentioned so often? Was she more to Lance than just his Teaching Assistant? But what right did she have for expressing concern or jealousy – she who had found it impossible to move out from the flat she shared with Howard after all, once she heard Lance was going to America.

So she replied to Lance's e-mails with enthusiastic sounding messages of her own. But one day, when the worry felt overwhelming, she did what she thought she could not do. She bought film for her camera, loaded it, and went out for a walk on Hampstead Heath. It was a bright, chilly, windy day. She climbed the hill, looking about herself at the skeletal trees denuded of their leaves. As she walked, she snapped pictures here and there, hesitant at first, but gradually growing bolder. She now wanted to know what the future had in store.

She found that she was near Spaniard's Inn, and walked over to Whitestone Pond. A childhood memory of when she was here on a freezing spring day with her cousin filled her mind. He had a little toy powerboat, but try as he might (and he did try for so long that their lips had turned blue and their fingertips bloodless) the engine would not stay revved up. The boat, instead of roaring across the water, floated sedately by the reeds, as if it was a prim little swan made out of paper. When she started whining that she wanted to leave, he became furious and pushed her up against a tree and told her to shut up. Next time she whined, he said, he'd push her in the water. Eventually they had returned to her aunt's house, where her cousin had tried once more to start the motor, and that time the toy boat had responded promptly, and had torn away across the carpeted floor, leaving a burnt trail behind it.

Florence took a lot of photos of the pond, and when the film was used up, she walked to the shops to have it developed. She almost did not dare look at the pictures when they were ready, but the first batch was simply of the Heath itself, on a windy day. She nearly overlooked a photo, which was of two children playing at the water's edge of Whitestone Pond, until she realized that when she had taken the photo no one else was at the pond, least of all children. Looking more carefully, she had a jolt of recognition that the boy was in fact her cousin Jack so long ago, and entangled in the reeds close to the shore was a little boat, which looked much tinier to her now than her memory of how it had looked on that blustery day of her outing with her cousin. So the girl, though further away and indistinct, was probably her as a child! This must mean, then, that the camera could go back in time, as well as forward! It was remarkable! She must tell Lance!

The next several pictures were of her preparing for her wedding. Oh no! Not that again! In one she was brushing her hair; in another she was holding out her hand to take some flowers; in another she was standing in front of a full length mirror, so it was possible to see her back as well as part of her front. But what was striking about these photos, in contrast to the previous wedding pictures she had seen last summer, was that in these she looked much more joyful. What could these mean? Would she be happier about marrying Howard, after all? He had seemed a little less impatient recently. Could she grow genuinely fond of him?

She had one more lie to tell him, and after that she would not lie anymore.

They had gone to a restaurant, and she leaned across the table and informed him that Elizabeth Carlisle wanted her to go to New York in April to work on a story. This was partially true, as Elizabeth did indeed want her to write a story about New York, and also meet a certain editor, but this was all only in reaction to Florence having asked her for some time off to travel there. For one ghastly moment, Florence had the impression that Howard was about to suggest going with her, but he did not.

Or not quite. It was now Howard's turn to lean across the table.

"I hope you realize you don't know a thing about New York, so I'm at a loss to see how you will write a story on it. But be that as it may, I assume you won't come back ill, as you had last summer after being in that ghastly place in the Lake District. You do remember, don't you, that it was I who nursed you back to health! I had to take several days off work for that."

"Yes, you were so helpful!"

"And what occurs to me is that it would be nice if you and I went away somewhere together. I'm not having you gallivanting around all the time without me! So, what do you say to us taking a trip to Paris? Paris in the springtime!"

"Yes, Howard; that would be nice!" She felt that she owed that to him, and besides, she did love Paris.

--------

It was Friday, April 13th, and after settling down in her seat, which was in the tail of the plane probably because she bought her ticket so late, Florence realized she could hear the air hostesses, who were seated just behind her and separated by a maroon curtain, chatting to each other in broad Cockney accents before the plane took off. At first she vaguely heard just the rhythm of their voices, but then something one of them said caught her attention and caused her to start to listen closely.

"Yeah!" said one. "Just imagine! This plane's only four days old! Who knows what might go wrong with it!"

"That's right!" another answered. "'Snot like a car what you take out for a test drive, is it!"

"Wewl, let's 'ope we make it! That's all I can say!"

Just as Florence was starting to feeling exceedingly nervous and wishing they would stop talking, and thinking that maybe she deserved to perish for lying to everyone so that she could surreptitiously see Lance, she heard some chimes. One of the air hostesses behind the curtain said, "Right you are, then!" into what was presumably a phone, and immediately followed this, in a posh voice in surprising contrast with her former Cockney tones, with an announcement over the loud speaker; "Ladies and Gentlemen, welcome to Virgin Atlantic's Flight 001 to Newark. We will shortly be towed from the gate. The captain has asked me to tell you to fasten all seat belts and make sure your seats are in an upright position in preparation for take-off!"

Despite the newness and apparent unpredictability of the plane, the flight was uneventful. Nevertheless, Florence didn't dare sleep but felt irrationally that if she stayed awake the captain would stay awake and alert, and be able to concentrate and fly the plane safely.

The plane landed about twenty minutes early. And there Lance was, waiting at International Arrivals, standing alongside what Florence assumed were a group of Indian taxi drivers as they all held up large signs with the name of their passenger, and likewise Lance had a sign, but his was smaller and said *Fleur!* in his squarish style of writing, in Royal Blue ink. He was clearly quite amused at his little joke, and had that excited, intelligent glow in his eyes that Florence always found so attractive. They hugged and laughed and hugged again.

"My sweet Fleur!" Lance exclaimed, holding her back in his arms and looking at her. "How amazing to see you. Despite a long flight, you look lovely! And what is it about your hair that looks a little different?"

"I'm growing it," she said, swooping down to get a little present of a book out of her bag and giving it to Lance. And straightening up again and tossing the hair out of her eyes, she asked, "Do you like it?"

"I most certainly do! You look so pretty. I hadn't realized your hair is so curly. And what is this?" he asked, looking at the book.

"Just a small thing. You can look at it later. Oh Lance; I'm so pleased to see you!"

Still laughing they went to Lance's car, and then he drove them a short distance from Newark Airport to an area called Exchange Place. After parking the car, they strolled along a pier that projected far into the water, and from there they could look across the Hudson River to Manhattan. It was dusk, and lights were beginning to come on in all the skyscrapers, and the view was breathtaking.

"I can't believe I'm here!" Florence exclaimed.

"Well Fleur; together you and I will explore every inch of this city!"

"Do you know what some of these buildings are that we're looking at?"

"Yes, this is Lower Manhattan in front of us. And the tallest twin towers over there are the World Trade Center. We'll go to the top of one of them, and eat in the restaurant, which might be the highest in the world, with the wonderful name of 'Windows on the World'. And those buildings clustered in front of the World Trade Center are the World Financial Center. These centers are interconnected by a lovely winter garden, which I'll take you to as well! It has a glass dome – can you see it? – and palm trees. Imagine palm trees in this area! And behind this complex is Wall Street. And then if you look slightly to your left, going uptown a bit, you see that white and green spire? That's the Woolworth Building, which, when it was built, was the highest skyscraper! And further uptown, where the buildings get lower, that's Greenwich Village where I live …and then further to the left still the buildings get taller again, and that's Midtown. Can you see the Empire State Building? It's the tallest of that cluster. Oh look, it just put its lights on! It seems to light its spire in different colors on different occasions."

All of Lance's excited words seemed to have been delivered in one breath.

"You're so knowledgeable, Lance! And look at that lovely suspension bridge all the way up there! The way it's lit up it looks like a delicate pearl necklace."

"Yes! That's the George Washington Bridge. And look, Fleur, if you turn your head in the other direction, you'll see that there's the Statue of Liberty! We'll take a boat out there, and then climb inside the statue, all the way up inside the torch!"

"Wonderful! There's so much to do in a week!"

"Yes, and we'd better start now! So let's return to the car, and go first to my apartment (they don't say 'flat') to drop off your luggage."

"Is this *your* car, Lance?"

"No, I haven't really driven much since getting here. I walk everywhere, or take the subway. I borrowed this car from Marissa – my Teaching Assistant - and I must say, it's an exciting challenge to drive in Manhattan."

"Because of driving on the other side of the street?"

"No; because of the density of the traffic, the mad taxi drivers who swerve in and out of lanes at great speed, and the excitement, even in your car!" He pulled out from the parking space, and suddenly said, "By the way, Fleur, did you bring your camera with you?"

"I didn't," she said simply. "This time I have a disposable camera, as I really want to be confident that my photos of New York will come out. So many people will ask to see them. But Lance, I did use my camera recently. Oh, and I wanted to tell you about it, because something quite odd happened."

"Given your camera, nothing is too odd! What happened?"

So she told him about the photo of her cousin and herself at Whitestone Pond when they were children. "So it seems that the camera can also go back in Time!" she concluded. "Which of course means not every photo it takes might be a prediction of the future."

"How fascinating!" Lance said, as he edged the car through slow moving traffic towards the Holland Tunnel. "Perhaps it's pointing out the possibility that Time can travel backwards as well as forwards!"

"As a matter of fact, if I remember correctly, that was one of the things we said in our 'forgotten' conversation about Time! Yes, we did! We said why assume Time only moves forward!" Florence said, her tiredness from the flight making her dreamy and close to her subconscious thoughts, and this, combined with the terrific intellectual stimulation of being with Lance made her feel that her mind was still flying high, punch-drunk with all the excitement and her ideas coming to her bathed in a glorious glow.

"That's terrific, Fleur! Yes; you're right! We *had* spoken about how Time could go backwards as well as forwards! I remember that now. What propels it to only move in one direction?"

"We can measure Space in all directions, so why not Time?" she asked, the car passenger window steaming up as she spoke, which she imagined was caused by the warmth of her passion.

"True, but Space is three dimensional," he replied.

"Perhaps Time is too."

"So much, then, for parallel Time axes. It might be even more complicated than that."

"We'll get there, Lance!" she said. "And meanwhile, the fact that my camera gave a photo of the past is, when we think about it, the one true certainty we have, as I *know* my cousin and I took his boat down to Whitestone Pond. All the other photos are still pure conjecture in terms of whether they're the future or not."

"Fleur! You're amazing! Thanks for coming to see me! I'm so glad you're here!"

They were by now emerging from the Holland Tunnel onto very congested streets in Manhattan. Florence could not believe the noise! Cars were constantly hooting ("honking", Lance corrected her) and the pavements ("No, sidewalks") were teaming with pedestrians. It took a very long time to drive the short distance to Greenwich Village, and an even longer time to find a place to park. They went briefly to Lance's apartment on Cornelia Street – "It's not much more than a bedsit" he told her – and it certainly was a tiny space with a window facing the brick wall of the adjacent building. From there they walked to a cramped but cozy restaurant on MacDougal Street. It was noisy and crowded, but energetic and attractive, and the food, as Lance had promised, was plentiful and of excellent quality. They sat at a table in the window, and as they shared an enormous chocolate devil's foodcake, they looked out at the brightly lit, narrow street, still thronged with people.

"This is the city that never sleeps!" Lance commented. "But speaking of which, it's five hours ahead for you. Are you very tired?"

"No! Not at all! It's all so exciting!"

A little later they returned the car to Marissa in a poorly lit parking lot (they never say 'car park,' Lance told her), and all Florence, who was now starting to feel sleepy, saw of Marissa, was a shadowy figure with a broad smile and perfectly even teeth.

Over the next few days Florence and Lance did so much. They ate at Windows on the World, at the top of the World Trade Center. Florence was enchanted, and loved looking down to the street below to the matchbox size cars, cabs, and buses. They also took a ferry to the Statue of Liberty and climbed inside the torch. And they visited Ellis Island, and were struck by the soulful photos of immigrants with their stories of the difficult journeys they'd made to come to the US. They strolled hand in hand round Greenwich Village and the Lower East Side, eating delicious food in Chinatown and Little Italy. They visited the Empire State Building and Rockefeller Center, and then walked round the sweet little zoo in Central Park, especially delighting in the polar bears and the penguins, which they could see swimming underwater through the glass walls of the tank. And then they would rush back up the steps and see the penguins again above ground.

The only time Florence and Lance were apart was when she met Tom Skates, who was the editor Elizabeth Carlisle asked her to see. She arranged to do this while Lance was teaching a class. She met him at the mezzanine level of Number Two, World Trade Center. Just as when they'd eaten at Windows on the World, she delighted in the beautiful upward graceful soaring of sleek whiteness of the Towers, which sparkled in places with the reflected sunshine. And when she stepped inside, she marveled at how modern and graceful it was, loving the purple carpets and chrome lifts, and the enormous Miro tapestry. She went with Tom to the immense shopping area on the lower concourse, where they both had a cup of frothy cappuccino. They easily struck up a conversation, and Florence was pleased to discover that they had a lot of work interests in common, and plenty to report back to Elizabeth Carlisle.

A few days later, Lance suggested that they visit the Catskills, as he'd been told that it's a beautiful, rustic part of New York State, easily accessible from Manhattan. He phoned Marissa and asked if they could borrow her car again, and she readily agreed. Then Florence and Lance did an Internet search, found a nice looking inn outside a town called Kingston, made reservations for two nights, and they set off.

They loved the drive up the New York Thruway with its open views of green mountains either side, and were so delighted when they arrived at their inn, which was very pretty. However, the inn keeper was in a fluster, as she realized she only had one room available after all. Lance requested a few moments to discuss it, and lead Florence a little way down the hall so that they could speak privately.

"What do you think, Fleur? I am perfectly fine with sharing a room, if you are," he said. In Lance's tiny flat, he'd given her his bed, and arranged cushions and blankets for himself on the sofa in the living room, so she was surprised, but also quite pleased.

"Well, yes; especially if there are no other rooms available," she replied. "It seems like a lovely place to stay."

"Yes, and just think! We'll save a lot on the expenses if we have just the one room!"

"True."

So they dropped off their bags in what was a charming room with dormer windows in the top of the house, and went, on the recommendation of the inn keeper, to a lovely French restaurant with wide verandahs, where a very French woman was not only the chef but also the mother of several little children who had been happily chasing some geese outside when they first arrived. After a sumptuous meal of *coq au vin, pommes dauphinoise,* and *tarte tartin,* they strolled around outside, looking up at the now dark sky that was spangled with stars.

"It reminds me of skies in the Lake District," Lance remarked.

"Yes, you certainly can't see anything like as many stars in the city."

"Too much artificial light."

"Too much pollution."

"It's amazing, though, isn't it Fleur," he said. "Here we see such a vivid representation of Time. What we see when we look at these stars is very, very old news. Because of their immense distance from us, it takes millions of light years for the light from the stars to travel here to our eyes. We are in fact looking at the history of these stars!"

"And we can't know what they really look like now?"

"No. Impossible. Some of these stars that we're looking at might no longer be in existence!"

"And other stars might have been born?"

"Absolutely! Yet their light hasn't yet reached our eyes." He clutched her hand. "Isn't it marvelous here! What a perfect visual depiction of the relationship between Time and Distance! You know, Fleur, I love Manhattan, as that is all about the up-to-the-minute dynamic present, but it's also nice to step away to the countryside, and drink in the marvels of the universe, and watch the profundity of Time."

"It's terrific that you have both extremes within easy reach of each other!"

They returned to their room in the inn, and climbed a little shyly into bed together, both still invigorated from their walk and their observation of the night sky. Lance started to fondle her, and then paused as if to check with her that this was acceptable. In reply, she put her head on his chest and hugged him tightly. His warmth reminded her of her last night at Landsdowne's Guest House. It inflamed her passion. Now not weakened as she had been then, she fully expressed her longing, desire and love for him. And he reciprocated. At first they were frenzied and wild from a passion stored up and hitherto unexpressed, but later they grew more tender and gentle, looking longingly into each other's eyes. She felt so happy to wake the next morning to him beside her.

Over the next day and half of the next, Florence and Lance looped their arms around each other, and walked and walked. They passed banks of golden daffodils that nodded in the breeze, and weeping cherry trees, their branches full of heavy clusters of pink blossoms, sweeping gracefully down to the ground. A little further along they came to a pond, on the banks of which were more cherry trees but these were of the upright variety. They were also replete with pink and white blossoms, and Florence ran beneath the branches, looking up through them at the blue sky beyond. Some petals drifted down into her hair, and she laughed and let them stay, breathing in their sweet fragrance.

"Fleur, come and look!" Lance called to her, and she went to him and they saw a goose slip into the water, and then five fluffy goslings plopped into the water after him, followed at the end, after a thorough survey that all was well, by the mother goose. Together they swam majestically away, all in a straight line; the father, then the babies, and last the mother. Without a ripple.

Around the pond trees were starting to cover themselves with small, still slightly folded leaves, which were a fresh, bright green, not the darker green characteristic of the leaves later in the summer. Hearing a rustle in the thicket, they looked up and thought they saw a large slim dog before realizing that it was a deer. The deer was quite close, but then it darted away.

They returned to the City the following afternoon, as Lance had a class in the early evening. They sat hand in hand in Washington Square Park, under a magnolia tree in full, heavy cup-shaped blossom. Florence felt so happy to be with him, but sad, too, as she was leaving the next day. A little later, when it was close to the time for his class to begin, they walked diagonally across the Square, still holding hands, and entered an NYU building bustling with students. They descended two flights of stairs, and walked along a crowded corridor lined with metal lockers, to a rather dim corner classroom that had no windows. Here Lance lit up the room, which was thronged with animated students despite it being late on a Friday, with his passion and brilliance, and sparked energetic and enthusiastic responses from most of them in a manner that Florence, sitting discretely at the back of the room, had never seen in any classes she had attended when she'd been a student.

After class, several students, clearly reluctant to leave his presence, clustered around Lance at the podium, pressing him with more questions. This went on for quite a while; so long, in fact, that a new group of students was starting to arrive for their next class.

"As a suggestion," Lance said, "for those of you who might be interested, let's continue our discussion at a restaurant."

"Hey, great!" one of them said. "I know a real cute place in SoHo. I forget the name, but I know how to get there. They serve all kinds of New Age food."

"Hey! I bet I know where you're talking about," another said. "It's called Café Gitane and it's meant to be delicious!"

"Yeah, that's the one! How did you know which one I meant?"

"Wasn't that the one Cindy went to last week, and she wouldn't stop talking about it!"

"OK; let's go there, then," Lance said. "And before we go, I would like to introduce you to Fleur, who is my special friend visiting from England."

All eyes turned to Florence, who was standing too at the podium, but had hung back a bit, to let the students talk to their favorite professor. "Hi!" many of them said, giving her a welcoming smile.

The group that went to Café Gitane consisted of a tall Asian man with a strong accent, who mostly kept quiet; a blond tanned young woman apparently from California, dressed in ostentatious designer clothes; two Asian-American women who talked and laughed a lot; and Marissa, Lance's Teaching Assistant, or "TA," as they called her.

They walked in an unwieldy group, down streets much darker than those in Greenwich Village, and lined with different architecture that looked more like warehouses.

"This is a yuppy area of loft conversions," Marissa told Florence, and when she looked confused, Marissa went on to explain, "You see, lots of artists moved here when it was cheap, as they liked the light from the huge windows and the high ceilings. Probably most of them can't afford to be here now, though. You have a Soho in London, don't you?"

"Yes, but it looks very different from this!"

"Sure. Well, you remember that soon after leaving NYU, we crossed a wide street? Well, that's called Houston Street, so SoHo means 'South of Houston'. There's also a NoHo, and some even say there's a NoNo!"

Florence found that she liked Marissa, despite initial feelings of wariness and jealousy that Lance might find her attractive, and despite the fact that this was her last night and she'd expected to spend it alone with Lance.

"There's even a DUMBO," added one of the Asian-American students, whose name was Susie Wang. "And that stands for Down Under the Manhattan Bridge Overpass."

"I love how playful Americans are with words!" Florence said.

"Not Americans. New Yorkers. There's a world of difference between New York and the rest of the country. Take Cameron, the Californian one. She's so ditsy!" Susie Wang said conspiratorially.

"Ditsy?"

"Yeah! You know; flaky! And then Midwesterners; they're a whole different story. Oh look, I think that's the restaurant over there. Hey, Dr. Ramsey!" Susie called to Lance, who was up ahead of them with the quiet Asian man. "You're going too far! It's over there, on the other side of the street!"

They were fortunate to find a sufficiently large table to accommodate them all, and as soon as Lance sat down, he was surrounded by his students, so Florence sat at the opposite end of the table.

"You see," said Lance, looking around the table benevolently and continuing the topic from the class, "We simply can't ignore the philosophers who have made such a profound impact on our current thinking. Take Hobbes, for example-"

"Hobbes?" said Cameron, the Californian girl, who had absent-mindedly been swirling a slice of lime around in her glass with bejeweled fingers, each one ending in a long, painted fingernail, some purple and some turquoise. "Isn't that a department store?"

Susie Wang stifled a laugh behind her hand.

"What did you think of the walk over here?" Susie's friend Twyla asked Florence, trying to deflect attention away from Susie.

"Fascinating," Florence replied. "I love the contrasting neighborhoods of Manhattan. I particularly like Greenwich Village. After being so used to every street being on a grid system, it's nice to see streets that are so higgledy-piggledy."

The table erupted in laughter.

"Higgledy-piggledy! What a great word!" Susie Wang said. And turning to Lance she added, "You Brits and we Americans definitely don't speak the same language!"

"I don't know about you guys," Cameron said, squelching some iridescent blue chewing gum between her parted lips, "But I could listen to Dr. Ramsey all day!"

"Yeah! Me, too!" several others echoed.

They ordered their meal, which was served on huge square white plates, each dish covered with sprouts of varying types, and they ate with chopsticks, frequently dipping their chopsticks into each other's plates to sample different kinds of food.

After they'd eaten Lance said, "Well, this was very pleasant! We will do this again. But now I'm afraid that Fleur and I must go, as she's flying home tomorrow so she'll have a very long day, and I don't want her to feel too knackered."

"Knackered? Is that a word? I love it!" Twyla laughed.

"What would you say?"

"I'm 'pooped'. But I'm going to start saying 'knackered' from now on!"

"Me, too!" Susie agreed.

Florence and Lance returned to his flat on Cornelia Street, and this time there was no preamble of arranging cushions and blankets on the sofa.

"You have nice students and they really love you," Florence remarked as she climbed into bed.

"Shhh! Let's not speak of them now," Lance said, his hand reaching down gently to caress her. They made love tenderly and affectionately, and feeling so contented, Florence slept blissfully the rest of the night.

She awoke to a repetitive blaring of a car alarm from the street below, and then a feeling of chilly emptiness. She realized Lance was no longer in bed, and rolled over on to his pillow so as to inhale the scent of him there. She then padded into the living room where she saw him at the computer.

"Good morning, my sweet!" he said cheerily. "Sleep well? I didn't want to wake you."

"Marvelously, thanks. How long have you been up?"

"Just a short while. Thought I'd check my messages, which will only take a moment. Then let's go out somewhere nice for breakfast, and stay in Greenwich Village until it's time to go to the airport."

"That sounds nice. I love Greenwich Village."

"Yes; we'll do something 'low key,' as the Americans would say."

He smiled and returned to looking at the computer screen. Then they both heard the 'ding' of a new e-mail arriving, and Lance's face momentarily changed in a complicated way that she could not interpret.

"Anything the matter?" she asked.

"No, no; not at all. Just an annoying question from a student," he said in a rushed sort of voice. He clicked out of the program. "Come," he said, looking up and smiling again. "Let's get ready and go and enjoy this lovely day."

They went to a restaurant the name of which amused them both - the Elephant and Castle (after the London neighborhood) – and seated at a round table, they ate poached eggs on an English muffin (also amusing as neither of them could find anything remotely English about the muffin) smothered in Hollandaise sauce, and ended by sharing an Indian pudding, which was delicious.

"I wonder if this pudding is as Indian as the muffin is English!" Lance said.

"It's phenomenally good, whatever it is," Florence replied, licking her spoon.

Before leaving, Florence drew a sketch of an elephant on a paper serviette and handed it to Lance, telling him that an elephant never forgets. She wanted him to remember their lovely time together always. They later strolled arm in arm down Fifth Avenue to Washington Square. As they approached the arch, they could see the gleaming white towers of the World Trade Center beyond. They sat down on 'their' bench under the blossoming magnolia tree, the base of which was bordered by a multitude of freshly colored little pansies. Around the Square stood the buildings of NYU, their purple flags with the white torch logo billowing in the gentle breeze.

"Fleur," Lance said, turning to her with that unreadable expression that she had seen on his face that morning. "Frankly I am in a dilemma."

"Why? What is it?"

"That e-mail I received earlier today…it wasn't from a student. It was from Bob, who is the Dean of faculty."

"Oh?"

"Inviting me to stay on here for another three years."

Florence felt every part of herself shut down, and a feeling of nausea hitting the back of her throat. Of course it had not been a troubling e-mail from a student. His students clearly adored him. Involuntarily and subconsciously she withdrew her hand from where it lay on his thigh. But she must not make a scene; must not behave as she had in East Anglia when he'd told her he was coming here.

"What will you do?" Her voice sounded strained, even to herself.

"I haven't decided yet. It's so complicated. I don't know what I should do."

She made every effort to sound helpful and neutral. "What are some of the factors that are swaying you one way or the other?" she asked.

"Well, clearly you can see why I love it here. And besides which, this is an excellent experience for advancing my career. But then there's Mother to consider. And my job at East Anglia. I don't know if they'd hold it for me if I stayed away longer than a year."

He hadn't mentioned her.

Tears sprang up in her eyes, making it feel as though she was looking at everything through a goldfish bowl.

"Don't look so sad, Fleur," he said, noticing. "I haven't agreed to staying here yet."

"No," she said, shuffling her foot through some dry, dusty leaf fragments that had collected near the bench.

They sat quietly for a moment. When she could stand it no longer, she said, "I don't want to sound presumptuous, but I just wondered if I am included in part of your equation or not."

"Fleur," he said, slowly exhaling. "There's obviously so much ambiguity there. I can't pretend to know or understand-"

"Oh Lance, as far as Howard is concerned, if that's what you mean, I-"

"All I can say is that I don't want to share you with him."

"But we've already - I mean, you and I - we enjoy-"

"Yes, it's true. And maybe we shouldn't have." He looked terribly sad.

"Oh Lance, don't say that! This time we've spent together, haven't you-?"

"No; let's not do this! Please, Fleur. We've kept away from this topic; we've refrained from mentioning Howard's name, and I don't want to bring him up now."

"Neither do I. I don't want to even think about him!"

"That's good. And don't misunderstand me. I have no regrets for what you and I have done. You've made me radiantly happy. Now please let's change the subject. There are only a few hours left until your departure. Let's try and make the most of them."

Florence forced a smile, even though all she felt like doing was weeping copiously.

"Well, it's a great honor that the Dean invited you to stay," she said at last because she felt she should.

"Yes, it's a great honor," he echoed wistfully.

By the fountain some Asian students, clad in white trousers and black tunics with brightly colored bands tied around their middle, were squatting on their heels on the ground, rhythmically beating drums in time with each other.

"That's Korean music," Lance told her. "I've heard them before."

They rose from the bench and went closer to the drummers. Then they wandered over to the Dog Run. Everything was ruined. Although they stood hand in hand, and chuckled at a German Shepherd colliding with a Golden Lab as they bounded joyfully around the enclosure, it was just a façade.

"When do you have to tell the Dean your decision?" Florence asked.

"He's given me twenty four hours to think it over," Lance replied.

They stood longer at the Dog Run. There was nowhere else worth going to.

"As soon as I get my thoughts in order, I'll let you know," he added. "In fact, you will be the first to know, especially since you are the first to hear of my quandary now."

He sadly put his arm around her. What did it mean? She noticed for the first time a small white dog, which, when another dog approached and sniffed at it, cowered, trembling, before slinking off to be alone in a corner that the other more rambunctious dogs ignored.

"Shall we go back to Cornelia Street and get your things?"

"Might as well."

It was earlier than necessary to leave for the airport, but it seemed pointless staying any longer in Greenwich Village. There was nothing left to do. And perhaps, Florence thought neurotically, that he could not wait to get rid of her, even though she hadn't made a scene.

As he gathered her into his arms at Newark Airport, before she left for the gate, he said, "Let's not focus on these last few hours. Let's just think of everything else we did together this week!"

She nodded, the corner of her passport in her mouth as she pretended to be looking in her bag for her boarding card, although in reality she bit down hard on her passport as she couldn't trust herself not to start crying.

"And Fleur," he added. "I saw in my diary that the clocks go forward in England tonight, so you coming here this particular week meant that we had an extra hour together. Sort of like a clock striking thirteen!"

He was back to conversations about Time. Always a comfortable footing for him. For them. He was trying to cheer her up. She nodded again, and taking the passport out of her mouth, they kissed.

"Thank you, Lance," she said. "For everything."

"Cheerio, Fleur! I'll e-mail you!"

"I love you," she whispered, and turning away quickly, she blended in with the crowd going through the gate towards Security.

The woman next to her in the departure lounge kept offering her hankies, as she couldn't stop crying.

# NINE

*SHE WAS AT ANOTHER AIRPORT* – London, Heathrow – with a stupendously happy Howard. They were waiting for the call to board their flight to Paris. In contrast to Howard's light-heartedness, she was strenuously depressed.

Her first morning back from New York she had been tired from jetlag and a virtually sleepless night on the plane, and had not thought too much about the fact that Lance had not yet e-mailed her. In fact, when she calculated the time difference, she told herself it would still be too early in New York for him to be awake, let alone to have made his decision. But by seven in the evening, when she thought she could no longer stay awake, she found ironically that she felt completely restless. Four times after going to bed, she had tossed off the duvet and gone to her computer to check her e-mail. Nothing. Not wanting Howard to continue asking her questions about what she was doing and not wanting to continue lying by saying that she was awaiting an e-mail from the New York editor with whom she'd met, she returned to bed, but was sleepless most of the night.

When finally she slept, she dreamed that Lance was sprawled out along the sofa in his flat at Cornelia Street, and she was bending over him trying to comprehend what he was saying as he seemed to have acquired a strong Chinese accent. Through the jumble of words, she made out, "I'm swaying towards staying here, Fleur." It was so real. She awoke and didn't immediately recognize where she was. She saw the dim dawn sending a feeble shaft of light through the window and first thought it was the airshaft of Cornelia Street.

Realizing that she was back in London, she quickly rose from her bed and went to her computer. Her fingers fumbled so much she could hardly log on. She was convinced that there would be an e-mail by now from Lance. After all, he only had twenty four hours in which to make his decision, and he told her she would be the first to know his choice.

"You've Got Mail. 1 New Message," her computer informed her. The e-mail seemed to take so long to download. And now she dreaded that this e-mail would be from him, as she intensely feared that her dream would be true, and he would be informing her that he had decided to accept the Dean's offer to stay, especially since he knew she had returned to Howard. But her dread turned to disappointment when she saw that the e-mail was not from Lance, but from Elizabeth Carlisle, asking her about her meeting with the New York editor.

Why wasn't he writing to her? *Was* it because of those last awful, awkward hours together, when they were essentially questioning, yet also avoiding asking, what their relationship was about; when they had also mentioned Howard? She wished so much that they hadn't had that conversation. In fact she wished that he had not received the invitation to stay longer at NYU until after she'd left. But there again, Lance had told her that they shouldn't think of those last tense hours, but of the rest of the week that they'd spent together; he told her of how she'd made him "radiantly happy". And they *had* been happy. She'd had an exceptionally wonderful time. Why didn't he write?

Should she e-mail him? No, because she'd still be waiting for his reply, only now it would be worse as he'd know her level of anxiety. But that was ridiculous! She could send him a bouncy, happy sounding e-mail thanking him for the incredible week they spent together, and in fact many times she started to compose just such a message, but it hadn't sounded right.

He might even feel that she was trying to influence his decision. Besides, he said he would write, so she must stop being compulsive and should wait for him to do so.

Her body was heavy with exhaustion, yet at the same time filled with a nervous energy which intensified when she decided to phone him. She dialed his number, trying to calm herself so that her voice would not give away her deep anxiety, but then sat listening to the series of long single rings of the American phone system. No answer. He was not in. She imagined his little apartment on Cornelia Street, with the black phone on his desk in the living room, ringing into emptiness. She heard his voice come on the answering machine; friendly and bright sounding, a voice with a smile, requesting the caller to leave a message and he would phone back. She put the phone down.

That night, after continuing to check her e-mail frequently throughout the day, she went to bed, and slept, though her sleep was superficial. And in the morning, though scarcely refreshed, Howard kept nagging at her to hurry and pack, as the taxi was coming soon. Unselectively she threw clothes into the suitcase, barely folding them.

And so here she was, at Heathrow again, and now they were being called to board the plane.

How quickly they arrived in Paris! They booked into an attractive hotel, with a circular staircase with wrought iron banisters, and then, leaving their suitcases in their room, went out to a café in a nearby street. They sat at a table out-of-doors, and drank strong coffee and ate *baguette* with ham and salad, pate and cornichon. During the meal, she listened with fascination to how quickly people seemed to speak in a foreign language, while Howard, oblivious of his surroundings, sat studying the guidebook and planning their itinerary even though she had been a much more frequent visitor to Paris than he was and knew the city well. He deliberately ignored the suggestions of places to visit that she offered. As soon as he had finished eating he said that they should immediately start to explore the city, despite the fact that she still had quite a bit of her sandwich left to eat. Perhaps to hurry her up, or perhaps because of his natural greediness, he put his fingers into her plate, and broke off a large hunk of the sandwich for himself.

The meal finished, Howard said they should go to the Seine and walk along its banks. They got lost finding the way, but Howard refused to ask anyone for directions. "Listen, if I could find my way around Hong Kong when I lived there, I can certainly manage Paris!" he said, consulting the guidebook again and leafing rapidly through its pages. And when, on recollection despite her extreme fatigue, she suggested that they turn down a particular street, he flatly refused and insisted on a much more convoluted way to get there. Later in the afternoon, they went to Montmartre, climbing its windy streets, and looked at the goods sold by street vendors. Howard bought a Toulouse Lautrec poster. They found a nice restaurant, where she ate a *croque monsieur* and he had *moules marinieres* and *bouillabaisse*, before returning to the Hotel and realizing that they'd left the poster behind. For the first time in many nights, Florence slept soundly, yet still woke with a melancholic feeling and a depressing exhaustion.

After breakfast, they went out into the bright sunshine and walked to L'Arc de Triomphe, and when Florence saw it she felt such a punch of sadness for the stately white arch mimicking it in Washington Square Park, which now seemed to be a place she had visited so long ago. Howard insisted that they visit both the Pompidou Center and the Monet Museum, which she thought would be too much to take in to fully appreciate, but he would hear of nothing else, and ultimately she did feel gratefully distracted from her despair as to why Lance had not written to her.

She suggested that they return to the restaurant from the previous night, in the hope of finding the poster, but Howard replied that they should first stroll through the Jardin de Tuilleries. They walked along its main path, and then he stated that they should rest for a while. Most abruptly and ludicrously he plummeted to his knees in front of her, as she perched primly on a bench, which interrupted her thoughts on how park benches in the Tuilleries were not unlike park benches in Hyde Park. Seeing him in a knelt position, his ample belly sagging over his belt even more than usual, made her think that the chic Parisians would consider just how clumsy and ridiculously ungainly the English were.

"Flo, I asked you to Paris now - in the springtime - as Paris is the city of lovers. Will you marry me?" he asked, tugging at something in his pocket, which was pulled tight over his squatting form, and produced a small, brown velvet box.

"Howard!" she exclaimed in surprise.

"Well, will you?"

She turned her head away, looking along the path towards the distant trees. A squirrel was busy with an acorn; a group of children went running by, bouncing a red ball; two women, *baguettes* tucked under their arms, were strolling towards them. She did not know what to say, and what she did say when she turned back to look at him, was as if a ventriloquist was speaking through her.

"Yes."

It was the devil of self-torture that afflicted her, that visited her at highly emotional moments, which though she wished with all her heart to be rid of Howard, pushed her into agreeing to bind the rest of her life inextricably with his. She was incapable of doing otherwise, and was much too tired to think.

He awkwardly hoisted himself to a standing position by using his free hand to push himself up from the ground, only narrowly missing a small pile of dog crap, snapped open the lid of the brown box, and slipped a diamond ring flashing in the sunlight, on the finger of her wrong hand. Roundly sitting down next to her and bumping into her hip, he kissed her wetly and ardently, and then put a heavy arm around her shoulders. His evident delight repulsed her, making her want to pull off the ring, making her want him to be kneeling down in front of her by the dog crap, making her want to hand the ring back to him as in an old cine film played backwards. But instead, driven by her devil that she perceived in the blurry periphery of her vision, which was jabbing its thumb at her and smiling with cruel mirth, she started to laugh. She laughed quietly at first, which encouraged Howard no end, but her laughter became hideously out of control, hysterical, macabre. She had done it now. With one tiny word she had sealed her fate. She was scorched by the panic that smoldered within her. She forced herself to stop laughing. Bright tears stood in her eyes, deliciously cooling down her burningly hot eyeballs.

"Have you finished now?" Howard asked, looking slightly perplexed. "Well, I certainly am glad I made you so happy."

He pulled her towards him, and weakened, she lay back against him. She was not as comfortable in his arms as in Lance's, and his smell was different, less appealing.

It was only much later that she started to miserably rationalize what she had done. Yes, it seemed that Lance had failed her. He had not come through. And now all that anxiety and sadness she had felt when he did not write, turned to fury. All that loving time together in New York, all the incredible things they did; what did it mean to him? How well did she even know him? Perhaps, all along, he was more attracted to Marissa. Howard, on the other hand, was more dependable. And her parents would be thrilled! And she was already living with him, so how different could it be? It was perhaps presumptuous of him to have already purchased the ring, but, quickly slipping it on to the right finger, she realized it was kind, and he even knew the right size!

"How did you know what size ring to buy?" she asked.

"Because I know you perfectly. In fact, I know you even better than you know yourself!"

That night they ate a celebratory dinner in a restaurant in which the tables were exceptionally close together. On the next table sat two Americans, and Florence was saddened to hear their exciting accent now. Still, they struck up a conversation, and it turned out that the Americans were from Philadelphia but traveled frequently to New York. Florence told them she'd just returned from a trip there, and when they started to ask her about some of the places she'd seen, Howard, who hated to be excluded from any conversation, told them how she was lucky not to have become ill while she was there, as she usually got ill when she was away without him, just as had happened the previous summer when she'd gone to the Lake District. He spoke with great drama about how he had to drive there twice; once to visit her and try to cheer her up, and the second time to take her back home, and then how he took so much time off work to nurse her back to health. Trying to redirect the conversation, she told the Americans that if they were thinking of going to England they should definitely still consider going to the Lake District, and not to be put off as it was so lovely there. "You bet!" the man who was called John said. "Didn't I say,

Martha, that we should go to the Lake Country? Martha's a great fan of Wordsworth. Isn't that so my love!"

"That's right! I truly marvel at his words. Take for example, '*Knowing that Nature never did betray/The heart that loved her*'. So simple! So right on! Yes, we chose a tour group around England that will include the Lake Country. You Brits certainly know how, in your tiny island, to offer so much of cultural and natural beauty! We're traveling to England on Friday and we can't wait!"

When it was time for dessert, and they realized that they had all ordered *crème brulee*, Howard leaned over to them and said in a voice saturated with complacency, that they'd just made the decision, only a few hours earlier, that they were going to get married. "You're a real lucky man!" said Martha. "Yeah, you sure are!" John echoed. "You've got yourself a mighty fine bride!"

Later, when they returned to the Hotel, Florence noticed that Howard was pouting, and she asked him if anything was wrong.

"This is meant to be the happiest night of my life, and yet they really spoiled it."

"Who spoiled what?"

"Those stupid, superficial Americans. Why were they only saying I was so lucky to have you? What about you being lucky to have me?"

"Oh Howard, I'm sure they meant it. They were probably just about to say it when the waiter came to pour the coffee."

"Yes? Well, I don't think so! They could have said it in front of the waiter. It's made me really pissed off. And here we are; I had wanted to have sex with you, but now I'm not sure that it's possible. Damn Americans!"

They seldom made love, and when they did, it was often awkward – legs and arms getting in the way, and his bulky body on top of her making her feel that he was cutting off her circulation - just as it was this glorious night in Paris with the city sparkling all around them, when Howard finally felt in the mood again.

"There!" said Howard, pulling away from her. "I think I did rather well. I certainly know how to pleasure you, don't I! And soon we can stop the contraceptives, as I want you to give me lots of babies, Flo!"

Florence, who habitually put on an act when they made love, nodded and turned away from him onto her pillow, saying it was great but now she was a little tired. She stared out into the dark room, remembering how, when she was a child, her bedroom furniture at nighttime would assume odd, monster-like proportions. Now these unfamiliar bulks of furniture in this room in a hotel in Paris looked the same way. She remembered, too, her genuine passion with Lance, when they'd made love in the Catskills and then back in his tiny flat on Cornelia Street, and how their bodies had melted into each other's and fitted together so perfectly.

The next morning Howard phoned his parents and told Florence to do the same. Both sets of parents were overjoyed and wedding plans were immediately set into motion. In fact, when they returned from Paris the following day, there were several messages from Howard's mother, asking if they'd decided upon a date; how they must book a hall immediately "as you never know, and the popular places fill fast;" suggesting a time to go with Florence to purchase the wedding dress; telling them that she herself would personally write up the list of desired wedding gifts as well as the guest list; and saying she was so thrilled that soon there would be lots of little Howards running about. "They're bound to have his green eyes," her message had said emphatically. "It might be considered a recessive gene, but in our family it is really powerful and has been passed down from generation to generation!"

Florence, who could not take all this, went over to her computer and logged on. Surely there must now be a message from Lance, whatever its contents. Still nothing. That was that, then. Such finality. She'd learned what he intended to do through her dream, and he seemed not to even have the courage to tell her directly. Angrily she shut down the computer and went over to Howard, placing her hand on his shoulder.

"Your mother's right," she said. "We should start making plans."

"Of course she's right! My family's always right! You should know that by now. Stick around with me, kid, and you'll learn a thing or two! We'll get married this summer. I like a summer wedding. And I know of a good place, a boathouse down by the Thames. It's where Ricky and Sylvia got married."

He phoned the place. It was booked solidly all summer. He tried other places. It was the same story.

"Let's try for late summer, then," Florence suggested. "We could wait a few more weeks."

"No! I wouldn't hear of it! The weather will be lousy and it will all be ruined."

"Not necessarily. Remember there is often an 'Indian Summer' in early September."

"All right, then," he said reluctantly, and redialed the number of the boathouse. It turned out that they had a vacancy for September 15th, so they made their reservation and put down a sizable deposit. "But if it rains, I'll kill you!" he told Florence.

Later, on the phone to his mother, he said, "I decided to book the place for after the rush of the summer, and I convinced Flo to agree with me. She's in such a hurry to marry as fast as possible, the gorgeous girl that she is, but she saw my reason when I explained that a lot of people might be away on holiday if we had it in the middle of the summer season."

"Good thinking!" his mother said. "Your head's always in the right place. Now let me speak with your dear fiancée."

Florence came to the phone.

"Congratulations again, dear girl! We're so happy for you both. You're very lucky to have the privilege of marrying Howard. Now, when would you like us to go shopping for your wedding dress?"

"Thanks, but I don't think that will be necessary. My mother and I were planning to go together."

"Nonsense! We can't put all the responsibility on her! I'll be there, too. Three heads are better than two when it comes to a decision as important as this one. After all, we want you to do all you can to look your very best!"

And so it was agreed, and when Florence did go out with her mother and Howard's mother, and stood as a mannequin, being turned this way and that as both older women argued over different designs, her patience was finally depleted, her body too tired to try on yet more frothy white dresses, and so she insisted on one dress in particular, though she could no longer tell them apart.

Then it happened. On the Sunday, four days after their return from Paris, she received an e-mail from Lance. It read:

*Fleur, my sweetest. I am at a loss to understand your silence. Every few hours I rush to my Inbox to see if there is a message from you, but there has not been. I recall you telling me that you were going to be traveling to Paris, so I have waited until I could wait no longer to write to you. I think you should be back by now, and hope Paris was to your liking. Are you well? I do hope so.*

*Perhaps, Fleur, you did not like my decision. Perhaps you feel this will complicate things for you. If this is the case, I truly apologize. I tried to balance all the factors, and feel I have made the right choice. I'm eager to hear from you, my love. Lance*

Without hesitation, Florence clicked on 'Reply,' incredulity absorbing her entirely.

*What WAS your decision, Lance? I hadn't heard from you, and have been longing to know.*

She added, "I miss you so much" but deleted those words, as she was still not wise to his decision. She clicked on 'Send' and hoped she would not have to wait too long for his reply.

His response, in fact, came quickly. Her eyes rushed over the words expressing his wonder as to why his initial e-mail had not reached her; how his mind was made up even at the airport as he was seeing her off; and how he had returned to Cornelia Street immediately and had gone straight to his computer to e-mail her. His intention, in fact, had been for his e-mail to arrive before she did, to greet her on her arrival. He was forwarding below the very message that he had sent then. Her eye glanced lower down on the screen, and yes, the time and date accurately reflected the evening of her departure from New York. And what he wrote in that e-mail made her feel both ecstatic and desperate, and caused her to reread it several times.

*My lovely Fleur,* (he wrote) *I could not get back from the airport quickly enough! I hated every red traffic light, every slow car in front of me, that kept me longer from the computer and from communicating with you. I want you to know that I cannot acquiesce with the Dean's invitation. If missing you then as a consequence of continuing my stay here were to be as painful as my feelings of missing you now, I simply couldn't endure it. And so I will tell Bob (the Dean) in the morning that I very much appreciate being asked, but that I am unable to accept his offer of extending my stay here.*

*Love always, Lance*

Florence heard the door open, and quickly minimized the screen. Howard entered the room, a donut in one hand and his laptop in the other.

"I saw the wedding invitations that you and my mother chose," he said, biting into the donut. A little squiggle of red jam oozed out and deposited itself below his lower lip. "Boy, when you two get together, you're like dynamite!"

"You like them?"

"Like them? They're bloody marvelous!"

He popped the remainder of the donut in his mouth, and chewing loudly, he carried the laptop into the bathroom. He generally spent an enormously long time in there, always with his laptop, which he said was the modern-day equivalent of a magazine. She hated this habit of his, but today it would be an advantage for him to be locked in there as long as possible.

She returned to Lance's message. So he had felt as she had, and their week together was as profound for him as it was for her. How could she have doubted him?

But now plans for her wedding were moving forward so rapidly. It felt as though she had been coerced into it. If only Lance's e-mail had arrived on time! It was inexplicable that it could have been lost, and now caused such major havoc. In fact, she wished he could have made his decision before she left New York. Maybe he needed time to think. Maybe he was a slow thinker.

157

She was a slow thinker, too. What could she do, now? She must think of some way of telling Howard, before he came out of the bathroom, that she could not go through with the wedding. But how could she put it to him? Quick; she must think of something! But her panic and her anxiety closed off her ability to think. All rationality was clouded in a tangled fog of emotions. She felt paralytic.

Must phone Anna. Anna would help her, would calmly know what she should do. But the phone just rang and rang. *Pick up, Anna; please pick up!* Then she remembered; Anna was away on a retreat. No! She must think this through for herself. But she was too afraid. Not only afraid that if she called the wedding off, Howard would tell her parents about the grotesque abortion she'd undergone. No, not only that. She was also profoundly terrified at the thought of how angry, and maybe vicious, he would be if she told him she could not marry him. She absolutely did not dare tell him that. Not now. She had no strength for that. Her fear of his anger was too great. And besides, it would not only be *his* anger, but his parents would be furious as well. And her parents – oh no – her parents would be livid, and so disappointed in her. They would also be appalled if they learned of her abortion. How could she risk all of this? And Lance was not physically there by her side to protect her against them all.

And now here was Howard emerging from the bathroom, smelly and complacent. Quickly again she minimized Lance's e-mail, and exceptionally frightened, she smiled nervously up at him. No time to think. No time to formulate a change of such proportion. She tried to suppress her panic. Perhaps she would tell him another time, when she had had more time to prepare what she would say. No; not perhaps! She *would* do this. But if for some reason...well, if for some reason she couldn't tell him, perhaps not that much would be changed if she did go ahead with this wedding. Perhaps it wouldn't be so bad, and she would avoid all that fury directed at her. And with Lance back in England, she could continue seeing him as before.

Howard said he was popping out for a newspaper, and ludicrously she felt compelled to grab this opportunity and immediately write back to Lance. She sensed his waiting for her reply to his monumental decision, after so much delay in her receiving it. But what should she say? She didn't have much time, as the newspaper shop was only on the next corner. The first part of her e-mail was easy, as she described her delight at his decision to return in January, and how she, too, had found the time they spent together in New York profoundly exquisite and inspirational. She lamented that his first e-mail conveying his intentions had been lost, and like him, she had made such frequent trips to her Inbox hoping to hear from him. What a protracted period of anguish they had both endured!

But now she paused. She was uncertain about how to write what she felt she needed to tell him next. But Howard would be returning any moment, and she must hurry. So, taking a headlong plunge into murkiness, in a swift second paragraph she slipped in the fact that she and Howard had plans to be married on September 15th. Wasn't it always best to be honest? And she deliberately used the word "plans," as aren't plans sometimes broken, and wouldn't Lance intuit that? She continued hastily, formulating her thoughts as she was writing and feeling that perhaps she was reaching a solution, that she saw that this would cause no difference between him (Lance) and herself. After an initial fuss and flourish when she and Howard married, things would settle down and she'd merely be living with him as she was already. Then, when he, Lance, returned to England the following January, they could climb back on their parallel Time axis - remote, separate and undisturbed - and since no one would know, this could not hurt anyone. In fact, she added, this would be better than before, as now they knew they loved each other, and she would always love him. The front door was opening, and she clicked on 'Submit'.

She waited two days for Lance's reply, and when it came, before even reading the words, she was struck by its brevity.

*Congratulations! Good luck. And goodbye.*

She was meant to be going to the bridal shop for another fitting of her dress, but quickly she wrote,

*Thanks, Lance! But why did I get an impression of finality? Why did you say goodbye?*

159

She knew e-mail could be subject to misinterpretation, devoid as it was of tone of voice or body language, so she was pleased with herself for writing to seek clarification. She read his reply that evening.

*Finality? Yes, unfortunately so. As I told you before, I cannot share you with Howard.*

# TEN

*THE WEATHER GREW WARMER AS* summer approached. Florence felt burdened by her sadness and sobbed secretly yet frequently, so that her eyes were permanently underlined by baggy gray shadows. Months had rolled thunderously by and she and Lance had exchanged not a single article of correspondence. The wedding date was looming increasingly close. She viewed it with dread. When she had been a student and had felt nervous about impending exams, she had comforted herself with the thought that the sooner the exams came the further they would be away, because as they approached, so too would they be sooner completed and would recede into the past. But no such comforting thought could be applied to the wedding. The sooner it came, the sooner it would change her state permanently. How could she have been so naïve as to think otherwise? Lance was right. Just because she and Howard already lived together made no difference. Frequently there was talk about children, and her future mother-in-law, loquacious as ever, wasted no time in telling her how she should hurry to procreate, as none of them was getting any younger.

She dreamed frequently of Lance; swift, surreal impressions that he and she were still together, enjoying their always fascinating conversations, laughing, holding on to each other. But one night her dream of him was more concrete, vivid, and certainly more disturbing. She dreamed that he was in trouble of some kind, and that he was calling out to her. She could not shake off thoughts of that dream, and although she tried to go about her business, completing work assignments, and attending to wedding preparations, the dream became a worrying obsession. She would go to sleep at night and try to reconstruct it, change the ending, so that whatever troubled him he'd managed to overcome, and he was happy once more.

But the dream continued to plague her waking state, and one day at work she logged into her e-mail account, and sent him a message. She asked him how he was, and said she was concerned because she'd dreamed he'd been clearly upset by something. She also confessed that she was missing him appallingly.

He wrote back immediately.

> *Fleur, even at a distance (of space and time) you continue to amaze me. When did you dream that dream? I ask this as it seems to have been prophetic. I had experienced some upsetting difficulties, but things are more manageable again now. Thank you for your concern.*

Florence knew she had dreamed that dream several weeks ago, but she then remembered the exact date as she knew that it coincided with a deadline she had to meet at work.

> *Lance,* (she wrote) *I am so sorry to hear you really did encounter some problems, and am glad that you indicate that they seem to be resolved now. My dream was so realistic – in it I heard you calling out to me and you sounded so agitated - and I felt extremely worried. I didn't know if you welcomed hearing from me again, so I've been hesitant to intrude, but I couldn't hold on to this worry any longer. I remember that the exact date of this dream*

*was August 2nd. I know this as I had to submit an article that day to my boss, so that was a clear marker. Your friend, Fleur.*

Lance wasted no time in replying.

*Good God! That was the very date my acute worries began! Fleur, before I came to America, you once argued that our concept of a parallel Time axis exclusively for us was fallacious, and recent events between us made me start to doubt its possibilities, too. But your dream proves otherwise. It could well indicate that you and I met in a different Time dimension and a different state of consciousness, and you saw how troubled I was. And because you had witnessed that, you could dream about it, which informed your conscious mind. I remember we once spoke about how having prophetic dreams could be proof of being on a different Time axis and experiencing something that had not yet happened on the dominant Time axis. Some might interpret the timing and nature of your dream as being due to telepathy, but maybe this itself is an exact explanation as to how telepathy can occur.*

*Don't worry any more about me. All is indeed well again. But let me tell you what happened. I've just returned to New York after having spent several weeks at Landsdowne's. Mother likes her routine, and so apparently do Rose and Allison. We were all there. Rose spoke frequently of you, asking me if I remembered you from last summer. Couldn't she see the pain that her random questioning inflicted! Even though all of us have been going there every summer for years, it now felt so different without you being there. Who, Rose wanted to know, should we include in our Scrabble game? We made up a pathetic threesome on several evenings. Remember the interminable amount of time Rose takes at each turn? And with no one to send secret messages to, as you and I had done last year with our messages contained in the words we made, the game felt strictly tame and two dimensional. Allison was slightly less quiet than at previous times, though Rose still shuts her out from most conversations. It seems that they are most excited about your upcoming wedding, and are very much looking forward to attending. At the mention of this, I had to make a huge effort to hide my emotions. But I could not help sliding my chair back from the table, and pacing about the room like an angry tiger, pleading dyspepsia as my excuse.*

*But I digress. One day at Landsdowne's, which happened to be August 2nd, I was about to embark on some work. My aim was to continue the project I had brought with me from NYU, that I had been researching and writing about since my arrival in America. And Fleur, it was all gone! Somehow the files were completely deleted from my computer. My computer had had a virus, but I hadn't known it could do this. And what's more, I stupidly had made no backup copies.*

*I was at a loss as to what to do. You know all about deadlines, so you'll appreciate how I felt. I had set time aside to complete an important phase of my research while at Landsdowne's, which was due on my return to NYU. You once commented on how impressive it was to have a one-hour photo development facility in an area as remote as the countryside around Landsdowne's, but I'm afraid that's the extent of their embrace with modern technology. I badly needed to find a place that could restore information on the hard drive of my laptop, but I wouldn't find it there. At the same time, I couldn't leave Mother as she had been so looking forward to my arrival and was counting on me being there.*

*So I stayed, Fleur, all the time worrying not only about losing time in terms of not getting my work done, but also whether that work that I had already done would be recoverable, or whether I would have to entirely repeat my efforts, which had involved such extensive research, as you know.*

*But all is well now. I cut my stay in the Lake District short by two days and found someone in London who worked on my computer, and for a considerable fee, restored all the data. I didn't begrudge the expense. I was just so relieved to have my work visible to me again. And while in London I visited the restaurant that you and I had dined at the day of the freak storm last October. I looked around to see if you were there. Of course you weren't. I was tempted to call you. Instead, though, I flew back to New York, and your e-mail was the first thing I saw...so we were both contacting (or intending to contact) each other on the same day, after so much time!*

*Forgive me for rambling. It feels good to be in touch again. L-*

She replied at once, empathizing with the problems he'd encountered; delighted that they'd been happily resolved; delighted and intrigued that the discovery of the problem had indeed happened on August 2nd; delighted, moreover, that they were back in touch. In fact, if the parallel Time axis hypothesis was anything to go on, they had never been out of touch. And incredible, she wrote, that they contacted (or thought to contact) each other on the very same day! Even so, she could not help lamenting that they had been so close in London, and could have met, and now he was 3,000 miles away again.

*Oh Lance,* (she wrote). *Oh Lance.*

And to this he replied,

*Fleur, now it's as if we were never out of touch. We have picked up again mid-sentence from where we'd left off, and this feels right and as it should be.*

They continued to send e-mails to each other, even more frequently than before her visit to Lance in the Spring. The day of the wedding was now very close, and activities and last minute details related to that event were even more intense, so it was a joy and a relief to read Lance's chatty e-mails, informing her that he had caught up with his research and had made up for lost time, that he had taken up jogging in Central Park, and describing the intensive three full day course he had just taught ("Imagine, Fleur; an entire semester's course spewed out, digested, and thrown back from Friday at nine, until Sunday at four!") and what he would be teaching "in the fall". He also mentioned the sights he was visiting in New York, though quite how he had time for that, she did not know. She could visualize most of the places he talked of, and shared his excitement vicariously. He described how different Washington Square looked now it was no longer Spring, but hot and humid, yet still thronged with people. He said he often bought food from a nearby salad bar, and ate it in the Square. He talked of how his work necessitated him making more frequent trips to the Wall Street area, and in particular how he'd met a man who worked at the Port Authority in the World Trade Center, who was extremely informative. In fact, he wrote, he had plans for a breakfast meeting with him the following Tuesday.

She loved these conversational e-mails, and the anticipation of their arrival is what sustained her, as the wedding day was now just one week away. She was so pleased that she and Lance were back in steady contact, and she so looked forward to his return in January. She knew these were not the right thoughts to have just before getting married to Howard, but she couldn't stop her thoughts, now could she! January was not so far away; there was the wedding to get through, then a few months of work, then she and Howard planned to take their honeymoon at Christmas (they were spending so much on the wedding that they could not afford an immediate honeymoon straight after it), and right after that Lance would return. She had decided not to work during the week leading up to her wedding, as there were so many last-minute arrangements, and also some out-of-town friends would be arriving, and she was planning a special garden party luncheon for them on Friday.

She did not dream what happened next. Only two long forgotten photographs, inexplicably taken and developed eons before the tragic events actually occurred, bore witness to the brutal scene of chaos, terror, destruction, injury and death that happened on Tuesday, September 11th. She was baking a batch of mini quiches for Friday's garden party, allowing them to cool before putting them in the freezer, when some news on the radio, which she had hardly been listening to before, split through her thoughts and shattered her albeit unstable equilibrium. An airplane, it was saying, had flown straight in to the North tower of the World Trade Center. It happened at 8.46 am, New York Time. It was thought to be an accident, though it was unclear how that could happen as it was a clear, sunny day, and it was not yet understood why the plane was flying so low, or indeed on that flight path, as planes were banned from flying directly over Manhattan.

It was Tuesday! Lance was going to a breakfast meeting at the World Trade Center on Tuesday! She ran to the phone to call him. An American woman's computerized voice informed her that all circuits to New York were busy. She did not know what to do. She spun around and turned on the television. A second plane hit the South tower of the World Trade Center at 9.03 am, and a short while later the Pentagon had been hit, also by a plane. As she was watching, completely stunned, an update informed viewers that a plane *en route* to California from Newark – Newark, the very airport that she had flown out of – had crashed in a field in Pennsylvania. Cell phone messages from passengers to loved ones. All flights grounded. Both towers of the World Trade Center in flames where the planes had dived in, at about the seventieth floor. By now it was clear that this was no accident. America was under attack.

She tried again and again to phone Lance. Then she tried his department at NYU, tried Marissa whose phone number she inexplicably recalled, tried Lance again. All circuits remained busy. No communication could get through. Maybe his mother knew something. She wished she could call her. How absurd that she could not; how absurd that his mother did not even know of her existence, as if she was his guilty secret. As if she did not count. As if a door was slammed in her face. Had she known his mother's phone number, she might have even phoned her, but she did not know it.

She yelled his name into the emptiness of her flat, out of the open window into the gray, rain soaked street, to the God who she wanted to save him. Why, why, did he go this very day to the World Trade Center? But maybe he had not gone. Maybe his plans changed. Or maybe he had not yet arrived. 8.46 *was* early in the morning. Maybe he heard of this calamity before venturing out, so did not go.

She switched on the television again. A beautiful, bright blue, sunny day mocked the horror of two white towers billowing flames and ugly black smoke. Views of the disaster were being shown from a helicopter slightly north of the Empire State Building. Would this be the next target?

Now there was a closer look at the World Trade Center. Some people trapped at the top of the towers, in what had been considered the most desirable space, with flames engulfing the floors below. Tiny people. Tiny. Who had had whole lives, complexities of daily living, now dropping from the buildings, plummeting down, jumping, falling. A murderous descent. Tiny people who had left for work that morning, perhaps kissing a husband, a wife, a girlfriend, a boyfriend, perhaps kissing children goodbye and saying they'd see them that evening. Tiny people who had thought up their agenda for that day of work; work that had seemed so important. But it wasn't important. Not at all. And as she watched these tiny people flutter down from the towers, she was pierced with the thought that one of them might be Lance. Perhaps his breakfast meeting was at Windows on the World. She couldn't breathe. But no; she did not think his meeting was there, as surely he would have mentioned that.

And now the South tower, though second to be hit, was collapsing. Collapsing in on itself. Imploding. The phone rang. It startled Florence. Maybe it would be Lance. But it was Howard.

"Christ! Did you hear what's happening in New York? Lucky this didn't happen when you were there last spring!"

"Howard," she started sobbing, "what's going on? All those people… how can *they* ever-?"

"Flo, you're always so sympathetic with everyone. Don't worry; you're quite safe where you are. I'm coming home now. No one is getting any work done here. You'll feel better once I get home."

"They're jumping from the building, Howard. From the ninetieth floor. Those people-"

"Flo, I know. I know. I'm watching it too. But I'll be back soon."

As soon as he rang off, Florence repeated her attempts to phone Lance at his flat, at NYU, to phone Marissa. Nothing.

The North tower was now collapsing. Terrible scenes of people running into the streets; an enormous cloud of white dust chasing behind them. Overtaking some who could not run fast enough.

Over and over all day the television showed footage of the planes, distinct against the clear blue sky, crashing into the World Trade Center. And it was emerging that the plane that went down in Pennsylvania was hijacked by terrorists who were intending to crash that plane into governmental buildings in Washington. Brave passengers on that flight gave up their own lives in order to save the lives of others.

"It's unreal," Howard kept saying, as he watched and re-watched the scenes of the planes flying into the World Trade Center. "It's like some sensational rubbish American film."

"Howard," Florence said. "Lance is there in New York. I'm really concerned about him."

"Who's Lance?" he asked, scooping up a handful of peanuts.

"Lance, remember, who I met last year in the Lake District. I just happen to know he went to teach at New York University. I'm very worried."

She tried to sound calm, but burst into tears.

"There, there! No need to get so emotional. New York's a big place. I don't need to tell you that. My, my; you're so sensitive. If I told you someone's tortoise got run over, you'd probably cry about that, too."

She turned back to the television screen. She had never heard reporters sounding so panicked before; they usually sounded calm and professional, even when reporting catastrophes. Some people from the World Trade Center who had managed to escape were now swarming across the Brooklyn Bridge, walking uptown, or taking ferries to New

Jersey and Staten Island. But statistics started coming in about the number of people estimated to have been killed. Nearby hospitals, they were told, were standing by ready to help those in need, but pitifully few people were being admitted. Also therapists and other helpers were on the scene to offer emotional assistance.

"I'm going to try to phone Lance," Florence admitted to Howard. This time the circuits were no longer busy, but his phone rang and rang, and then his voice came on the answering machine. After several attempts at also phoning NYU, and turning her back and ignoring Howard's questions as to how she knew Lance's phone number, she got through. An agitated sounding secretary answered, saying she was on her way out; that everyone was leaving; that there was a strange smell in the air. She knew Lance, but had no idea as to where he was now. In fact, she did not know where most people were. Because this happened early in the morning, very few people had yet arrived at work, and hearing the news they would stay at home, or if they were already traveling they'd no doubt have turned back.

Somehow, having made contact with someone at NYU, Florence felt marginally better. But as the sky darkened over another evening in London, her terror increased again. What was happening in New York? Where was Lance? Maybe he'd e-mail her and tell her. There were no messages from him, but she sent him a brief e-mail asking him to respond to her as quickly as possible to reassure her that he was safe.

She kept checking her e-mail, and listened to the news throughout the night; how rescue workers from all five boroughs of New York City were on the scene, brave 'firefighters' who had entered the burning buildings to help those who were trapped to find a means to escape. Many of those firefighters were themselves now missing. And now that both towers had collapsed, firefighters and other rescue workers were sifting through immense piles of white rubble, despite the fact that it was still burning. Thousands of citizens had come to Ground Zero – some to pay their respects, some out of curiosity, and others to offer assistance.

The next day's newspaper was full of coverage about the terrible events. Florence, turning to an inside page to continue reading the cover story, was totally shocked to see a grainy black and white photo of a person being lifted onto a stretcher while others ran past, a dense white cloud above their heads. It was the same picture that her camera had shown all those months ago! She retched and let the paper drop from her hands. Then she picked it up again, to see if the person on the stretcher was Lance. It was impossible to tell.

She stumbled around her flat, dazed from the coincidence of the picture in the newspaper and her photo from her camera. She tried phoning Lance again and again. Then she tried Marissa, who was home!

"Have you heard from Lance?"

"No, sorry. But have you heard what's going on over her? It's terrible! I stood on the roof of my East Village apartment, and saw the towers fall. I can't begin to tell you-"

"Marissa, I think Lance was planning to see someone at the World Trade Center yesterday morning."

"Good God! You mean Irv Sterling? Are you sure they were meeting yesterday?"

"Yes! At least I think so. Can you please get hold of him, and ask him to phone or e-mail me? I've been trying and trying to phone, and either all circuits are busy, or I get no answer."

"Jesus! I'll go right over to his apartment. No one's going to school today."

"Thank you! Please call me back straight away, if you don't mind."

"Right! Talk to you soon!"

But it was not soon. Howard, before leaving for work, reminded her that she had a dinner party to cater. "And what's more," he said beaming. "You've got the weekend to look forward to. The future Mrs. Howard Feldman!"

He waited for her jubilant response, and then, angered by her continued sad expression, and the way she sat slumped at the kitchen table, said, "Pull yourself together, Flo! Come on; snap out of it!"

If there was anything guaranteed to make her feel worse, it was someone telling her to 'pull herself together.'

"I'm trying, Howard," she said.

"Well then, stop moping. Anyone would think you're going to a funeral rather than your own wedding!"

"God forbid!" she shrieked to his receding figure as he walked out of the kitchen.

As a batch of biscuits was smoldering in the oven, Florence watched interviews with survivors on the television. No one was crying. They were all too stunned. One man spoke of how he took the ferry to New Jersey, and how he and all the other passengers were individually hosed down before being allowed to proceed, as the white powder covering each of them was suspected of being a dangerous substance. Another told of a coworker on the fifty fourth floor who was blind, but whose guide dog helped him out of the building. One spoke of how the elevator was so crowded that she was forced to descend the stairs, which were also jammed with people and smoke, but how she made it down from the nineteenth floor.

Florence cried, baked some more biscuits, listened to the news, called Lance's number, and waited for Marissa. Eventually Marissa phoned back. She'd been to Cornelia Street. No answer. Frankly she had no idea where Lance was, and did not know how to find him.

"I'll contact the chair of our department at NYU, and some other guys on the faculty, to see if anyone there has heard anything," Marissa said. "I have a directory somewhere that lists their home numbers. By the way, some folk are putting up photos of missing people on the walls of subway stations, bus shelters, anywhere, asking if anyone had seen this person. Do you want me to do that?"

"Oh God!" Florence said.

"Hey, let's not get too worried at this point. Rescue workers are at the site working around the clock. And they are still calling it a rescue mission and not recovery yet. Hang in there! I'll call you right back as soon as I hear anything."

The phone rang several times, always for a reason related to the wedding; timing of the flower delivery, dress fittings, changes of the time of arrival of certain guests. To each she said, "Isn't it terrible what's happened in New York," and started to cry. Most reassured her briefly, putting her heightened emotional state to pre-wedding nerves. Only the florist took her more seriously. "My cousin's got a daughter what lives near there," she told her. "My cousin was right worried, she was. But it's OK. She got a phone call last night. Best call she could get, if you ask me."

"Yes," Florence gulped.

"You got someone over there, have you?"

"Yes, a very close friend."

"I'm sure she's fine, love. You'll see."

On Thursday guests started arriving. Some were staying with each set of parents, and Rose and Allison were coming to stay with her. Over a cup of tea, Rose said, "Do you remember that dear Dr. Ramsey from when you were staying at Landsdowne's last year? Well, I hear he's teaching at a university in New York. Exceedingly bright young man. But now with this awful news from over there, I do hope he is all right. I, for one, can't understand why he went to New York in the first place. Such a dangerous city! America is not at all civilized. Just look at all those dreadful cowboy films. His mother is quite frantic, I hear. She simply can't get through to him."

Florence nodded, her eyes brimming. "I do hope he is all right," she said. What a platitude masking so much emotion! And if his mother also knew nothing, then this was indeed terrible. "I pity his mother. What will she do?" she added.

"The same as everyone else, I should think. Sit and wait. What else is there to do? To think, they were so devoted to each other. And he was so good to her; always patient and helpful. Ah dear; it won't be the same without him!"

Hearing Lance being spoken about in the past tense, Florence could not keep from crying. "It's so hard to hear from anyone over there," she sobbed. "It's really difficult to get through."

"You also have loved ones over there, do you, my dear?"

"Yes!"

"Dear, dear, dear," Rose tutted. "Well, enough of this morbid talk just before your wedding! I'm sure everything will be fine with the person you know there! And just look how beautiful you look! Allison, you did pack the camera, didn't you?"

"Oh dear, no Rose. I thought you took it."

"How preposterous! Of course I did not take it! Whatever would make you think such a thing? But-" and here she looked saucily at Florence, "I

173

did pack the Travel-Scrabble, as I remember you enjoyed the game. If there's time, do let's play."

Florence managed a polite smile. "Yes, if there's time," she echoed.

"But what's that over there?" Rose asked, rising and walking over to the sideboard, dense with papers, envelopes, bags and even a hairbrush.

In the corner was her camera. It had been there for so long that Florence did not even notice it any more. Its brown case was covered in dust, reminiscent of how it had looked when Florence first saw it in the shop.

Rose, being naturally inquisitive and with her usual sense of entitlement, went and picked up the camera and opened its case.

"Well, it appears to have film in it," she said. "How nice! Do let us use it to take pictures of you, dear Florence, at this lovely time!"

"No, Rose; I'm sorry but you can't."

"Can't! Why ever not?"

"It's broken, you see. It's a complete waste of time. Quite useless. And absurdly heavy. I don't know why I haven't thrown it away."

Ignoring Florence, Rose advanced the film, pointed the camera at Florence, and clicked.

"There, my dear! It seems to be working fine. I don't see any difficulty with it at all. And consider, what do we have to lose? Allison stupidly forgot to pack our camera, so we'll use this one. If the pictures don't come out, we're no worse off than if we didn't take them in the first place. Here, Allison! You take a picture of Florence and me together!"

Allison took the camera, and hoisted the strap onto her bony, pigeon-like shoulder.

"But we do have a professional photographer coming," Florence said, "And we'd be all too glad to give-"

Just then the door opened and Howard walked in.

"What's this I hear about a professional photographer? Oh, Rose and Allison! How delightful to see you both again! How are you? So nice to see you both looking so well!" And he shook hands congenially with both of them.

"Good day, good day, Mr. Feldman!" Rose said. "It's so kind of you to let us stay here on this happy occasion. What a beautiful bride Florence will make!"

"Yes, I think so!" he said, patting Florence's arm possessively. "And permit me to say that I believe I'll make a dashing groom! Yes indeed, and I think we'll have a great number of photos to show ourselves off. Now, about Flo's camera – of course you can use it. It's just a bit dusty, as it's not been used since she was in the Lake District last year – where she met you, of course – so it would seem only right for you to use it now."

On Friday, Florence awoke to the frothy edges of her dream, which she could not recall, but which had left her with a lingering feeling of happiness. But then a clear message clamped down in her head, "Lance is dead", and the happiness and relaxation were chased away. He must be dead. That would account for why she could not connect with him, either by phone or e-mail, or even telepathically. He must have been blown off their parallel Time axis, in fact blown out of all conscious dimensions of Time, when the towers fell. And she, the person he was closest to, who loved him more than anyone, would be the mystery mourner at his funeral, finding solace nowhere. For how could someone, with no recognized existence and no known relationship to Lance, be comforted?

During the day, events relating to the wedding were escalating in Florence's flat. News from New York was similarly escalating. But with no specific information from Lance, Florence started constructing fantasy dates in her mind. Next Friday she would hear one way or another. By Saturday of next week she would certainly be fully informed. In the absence of real data, it was all she had to go on.

Guests arriving for the garden party ignored events on the other side of the Atlantic, and seemed deliberately jovial. Florence sought out Anna, to find solace in her, and was actually pleased to see that David had not yet arrived. Anna was to be her maid-of-honor, so when Florence asked her if they could come inside to talk privately, no one thought a thing of it.

"What is it?" Anna asked, her intelligent face looking concerned.

"I don't think I can go through with this wedding, Anna. I don't!"

"Why are you feeling this way now, Florence?"

"I can't stop obsessing about the dreadful things that are going on in New York. What right do I have to celebrate, with extraordinary excesses of everything from good will to expensive gifts, while there's so much suffering going on there?"

"You *are* a good person, Florence! That's why I love you. You are filled with empathy and compassion. But you can't do anything about what's happening over there. It's far removed. Right now this is about *you*. And we're all here because we are so fond of you, and you deserve happiness. And also, another angle on this that you might not have considered is that you might be feeling the jitters before getting married, which is very natural. I certainly remember feeling that way. That could be heightening your sensitivity to everything else, although admittedly what happened in the US is unbelievably horrific."

"There's one other thing I haven't told you, Anna," Florence said, needing to unburden but still unable to confess completely. "There's someone who is in New York, who I love. And I don't know what's happened to him. I can't get through to him, and others who I've spoken to in New York don't know where he is either. All I know is that he was planning to be at the World Trade Center that morning, last Tuesday, and no one has heard from him since."

Anna, tactfully not questioning who this person was, and looking directly into Florence's eyes, said serenely, "Under Jewish law, a *mitzvah* such as a wedding or Bar or Bat Mitzvah, will go ahead, even if a loved one is ill or has died. Celebrate first; that is the ordained priority. Then do whatever else needs to be done. My darling Florence, I am so sorry you are personally connected with the tragedy over there, and I can see how pained you are, but I will always be here for you. You can count on me. And we can pray, too."

"But how can praying to ask for him not to be dead be realistic if a building of over one thousand feet collapsed on him?"

"But consider that there are actually an incredible number of survivors from a complex of that size! Poor Florence; I know that waiting for news like this is extremely hard. But don't assume the worst just yet. Let's still assume he's alive. And certainly in the meantime you and I can pray. It gives you something active to do, which is good, as one of the reasons why waiting is so hard is because it is passive and one feels one has no control. So Florence, we'll pray. There's a wonderful American rabbi, Rabbi Kushner, who said that the best, and most realistic things to pray for are courage, strength and hope. So let's pray for these, for you and for him. All right?"

Florence nodded, and they hugged. Just then Howard entered the room.

"What's this? My fiancée in tears? Quick, give her some champagne!" he said sarcastically, and went back out into the garden to fetch a glass.

"He doesn't know about this," Florence whispered.

"I thought not," Anna replied. She squeezed Florence's fingers. "We'll talk again. I understand, Florence. Believe me, I understand."

"He's called Lance," Florence murmured.

"What did you say?"

"I said he's called Lance. Lance is the person in New York. Now you will know the name of the person you are praying for."

"Lance. Good. We'll pray for him and for you. Ah! Here's your drink!"

"Thank you, Anna," Florence said, again hugging her friend.

Howard had entered the room, a champagne glass in each hand, and from the way he moved in an exaggeratedly delicate fashion between the bed and the chair, Florence could tell he was slightly tipsy.

"Come on! Wipe away those tears and come outside," he said, handing a glass to each of them. "Everyone will be wondering where you are."

They stepped out into the garden. Friends and relatives swarmed around Florence, and Allison held up the camera and clicked and clicked.

"Don't use up all the photos now!" she heard Rose chiding. "Save some for the wedding itself!"

"Yes, Rose."

*Courage, strength and hope.* Florence kept chanting these words to herself as if they were a mantra.

By late afternoon, the guests started to leave, and so did Howard. He was to spend the night with Roger, who had been a friend of his since public school, and who was to be best man. Florence's mother, her cousin Sally, and Anna helped to clear up, and then stayed on a while longer for some quiet women's chatter, which was embracing and comforting. They eventually left, advising Florence to have an early night.

Florence remained with Rose and Allison in the garden, and they succumbed to Rose's Scrabble game. The early evening sunlight was soft and golden.

"I have an idea!" Allison said, uncharacteristically initiating conversation. "Why don't you put your wedding dress on now, Florence!"

"What on earth are you suggesting?" Rose asked, clearly annoyed to have the Scrabble game interrupted.

"Well, dear Rose, I only thought I could take her picture now while the light is so nice, and also there is not the crush of people that there'll be tomorrow."

"No, no! Take the photos tomorrow, Allison, for goodness sake!"

"Well, if truth be told, I just have the one picture left. I used up all the rest so quickly in all that excitement this afternoon. So, if you don't mind, Florence-"

"Well, of course she minds! And whatever do you mean by using up practically all the pictures, and the wedding has not yet taken place!"

"Actually, Allison has a great idea!" Florence said, rising. "I'd be happy to put the wedding dress on now. There's really no point in lugging the camera around tomorrow. I'll be back in a jiffy!"

To a background of protestations from Rose, Florence left the garden and went inside to change. She returned quickly, appearing to float in her cloudy layers of whiteness.

"Ah, my dear! Charming, quite charming! Isn't she, Allison?"

To which Allison burst into tears. "It's so lovely," she managed to say.

"For heaven's sake, Allison! If you are going to take a picture, take it now before the light fails, and stop your sniveling. If you are like this now, what *will* you be like tomorrow?"

"Yes, Rose." Allison obediently stopped crying, pulled out a lace handkerchief that had been tucked up her sleeve, and blew her nose. Then she stood up, pointed the camera at Florence, took an amazingly long time focusing, and finally snapped. She advanced the roll of film, discovered there was one more picture, and then took that, too. Then, when the film would advance no more, she handed the camera back to Florence.

"Thanks, Allison!" she said. "I'm going to change back into comfortable clothes, and then I'll nip round the corner and get this film developed. There's a one-hour photo place really nearby."

"What? Go out now? Isn't it a bit late?"

"Don't worry! I'll be fine. In fact, I can drop it off, and then return to our Scrabble game, and then I'll just go back and pick it up later."

Shortly before 9.30, Florence picked up the film. She had to look at the pictures before showing them to Rose and Allison, for, if the camera behaved as erratically as it usually did, she must remove any suspicious pictures. With heart thumping, right there in the shop she slid them out of the envelope. She leaned heavily on the counter. Every single picture was of her with Lance! She nearly cried out loud. They were holding hands, walking together through green, open countryside.

"We're closing now, dearie! Just got this batch on time, you did," the woman behind the counter cooed. "Better go and look at the rest of 'em at 'ome, if you don't mind."

"What? Yes, of course."

Gripping the pictures tightly, she went out into the street. Under the neon pool of light of a lamppost, she studied the pictures again and again. Lance! He was alive! And they were together. She tenderly kissed his picture, letting her lips linger on the photo until the taste of the chemicals made her pull away at last.

But then a dreadful thought. She'd discovered that her camera displayed pictures of the past, just as it had done when she saw that photo of herself and her cousin when they were children, playing with the toy boat at Whitestone Pond. So these pictures of her and Lance together might be views of when they were exploring the Lake District or even the Catskills. Either way, they could be pictures of their shared past, rather than an indication of the future.

She returned home bleaker than ever.

"How did the pictures turn out?" Rose enquired. "Do show them to us!"

"They did not turn out," Florence replied. "I warned you that I thought the camera was not working."

"What, none of them?"

"Not a single one."

# ELEVEN

*HER WEDDING DAY.* No time to listen to the news on the radio or television. As she stood under the *chuppah*, mourning a man she secretly loved, and ostentatiously marrying another man who she did not, she maintained a state of complete *sang froid*. In fact, she felt so removed from everything, that she could not understand the structure of the service, and all seemed nebulous to her. What kind of ridiculous mockery of all she held sacred was this, that people overflowed with joy for her, yet she felt no joy herself? All that she noticed, irrelevantly, was that Rose, sitting in the second row and beaming up at her, was wearing a fascinating dress the color of dead roses, which had a low scooped neck and bunched up material amusingly arranged to look like a rose, over her heart.

"My wife!" Howard said, pulling up her veil and kissing her triumphantly, after having slipped the ring on her finger.

The photographer flashed his camera at them incessantly, and large, happy faces came up so close to her as if she was suddenly myopic, congratulating her. As soon as the service was over, they drove to the boathouse for the reception. It was a splendid place, and the weather remained cooperative. Round tables covered with creamy colored cloths and adorned with flowers, were set up on the gently sloping lawns, and handsome waiters in tuxedos decorously served the food.

Perhaps Lance was safe after all. Maybe the reason for his lack of communication was because he knew she was busy this week with her wedding. *"I do not want to share you with Howard."* She would accept coldness from him, even hostility, if he could just be alive. She ate the food, mingled with the wedding guests, danced, was witty, smiled. *Courage, strength and hope,* she kept chanting. *Courage-*

"How are you feeling?" It was Anna who had come up to her. "This is really a beautiful wedding. And you're holding up really well."

"You really helped me by what you said yesterday, Anna. Thank you."

"No need to thank me! And did you hear on the news that they're now thinking that they overestimated the numbers killed at the World Trade Center? People who had been unaccounted for are showing up. It seems that many had fled the city and were presumed dead, whereas they are in fact safe. Also, the attack was quite early in the morning, so many had not yet arrived at the buildings. So things are looking a little more encouraging over there."

"Thanks, Anna!" She inhaled deeply.

A large boisterous crowd of Florence's friends came over to join them.

"God, you're gorgeous, Florrie!" Joe, an old boyfriend told her. "I always thought you should have married me, though!" he chuckled, having seemingly forgotten that he was the one to have broken up with her.

"Nah!" Tony said. "What would she want with you, Joe? We all know it's me she fancied, right Florrie!"

"Well, she's done bloody well for herself without either of you, I should say," a woman's voice said from the back of the crowd. The voice was familiar, but for a moment Florence couldn't place it. Then she saw her!

"Bess!" she screamed. "I thought you were in Australia!"

"What? And miss your wedding? Not bloody likely! We kept it a secret about me being here – I'm staying with Anna and David, and made them swear not to tell you – as I wanted to see the expression on your face when I turned up!"

"This is incredible, Bess! It's marvelous to see you! You came here specially; I mean, Bess, really!"

They hugged, warmly clutching on to each other and holding the embrace.

"Let's come and sit down and catch up a bit," Florence said. The three of them, Florence, Bess and Anna, all walked over to a bench by a clump of weeping willow trees, near the water's edge.

"Not that that amazing hunk of a husband knows me yet," Bess said, "But he's got me entirely to thank! If I hadn't suggested going to Andy's party – you remember, right? – because I fancied some bloke, and you being so typically contrary-"

"I'm not generally contrary."

"As I was saying," Bess laughed. "If I hadn't asked you to come to that party with me, you would *never* have gone to see your parents that weekend! So I go to the party, alone mind you, and meet *no one*, and you, you devil, go to your parents, and come back with your future husband! He's really quite OK, isn't he, Anna!"

Anna, who had been smiling benignly throughout this exchange, said, "Oh yes, Howard's very nice. But look, Bess, you might not have met anyone at that particular party, but you didn't do too badly for yourself after all, did you!"

"Is Bruce here, too?" Florence asked.

"No, but he sends his best wishes. He'd have liked to have come, he really would. It would be great for him to spend time with all you people I talk about incessantly!"

"How long are you staying in England?"

"For as long as Anna will have me! No, not really! Actually, I've already been here almost a fortnight, as I had to make the dutiful visit to see *my* parents. I'll stay the rest of the weekend with Anna, and then I'm scheduled to leave on Monday. But now, what with that terrorist attack in New York, I'll have to check that my plane will still be flying."

Florence swallowed awkwardly. For a few moments, in the surprised excitement of seeing Bess, she'd had a reprieve from her fears.

"Don't look so anxious, Florence! I'll be fine. The flight might be bloody long, but they feed you and show you films, and I bought this super new novel to read, so it can't be bad. I hope you and Howard will come over to visit the old B and B!"

"B and B? Bed and breakfast?"

"No! Bess and Bruce! Do come!"

"I'd love to. But look, if you're here only till Monday, we must see each other tomorrow. Come over for brunch!"

"What? No honeymoon? Won't you be away somewhere exotic?"

"No, we're planning to have our honeymoon at Christmas."

"I see. But surely you're not going to want me over tomorrow, your first day of married life!"

"Of course I do! Especially if it's the only opportunity of seeing you before you return. You can come and get to know Howard a bit more. Anna, you and David come too!"

"That's sweet of you, Florence, but no. You don't have much chance to talk to Bess, so you and I can see each other another time. Incidentally, though, you should really take Bess up on her offer of you and Howard going to visit. David and I decided to go at Chanukah. I love the thought of swimming while it's warm and sunny at that time of the year! Speaking of sunny, you're really lucky with the weather today, Florence! What a gorgeous day!"

A gorgeous day.

Gradually, as the sun's rays changed to amber, causing the quiet ripples on the river to sparkle in golden merriment, the wedding guests started to depart. Best wishes were exchanged, gratitude expressed, plans to visit were declared. And if anyone found it remarkable that Florence and Howard spent virtually no time together throughout the party, and only danced the first dance together, they did not mention it. At least, not within earshot of the bride and groom.

Florence and Howard drove home, the car heaped with brightly wrapped and beribboned boxes. Once they'd unloaded their loot into the center of the living room, Howard, eying the presents with satisfaction, clasped Florence around the middle and said, "Well, Mrs. Feldman! Now we can start to reap the benefit of married life."

"Do you mean because of all those presents?"

"Yes, of course. We've done pretty nicely for ourselves, I'd say. And not only that. Just think how much money we'll now save on our taxes! We can file jointly. What better incentive to marry is there than that!"

Florence studied his face to see if he was joking. He was not.

Bess came for lunch the next day as planned, and chatted quite pleasantly with Howard. At the completion of the meal he rose saying, "You'll have to excuse me, ladies," and went with his laptop into the bathroom. Florence, assured that he would be in there quite some time, and knowing that Bess would soon be far away in Australia, decided to confide in her about her relationship with Lance.

"Well, we're going to have to hope he escaped, if he was even there at the World Trade Center last Tuesday," Bess said. "My guess is he probably left the city when he heard what happened, same as countless others. And that being said, he'll soon be back in England from what you told me."

Florence nodded uncertainly.

"And then it seems your biggest problem once he's back will be that you just got married to someone else. You'll have to become what I am, Florence. An actress!"

"What?"

"It's a fact that some of the best actresses are not those who are actually on the stage. Look. I see no harm in it. You're married now. Lance returns to England. You *act* the perfectly loving wife to Howard – who's OK, by the way, but a bit of an egoist. But, come to think of it, that's to your advantage. Tap into that endearing feature by flattering him immensely. That will keep him happy. Meanwhile, off you go with Lance whenever you can."

"It seems so wrong."

"To hell with that. One can't be naïve, Florence. Look, I heard all those people at your wedding yesterday wishing you luck. But the French understand this better than we do. The way they say good luck is *bonne chance*. Chance, Florence! Chance! In fact, that is all that luck is. A random chance. One can't leave one's life to something so random. You have to be more deliberate than that. So act! Act deliberately! Give the performance of your life! And you'll get through. It'll get easier and easier."

"It's all very well for you to say, Bess. You're a professional actress!"

"But look, sweetie. I didn't start that way. The first acting part I had

184

– for which I attended all the rehearsals without fail although they were shit for me and unbelievably boring – was to carry a chair on the stage at the middle of the second act. Think about it. Weeks of rehearsing and coordinating with others, just to carry that ridiculous chair on stage. But I carried that chair with such character and conviction, that by the next play I was given more of a part, and more and more, in subsequent plays. Anyone with imagination can act, Florence, and you've got plenty of that!"

"Bess, I hope you don't mind me asking, but do you 'act' with Bruce?" Suddenly Bess looked completely intent and serious.

"No," she said. "Bruce is my soul mate and my constant source of inspiration."

--------

The next day, Monday, Florence dialed Lance's number again and again and again. His voice on his answering machine was so alive. She did not believe in ghosts, but knew that if Lance had been killed, he would haunt her always. Her mind would be forever filled with obsessive thoughts of the horror of his being excruciatingly wounded, with shrieking bolts of pain, of dying alone in a foreign land. He'd not gone to fight in some war-torn nation, but had gone to give of himself, of his wisdom and intellect. Who would have thought that New York could have been attacked? She knew his agonized, solitary death would forever be with her, just as the words of her friend, Lizzie, who had died of cancer at a young age and who had described in minute detail every symptom, stayed with her.

On Tuesday, after she'd returned from a half day back at work, she started writing thank you cards. The phone rang, and she went slowly to answer it.

"Hi! Is this Fleur?" An American voice.

"Yes." Her heart was starting to hammer furiously.

"Hi, Fleur. This is Abe Siegel from NYU. I've been informed that you're a close friend of Lance Ramsey. I'm afraid I have some pretty bad news for you."

"Yes." It had come at last. Closure. That's it, then.

"Lance was injured last Tuesday when the World Trade Center was attacked. He's at St. Vincent's Hospital."

"Oh, thank God!"

"Excuse me?"

"I mean, thank God he's alive! I hadn't heard. I've been trying to contact him. I was afraid he might've been killed."

"I'm so sorry for not contacting you earlier. We heard last week, and I notified his family. Then I went out of town for a few days. This morning Marissa Barduccio came into my office, and I told her the news as she'd been his TA and she's been wondering what's going on. She was the one to ask me to contact you."

"Thank you! Thank you for telling me! How is he?"

"Not so good. Two broken legs. But I'm sure he'll be getting better soon. St. Vincent's is a good hospital."

"Thank you! Oh, thank God! And please thank Marissa, too."

"Will do. We're all so shocked that this attack happened, and affected our visitor from England, too. Please let us know if there's anything we can do to help."

A little later Howard returned from work. She informed him that she was going to New York the next day.

"You're what! You'll do no such thing!"

"I have to, Howard. Lance was injured at the World Trade Center attacks. He's all alone in a hospital there. I must go!"

"And if you go, I'll be all alone here! Your husband of just a few days. Hell, the icing hasn't even hardened on the wedding cake yet. Why do you keep talking about this fellow, Lance? I thought he was just a casual acquaintance from your holiday more than a year ago. I'm by no means doubting that what happened in New York was a terrible tragedy. But it's a play on another stage. You're the star of the play here, 117 Aubrey Street, as the new wife of Howard Feldman!"

"Howard, I'm sorry. This, I know, is a totally strange thing to do. But he's been hurt, Howard, and-"

"For Christ sake! Just because you're called Florence it doesn't mean you have to play Florence Nightingale to every Tom, Dick and Harry. You don't even know the first thing about nursing, let me remind you!"

"But, Howard-"

"Florence, no! Let me also remind you we could be on our honeymoon now. No disturbances from the outside world. Yeah, I know we're not actually on our honeymoon yet, but we agreed it would be a sort of honeymoon here at home, immediately after the wedding."

"You're right, Howard, but you must see that these are highly unusual and unforeseen circumstances."

"But they're over *there*. And we're here. And I'm your new husband!"

"Howard, I'd never dreamed that I'd go away immediately after our wedding. Of course not. But I'll make it up to you later."

"You're not going, Flo!"

"I am. I already bought my ticket on the Internet."

"You did what? For fuck's sake, we don't even know if it's safe to fly. They used those planes as missiles. How do we know that won't happen again? It points to a bloody lack of security, and that's not something that can be corrected overnight. It would be suicide to fly now."

"Bess just flew yesterday. She flew much further, all the way back to Australia."

"Yes. And back to her husband. And you'd be flying away from yours. And into a bloody war zone."

"Look, Howard. I know everything you're saying is valid. And I'm truly sorry, but I must go."

"I won't let you."

"You can't stop me."

"How long will you go for?"

She knew he had started to accept her plan. "Only a week."

"Well, something else you haven't thought about, little Miss Sainthood. What will Elizabeth Carlisle have to say about this? Sweet little woman, isn't she! I got a chance to talk to her quite a bit at our wedding. Remember we had a wedding? Let me think. That's right! It was three days ago! As I was saying, Elizabeth Carlisle highly praised your work, but I think the subscript is that she's getting pretty sick of all your absences. And so am I! You took off the week before the wedding, which was reasonable, but now this!"

Act! Carry that chair on stage. This is only the beginning. She went over to him and placed a finger on his lips.

"Howard! My husband!" She lightly kissed his cheek. "I will miss you every moment I am away." More kisses. "And please believe that this is not a trip of my own choosing. But I feel compelled to go and help."

Howard looked smug and pleased at the attention. But then he became more alert, as if shaking off the trance.

"Help? What do you mean? And I hope you know that the air quality will be like shit after the collapse of two huge skyscrapers. You'd be a fool to go."

"Thanks for worrying about me. But don't be too concerned. I will-" Kiss. "return soon." Another kiss. "And having done this thing-" Kiss. "that I feel compelled to do," Kiss, kiss. "I'll return to you lighter and freer in mind and conscience." Kiss, kiss. "And devote all my attentions to you, my sweet husband." Full kiss on the lips.

--------

Florence was on the plane heading for New York, and feeling terrified. The engines had made all the right sounds going down the runway, but then it sounded as though they'd all cut out and failed as there was no sound at all. She imagined their plane as momentarily suspended before plummeting to the ground. She glanced over to the airhostesses, who were behaving normally. Even though slightly reassured, she still wanted to grab the arm of the fat man in the seat next to her for comfort. Perhaps Howard was right, she thought, and security was still an issue. Maybe this flight wouldn't make it. And after all, she thought, perhaps this is what she deserved for leaving her new husband in such a callous way.

But the plane didn't plummet to the ground, and they made it safely over the Atlantic. It felt so different for Florence landing in Newark again, only five months after her last visit, and without Lance there to welcome her as she came through the customs area. She took a taxi to the Washington Square Hotel, which is one hotel she remembered from before. She'd made no price comparisons with other hotels, but was just relieved to be able to stay in the right neighborhood.

After checking in and putting her bags in her room, she decided to visit Lance straight away and not wait until the next day, as it was only about five o'clock New York time. She crossed Sixth Avenue and walked slowly along Greenwich Avenue towards St. Vincent's Hospital. Walls of buildings, bus stop shelters, even the poles of street lights, were plastered with photos of the staring faces of missing people, with desperate messages underneath, such as "Have you seen me?" and "If you have information, please call-". She felt choked with emotion; she empathized with how these people felt, not knowing, and how terrible was the waiting, the pleading and despairing, the hoping, the giving up. And now the miracle had occurred for her and Lance; her prayers for courage, strength and hope answered. Lance was alive, and after all that only had broken his legs! Why, people broke their legs all the time! A simple tumble might do it, a roll off a horse, a skid on a banana skin. That thought made her feel almost merry as she approached the hospital.

She asked at the reception desk where she could find Dr. Lance Ramsey. The woman behind the desk must have thought she was referring to a medical doctor, because after looking through her records, she said there was no one of that name here. Florence felt a moment of panic, then of hope that he'd already been discharged, but when she thought to explain that he was a patient, she was told the room in which to find him. She took the elevator up to the fourth floor, and started heading along the corridor. A little blond haired girl, of about seven or eight, was holding the hand of a plump African American woman, and crying. "There, there; don't you cry no more, Jessie. Your mama want you to be a strong little girl, now don't she!" the woman said.

Florence hurried past. A patient was being wheeled rapidly along on a stretcher, an anxious cluster of people peering down at him, and hurrying alongside. A tall woman in a lilac suit was coming out of one of the rooms, saying loudly, "No amputation! Please, Dr. Mezzinger. He's not in a state to decide for himself, but please not that!"

"Rest assured we'll do everything we can to avoid such drastic measures," the white-coated doctor told her. "But we ask you to be patient. Time will tell."

Florence hurried on down the corridor before realizing she'd gone too

189

far. She turned around and retraced her steps. She found the right room number, and placing her hand on the doorknob, she suddenly wondered whether this was the room that the woman in the lilac suit had come from. No, it was impossible to tell. Such a long corridor. She slowly and quietly entered the room, after softly knocking on the door. Her heart was thudding. It took her a moment to realize that the pale, gaunt, bearded man, lying there asleep and pierced by so many tubes, and with both legs in traction, was in fact Lance.

She was relieved that he was asleep. It gave her time to familiarize herself with how he looked, so that when he woke he wouldn't see her shock. She tried to steady herself, and calm her rapid breathing. She went over to the window where some yellow daisies flopped limply in an orange plastic beaker, and in doing so she accidentally knocked down a magazine. The noise woke Lance, and he opened his eyes blearily.

"Fleur?" It was little more than a croaky whisper.

She rushed over to him, and bending over the bars along the side of the bed, she touched and kissed his face. His prone body remained inert, unresponsive, though the smallest trace of a smile was apparent through his bearded lips. His familiar smell was gone, replaced really with a statement in the air that spoke of institutions, of floor wax, of the laundering of hundreds of sheets, of the vinegary odor of sweaty feet, of sickness and invasion into the intimacies of private life.

"Fleur? Did they bring me back to England?" He spoke very softly, as if from a great weakness and heavy sedation.

"No, Lance, no. You're still in New York. I came over to see you as soon as I heard. How are you? How are you feeling?"

He groped for her hand and gently stroked it. His thumb rubbed up against her engagement and wedding ring. What a fool she was not to have taken them off before coming to see him. At the first opportunity she would.

With her free hand she lightly brushed the hair off his forehead, which felt burning hot and clammy. His eyes fluttered shut again.

"Are you feeling OK, Lance?" she whispered, close to his face.

He didn't answer for some time. Just breathing deeply in and out.

Then he seemed to slightly rouse himself, to a state of alertness that he could not maintain.

"So sorry. You've come all this way. Rude of me. I won't be so sleepy in the morning."

He continued to gently rub her hand, but soon his hand went limp and he seemed to be deeply asleep. She sat at his bedside for a while longer, but then rose, lightly kissed each of his eyes as they darted back and forth under closed lids, and tiptoed out of the room.

As soon as she was in the corridor, she pulled off her rings and stuffed them deeply into her pocket. She felt very concerned about why Lance was so tired. Then she realized she'd eaten nothing since leaving England, and not wanting to return yet to the hotel, or eat alone in a restaurant that she'd eaten in so happily with Lance on her previous trip, decided to visit the hospital's cafeteria. She took a wet plastic brown tray from the pile, and slid it along the rack, considering her options. Grayish mounds of food steamed unappetizingly, so she settled on a Sarah Lee slab of pound cake and a cup of tea.

She went to look for a table, and noticed the same woman in the lilac suit she had seen upstairs, seated with a man who she presumed was her husband, at a table near the window. In this frightening, alien place, where emotions ran so high, this woman clad in lilac, though a stranger, was a point of reference, so she decided to sit at an adjoining table which was unoccupied.

But, as if on a seesaw, as soon as she sat down, the woman in lilac rose to go. Florence felt disappointed, until she realized that the woman was refilling her cup and returning to her table. She ducked her head to fiddle with the plastic wrapper of the Sarah Lee cake as she walked past, and when she looked up again she noticed that the woman in the lilac suit was cupping both her hands around her Styrofoam cup, as if its warmth provided some comfort. Her eyes were dark and troubled, and when she started to speak, Florence realized that she had an English accent.

Florence's body seemed to react before her mind did. She watched herself rise, move over to the table occupied by the woman in lilac and her husband, and ask if she could join them. The woman seemed momentarily startled, but the man, who was chubby and friendly looking, and who wore wire rimmed glasses with smudges on the lenses, said, "Sure!"

They talked for a while about the terrible events that had occurred. They said how they hoped that more people might still be found alive in the wreckage, though the chances were so slim, but you never knew, miracles did happen. And they talked about the patients upstairs and how they hoped they would soon be well again.

And then an incredible thing happened. Florence felt, as she spoke with the woman in the lilac suit, that she was looking at Lance. They did not look alike, Lance and this woman, but many of the woman's gestures and mannerisms were the same as his, and her occasional smile spoke sincerely of the way Lance smiled from his eyes.

"Excuse me for asking. This is really a long shot. But do you, by any chance, know someone called Lance Ramsey who's English, but has been teaching here in New York?"

"Lance Ramsey! Do *you* know him? I'm his sister!"

"What? Are you? You're Juliet? I'm his friend, Florence-!"

"Fleur, is it? Yes, my brother has spoken about you! Goodness! What a coincidence that we found each other here in this cafeteria! And this is Irv," Juliet said, indicating the chubby faced man.

He partially rose and shook Florence's hand. "Irv Sterling," he said. "Pleased to make your acquaintance."

"Irv! Are you the man that Lance knows from the Port Authority? He e-mailed me about you."

"He did, did he?" Irv said, managing to look happy and sad at the same time.

"How long have you been here?" Juliet asked Florence.

"A few hours. I checked into a hotel nearby and came straight here. How about you?"

"Since last Friday, I think it was. I don't know. The days blur into each other. Have you been up to see Lance yet?"

"Yes, I was just up there. He was very tired."

"Tired? He's half dead! It's amazing he's alive at all."

"Thank God they saved his life," Florence pursued optimistically, masking the shock she felt from Juliet's statement.

"Yes, but what about the *quality* of his life now? He's been very badly injured. One of his legs is broken. The other is essentially smashed, with deep lacerations and some second degree burns too. His wounds became horribly infected, causing him to have a high fever. And he lost a lot of blood. Thank goodness he had the presence of mind to refuse a transfusion, so they pumped lots of fluids in him to maintain the pressure. Naturally he's very anemic, so he's taking enough iron to build a railway from London to Norwich!"

Florence put her hand to her head. "I hadn't known the extent of it," she murmured. "He must have been in agonizing pain."

"Well, naturally he's being given a mountain of pain killers. They operated on him for the second time a few days ago. They put some pins and plates in his shattered leg, to see if that will work. There's still a chance, though, that he might become an amputee."

"No!" It was almost a shriek.

"Let me tell you, if that doctor so much as gets out his knife, I'll demand a second opinion! One wonders if what they do is for the sake of expediency or the best interests of the patient."

"I guess it's kind of irrelevant to say this," said Irv, speaking for the first time. "But I feel so lousy. I guess you'd call it 'survivor's guilt.' It all could have been avoided, if only I'd got to the phone on time."

"What do you mean?" Juliet demanded.

"I had scheduled a breakfast meeting with Lance in my office that morning. My office is – I mean, was – in the World Trade Center. On the fortieth floor. Boy, he loved that office! Great view of the harbor and the Statue of Liberty. He'd always look out of the window and comment on the quality of light, and the view, before we'd get down to business. The Port Authority had collected some data, you see, that he found useful for the research he was conducting. Well, that day, last Tuesday, I guess exactly a week ago-" and here Irv gave a sort of choking cough, "that day, we were going to meet at 8.30. Only my wife woke that morning feeling sick, so she asked me to take our daughter to her orchestra rehearsal at school instead of her. We live in New Jersey, and I knew if I did that, I wouldn't be able to get to work until later. So I tried to phone Lance to see if we could postpone our meeting, and meet instead at 10.00, but when I called his apartment, there was no answer. I felt kind of bad about him having to hang around and wait for me all that time after I'd dropped off my daughter at her school, so I tried calling my secretary as I wanted to ask her to explain to Lance when he arrived that I was running late and I'd be there as soon as I could. I also intended asking her to get out some of the data, and let him start looking through it while he was waiting." Irv picked up his cup and swirled the filmy coffee around so that it made spiraling rings. "But I couldn't get through to her. All lines were down. Of course I didn't know yet what had happened. After repeated efforts, I managed to get hold of her on her cell, and that's when I heard about it."

He chucked the rest of the cold, filmy coffee down his throat. Then, banging both hands on the table, he stood up.

"That's it for my story. I expect you ladies have a lot to talk about. I'll swing by here again later this week. You'll still be here, right, Juliet?"

"Yes, I plan to stay until Saturday," she said frostily.

He shook hands with both of them. "I hope we'll meet again," he told Florence.

Florence, touched by the smudges on his glasses, and his wide dark eyes blinking rapidly behind them, said to Juliet after he had left, "Poor man. He feels terrible. It's true he had a fantastically lucky escape, but I don't think he should blame himself for what happened to Lance."

"I'm not sure I entirely agree with you," Juliet replied. "If he'd phoned Lance a little earlier, it might have spared him this."

"He just seemed so sad. Well, of course we all are."

"Look, I'm going back up to see Lance in a minute. I imagine you'll want to be returning to your hotel and going to bed soon, since you've just flown in, but from tomorrow onwards, I think it's best if we take it in turns to see him. It might overwhelm him if we both go in together."

"Yes, let's do that. And Juliet, I had no idea of the severity-"

"Yes, well it was touch and go for a while."

"And now?"

"And now they say his condition has stabilized. I don't know, though. He still looks bloody awful to me."

Florence pulled a handkerchief out of her pocket to wipe her eyes, and in doing so, her diamond engagement ring dropped to the floor and rolled away. She bent down, fumbling around to find it.

"What did you drop?" Juliet asked.

Just then a man at the next table tapped Juliet on the shoulder and handed her the ring. Juliet passed it impassively back to Florence, her expression unchanged.

"Well, I'll go up now." Then, noticing that Florence was stuffing the ring back in her pocket, said, "Aren't you going to put that ring on? It looks fairly valuable to me, and if you put it in your pocket, it might drop out again, and you might not be so lucky next time in terms of finding it."

"No, no. I'll put it in my pocket for now, and put it away safely when I get back to my room."

"I see. Well, as I was saying," Juliet continued in a supercilious voice, "I'll go up and see how Lance is now, assuming he's awake, which he isn't very often. Good night. I'll see you, I expect, in the morning. I usually arrive by 8.30."

And so saying, Juliet went to the elevator and Florence left the hospital and walked down the dark and quiet streets to her hotel. But she couldn't sleep. In her immense relief that Lance was not killed, or still missing and presumed dead, she realized she'd trivialized his injuries, and had not realized he'd been in so much danger and still was. Whimpering, she summoned up Anna's words of "Courage, strength and hope" and with them ardently prayed for Lance to be well again. Please. Please be well again.

And so started, over the next few days, a collaborative arrangement between Juliet and Florence, in that they would alternate seeing Lance, leaving the other waiting in the cafeteria for her turn. This might sound chummier than was in fact the case. If Florence had detected similarities between her and Lance initially, now she only saw differences. Juliet was prim, austere, and in many ways inaccessible, which was such a contrast to Lance. But what was Lance like? She could hardly remember. Now she saw only his dimmed eyes, his face chiseled into bony unfamiliar angularity. He slept most of the time, and when he was awake was subdued and completely diminished.

Florence felt an overwhelming sadness when she was with him, for his frailty and vulnerability; and a piercing, exhausting anxiety while awaiting her turn in the gray, Formica cafeteria. The days indeed blurred together, as Juliet had said they would. She particularly hated waiting in the cafeteria, and developed a strange habit of not wanting to touch anything for fear of contamination. And once upstairs, walking along the corridor, she tried to avoid looking at any patients through their open doors, as she did not want to see their suffering. She couldn't wait to see Lance each time, but knowing he was so ill and might still be in danger, filled her with such panic. She concealed this from him, and sat with him, holding his hand and speaking a little to him. But she doubted that he even knew she was there.

Juliet, on the other hand, was filled with anger; anger, not only at the terrorists, but also at the doctors and nurses who attended him, and at Lance himself for having the knack of being in the midst of someone else's fight. This was particularly clear on Friday night when she suggested to Florence that they have dinner together at her hotel, the Hotel Stanhope, which was uptown.

After leaving St. Vincent's hospital that afternoon, Florence decided to walk around a little first before taking the subway. Crossing Fourteenth Street she was momentarily panicked at the sight of a succession of police cars and ambulances rushing along, sirens blaring and lights flashing. Had there been another attack? But then she rationalized that it was not unusual to see emergency vehicles in large cities.

She wandered into Union Square, and saw the stunned faces of people holding a candlelight vigil. Their sadness was palpable. The wind had changed direction, now blowing uptown from Ground Zero, and there was an acrid stench in the air. At the first subway entrance she found, she ran down the stairs, grateful to substitute the dusty, metallic smell of the subway with the rank odor outside. But inside the station, the walls were plastered with the faces of the missing. Dozens and dozens of them. Bright patchworks of color, reflective of unspeakable tragedy, that inescapably echoed and re-echoed around New York.

A short while later, seated opposite to Juliet in the elegant dining room of the very posh Stanhope Hotel, she said, "So you're going back to England tomorrow?"

"Yes, I have a big case on Monday that I can't miss. And of course I must see Mother and offer some reassurance. But I'll return here soon enough."

"Are you a lawyer?"

"Yes, a barrister."

"Oh."

They ate their grapefruit in silence.

"How much longer are you staying here?" Juliet eventually asked.

"Until Wednesday. Then I must return to work, too. I'm a writer for - magazine."

"I see."

More silent scraping of the grapefruit pulp from its skin.

"These doctors are butchers. All of them," Juliet suddenly spat. "I hope they have the sense to let Lance heal and not amputate. Can you imagine? What a loss to human dignity! He's just one more body in a hospital gown lying in their hospital bed, as far as they're concerned. Just like bringing in a car for repair."

"Are they still talking about amputation?"

"Don't be silly! They don't tell us anything."

"Oh God, I hope he'll be all right. To think how much he loves roaming around the countryside. And he'd recently taken up jogging. Did you know that?"

"Let me tell you this. It might sound heartless, but if they amputate, or if for some other reason Lance doesn't make a full recovery, I can't put up with two invalids on my hands. It's enough with Mother. I've had to look after her practically all my adult life!"

They had moved on to their entrée and Juliet was angrily spearing her chicken. Florence was appalled. She hated Juliet! What a nasty, selfish person she was, only thinking how she'd be affected, and completely devoid of any sympathy for Lance.

"Lance has had to look after Mother since he was a child. He never told you any of this?" she questioned, a big slab of chicken breast glistening on her fork.

Florence shook her head. "He told me you and he share a house, but that's the extent of what I know."

"Well, as you no doubt surmised, Lance is quite a bit younger than I. In fact by twelve years. So I was an only child growing up, and would've been happy, I expect, especially as Mother was always so sweet, but my father was a difficult man." She sat back in her chair, and sipped her red wine. "And he became more so after Lance was born. Mother said that was how he behaved when I was a baby, too. He didn't like not being the center of attention, and hated, for example, having to wait for his dinner while mother attended to the baby, or for anything else, mind you. Inexplicably, though, Mother was quite dependent on him. You must remember that I was a teenager by then, and sufficiently sophisticated to accurately perceive the family dynamic."

Florence felt amazed at how willing Juliet seemed to be about mentioning intimate details of her family history. It was certainly unusual for the English to show such a lack of reserve, and this made her shift uncomfortably in her chair, but even so Juliet continued to talk.

"Well, when Lance was about four or five, my father left us. He completely vanished," she continued, glancing over coldly at Florence. "And Mother's personal development was totally arrested from that day. She always maintained her sweet disposition, but she aged terribly. I believe you've seen her, haven't you? Well, how old do you think she is? Never mind! You don't have to answer that question. But I'll tell you. She's now in her early seventies. No spring chicken, certainly, but not as ancient as she appears, as I'm sure you'd agree."

Florence's eyes widened as she recalled Lance's tiny mother, her sweet smile, her excessively wrinkled face, her deafness, her need to be helped up the stairs.

"And her lack of independence that she'd always had," Juliet said, "even when my father was around, was aggravated and all directed initially to *me* once Father left us." Here she studied Florence angrily for a few uncomfortable moments. "Oh yes, she *wanted* to look after Lance herself when he was a child, but her energy waned and she was not always clear as to what to do. This all coincided with when I was meant to be going away to University, so I had to turn down an offer I received from Oxford, and stay at home and attend the local university, so that I could help to raise Lance. It's as if he had two parents after all, Mother and me, though Mother was pretty helpless."

Florence put down her knife and fork, even though she had some chicken left on her plate, and stared at Juliet, who was now pouring herself some more wine.

"Whenever I did go out," Juliet continued, picking up her wine glass, "I heard that Mother would not let Lance out of her sight. I think she was afraid of losing him, just as she'd lost Father. And Lance acquiesced. He could sense her need, so as he grew older, he became increasingly attentive to her, and *he* looked after *her*! It was an extraordinary role reversal. What's amazing is that he did so willingly. Or at least he was uncomplaining. For me, though, it was different. I wanted to live my own life, and it felt like having an albatross around my neck."

Juliet sighed deeply, and seemed momentarily lost in her recollections. But sure enough she had more to say, and Florence continued to listen obediently.

"As far as I can tell," Juliet said, waving away the waiter dismissively who had come to ask if they wanted dessert, "Lance was well liked at school, but he never socialized much. He did walk home with Alistaire and Wilkie, though they weren't real friends. In fact, that's a story, too. Alistaire and Wilkie were always having fights about something, and my brother would always get in the middle, even though it never had anything to do with him, and then he'd come home hurt. Just like now. Someone else's fight…

"So Lance spent a lot of time at home, keeping an eye on Mother, and he developed the habit of reading. Sometimes he'd read aloud to her, or tell her about what he'd just read. By the time he was twelve or so he'd become a very studious young man indeed. And by then I was twenty four and due to be married. Two days before my wedding, it was discovered that Lance had a heart murmur. Nothing very serious. But it terrified Mother, who was convinced that he'd have a heart attack at any moment. She was so hysterical that she could not walk, and had to be carried in to the wedding ceremony. Not a good way to start a marriage. Still, that didn't make any difference. It's said we marry the equivalent of someone in our family, so I foolishly married a version of my father. I was divorced

– on my instigation, mind you – and home again with Mother and Lance, after a year and a bit. It's no wonder I took up the profession of Family Law. Families can be the biggest battleground there is."

"But Juliet! Lance has a heart murmur? I didn't know that. Is it something to be concerned about now? Do the doctors know about it?"

"My goodness! You're awfully naïve. Haven't you seen how Lance is hooked up to every medical machine and monitor known to the medical profession! Don't worry; they're measuring his vital signs, and, I expect, a good deal more besides. Personally, I think that whole heart murmur nonsense was a hoax. I think he was putting it on, subconsciously of course, as he didn't want me to leave home to get married. Remember I was like a parent to him. He's never had a problem with his heart since."

"Well, that's a relief, as long as it doesn't complicate his condition now," Florence sighed. But again she was forcefully struck by Juliet's hardness and lack of sympathy for Lance, then and now. Just because she's an astute Family Law barrister, with big cases and a sharp tongue, it didn't mean she had to be so brusque.

"No; that's the last thing we have to worry about," Juliet said, impatiently spiraling her finger abstractly around a circle in the pattern on the armrest of her chair. "But in any case, now you know our family background. I must say I'm surprised that Lance hadn't told you. And now perhaps you can better understand why I would be full of fury and resentment if Lance becomes a permanent invalid, too. I think in this I'm being a realist."

"I'm sure that Lance will be completely better soon," Florence replied optimistically. "I've been told St. Vincent's is an excellent hospital, so I think he's in good hands."

"We'll have to see about that, won't we."

"It's interesting, in light of what you've told me, that Lance came to America at all," Florence said, deliberately changing the angle of the conversation, but also wanting to counter the picture Juliet had painted of Lance.

"Well, it surprised all of us. But I think it was a good thing for him to do. I encouraged him to go, although, in all fairness to him, he was very enthusiastic as he thought it an excellent opportunity. He's married to his career, you know."

At this, Florence winced. But then again, maybe Juliet was just trying to hurt her, and she would certainly not give her the satisfaction of showing her that she'd achieved her mark, so she looked at her and gave her a simple smile.

"What's more," Juliet continued, clearly with an agenda of points she wanted to cover, "we've both been prisoners of our childhoods. We've scarcely left home, either of us. We both attended the local university. Of course I left briefly when I was married, and some years after that went to Law School in London, but that's the extent of it. In the end, ironically, it was Mother who moved out two years ago, when she went to live in that Home in the Lake District. And do you know how that came about? It was thanks to me! I could sense that Mother wanted to move, just as I could sense that Lance was beginning to think it would be a good idea if she did so. But each made assumptions about the other, thinking the need was so great to be together and preserve that wretched *status quo*. It was all because I told each of them individually to be honest with each other, to express their true needs, that change could be implemented – guilt free from both sides!"

"I'd had the impression that your mother had moved much longer ago than two years, as I thought you'd been going to Landsdowne's for ages," Florence said.

"And so we have. In fact, Landsdowne's is one of the reasons that Mother knew the Lake District and wanted to move there. That, plus the fact that she vaguely knew someone at the Home. That doesn't stop her being totally needy, though." She sighed deeply. "Well, it's getting frightfully late. We'd better ask for the bill. I presume you'll be taking a taxi back to your hotel."

"No, I think I'll go on the subway."

"Rather you than me."

That night Florence had a disturbing, horrible nightmare. She was going into Lance's hospital room. The floppy yellow daisies were back in the orange beaker on the windowsill, even though a part of her rational, non-dreaming mind knew they'd been thrown away a few days ago. She went to the window to look at them, and was surprised at the view outside. Instead of overlooking a courtyard, as she knew was the real view from his hospital window, she saw many skyscrapers. And, as she looked at them, she saw that the sky was full of low-flying planes. They skidded around the buildings, then crashed right into them. The sky turned orange with the glow of exploding skyscrapers.

As Florence, in her dream, continued looking out of the window, she realized a nurse was in the room, and was wheeling out Lance's bed. She spun around.

"What are you doing? Where are you taking him?" she cried.

"To pre-op."

"What's that mean?"

His room was very dark. All the walls were black and hung with mirrors. The nurse was standing at the head of Lance's bed, holding up the IV and the bottle of pale, shimmering liquid. Only the whites of her eyes showed.

"We're going to chop off his legs."

"What? No!"

"Oh well, perhaps it's only the right leg. No. Perhaps it's the left one. Beats me."

Then the nurse started to wheel Lance's bed at amazing speed down the corridor.

"Wait!" Florence heard herself shouting. "Wait!" She couldn't run as fast. Her limbs were flailing, like a hand-puppet without a directing hand. The little girl in the corridor, holding her black nanny's hand, was crying and crying. Then Florence woke up. She realized it was she, herself, who was crying.

She knew she wouldn't be able to go back to sleep. Wouldn't be able to eat. She was so frightened. Everything was terrible. She didn't think she was strong enough to cope with this.

That morning, despite feeling tired and jittery, Florence walked around Washington Square before visiting Lance, giving Juliet time to say goodbye to him. She tried to avert her eyes from the massive plume of smoke rising into the air from where the Twin Towers had once stood. She wandered down along MacDougal Street, and noticing a flower shop, walked in.

Behind frosted glass doors her attention was caught by a pot of morning glories. She remembered Lance once telling her that they were his favorite flowers. "Time is embedded in nature," he'd told her then. "See how the morning glory opens its petals with the rising sun and closes them when the sun sets." The florist, noticing Florence looking at them, told her they were from Northern Australia, which sounded close to where Bess lives. The florist smiled so kindly when she spoke, that Florence, purchasing them at once, thought this must be a good omen.

As she pushed open the door to Lance's room later that day, she heard the murmur of men's voices. Upon entering, there was Lance, clean shaven (apparently a parting gesture from Juliet who'd helped him shave) and clear headed as his fever had lifted. So he was getting visibly better, after all! She felt almost faint with relief. He was involved in conversation, but he stopped and beamed at Florence as soon as he saw her.

"Fleur!" he said in a stronger voice than she'd heard him use since the attack. "I'm pleased you're here. And what are these? Morning glories? Thank you! Fleur, I'd like to introduce you to two of my colleagues from NYU. This is Abe Siegel, and this is Dave Burton."

She stepped forward to shake their hands, and to Abe she said, "It was you, I believe, who phoned me in England to let me know that Lance was here. Thank you so much for doing that."

"You're welcome!" Abe said. "I sure am glad you could come over and be here."

They all spoke amiably for a little while, and then the two men left. Florence immediately went up to Lance and kissed him.

"You look so much better today!" she said.

"I feel it. I'll soon be out of here and going home!"

"Did they tell you that?"

"No, but I feel it."

"That's wonderful! When you say, 'going home', do you mean back to England?"

"Good God, no! I have a year's contract with NYU, and I intend honoring that contract. I can't wait to get back to the classroom."

She really admired his spirit, and squeezed his hand encouragingly.

Just then there was a rapid knock on the door, and a nurse swiftly entered with a tray of food.

"We're starting you back on solid foods today," she told him. "But at the beginning we just want you to eat foods that are real easy to digest. So here! There's jello, apple sauce, ice cream, and a glass of juice."

"That sounds good to me," he said.

The door opened again, and in came Marissa, Cameron (who was the Californian student who wore designer labels), and a tall, serious looking Indian man, apparently called Nikhil, who Florence had not seen before. There was extreme excitement and chatter. The young man, it turned out, was to be Lance's Teaching Assistant this semester. Cameron handed Lance an enormous purple envelope, saying, "I swear every guy in the dorm signed it!" and then started to cry noisily.

"Please don't upset yourself," Lance told her kindly. "I'm getting better all the time. It was extremely thoughtful of you to give me this card," he said, tearing open the envelope and running his eye down all the messages inside the card with a smile.

"But you're like the most popular professor! It's just so unfair that this happened to you!"

"I consider myself lucky," Lance said. "I'm extremely grateful that it was just my legs that were hit, and not my heart, lungs, or head." Florence was amazed to hear this, and admired him even more.

"Jesus!" Cameron snorted, very splashy tears running down her powdered cheeks.

"I'm not saying it wasn't frightening. But it's over now. It wasn't my time to die. I'll be back in the classroom soon! I don't intend to be out for much longer."

At this it became apparent that Cameron was crying as much for herself as for Lance, as she said, "Daddy wants me to come home to California immediately. He doesn't want me here. He says with a last name like mine-" She turned to Florence. "My last name's Schwartz – well, with a name like Cameron Schwartz, he thinks I'm too much of a target."

"How long do you expect he'd want you to stay in California?" Marissa asked.

"I dunno. Actually, being real honest, I've gotta admit that I'm scared here. I'm very young. Probably the youngest student at NYU. I was accelerated through middle school and skipped grades five and seven."

"Well then, perhaps it would be best for you to return to your family for now."

"Yes, but if I do come back here after a semester, you won't still be here, right, Professor Ramsey? You're just here for the year, aren't you?"

"That's right," Lance replied. "I'll be returning to England in January."

"I know!" Cameron said, brightening. "I can come over to England and visit you guys!"

"An excellent idea," Lance said. "By the way, would anyone like a chocolate? Abe Siegel was here earlier, and brought some in."

Cameron took three chocolates in one handful. Florence marveled at how she could remain so skinny.

"And Nikhil, we'll need to talk soon about my lesson plans. Meanwhile, I hear James is substituting for me. Is everything going well?"

And so they all continued to talk until it became apparent that Lance was growing very tired. He'd hardly touched his food when the nurse re-entered to take his tray. Florence told herself that she'd look in Jefferson Market and Balducci's, and find him some easily digestible yet more appealing food. By the time they all left, it was mid-afternoon.

In the corridor, Marissa turned to Florence, and said, "So glad you came over, Fleur! Abe told me he'd called you."

"Yes, he did. Thank you from the bottom of my heart for asking him to." And so saying, Florence realized that she really liked Marissa now. She almost felt like crying when she again remembered the agony of waiting for news and thinking Lance was dead. Yet Marissa had been there for her, and so supportive.

"Sure. Hey, do you have plans right now? Some friends and I thought we'd grab a hamburger and then go down to Ground Zero and pay our respects. Want to come?"

"No! Thanks for asking me, but I couldn't go there." She absolutely didn't want to be at the site which nearly killed Lance; didn't think herself capable of looking at the bulging amounts of rubble, with people or body parts of those less fortunate trapped inside. Instead she wanted to preserve her beautiful memories of five months ago, of the sleek, shiny, silver and white elegance of the Twin Towers, and the glorious time she had there with Lance.

"I understand. How do you think Lance is doing? He looks pretty lousy to me."

"Does he? Oh, he's so much better today. Actually the best I've seen him so far," Florence replied, though she felt the upsurge of a new worry based on Marissa saying he looked lousy. Maybe he still was dangerously ill, and she was just growing accustomed to the way he looked.

"God, what an awful thing! I don't think New York will ever be the same. How long are you staying?"

"A few more days."

"Well, I expect I'll see you around here. Bye now. Take care!"

Over the next few days there were frequently other visitors coming to see Lance, including NYU faculty members and students. Florence grew comfortably acquainted with Abe, and she also saw Irv Sterling again from the Port Authority, who was friendly and chatty. Lance had good days, and some that were far from good, but he *was* generally improving, as was evidenced by the fact that he was attached to less machines and monitors.

On her last night, Florence was in her hotel room, reluctantly putting the few things she'd brought with her back in the case, when the room phone rang, completely startling her.

"Come over!" It was Lance. His voice sounded warm, rich, inviting.

"Lance!" she exclaimed.

"Hello Fleur. Are you able to come here now?"

"Well yes!" she said. She looked at her watch. It was after nine o'clock. "Will they let me in at this hour? Isn't visiting time over?"

"They *have* to let you in! If they don't, I'll get out of this bed and insist upon it!"

"Oh, Lance! I'll be there straight away!"

She rushed to St. Vincent's. Sixth Avenue was still crowded, but there was a palpable mood of lingering sadness. Gone was the fun-loving vivacity she'd seen when she first came to New York. Fortunately she did not encounter any difficulty in going up to Lance's room. He lay stiffly in bed, though smiled so radiantly when she entered, with that familiar smile and sparkle in his eyes, as well. She went over to him and kissed him gently.

"Bring over the chair, right up to here, Fleur," he said, tapping the side of the bed. "Really close. And please pull down this ghastly rail along the bed."

"Should I?" she asked, a little afraid.

"Of course! I'm not likely to fall out! And if I do, you can catch me!"

She laughed and did as he requested, and tightly held his hand that was free of the IV.

"Fleur, it means so much to me that you came to New York to see me."

"I *had* to see you, Lance. When I heard about what happened at the World Trade Center, and knew that you'd planned to be there that morning…Every day, not knowing where you were, if you were alive, was torture. So when Abe phoned – God, I was grateful for that, and so grateful to Marissa too, for asking him to call me – I came straight away."

"Thank you."

"How are you feeling?"

"I'm alright. A bit sick of being here. Let's talk of other things. In fact, let's be perfectly British and talk about the weather. What's it like outside?"

"Every day since I've been here has been about 75 degrees, with a clear, blue sunny sky."

"That sounds lovely."

"How *can* it be lovely? Doesn't it *know* what happened? To produce this glorious weather relentlessly, day after day…It seems like a cruel mockery of what happened."

Lance was silent.

"Lance, you haven't spoken about what actually happened *to you* that morning. Do you want to speak about it now?" Florence asked.

"Well, as you know, I was going to meet Irv in his office at 8.30. I took the elevator up…Up…No! I can't! I can't talk about it, Fleur! I can't."

In his eyes there was a wild, almost savage expression, and his face was very red.

"It's all right, Lance," she said, panicked by his level of emotion. She stood up and wrapped her arms around his shoulders and held him tightly. His body felt rigid with tension. She continued to hold him, whispering, "I'm so sorry," from time to time, until gradually, with the occasional jolt of his body, she felt the tension subside and he slept. He must have slept for about twenty minutes, and she continued to hold him, kneeling now on the edge of the chair, despite getting pins and needles in her arms.

He woke with a beatific expression. He looked so calm and relaxed.

"It's so good," he told her, "to wake up and see your face. Sorry for dozing off like that. Did I sleep for long?"

"No. Not long. It seems to have done you good. Did you sleep well?"

"Mmmm."

They kissed. "It's a shame," he said, "that there isn't enough room on this bed for you to lie alongside me."

"Just as we'd done in the Catskills," she said. "Remember that lovely bed we had there, that was so high off the floor? And it had that beautiful patchwork quilt on it, remember?"

"Yes! And remember how it squeaked every time one of us moved!"

"I do! And how it sloped down to the middle, but that was alright as it meant we kept rolling closer together!"

"That was a phenomenal place, Fleur. We should go back."

"That would be great! And do you remember that lovely lake we discovered, with the cherry trees growing on the banks, and how they were blossoming when we were there?"

"Yes. They wouldn't be blossoming now, of course, but we could go there, Fleur, and run around between the cherry trees, chasing each other. You could wear that long skirt of yours that I love, and that shawl, and we'd both be barefoot. That's how I picture us."

"And you'd catch me in no time, what with all the jogging you've been doing!"

"And then, when I'd caught you, we'd fall together to the ground, Fleur, and lie in each other's arms."

"And somehow there would be a bed of fallen pink petals, that would provide a soft and fragrant carpet for us."

"Yes! And later we'd return to the hotel, and pull back the patchwork quilt-"

All this while, Lance lay completely still, clasping Florence in his free arm, and she, still kneeling in the chair, had her head on his chest, hearing the banging of his heart. She ran her hands lightly over his body, as if the power to heal was radiating from her fingertips. Then she looked up at his face, more familiar again now that he was no longer bearded, and moved towards it, placing her head in the remaining space beside his on the pillow, and they lay there, holding each other, and they kissed for what seemed to be a glorious eternity.

At 1.30 am a nurse bustled in to take Lance's temperature, measure his pulse rate, and check the IV.

"Hey there! What you doing here?" the nurse asked, officious but slightly amused. "It's way past visiting time!"

"I invited her in. Please, LaToya," he said, reading her name off her badge, "let her stay a while longer. She's going back to London tomorrow."

"Well, just while I complete my rounds. Then she's gotta go, OK."

"Thank you," they both said.

LaToya jolted up the rail of the bed, and then moved down to the other end, pulled up the sheets, and inspected Lance's legs.

"Hey, this dressing should be changed," she said. "It's started oozing again under there."

Florence rose from the chair, and keeping her eyes focused on the tightly shut petals of the morning glory plant on the windowsill, moved towards it. Peripherally, she could see that the nurse seemed to produce from nowhere the necessary supplies, and was tending to Lance's wound.

"Is it normal for it to still be oozing now?" she asked nervously, avoiding the sight of his leg.

"Oh sure! He's doing real well. This oozing is all part of the healing," the nurse replied, (which Florence did not know whether to believe or not) and then she efficiently covered the affected area with a new, bright white bandage. "There. That should do it."

"Thank you. That feels much better," Lance said.

"You English are so polite! I want to go to your country!" the nurse said with a chuckle, as she pulled the sheets back over Lance's legs. "OK, I'll be right back."

With that she left, and Florence went back to Lance's side, sitting really close to him in the chair and holding his hand through the bars. She didn't want to show him she'd felt afraid. Instead she asked him about the courses he was planning to teach when he returned to NYU.

A short while later, the nurse put her head round the door and said with a smile, "OK girl. Time's up. You outta here now!"

"OK, I'll go now," Florence said, pulling reluctantly away from Lance and standing up.

"Thank you. Good night!" the nurse said, shutting the door behind her.

"Will you be all right out on the streets alone so late?" Lance asked Florence.

"Of course! I don't have far to go. Good night, my love. I'll be back in the morning to say goodbye."

He held out his arm to her and she leaned over him.

"Fleur, this evening – you being here – this has made me feel better than any treatments, any medicines that they've given me. It's reminded me about what's good in life."

"Thank you! For me, too. I love you, Lance. Now you should get some sleep."

--------

Florence asked her taxi driver taking her to Newark Airport to first park briefly at Exchange Place in New Jersey. She got out and looked across the Hudson, as she'd done with Lance in the Spring, but now she saw the wounded Manhattan skyline. Without the Twin Towers as a focal point, the skyscrapers of lower Manhattan looked smaller and stubby. By contrast, in midtown, the focal point was the Empire State Building, with the neighboring skyscrapers clustered around it, but now the downtown area had instead two smoky parallel shafts of empty air, which had once been vertically thronged with people, desks, computers, filing cabinets, phones, fax machines, stacks and stacks of paper, memos, envelopes, photos, artwork, flowers on desks, wallets, keys, pens, pencils, postage stamps. She was getting sad. She must stop this.

It was hard to stop, though, because at the airport bookstand she'd been attracted to the very black cover of the *New Yorker Magazine* designed and executed by Art Spiegelman, and spent much of the flight looking at photos and reading articles about the attack on the World Trade Center.

And of course she kept thinking about Lance. But she told herself he'd be all right now. Juliet was returning to New York soon. And he had lots of visitors. And he was clearly stronger every day. Hopefully he'd soon be discharged and would return to Cornelia Street and be back to teaching in no time.

She did think, though, that it was strange how he hadn't mentioned Howard, nor had he asked about the wedding, either. Of course she was grateful for that. And then, turning comfortably in her seat, she contemplated how perhaps the beautiful and tender expressions of love between them the previous evening showed how Lance was prepared, after all, to share her with Howard.

The captain made an announcement that they were going to be landing soon. And thinking of Howard reminded her to quickly put back on her engagement and wedding rings, which were lodged at the very bottom of her handbag.

# TWELVE

*AS SHE WALKED INTO THE* Arrivals Lounge at Heathrow Airport, two and three quarter hours later than the estimated time of arrival due to delays caused by heightened security, Florence was surprised and perhaps a bit pleased, to see Howard waiting for her. Maybe this was what married people do.

"Howard!" she exclaimed, going up to him. "How nice that you came to meet me! Sorry. You must have been waiting an awfully long time."

"Hello Flo," he said, with what looked strangely like a malevolent smile. "I trust you had a good flight." He seemed detached, and did not kiss her, neither did he offer to carry her bag.

"Yes, very. How are you?" she asked, giving his cheek a quick kiss.

"I'm very well," he said. "Very well indeed. Never felt better, in fact." Still the malevolent, sour smirk. Perhaps she was just tired.

They found his car and Howard drove off rapidly. Florence, who had been starting to doze, woke when he braked suddenly for a red light.

"Where are we?" she asked, not recognizing the street.

"We're on our way to Harrods," he answered shortly.

"Oh? Why are we going there now?"

"Because it's your turn to do the food shopping! Remember? I did it last time, and *all* the bloody time you were gallivanting around New York enjoying yourself! So I thought it only fair that you pick up something really special in Harrods' Food Hall now."

"But Howard, I'm very tired, and would just as soon go straight to bed. Let's go to our local Tesco's and I'll pick up something quick for today, and I promise I'll go to Harrods tomorrow."

"Well, hard luck there. To make up for your absence, the least you could do is oblige by doing what I ask, and pick up some frigging food from Harrods today!"

They drove on to Harrods mostly in silence. They could not park close to the store, so had quite a way to walk. Florence plodded along the street, and then around the Food Hall, with Howard darting around between the display cases, telling her to purchase this and that. It came to a frightful amount of money.

Once home after shopping, Howard said, "Now lay the table. Remember, we have our beautiful plates – those given to us as wedding gifts – to eat off. You do remember we had a wedding, don't you! So, just set everything out on the table while I go to the loo."

"Howard, you eat it. I think I'll go to bed, and have it later."

"No, you don't! We'll eat together now!"

"Howard, you're very kind, but-"

"Have you considered that I might *want* us to eat together? After all, you've been away so long."

"OK."

She draped the table with a deep blue tablecloth, and then put out the purchases from Harrods – a huge platter of salmon surrounded by an arrangement of thinly sliced cucumber, tomatoes and egg, as well as a luscious green salad, a potato salad, a couscous with vegetable salad, various dips, several French cheeses and a baguette. She laid a place for Howard and herself with their new and very fancy wedding plates and crystal glasses, and for added flair, she set out two beautiful new candlestick holders of brightly painted pottery. And she put in the fridge the tempting chocolate, cream and strawberry cake that Howard had also insisted she purchase.

Howard returned from the bathroom still zipping up his flies. "I think we should have wine, too," he said. "Fetch a bottle of Liebfraumilch from the cupboard. We have much to celebrate."

Howard tied his serviette around his neck. They started to dine magnificently, only Florence was forcing it down, not only because of her lack of hunger and fatigue, but also because she felt uncomfortable with this eccentric malevolence that Howard seemed to emit.

"This is superb, Howard!" she said.

"Well, make the most of it. It won't happen again. I bet you didn't dine like this in New York."

"No, how could I? I was mostly at the hospital. The food was really dingy there, as you can imagine, but sometimes I bought food in-"

"Did you? How very compassionate! And how was your dear patient?"

"Lance? Much better now, thanks. But he seemed dreadful at first. One of his legs was so mutilated that they threatened amputation."

"Threatened? Who was speaking threateningly?"

"The doctors. I mean, he was-"

"How very touching that your little friend was so badly injured." He had picked up a section of the salmon's backbone and was squeezing the flesh from it with a moist thumb and finger before placing it into his salivating mouth. "Pass me more couscous salad! Didn't I make a good selection telling you to get these foods!"

"Yes, delicious! Well, as I was saying, Lance had two operations-"

"So you, my little Ms. Nightingale, were his nurse. Very touching. Tell me, how would you have behaved if your parents had named you Helen?"

"What?"

"Nothing. Just a little joke of mine. You wouldn't understand." He was drinking heavily, and now asked her to open a second bottle of Liebfraumilch.

"Do you think you should?"

"Rather! Just start perking the coffee. Ah yes, another wedding present. And it makes such satisfying coffee!"

Florence rose to clear the plates. She was feeling light headed and a little wobbly, and badly needed to go to bed. She opened the door of the fridge to take out the milk, and saw the cake peering through its plastic window at the top of its huge white box.

"Howard, that's such a beautiful cake. Let's leave it for tomorrow. Or maybe later this evening. I couldn't do it justice now."

"Nonsense! Come on! Put it on the table at once!"

"No, really."

Howard kicked his chair back, and lumbering to the fridge, grabbed the cake box and banging it on the table, tore off the lid. "Start slicing it!" he commanded. "I seem to remember that we were even given a silver slicer as a present. Go and fetch it now! 'What a lot we got!' Pity you won't be seeing all these presents anymore."

"What did you say?"

In answer, he delicately picked up the cup that Florence had placed before him, and said, "Look! Isn't it pretty! Weren't our friends generous to us!" And so saying, he violently flung the cup into the corner of the room, where it made a thud on impact and then a delicate tinkling sound as small sharp pieces of bone china shattered, piercing the walls and floor like a thousand tiny needles.

"Howard! What are you doing? Stop it! You're drunk!"

"Oh no, my dear. I'm very sober," he said straightening up. "And why should you care about these ridiculously dainty cups? As I just told you, you won't be seeing them again. They're mine to do with as I wish!" And with that, he flung Florence's cup into the corner, too.

"I don't understand. Why are you saying that I won't see them again? What do you mean?" Panic was mounting in her, and was hard to control as she was so tired.

"I hope you enjoyed your meal as it's the last one you'll get here. 'The last supper.' Oh but wait, let's not forget the chocolate cake! Go on! Eat it! I picked it out specially!"

"No, I don't want it now."

"Eat it, I tell you!" he said, digging into the whole cake roughly and deeply with his silver fork, creating an ugly scar on its side where it had once been perfectly decorated with light chocolate frills and twirls. He had scooped up a large amount, and violently ramming it into Florence's mouth, brutally poked her upper lip with the tines of the fork and ripped downwards through her flesh, while holding her down by the shoulder with his other hand.

"Howard, stop it!" Her lip felt a searing pain, and she was practically choking from being force-fed, but already he was shoving in the next forkful. "I can't eat it like that! Stop!"

"You'll regret it later when you won't be able to have any more."

She wriggled free of his grasp and coughing and spluttering, stood up.

"That's right! Leave me! That's what I want you to do, you whore! You slut! I should have taken notice of the red flag when I heard about you and your disgusting antics with Renard. True to form, you can't stop now, can you? You pervert!"

She froze, one hand clasping her mouth.

"See! You don't deny it. You've been trying to leave me ever since you first flirted with me. I was just another conquest to add to your disgusting list. Spilling wine down me at your parents' table! Pathetic! What a ploy. I should have seen through you then!"

"I don't know what you're talking about!" she gasped.

"Just fuck off! Leave! Go!" he shouted, thumping down on his seat at the table, and putting his hands over his face. She felt momentarily sorry for him. Then, looking up and raising his voice once more, he said, "You infidel! You think I don't know why you *had* to go and see Lance in New York! And not for the first time either, it turns out! You think I'm *that* stupid! Well, your game's up, girl! I've found it all out."

Florence flopped down into her seat. Her hand up against her mouth felt wet. She looked down and saw that her fingers were covered in blood. It was then that she realized that her lip was bleeding profusely from where he'd jabbed it with the fork, and that the lingering dense, dark, sticky sweetness of the chocolate cake in her mouth had combined with the old metallic taste of her own blood. She tentatively ran her tongue over her teeth to see if any were missing. They were all there.

"I'm sorry," she said.

"Really, Flo. It's hard to see what you see in him. He strikes me as a most peculiar fellow. He takes filial devotion to a whole new level. I wonder how you can stand it, given how impatient you are when my mother phones. Oh, and speaking of my mother, I naturally had to put her in the picture, and she's utterly incensed. She swears she'll never speak to you again. And of course she's told everything to your parents. You'll have to deal with that, but I hear your mother became quite hysterical, and your father is in a total rage."

"No! I'll have to phone them," she said, terrified.

"Not so fast. We haven't finished yet. Besides, it's doubtful that she or your father wants to have any more to do with you. In fact, I seem to remember your mother saying something like, 'She may be my daughter, but to me she's become a complete stranger.' Oh, but let's not get distracted. I believe we were talking about you and this chap, Lance."

Florence felt weak. "How did you find out?" she asked, reaching for a napkin, dipping it into her glass of water, and holding it up against her lip.

"I have my sources."

"Who?"

"Well, if you must know, your dear Rose and Allison are sharper than they appear. In fact, they are quite treacherous old ladies. A regular Miss Marple, is Rose. She phoned a few days after the wedding wanting to speak to you. A not unreasonable request, and a most thoughtful one, considering she wanted to thank you for accommodating her and Allison over the wedding period. Imagine her utter surprise when I told her that you'd gone away. 'What? So soon! But you've not yet been married a week!' she exclaimed. 'Precisely,' I told her. 'But Flo wanted to go to New York. A certain Lance Ramsey was apparently hurt at the World Trade Center disaster. Oh yes, maybe you know him. I believe he was staying at Landsdowne's at the same time that Flo met you.'"

He leaned back in his chair and glared at Florence, who looked back at him, the blood soaked napkin at her mouth, in muffled horror.

"Well, Rose became all a-twitter," he continued. "At first she said that she had no idea that you and Lance (Dr. Ramsey, as she called him) knew each other that well. And she was, naturally, concerned that he'd been injured, but on that score I comforted her by mentioning that you'd told me when you first arrived that he had only suffered a broken leg. Strangely, she then said, sounding conspiratorial and rather pleased with herself, 'Well, I really oughtn't tell you this, but something odd happened on the eve of your wedding, that made Allison and me rather curious. You will remember that Allison was using Florence's camera, as she had forgotten to pack mine.' 'Yes, yes,' I said impatiently, beginning to think the woman was quite dotty as she seemed to have completely gone off track. 'Well, Allison entirely used up the film the night before your wedding, by taking the remaining pictures of Florence in her wedding dress. Yes, we asked her to put it on then to show us. Quite gorgeous, she looked, didn't you think!' 'Yes, my mother picked out that dress for her,' I replied, 'But I'm afraid I'm having some trouble following you. I thought we were talking about something else.' 'I'm getting to that, dear Mr. Feldman,' she said, and she did."

Howard stood up roughly from his chair, making it rock precariously backwards, and paced around the table. Florence, though hopelessly distraught and in considerable pain, could not help being impressed with how accurately Howard could mimic Rose's voice and manner. It was irrelevant, of course, but she never knew he had any acting skills.

"Yes, she did," he continued, pouring himself some more wine. "She said that since the film was used up that night, you'd told them you'd get it developed straight away in that one-hour photo place close by. I then had to hear the details of the Scrabble game you played while waiting for the film, and then how you'd gone out to collect that film just before the shop closed. 'When she returned,' Rose said, 'your wife looked a bit peculiar. We asked her if the pictures came out nicely, and she said, in a strained voice, that not a single picture had come out. We said it was a shame, and she reminded us that she'd said that the camera wasn't working. Her behavior was very strange and flustered, but Allison and I put it down to pre-wedding nerves.' God, your friend Rose is long-winded, but she is thorough, I'll give her that."

He took a long swig of wine. Then he started walking towards Florence in a threatening manner, and she nervously edged her chair away from him. Her lip, she knew, was still bleeding.

"But even those who like to spin out their tale eventually reach the punch-line, and Rose certainly reached hers. In a very confessional voice, she said, 'The following morning your dear wife took a long time dressing, which of course is understandable. It's not every day we put on a wedding dress, now is it? Well, Allison and I were waiting in the kitchen, and all of a sudden Allison noticed the camera on the sideboard and the envelope from the photo development shop beneath it. And we noticed that the envelope looked full, not empty as Florence had had us believe."

Florence inhaled sharply; how could she have been so idiotic as to not carefully put those photos away somewhere safe before the wedding?

Howard, delighting in Florence's heightened discomfort, continued to act the part of Rose telling him all on the telephone, "So Allison asked why Florence said no photos had come out, Rose told me. But of course our dear Rose is a sharp woman. 'I surmised,' she said, 'that probably she'd told a fib as she hadn't liked the way she looked in the pictures,' which, as an aside, was rather witty of her, especially as you managed, despite the gorgeous dress my mother chose for you, to look slovenly and unkempt," Howard told her. Then, back to his 'Rose voice' he said, "'...and I urged Allison to open the envelope and we'd see for ourselves,' Rose said. 'Now Allison has always been such a meek person, and she couldn't bring herself to do it. So I marched up to the sideboard and opened the envelope of photos myself! Imagine my surprise!'"

Florence could hardly breathe. She glanced towards the sideboard, but neither her camera nor the envelope of photos was there.

"'What?' I asked her," Howard continued. "'What did those photos show?' 'Well,' she said, 'I don't quite think I should be telling you this, but since we've got this far…they were of Florence and Dr. Ramsey. They seemed very much together, hand-in-hand, laughing, even kissing, I'm afraid. It looked like they were in the Lake District, as it was very rural. But what I simply can't understand is how they found the time. Dr. Ramsey was always at his mother's side. Apart from an occasional game of Scrabble, they hardly spoke. So how did they do it?' There! That's what she told me. So how did you do it? Oh, but I forget. Sluts don't speak. They're only interested in lusting after the body. But when did you have time for that with our most upright Dr. Ramsey?"

"Where's my camera now?" Florence asked. "And where are those photos?"

"Ah, so you deny nothing!"

"I only ask where my camera and photos are," she asked, rising, and

219

feeling incredibly dizzy. Blood poured anew from her lip, and she sucked it into her mouth and swallowed it.

"You'll find your camera with all your other belongings. In a heap on the floor in the bedroom. I emptied all your stuff out of the drawers and cupboards."

Florence started to move to the bedroom door.

"Not so fast!" he said. "There's something else I have to tell you, that I think you'll find of interest, and that's Elizabeth Carlisle's reaction."

"Elizabeth Carlisle? What's she got to do with any of this?"

"Well, I decided to phone her."

"You didn't!"

"Why yes, as a matter of fact, I did. Sweet little woman. I had spoken quite a bit with her at our wedding, so I was quite comfortable giving her a call."

"What did she say?"

"You mean, what did she say besides the fact that she's made you redundant?"

"Redundant?"

"Well, I'd think so. It seems you lied to her, too, and bosses, like husbands, don't like to be lied to."

"I didn't lie to her!"

"All right. Perhaps 'lie' is too strong a word. But you told her you were going to New York last April, and she, being the kind person she is, found some work for you to do out there to justify your absence from the office. So you met up with some editor. Big deal, if you ask me. But you're right. You didn't exactly lie to her. It was me you lied to, as you had told *me* you were going to New York for an assignment, whereas Elizabeth Carlisle told me it was entirely the other way round. And now you took more time off work, and well, it's just too many absences and she senses a certain lack of commitment. But that's your business. It's nothing to do with me. I'm sure you'll find this out from her soon enough. In the meantime," he sneered, "I hope you enjoyed your meal. Clean up the plates now, and then pack your bags."

"Pack my bags?"

"Yes, I want you out of here!"

She glanced at the clock. "But where can I possibly go at this time?"

"Do you think I care? You've been constantly going away when I *did* care, but that didn't stop you. So get out after you've cleaned up. I'm not having you here! Oh, and another thing," he said seizing her hand. "Give me back that wedding ring! Go on! Take it off your lousy finger." He started bending her finger back and pulling viciously, causing her to shriek. "You won't need this anymore. I've filed for a divorce! Yes, fuck it! The shortest marriage known to man!"

"Please, Howard. Let's both try to calm down and talk."

"There's nothing more to talk about. I've said all I needed to say."

"But give me a chance to talk, too. What I want to say is not a justification for my behavior, but an explanation. Please let me do that, so that perhaps you'll understand."

"Not that I give a shit about your welfare, but the longer you delay your departure with idle chatter, the harder it will be to find a place to stay tonight."

"Thanks for being considerate, Howard, but I need to tell you why I did what I did."

"It won't make a difference, even if you do tell me. I still want a divorce."

"Howard, when I went to the Lake District last summer, I just wanted some time alone. I needed a break. I didn't think you and I were getting along so well, as I think you'll agree, so I wanted some time to replenish myself. I didn't expect to meet anyone, romantically I mean, and I certainly wasn't looking. But Lance helped me with my camera when I first arrived as I thought it was jammed, and he and I found that we could talk to each other so easily. Instantly we had all sorts of fascinating conversations."

"You realize this is just weakening your case, don't you! You had pretended to have nothing to do with him, when I had to go up there and bring you home as you were ill, so you were a liar as well as an ingrate. But I'd suspected you'd been speaking with him on the phone after you'd returned, and I even caught you once, remember? And you flatly denied that it was anything other than casual and very occasional. God, you hideous deceiver!"

"We were just extraordinarily close friends."

"And we're not, you and I?"

"It's different, Howard. Lance and I have lots of interests in common. And yes, I did go to New York last April specifically to visit him, and I expected it would just be a visit to a friend, but that you wouldn't understand, so I didn't tell you. I'm so sorry about that."

"I must say, you've got a very odd definition of a friend," he said in a peremptory manner. "What about those photos of you and him in the Lake District kissing away! Cameras don't lie, Flo, even if you do!"

"Actually, that camera-" But no! She couldn't tell Howard about the inexplicable mysteries of that camera. That was a precious secret, shared only with Lance. "We're warm, affectionate friends," she continued limply. "I'm sorry if these photos gave you a different impression." She sighed. "But then, when the World Trade Center collapsed, and he'd told me he'd be there that morning, and then I heard nothing from him for day upon hellish day, I was naturally frantic, as anyone would be for a friend."

"Very sweet story, Flo. I just have one question."

"What?"

"Why did you agree to marry me?"

"I-"

"Why, Flo? Answer me that! After all, you had so much of a better friendship with Lance. Was it because Lance couldn't ask you to be his wife because of his unnatural tie to his mother? Was he too busy fucking *her*? Was that it, Flo? Was it? Or was it that he was so physically incompetent, on account of still being a 'Mama's boy,' that he couldn't get it up? Well, answer me! Was that what it was?"

Enraged, Florence shouted, "I said yes to your marriage proposal when I really meant to say no!"

"What?" he thundered. "You said yes when you meant to say no! Consider yourself lucky that it was the teacup that I broke rather than your neck!" At that he took the wedding ring that he'd been twisting around his little finger, and stepping quickly to the window, flung it out into the bushes.

"There! Satisfied? You've had your little talk now? You've put me in the picture? In light of what you've just told me, I'm glad that I told my mother about you having had an abortion."

222

"You didn't!"

"Oh yes, I did. When I told her about you having gone off to New York to see your man immediately after you and I had just married, and she was incredulous, I thought I needed to reinforce the image of the type you are, so I told her about the abortion. Oh dear, shouldn't I have done that? You think it might have upset your Mama and Papa too much when she told them, do you?"

"You horrific twister of information!"

"Is that the best you can do! Now pack your things and leave! And there's no point trying to sneak back as you won't get in. I've changed all the locks. So take everything now. But mind you don't take a single wedding present. They're for me. After all, it wasn't me who destroyed this marriage."

"I won't take the wedding presents. I think we should return them to everyone."

"Nonsense! I wouldn't hear of it! They're mine! All mine."

Florence went to the bedroom to gather together her belongings, which, as Howard had said, he'd dumped on the floor. It would be impossible to take it all tonight, but she took what she could. And with all the bending and lifting of heavy objects, her lip was bleeding again, and felt oddly numb and large. What she could not find, though, was that recent envelope of photos that Howard had been speaking about, and she searched for as long as she could until she had no drop of energy left.

She couldn't calculate how many hours since she'd last slept, but it must have been quite late at night when she knocked on Anna's door. The rapidly packed bags and her laptop were excruciatingly heavy. Anna opened the door at the second round of knocking. She'd clearly been asleep, but, Florence hoped, in her training to be a rabbi, she must surely be used to some nighttime emergencies.

"Anna, I'm sorry to disturb you so late at night, but-"

"Florence! Are you all right? Come in!" And then, as Florence stepped into the lighted hall, Anna took a sharp intake of breath and said, "Whatever happened to you? You look as though you've been hurt!"

"I'm OK."

"But your lip! It's all swollen! It looks like you have a deep cut above it. Let me help you! Come into the kitchen and sit down! What caused this?"

"Howard jabbed a fork into my mouth."

"He did what to your mouth?"

"He was trying to force me to eat some cake. He was very drunk. And hideously angry. He said vile, threatening things to me."

"But that's terrible. You've got a deep cut there. Does it hurt?"

"Not anymore. It just bled a lot."

"I'm really concerned about this, Florence. You probably should've had stitches, though I think it's too late now," Anna said, while gently sponging Florence's mouth with a soft, warm cloth. "Why was Howard so angry?"

Florence told her everything. "I spent a week in New York. I've just returned. I know I just got married, but I had to visit Lance. Lance was the person I'd been referring to at the party before the wedding, when I told you I was so upset and worried and frightened. I received a call on the Monday after the wedding that he'd survived, just as you said he might. But it turned out that he was indeed seriously injured at the World Trade Center. Though not killed, thank God. He's recovering in hospital. I had to go, Anna. I had to. Just for a week. I thought Howard understood. But he didn't."

"Wow! Well, I see that this would be hard on him."

"He picked me up from the airport, which I thought was quite nice of him, but then he made me go food shopping at Harrods-"

"He made you go food shopping! Wouldn't it have been easier, since you-"

"It was my turn. Howard is a great believer in taking it in turns."

"Well, even if he was so inflexible as to insist on you doing the shopping, why didn't you shop somewhere closer to home?"

"He was acting very strangely. He definitely wanted me to buy food at Harrods as he kept saying this was 'our last supper'. And he made me buy tons of stuff, and then insisted that we eat it all once we got home. And we started having a terrible row about me having visited Lance, and, well Anna, he said he's filed for a divorce."

"Divorce? How do you feel about that?"

"Shocked. Surprised. Relieved."

"Yes, I think you should feel relieved to be away from anyone who could be verbally and physically abusive to you."

"But I'm to blame for that, Anna. He did it as a reaction to what I did."

"I won't accept that. No one deserves to be treated with violence. Your behavior made him extremely angry, yes, but you didn't make him hurt you. He is responsible for his actions."

"I feel so ashamed. So many people were so generous and lavish with the presents they gave, and I, all along-"

"You'd told me you had doubts about Howard, Florence. I wish I had listened to you more about that. Is Lance American?"

"No, English." And she told Anna all about how they'd met. "I hadn't gone looking for anyone else when I went to the Lake District. And I've always considered myself a moral person, but clearly I'm not! I've done a dreadful thing!"

"Well, truth to tell, you've never been that enamored with Howard, have you? So why did you agree to marry him?"

"He asked me that, too. I think I married him to please him, and my parents, as it's what they all wanted."

"But what about pleasing yourself? Isn't that the most important thing here?"

"I thought I could get used to him, that I could grow to like him more. Isn't that what happens in arranged marriages?"

"But why think that way? Why did you want to pretend that you had no choice in the matter of your own marriage?"

"Well, because in some ways I didn't. You see, I've always been a bit scared of Howard. He has power over me, and he knows it. It turns out that he knew -"

"What? What did he know?"

"Well, he knew Renard made me pregnant. He'd heard about it from some distant relative of his ex-wife who happened to know Renard. This was basically the first thing he said to me when he and I first met. Do you remember Bess saying at the wedding how lucky I was not to have gone to some party with her ages ago, but to go and visit my parents that weekend, and come away with my future husband? God, how I wish I'd gone to that party instead! Anyway, Howard surprised me so much by knowing that I'd been pregnant – he even asked me how my child is now - so I'd stupidly blurted out to him that I'd had an abortion, and that I'd kept this information about the pregnancy and the abortion from my parents. So he's always been obliquely threatening to tell them about it. Or more accurately to tell his parents, who are good friends of my parents, and so they'd be bound to tell them. I thought if I always did what he wanted, he'd keep quiet about it."

"Oh, Florence! You did nothing wrong by having an abortion. You were raped! I hadn't realized that your parents didn't know about it. It would've been better if you'd told them about it at the time. I wish you had never met Renard in the first place. But you're not to blame for what happened, and I'm sure your parents, however anti-abortion they are in their outlook, would have understood, given the circumstances."

"Well, they apparently know about it now, as Howard told me he told his mother and she's bound to talk. And he says my parents disown me and-"

"I sincerely doubt that. Yes, it wasn't the best way for them to find out, but I'm sure when you explain to them-"

"The whole thing's become so ugly, Anna. He apparently also talked to my boss, Elizabeth Carlisle, and turned her against me, so I might have lost my job!"

"Don't believe everything he says, Florence."

"You don't hate me, do you, Anna?"

"Of course not!" Anna said, cradling Florence in her arms. "I love you. You are my dearest friend. And you did nothing wrong in visiting a beloved friend who is in hospital. Why, visiting the sick and offering comfort to those in need is a true *mitzvah* - one of the loveliest gifts you can give, and certainly one of the most moral acts. And from what you told me, your visit made a huge difference to Lance in terms of his healing. The only thing that might be considered unfortunate is the timing, since you had just got married, and naturally no new husband wants to be abandoned so soon after he has just made up his wedding bed.

"But Florence, there's another way of looking at this too. The very timing, the fact that you flew out there when many people are now afraid to fly, shows remarkable bravery, as well, of course, as showing what abundant generosity you have. After all, New York is far away, and this journey must have been expensive, too. Not only that, but you were flying right into a city that had been under attack. Who knew if there were more attacks to follow? It's amazingly courageous of you to have gone out there. Few people would have done that. So in many ways your trip to visit Lance proves what a good person you are. Which is what I've known all along."

"Thank you, Anna."

"I'm so sorry for all you've been going through, Florence. But now come and get some sleep. The guest bed is already made up, so pop into it, and sleep refreshingly and well. And of course you know that you are welcome to stay here with David and me for as long as you want."

Florence went the following afternoon to see Elizabeth Carlisle. Her lip was still swollen and ugly, and she was pale with exhaustion and tension.

"We go back a long way, you and I," Elizabeth began from across her desk, glancing briefly at her mouth, but expressing no concern as she would have done on previous occasions. "And I've always been impressed with your work. But things change, and recently I've started to pick up on a general lack of focus in what you do. That, on top of your frequent and sometimes last minute absences. I've tried to be accommodating to you, but at the same time we have a business to run. Frank, our new editor-in-chief, was quite upset that you left for America again. Twice in a year! I had to give the story you'd been working on to Laura, and I must say she did an impressive job rescuing it, and turning it into something decent, even ahead of the deadline. Did you read her story? It was really quite good. But we can't keep rescuing you, Florence. The behavior you've been exhibiting could jeopardize the production of the magazine."

"I'm so sorry," Florence said sincerely. "I hadn't meant to cause such havoc. And no, I'm afraid I've not yet read Laura's piece, though I will do so immediately. But you see, I'd been so distracted by the terrible events at the World Trade Center as I have a close friend who was badly injured there."

"So I heard."

"Please, Elizabeth," Florence implored, detesting Howard for his meddling. "My most recent visit to New York was under exceptional circumstances, as I think you'll agree. It won't happen again. And that particular friend will be returning to England in the New Year, anyway."

"Far be it from me to get into your private affairs, Florence. But I am afraid I have bad news for you. Frank instructed me to tell you that he wants to end your association with this magazine. Certainly if your recent trip was the only time you'd taken a leave, it would have been viewed compassionately, but you have started developing a history. A trip to New York and then Paris last April, and the previous summer, an extended time in the Lake District, followed by sick days. Then a week before your wedding, and then, without warning, another departure almost immediately after that. It all demonstrates a lack of commitment from you. You must see, from our point of view, that these absences are becoming a pattern with you, and often you are away at the magazine's busiest times."

Florence felt herself growing nauseous, and took in a deep inhalation to steady herself. Elizabeth rose and came round to the other side of the desk, and pulled up an armchair facing her.

"However, with that said, I want to also acknowledge that your work has been indispensable to the magazine. Your stories are of exceptional quality, and I've often told you, haven't I, that you write with flair. Also you established a very promising relationship with Tom Skates, the editor I asked you to visit in New York. So what I propose is this - and mind you, I want you to be aware that I am going out on a limb for you - that you continue your relationship with us in a freelance capacity. That, at least, might motivate you to stay at your desk, rather than taking too many leaves of absence. Consider it a probational period, if you will. Then, at some future and as yet unspecified date, we will reassess the situation."

Elizabeth rose, the discussion over.

"Thank you," Florence said, also rising, mute to the ability to protest. "It's very kind of you to extend yourself to me, and I won't disappoint you again." And, thinking fast, though insincerely, she added, "And, as a matter of fact, I have an idea for a story right now! I'll send you a proposal by Monday."

The positive note she ended on belied the underlying feeling of deflation and despair that Florence experienced. But far be it for her to show her feelings to Elizabeth Carlisle. And she knew, too, that what her boss had said about her frequent absences was true. However, she also knew freelancers were paid next to nothing, and hovered in a constant cloud of uncertainty as to whether each of their stories would be accepted. She felt that so much of what she'd carefully constructed over time, in her work and personal relationships, was slipping away from her. And now she had the daunting task of following through on her story idea by Monday, because for the moment, if truth be told, her mind was completely blank.

# PART TWO

# THIRTEEN

*OVER THE NEXT SEVERAL MONTHS,* Florence tried to rebuild that which had been eroded. She was delighted to have found a very reasonable yet attractive flat off the Fulham Road, at the very top of a terrace of houses which had no lift, and although Anna and David had made her feel so welcome and had insisted that she stay as long as she liked, it was time to move, as Anna was in the early stages of pregnancy, with all the accompanying symptoms of exhaustion and morning sickness, and needed some privacy. As well as finding herself a nice flat, Florence had gratifyingly, through several attempts, started to smooth things over at least with her father; and she had managed to work hard on several stories simultaneously, her energy and intellectual excitement once again ignited. And the news from Lance was encouraging; he was back to teaching again at NYU, and feeling much better. All in all, apart from contentious letters from Howard's lawyer to her lawyer, which surprised her as she had agreed to an uncontested divorce, things were calming down.

Even though she and Lance exchanged frequent e-mails, there never seemed to be a right time to tell him about the divorce. His e-mails were chatty and pleasant, though once he did write something about how he was still having nightmares. She had not known about this before, and asked him about it in her next e-mail, but his subsequent e-mails never mentioned the topic again.

And then, around Christmas, an e-mail arrived from him with the title, "Coming Home". She clicked excitedly to open it, and read:

*Fleur, my love, I'll be returning to England on January 21st. I'd like you to be the first visitor in my new house. Yes! In true American style, I actually found my house on the Internet and bought it over the phone! Imagine that! I have rather a big surprise for you. I'll send details of address and directions once I arrive. Plan on coming two weeks after that, to give me time to get settled. Longing to see you. Lance.*

A later e-mail informed Florence that the house he'd purchased was actually in the Lake District, which made her think he might want to be closer to his mother, though she wondered why he would be so far away from his university in East Anglia.

The day she was to drive up there to visit him, she had received reassuring news that Elizabeth Carlisle loved her last two stories, and she also heard from a literary magazine, to which she had submitted a work of fiction, that they were going to publish it, and they expressed an interest in seeing more of her work.

So, feeling happy and confident, and breathlessly excited about seeing Lance, Florence packed a small bag with a few clothes, and set off early in her car for the Lake District, carefully following his directions. By the time she pulled off the motorway at Penrith, and headed for the country roads, it was just after 4.00 pm, and already growing dark. These local roads were narrow and quite steep, and in the dark the drive started to feel quite difficult and rather frightening. After some distance she saw a sign for the tiny villages of Applethwaite and Bassenthwaite, which surprised her as she knew they were close to Landsdowne's Guest House; funny that Lance had not mentioned this in his directions. She continued driving as directed, and then turned into an extremely narrow lane, wide enough for one car only, and at that point it started to snow. She turned on her high beam headlights so as to better navigate along the narrowness of the lane, and from their glare it looked as though all the snowflakes were enormous, and were all falling from a black sky diagonally from each side, onto the car. She turned off the high beam setting, so the snowflakes were no longer illuminated, but without the high beam she could not see where the next twist in the road would be. She slowed down to almost a crawl, and just as she felt that she was almost too afraid to go further, she realized that she had arrived.

And then she realized one more thing. The house! It was the very house, 'Fern View,' that she and Lance had snooped around that innocent summer afternoon, returning at nighttime when they'd been scared off by an eerie, ghostly glow from one of the downstairs windows. Only now from both downstairs windows either side of the front door there glowed a warm yellow light. She switched on the light inside the car and looked again at the directions to make sure this was the right house. Yes, it seemed that it was. Could Lance have really moved here? It seemed incredible. The only apparent architectural difference between the way the house looked now, and how it had looked that summer was that from the light over the porch she could see what appeared to be a long ramp, twisting this way and that, up to the front door. Florence's mind flashed back instantly to the photo of this house which incredibly showed this very same ramp, and was inhabited then by what seemed to be an elderly couple. Perhaps they were the people from whom Lance bought this property. But if that were so, they couldn't have lived there for very long!

She climbed out of the car, and walked carefully up the icy ramp to the front door in a state of excitement, bewilderment and fear. When she knocked it took a moment, and then a very tiny Asian woman opened the door.

"Excuse me. I'm not sure if I'm at the right house. I'm looking for Lance Ramsey," Florence said.

"Yes. Quite right. Come in!" the woman said in a light, high, little girl's voice with a strong accent. "You Fleur? Lance expecting you."

"Thank you," Florence replied, wondering who this woman was. Stamping the snow off her shoes, she entered the house.

"I'm Mei-Feng," the woman said. "Lance in this room. Come."

Florence followed Mei-Feng into a bright living room, and there, seated on the sofa, a laptop on his knees, was Lance! She rushed up to him, but he did not rise, though he gave his beautiful smile.

"Fleur!" he exclaimed enthusiastically. "I'm so glad you're here! How was your drive?"

"Oh, it was fine." She didn't want to tell him about her fear on the tiny local roads.

"You look terrific! And your hair has grown so long! Come and sit beside me." He put the laptop down on the table next to the sofa, and patted the cushion next to him.

She kissed his cheek and sat down.

"It's so fantastic to see you, Lance," she said, bubbling with excitement, yet at the same time feeling inhibited and confused by the hovering presence of Mei-Feng. "As for my hair, I decided not to cut it until you came back to England!"

"Well, I'm here now! And it really suits you. Keep it like that," he remarked, smiling more broadly. But then his smile faded, and she noticed that he was still quite gaunt and very pale, and he looked weary, apprehensive and ill at ease.

Mei-Feng went up to him and said, again in that high voice, "I'll go to village now for shopping. It snow again. Do you want me to get you anything?"

"No thanks," he replied. "Be careful you don't slip. See you later."

She put her hand tenderly on his shoulder, and left it there slightly longer than convention would imply.

"See you later," she repeated, and bowing slightly to Florence, left the room.

"That's Mei-Feng," Lance explained. "She was at NYU. She wanted to come to England. She'd been helping me with a few things in New York once I was discharged from hospital."

All sorts of complicated feelings and questions were running through Florence's mind. If Lance were to have brought any woman back with him from New York, she thought it would have been Marissa. What was his relationship with Mei-Feng? And was she living in his house with him? But instead she asked, "Had she finished her degree, or did she interrupt her studies to come over here?"

"Neither. Mei-Feng worked in a technical capacity at the Faculty Technology Center. I met her when I needed help with a PowerPoint presentation I was giving. She's very good at what she does. People with her skills can get a job in five minutes these days. In fact, she's already found a job here, working from the house through the Internet."

"That's good." So she did live here! "Where's she from originally?" This was not at all what she expected to be talking to Lance about when first seeing him again after all this time, and all that had happened.

"Taipei, Taiwan," he said. Then he tenderly took hold of Florence's hand, and kissed her gently. "Thanks for coming all the way up here, Fleur," he said. "I hope the drive wasn't too awful."

Ah! This was better.

"It's so wonderful to see you again, Lance," she said again. "And not in a hospital bed. You look great! How are you feeling?"

"I'm feeling much better all the time. And you?"

"I'm feeling much better all the time, too! I'm getting a divorce from Howard!"

Lance's face was full of consternation. "Fleur, did you marry him? I didn't know that."

Florence was surprised, and also concerned. "Yes, Lance. We married last September. September 15th, in fact."

"How could I not remember a thing like that! I completely did not know, Fleur."

"Well, perhaps it's not so surprising, after all. It happened around the same time that you were injured at the World Trade Center."

"My God! I absolutely don't have any recollection." He pushed up his glasses and rubbed his eyes. Then he looked at her again. "But you're getting a divorce now, you say. Is that why you moved to a new flat, Fleur?"

"Yes, that's right. And I love it there."

"I hope this divorce hasn't been really hard on you."

"No, I'm fine. It was a little hard at first, but now things seem to be moving quite quickly. It should all be finalized in a month or so."

"How long has this been going on for?"

"We started divorce proceedings at the end of last September. We really weren't married very long! The whole thing was a huge mistake."

"No! You were only married a few weeks! And some of that time you were with me in New York! Oh God, Fleur, I hope things weren't too terrible for you! Why didn't you tell me anything about this?"

"I don't know. There never seemed to be a right time. And besides, I think it's because whenever Howard comes up in the conversation, things get tense between you and me. I didn't want to risk that by e-mail, and preferred to tell you when I saw you instead."

"If indeed things ever were tense between you and me, it's only because I thought you entertained some kind of unfathomable fondness for Howard. But telling me you are leaving him is a completely different thing, and as long as you're fine, then I'm delighted!"

"Yes, I am fine. But let's not talk of Howard, Lance. It's so lovely here! This house is beautiful on the inside. You seem to have settled in really quickly."

"Well, Mei-Feng has been an enormous help," he replied, which made Florence wince silently. "And of course," he continued, "I had movers transport my belongings here from East Anglia, as well as two friends who came along to help unpack. And some of the furniture actually came with the house. You might even recognize some of it from our window-peeping days! All I needed was to hire a carpenter to hammer a few things together, and we were all set."

"Actually, Lance," Florence said slightly mischievously, "I can't believe you moved here!"

"You mean, you can't believe that I'm no longer living with my sister, or you can't believe that I chose to live in this particular house?"

"Well, both really."

"Ah! In the first place, I realized in New York how much I value my freedom and independence. Juliet is kind and well meaning, but she can be a bit domineering at times. Well, you saw her, so I think you'll understand what I mean."

Florence nodded.

"Besides, I'm much closer to Mother here, which she's glad about. And as for living in *this* house in particular, you're referring no doubt to how you and I believed it to be haunted. Well, I'm little more than a ghost myself, so these things no longer scare me."

"You? A ghost? No! You've been through a terrible trauma, but you've survived! You're healthy and strong, and have resumed teaching, and- Actually, when will you be returning to your teaching in East Anglia? Isn't it a bit of a commute from here?"

"I'm not going back for a while. I'm going to be writing a book, Fleur, and also I'm doing some online teaching for East Anglia. Mei-Feng has been showing me the technical aspects of that. It's really fascinating as I can connect with my students without leaving home. I was just doing some online teaching when you arrived."

More mention of Mei-Feng. This was unsettling, to say the least. But determined not to show any concern as this was certainly not the right time for it, Florence said eagerly, "Great! And what will your book be about, Lance?"

"It's going to be about general issues of globalization. And I plan to have a chapter on Time, which I would like to write with you, actually. I've been giving it a lot of thought, and perhaps we can talk about it later."

"Definitely! I'd love to collaborate on a chapter with you!" This felt better again. "Meanwhile," Florence said, "where's the loo? These long car rides-"

"Just go back into the hall, face the grandfather clock, and you'll see it on your left."

"You have a grandfather clock? How nice!"

"Yes, I inherited it with the house."

Florence bent over and kissed him, despite her lingering uncertainty about what Mei-Feng was doing here in the house, and what her own relationship now was with Lance. But since she couldn't ask this now she jumped up and rapidly left the room. As she walked towards the bathroom she saw a wheelchair pushed into a corner of the hall. A wheelchair! She gasped involuntarily, and rushed back to the living room.

"Can't you walk, Lance? Can't you?"

"I thought you needed the bathroom."

"I don't need it any more. Lance, can you walk? I just saw a wheelchair in the hall." Of course! That explained the ramp leading to the front door. That explained why he had not opened the door himself when she arrived, nor stood up when she entered the room. It might even explain why Mei-Feng was living with him, as surely a man who had recently lost the use of his legs would not be able to manage on his own, especially in a place as remote as this. "Mei-Feng has been an enormous help," he'd said. God! Poor Lance.

"Why didn't you tell me?" she cried.

"What would have been the point?"

"But Lance, you kept writing to me that you were better. All your e-mails said that. And you went back to teaching at NYU!"

"Yes. And yes. I am much better than I was. And I did return to NYU as quickly as I could. As you know, it was only a few blocks away from my apartment. And my classes are largely discussion based, so there was never any reason really for me to stand. On the odd occasion in which I needed to distribute handouts, or write on the board, or show a PowerPoint presentation, my Teaching Assistant Nikhil was very obliging. You remember Nikhil, don't you?"

"Oh, Lance!"

She hugged him, burying her face in his neck. When she looked up at him, he gently parted the hair from her face, and then, with his hands on her shoulders, he said, "It's OK, Fleur. You're so sweet and naively optimistic. That's one of the things I love most about you. You heard my left leg had been crushed, yet you held onto the belief that American doctors could implement a magic cure and that I'd be back on my feet in no time. I had the impression that's what you thought from your e-mails, so I didn't want to disillusion you."

"But Lance, your bones are fusing back together, aren't they?"

"I expect they have done so, yes, with the help of a few pins and plates. But apparently there's a little bit of nerve damage in my left leg. Don't fret, Fleur. As I said, I'm getting better all the time. And everyone was so good to me at NYU. What a marvelous crowd. I even got used to seeing everything from my wheelchair at the eye level of a six year old, and of everyone standing over me looking down. The only problem was using the subway, which was close to impossible, as most stations don't have lifts. But it was OK; I was relieved to be living in Greenwich Village as it's the heart of everything, as you know."

It took a while to digest all this information, of Lance a diminutive presence in a wheelchair out on the streets of New York with crowds jostling past him; of him trying to cross the broad and busy avenues; of him barred from taking a subway; of him probably avoiding taking buses as it would be so arduous for him to get on and off and would incite impatience on the part of the commuters. Even going from his flat on Cornelia Street and across Sixth Avenue to his NYU building on Washington Square was probably a terrifying and time consuming endeavor.

"Do you have any pain anywhere? Does anything hurt?" she asked.

"Only in my mind. Physically my right leg no longer hurts, and my left leg is partially numb, which is part of the problem, I suppose. But I do have nightmares, Fleur."

"I'm so sorry. What are they about?" she asked. It was only later that she remembered that he'd once written in an e-mail about having nightmares, but this was some time ago. She was still adjusting to the idea of Lance in a wheelchair. That's why he still looked so gaunt and strained. He was not better at all.

"There's one in particular. I keep dreaming it all the time, I check into this lovely inn. Someone's telling me I'm lucky to get a room. It's the last in the inn. I make a lunch reservation for myself, and again they tell me they're completely full and I'll have to wait until 1.19."

"1.19? That's a funny time."

"Yes, but apparently numbers have great significance in dreams, and aren't necessarily meant literally. So I've been trying to think what it might mean."

"Yes, that's true," Florence said thoughtfully. And then suddenly she exclaimed, "Oh Lance, I just realized something! The digits 119 are the date of the attack on the World Trade Center! The 11th of September!"

"Good God! I hadn't thought of that! How amazing, Fleur!" Lance said, pausing and rubbing his eyes, perhaps to take that in. Then slowly he resumed speaking about what happened in his nightmare. "Anyway, I go to the dining room at the inn at 1.19, and it's completely empty except for one woman who's about to have a baby. I'm eating my lunch, which somehow has become my breakfast, and then I go up to my room, and there are pretty little chamber maids in crisply starched aprons, behind open doors of every other bedroom in the inn. They are busy making beds and folding towels. And every morning it's the same thing. Only there are never any guests. I'm there all alone, except for the woman now giving birth in one of the rooms, and she's swearing loudly. I help deliver her baby – a helpless, wrinkled thing – and when it opens its mouth to cry, I see its tongue is black like a giraffe's."

"What a disturbing dream, Lance."

"Yes! I wish I wouldn't keep dreaming it. What you said about 119 is fascinating, but I feel there's so much more to understand in it."

"I wonder if this dream is recurring because on some level you feel stuck, trapped in that awful time, and in that hospital room. But you're no longer there, Lance. You're free now, and you're so much better."

"Maybe. But that baby. That baby, I'm sure, was representing me. Like all babies, it needed to learn to walk. But the black tongue. Ugh! That was so revolting. That baby was a freak. And so am I. People stare at me when I go out, and as soon as I notice them, they politely avert their eyes. It's easier to stay at home."

"Of course you're not a freak, Lance. People who behave that way are just stupid. And you need to go out from time to time. You shouldn't stay at home all the time."

He did not answer, and Florence rubbed his hand.

"I'm thinking about those chamber maids," she pursued. "Do you think they might have represented nurses?"

"That's fascinating, Fleur! I hadn't thought of that. Actually it could make sense as I was told that St. Vincent's had been preparing for a huge influx of patients after the towers collapsed – just like those chamber maids preparing for a lot of hotel guests to arrive – but I was amongst the very few who were brought in. So many people perished that day. I think I might have survivor's guilt, Fleur."

"Don't feel guilty, Lance. You have nothing you are guilty of. And as far as I am concerned, I thank God that you survived!"

Again Lance was silent, and hung his head.

"Do you feel disappointed in the hospital care you were given?"

"No, I don't think so."

"But I wonder, deep down, if you feel you were ignored; that somehow, if you'd had more attention or even better treatment, you'd be able to walk now? I mean, it's so striking in your dream that those pretty little chamber maids kept making beds and changing towels for guests who never arrived, and yet from your description it seems that they had their back to you and the pregnant woman."

"That's interesting. You could be right. I suppose I'm bound to be disappointed on some level, though it's not rational to blame the medical staff. They did all they could for me."

"I'm sure they did, Lance. That was the impression I had, too. But our feelings aren't always rational."

"True. But one other thing," he said hesitantly. "Sometimes the way a dream is interpreted might tell more about the person making the interpretation than the content of the dream itself. So, if that's the case, are *you* disappointed in the medical care I received, and do you feel they could have done more for me? Actually, more to the point, do you feel disappointed in *me*?"

"No! Of course I don't. I feel sad and disappointed *for* you, as I know how active you are – how much you enjoy romping around the countryside, or strolling through city streets, or jogging – but I could never feel disappointed *in* you. I love you, Lance."

"Thank you," he said softly, kissing her hand. She wrapped her arms around him, and kissed him back. Suddenly he pulled away, his face full of anguish.

"Fleur, you having reminded me that you married Howard has stirred things up in my mind. It's like a catalyst! All sorts of memories from that time seem to have been reawakened! God, Fleur, I feel I might burst! How could I have forgotten about you marrying Howard? It made me so depressed at that time!"

"Oh, Lance. I'm so sorry. I didn't mean to upset you. I hadn't realized-"

He took her hand again. "Fleur," he said, and faltered. "Fleur, you haven't upset me by telling me you're getting a divorce. Not at all! Though

243

I'm sorry for any difficulties you've had to endure. But when I remember back now to the time when you were about to be married-" And now he clasped her hand so tightly that his knuckles were white. "Frankly that was almost unbearable. I saw it as the end of you and me."

"But no, Lance! Never that. I thought we could climb onto our parallel Time axis and continue as always."

"It wouldn't have been possible, Fleur, if you'd married Howard. Remember how we stopped communicating for months? That's what I'd been thinking when you e-mailed me after your stay with me in New York to say you were marrying Howard. But then – and this is the strange part and shows you might in fact be right that we do indeed have a parallel Time axis exclusively for us - there are forces, forces so great that even you and I don't understand them, as we both tried to contact each other on the very same day! And after such a long time of being out of touch! That did it for me! It felt as though we were bound to stay connected. I was so pleased that we were back in touch. But I can't pretend that I wasn't intensely distressed about your wedding. I remember now that the week leading up to it I felt sick with passionate disappointment. Of course I couldn't tell you this. How could I? I think perhaps when one is frantic, one is more likely to behave irrationally. Don't you think so?"

"Yes, I do. I was frantic, too, Lance, thinking of you, being so relieved and delighted that we were back in touch, and detesting the very thought of marrying Howard. I didn't want to marry him. I never meant to say yes to his proposal. Oh, it's hard to explain. But the very thought of Howard as my husband was revolting and I absolutely thought I could *not* go through with the wedding, though I knew I had to. I cried for weeks leading up to it. There was such momentum towards our wedding date, such social pressure, such family pressure, that I felt I was propelled towards it on a huge, violent wave."

Lance looked perplexed. "I'm not sure I'm completely following you," he said.

"Forgive me, Lance. I'll tell you more about this some day. But for now perhaps all I can say is that Howard had some sort of detestable power over me. I couldn't fight it off. He terrified me." Then, looking up at Lance, whose expression she could not read, and thinking that he might abhor her now that she'd reminded him that she was a married woman, and so passive besides, she said quietly, "If you'd prefer for me to leave now, Lance, I understand."

"What? Leave? Why on earth should you leave? No, of course not. But what torment it seems we were both going through parallel to each other. It makes no sense."

"It doesn't," Florence agreed.

"But speaking of being frantic, what I'd planned to do, Fleur – I might as well confess it now - during that week leading up to your wedding, was to go to Mei-Feng's apartment as I was too distressed to be alone."

"Mei-Feng? Is she your lover?" She blurted it out. She couldn't stand avoiding that subject any longer. Better to find out now, even if that would be the final straw, and would mean leaving and going to the nearest hotel was inevitable. She could even go to Landsdowne's. God, no! She could not do that. All those associations with Lance there.

"No, Fleur. She's not. I wanted her to be at that time, and she wanted it, but I couldn't bring myself to do it. The reasons were all wrong, and it would have been unfair on her. I told you, I was frantic and irrational. But Fleur, the awful, dreadful thing is…that's why…that's why I didn't receive Irv's phone call about delaying our meeting at the Port Authority that morning. But how can I tell him I wasn't home as I was staying with a woman?"

Florence felt overwhelming relief that Mei-Feng wasn't Lance's lover. But realizing that Lance was waiting for an answer to his question, she quickly adjusted her thoughts and said, "You could tell Irv that, Lance."

"What?"

"You could tell him. Irv was one of the first people I met when I came over to see you at St. Vincent's. He was in the cafeteria with your sister. He seems like such a kind, chummy man. And he was so sad. He immediately told us that he was racked with guilt that he had not prevented you from being at the World Trade Center, seeing that he had managed, unintentionally of course, to have avoided being there then himself." Lance looked at her with surprise. "But it's up to you," she added.

"Thanks. I will tell him, then." He paused. "Fleur, talking about this has started reminding me about…about everything else. You'd asked me, when you visited me in hospital, if I wanted to tell you about that morning at the World Trade Center. Until now, I couldn't, as all I remembered were vague impressions which were fleeting and couldn't be talked about as they didn't even have words; just strands and wisps of images and smells, really. But now I'm starting to remember! It's all coming back. I've got to tell you of this. Can I?" he asked, visibly distraught.

"Yes, Lance," she said, alarmed. "But you don't have to if it's too upsetting."

"No! I must speak now that it's back in my mind again. It's worse to hold it in." He looked wild, almost savage with emotion. She put her arm firmly through his, hugging him closer to her.

He initially seemed unable to speak, and looked down at his thin bony wasted knees. "That Tuesday morning, Fleur," he said at last, "I left Mei-Feng's apartment early. She lived in the East Village, so it wasn't a long subway ride downtown. I walked through the underground plaza of shops at the World Trade Center thinking about how much you'd enjoyed this area; remembering how you loved to look in the window of Godiva's, and how I'd always intended to buy you chocolates but never did – too late now; how you liked to try on samples of perfume at the Body Shop; how one day, after you'd met with that editor, you brought back to Cornelia Street the most delicious pastries from Ecce Panis. I'd even been listening on the subway to the Vivaldi Lute Concerto that you'd bought me from the Borders down there. And now, I thought bitterly, you were happily preparing for your wedding, which was then in four days' time."

Florence started to cry. "Whatever happened to our telepathy then? Our traveling on the same Time axis? We normally know and understand each other so well! 'Happily preparing for my wedding?' No! I thought only of you."

Lance looked at her, tears in his own eyes too. "What a tragic time for us to have our lines crossed, as it were. Yes, as you say, it's terribly unusual for us." And then gazing into the corner of the room, he continued. "Well, from the underground shopping plaza I entered the North Tower, and took the elevator up to the fortieth floor, to the Port Authority offices. There was no one in the reception area, so I went to Irv's office. The door was open and it was clear that he hadn't yet arrived, as it was still early, so I decided to sit down and wait. I'd done that once before, as he was very informal about that sort of thing. I plugged myself back into my Discman – I wonder where that thing is now? - and continued listening to the Vivaldi.

"After what seemed like quite a long time, and Irv still hadn't arrived, I thought I'd turn off the music and go and see if anyone could tell me if they'd seen him yet. And that's when I heard shouting and great agitation. I hurried to the reception area, and saw it was filled with confusion. People were running everywhere, and in the open area behind reception, where the secretaries usually sat, I saw that they were fleeing from their desks, not stopping to take bags or jackets, although I did notice one secretary was on the phone. Someone told her to stop talking and get out. Someone else said her phone line was dead. I went up to a man as he was marching towards the door and asked him what was happening. He told me a plane had crashed into the building about forty floors above us."

"Oh Lance, how terrifying," Florence said, rubbing harshly away the tears on her cheek, and sitting bolt upright. "Were you terribly scared? What did you do?"

"I don't know how I felt. Only that there was total mayhem. Someone shouted that a second plane had crashed into the South tower. People were shrieking, and pushing past each other. I was by the elevator. You can imagine how many people were crowding on to it. There was a pregnant woman at my side. She was hysterical, and paralyzed with fear. She couldn't get on the elevator, and refused to do so when the next one came, even though she and I could have squeezed on. People were shouting at her for delaying their transit, and this paralyzed her more."

"The pregnant woman in your dream!"

"Yes, I think so!" Lance said, looking momentarily at Florence again. Then, fiddling with his hands in great agitation and again staring off into the corner of the room, he said as if almost to himself, "Well, how could I leave her? And since she wouldn't take the elevator, I convinced her to take the stairs with me. I held her hand and didn't think I could do it, but somehow I encouraged her to come with me. It was very slow going down. The stairway was relatively narrow, and jammed with people, shuffling and pushing, and more cramming on at every floor. There were no lights, and the air smelled smoky. It was a slow and somber descent, but I tried to talk to her all the way down. Eventually, though, my voice gave up straining to be heard over all that noise of shouts and screams, and the smoke was making me cough. And firefighters were trying to push their way up the stairs as we were coming down. My legs were beginning to ache. I can only imagine how she must have been feeling. Also, the stairs did not go continuously down, and on some floors we had to traverse that level, looking for the next stairwell and trying to squeeze into the downward march."

"But Lance! You could have left the building much faster, possibly on the lift, if it wasn't for this pregnant woman? Did you even know her?"

"No, I'd never seen her before. But I couldn't abandon her once I'd noticed her beside me. It was the only ethical thing to do. I think if you'd been in my position – and God forbid that should ever be the case - you would have done the same thing."

"I'm not sure I would have. Especially if I did not know her. It's hard to say. It's too hypothetical."

"I think you would have, Fleur."

"Lance, I don't know. Was there an obligation for you to be a hero? Yes, I see that it was compounded by the fact that she was pregnant – two lives rather than one. But didn't you also have an ethical obligation to yourself, and even to your loved ones, and wouldn't that make you want to rescue yourself first?"

"They're tough questions, Fleur. And one doesn't really stop to think at times such as those. I acted instinctively."

"Well, it shows what a good person you are, Lance, endangering yourself to help another."

"I'm not sure, Fleur, if it really was endangering myself any more than if I'd left the building sooner. The South tower collapsed more quickly than the one we were in, so it might have been even more unsafe to be outside earlier. I might have been hit and killed on the spot."

"Don't!" Florence shuddered. "But the tower you were in was collapsing, too. Time was of the essence to get out quickly."

"Yes, but I didn't know that at the time, though I could have guessed."

"What happened to that pregnant woman, Lance? Did she escape unharmed?"

"That's just it, Fleur. I don't know what happened to her once we eventually got outside. You know, it strikes me that it's wrong to think of the survival of the fittest. I heard a story about how a blind man escaped that day from the World Trade Center, with just the help of his guide dog."

"I heard that story, too. It was on the news."

"Was it? So you see, I think Darwin had it wrong. Fitness does not enter into it if there's some form of help and collaboration, rather than competition as Darwin would have us believe. Location relative to the position of a sudden and ferocious natural disaster makes a difference, too, and a very large part of both location and the likelihood of help is luck, or lack of it."

"Or destiny."

"Yes, or destiny. If you believe in that."

"That's all really fascinating on a philosophical level, Lance. But what happened to you once you got outside?"

"That's even harder to talk about, Fleur, though I must say that it's fantastic that you're here, talking with me about all of this." She noticed his hands were shaking, and she pulled him closer to her to comfort him. "Well, I came out of the building at Vesey Street," he continued, "and I was going to walk along it to Church Street, and then head North back to the Village. But the air was filled with a choking white powder. And so many papers drifting down. I happened to see a Memo float through the air towards me. I grabbed it, for some reason, and saw that it was marked 'Important'. How trivial whatever had been important was now! What had previously seemed to be such highly important business matters now amounted to nothing! I doubt whether anyone who returned to work the following day, assuming they had an office to return to, found anything they'd previously been working on was worth the effort now."

Lance pulled a handkerchief out from his trouser pocket and mopped his forehead which was glistening with sweat. Then he inhaled deeply, and continued.

"Anyway, back on Vesey Street, there was a huge crowd of people and they were all running. Have you ever seen an entire crowd run, Fleur? It's like a wild stampede of animals. The pregnant woman had gone. I don't know where. She'd darted out into the crowd. So I started running, too.

And it was then that I saw the best of human nature, and the worst. My assistance to the pregnant woman was by no means unique, as I saw plenty of people helping others. But I also saw people falling and being trampled underfoot by others in their desperation to get away.'"

"Oh!" Florence said, visualizing the scene he was painting and feeling disgusted.

"The white dust in the air grew thicker, and I could hardly see. I followed others blindly, and turned on to what I thought was Church Street. I was moving with the crowd, holding my shirt over my nose and mouth to filter out the dust, when a black man, his face covered in dust, stopped and told me my leg was bleeding. He had a marvelously deep, melodic voice. I was surprised as I hadn't felt anything. I looked down, and sure enough, there was a spreading bloody stain on my right trouser leg."

Lance looked down at his leg now, and rubbed it instinctively. Florence nestled even closer to him. "When I looked back up at him," he continued, "I saw he had a cut on his chin. Deep red blood against the chocolate brown of his skin, which was congealing in the white, dusty powder plastered over his face. 'It looks like you're bleeding, too,' I told him. 'Nah, that ain't nothin', man,' he said. 'Just cut myself shaving, is all. But your leg, now; looks like a mighty deep cut to me from the amount of blood spilling out of it. Here, I saw an ambulance a block over. I'll take you to it.' That man was so kind, Fleur! I felt euphoric that he was rescuing me, that I was going to be helped to get away from that awful place."

"How marvelous! What a kind man to stop and help you. Though it's amazing you felt no pain in your leg. You must have been in shock," Florence said.

"Yes, maybe. Anyway, that man came and visited me in the hospital a few times. Can you believe that? I don't know if you ever saw him."

Florence shook her head. "No, I don't think so."

"Do you know, Fleur; I feel an almost unconditional love for him. I quite frequently write him letters, and will continue, even from here. He told me his name was Lovey Barker. What an appropriate name for him! When I asked him the derivation of his wonderful name, he said his grandmother was there at his birth, took one look at him and said to his mother, "What a lovey!" and he's been called that ever since!"

"How sweet!"

"Yes. Well, Lovey was a security guard for Deutsche Bank, which was close to the World Trade Center. He was a giant of a man, so it was hard to tell his age, but I think he was quite young. He'd had such a hard life, but he still had room to be helpful to others. One day when he visited, he told me he was starting a college course. It had been his father's wish before he died. His father had been shot dead when trying to break up a fight between two friends. Lovey had been a high school dropout, and he returned to get his diploma after his father was killed, and is now at college. He wished so badly his father knew. I told him I hoped to have him in one of my classes one day," Lance said dreamily.

Then Lance adjusted his position, pulling away from Florence, his face distorted with terror. "But, back to that morning…He asked me if I could walk on my leg since it was bleeding like that, and I could! Maybe it *was* the shock, as you said. I don't know, because, as you know, that leg was broken. I don't even know how that had happened. We rounded a corner, and saw the ambulance a little way up the street. Lovey told me he wanted to make sure that I didn't miss it, so he hurried ahead faster than I could go. I saw him obscurely through the dust, and then I looked up and saw a steel girder falling towards me. It all seemed to happen in slow motion – something for us to consider in our exploration of Time – and I keep thinking that since it did happen so slowly, why didn't I get out of the way? Through the white cloud I could see this rusty steel girder in all its intricate detail. I could see how it had been ripped away from where it once stood, as the left side was buckled open showing three huge holes, arranged vertically, where once I imagine they must have been the means of attachment to the building. And I saw black, indecipherable squiggles on the girder, resembling graffiti, though were most likely the result of scorching. And a sharp, twisted flap stood out on the right side of the girder, and contained one very bright yellow and very large screw. This girder was falling towards me with inevitability, and I was resigned to it. I felt it momentarily rip through my left leg. I don't know what else happened, but later I was in hospital, so I suppose that ambulance, or some other ambulance, took me there." Lance's face was pinched and his body trembled uncontrollably.

"Oh, Lance," Florence said. "This is so terrifying."

"And of course then I was there for so long," he continued after a pause. "And you, my sweet, came to visit me, and so did Juliet, and others too, but everything about that time is hazy. They pumped so many medications into me, that once I finally left there, I threw away everything in my bathroom cupboard. Even the aspirin. I don't want to take another pill. Not for anything."

His face was drained of the little color it had had, and he leaned back on the sofa, and rested his head. Florence felt sick. "What a terrible, traumatic experience, Lance," she said. "There are not even words to describe what you went through. Or how sorry I am."

He gave a flicker of a smile, and she leant over and hugged him. Then from nowhere her mind thought back to the photos!

"Lance!" she exclaimed. "My camera! Those strange photos!"

"Which photos? What about them?"

"There were two grainy photos, looking like photos in a newspaper, of a dreadful street scene. Of chaos and despair and mass injury. In one, the even more horrible of the two, a man was being put on a stretcher, and I realized it was you! Your trouser legs were dark with what I presume was blood."

"No! That's impossible! I never saw them! You never told me about them! When did you take those pictures?" His bright eyes looked very alert and frightened.

"I didn't. You did."

"What?"

"You remember that I asked you to use up the last roll of film for me just before I left Landsdowne's? And do you remember, too, that we didn't look at those pictures together until weeks later when you came down to London to visit me? But I actually decided to look through those pictures first, the evening before your visit, and when I saw those two horrific ones, I instinctively pulled them out before showing the rest of the pile to you the next day. You, being as bright as you are, immediately detected that there were fewer photos in the batch than you would've expected, but I got round that somehow."

"Why did you hide them from me?" he asked sternly.

"Shouldn't I have done that? Are you angry with me?"

"No, Fleur. Of course I'm not angry. I just want to understand."

"I'm so sorry, Lance. You had never wanted to use that last roll of film. You had wanted us to stop using the camera. But I urged you to take the photos for me! How I wish I hadn't!"

"Don't be silly, Fleur! It seems we took it in turns having fears and doubts about whether or not to use your camera. I had convinced *you* to keep using it at times when you hadn't wanted to."

She said, "I'm so angry with myself, Lance, for keeping those photos from you."

This was it. This was the usual trigger that would cause the angry man to explode. Howard; her father; Renard; her cousin Jack, whose behavior at Whitestone Pond was just one episode in a lifelong habit of impatience and irritability…any of them might have heard this, and if not already angry, would certainly have become furious at this admission of her own guilt and vulnerability. But she remembered now that Lance did not seem to grow angry. He shifted himself with some difficulty on the sofa, and turned to face her more fully, his expression full of gentleness.

"There's no reason to be," he said simply.

"But there is! Once I saw those dreadful photos, I should never have thought that I could control the situation! I should have shown them to you, and let you decide."

"Decide what?"

"Whether you wanted to go to America."

"I don't understand. What does that have to do with it?"

"I'll get to that. But when I first saw the photos, just before you came down to London that first time, I didn't know what was happening in them at all. Only that there was something irreparably terrifying. Something that I wanted to protect you from knowing about. But how absurd! If it was something happening in your future, surely you had a right to know!"

"Fleur, in the first place we have to put our minds back to that time. It was pure conjecture then, on both of our parts, that the photos from your camera had any predictive validity. We both rather suspected that they did, but we didn't know. But even assuming that we knew 100% that they were accurate, you were confronted with an ethical dilemma – yes; you too, had a tough ethical choice to make! - and you chose what you thought was best for me. And Fleur, I really appreciate that. In fact what you did for me is similar to what I did for the pregnant woman. We both had the best intentions when we each made our choice. But we can't ever know final outcomes when we decide on a course of action. Look, in rescuing the pregnant woman by helping her down the stairs, the stairwell might have crumbled and we'd all have been crushed. We don't know. We take a risk. It's like the philosopher, John Rawls, said in a different context; that we make our choices within a 'veil of ignorance.'"

"But Lance," she persisted, more lucid now in her relief that he was genuinely not angry, as angry men made her confused and tongue-tied and afraid. "If we are to be speaking about ethics and rights, don't you think it can be argued that each of us has a right to know information, even frightening information, that someone else knows about our future, assuming, as you said, that the information was 100% accurate, which it turned out to be?"

"Not necessarily. An argument can be made for letting a person live in contented innocence, rather than in dread and avoidance attempts all the time. Because if it really is that person's future, then it would be inevitable, and unavoidable."

"That's just it! I thought, so foolishly, that I could interpret these pictures as a warning, and prevent that awful event from occurring. You see, after your Award Ceremony I looked at those photos for a second time. Do you remember how Dr. Erikkson's pompous, doubting attitude made us decide to have another look at our photos, in a more scientifically rigorous way? So I forced myself to look at those two abysmal pictures when I got back to London that night, and that's when I realized that the street scene I was looking at clearly appeared to be in America! But by then I was afraid to tell you this. Remember how badly I'd behaved that day, when I first found out that you were going to New York? I didn't want it to seem that I was trying another tactic to prevent you from doing something you clearly needed to do."

"But really, Fleur. You didn't-"

"No, please listen," Fleur said, interrupting him. "As I saw it, I had protected you from the shock of seeing the photos. But now I had a duty to protect you from the awful event itself. I have to admit that at first I tried to comfort myself, Lance, in absurd ways. I even started hoping Dr. Errikson was right that Time was only unidirectional, and there were no parallel axes of Time, implying that the future must be unknowable, and therefore those awful pictures meant nothing. But I found no comfort in that. How could I? His outlook was arguing against the very ways of interpreting Time that had made us so excited!

"I was convinced that these photos spoke of a grotesque evil, a truly macabre event. So the only thing I thought I could possibly do to heed the warning and prevent the event from happening, was that when I came to visit you, I was going to look carefully at every street we saw, and try to identify the street in the photo. Then, without telling you why, I'd somehow warn you never to go to that area again."

"Fleur, my sweet-" Lance started to say, but Florence held up her hand and hurried on. "But, and this is the most deplorable part of all, I had such an incredibly terrific time when I was with you in April, that I'm afraid I actually *forgot* about those dreadful photos. And, what's more, I believe that even if I had remembered them, I would not have related the streets in the photos with the area around the World Trade Center, as this was my absolutely favorite part of Manhattan. I'm so sorry, Lance. I had meant to protect you! I should never have assumed I'd have such competence as to bend and alter events. I should have shown you those photos as soon as I'd seen them so you could decide yourself if you wanted to still go to New York, or not. God, I wish I had!"

"My sweet Fleur! Don't be so hard on yourself! It pleases me so much to hear about how much you enjoyed yourself when you visited me in New York last April. I, too, had a phenomenal time when you were there. And it pleases me no end how you wanted to protect me. Thank you, my love, for that. And I dare say that if you *had* shown me those two photos before I left England, I might have had them in the back of my mind at first, but then I would also have completely forgotten about them, too! Don't worry! You could no more protect me from the calamity at the World Trade Center, than it seems I could protect you against marrying Howard. If we could, it wouldn't be our future, so it would all be wrong. The future is inevitable, and we must accept that. Those events were bound to happen, and we can't dodge around them."

"That's true. Thank you, Lance. Thanks for pointing that out."

"And consider, Fleur; the stuff of many Greek tragedies is the irony of trying to protect against an evil future event, and by so doing, inadvertently causing that despicable event to actually occur. It's far better that you forgot all about it, so that we were free to enjoy ourselves."

"Yes."

"What is amazing, though, is your camera's ability to take these photos of future events! That's the part that's really perplexing, and what we really need to be addressing." Lance started to look more himself again, dedicating himself to his favorite topic about Time and her odd camera. He sat up straighter on the sofa, rubbing his hands together, and said, "Actually, I've been doing some reading about early cameras, and according to what I read, there'd been an idle bet between a man named Leland Stanford – of Stanford University – and someone else, about whether all four of a horse's hooves leave the ground at the same time when it's galloping. Stanford was a railway tycoon, but was also very keen on horse racing, as I suppose he was a man who liked fast means of travel. Anyway, the horse's hooves move faster than the eye can see, so it was necessary to invent a camera with an amazingly fast shutter speed. A certain Edweard Muybridge did just that, having built a camera with a shutter speed of a 500th of a second, and with this camera it was possible to determine that indeed all four of the horse's hooves did leave the ground simultaneously. You see, the camera freezes the moment of time, and unlocks any secret that was contained within it – in this case, the motion of the hooves."

Florence really admired Lance for being able to move beyond his horrible physical limitations and use his mind so admirably, but she didn't want to interrupt as he was so clearly mentally stimulated.

"Now, what does this have to do with your camera?" Lance continued rhetorically. "Well, it seems that your camera, like all other cameras, freezes the moment in time, but somehow it peculiarly transfers that moment in time to *another* date, so that when we see the developed photo the time is other than the time at which the photo was taken. How it does that is completely unclear, but what is fascinating, Fleur, is that it happens!"

Here was the old Lance speaking, the Lance who grew animated over the pursuit of intellectual ideas, whose eyes shone with curiosity and excitement. And for a moment Florence forgot about the physical state of his legs. She, too, grew excited at the connection between her camera and Time.

"Yes! My camera seems to more often shift to a future time, although on rare occasions it moves backwards, too. One day I hope you and I will discover how my camera is able to skip a beat, or jump ahead a beat, to change the temporality of the picture. It seems to do so with particularly highly charged events."

"Fleur, I'd like to see that photo of me on a stretcher. And the other one of the street scene, too. In a gruesome way, they fascinate me. Will you come and stay again next weekend and bring them with you? I know that this might be a ridiculous thing to ask, as you've scarcely arrived this weekend, but will you come again?"

The length of the drive, and her fear on the dark, snowy local roads notwithstanding, she immediately replied, "Of course, Lance! There's nothing I'd want to do more!" Besides, she would leave even earlier next time, and also the days were lengthening now, so it would be increasingly easier. "And I'd like us to look at those initial photos that showed my wedding, too, because I think there was more on my face than just unhappiness at marrying Howard, even though that alone would've been bad enough."

"What do you mean?"

"I think my face also showed how terrified I was about what might have happened to you."

"To me? Why?"

"You'd e-mailed me that you were going to have a breakfast meeting with Irv on September 11th at the World Trade Center. As soon as I heard the news that day about the attack on the Twin Towers, I kept trying and trying to phone you, but first I couldn't get through as all lines were down or jammed, and then, when I could, I just repeatedly got your answering machine. That connection between us that you'd spoken of earlier when we'd contacted each other on the same day after being out of touch for months, seemed to be completely severed, as we just said. And I thought that could only mean one thing – that you were dead. I was desperate,

Lance. Not knowing for days – actually a week in fact - was the worst torture I have ever been through. And trying to appear to be the smiling bride on top of it all-"

"My love," he said, looking shocked. "I don't remember having sent you an e-mail telling you I'd be at the World Trade Center that day."

"Yes, you did! And when I looked at the newspapers the next day, and saw horrific photos of the scene there, with one in particular of a man lying on a stretcher with his legs twisted horribly and soaked in blood, that was when I remembered my photo of you on the stretcher, and I was almost sick. It seemed to be proof that you hadn't survived, and if that was the case, I didn't know how I could survive either. I read once that Simone de Beauvoir, desperate at the thought that Jean-Paul Sartre hadn't survived the war, thought of taking her own life, and the only reason she didn't was because of the glimmer of hope she had that he might not have been killed. Well, I felt the same way. But I certainly didn't know how I could go through the farce of the wedding. I was tortured."

They hugged shakily as Lance was trembling again, and felt weak and bony in her arms.

"Lance!" Florence said suddenly. "Another photo! Another one that predicted correctly!"

"Yes?"

"On that same roll of film, there was one of this house – your house now - showing the ramp up to the front door outside! Do you remember it? You saw that picture!"

"I'd completely forgotten it! That's incredible! I only just had the ramp built. That was the main reason for employing a carpenter when I moved here. That, and putting some rails up in the bathroom. How had you interpreted that ramp when you saw that photo of it?"

"Of course, when I saw the photo, I had no idea you were going to buy this house. I thought that an elderly couple had lived here. There were in fact two people in the photo, but they were in silhouette, so it was hard to see what they looked like. Even when I arrived just now, and saw that the ramp did exist, I concluded that you'd bought the house from this elderly couple."

"Ha! An elderly couple indeed! Instead of an approaching-middle-age cripple!"

"No, Lance! Please don't talk that way."

Just then they heard the front door bang. Mei-Feng had returned from her shopping trip.

"I got you nice dinner from the village," she said, entering the room and putting the bags down in the corner.

"That's splendid!" Lance said kindly. "Thank you. I hope it wasn't too snowy outside."

"Snow finished," she said, going over to a fold-out table in the corner of the room, and sliding it in front of Lance.

"No, stop!" he said gently. "I think in honor of Fleur's visit, we should eat in the dining room tonight."

"Are you sure?" Mei-Feng asked, at the same time that Florence said, "Please don't go to any extra trouble on my account."

"Yes, definitely!" he said.

"I bring you your wheelchair," Mei-Feng said.

"No, don't worry about that. Why don't you start putting the dinner on the table, please, Mei-Feng. Fleur and I will join you in the dining room in a minute."

"Yes," Mei-Feng said, and picking up her bags, she left the room.

"It strikes me, talking to you," Lance said to Florence, "that I've allowed myself to become somewhat lazy. I haven't actually tried walking for some time. I'm sure I can do it now! Speaking with you has re-energized me! Will you be so kind as to just help me to stand, and then I should be on my way."

"Of course, Lance!"

Lance needed a great deal of help levering himself up from the sofa. Finally he was in a standing position, but leaning heavily on Florence. She was reminded anew, with a fresh pang of concern, as to how bony his body felt. He'd always been slim, but now he felt skeletal. He put his right leg forward quite deliberately, but his poor, smashed left leg trailed pitifully behind. He managed to shuffle it forward a marginal amount, but then it buckled, and he flopped forwards, but luckily Florence managed to pull him backwards onto the sofa. His face had a ghastly pallor, and his forehead was beaded with sweat.

"Please ask Mei-Feng to get my chair," he panted. "I'm afraid I can't make it all the way."

A little later they were assembled round the dining room table, studying the contents of several white cartons of rapidly cooling, congealed, greasy Chinese food that Mei-Feng had purchased. Lance's inability to even walk a few steps had a depressing effect on all of them, and no one found anything to say. For a while the only sound was that of forks scraping against their large white dinner plates.

Suddenly Florence had a realization.

"Lance, I thought I remembered the dining room to be at the front of the house, on the other side of the front door than the living room. I didn't remember it being in this location at all."

"You're quite right, Fleur. This is the newer extension at the back of the house, which the previous owners had intended as a sun-room. I've taken the former dining room as my bedroom." He took the serviette off his lap, and put it folded on the table. "Now, if you'll excuse me, I think I will go to bed. I'm a little tired."

He'd hardly touched his food.

"You had lot of excitement today. I take you to your room now?" Mei-Feng said.

"I think so."

She sprang up, grabbed possessively onto the back of the wheelchair, and giving Florence a defiant look, pulled his chair away from the table, and wheeled him towards his room.

"Fleur," he called over his shoulder. "Please come and say good night to me once I am ready for bed."

"Certainly!"

Mei-Feng was with Lance a long time, so Florence cleared the table, washed the plates, forks and glasses, and put the leftover food in the refrigerator. Still Mei-Feng was not back, so Florence went to look at the books on the bookshelf. Maybe she'd find the one on early cameras that Lance had mentioned. She could not, so instead she took down Graham Greene's novel, *The End of the Affair*, and settled down to read.

She'd read several pages when at last Mei-Feng returned, saying Lance was ready to see her now, but first she must show her the guest room upstairs. Florence followed her up the stairs and into a small room with a dormer window. There was a little vase of flowers on the dresser, and the room, though crowded with furniture, was very neat.

"How lovely!" Florence exclaimed. "You've made this very cozy!"

"I hope you like. I leave you now. I have work on computer."

"Well, thank you, Mei-Feng. Good night!"

Florence spread a few of her belongings on the bed, and quickly went back downstairs to see Lance.

"I'm sorry, Fleur," he said from his bed when she entered the room. "You can't be having much fun tonight."

"Of course I am! Just being with you is all I wanted."

"Thank you for that, Fleur! I'm so tired, but I don't want to sleep yet."

"Don't feel you need to stay awake on my account. We have a whole day tomorrow, and even part of the next."

"It's not only that. Frankly I just don't want to have that nightmare again."

"You might never have it again, Lance, now that we've talked about it."

"I hope you're right. Come, climb into bed beside me. There's a lot more room than in that hospital bed."

He moved over, and pulling off her dress, she slid in beside him. She avoided putting her legs near his legs, not only for fear of hurting him, but also because she did not know what they looked like – she remembered the oozing beneath the bandage while he was in hospital - so was scared to touch them now. He was wearing freshly laundered pyjamas; she could tell by their scent and their crispness. She had never seen him in pyjamas before.

"It's lousy that I'm so depleted," he said, "and have no energy to express how glad I am that you're here."

"I'm so happy to be here, too," she said, putting her head against his shoulder. "Don't worry about being so tired now. I completely understand. But would you like to talk a bit? I love to cuddle you and talk."

"I love that, too." He took off his glasses and switched off the light,

261

and Florence noticed that a small night-light was plugged into the wall, giving just enough light to see his face. He put his arm around her.

"Do you miss New York?" she asked.

"Yes, as a matter of fact, I do. Of course everything changed in the second semester, but even so I met some tremendous people there. I loved NYU and New York in general."

"Will you stay in touch with many people?"

"Definitely! And Abe told me – you remember him? – he's the department chair, he told me they'd welcome me back as a Visiting Scholar whenever I'm ready to return."

"That's great! You really impressed them! They could see what an extraordinarily fine teacher you are."

"Thanks. But it might be because they feel sorry about what happened to me."

"Well, that might come into it, too, but I could tell when I visited you in April, how highly everyone thought of you, and what an amazing teacher you are."

"You're so kind, Fleur," he said, gently kissing her and running his fingers through her hair.

"How is Marissa?" she asked.

"Marissa? She's great! She finally found love."

"Really? Who is he?"

"Actually, it's a 'she'."

"I didn't know Marissa was a lesbian!" Florence said, genuinely surprised.

"Didn't you? Couldn't you tell? I thought so straight away. Anyway, it seems she's the only one who benefited from '9/11,' as they started calling it. She was volunteering at the World Trade Center site, serving food to the rescue workers and firefighters, and she met Kaitlin there. They became inseparable. Marissa's very happy."

So! All that time worrying that Lance and Marissa were attracted to each other, and Marissa was a lesbian all along!

"I'm glad she's happy. She seems very nice. How about your new Teaching Assistant? How's he?" She felt this light chatter was doing Lance a lot of good, and helping him to relax.

"Nikhil? Yes, he was very good. Quite unlike Marissa, but extremely helpful in his own way. He was always so serious. It's impossible to tell, of course, if he would have been less serious were I not disabled."

Florence swallowed at the sound of the word 'disabled,' but she continued the rhythm of the conversation. "Was it hard for you to teach in the second semester?"

"No! I was really looking forward to returning to it, if you remember. It was a terrific distraction, actually."

"What exactly does a Teaching Assistant do?"

"Lots of marking, thank goodness! That's the one part of teaching I could do without. Also taking attendance. Sometimes meeting with students to answer a few questions."

"It sounds like you'd like to return to New York," she said.

"Yes! I'd love to. I felt really alive there. There's just one thing I regret. I always wanted to walk across the Brooklyn Bridge into Manhattan. I don't suppose I'll ever be able to do that now."

"Yes, you will, Lance!" she said with determination. "It's a great goal to have, and to try to accomplish. You *will* be able to do it! Just give yourself some time. Both you and New York are healing."

He sighed and flopped back on his pillow listlessly.

"How's Juliet? Does she mind very much that you moved out of your family home?"

"Oh, she pretended to be a bit cross, of course. And she insisted that I have help. But I could tell that she'd really resent it if I moved back in with her, and she'd have to be the one looking after me. She'd never have admitted it, of course, but after years of being with Mother, I don't think she could stand to add me to her plate. So actually I think she's secretly relieved that I moved here."

"But you didn't decide not to live with her for that reason, did you?"

"Definitely not!"

"Did she visit you many more times in New York after I'd gone back to London?"

"Yes, she came three times all together, which was kind of her. She was there when I was discharged from hospital, and she helped me settle back into Cornelia Street. That's when she said I would have to have help after she left, which of course was essential, so I decided to employ Mei-Feng. Of course, Juliet stayed on a while after Mei-Feng arrived, to boss her around a bit, but I think she was generally satisfied."

"Lance, what did Juliet think of me? Did she ever say?"

"Oh, she liked you well enough, but she had some reservations. Oh! I understand it all now! She said something about picking up your ring from the floor. I didn't know what she meant at the time. I suppose, in retrospect, she wondered why you were so concerned about me if you were married!"

"Oh dear."

"I wouldn't worry about it. You know she's a lot older than I am, and I think sometimes she thinks she's my mother rather than my sister. What she fails to recognize, though, is that I'm a grown man, and have been for quite some time!"

He closed his eyes and started to breathe more deeply.

"You're tired now, Lance. Why don't you sleep a bit?"

"OK," he said, his eyes remaining shut. "And don't forget," he said, his speech starting to slur a little. "Don't forget to-" His voice trailed off.

"Don't forget what?"

"Don't forget to bring that photo," he said dreamily. Then suddenly opening his eyes, he said, "In fact, bring *all* the photos next weekend. Let's look at every single one of them!"

"Good idea! Let's do that!"

He settled back against his pillow, and seemed to be truly asleep. Then, just as suddenly, he jerked awake and said, "Would you like to cook next weekend?"

"Certainly! I thought you were asleep."

"No. Not asleep yet. Yes, you cook. Like you did sometimes on Cornelia Street. It would be good. I enjoy your cooking." He closed his eyes, and added sleepily, "Mei-Feng is a terrific person, but she doesn't cook. That was of no concern in Manhattan, with the abundance of take-out places. But here, one can get awfully tired of Chinese food from the village."

"Oh Lance, I'd *love* to cook! I'll start tomorrow! I'll make all sorts of nourishing things, and all your favorite dishes! I'd be really happy to do that."

But he was already asleep. Quietly Florence lightly kissed his cheek, climbed out of bed, slipped her dress back over her head, and left the room. She went up to the guest bedroom, put on her nightdress, and climbed into bed, which creaked as she did so. She was tired, too, from her long car journey. She switched off the light. The room was extraordinarily dark; the sort of darkness that can only be found in very rural areas. She closed her eyes. Horrific images of the September 11th scenes that Lance described filled her mind. She snapped her eyes open again, but since the room was so dark, it was as if her eyes had remained shut.

She turned over and the mattress creaked again. The grandfather clock downstairs chimed mournfully. The room was exceptionally cold, and the sheets felt so damp and frigid that she kept her legs bent close to her body. Despite herself, she started to feel fearful. She and Lance had convinced themselves two summers ago that this house was haunted. When she had first arrived today, that idea had seemed ridiculous. But now it didn't. Lance had said he was not much more than a ghost himself. What if he were really dead? That he had died essentially, but St. Vincent's had recharged just a small part of him? Or what if he died now, tonight?

Just then she heard something bump into the windowpane. What could it be? She sat up in bed, startled, but then lay down again, pulling the blankets over her head. Perhaps it had been a bat? Or a tree branch blowing in the wind? Or could it have been a ghost? She had never taken the idea seriously before; even when she and Lance were scared two summers ago, she thought perhaps that she had let herself be influenced by him, and had not originally been genuinely frightened herself. Now she wasn't so sure. What if she saw that ghostly ball of light again? Actually, hadn't it glowed from the dining room window, and wasn't this the room that Lance had now chosen to be his bedroom? Was this a forecast of his death?

The grandfather clock chimed again. It must be set to chime every fifteen minutes. How could she possibly fall asleep before the next round of chimes? She turned over again, into a new area of bitingly cold sheets. And then she heard the sound of a dog snarling and barking ferociously outside, as if it was under her very window. She went deeper down inside her bed, and tried to calm herself. She must fall asleep! But again the despair of the World Trade Center collapse flooded her mind.

She was so worried about Lance. Nothing for it, but to go downstairs and check on him. And in truth, she couldn't remain in this room much longer.

Shivering profoundly, from fear as well as the cold, she went downstairs and softly entered Lance's room. In the dim illumination of the night-light, grotesque shadows played on his face.

"Fleur! Where have you been? I woke up and you were no longer here!"

She felt so relieved to hear him speak. She went up to him. "I thought you were asleep and would be more comfortable if you had the bed to yourself." After all, why else had she been shown the guest room?

"No, Fleur! No. I thought you'd gone to the bathroom. I waited and waited for you. My wheelchair isn't in the room, otherwise I would have come to look for you! Where were you?"

"I was in the guest room. Mei-Feng had shown me where it was, and had made it ready for me."

"Mei-Feng doesn't understand. Please come into bed with me now. That is, as long as you want to."

"Yes, I do!"

She climbed into bed beside him. She was still shivering and her teeth were chattering.

"Why, you're so cold! Come, let's cuddle, and you'll soon be warm again."

Gradually, lying in his arms, she grew warmer and calmer. And then eventually she grew incredibly hot, and wished to take off her nightdress. But she knew she could not. Lance had on his pyjamas, and she had to respect that fact. Finally, as she was almost dropping off to sleep, Lance said, "Fleur, what made you come into my bedroom again now?"

"I needed to see you, Lance. I needed to see you very badly."

"I'm so glad you did," he said, and soon after they were both asleep.

She awoke abruptly hearing Lance yell. His body was twitching. She put her hand on his back to steady him, but he wouldn't wake up, and instead continued, in a twisted frenzy, to dream a dream of what must have been horrific content. She held him tightly and nuzzling up to him, he eventually slept more serenely, and she fell back to sleep, too.

"'The darkest hour is before the dawn,'" he quoted, waking her from a dream she no longer remembered. She had no idea how long she'd slept. She turned and stretched.

"Yes," she said sleepily.

"It's true, Fleur. Especially in these rural areas, so far from city lights. It'll be the dawn chorus soon. Actually, I think that amounts to one resilient bird that chose not to migrate for the winter."

"Uh-huh."

"Fleur, are you awake?

"Yes."

"I thought so, Fleur. I hate the nights. That's when the very worst thoughts come to me."

"What were you thinking about now, Lance?" she asked, still somewhat befuddled, and trying to shake the sleepiness from her.

"About a dream I just had."

"What was it? Do you want to talk about it?"

"I was on the New York City subway. It was rush hour, and very hot and crowded. And then, without explanation, the train stopped between stations, and the lights and air conditioning went out."

"How horrible!"

"And then there was some sort of emergency announcement that everyone had to leave the train and walk carefully down the track to the next station. 'Don't you remember, you fool!' I thought to myself. 'You're no longer ambulatory! So what are you going to do now?' And then I realized that it was not the subway in New York, but I was on a British train stuck in the tunnel on its way to Norwich. And people were shouting and pushing each other out of the way, to reach the one tiny door to get off the train."

"Oh Lance," she said, hugging him. "It was a terrible dream. But it's OK now."

"I tried to change the dream, Fleur. I wanted to make it so that I'd get home. And so the train started up again, and I thought all would be well. But then, as we were approaching Norwich, instead of decelerating, the train actually picked up speed, and we flew through the station without stopping."

"Lance, don't worry any more. You *did* make it home. Not to Norwich, but to your lovely new house. And you're perfectly safe here. Don't be anxious anymore."

His eyes looked from her to the window where the sky was visibly lighter, and back to her again. "I've gone from 'helper' to the one always needing to be helped."

"Many people perform both roles constantly throughout life, Lance. Even now, you're still a helper. You're helping your online students to gain knowledge and you're inspiring them with a love of learning. And you're helping me to find happiness again."

"You really do love me, don't you, Fleur," he said incredulously.

"Absolutely and completely and whole-heartedly!"

"I've been feeling so useless. And that I'm no longer who I was. I look at my left leg and don't recognize it as part of myself, and the way it functions is now so different that that doesn't feel like me, either."

"Lance, I'm convinced you are getting a little better all the time. It's bound to be a slow process given how severely you were injured."

"When people look at me," he continued, "they don't see me, but instead they see a disabled man in a wheelchair. I have a new identity; I'm no longer defined by my personality or my job, but by my personal tragedy."

"I'm sure that's not true for the people who already know you, Lance."

"Maybe not. But then they feel pity, and I can't stand to feel pitied, Fleur."

"I've been thinking about this in a different context. Knowing I'm going through a divorce, some people might pity me, too," Florence said, pulling up the duvet a little higher over her shoulder, as she was starting to feel cold again.

"Yes, we all have our stories. And admittedly many of them are bad. But it just seems that I wear mine more explicitly than most."

"But Lance, we all have a tendency to label people and make assumptions about them based on superficial appearance, but often we know very little about their private lives and what they are really like."

"True. It's one of the reasons that I find online teaching appealing. It levels the playing field as none of us can make judgments about any others based on appearance. But Fleur, even if people can't see me and make assumptions about me, what I feel inside still has an enormous impact. When I was first injured, I didn't feel a thing emotionally. Perhaps it was because I was too involved with the business of staying alive. Or perhaps because my feelings hadn't yet caught up with events. Then, when I had recovered a little more, I felt so grateful to be alive and not more seriously injured."

"I remember that. I remember you saying that to your student from California."

"Ah yes, Cameron! She was a character. And yes, I did feel grateful then. But now I ask myself, what do I have to feel grateful for? I'd have a right to be grateful if I had escaped unharmed. Or better yet, if I had not visited the World Trade Center that morning. Especially if I had been in my own apartment on Cornelia Street to receive Irv's call, rather than running like a traitor to be with Mei-Feng. Or, of course, if the attack had not happened at all. But grateful now? For this? For feeling like a partially squashed giant insect?"

The windows rattled from the strong wind outside, and they heard what sounded like an owl hooting. Florence ruffled Lance's hair in a feeble attempt of comfort.

"Do you know, Fleur," he continued, turning slightly. "When I was eleven and attended my new school, there was a boy there called Andrew, who was in a wheelchair. In a wheelchair at the age of eleven! And do you know what I thought to myself then? I thought, surely not! Surely that should not happen to someone so young. At least wait, I thought, until they're really old, like thirty or forty. But now I'm thirty-six, and I consider myself not old at all, but still quite young! And so I think, surely not! This shouldn't happen to someone until they're sixty or seventy. But it would be the same then. There's no right age for infirmity."

"You're right, Lance. There is no right age. This should never have happened. And calling it a tragedy probably doesn't help how you feel. But I think there are bound to be many stages of grieving to go through. I'm sure it's natural. But let me tell you one thing that might help you, as it certainly helped me the day before my wedding, when I was tortured with anguish and despair having heard about the attacks on the World Trade Center and not knowing anything about whether you were safe and not being able to contact you. I spoke to Anna, who's extremely kind and empathic - I'd like you to meet her one day – and I told her a little about the despair I was feeling and why. And what she advised was to pray for "courage, strength and hope." Whether one is religious or not, a sustained belief in those three words really helps. I asked for it for myself and I especially asked for it for you. And I kept on asking. And a few days later Abe from your department phoned me, telling me you were alive! I could have kissed him down the phone! So Lance, let's focus on those three words for you now."

By now early shafts of sunlight were streaming through a chink in the curtains. Lance, nestled against her, was smiling inwardly, and dropping back to sleep. Florence could not sleep again, and when she a little later heard sounds of Mei-Feng in the kitchen, she slipped quickly upstairs to dress, and then went to join her.

"Good morning!" Mei-Feng said. "You want breakfast? Bowls over there and kettle still hot."

"Thank you."

Florence sat down opposite her and started sipping the tea she had just made.

"You not hungry?"

"No, not yet."

"You know, it not right that you make Lance try walk yesterday. He not walk again. Doctors say so."

Florence was surprised at this swing in the conversation, and that Mei-Feng seemed more outspoken than she would have expected. "Doctors don't always know everything. I think it's important that he still has hope," she replied.

"No. Because it lead to disappointment. He very sad and disappointed last night. I see that."

"And you don't think he's sad and disappointed to be confined to a wheelchair?"

"No. He accept he need wheelchair. I know. I see him in New York."

"If we all give up the moment we fail to do something, where would we be? I think it's very important that he has determination and a goal of recovery."

"No. That not real. That make him sad."

"I can't agree at all!" Florence said, rising from the table. She tipped away the remainder of her tea and started washing her cup, hoping the sound of the running water would literally drown out Mei-Feng's clipped, infuriating, little girl voice.

"I see his leg," Mei-Feng continued, a cold, hard look in her eyes. "Half of it blown away. How it possible for him to walk?"

Florence felt the return of that old nauseous feeling. "I think I'll go out and explore the area a bit," she said.

"Yes; go! Lance sleep late each day. He sleep a lot."

"I'll see you later. And, if you must know, it was not me that told Lance to try to walk to the dining room last night. He had that idea on his own. And I think it's tremendous that he did!"

Taking her coat and scarf that she had draped on a kitchen chair, she left the house quickly, before Mei-Feng could reply. Despite the icy patches, she walked rapidly down the ramp from the front door. The ground was sparkling with a crusty layer of snow, and the air was crisp and very fresh.

As she walked, she thought about her conversation with Mei-Feng. Half of Lance's leg blown away! Was she exaggerating? She herself had not yet seen his leg to know, and the very thought frightened her. But could it still be feasible for him to walk? Or was Mei-Feng more of a realist than she herself could be? But how could it be right to passively accept things as they were; for Lance to remain listlessly resigned, while his inner-self experienced tortured memories and nightmares? Where did courage, strength and hope come into this? Perhaps one needed courage and strength to come to terms with the fact of being crippled for the rest of one's life, but then what about hope? What part could it play? Surely it would be better, wouldn't it, to seek courage to overcome the trauma of despair; strength quite literally in the physical sense; and hope that each day – yes, each day, and not some distant horizon – would bring normality back to his everyday life, and an end to disability, deprivation and depression.

Was Mei-Feng's negative attitude good for him? She was the one who was constantly with him. Surely her attitude would be bound to influence him. Was there an edge of cruelty to her? Was she acting out of self-interest? Why, if Lance recovered, she would be out of a job and a place to live and a car and his company. Most of all, his company. After all, hadn't Lance said she had wanted him to be her lover? Maybe she still clung on to that hope. Florence tossed around these inner voices, and then deliberately tried to control herself.

As she continued to walk along the public footpath, a plume of tobacco smoke uncoiled towards her, reaching her nostrils first before she saw a heavy set man puffing at a pipe, standing just off the path, allowing his dog to sniff amongst the leaves. Was this the deranged dog she had heard barking last night? But no; it did not seem to be, as this dog was a Chow, and she knew they do not bark.

With a brief "Good morning!" she turned quickly around, and retraced her steps back to the house. Angrily kicking the ramp before walking up it, Florence reached the front door and knocked. Wouldn't it be wonderful if Lance answered the door, but she knew this could not be.

The three of them were going on a walk. Mei-Feng pushed the wheelchair. Her tiny body was lithe and very powerful, and she moved surprisingly quickly for someone of her stature. Florence could hardly keep up with her. Then Florence had to stop to tie her shoelace, but Mei-Feng did not wait for her. Instead, she started to run, roughly jostling Lance up and down over the bumpy, uneven path.

Florence's shouts of, "Stop a minute! Wait for me!" turned to, "Mei-Feng! You're going too fast! Don't you see how you're bouncing Lance around too much, which can't be good for him!"

"Mei-Feng is a jogger!" she heard Lance shout back to her, over the sound of running feet slapping the ground and the wheels of the chair colliding with stones on the path. "We used to jog together in Central Park," he added, his voice receding as the gap between them widened.

Florence noticed that the path they were on started to descend steeply to the lake. It was getting steeper and steeper. Mei-Feng's speed increased; the sound of the slam of each footstep getting louder. To Florence's horror, she saw that ahead of them, the path swerved sharply to the right. There was a precipitous drop, covered by dense thicket, down to the lake. She was terrified that at such a speed, Mei-Feng would lose control completely, not be able to maneuver around the bend, and Lance and the wheelchair would hurtle down into the lake.

She couldn't catch up. Rousing herself from this horror, she deliberately changed her dream, so that she would be the one pushing the wheelchair instead. She would do so with one hand on the handlebar, and the other on Lance's shoulder. They'd amble along slowly in this manner, and then he'd lift his hand to clasp hers.

# FOURTEEN

*IT WAS CLEAR FROM THIS DREAM,* and others like it that Florence dreamed after having stayed with Lance, that she did not trust Mei-Feng. Also she was concerned that Lance spent too much time at home, on that end of the sofa in which she'd found him when she'd first arrived. He'd talked about how teaching at NYU was such a good distraction, and she felt strongly that he needed more distractions now.

So, as she was preparing to visit him again the following weekend, she also included in her suitcase, besides all the envelopes of photos, some art supplies, as she knew he was keen on drawing, and had seen some of his sketches, which were quite good. Driving to the Lake District, Gluck's "Dance of the Blessed Spirit" came on the radio. It was a piece they both loved, and she took this as a good omen.

It was twilight when she arrived several hours later, and Mei-Feng opened the front door to her. Lance was in the hall behind Mei-Feng, and as soon as he saw Florence he made several little swivels of his wheelchair back and forth, much as an ambulatory person might hop up and down as an expression of emotionality. She put her bag down and rushed to him, placing her hands on his shoulders and bending down to kiss him. And she was glad when he suggested that they go into the living room, as that way they sat down together on the sofa, and she was no longer towering over him. While waiting for the Chinese meal that Mei-Feng had gone to the village to purchase, he asked if she'd remembered to bring the photos.

"Yes, I have them with me," Florence replied. "But we might not have time to look at them now."

"Let's make a start anyway," Lance said. "Mei-Feng usually spends quite some time in the village. I hope you're not too hungry." His eyes looked animated, and he shifted position in excitement as Florence started to take the bulky envelopes from her bag and place them on the coffee table.

"Are they all here?" he asked. "Is this everything?"

"All except one roll of film," she said. "Howard has that."

"How come? What are they of?"

"They're of you and me in the countryside somewhere. I'm not sure if it's around here or in the Catskills. Either way, we seemed to be – how should I put it? - enjoying each other's company a great deal."

"They sound lovely. But why does Howard have them now?"

Florence explained how Allison had used her camera the day before the wedding, and when she'd immediately had the photos developed and saw how delightful they were and had nothing to do with the subjects Allison had taken, she'd of course told Rose and Allison that none had come out. Then, her voice sounding shaky even to herself, she said, "I glimpsed such happiness in those pictures. I only saw them so briefly, under the light of a lamppost as the shop was shutting. They were such a comfort to me, as they told me you were alive, even though I still hadn't been able to contact you. But then, when I got home, I remembered how the camera had once swung back in time, as had happened with that photo of my cousin at Whitestone Pond when he was little, and if this was the case, these photos could have been of our visit to the Catskills last spring, and were therefore no proof at all of you still being alive. Seeing what might have been extraordinarily happy memories instead of a promising glimpse into the future made my anguish and grief that much more deplorable."

"My sweet love," he said. "I'm sorry you were so dreadfully unhappy then. But it's all worked out now."

She nodded.

"But what I still don't understand is how Howard ended up with those photos."

"Well, it seems that the following morning, while I was dressing for the wedding, Rose and Allison saw that envelope of photos in the kitchen. I must have been so distracted that I hadn't remembered to put the photos safely away with the others. How careless of me! Something made them open up the envelope. Well, as you can imagine, they were so surprised to see the contents! Then, later that week, Rose had apparently phoned to thank me for accommodating her and Allison before the wedding, and when Howard told her that I was in New York visiting you, she at first expressed surprise, but then went on to tell him about those photos, which apparently were *still* where I'd left them in the kitchen."

"So he saw them? How did he react?"

"Yes. He told me later that he'd at first thrown the photos away in disgust, but then later fished them out of the rubbish to use against me in the divorce proceedings, only after he'd thrown the remains of some spaghetti in tomato sauce on top of them. So I imagine that they're now all defiled and smeared with red stains."

"What a shame! I'd really like to have seen them."

"Me, too. He told me all this after I'd returned from visiting you in New York, and of course by then he had a whole different understanding of why I'd insisted on going to see you in hospital. He was awful. Really violent and threatening." She hadn't meant to disclose this, but it was out now.

"Violent?"

"Yes. I don't really want to talk about it."

"Wait a minute. I'd wanted to ask you…I noticed a faint little white line, like a scar, above your lip that I hadn't remembered seeing before." He gently ran his thumb over her mouth. "Is this anything to do with him?"

"Yes." She told him sketchily about how it had happened.

"The bastard!" he said hotly. "How dare he hurt you? Did it hurt a lot? What a terrible way to treat you! Now I'm beginning to understand what you'd said obliquely last weekend about being terrified of him. Did he often hurt you?"

"Not often physically. But he'd hurt me mentally and emotionally really rather frequently."

"My sweet love. What a good thing you've left him. It's so odd; he knew how to switch on the charm when he visited Landsdowne's. No one would guess he could be capable of behaving this way to you. What a sociopath! My poor love."

Without meaning to, Florence started to cry. Her little scar, her moment of pain and fear, was nothing, was so insignificant compared to the terrible hurt and terror he had suffered; the atrocious scars he must surely have on his legs! And yet he was comforting her. The pathos of this made her start sobbing uncontrollably for him. All the pent-up shock from discovering last weekend how he was now unable to walk, that his life was completely changed, that half his leg had been blown away, flooded over her. The grief she felt for him could be held in no longer, and finally needed expression. And he was sad for her, for a little scar that measured less than a quarter of an inch!

And the more she cried, the more he comforted her, completely unaware that it was his wounded state that was the reason for her unremitting sobs. But she could not tell him she was sobbing for him, as she knew he didn't want pity. This fact, that she was crying for him, and he, not knowing it or understanding it, was comforting her the more because of his dear kindness, struck her as being so pitiful, that she cried it seemed, without limit.

At last, with just a few lingering shudders, her crying episode was over, and she managed to say, since it was important, "It's nothing, Lance. I'm just a little tense, I think. Forgive me."

"I'm so sorry you went through all of that, Fleur. And I feel responsible."

"Nonsense! I *had* to come to New York to see you, Lance. I did it for myself as well as for you. It was worth any risk."

He gently pulled her to him, and kissed her. "I love you," he said into her hair. "Thank you for being with me in the hospital, despite the dangers, both political and now I realize personal as well." He ran his fingers through her hair and then hugged her again. "And I don't think," he added, leaning back on the sofa, "that Rose and Allison were deliberately malicious. They have so little excitement in their lives, so they probably love to spice it up with a little gossip. It's actually quite funny, when you think about it. Imagine the look on their faces when they saw photos of you and me together!"

"Yes. Presumably you're right. But I can tell you, that's the last time I play Scrabble with them again!"

"You won't be missing much!" he laughed.

Hearing Mei-Feng at the front door, they quickly gathered up all the envelopes of photographs, and Florence, giving one last sniff, stuffed them in her bag, just as Mei-Feng entered the room, her purchase of Chinese food apparent from the greasy, garlic smell even before she unloaded the white containers from her bag.

The same routine, only in the living room with fold-out tables this time, and not the dining room. Ah! It took so long. Dinner. Small talk with Mei-Feng, with her bright, cruel smile, and her high, little girl voice. Her wheeling Lance peremptorily into his room and being with him for such a long time. Longer, still, than that. Florence was convinced that he'd be asleep before she was 'allowed' in to see him. Why couldn't she herself help Lance prepare for bed? She'd offered. It would give Mei-Feng a break, but neither she nor Lance seemed to want that. This was inexplicable to her.

At last! At last she was entering Lance's room, but Mei-Feng came in behind her. Really, this was too much! Lance indeed seemed practically asleep. Mei-Feng busied herself with straightening his sheets, and giving him a glass of water. She also spent a long time fussing with the window as she said it was not fastened properly and that it was a chilly night.

And now Lance was asleep.

"Come!" Mei-Feng whispered. "We let him sleep."

"I'll just stay a little longer," Florence replied.

"Why? There no point. You disturb him. Is important he sleep."

Florence could not disagree with that, and looking back at Lance, she prepared to leave the room when she saw him open one of his eyes, smile quickly and wink, and then close his eyes again, just before Mei-Feng turned off the light.

Mei-Feng climbed the stairs to her room, and Florence did the same.

She sat in the guest room for about fifteen minutes, reading her book. Then she crumpled the sheets, turned out the light, and went quietly back downstairs to Lance's room.

"At last, Fleur!" he said, switching on the bedside light and putting on his glasses. "I thought you weren't coming back."

"Lance, really! What is going on?"

"I'm recognizing a characteristic in Mei-Feng that I hadn't seen in New York. She can be quite bossy, it seems. But look, never mind about that. You're here now."

"Why do we have to go through this pretense, this charade with her, in your own house? Why can't we be open?"

"It's a fair question. But it's a bit awkward. You see, I think I'm quite a private person."

"Well, I certainly respect that. And perhaps she's right about this evening. You do seem tired, in which case I shouldn't disturb you."

"No! How could you be disturbing me? I want to be alone with you here, Fleur. Please don't ever have any doubts about that." He reached out for her hand, and smiled up at her. She smiled back.

"Did you bring the photos?" he asked.

"Yes."

"Good! Come into bed with me, and let's look at them!"

She didn't know why she did it, but she took off all her clothes.

"Fleur, you're gorgeous! How am I going to be able to look at the photos with such a major distraction?"

"Should I undress you, too?" she asked.

He nodded sheepishly. She gaily lifted his pajama top over his head. As soon as she reached down to pull off the pajama bottoms, she saw his penis, and it was large, swollen and erect. And because this was the focus of her attention, and her desire for him so urgent, she only seemed to notice peripherally his legs, pathetically thin now since the muscles had atrophied, and how his left leg had a long hollowed area reaching the length of his calf and above the knee a little, of an angry red and purple color, where the hair had been denuded.

She climbed into bed and hugged him tightly. He rolled on top of her, and in this position his body felt so unfamiliar to her. It wasn't only

279

that it had almost been a year since they last made love - and then it had only been on three occasions - but it was also because the bones of his ribcage and hips were protruding so much, jamming into the soft tissue of her body; and his legs, well his legs... But the strange, shiny feel of his scarred left leg as it brushed against her, filled her with waves of tenderness for him, bordering on an erotic thrill. And when for the second time he lurched slightly sideways after attempted yet unsuccessful penetration, because his left knee could not support him, she rolled with him, pulling him to her, pressing firmly on his buttocks while giving little moans of ecstasy, and he responded so that he was now moving rhythmically inside her, and now it was no longer strange but good and familiar, and all around her swirled concentric, radiating circles of beauty, goodness, thrill and deep contentment.

And when their lovemaking was complete, he lay quietly for a moment, and then opened his bright, clear, articulate eyes. "God, that felt good," he said.

"I'm ecstatically happy, Lance!" she replied. "I love you."

He lightly cupped her chin with one hand and looked directly into her face, and he smiled for a long, steady minute. But gradually, with his lips still pulled over his parted teeth, he started to weep. He wept happy tears from his smiling face, still looking into her eyes.

"I was so afraid that this would be one more thing that I wouldn't be able to do any more. But you; you make it all possible. Thank you so much, Fleur, for giving me such happiness."

Overcome with emotion, she clung to him, her eyes also wet. "It was marvelous, Lance."

"I love you, Fleur," he breathed. Their crying gently subsided, and they were quiet for a while; just trailing their fingers over each other's arms, back, shoulders and hair, and giving little kisses. Then he sniffed, ran his hands over his eyes, and turned on his elbow and looked at her.

"It doesn't disgust you, then? My leg doesn't disgust you?"

"What? No, no; of course not."

"It disgusted me. I could hardly look at it at first. Actually, I still can't really. It's repulsive. I'm still disgusted by it."

In answer, Florence moved down the bed towards his left leg. The newness of its appearance would take some time to adjust to, the devastating degree of raw injury filling her with a squeamishness that made a catch in her throat and nearly induced a feeling of nausea. But it stabbed into her sense of pity and aroused her feelings of nurturance, so she gently kissed and stroked the long indented expanse of red, shiny skin. She knew, sadly, that he could not feel much of what she was doing, but he could see. And the look on his face, though sad and somewhat embarrassed by what was left of his leg, was also deeply appreciative.

"Don't be disgusted, Lance," she said. "It's bad enough that such cruelty happened, let alone that it's left its mark. But it's not repulsive. Your leg is part of you. And I love you. And," she said, moving back up the bed, "I think you should try to look at it as much as possible. Become familiar with the way it looks. That will eventually lessen the pain of seeing it."

"Will it? I don't think such a thing is possible."

"It will be, Lance. I'm sure it will be."

He smiled and stroked her hair. "Well, if you can tolerate my deformity, then perhaps I can grow accustomed to it, too."

"It's not just 'tolerate', Lance. Tolerate sounds to me as if there is still a bit of a problem, but that I will have to put up with it. No, that's not the case at all. I totally accept you in your entirety."

"Thank you," he said. "Thank you, Fleur." He sighed, shut his eyes and his breath became slower and deeper. Florence, convinced he was asleep, murmured a reassuring comment, and turning off the light, started to drift off to sleep herself.

Suddenly, though, Lance said, "Let's look at the photos now, Fleur! We still haven't looked at them yet!"

He rolled over, switched the light on again, and put on his glasses. Florence, quite startled, tried to pull herself back to a waking state.

"Perhaps it would be better to see them in the morning," she said sleepily.

"No; let's look at least a few now!"

"OK." She bent out of bed to get her bag, and taking the photos from it, she spread them on the bed. He pounced on an envelope hungrily and emptied its contents.

"Look, Fleur!" he said enthusiastically. "Me boarding a plane! We hadn't known it then, but that must be the plane I took to New York, so that one predicted correctly!"

"Yes!" she said, more awake now, and realizing how amazing this was.

"We never did find that one of the handshake, did we? Did it ever turn up?"

"No, it didn't," she said, remembering with shame how she had thrown it away.

"Ah, your wedding, Fleur. Let's not look at those. But wait! What's this? Who are these people?"

"That's the strange one that I told you about, where the camera went back in time. That little boy is my cousin, and over there, by the other side of the pond, is me."

"You, my sweet? How old were you then?"

"About seven or eight."

"What a delightful little girl you were. Oh, and Fleur, look! Look at this one! This is really incredible! Look, here you are reading by that unusual light in the living room! I inherited this light from the previous owner as I love the way it looks."

"Let me see! Oh yes! I remember when we saw this one before, and you said I was reading inside this house, and I said it was impossible, as even snooping around looking through the windows was enough for me! Little did I know that you'd move here, Lance!"

"Exactly, Fleur! Can you believe it? This camera of yours is incredible. Did you bring it with you now?"

"No, not this time."

"But you will keep using it, won't you? Why don't you bring it next time!"

"OK."

Then she saw his expression change. She put down the picture of her reading in the living room, and looked with alarm at the photo he was holding. It was the grainy black and white photo of him on the stretcher, his legs soaked in blood, and his face a mask of agony. Without saying anything, he picked up the next one, of people running, of a cloud of white smoke in the air seemingly chasing them, of fire engines and ambulances and halted cars at all angles.

"Oh God!" he gasped, putting his hand over his nose and mouth. "God help all of us. All those people."

"Lance, don't look anymore at those photos. They're too upsetting."

"No, Fleur. I must. It's what's in my mind the whole time."

"Lance, this can't be good for you. Let's please put these pictures away. I shouldn't have brought them," she said, now fully awake and alarmed at his reaction.

"Nonsense!" He turned back to the one of him on the stretcher. "You were right not to tell me about these pictures, Fleur." His face started to twitch convulsively. "Who knows?" he continued, his voice strange and shaky. "Perhaps if I had seen these I would not have been so brave after all. Perhaps I'd have chickened out of going to NYU, and what a rich experience I would have missed out on! So you did me a favor not telling me." He gave an odd laugh and squeezed his eyes tightly shut. "But we both know we can't sidestep Time. So, if I hadn't gone to NYU then, I might have traveled to New York at some other time and for some other reason, and some other type of calamity would have caused me to become injured instead. Time moves inevitably forward, delivering its blows."

He sank back into his pillows, his face white and looking completely spent. "Are there more photos showing me being injured?" he asked eventually.

"No," she whispered.

"Well then, let's look at the rest. But do you mind, Fleur, if I keep these two pictures?"

"Certainly you can keep them, if you wish. But do you think it's good for you?"

"Good for me? That's surely irrelevant! Let's not pretend this didn't take place. These are photos of what happened to me; what my memories are made up of; what my nightmares hinge on." Then, glancing at Florence, he said more softly, "But enough of that for now. Don't look so upset, Fleur."

"I'm only upset if they add to your suffering. On the other hand, it could be very healthy for you to get it all out. But I just can't stand to see you relive this."

"I relive it all the time, Fleur."

They hugged, but found no comfort.

"Let's not look at any more of these photos now, after all," he said. "Let's save the rest for tomorrow."

"Good idea!" she agreed. He separated the two photos from the rest that she was putting back in her bag, and put them in his bedside drawer. Then he took off his glasses and switched off the light. They moved into each other's arms, their naked bodies touching and intertwining, no longer stiffly held at a distance as had been the case the previous weekend, and with no layers of clothing on to act as barriers to true unity. It was amazing how quickly Florence fell asleep, especially as she'd felt so emotional moments earlier about Lance seeing the photos of himself after the World Trade Center attack. But she slept soundly until morning. Lance was still deeply asleep when she awoke, but she noticed a folded square of paper on her pillow, folded and refolded as was his fashion. With fingers still clumsy from sleep, she unfolded the paper and read:

*Fleur, my love: Your camera is a remarkable thing and you are certainly a remarkable person. I can't comprehend how your camera displays what it does, or why we have the privilege of seeing its photos, for privilege it is, despite our fears. I'm wondering if it could be because of your camera's mirror-lens, which is designed to fold the light. Perhaps, in folding the light, it switches over to a different Time dimension by mistake. Am I making any sense? All Nikon F models have the mirror-lens, though, and I sincerely doubt they are yielding the same perplexing photos as your camera does.*

*But that aside, my sweet — we must not worry about the future, as it must be comprised of many things. They're certainly not all bad. As I lie here now I think of the picture of me boarding the plane. And the one in which I am receiving the award. And my favorite of all — you, my love, reading in the living room, here in my house! I'm so grateful that you are here with me, Fleur. Really*

*I'm overjoyed. That happiness chases away the fears from the dark events, at least for a while. Lance.*

The following afternoon, straight after lunch, she enticed him to go food shopping with her. He was reluctant at first, but she pretended that she was afraid of losing her way without him. It felt good to be out and driving around, and they drove well beyond the village to look at the countryside, which was bleak and desolate in this wintry weather. But the lake, which appeared as a broad, rippling gray body of water, had a luminescence and beauty of its own.

After driving for a while, Florence suggested that he take over. He was surprised, but she urged him to try, saying that his driving leg was his right one, which was probably sufficiently strong to be able to use the accelerator and brake pedals. It was awkward shifting seats, but worth it! He pulled out hesitantly at first, but then drove with increased confidence. It felt like old times! Lance behind the wheel looked as he had always done, and it was almost possible for both of them to forget what had happened. They wound the windows down, despite the cold, and felt the wind in their hair, which made them both feel gloriously happy and liberated.

Then a thought struck her. "Lance," she said. "Let's go to the teashop in Portinscale before we do our shopping, and look at the rest of the photos there!"

He gave her a quick glance. "Do you have the photos with you?"

"I do! I think it would be fun to go there again, just as we had two summers ago! Besides, it was the place in which we first discovered the peculiarities of my camera."

"Actually, Fleur, I'd rather not."

"Why not? Don't you like it there anymore?"

"It's not that," he said, slowing down the car. "It's that I'm not ready yet for people to see me."

"But why, Lance? In New York, you couldn't wait to return to teaching. You didn't seem to mind people seeing you then."

He pulled over on to a flat, grassy patch beside the road, alongside a gate into a field which marked a break in the hedgerow, and put on the hazard lights.

"Somehow, Fleur," he began slowly, "it was different there. There in New York, we were all in it together. What had happened left us all shocked, stunned, and scared, too. We'd all been 'damaged' to different degrees. Many of us felt fearful at the sound of a low flying plane, or if we saw a group of people running – even if they were commuters running for a train! One of my students told me she was scared if she heard static on the radio, because that morning, September 11th, she'd been listening to WNYC, the public radio station, and suddenly lost the reception. She wondered why they took so long correcting the error, until she realized that the World Trade Center, that had their radio antenna on the top of one of the towers, had been hit. There are so many stories. But it's a completely different world here, Fleur. Literally it feels as though I've stepped on to a different planet."

She put her hand on his thigh. She now understood better why he'd stopped feeling so grateful and instead felt more depressed. It had coincided with his move back to England. A reverse culture shock, complicated by the loss of a shared experience, even if that experience was so traumatic.

"But you can't hide yourself away," she said. "You can't deprive yourself of things you enjoy just because of what you assume people will think. You do enjoy the teashop, don't you?"

"Yes, of course I do. All right, Fleur! I know you're right. We'll go to the teashop!"

He switched the car engine back on and pulled out. They arrived in Portinscale a short while later, and Florence helped Lance out of the car and into his wheelchair, which she pushed into the teashop. The little bell sounded on the steamy glass door as they entered.

"Well, if it isn't Dr. Ramsey!" the teashop owner declared. "But Lord, what happened to you?"

"Good afternoon, Mrs. Brown. I was unfortunately at the World Trade Center in New York when it was attacked."

"Heaven help us!" she cried. "I knowed you was in America, but no one told me you was there! We saw it all happen on TV, we did. The whole thing. Glued, we were, to the telly. Glued. Couldn't take our eyes off it, even though it kept repeating itself. Those films of them planes coming out of the clear, blue sky and diving straight into them buildings. My word! You was there then?"

"Yes."

"It's a miracle you's still alive, is what I say. Look, I'm sorry, dearies. I'm keeping you by the cold door while I can't stop yakking. You find yourselves a nice, comfortable table. Any one will do. And I'll go and fetch me old man."

"Mrs. Brown, do you remember Fleur? She was here with me two summers ago. In fact, it was her idea to come for tea here this afternoon."

"I thought you looked familiar, dearie. Nice to see you again. Was you in New York, too?"

"No, I was in London at that time. It's nice to visit your teashop again now."

"Thanks for coming again, I'm sure." Then, seeing Florence help Lance from his wheelchair to a seat at the table, Mrs. Brown asked, "All alright, are you? That's nice. I'll be back in a jiffy. Cooey! Freddie! Freddie, come 'ere. Look who's come for tea today!"

"I'm sorry, Lance," Florence whispered, sitting down on a chair beside him and touching his arm.

"It's all right, Fleur," he replied, giving his glorious smile.

"It's another Noah's Arc situation, if you ask me," a stout woman who was delicately picking up an egg-and-watercress sandwich said, from a table at the corner of the room. "We're all corrupt, especially in America. Too much greed. That's what it's all about. So God gave us a warning."

"That's an interesting interpretation," Lance said.

"Yes, greed," she said, pushing another sandwich into her tiny, round, crimson painted mouth, her cheeks bulging on either side. "Especially in America. They think they've got it all. And the bigger the better. Big cars, big wallets, big buildings. Lost touch with God and with nature, if you ask me."

Just then a merry looking man, with an apron covered in flour, came up to Lance and Florence's table, accompanied by a very excited Mrs. Brown. The story was dutifully repeated, and while they were doing so, the stout lady paid noisily and bustled out of the tearoom.

"It was like a film," Mr. Brown said, "watching it on the telly. We couldn't believe it was really happening. Just like a film, you know, with all them explosions and fires and chases. We couldn't believe it was real, could we, Margie?"

"No," she said, shaking her head.

"Remember 'ow I said the Empire State Building would be the next to topple. Remember 'ow I said that, Margie."

"Yes, yes; you said that, Freddie."

"All them lovely skyscrapers. I thought they'd all go down. Just like dominoes. Never knew Dr. Ramsey was in the middle of all that, did we Margie?"

"Oh no. We knew Dr. Ramsey was in America, but America's a big place. We didn't know he was there."

"What do they want with all them skyscrapers, anyway?" Freddie continued. "Want to be high up, go up a mountain! That's what I say! Not for nothing do we live where we do."

"But it's exciting going up to the top of skyscrapers too," Florence said. "There's something magnificent about being so high up and looking out of the window at the city life below."

"Not any more, though," Lance replied. "It's true that the upper floors of skyscrapers had the highest rents, but I think that's all going to change now."

"They had a problem with them stairs, didn't they?" Freddie said, pulling out a chair, and sitting down at the table with them. "Not wide enough staircases, or something."

Florence worried that talking about going down the stairs would be too difficult for Lance, so she cast about in her mind to find another topic. But she did not need to as Freddie immediately said, "So what do you reckon they'll build on that land once it's cleared?"

"I have no idea," Lance said.

"I'll tell you what they'll build," Freddie replied. "You mark my words. They'll build the highest skyscraper in the world, that's what! People have got short memories, they have. They'll soon forget how dangerous it can be up there on those floors way in the clouds. The highest skyscraper in the world! That's what America is all about. Don't know if you'd call that foolish pride, or undefeatable spirit. Either way, that's what they'll build."

"You wouldn't catch me at the top of no skyscraper," Mrs. Brown said.

"Nah! But there's plenty that would be up there in a minute. Isn't that right, Dr. Ramsey?"

"Yes! I'll go up to the top of whatever new building is erected there, big or small," Lance said. Florence looked at him admiringly and put her hand on his thigh under the table; Mrs. Brown said, "You've become a right American, you 'ave!"; and Freddie Brown, clapping him firmly on the shoulder, said, "That's me lad! So, what will you be 'aving? We've got some hot buttered teacakes, which came out lovely today, if you'd like them. And it's on the house, it is!"

"Thanks, you're very kind. But I'd really rather not," Lance said. "I'd prefer to pay."

Later, after Freddie had returned to the kitchen, the tearoom started filling with people, and Mrs. Brown was kept busy bustling around. She gave extremely generous portions of teacakes and sugar buns to Florence and Lance, with a wink to Florence when Lance was looking elsewhere. And when they'd eaten, Lance bent over the two photos again, that he'd remembered to take from his bedside table drawer. Florence started looking at the other photos, but Lance did not express much interest in seeing them.

But suddenly a group of pictures caught Florence's eye, and she exclaimed out loud.

"What is it, Fleur?" Lance asked.

"Lance, look! I had never understood this before, but I do now! Here are some photos of me preparing for my wedding, and I'm smiling! I couldn't reconcile these pictures with those others we've seen of me looking so devastated. But, Lance, I've just realized! Look!" she said excitedly, scrambling through some other photos, and then placing one down alongside the picture she was already studying. "I'm wearing a different dress! Don't you see! It's a *different* wedding!"

"Better luck next time!" he said, somewhat absent-mindedly.

"Lance, I'm getting married again!" she exclaimed.

But he was back to staring at the horrific pictures of September 11th. In all likelihood, it was the conversation with the Browns, or perhaps general exhaustion from over-exertion. They were both quiet on the way home, each locked into their own pattern of thought. Florence couldn't help realizing that as Lance looked repeatedly back to the past, she was increasingly looking to the future, and to that of a solid union with the man she loved.

# FIFTEEN

*THAT LANCE WAS OBSESSIVELY* continuing to think of the attack on the World Trade Center was apparent not only in how he frequently stared at the two photographs that he now carried around in his wallet, but also in the series of sketches and paintings that he did over the next several weeks. Rather than serene pictures of the landscape, which was what Florence anticipated and hoped for, Lance did a series of pictures of crowds of agonized people surrounded by jagged, uncompromising lines, in blacks and grays, with splatters of red and orange.

She continued visiting Lance every weekend, and each time she tried hard to help him to feel less depressed and traumatized, and it was true that he was so pleased to see her and even had times when he was his old self, full of energetic curiosity, but more often he was apathetic and trapped in his downward spiral of thought. He frequently spoke almost exclusively about his withered leg, and she was aware at these times that her presence did not seem to cheer him up. She had printed out and brought with her the early e-mails he'd sent her when he'd first arrived in New York, e-mails that were full of awe and excitement and delight about the incredible energy of the city, as she thought these might be pleasant reminders of how he had felt then. But these e-mails, like those white cartons of cool, congealed Chinese food that Mei-Feng purchased, remained largely untouched.

Then, one extraordinary weekend in June, two remarkable events occurred. She was sitting one dull, soggy afternoon in Lance's living room, lashings of rain beating against the windowpane, reading under the puddle of amber luminescence from the unusual light that Lance had inherited with the house; the very light, in fact, that she had appeared to be reading by in one of the photos from her camera. Lance was across the room, in his usual position on the sofa, laptop on his knees and surrounded by a pile of books on the sofa, adding some responses to his students in his online class, when he suddenly piled the books neatly in one corner, put the laptop on the table beside him, and said, "I've got something for you, Fleur! It's a surprise! Shut your eyes!"

"A surprise?" she asked, genuinely intrigued and pleased.

"Yes!" he said, looking oddly excited. "Shut your eyes."

She shut her eyes.

"And cover your ears," he added.

She opened her eyes again enquiringly.

"Keep your eyes shut, Fleur. And cover your ears. Oh, and hum a little tune," he said playfully.

She couldn't help opening her eyes again. "Hum a little tune, you say?"

"Yes!"

So she sat there, eyes closed, hands over ears, and her voice humming 'The Dance of the Blessed Spirit' sounded different, coming from completely inside herself. She could feel her body vibrating from the humming. And then she felt something else. Something quickly touching her shoulder. Instinctively she looked up. There was Lance, standing above her, leaning on crutches and wobbling slightly, but grinning triumphantly.

"Lance!" she exclaimed, jumping up. "You walked! You did it! You walked across the room!"

"Yes!"

"This is the most amazingly wonderful surprise, Lance!"

"Yes!"

"You walked!"

"Shall we walk together back to the sofa?" he asked breathlessly.

"Yes, definitely!"

Keeping right beside him, Florence took tiny steps, measuring the slow, awkward progress, the shuffle of his wasted left leg, and seeing the vast, shaky distance through his eyes. Her heart beat as rapidly as if she'd been sprinting. They arrived at the other side of the room, and he dropped the crutches and clung on to her, and they almost fell together on to the sofa, upsetting the pile of books which clattered noisily to the floor.

"Lance, that's so wonderful!"

He closed his eyes for a moment. He was breathing heavily. Then he opened his eyes, looked directly at her, and nodded happily.

"You *can* walk again, Lance! You've proved Dr. Mezzinger wrong!" And Mei-Feng too, she thought to herself.

"I can actually walk a little better than that if I strap on a sturdy metal leg brace to my left leg. But I had a sudden impulse to show you now! Right this moment!"

The little boy pathos of his words and tone of voice made her hug him to her tightly. "Thank you for being so spontaneous! I had no idea! Have you been practicing a lot?"

"Well," he said, rubbing his arm across his sweaty brow. "Mei-Feng has been taking me to Yoga or swimming about twice or three times per week. There's a nice sports facility on the way to Mother. I think that's been helping a lot. I wanted to keep it a secret until I could show you that I could do it!"

He closed his eyes again. The effort had certainly cost him a lot.

"It's phenomenal, Lance! It's absolutely phenomenal how much you have achieved!"

"I didn't want to passively accept my infirmity, as my mother did about herself albeit in a different context." He stared down at the crutches lying crisscrossed on the floor. "That part hasn't been easy. It's hard to shake off the demons ingrained since the formative years of childhood. I don't mean to sound as if I'm blaming Mother for her passivity and dependence. I'm not at all. She is a sweet and lovely person. You know; you've seen her. But I started wondering whether we can help the way we feel. I mean, can we control our feelings? Can we force ourselves to feel a different way? I don't know. I still don't know. It's certainly a difficult struggle for me.

"But then," he said, and now Lance looked away from the crutches and up into Florence's eyes, "I thought how it's not my feelings that are important, but my *reactions* to them. My feelings are going to come anyway, and they do. They've become habitual. But I wanted them to have less power over me. And that means that I should react to them less. It's like a person who is extremely shy. Should he keep giving in to that shyness, or should he make an effort to speak to people, even if the thought filled him with fear? I don't know if I'm making myself clear. Do you see what I'm trying to say, Fleur?"

"I think so."

"Good. Well, I thought about you; about how you risked personal and professional relationships to come and see me immediately after September 11th. Not only that, but you risked your own personal safety, too, in the face of what you know to be Howard's uncontrollable anger. You marched right into the midst of the turmoil to visit me. As Cameron and plenty of others were leaving the city, you arrived for me. And now, back in England, you're prepared to drive miles upon miles every weekend to see me. And God knows, I haven't been great company! So, don't you see, Fleur, the way you're reacting to me is inspiring me to change my reactions to some of the feelings that plague me, and ultimately, I very much hope, to even change the feelings themselves."

"Lance, I come to see you because I want to. Because I can't do without-"

Heightened emotion prevented her from saying anything else. They kissed deeply and lovingly. It gave her time to compose herself.

"It's excellent that you aren't giving in to feelings of failure, Lance. And it's not only battered emotions that are so understandably there, but also real physical difficulties. You have such strength and determination! I admire that about you so much!"

"Well, as you saw, I still have a long way to go before what I just did could really be called 'walking'. But it's a start. And I keep thinking of those three words you told me, Fleur. 'Courage, strength, and hope.' 'Courage, strength, and hope.'"

"Thank you, Anna," she muttered.

"My right leg has to be the dominant one, and sort of do the work for both legs. It's ironic because had my right leg been the only one injured, I suspect it might well have caused me to have a limp. But it has to be strong now, because my left leg will never be of any use."

She knew this to be true. And yet she said, "Who knows? With the progress you're making, your left leg might well recover more and more." And she knew this could be true, as well.

The next morning it poured outside, and although Florence loved walking in the rain and knew Lance, prior to his injuries, enjoyed it too, now it was of course out of the question. He was seated in his corner of the sofa, and although he did not complain, the red tartan blanket over his legs was a sure indication that the sustained damp weather made his joints ache. She was reading a section of the Sunday newspaper, and Lance was working in his online class. She looked up at him, marveling at his concentration and evident enjoyment of teaching in this new way online. He caught her eye and smiled.

"How's your class going?" she asked.

"Very well, thanks. It doesn't fail to amaze me how asynchronicity does so much to enrich the discussion. I suppose it makes sense, though, as it gives all the students time to think at their own pace, and respond when they have a good idea."

"I like the idea of people doing things at their own pace, rather than having a rigid system of Time, or 'timing' imposed upon them. Somehow that imposition of Time moving relentlessly forward feels even more to be the case in London than here."

"Good! That shows you're feeling more relaxed."

"That's certainly true," she replied. "But also in London our lives seem to be so governed by the clock; we wake up to the sound of our alarm, we rush to work at the same general time as everyone else, we eat when our boss allows us to have a lunch break rather than when we're hungry, we work at regulated hours rather than when we're inspired, and then we all rush home again at about the same time. At least, that's what it's like for the vast majority of people, and used to be true of me, too, before I became a freelancer."

"You're absolutely right! What a contrast that is with being here in the countryside where we're so much closer to nature. As you've no doubt noticed, nights are really dark here, as opposed to the constant amber glow of lights all night long in the city. And here we can see flowers opening and closing, just like the morning glories you so kindly bought me while I was in hospital."

She rose and went to sit next to him on the sofa, and he placed his laptop on the table and put his arm around her. "Did you know, Fleur," he continued, "that there wasn't just one Greek god of Time, Chronos, but there was also Kairos, the god of opportunity, chance, and – well – timing, which was the very word you just used. And in fact your thinking about sleeping and eating according to your body's needs and desires rather than having a strict system of Time imposed on you, is Kairological rather than Chronological, just as is working when you're inspired rather than when you're told to produce something. It's what you said you do as a freelance writer and it's what I do, too, in my online teaching."

"Yes! And this obsessive compunction that many of us feel we need for punctuality is really robbing us of our spontaneity and creativity. I suppose, though, to a degree it's inevitable, as we do need to coordinate with others."

"Yes and no. We're coordinated with each other in my online class, even though it is conducted in virtual time. Some call it asynchronous. But why call it by what it's not – not synchronous - instead of simply calling it Kairological!"

"I think you and I both function better when we don't have a rigid schedule."

"Yes, you're a free spirit! I could tell that about you the moment I first met you, and think I told you."

He ruffled her hair and she laughed.

"Oh Fleur," he suddenly said. "Speaking of Time – though from a rather different angle - I believe Mei-Feng forgot to wind the grandfather clock yesterday. Would you mind winding it, please? The key for opening the cabinet is on the mantel piece over there."

"Of course!" Florence replied, and without knowing it, this was then to become the occasion of the second remarkable event of that wet and soggy June weekend.

She went out into the hall, the small key in her hand, and looked up at the ancient grandfather clock, proudly positioned against the wall near the staircase. She had never really looked at it before. She ran her hand over the details of its fine carving. It was a beautiful piece, a rich shiny mahogany carved into flowers and what looked like angels with trumpets above the clock face. She now no longer minded its incessant chiming every fifteen minutes, as she had on the occasion of her first visit. No wonder Lance had wanted to keep it when he purchased the house.

As she was inserting the key into the lock, she glanced up at the clock face to check the time, but saw something that startled her. She ran back to the living room.

"Lance!" she cried, "Have you looked at that clock? I mean, really looked at it up close? Have you seen its face?"

"Yes, of course! Why?"

"Have you seen what's written on its face, Lance?"

"No," he said. "I don't recall having seen anything written on its face. But then, from the wheelchair-"

"Lance, let's come and look at it together now! Do come! Anyway, wouldn't you like to watch me wind it? After all, we're both fascinated with clocks!"

All the while she was saying this, she was excitedly taking the laptop which he'd resumed looking at from his hands, and removing the blanket from his knees.

"What is written on the clock face?"

"Come and see!" she said to him, handing him his crutches.

"I think I'll go in the wheelchair, Fleur."

"No, Lance; no! Please try to walk. It was so wonderful seeing you standing yesterday. Seeing you at your full height! And you'll be able to see the clock face better. And then you could sit on the bench in the hall while I'm winding it."

"Very well!" he laughed, pretending to be cross, but catching her excitement. "You're a hard taskmaster, you are! I should never have shown you my latest accomplishments!"

She pulled him up, laughing too, and he positioned himself on one of the crutches. Just before putting the other crutch under his other arm, Florence said, "No! Use me as the other crutch. Lean on me!" And he did, so together they made their way slowly into the hall. When they reached the grandfather clock, they looked up at its face gazing solidly down on them.

"'*Only a man who lives not in time but in the present is happy,'*" read Florence excitedly from the clock's face. "Wittgenstein, it says. A quotation from Wittgenstein!"

"That's so fascinating, Fleur!" Lance said. "I'd never noticed that before, all these months of living here." He lurched a bit, as if his legs could not support the excitement in the rest of his body. "I need to sit down."

"Of course!" Florence said, helping him to the bench. It was made of a hard, polished wood, and was unyielding and very upright, but Lance seemed grateful to sit on it.

"We must think about this further, Fleur. It mirrors our thoughts so exactly about rejecting conventional measurements of Time."

"Yes, and how ironic that a clock itself should say that!"

"Somehow, Fleur, I feel it ties in completely with this house. With the atmosphere here."

"What do you mean?"

"I'm not sure. We'll have to think more about it. How terrific that you showed this to me!"

Florence opened up the cabinet to wind the clock.

"Lance!" she exclaimed. "Did you know that there seems to be some paper tucked in behind this slot of wood?"

"No! What is it?"

"I can't really see. It's very dark in here. Wait! I think I can pull it out without ripping it. Oh, it's an envelope!"

"An envelope, Fleur! Is it addressed to anyone?"

"To a Mr. Throgmorton. Who's he?"

"I don't know. Maybe he lived here once. Let's open it!"

"Do you think we should?"

"Of course! This clock belongs to me, now. Who knows how long this envelope has been in there."

"What a strange place to put a letter!"

She sat down on the bench beside Lance, and slit open the envelope. Inside it was a note scrawled on a piece of paper, and behind that a stack of old photographs. They first looked at the note together. It read:

*"Time present and time past*
*Are both perhaps present in time future,*
*And time future contained in time past.*
*If all time is eternally present*
*All time is unredeemable."* (T.S. Eliot, 1888-1965)

"This is incredible! Whatever does it mean?"

"I'm not sure."

"Perhaps a clue would be to find where this quotation is from."

"Yes. But let's think about that later. Let's see these photos first!"

The photos were turning yellow, and curling up slightly at the corners. The first one that they looked at was of a young woman with billowing dark hair, and judging from the way she was dressed, the picture might have dated from at least half a century ago. Her face was full of merriment, and she looked replete with vitality.

"What an attractive young woman," Florence remarked. "I wonder if she's still alive today."

The next photo showed a group of three warmly clad people, standing by the front of what was now Lance's house. The same young woman was part of the group. An old fashioned car was parked nearby on the drive. Snow lay thickly on the ground, and everyone looked cheerful, as if they were anticipating coming inside to a Christmas dinner.

"These are amazing!" Lance commented. "I wonder who these people are."

They turned to the next picture, which showed an adolescent boy and an older man, both of whom had been in the group photo. The youth had a fresh, pleasant face, and the older man, presumably his father as he had one arm around him, was gazing at the camera, though had a look of impatience, as if he wanted to hurry and get all the nonsense of taking photographs over in his evidently greater desire to go fishing. And sure enough, in his other hand he held a fishing line, and there was a bucket at his feet.

The last photo in the batch was of a woman, who Florence guessed was the mother. She had a tight, unexpressive face; wide, flat cheeks; and crinkly gray hair which stood up all around her head.

Lance let out a little gasp when he saw this picture.

"I've seen her before," he said.

"What? What do you mean?"

"She's in my bedroom sometimes. At night. Over by the wardrobe."

They both suddenly felt icy cold.

"What a cold draft from under the front door! Hard to believe this is June," he added.

"How can she be in your room? Why didn't you tell me? What does this mean?" Florence asked, greatly afraid.

"I see her often. I thought I was going mad. Or hallucinating. That's why I couldn't tell you. Or perhaps she was part of some recurring nightmares, though I was sure I was awake. But now we have evidence! She must have lived here! And she's still here now."

"Lance, I'm frightened. Let's put the photos away!"

"Yes! And let's go back to the warmth of the living room."

She helped him up, but after taking one step he shook his head. "I can't do it! Please fetch me my wheelchair."

Trembling, she ran to get his chair and then helped him into it. She realized he was shivering, too. They went quickly into the living room, and Lance sat back in his corner of the sofa. She pulled the red tartan blanket over him, right up to his chest, and tucked it in tightly all around. Then she sat down next to him.

"Fleur, you're freezing, too! Let's share this blanket," he said, tugging out some of the blanket from beneath himself, and holding out a corner to her. She wrapped it around herself, and he put his arm around her. They half-reclined together, cuddled against each other, and extraordinarily both fell asleep.

Florence awoke to the feeling of Lance fingering ringlets of her hair;

twirling them around his finger, gently pulling them straight, and letting them spring back into their usual curled position again. She opened her eyes, momentarily wondering what time it was, and what they were doing in the living room. Then she remembered the photos from inside the grandfather clock, and the bitter cold sensation.

The rain had stopped, and a watery sunlight was streaming through the windows. She looked up at Lance. He was smiling down at her. Every trace of the terrible stress he had endured since September 11th, that had blotched and tightened his forehead and cheeks, and troubled his eyes, seemed to have been smoothed away. He looked as he had done when they first met, by the green shaded light in the drawing room of Landsdowne's Guest House, when he'd first helped her with her camera.

Sitting up straighter, she took his face in both of her now warm, tingling hands, and gave tiny, soft kisses first to one cheek and then the other; then to his forehead; then carefully removing his glasses, to each of his bright, clear, intelligent eyes; then to his chin; and finally to his mouth. It was a seal. He laughed playfully and reciprocated the kisses on her face, in each of the areas and in the same order that she had kissed on him.

"What we've just seen and felt was extraordinary, Fleur," he said, once again fingering her hair. "But you and I don't think in conventional ways; we don't mindlessly go along with the prevailing ideology handed down to us by those with power in society. We don't go in for woolly thinking. That's one of the reasons why I've always found you so remarkable. You're too much of an original, intelligent thinker to slip into the convenient, well worn pattern of socially conventional thought. So I don't think we should be afraid of what we've just experienced. Instead, we should think, really think, about what it all means. I want us to do whatever it takes to explore and understand all of this."

Despite his words, Florence did feel afraid when she thought back to the photograph of the woman and how Lance saw her frequently in his room at night. But then she remembered what Lance had said the day before, about not giving in to an automatic response to one's feelings. On the other hand, wasn't it important to recognize one's feelings and pay them some respect? Didn't they serve to protect the body?

Lance saw her hesitation. "Please, Fleur!" he said simply.

That did it! She had to ignore her fear, because this meant so much to Lance. He was finally ignited, fully alive, excited, and inquisitive; the very features that made her love him in the first place, and that she had not consistently seen in him since her stay with him in New York the previous April, more than a year ago! By fully inquiring into this together, which is what he wanted, perhaps her feelings of fear would change in a way that avoidance could not make possible.

"Yes, OK Lance," she agreed, and in trying to compensate for and cover up her fear, she hurried on to add, "You tell me when you see that woman again! Wake me up and let me know she's there. And let's try and find out who she is, and the others in the photo, and the meaning of the piece from the Eliot poem and why it was there with the photos, and - why – we might even reach a new understanding of Time itself!"

"Steady on, Fleur! One step at a time! But your statement about hoping to grasp a better understanding about Time indicates that we're both approaching this in the same way. I don't want us to think of this woman as a ghost. I think she's somehow crossed over into our Time, or we've crossed into hers. I don't know why I think this, or how it could happen, but this is what I conjecture."

"Wow! Do you really think so?"

"Mmmm," Lance replied. "It certainly seems possible."

Glancing down, Florence unexpectedly saw the envelope from the grandfather clock, which oddly lay beside her on the sofa, though she hadn't remembered bringing it with her when they fled back to the living room. She snatched it up, and taking out her notebook from her bag, she copied down the passage from the Eliot poem. Then, rushing to the hall, she also copied down the Wittgenstein quotation from the face of the grandfather clock, before stuffing the envelope securely back inside the cabinet of the clock, and her notebook in her bag.

Coming back into the living room, Lance looked up at her and smiled. "Actually I've just had a thought," he said. "The weather seems to have cleared up now. The sun's even trying to shine a bit. Let's go out! I know you've been wanting to do that. And there's a very special waterfall I want to show you. I think it might even have some relevance to some things we've been saying about Time, as I think you'll see."

"Yes, let's do that!" she replied, suddenly aware that she was anxious for some fresh air. "The only problem is that, since we'll have to take my car as Mei-Feng has yours, how will we fit your wheelchair into it?"

"Let's not take the wheelchair. There are no real paths there anyway. I'll walk!"

"Is it quite rocky and uneven?"

"A bit. But exquisitely beautiful and well worth it, as I think you'll agree."

"Is it far from where we'll park the car?" She was worrying how he could possibly manage it, though at the same time did not want to discourage him. "Because perhaps you should wear that leg brace that you told me about." As she said this, she feared that he might think she was being too controlling or over-protective.

"No! No! Let's go now!" he said, starting to try to rise.

"Lance, you can certainly lean on me if you wish. I love that. But I really do think you should put on the leg brace if it's a rough path. Also, since it's been raining, it might be slippery."

"Very well!" he said with a short sigh. "Can you please get it for me? It's tucked away at the back of my wardrobe."

She went to his wardrobe, nervously looking around to see if she could detect the woman from the photo, but to her relief nothing seemed extraordinary. A few minutes later they were ready to leave. The brace made tiny clicking noises whenever Lance swung his leg.

"How does your leg feel?" she asked.

"Actually my leg feels wonderfully supported, Fleur." And he did seem to move more easily with it strapped on.

"I'm glad. Will you drive?"

"Love to."

Lance drove more quickly and confidently than before, and remained animated in his conversation.

"Here it is!" he exclaimed after having driven for quite a while. He pulled the car to a halt and they got out. Florence could hear the splash of gushing water before she could see anything.

"Over there!" he said, pointing with the white rubber tip of his wooden crutch to a place beyond some trees.

The air was beautifully fresh and clear, as it is after prolonged rain, and the leaves on the trees glistened with tiny droplets of moisture. Florence and Lance moved along a short distance, and then they saw the source of the sound; a magnificent waterfall of crystalline water dashing headlong down, rushing past rocks and boulders, and plunging into the lake below.

"It's beautiful!" Florence breathed.

"Do you mind if we sit down on those rocks over there and watch it for a bit?" He was panting slightly.

"Absolutely!"

They sat quietly on the wet rocks and watched.

"Have you heard of a clepsydra, Fleur?" Lance asked at last. She shook her head, so he went on to explain that it was device which used water flowing from one bucket to another below it to measure Time. He said that they had been used in rural China.

"But there's another aspect to this," Lance continued. "We can clearly see the rushing movement of the water in the waterfall, and yet, when we look out at Lake Crummockwater where this waterfall cascades into it, the lake looks perfectly still. If we were to return to this lake tomorrow, it would look exactly as it does now, but in fact it would contain completely different water, as the water now in it would have flowed away. It's as Heraclitus said, 'You cannot step into the same river twice, for fresh waters are ever flowing in upon you.' Everything is changing. Nothing is permanent. I think Time is like this; it flows but is always present."

"But that's exactly what T.S. Eliot said!" Florence said, excitedly taking out her notebook and reading from it the line, "'...all time is eternally present.'"

"Wow! You're right, Fleur!"

"Yes, and speaking of the 'present,' isn't this what the Wittgenstein quotation on the grandfather clock also meant, when it recommended living in the present to find happiness, and not in conventional time?"

"True; that's actually a very Buddhist philosophy, and maybe now we can see an explanation of it, if we think of the eternal present as being made up of all Times in the past and future as well. Because, continuing our analogy with this waterfall, tomorrow – the *future* - there will be new water in the lake, as we said, but water eventually evaporates, then falls back to earth as rain, and contributes to the waterfall, so this was water from the *past*, too."

"I like that! And by the way, you speaking of the 'eternal present' reminds me of when we had that wonderful, really exceptional kiss, which seemed to last for ever, when you were in hospital. My last night visiting you. Before the nurse came in. Do you remember?"

"How could I forget it? That marvelous kiss is still with me. It's why I'm here today," he said simply. They held on to each other and hugged strongly.

"Oh, but not to get distracted" she joked, "When you talk about the eternal present being made up of the past and future, this is *also* something T.S. Eliot said."

"I should've been a poet!" he said facetiously.

"Yes!" she smiled, and then reading again from her notebook, she said, "Because before he talked about time being eternally present, he'd written, "Time present and time past/Are both perhaps present in time future/ And time future contained in time past.'"

"Perhaps Time is circular, and would be, if the Water Cycle that I just spoke of is really applicable. Perhaps the future is contained in the past, and flows back into it," Lance replied, his good leg jogging up and down, just as she remembered it had done when they'd first spoken about Time that night at Landsdowne's. She was thrilled that his mood was so improved, mirroring the sun cracking through what had been dark clouds overhead earlier that afternoon. She squeezed his hand.

"Do you know, this reminds me of something you wrote to me from that impossibly slow train you took to Heathrow Airport before leaving for New York. You'd said something like 'the Future can influence the Past, and that you think that's what's happening between us, though you didn't know why you thought that.'"

"Yes, I do remember writing that. And I still feel it, too."

"Maybe that explains why you and I were drawn to each other at Landsdowne's. Maybe we've always known each other."

"And always will."

Savoring that comment, Florence said, "And Lance, speaking about how the future could influence present actions, or perhaps even the past, isn't that exactly what my camera is often picking up?"

"Very true! Even more reason to believe in the possibility of Time being circular. In fact, if this is true, it offers a good explanation as to why we can think that Time is infinite, because of the infinite number of points on the circumference of a circle."

"So, if we think of Time as circular and infinite, it means that there was no beginning and there won't be an end, either?"

"Right! But the idea of no beginning might upset your friend, Anna, and others who hold strong religious convictions."

"Yes; I remember that *Genesis* starts by saying, '*In the beginning God created the heaven and the earth. And the earth was without form, and void; and darkness was upon the face of the deep.*'" And then laughingly she sang, "*And God said 'Let there be Light!' And there was light!*" from Haydn's *The Creation*.

Lance smiled. "And then, of course, we have the scientists and other rationalists, who believe instead in the Big Bang Theory, as the way in which everything began," he added.

"Well, between the rationalists and the religious people, that includes nearly everyone then! Nearly everyone believing that Time had a beginning."

"Yes. Or maybe not," Lance said, his eyes looking particularly luminous. "Maybe the Big Bang, or God's Creation, are just one of the infinite points on the circumference of the circle of Time. They each are eternally present."

"You know, this reminds me of Douglas Adam's book, *The Restaurant at the End of the Universe*," Florence said excitedly. "The restaurant is the gathering point one evening for the characters in the story to watch the spectacular show of the demise of the universe, only to be repeated the following evening and every evening after that."

"Yes, that's a great book, and certainly makes a point about the circularity of Time. But for those who do believe in a beginning, what was there before the beginning?"

"It's too complicated. And hard to imagine. But perhaps it accounts for that other Time that Anna spoke about – you remember – the Time before the Sun and Moon were created on the Fourth Day to create a measurement of Time."

"Terrific thought! Yes, Fleur! How was Time measured on Days One, Two and Three? It's so intriguing. I've continued to think about that since you told me about that conversation you had with Anna, but I keep coming up with a blank. I don't have an answer for that yet."

"Neither does Anna. Nor I, for that matter. But for now, if we get back to thinking of Time as circular and infinite, perhaps we can assume there are an infinite number of present moments, made up of all of Time converging. A confluence of Time; Past, Present, and Future," Florence said, subconsciously drawing a circle with her finger on the surface of the damp rock she was sitting on.

"But there's just one thing that troubles me, Fleur, when I think of Time this way," Lance said, "and that is that we seem to definitely know that the Past is 'behind' us. That we have memories of what happened before, tucked away in filing cabinets in our mind."

"Not necessarily, Lance!" Florence replied. "I've read that there is new research on memory formation, and that neuroscientists are beginning to dismiss the idea that our memories are logically filed and stored, but that instead when we have a memory of something, it is created freshly each time."

"Is that so?" Lance exclaimed excitedly. "In that case, this is great! And it shows me how I've been guilty of adhering to the very paradigm of the steady marching forward of Time that I claim to have been rejecting! If we create our memories freshly each time, then the Past can be present now, and not necessarily behind us!"

"Yes!" Florence said, catching his excitement.

"Which shows how it's more than possible for a past event to enter our present time!"

"Which is also what you said could happen if we believe in parallel axes of Time. That we could jump over from one Time axis to another, which might be the Future, or the Past."

"You're right! Both explanations are plausible, and either could account for why the Past, Present and Future could converge. So it could, in fact, give some explanation as to how the woman in that photo from long ago is by my wardrobe now!"

"Lance, this is incredible!"

"It is! And I can't tell you how glad I am to have seen her photo! To know she actually existed! And I'll be even more delighted when you see her, too, Fleur."

"Yes!" she agreed, though she still felt afraid at that thought, but that seemed so insignificant against the joy she now felt that here she was, in this enchanted place of sparkling light and rushing sounds of the waterfall - with Lance! Yes, that Lance was well enough to show her this beautiful place, and they were having this wonderful conversation. It was unbelievable that he'd walked! Granted that this was only a tiny distance from the car, and thank goodness the path wasn't as rough as he'd implied, but he'd done it!

"Lance, I've just had a thought." Here Florence started talking more slowly and carefully. "If we find that woman had died – if that is the case – and if we believe she's apparent now because of the circularity, or confluence of Time, then this would also apply to all those people who lost their lives at the World Trade Center. They're still present, too. After all," she added, tossing a little stone into a puddle close by and watching the concentric circles radiating out from where the stone plunged in, "time continues. If we believe it stops when someone dies, then we are implying that Time is consciousness. That it is snuffed out at the end of a life. But isn't Time more than that? After all, we were just saying it's infinite."

Lance looked troubled and then perplexed. "God, Fleur; I hope you're right!" He ran his thumb over a leaf hanging on a little branch close to him, spreading out its droplets of moisture. "Time is consciousness. Hmm. That is interesting. I think that might've been one of the things we talked about late into the night at Landsdowne's that time. But yes, you're right. Time is more than that. It's whirling around us in a circular motion, creating the eternal present." He still looked somber. "I hope you're right that the people who died at the World Trade Center are still present."

"I hope so, too" she said softly.

"Come, Fleur," he said after a while. "I think that's all the sunshine we'll get for today. I wouldn't be surprised if it rains again soon. Let's get back to the house."

# SIXTEEN

*ON TUESDAY OF THE FOLLOWING WEEK,* Florence did an Internet search, and traced the full T.S. Eliot poem from which they had read the excerpt. It was called 'Burnt Norton,' and was the first of his *Four Quartets* published in 1936. She was delighted to have located it, and e-mailed Lance the URL. A particular passage in it both amazed and shocked her, as it spoke about a "white light" and said how, being seen in the new world, it made the "old [world] explicit," and generated feelings of both "partial ecstasy" and "a resolution of partial horror."

> *Lance!* [she wrote in the e-mail] *Can you believe this? A white light! I wonder what Eliot was thinking when he wrote this passage, and whether he saw anything like what we saw, two summers ago - that white glow from the downstairs (now your bedroom!) window. But doesn't it seem to be exactly what we've been wondering about? Doesn't it! "Both a new world and the old made explicit." The Past and the Present! Isn't this what we are trying to comprehend! The light, the woman by the wardrobe;*

*aren't they aspects from the 'old world' brought into our present new world? And yes, Eliot seems to be describing our feelings exactly; both how we are trying to resolve a possible horror, and how we are at times ecstatic about doing it!*

As she typed this, she felt incredulous. How did Eliot know? He seemed to be describing their unique experience. And who put that excerpt from his poem in the grandfather clock, and why? Her heart beat with excitement. She couldn't wait to hear back from Lance, to see how he interpreted this.

She reread the poem. It was so long and complex; it would take several readings to fully comprehend it, and even then maybe each time, on a different level and in a different way. And now she saw a passage about how love is timeless, causing and ending all movement, and it made her think again, with heightened emotion, of the way she and Lance had kissed the last night she saw him in hospital at St. Vincent's. There had, of course, been many kisses before, and especially since, but there was something about that particular kiss that did indeed feel timeless.

Her eye ran over more of the poem again, and she stopped at:

*"Footfalls echo in the memory*
*Down the passage which we did not take*
*Towards the door we never opened*
*Into the rose-garden."*

No! she thought. We must never let our love slip away. We must never avoid unlocking the door to our rose garden. How she loved Lance, and wanted to be united with him always. After all, wasn't it the case that when she suggested that perhaps they had always known each other, he'd said "And always will"? She tried to run the conversation back through her mind. Yes, he had said that! Oh lovely, wonderful Lance! She stood up and walked away from the computer; first to the window where she glanced contentedly down on the busy, narrow street far below, and then to the bathroom. She caught sight of her face in the mirror. Love had transformed

her. She noticed now the peachy glow of her cheeks, the brightness of her
eyes, the energetic radiance as an aura surrounding her.

The phone rang, startling her. Perhaps it would be Lance, responding
in excitement to her e-mail. Too much to say to type into a reply e-mail.
Fingers would not work fast enough. Better to talk.

"Florence?" A man's voice, but not Lance.

"Yes?"

"Don't tell me you've forgotten me so quickly. It's Howard!"

"Howard! Gosh! How are you?"

"I've been doing a lot of thinking, Flo. I know this divorce is dragging
out, and is still not over yet, despite earlier predictions. But I still want us
to be friends."

"Howard, I don't know if we should even be speaking to each other!"

"That's nonsense, Flo, and you know it! Of course we can speak! And
we can be friends again, too. We've known each other for years. In fact, I'm
phoning to see if you'd like to meet me for a drink this evening."

"No, Howard. I couldn't possibly."

"Why? Aren't you free then? We can make it another evening, if you
prefer."

"It's not that. I-"

"Flo, listen; I've got something to give you that I think you'd particularly
want back."

"What are you talking about?"

"You'll see, if you meet me."

"Howard, this is ridiculous! Tell me now!"

"OK. It's that set of photos that I 'confiscated.' I'm prepared to give it
back to you, as a gesture of my friendship."

"Oh."

"So you will meet me, then! Shall we say in an hour's time, at 7.00, at
that wine bar you've always liked, at the corner of-"

"All right! I'll see you then."

"Good girl!"

She didn't have much time to think about it. It wasn't right to see
Howard; they were adversaries. But she desperately wanted those photos
back. She wanted to show them to Lance, and see them together in the

countryside, see him walking normally, unassisted. She was still wondering whether this was a vision of their future or scenes from their past. Together they'd look at them and determine that.

She got ready quickly, deciding that she would receive the photos, have a quick drink to be polite, and then leave promptly. No harm in that.

Howard had arrived at the bar before her, and was seated at a table. He had lost some weight, and she had to begrudgingly admit to herself that he looked quite nice. He stood up when he saw her arrive, and kissed her cheek.

"Wow, Flo! You look terrific!" He could detect, she was sure, her glow of love. Everyone could. The radiance of her love could not be contained.

He bought her a drink.

"So how are you?" he asked.

"I'm fine. And you?"

"Still working for Elizabeth Carlisle?"

"Yes." She did not intend to tell him how he had nearly cost her her entire job, and how she had managed to hang on as a freelancer.

"Come on, Flo! Relax! I'm not going to bite. You don't need to speak to me in monosyllables!"

She smiled quickly.

"Still in touch with that chap you met in the Lake District? The one who went to New York?"

"Yes, though he's back in England now." She immediately wished she had not volunteered that information.

"How nice! All recovered from his broken leg, I take it?"

"No, he's not completely recovered yet. His injuries were more extensive. He's been in a wheelchair for ages, but he's trying to learn to walk again."

"Nasty! Very nasty! We're none of us safe anymore. London might be the next place to be hit, because of our alliance with the U.S. Of course, we're made of tough mettle here, and we're used to terrorism, what with the IRA, but still…So, he's back in East Anglia, is he?"

"No, he moved. But enough of that! What about you? How are you doing?"

"Still seeing him, are you?"

"Look, Howard," she said, finishing her drink, "I really have to go. Thanks for the drink. If you could please give me the photos, then I'd best be on my way."

"Flo, we've hardly seen each other yet. Come on! I've got so much to tell you. You asked how I was doing. Have you eaten yet? Let's order a curry! Remember they're quite good here?"

"Honestly, I don't think so."

"Waiter! Two curries! And some more white wine? Yes! Two more glasses of white wine!" As soon as the waiter had left, he said to her, "Remember they're very quick here. It'll actually save you time to eat here rather than to go home and start cooking. I promise we'll be out of here by 8.15!"

She sighed. "Howard, we're adversaries! Your lawyer has been sending my lawyer-"

"Yes, I'm aware of that correspondence. But don't you think the whole thing could be simplified if we're friends again? I'm not angry with you anymore. See! Here comes the curry! That's nice and quick!" he added to the waiter.

They started to eat.

"Mmmm; delicious!" He still ate in that greedy way. "I've been on the Atkins diet, Flo," he told her. "I've lost almost a stone!"

"I can tell," she said politely. "You look good."

"Thanks! Now that's better! That's the first kind thing you've said to me. Now you're back to yourself again!"

They ate in silence for a few minutes.

"Flo," he said, after deliberately shoveling the rice off to the side of his plate. "Did you know I moved?"

"No! Where did you move to?"

"I didn't want to stay in our old flat. Too many memories of times together with you. So I found a great new place in Camden Town. It's actually not far from Camden Lock, so it's very nice."

"That's good. I hope you enjoy it there."

"You're getting nicer and nicer! Thank you! Yes, my new pad is really very attractive; skylights, stark white walls, high ceilings, ultra-modern. In fact, that whole place is on a couple of levels."

Florence thought of her own cramped, but charming little flat, on the fourth floor of a terrace of old, Edwardian houses.

"It's a good place for parties!" he continued. "Actually, that's how I met Stephanie."

"Stephanie?"

"Yes. She lives in the building. She's an architect. We've been going out a bit. She's independently wealthy. Inherited, of course! You don't get rich from architecture!"

Florence felt relieved that Howard had a girlfriend.

"I'm pleased for you," she said simply.

"Are you?"

"Yes, of course I am. Now, I think we'd better ask for the bill."

"OK, OK! Look, it's not even 8.15 yet! Even faster than I thought!"

The waiter brought them the bill. Howard insisted on paying.

"Thank you, that's kind!" Florence said, standing up. "I must be going now. If you could please give me those photos, that would be great."

"Yes, it was fun seeing you again," Howard said. He opened his briefcase, and started rummaging through the contents. "Now, where is that film envelope?" he muttered. "That's odd," he said, finally. "It doesn't seem to be here." He clicked shut the lid of his briefcase and patted his pockets, looking for the bulge of the photos in there. "How silly of me! I could have sworn I brought them with me. I'm afraid I don't seem to have them."

Florence felt profoundly disappointed. She waited patiently while he continued fruitlessly searching.

"Oh well," she said. "Perhaps I can drop into your office one day and pick them up."

"Well no, that would never do!" Howard replied.

"Why?"

"Well, what with the new security in the building, it would be next to impossible to get in. And then we're working on a new project at the moment that involves quite a bit of travel. I haven't told you yet about that project, but it's great! It's-"

"Howard, I'd love to hear about your work, but not now, I'm afraid. Let's arrange when I can get the photos from you, and then I have to go."

"I know!" Howard said, his face enthusiastic. "Come to my new flat with me now! It's not far from here. Only a few stops on the tube. That way I could show you my flat, which I'd love to do as I'm sure you'll be impressed, and I can also give you the photos."

"I don't know."

"Come on! It won't take long! And you want those photos back, don't you, and there doesn't seem to be any other opportunity any time soon."

"But, Howard-"

"Oh, come on! If those photos mean so much, you'd better come now and get them, before I change my mind!"

And so, twenty minutes later, they were entering Howard's new flat. It was indeed hugely attractive and vastly spacious. The furniture with which Florence was so familiar, took on a completely different look in its new environment. Howard turned on some spotlights, and dimmed them so they shone softly.

"Sit down!" he said. "I'll get you a drink. What would you like?"

"Nothing for me, thank you."

"Come on; keep me company!"

"Well then, just a cranberry juice, please."

He gave her one, and poured some whiskey for himself.

She sat in the armchair, and he splayed himself out comfortably on the sofa.

"So how do you like it here?" he asked.

"It's very nice."

"Why are you sitting so stiffly in the armchair? If you come and sit next to me, you'll see there is a great view through the skylight up there."

"I'm comfortable here, thanks." She finished her cranberry juice and stood up. "Thanks, Howard. But now I'm definitely going home, if you could please give me the photos."

"A minute, a minute," Howard said, also standing and pouring himself some more whiskey. "I can't think where I put them. You'll have to help me find them!"

"But Howard!"

He started pulling open drawers of the wall unit. "Not in there!" he remarked. "Let's try the kitchen."

So they went into the kitchen, and Florence stood there as Howard looked through a neatly stacked pile of papers, and then started opening cupboards and drawers.

"I know!" he said, grabbing hold of her hand, and pulling her back into the living room. She struggled to free her hand, but his grip was tight.

"Relax, Flo!" he said, walking in a mock stealthy way over to the bottle of whiskey and refilling his glass. "We're just holding hands. It's all right to hold hands with a pretty woman. There's no law against it. Besides, I've just remembered where the photos are! They're in the bedroom! Come on!"

Still with the iron grip of his hand crushing hers, he pulled her down the stairs and into his bedroom on the floor below. He pushed her roughly on to the bed.

"No!" she screamed, trying to rise. He came down on top of her, his wet mouth seeking hers. She managed to wriggle free and ran back up the stairs to the front door, but he was too quick for her, and turning a key in the lock, he rapidly put it in his pocket. Florence was petrified. He pushed her down on to the living room sofa, saying, "Hah! I've got you now!"

"Howard, stop it!" she yelled. "This won't help the divorce at all. Let me go now, and we'll say nothing about this."

"Never!" he bellowed, his weight bearing down on her. "You haven't got a leg to stand on. You came to my flat willingly. There's nothing you can do."

And again his salivating mouth sought hers.

"Howard, please! Please!" she shrieked, rapidly turning her head from side to side to avoid his lips.

"No!" he said, savagely ripping open her blouse and feeling for her breasts. "I've no intention of letting you go, Flo. You promised me babies, remember! You promised me lots of babies." He roughly pushed his other hand under her skirt and pulled aside her panties. She tightly clenched her legs together.

"But you filed for divorce!" Florence panted, squirming to free herself from him.

"Well then, I'll drop it. I'll tell my lawyer in the morning. We're still married now, my little Flo, and I have every right to have you pleasure me." Quickly he unzipped his trousers, and kicked them off, along with his briefs. His penis was spluttering little drips of liquid.

"No!" Florence screamed. "Stop it! You know we're in the midst of a divorce!"

"Need I repeat, my little one, that you came willingly to my home?"

"You tricked me! You tricked me into coming here. Now let me go! I don't care anymore about the photos. Keep them! Just let me go!"

"No, I won't! What is it, Flo?" he said, jabbing his hand into her vagina. "You prefer your limping lover to me? Is that it? Tell me, is he as impotent sexually as he is physically? Ah, my heart bleeds for the poor, wounded man!"

"Shut up!"

"I bet he doesn't have my sexual prowess. Probably never did, even when he was an able-bodied man. But of course, you wouldn't know about that, now would you?" he sneered sarcastically, jabbing again at her vagina.

He tried to spread apart her legs. What happened next surprised them both. Florence vomited. Howard jumped aside.

"Now that wasn't nice," he said. "Go quickly to the bathroom and clean yourself up. And be quick, because then you'll have to clean my sofa, too."

Trembling, Florence grabbed her handbag and went to the bathroom. She intended using her mobile phone to call the police, or Anna, or whoever would help her now. But agony and irony! She had forgotten to recharge the battery, and it was completely flat.

She took off her twisted and stained blouse, and washed the soiled area under cold water. Then she removed the rest of her clothes and stepped into the shower. She noticed an ugly bruise developing upon her breast and scratches around the triangle of her pubic hair where he had clawed her. She let the water run for a long time over her bruised and battered body. It stung at first, but the longer she let the water fall on her, the better she felt. She thought of the crystal clear water of the waterfall that Lance had taken her to last weekend, and she closed her eyes and tried to imagine herself with him there now. In her mind, she constructed that he was beside her on the rock, and then she had stood, shed her clothes, and was standing under the waterfall itself. Then, dripping beads of shimmering water, she had come back to him, helped him undress, and together they stood in the cool, refreshing splash of the waterfall.

Howard's rough hammering on the door interrupted these healing thoughts, and she was unable to return to them. She took the soap and rigorously scrubbed her body and soaped her hair.

"God damn you, Flo! Come and clean the sofa!" she heard him shout over the running water. She ignored him and lathered herself all over again. It was only when her fingertips started to crinkle from immersion in water for such a long time, that she stepped out of the shower, dried herself and dressed. Her blouse was still wet, and smelled vaguely of vomit, but she put it on anyway.

"Come out now, Flo!" Howard yelled, again hammering on the door. "I need a pee!"

She sat on the toilet lid and put her hands over her ears. She sat there for a very long time. She wished there was a window in the bathroom, not to climb out of – she knew they were too high up – but to open and provide fresh air. She felt horribly claustrophobic in that small bathroom. How long would the oxygen last? But it was preferable to be in there, even if the oxygen level was becoming depleted, than to go back out to Howard.

Gradually his banging on the door ceased, and his yelling stopped, too. Still she continued to wait. She couldn't stand it, but she forced herself to stay still longer. Her watch said it was 2.20 am. She bargained with herself to wait until 2.45. She almost made it.

With heart thumping extraordinarily, she quietly opened the door and tiptoed out. The lights were still on in the living room. She could see the back of Howard's head as he sat motionless in the armchair, the bottle of whiskey at his elbow. She had prepared a speech to make to him, something about how they should move on with their lives, how she wished him luck with Stephanie (was that the name?), and how she would not tell anyone about what happened this evening if he would be reasonable and let her go now.

In her terror, she forgot every word of what she was going to say to him. But as it happened, she did not need to. He appeared to be asleep. Now all she needed was to see if the key was still in his trousers' pocket – he had put his trousers back on again – and if so, she would have to take it out with exceptional care not to wake him.

She crept towards him, noticing the large, cranberry colored stain of her dried pool of vomit on the sofa opposite him. Even though Howard had lost some weight, he still filled the armchair fairly amply, so she could see no way to reach inside his trousers' pocket without disturbing him. But she simply had to do it. There was no option. Before making a move, she thought carefully as to what pocket he had used. No sense in increasing her chances of waking him by searching in the wrong pocket. She tried to visualize the scene, but it was hopeless. It had happened so fast, his springing up behind her and swiftly locking the door and removing the key. Logically, since he was left handed, he probably put the key in his left pocket. She'd try there, and have to hope she was right.

Extremely nervously, she slipped her hand down his left side. At first she couldn't even feel the entrance to his pocket. He groaned slightly, and shifted his weight. She was terrified and sprang back. After a minute, she tried again, more deliberately this time, despite her rapidly beating heart. She felt as though she were in a film. This had no reality at all.

She felt the entrance to the pocket and tried to move her hand inside. It was hard as he was wedged up against the armrest. Also, she did not want to apply any pressure that might wake him. Then her fingertip felt metal! Continued little tentative pokes just elongated the process and were more likely to wake him. She needed to be quick and deliberate. She dug down, took the key between two fingers, and pulled it out! He groaned again, briefly opened his eyes, said her name, and was then back to sleep again, his head against the wing of the headrest.

She noiselessly made for the door, inserted the key, turned it, opened the door, and she was out! She ran down the corridor – no time to wait for the lift – and down the stairs. She let herself out of the building, and kept running, even though she felt sore, and her wet, ripped blouse flapped in the cool night air. She wasn't sure which direction she was going in as she hardly knew the area, and she suspected that it was still too early for buses and tubes to be operating yet.

When she was too breathless to run any further, she stopped and practically doubled over. The sordid repetition of history, of the way this incident mirrored that with Renard many years ago, only that first time he had actually penetrated her with his penis whereas Howard had attempted to…The thought made her vomit again, though she had little left. Mostly it was dry heaves. What was the matter with her? Why did this keep happening to her? Was she to blame? Too trusting? Too naïve?

She leaned weakly against a wall. When she felt a little stronger she started walking. She couldn't run anymore, and besides she was now thankfully sufficiently far from Howard's flat that even if he came looking for her, he'd be unlikely to find her. She looked around. There were a lot of shadowy doorways and alleyways. She knew she must find a main street…

Just as she was about to become panicked, she saw the glowing yellow lights from the interior of a double-decker bus swing around a bend, coming towards her. She didn't know where the bus stop was, but stepping out into the road itself, she held out her arm, requesting the bus to halt. To her surprise, it did, and she leaped on, not even having read where this bus was heading.

"Shouldn't stand in the road like that, miss," the bus driver told her. "Could've got yourself killed."

At this point, she almost didn't care. She was desperately tired, cold, and her body ached and felt filthy. The bus went to Victoria Station, where she knew she'd have a long wait for a connecting bus at this hour. When she finally arrived home, it was close to 6.00 in the morning. She took off her blouse and threw it in the peddle-bin; the rest of her clothes she put in the laundry basket, promising herself she'd go to the launderette as soon as she could. Then, as though the water and soap in Howard's shower, and his towel too, had polluted her, she had another long shower before stumbling into bed.

She didn't know how long she'd been asleep before the sound of a ringing phone penetrated her dream. At first she mistook the sound for her alarm clock, and was going to reach out to turn it off, and then she realized that someone was calling her. She picked up the phone.

"Hello?" she muttered thickly.

"Fleur! Fleur, it's Lance! Are you all right? I tried phoning you so many times last night. I wanted to thank you for sending me the whole of Eliot's poem. It's amazing! I want to talk to you about it!"

"What time is it?"

"I don't know. About 9.00-ish, I think. Fleur, you don't sound yourself. Are you OK? Did I wake you up?"

She was more awake now. "Lance, oh Lance. Last night-"

And she told him what happened.

"Fleur, the bastard tried to rape you! For God's sake, he tried to rape you!" He was almost shouting. "Listen, I know you're tired and haven't had much sleep, but you must go and see a doctor. Promise me you'll do that."

"Oh, it's OK, Lance. I'll feel better when I've had some more sleep."

"No! You must make an appointment to see a doctor today. This morning! It's extremely important that you do that! We have to make sure he hasn't hurt you in any way, the filthy louse! Now I understand why you've been afraid of him. He's a dangerous man!"

"Lance, I think I'm fine. You don't need to worry."

"I sincerely hope you are fine, Fleur. But you need to be checked. This is not something to be trivialized. That's one thing I'm getting to know about you; you're so wonderfully kind and attentive to others, but you often seem to ignore yourself. You ignore your own needs. If this had happened to someone else, you'd be the first one to take her to the doctor. Now, all I'm asking is that you are equally kind to yourself."

She paused.

"God, I wish I were with you now!" he exclaimed, giving the sort of cry that speaks of extreme frustration, and which is normally accompanied by kicking a table with a steel-toed shoe.

And then she remembered. "But you *were* with me. Last night, I mean. When I stood for ages under Howard's shower, and the water was splashing and splashing down on me, I imagined so deeply – so deeply that it felt real – that I was with you, and we were both standing together under that waterfall that you took me to last weekend. We had taken our clothes off, and we stood under the cool flow of water, with the sunlight sparkling on it, bending a prism of light into a rainbow."

Lance was quiet. She thought she heard him sigh.

"That's lovely, Fleur," he said at last.

"Yes." She felt so moved by his tone of voice.

"I can't bear the thought that you were violated. That you were hurt.

Please see the doctor to remedy that. And besides," he added, "You'll definitely need this to come to light in your divorce proceedings. In fact, you absolutely should call your lawyer and let her know what happened, too. Fleur, my sweet, I know you are in desperate need of sleep, but you must do these things first. Promise me you will. And please phone me after your appointments, and let me know what happened."

Later that afternoon Florence reported to Lance that she was fine. Her scratches and bruises were superficial and just needed some antibiotic ointment and a healing balm. There was some inflammation around the vagina, but this was not serious. The doctor had suggested some pills to calm her after this trauma, and had also given her the name of someone to go to for counseling, but she had declined both. As for her lawyer, she was not there, but, she told Lance, she had sent her an e-mail describing the event.

"Well, if you're really fine, then I'm relieved," Lance said. "Are you sure you don't want the counseling."

"Yes, quite sure."

"Fleur, tomorrow's Thursday. Do you want to come up here then? I know it's one day earlier than usual, but would you like that?"

"Yes!"

"And Fleur, listen; it's summer time and you've had no holiday. Would you like to stay here until the end of the weekend after this?"

"Yes, I'd love to."

"You don't have any immediate deadlines on any stories, do you?"

"No."

"Good! And even if you did, now's not the best time for you to be working. You need to replenish yourself after what you've been through. And by the way, if you're too tired to drive, why don't you take the train? Mei-Feng can pick you up at the railway station at Penrith."

"It's fine, really. I'll drive."

"If you're sure. And Fleur, I'll take you out for dinner tomorrow night. It's been a very long time since we've done that."

The following evening, sitting in the very lovely, rustic dining room of the Ouse Bridge Hotel, Florence felt so happy. Something that she'd thought could not happen – that Lance and not Mei-Feng, would be at the front door to welcome her when she arrived – actually did happen. In fact, he'd opened the door so quickly that he must have been seated on the wooden bench in the hall, anticipating her arrival. And when he opened the door, his smile for her was so exquisite, sincere, gentle. So full of kindness.

And now, sitting at a table overlooking grassy lawns descending to the water, and with Lance treating her so tenderly, not mentioning the ugly events she had been a part of, she felt so privileged. Nothing should be taken for granted. They had not been out to a restaurant together since her visit to him in New York two Aprils ago. It was only later that evening, when Florence climbed into bed alongside Lance, and he saw her bruised breast, turning now the gray-yellow color the sky becomes when a hurricane is approaching, that he cried out. He insisted on exploring the rest of her body, wincing when he saw the scratches and sores on her stomach and the top of her legs.

"What a fucking bastard!" he said again of Howard. "Look how much he hurt you."

"Lance, it's fine. Really, it's nothing much." She glanced down at his legs, so much more profoundly and permanently injured than she had been. Even though his right leg was visibly strengthening, and the scars on each leg were much less vivid than before, his left leg remained scarcely more than a pitiful stick.

He saw her glance, and said, "Fleur, just because something traumatic happened to me, it doesn't mean that any new upsetting situations which unfortunately will continue to arise, are any less valid. Upsetting things happen, and will continue to do so, just as happy events happen, too. We need to face each situation honestly, and experience the accompanying emotions rather than denying them."

"It's true. But really you're making more of this than-"

"No! I'm not! Look; this man tried to rape you; he hurt you; he held you captive; he scared you! Who knows what else he might have done to you if you had not managed to escape? And what about this scar on your upper lip that he's responsible for? Another incident when he was enraged, and at these times, it seems, he turns to excessive drinking and violence."

"But I had upset him."

"So what? There were plenty of other things he could have done with his anger. You must realize you didn't deserve any of this."

He tossed back the hair from his forehead. "I'll be interested to see what your lawyer says," he added.

"I didn't want this divorce to be contentious. I just wanted to get it over and done with as quickly as possible."

"But it *is* contentious. You can't ignore what's been happening. And it doesn't seem likely that this will slow it down any more than it is already slowed down. I thought the initial projection was that it was meant to be over by March or April. What happened to that? It looks no closer to finalization now than it did then."

"I think Howard has been dragging his feet, though why I don't know. It's hard to account for his motives."

Lance took her hand that was lying loosely on the sheet, put it to his lips and kissed it. "Fleur, you are an inspirational thinker and you discuss abstract and philosophical ideas with amazing elegance. But – and please excuse me for saying this – when it comes to practical matters concerning yourself – not others, mind you, but yourself – you can at times be remarkably naïve. You're like a little girl; wide eyed and with a clear complexion, and that's one of the things that I find the most appealing about you, as I think I've told you before. You've never become jaded by unfortunate events. But at the same time, this wide-eyed innocence, this trust you put in everything, this lack of *savoir faire*, can make you vulnerable. You expect everyone to be as nice and kind as you are, but I'm afraid that's far from true. You say you don't understand Howard's motives, but let's examine his behavior the other evening."

"Must we?"

"Yes, I'm afraid so. I really think we should. Look; he told you he'd give you back the photos he stole, but that was just a carrot. He knew you'd want them back, so this was his way of tempting you to see him, which you otherwise would not have agreed to. But think about it. Why would he give you back these photos? If he really wanted to go ahead with the divorce, this is an important piece of evidence about your infidelity to him."

"But Lance, he mentioned something about wanting us to remain married, so perhaps-"

"No! That would not make him want to return those photos. He'd hardly want to give you photos of you joyfully together with another man, now would he?"

"True. So why did he want to see me?"

"For information. And possibly, though this is conjecture, he's missing you and feels lonely. I doubt there really is a Stephanie, and even if there is, I'm fairly certain she doesn't match up to you. That could explain why he's been dragging his feet. He's now reluctant to let you go, or at the very least, is conflicted about it."

"He did say he wanted us to be friends."

"There you are, then. Incidentally, did he ask anything about me?"

"Yes, he did. And that was where I was such a fool. He'd been under the impression that you were still in New York, but I told him you'd returned to England. It just slipped out. I'm sorry. I should never have volunteered that information."

"Well, armed with that bit of knowledge, it probably increased his sense of urgency."

"Yes. He started saying absurd things, such as how I'd promised to give him babies. But I hadn't."

"He's a treacherous man, Fleur," he said. He rolled over and stared up at the ceiling. "In many ways, I can't help blaming myself for what happened to you."

"Why? You had nothing to do with this."

"Why? Because, for the last nine months, I've been so self-absorbed. You've been going through some pretty terrible stuff, too, with this divorce, and I hadn't even asked you about it. I'm afraid my behavior completely contradicted what I'd just said about other unfortunate or difficult things being valid, too. That, and the fact that you don't complain or even acknowledge difficulties that you're experiencing. But it was up to me! I knew you've been going through this, but I ignored it!" He turned back to her, his eyes full of sorrow. "I deeply regret that, Fleur!"

"No, Lance! You can't blame yourself. I hadn't wanted to talk about it. In fact, up until now, there was nothing to talk about. Just some boring, pompous letters written in hard-to-decipher legalese, from his lawyer to my lawyer, and vice versa, with copies forwarded to me."

"But you need to understand what's going on. Give the letters to me, if you're comfortable doing so, and from now on, I'll do my best to help you with this. My thinking now is that you might need some protection from him such as a restraining order, or some such thing."

"Thank you. I'd be grateful if you look at the legal correspondence. But Lance, please know that I don't think you've been self-absorbed at all. You experienced an unspeakable trauma, which you're still sadly affected by, and I'm sure it's perfectly normal for anyone, having suffered as you have done, to be preoccupied with the events. But even given that, you've been wonderfully sweet and kind to me throughout."

"Fleur, if I've been sweet and kind at all — and thank you for telling me this - it's all in response to you for coming up to see me, and being the loving person you are. And now," he said, taking her gently in his arms and caressing her hair, "let's sleep. Let's sleep in each other's arms."

The next few days were peaceful and serene. Florence overcame the jittery feelings that had been with her since her encounter with Howard, and Lance was even more attentive to her than usual. Each night and early morning he rubbed the antibiotic ointment into her scratches and abrasions with such a soothing touch that she felt she would have been healed even without the ointment. And he was making amazing progress with relearning to walk, and now no longer used the wheelchair in the house, but could move slowly between the downstairs rooms with the aid of the crutches and leg brace. A few times she even helped him slowly climb the stairs so that he could remind himself what the upstairs part of his house looked like and become familiar with it again.

Each day the weather was clear and sunny, and they went out in the car to different areas that Lance knew, and had very short walks. They did not speak again of Howard; neither did they speak of the Eliot poem, or the woman-by-the-wardrobe, or the strange photos. They just focused on the present, and how truly lovely it was to be together over an extended time.

One day, after having walked up a small incline, which Lance rather laboriously managed to do, he sat on a tree trunk that had tipped over at an angle, as its branches were intertwined with those from another tree, and was quiet for a long time. This was a quietness that felt different, that

327

somehow commanded respect, as he inhaled deeply and softly, and looked almost as if in a trance. Disconcerted at last by the continued silence, Florence started fidgeting and wanted to speak, and so eventually she quietly said, "Lance, are you all right? You have such a far away expression on your face."

"No, not far away at all. Just the opposite. I'm absolutely here. In minute detail."

"What do you mean?"

"Fleur, just being out here is so tranquil. I feel I am one with my immediate surroundings; that there is no separation between me and the environment. I'm not an outsider, but am gazing from within. It feels almost like a spiritual sensation. Do you see what I'm saying?"

"No, but I wish I did."

"Most people, myself included before my injuries, just rush along without really noticing anything. Just hurrying on to the next event, their minds on somewhere else. But look at this glorious spectacle that nature offers us every night and every day! Look at the breathtaking beauty of simple things, like the pattern of the bark on the trees; the delicate intricately woven system of veins on the leaves; the little tangle of tiny pure white flowers over there, a drop of moisture hovering on the petal; the reflection of the light on the water which in turn is shimmering on the branches of the nearby trees; the clouds tinged with the glow of the sun. And listen, Fleur; the air is full of sound if we are receptive to it. Did you hear that bird calling with such a sweet, clear high voice? Or the occasional insect buzzing? Or the leaves rustling in the little puffs of the breeze? Why, even the air itself is so full of sweet, fragrant freshness that I want to drink it in."

"That's exquisite, Lance. You're teaching me how to really perceive this beauty around us in detail."

"I had never appreciated it myself before, not truly, even though I'd always loved the Lake District. But now I have a slowed-down life, I have more of an opportunity to observe the details, rather than running past them as I had in former days. And when I perceive how profoundly marvelous nature is, it makes me feel soothed and also uplifted. The killing, the maiming, the *raping* - the ugly, pointless, unfathomable stuff that people do to others - loosens its grip when I'm out here."

When they returned home, Florence cooked as she did every evening, and Lance, now always ravenous, ate with such appreciation. In this way, they really fed each other and mutually benefited and felt replenished.

And then on the fourth or fifth night of her visit, Florence dreamed vividly that she needed to run from Howard who was close behind her, and shouting wildly and waving his fists. They were running along dark streets, illuminated only occasionally by a ball of light from a lamppost. A flight of steps lay ahead of her, and she started to mount them as quickly as possible, even though she was breathless. But at the top, they seemed to turn and she started to descend onto another plane, only to find herself climbing up them instead. It was like being in a giant Escher canvas. In her confusion, she ran madly up and down flights of stairs, yet knew all the while that Howard was gaining on her.

She heard his heavy panting, but then she heard something else, too – like a growl - that made her briefly turn around in her flight. And then she saw that it wasn't Howard, but a mad dog bounding towards her. The dog was salivating and snarling, and growling ferociously, and she knew she didn't stand a chance. Desperately, she fled up the next flight of shadowy stairs. Bam! She bumped into the wall at the turn of the stairs, and woke up.

But even when awake, she could still hear a dog snarling and barking. Was she still dreaming? And then she remembered. Wasn't this the same sound as she'd heard the very first night she'd visited Lance, and was cringing in fear up in the guest room? She turned over, opened her eyes, and looked at Lance. In the dim light of the night light, she could see that he was deeply asleep, one arm flung over his face. He didn't appear to have been disturbed by the dog, even though it sounded as if it was so close by.

And that is when she saw the woman! The 'woman-by-the-wardrobe.' Florence was petrified. Half sitting up in bed, holding up the duvet to cover all but her eyes, she noticed that this woman was gripping onto a leash, at the end of which was the dog that Florence could hear. The dog, which she immediately recognized as a pit bull with its square, ugly face, was tugging at the leash and frothing at the mouth in its agitation.

"Lance!" she whispered, nudging him.

"Mmm?"

"Lance!" she whispered again, more urgently this time. "Wake up!"

He opened his eyes, groped for his glasses and put them on, and was immediately alert.

"Fleur! The woman! You can see her, too! You can see her, Fleur!" he whispered excitedly.

"Yes, yes, I can. But you'd never mentioned a dog."

"I've seen the dog a few times, but never heard it before. It sounds quite fierce, doesn't it!"

"Yes, that's what woke me. I'd heard it the very first time I stayed with you, too, but assumed it was a dog outside somewhere."

"The woman's wearing a blue plastic raincoat. I've only ever seen her in green trousers and a pink top before."

"Lance, what's happening?"

"I'm not sure. I'm so glad you woke me! And that you can see her, too! But she seems to be dressed to go out. Let's quickly get dressed too, so if she goes out, we can follow her!"

"No, Lance! I don't think we should do that. And besides, that dog-"

"That dog can't hurt us. I think that dog lived many years ago. Quick. Pass me my trousers."

She gave him his clothes, and was impressed with how quickly he slipped them on. It reminded her of when she was with him on Cornelia Street. She, however, was more reluctant about putting on her own clothes.

"Come on, Fleur! Let's be ready quickly! This could lead us to some amazing discoveries."

She remembered her promise to him. To herself, really. But this was frightening. She needed time to digest the fact that she was seeing a woman and her dog from a different time.

"Quick, Fleur!" Lance urged, his voice rising a little above a whisper now. "Please hand me my leg brace and crutches. Listen to her! She's mumbling something. I think she's going to be leaving any minute!"

The woman was indeed speaking. She seemed as agitated as her dog. They could make out that she was saying, "Kitty! Kitty! Where the devil is that girl?" And then, in a sudden act that terrified Florence and Lance, she took a flashlight from her pocket and turned it on, shining it for a moment in their direction.

"Who's there?" she asked, beaming the light in their direction, but then swiveling the light past them in a jagged fashion along the upper part of the wall and then out of the window. "Is someone there? Oh never mind! Come on, Eloise; we've got to find Kitty!" she said to the dog.

"The white light!" Florence gasped.

"Yes!"

"The white light we saw from the darkened window when we first snooped around this house-"

"Very probably!"

"My God! And it was from the window of this room when it used to be the dining room! Oh Lance; that explains it! The flashlight created the white light!"

"Yes; Fleur this is incredible! Maybe we'll understand all sorts of other things too, if we follow after her and the dog."

"But do you think she saw us?"

"I don't think so. She seems very distracted and intent on finding someone called Kitty. Hey, quick Fleur! She's walking towards the door!"

As best as he could, Lance jumped to his feet, quickly positioning the crutches under each arm and starting to move more swiftly than she thought him capable of. "Quick! Let's follow her. We mustn't let her out of our sight!"

All along, the woman was muttering about where Kitty was, and how dare she stay out after dark when she knew it wasn't permitted.

"Come on, Eloise!" she said, tugging at the dog's leash. "And do be quiet!"

Then she and the dog vanished.

Florence and Lance quickly opened the bedroom door, and briefly saw the woman and dog in the hall before they vanished again.

"Quick! Open the front door, Fleur! They must have gone outside!"

Florence opened the door. The black sky was spangled with more stars than she thought possible, and a high moon cast a silvery light around them. Once their eyes adjusted, they could pick out certain things; the old elm tree in the front garden, and their two cars. And then they saw the darting white point of light from the flashlight that the woman held, and they followed in that direction. Instead of walking up the driveway, the woman turned up what presumably might once have been a little side path, but it was now overgrown with bushes and weeds.

"I remember now," Lance panted. "This is a shortcut that takes us higher up the lane."

Luckily the woman was walking fairly slowly, allowing the dog, which was quiet now, to stop and sniff in many places. Florence and Lance could keep pace and were following close behind, the moisture on the leaves of the bushes from an earlier rain shower, dampening their clothes as they brushed past them.

Soon they were out on the lane, higher along it as Lance had said, which meant that they were closer to the intersection with the road that led to the village.

"Let's see which way she chooses to go," Lance said.

But now the dog started pulling the woman more powerfully, and she picked up speed.

"Kitty!" she was calling. "Kitty!"

The dog pulled even more, and started snarling viciously again, and the woman walked in a highly sprightly fashion after her. Lance tried his best to keep up; crutches moving forward quickly at the same time as his good leg, but the other leg dragged behind so he couldn't move fast enough, try as he might.

The woman and the dog turned the corner in the opposite direction from the village, and the road started to slope steeply upwards. The distance between Florence and Lance, and the woman and her dog was widening.

"This damn leg!" Lance gasped, completely exasperated. "I can't keep up. Go after them, Fleur! See what happens!"

"But I can't leave you. We must go together."

"No! We'll lose them completely if you wait for me. You must go alone, Fleur. Hurry! I'll wait here for you."

Just at that point they saw the woman and her dog slip into a footpath off the road, and disappear from sight. Florence paused for a second, experiencing a kind of fear she had never felt before. Fear of going after this woman! Alone! And fear of leaving Lance, unsteady and unaccompanied, along a deserted, dark country road. But she quickly kissed him on the cheek, and sped towards the footpath.

She rushed down it. It was much darker along the footpath as it was like going through a tunnel of trees, and the light from the moon was largely shut out. She moved forward, stumbling a few times, and grazing her knee and the heel of her hand. Then she heard the dog again. It was like her dream, but in reverse. This time she was chasing the dog!

She caught up with them fairly quickly as the woman had stopped and seemed to be talking to someone. Florence could not see who it was, as the woman had the flashlight pointed downwards to the ground. The dog, though, seemed in a frenzy; it was pulling wildly and growling as ferociously as in the sounds that had penetrated her dream. With one sudden tug, the dog broke free. It rushed off along the footpath, and the woman, making rapid excuses to her companion, ran after it. Florence ran too, easily overtaking the woman. She saw the dog dash down into a ditch at the side of the path, briefly heard a man's startled voice saying, "Good grief!" before he rapidly left, and then saw, for an instant only, the bewildered yet imploring face of the young woman with the billowy hair who she recognized from the photo, watching the departing figure of the man.

In the next second the dog leaped at her, snarling, teeth sinking into her legs so that she collapsed, screaming, on to the ground. The dog gripped hold of her neck, plunging its teeth in and not letting go. Florence felt faint. She, too, sank to the ground on the bank above the ditch. And then she heard a tiny, electronic beep. It was only very occasional. She ignored it, as she was fixated with revulsion and absolute horror at the terrible scene in front of her. The dog was now tugging at the young woman's neck, shaking its head back and forth as dogs are inclined to do when playing with a toy. The young woman's shrieks had now turned to moans. The dog was pulling out something from her body in a long loop, and now appeared to be eating it.

Florence, still seated on the ground, put out her hands on either side to avoid collapsing. As she did so, her right hand touched something cold, hard and metallic. At the same time as touching it, she realized that this was also the source of those electronic beeps. She looked down. It was her camera! She was sure of it! There it was, on the ground, in exactly the location, she now assumed, that it had been in when she had tried to rid herself of it on a lonely, despondent walk that she'd had when she'd visited Landsdowne's Guest House two summers before!

Picking it up with shaking hands, not knowing what she was doing, she aimed the camera, and – flash! – with the last gasps of battery power apparently left, she took two photos of this appalling scene. Just as she was doing so, she was aware of the woman who had finally caught up with her dog, screaming "Kitty!" in a voice echoing with sadness and haunted by despair. But after the camera had flashed, Florence found herself sitting beside the ditch in total darkness, no sign of the mauled young woman, or the dog, or the other woman, any longer apparent.

Florence rose unsteadily to her feet, slung the camera over her shoulder, and trudged back along the footpath, and then down the steep descent of the road.

"Fleur! You've returned so quickly! Almost instantly. Splendid! So you decided to turn back, did you? In retrospect, I think that was the wisest decision."

She had not noticed Lance leaning against the dry-stone wall, along the edge of the road where she had left him. She was unable to speak.

"Fleur?" he said again. And then he noticed the glint of the camera lens. "You took your camera? I didn't know you had it with you. Very sensible."

Still she could say nothing.

"Wait! I think you did see something! What did you see, Fleur? Tell me!"

Florence felt that her face had become wooden. Only her eyes, huge and searching, seemed capable of movement.

"Fleur!" she heard him say again. "Are you OK? You seem shocked by something. Let's return home quickly!"

She plodded silently along at his side, one foot planted firmly after the other in an otherwise swirl of confusion. Once they were back in his house, she was aware that he was speaking to her again, but she couldn't quite make it out. They were in the kitchen, and it sounded, through the enormity of the fog and muddle, that he was suggesting that he'd make her some sweet tea. She felt intuitively that there was something wrong about him making tea, but she couldn't think this through. She was aware of him carefully removing the camera from her shoulder and placing it on the table. She heard the sound of water running, the lid of the kettle being clipped on, and later (A few minutes? An hour?) a cup and saucer being placed in front of her. Interestingly the saucer seemed to have as much of the tepid milky brownish liquid in it as did the cup. She lifted the cup to her lips and swallowed, wondering why her lap felt wet.

She vaguely sensed that Lance sat down, and was talking about the tea. That it was sweet. That was it. Then the tone of his voice seemed to change. Sounded more agitated. It caught her attention more, and she detected, through the mists of confusion, his jaw opening and closing more rapidly. But still she couldn't work up the energy or focus to respond.

"You were gone for virtually no time at all," he seemed to be saying. "I saw you run off to follow the woman and her dog. Then I adjusted the straps on my leg brace, and when I straightened up, you were back! There was no time for you to see anything that I didn't see, yet from the way you look, it seems that you *did* see something. Possibly something awful. Please, Fleur, tell me about it!"

Still nothing. She couldn't utter a word. She closed her heavy eyelids, but then opened them again when, as if from a great clouded distance, she heard him ask, "Are you angry with me? Is that it? Is that why you won't talk to me? I wouldn't blame you if you were. I should never have put you in such danger! I'm so sorry, Fleur."

Shadows moved, and she was aware that he was sitting close to her. Now hugging her. Now rocking her body backwards and forwards.

"Oh God. Fleur! Come back to me, Fleur! I don't care what happened. You don't need to tell me. It's not important. I don't care if we never crack what happened, or who the woman is, and why she's in my room. I don't care if we never crack the meaning of Time. What is important is that you are all right!"

She became aware that he was crying. Could feel his large, splashy tears wet her shoulders. His head buried against her neck. This alarmed her. But still she couldn't rouse herself.

"I shouldn't have made you go! I shouldn't have done that! I'm so sorry, Fleur. Talk to me! Oh please talk to me!"

Gradually the warm, sweet tea and the warmth of the physical contact from Lance's body, percolated through Florence, and her vision cleared. Slowly she lifted her arms, which had been stiffly at her side, and placed them around Lance's back. She felt his body hiccup into another sob.

"What is it, Lance?" she murmured. "What's the matter?"

"Fleur!" He lifted his head and looked at her. "Fleur! Thank God!"

"What's happened, Lance?"

"You…you seemed to have had a terrible shock. Your face was drained of all color and your lovely eyes were so vacuous. You've been incapable of talking, or responding to me at all. Oh Fleur, I was so worried about you. How do you feel now?"

"Me? I feel fine," she replied, rubbing her eye with a hand balled up into a fist.

"That's such a relief, my sweet Fleur! But what was it that you saw? Are you able to talk about it now? What happened after you followed the woman-by-the-wardrobe? What shocked you so much?"

"I…I don't recall," Florence said dreamily.

"Don't you? Try to think, Fleur. You do remember following the woman and her dog outside, don't you?"

"I'm not sure what you mean, Lance."

"The dog. It was snarling and growling. Remember?"

"Yes, I do remember that now. But I thought it was a dream. In the dream the dog was chasing me."

"But that woman! The one by my wardrobe! You woke me to tell me you saw her. Remember she was talking about someone called Kitty, and she seemed very annoyed?"

"Oh yes, I think I remember that. But it's so hard to capture dreams. The more you chase them, the more they escape."

"But that part wasn't a dream, Fleur! We both saw the woman and heard her speak! Oh, please tell me that you saw the woman, too! The woman by my wardrobe!"

"Yes, I do remember that now. She was in your room. But that dreadful dog-"

"Don't worry about the dog. But you saw the woman! That's so important to me. What else do you remember, Fleur?"

"Lance, I'm so tired. I can't be sure of anything," she said. But then her eyes caught sight of her camera on the table. "What's my camera doing here?" she asked, perplexed.

"I don't know! I asked *you* that. I thought you brought it along."

"No, no; I haven't used that camera since…since Rose and Allison used it at my wedding."

"You mean, you hadn't brought it here with you?"

"No, it's been in a drawer in my flat."

"Fleur, this is getting even stranger." He reached out and put his hand on her shoulder. "Please try to remember what happened."

"I'm trying, Lance. Really I am. But it's a bit like after we first met and had that discussion about Time. We couldn't piece it together afterwards."

"But you do remember that you and I followed the woman and her dog outside. That's why we're dressed now, even though it's 3.30 in the morning, and why our clothes are a bit wet as we brushed past wet bushes in the garden. The dog was called Eloise. Do you remember that?"

She nodded. "I think so."

"And they turned off the driveway and through that overgrown area with the wet bushes, which came out on the lane near the intersection with the road. Do you remember that?"

She nodded again.

"But they turned on the road away from the village, and up the steep hill. And I couldn't keep up, and so I told you to go on ahead alone. Do you remember that, too?"

"I'm not sure. I think so. But I don't know. I just have the feeling that something happened, something incredibly important, yet it's slipping away from me and I can't grasp onto it, as I said."

Just then the indicator of the low battery power in the camera started its series of beeps again.

"Lance! I remember that sound! That was the sound this camera made when I was staying at Landsdowne's Guest House, and went for that long walk and got lost. It helped me locate myself and find my way back. Do you remember me telling you that?"

"I most certainly do!"

"And it happened another time, too. Another time more recently. Yes! That's it! It happened tonight!"

"Tonight, Fleur? Tell me how."

"I'm not sure. I think I was sitting down on a bolder, and ferns were growing all around, and I reached out my hand and there it was! Yes! I do remember now. I remember thinking that incredibly it was in the same place as it had been when I found it, when I was at Landsdowne's. But it couldn't have been! That was two summers ago, and you and I have used it many times since then. And Allison was the last to use it."

"Fleur, this is remarkable! Truly remarkable. Did you take any photos tonight with it?"

"Yes, I think so. I think I took one or possibly two, and then there was insufficient battery power for more."

"Good! But you don't remember what the photos were of?"

"I'm afraid not."

"Well, we'll find out when the film is developed. Or maybe not, given the nature of your camera. But my sweet Fleur, let's get some sleep now. It's terribly late. There are only a few hours until morning. And then tomorrow, let's use up this film and go to the village to have it developed straight away. Maybe the camera really will give us a clue this time as to what you witnessed. Tell you what, let's even go to the teashop again while it's being developed. I think you'd like that."

"Good idea."

They rose from the table, and they helped each other to bed. As she was removing her own shoes, she gasped.

"What is it?"

"Lance, look! There's a little piece of fern stuck in my sandal!"

"Exactly as you said, Fleur!" he said, folding her into his arms when she had climbed into bed. "'The camera in a patch of ferns.' Maybe we'll understand more in the morning."

They snuggled into each other, and quickly fell asleep.

But when they woke at 10.15 the following morning, it was clear that they would not be going to the teashop, or anywhere else. Lance, who generally did not complain, was in a great deal of discomfort. When he tried to sit up, he winced and sank back down onto his pillows.

"What's the matter, Lance?" Florence asked him. "Don't you feel well?"

"I ache all over, Fleur. The sides of my rib cage hurt from the crutches. But mostly it's my back and right leg. It's agonizing."

What he did not also say, that Florence discovered later, was that several of his toes and the backs of his heels, which had reverted to being as soft skinned as when he had been a newborn baby from lack of walking, were now covered with sores from blisters that had burst.

Feeling extremely worried about how much pain he was in, she said, "Oh dear! You over-exerted yourself last night. Do you have any painkillers? Would you like to take something?"

"I threw everything away, remember? You'd better go and ask Mei-Feng. She might have some exotic herbal remedy."

"OK."

Florence dressed quickly and hurried out of the bedroom. Mei-Feng, probably pleased by being needed, was at Lance's side in an instant.

"I have special bath salts. From Taiwan. They very good. They help you quickly. I run bath water and help you in bath."

She was very tender with him. Florence, who felt redundant, left the room and went to the kitchen to make tea. She was just finishing her cup when Mei-Feng came in. In contrast to her tenderness to Lance, she was fiercely accusatory to Florence.

"What happen last night? I hear noises. You talking. And now I see Lance's clothes on chair. All wet! Wet makes his bones ache. Especially in cold night air. You know that. Why you go outside?"

"I'm sorry if we disturbed you. But there was a dog barking ferociously, and we-"

"I hear no dog. No dog nearby. I only hear you. It very foolish to go out in middle of night. Lance still weak. Can hardly walk. And it very dark. This very foolish. Very dangerous for him."

"Mei-Feng, I know you're right, but-"

"You very selfish lady. He just tell me now, in bathroom, you come in last night and you cold. He make you tea. He very kind person. But not right he make tea. He not walk well. Perhaps he spill hot water on his legs. This very serious. Skin on his leg very thin. Very scarred. You make worse."

Florence could not stand any more of this. Taking the camera, she went outside. She pointed the camera and snapped in any direction. Used up all six remaining shots. She returned inside and went straight to Lance's room. He was bathed and back in bed, and appeared to be asleep again. She went out and drove to the village, going straight to the post office to have the film developed. While it was developing, she walked up the High Street and purchased food for dinner.

Having returned later to pick up the photos, she decided to look at them immediately, before going back to the house. So she sat on the very bench that she had sat on two summers ago with Lance, when she had first discovered her camera's extraordinary powers by showing a picture – entirely accurate, as it turned out - of her utter dejection on her wedding day.

And now, one after another, she looked at these new photos, and excitedly, yet horror-struck, she exclaimed to herself, "Yes! Yes, now I remember!" She couldn't wait to get back to Lance to show these to him! She hoped that in her excitement and haste, she would not crash her car into a tree, causing the secret to be lost for ever.

She drove rapidly back to his house, pulling up the handbrake while the car was still moving forwards, and grabbing the bags of groceries, rushed up the ramp to the front door. Ignoring Mei-Feng's expression, she ran into the kitchen to put the food away, and then, seeing that Lance was not on the sofa in the living room, she went quickly to his bedroom.

She ran over to the bed where he lay on his side, his back turned to her.

"Lance! Are you asleep?" she whispered.

"No."

She kissed him lightly on the back of his head.

"How are you? I hope you're feeling much better! I've got something so enormously significant to show you! You know, you were right! The camera did indeed offer the clue as to what happened last night. It's all here! I remember it all now."

He turned slowly towards her. Instead of looking excited, as she was, his face was dull and full of pain.

"Fleur, we need to give up on this. We've been playing with fire for too long. It's too dangerous to meddle in such things."

She was incredulous. "Lance, you can't mean that. You don't feel well now, and I'm terribly sorry. But I'm sure you'll feel better soon, and then you'll definitely want to get back to this! We've come so far."

She sat down on the bed.

"No, Fleur. I'm serious. We need to stop this," he said, turning back again, and facing away from her.

"You've been speaking to Mei-Feng!"

"Of course I've been speaking to Mei-Feng! She lives here. But it's nothing to do with her. After last night, it's clear to me that we can't go on."

"But this isn't what you were saying last night."

"No. But now it is clear to me. We've been given enough warnings."

"What warnings? You mean, how you are in pain today? Lance, I wish I could ease your pain. I wish it were *my* pain instead of yours. But this topic, this topic of Time, is something that has intrigued and inspired both of us ever since we first met. And now we've started making some remarkable discoveries! Of course the acquisition of knowledge isn't easy. If it were, it would have been discovered already. But I really am convinced that we're making a breakthrough now! If you'll just look at these photos, you'll see what I mean."

"No! I don't want to see them, Fleur! Please take them away."

His voice, even though muffled slightly from the pillows into which he buried his head, was sharp. There! Even Lance was capable of anger – the thing that scared her so much. It was silly of her to assume otherwise. She did not know what she'd done to make him angry, but then she often had not understood why Howard had become angry with her at times. Perhaps Lance was furious with her for not speaking to him about the incident last night. Or could he possibly be jealous that she saw something that he did not? Neither seemed plausible. Perhaps Mei-Feng had influenced him against her. Or perhaps Mei-Feng had nothing to do with it, and the fault lay in the fact that she was not good company, and inadvertently got on people's nerves after a while.

Full of fear and self-doubt, she rose from the bed and walked over to the window and looked out. After a pause, she sighed deeply and turning back to the room said quietly, "Do you want me to leave?"

He slowly turned back to face her, and their eyes met at last.

"*I* don't want you to leave. But for your sake, I think you should go. You came here to recuperate after a horrific incident with Howard. Your scratches and bruises have not yet faded. And I failed you. I'm no better to you than he is. I can't even take care of myself, so why should I entertain such grandiose ideas that I can take care of you?"

"What are you talking about?"

"Such brave talk. Talk, talk, talk! That's all I've been doing. Telling you I wouldn't be like my mother. Oh no, I wouldn't give in to infirmity! But it's nonsense, Fleur, and we both know it. I am, after all, my mother's son. And there's no point in me going into denial. I have a partially paralyzed leg. I'm a cripple! An invalid! Disabled! I've tried them all on for size, all those labels, and they all sound equally appalling. As if they are describing someone else, and not me. But for God's sake, I need to accept that this is my reality now. And it makes me feel completely emasculated."

"But Lance-" Florence said, running over to the bed, but he held up a hand for her to be silent, and continued, "But none of that is really the point. What it meant was that although I wanted so badly to follow that woman last night - to see where she led us, and to try to understand why she's in my room and if there's a reason why we can cross over into her time and see her at all - I couldn't do it! And that made me so furious and frustrated! So I pushed you into going instead of me. That was completely reckless and foolish and entirely unthinking, and I never should have done it!"

"Lance!" So he was not angry with her, but with himself. And she was moved to pity for him for the frustrations he felt so deeply. She lent down towards him, as if to kiss him.

"No, Fleur! Stop! I don't deserve your kisses. What I did to you last night was absolutely terrible. I put you in such danger. I went as low as Howard, in my way. I *urged* you to go forward. Alone! I completely took advantage of you. Of your kindness. Your compliance. Your lack of what I've previously called, your *savoir faire*. You naturally said you didn't want to go, but you went anyway, as you knew I wished it. And when you returned virtually immediately, I was so relieved as I'd by then realized the folly of my expectation, and thought you had too, which is why I thought you'd so sensibly decided to turn back. But you hadn't. And you witnessed something dreadful. So dreadful that you completely shut down, for a terrifyingly long time. God! Now I come to think of all this, I'm worse than Howard! You deserve better than either of us!"

"No! You mustn't be upset with yourself, Lance! You have no reason to be. I wanted to pursue the woman and the story behind her as much as you did. Yes, I was frightened at first, but that was momentary. And you're not making any sense at all when you equate yourself with Howard! Please don't even speak of yourself and him in the same sentence!

"And Lance, I remember now, thanks to these photos, what it was that I saw, and although it was terribly shocking and awful, I personally wasn't in any danger. You said so yourself at the time, and when you told me that I was less scared. The dog couldn't hurt me, you said. And you were right."

"But even if that dog couldn't touch you, there were present dangers. It's not safe for a woman to be out alone at night in pitch black, remote rural areas. Besides, whatever it was that you saw – and no, please don't tell me! – whatever that was, it's undeniable that it gave you a profound shock. You were rigid with fright. You were like a zombie, Fleur. And if that isn't a warning to keep away from this, I don't know what is! Oh, I see! You thought when I talked about a 'warning,' that I was talking about myself lying here, unable to get up today. Well, frankly, fuck that! I don't care about that. As you said, it will pass. But don't you see, Fleur; I care about what it did to you! What if it had shaken your mind so much that you would never be capable of returning to sanity? I was terrified, Fleur. Terrified. I thought I'd lost you!"

At the thought, Lance's eyes clouded with tears.

"Oh, I do remember that now, Lance. I vaguely remember being aware that you were awfully upset. But it was as if I was coming out of a dream-like state, so I had forgotten about it later. But now you tell me, I'm so sorry that you were upset. I can't bear to see you upset."

"Fleur, you terrified me! I tried everything; talking to you, rubbing

343

your hand. I even attempted to make you some very sweet tea in the hope of reviving you that way."

"Ah! That's what Mei-Feng was referring to earlier. I hadn't remembered the tea, and didn't understand what she was saying. But she was furious that you did that, as she thought you could have scalded your legs. And she's quite right. You never should have made me tea!"

"But I had to do something! I was talking and talking to you, and getting no response. Fleur, as I said, this is dangerous."

"No, Lance; I've just understood something. Or at least, it's a possible explanation. You said I'd been gone for no time at all when I ran after the woman. But maybe it *was* no time at all *in our time*. But maybe, maybe, I had crossed over into *her* time. The woman-by-the-wardrobe's time. Also, quite possibly the reason I was stiff and unresponsive when I had returned to you was because I was still witnessing what was going on in their time."

"That's interesting, but I don't think so. After all, I had been with you and we both saw the woman and her dog, so by your argument, I would have been in their time, too."

"But no! Because you stopped. You stopped accompanying them when you stopped to rest at the side of the road. That could have been when you returned to our time."

"Hmmm."

"And immediately after I flashed the camera, they were gone, and I was back in our time, too!"

"Fleur, why don't you show me the pictures now, and then I'll have a better idea."

"Actually, Lance, let's not look at them yet after all. You've raised some really important concerns. In fact, we've both had our doubts about actively trying to grasp the meaning of Time, but it's occurred to each of us on different occasions. Let's wait until tomorrow, and give ourselves some time to reflect about everything you've said, and then we can decide if we want to continue pursuing this. You don't feel well now, and we're both tired. It's not the best time now."

"I don't know what to say."

"Lance, it's turned into a beautiful day. Are you able to sit up comfortably?"

"I'll try. Why, what do you have in mind?"

"I think the sunshine soaking into your body would do you good. Would you like to go outside in your wheelchair? We could sit in the garden for a bit."

"That sounds nice."

He started to sit up, and grimaced as he did so. Florence massaged his back, and then helped him into the wheelchair. He moved into the chair stiffly and as if in great pain. She placed pillows behind his back, and even though it was warm, wrapped a blanket around his legs. Then she navigated the chair to the front door, down the ramp, and outside, turning on to the lawn at the back of the house. She did as she had seen herself once when half dreaming; with one hand she pushed the chair, and the other was on his shoulder, and also, as in her dream, he lifted his hand to hold hers.

The late afternoon sun bathed the back garden in a golden light, suffusing it with a warm, drowsy feeling. She parked the wheelchair in a patch of sunlight, and she sat down close by on a swing that was strung by means of a long rope to a high branch of a tree. She gently rocked backwards and forward. She did not speak. Instead she listened to the breeze in the trees, the tiny cheep of a small bird, the plunging sound of ducks plopping into the stream at the bottom of the garden, the lazy buzz of a bumble bee, and far off the laughing sounds of other water fowl. All was very still and peaceful. The air was pure and fragrant, unlike the diesel-choked fumes of London. She looked around the garden, at the golden buttercups dotting the fresh green lawn, and over in the bushes, sprays of tiny white flowers amidst the foliage, and a flower she did not know, with one tiny petal, purple blue in color, in the shape of an '8'. She leaned over from the swing and gathered buttercups until they filled her lap. Then she looped their stems together, making a chain which she put around her wrist.

"It's idyllic out here, isn't it," Lance said.

"Wasn't it Henry James who said there were no nicer words in the English language than 'summer afternoon'?"

"Yes, I think it was."

They were quiet again, Florence gently rocking back and forth.

"Lance," she said at last.

"Yes?"

"I hope you don't sometimes feel tired of me."

"Certainly not!"

"And do you really want me to stay?"

"Fleur!" he exclaimed. "I took an enormous risk when I said that it might be better for you if you left. It needed to be said, though. I'd been agonizing all day about what happened to you last night as a result of me pushing you forward. But I can tell you this – if you *had* said you wanted to leave, I'd be the next ghost to haunt this house!"

"Oh Lance!" she laughed, jumping off the swing. And kneeling by him in his wheelchair, she looped her arms around his neck.

"Fleur, you genuinely do want to stay, don't you? You're not just doing this for me?"

She sat back on her heels, her hands on his lap.

"I used to think, Lance, that I didn't know what love was. It's odd; I've always known when I'm happy or when I'm sad. But I always used to wonder how I would know if I was in love. But being with you, Lance, I know! I love you with my body and with my soul. I love you with my heart and with my intellect."

Lance smiled his beautiful smile. Then he gently slid the buttercup chain from Florence's wrist, and placed it on her head.

"There!" he said. "A garland of golden flowers for my true love!"

# SEVENTEEN

*THAT NIGHT, DESPITE EXHAUSTION,* neither Florence nor Lance slept very deeply. And in the morning, Florence said to him, "I didn't see the woman-by-the wardrobe last night, even though I was awake a lot."

"Neither did I. It was strange not to see her, as she seems to have been here so regularly before now."

"It was quite disappointing, actually. Though I can't believe I'm saying that!"

"Yes, I was disappointed, too."

He turned over, put on his glasses, and pulled open his bedside table drawer. From it he took out a wad of folded papers. Unfolding them, Florence could see it was a printout of 'Burnt Norton,' the poem by T.S. Eliot, and he pointed out, rather glumly, words within it such as "perpetual possibility" and "a world of speculation."

"But no!" Florence protested. "There wasn't anything speculative about the woman-by-the-wardrobe. She did exist! She wasn't an abstraction. We both saw her!"

"You only saw her once. And at first you were even unsure about having seen her at all."

"But what about you? You've seen her lots of times!"

"True. But we need to remain rigorous in our approach. We need to be able to stand up in front of the likes of Dr. Erikkson, or any academic community for that matter, with irrefutable proofs. So really, then, we need to remember that what we've seen is thus far only a *possibility*. Or, as T.S. Eliot said, which more accurately can be applied to our case, a "perpetual possibility," since I've seen her a lot of times, but that still does not guarantee that a real woman was there. Who knows; perhaps I keep imagining her. And then perhaps you'd imagined her, too, if you'd been influenced by what I'd told you."

"Certainly not! Are you saying that everything I witnessed, all the horrors and trauma in the dark woods, wasn't real? Are you seriously saying I made it all up? And if you want irrefutable proof, what about my photos from that awful scene? I know you haven't seen them yet, but when you do I think you'll agree that they should provide sufficient confirmation to that smug, self-inflated Dr. Erikkson! And furthermore," Florence added, just remembering another important point, "as soon as you first saw the photo of her that we found in the grandfather clock, you told me you'd seen her before!"

"I know, Fleur! Calm down! I'm just trying to play devil's advocate."

"Well, I think we were really onto something when we spoke about the eternal present, and the circularity of Time."

"Yes, I agree. Honestly I do. Just sometimes, though, I try to anticipate how our literally incredible findings will be received. But enough of that! I am completely with you!"

"Good! So you do want, don't you Lance, to pick up where we left off? You do want to see the photos from two nights ago, and talk about what happened then?"

Before Lance could answer, the phone rang.

"Juliet!" he exclaimed. "What? You're at Landsdowne's with Mother? Yes. Yes, of course. Yes, that's nice. OK, I'll be there later on today. Yes, of course I can. You don't need to do that. Yes, it's all right. OK, then. Thanks. Goodbye!" Lance said and put the phone down.

348

"It seems that Juliet has arrived two weeks earlier than I expected, and has picked up Mother and taken her to Landsdowne's," he told Florence. "She asked if I could visit them there for an early dinner this evening. Will you come with me, Fleur?"

Florence felt awkward at the thought of seeing Juliet, and then embarrassed at the realization that Rose and Allison would be bound to also be there.

"Wouldn't you prefer for Mei-Feng to take you?" she asked.

"No, I'd like you to come, Fleur. That is, if you'd like to."

"Of course!" she replied, smiling. "Have you been to Landsdowne's since you moved here?"

"No, this will be the first time."

At that, she realized that any awkwardness or embarrassment that she might feel must surely be eclipsed by the awkwardness and embarrassment Lance might feel as a result of being seen for the first time since his injuries, by Mrs. Landsdowne and her guests. He had felt reluctant to go to the teashop. How much more difficult this outing must be for him!

Later that afternoon Florence had parked Lance's car by the entrance to Landsdowne's Guest House. She first took the wheelchair from the car, and bumped it up each step to the front porch, remembering, as she did so, how she had sat on this porch the day before her departure from there two summers ago, and how Lance had trotted up the steps towards her, a bunch of wildflowers for her in his hand. It was the first time he had called her Fleur.

Hearing the commotion, Mrs. Landsdowne came out.

"Why, if it isn't Florence Hamilton! I remember you! How are you, dear?"

"Hello, Mrs. Landsdowne! I'm fine, thanks. And you?"

"Are you coming back here for a holiday? I believe I do have a room available, although it wouldn't have quite such a nice view as the room you had before."

"Oh no, no thank you! I've come with Lance Ramsey. We're coming along to see his mother and sister for dinner here."

"Oh! You're here with Dr. Ramsey, are you, dear?" Florence could not tell if she seemed surprised or not.

"Yes, he's just down there in the car."

"Awful thing, that, about his legs. We haven't seen him since last summer. He was a strapping young man then. Terrible shame." So saying, and despite her enormous girth, she flew down the steps, and Florence ran after her.

"Dr. Ramsey! How lovely to see you!" she shouted through the open car door. "Your mother and sister will be so glad!"

"Hello, Mrs. Landsdowne! Good to see you! I hope you're well."

"Yes, yes," she said, bustling around him, as Florence helped him out of the car and up the steps. He was still in some pain, and it was evidently a relief for him when he reached his wheelchair on the porch, and sat down.

"And you," Mrs. Landsdowne remarked once he was comfortably seated in his chair. "Despite all that's happened to you, you look the picture of health! A regular phoenix rising from the ashes!"

It was in fact true. Lance had a fine color in his face, his eyes shone, and he no longer looked so gaunt. Hearing the excitement by the front door, Juliet, Rose and Allison came out. There were many animated voices, especially from Rose.

"Indeed you do look well, dear Dr. Ramsey!" she exclaimed. Then she saw Florence and her painted eyebrows shot up in surprise.

"Thanks. I feel well. And I have Fleur to thank for that. She comes up every weekend, and is invariably gentle, patient, and compassionate. And what's more, she's a terrific cook! You all remember Fleur, don't you?"

Juliet, having bent down to give her brother a brief kiss on the cheek, shook Florence's hand.

"We haven't seen each other since that awful time in that New York hospital. How are you?"

And Rose, looking disdainful, refused to shake her hand, but stood in a corner and sniffed, "Hello, Florence," before turning away. It was clear that she was thinking where she had last seen Florence. Allison, shy and obedient at her side, turned away too.

"Come inside! Let's see Mother!" Juliet commanded, and the party went inside. Florence returned to the car to park it in a proper space. When she entered the large reception area, she saw Lance, bending forward attentively talking to his mother, who looked even tinier and frailer, and seemed even deafer with her ear cocked close to Lance's mouth when he was speaking, than the last time Florence had seen her. She was about to go up to greet her, when she heard her say to Lance, "So, where's your little Oriental girlfriend?" Florence stopped in her tracks, and then heard Lance reply, "You mean Mei-Feng? She's not my girlfriend! I employ her. She helps me out." Then he looked up and saw Florence, and smiled at her.

"Mother, I'd like you to meet Fleur again. You might remember her from a few years ago when she came to stay here for a holiday. Fleur's with me."

"What's that you say? Fleur Wisley? How do you do? Not any relation of the Peyton-Wisley's are you?"

Just then the dinner gong sounded, and they slowly went through to the dining room, where Mrs. Landsdowne had pushed two tables together. As she walked in, Florence remembered how she'd been a solitary diner in this room when she'd first come to stay here two summers ago, the novel she'd been reading as her only companion. Now here she was with such a crowd, but again feeling like an outsider. Juliet busily took her place at the head of the table, and ordered her mother to sit at the other end. Florence helped Lance from the wheelchair into his seat, and as she did so, he pressed her hand for some extended moments. That gesture gave her reassurance and strength, and she smiled at him as she took her place across from where he was sitting, and next to Allison. The meal was formal and sedate, and they mostly broke into little clusters of conversation; Lance talking to his mother, Rose and Juliet speaking together, and Florence talking to Allison. However, as tends to happen when formal groups of people assemble, there were lulls in the conversation amongst two of the groups at the same time, while the other group continued their conversation. During one such lull, Juliet's voice could be heard loudly stating, "For heaven's sake, no! I shouldn't think I'll stay as long as a fortnight. Having to put up with *two* invalids is enough to drive me round the bend!" Florence immediately glanced at Lance who, though he must have heard, showed no outward reaction to such a hurtful comment. In her embarrassment, Florence hurried on to tell Allison about an amazing juggler she'd seen in Washington Square Park. A little later, another inevitable silence fell on all except Juliet and Rose, who were now talking about marriage. "I simply

351

don't understand young people these days. In my day, marriage was for life," Rose was saying, to which Juliet readily agreed, keeping the fact of her own divorce a closely guarded secret.

When they had finished their coffee, which was served in the living room with those truffles which Florence fondly remembered having devoured during her last stay, Lance announced that he had some family business to discuss with his mother and Juliet.

"Don't you imagine, dear Dr. Ramsey, that young Florence here would be greatly entertained by a game of Scrabble?" Rose said, taking Lance's hand briefly in her blue-veined one. Despite her obvious intentions of behaving frostily to Florence, the temptation of playing her favorite board game with an old challenger was getting the better of her.

"Indeed! I imagine that she would like that very much!" Lance twinkled mischievously at Florence as she sat on the familiar window seat. "And when I return, save a game for me!"

"Come on, Lance! Let's go into the library and get this business matter over with! Mother's already there. And don't expect me to push you! You can wheel yourself!" Juliet declared and rapidly left the room.

Florence jumped up, and placing her hands on the back of the wheelchair, started pushing Lance towards the open doorway.

"It's all right, Fleur; I'm not that feeble!" he said, starting to turn the wheels with his hands, and moving rapidly away.

Florence, having felt stung by Juliet's words to Lance, especially when taken in combination with her insensitive remark during dinner, now felt that she herself had overstepped the delicate and unspoken line. She was publicly treating him as an object of pity, in constant need of help. The very thing he was striving for so hard – to regain his independence – she'd now crushed as her insensitive attempt to help him just now was as bad as Juliet's blatant and repeated remarks about his disabilities.

As if reflecting her thoughts, Rose turned to Florence and said, "Poor Dr. Ramsey! It breaks my heart to see him so crippled like that."

But Florence, not wanting to give away her inner agitation and remorse, and anxious that Lance might have heard Rose's remark, replied loudly and brightly while trying to dispel her own worries, "Yes, but he's doing so well! His condition is improving every day."

"Is that so?"

"Absolutely! The doctor said he would never walk again, but he's proving him wrong. He can walk a little now. Just not today, as he had a bit of a setback. Just a temporary one. But overall he's not one to be defeated!" She said this, while at the same time hearing echoes in her mind of Lance's words, uttered in despair, "I am, after all, my mother's son."

Allison unfolded the Scrabble board and distributed the letter racks. Then she spilled the letter tiles face down on the table with a great clatter that made her apologize.

"Yes, well, just get on with it!" Rose said, and Allison responded by meekly sliding seven tiles over to each of them.

"Ah well, it's nice to know he's on the mend," Rose said, peering at her letters before arranging them on her rack. "But the world is not the same place any more. Not after those dreadful attacks last September. Although, out here in the Lake District, you'd never know. It still looks the same here now as it did when I was a child."

"I didn't know you came to the Lake District when you were a child," Florence said, while also arranging her letter tiles. "Did you come here for your holidays?"

"Gracious me, no! I was brought up in the Lake District by my grandparents. It was my parents who lived in India, and I went out to join them before the outbreak of war. But living here as a small child is why I've always been so fond of this area. Now look at that! All X's and Q's! Whatever word can I make from that, I ask you! Allison, you go first!"

Florence was interested in what Rose had said, and did not want it dropped, despite the Scrabble game.

"You lived here in this very area, did you, Rose?"

"Indeed I did. Very close by. But that was over half a century ago! Oh dear! Now I'm giving away my age!"

"Perhaps you knew, then, a family called Throgmorton, who lived in the house that Lance now lives in?"

"Oh no, the Throgmorton's didn't live there! They lived over in Wolvercote Hall. They were a splendidly wealthy family, with lots of children. Why, as a child I used to go over to the Hall to play with them!"

"That's funny. Recently we came across a letter in Lance's house, that was addressed to Mr. Throgmorton, so we assumed he had lived there."

"Now, let me see. At that time - when I was a child, mind you, so my memory might be a bit faint – there was a family called Lacey living where Dr. Ramsey now lives. Yes, that's right! The Lacey's. They had two children, and they used to play at the Hall, too, so I saw them on a few occasions. A son and a daughter. What were their names? I didn't know them well, as they were quite a bit older than me."

"Lacey," Florence mused quietly to herself. And then more loudly she asked, "Might the daughter have been called Kitty?"

"Kitty! Yes, that's right!" Rose said, quite startled. "How did you know that?"

"Actually, Lance and I have been looking up the local history of the area." And then, reaching into her handbag to the package of photos just developed, she leafed through and pulled out a picture of the woman-by-the-wardrobe, which was identical, in fact, to the photo stored away inside the grandfather clock.

"K-I-T-T-E-N-S!" Allison said proudly, laying down her first series of letters on the Scrabble board. "Your turn now, Rose!"

"Do you know this woman?" Florence asked Rose.

"Why, that's Mrs. Lacey! Virginia Lacey. Goodness me! That takes me back! I haven't seen her since I was…since I was…I don't know how old. Where does this picture come from?"

"Oh, I just found it. Who is Virginia Lacey?"

"Rose, it's your turn!"

"All right, Allison dear! Just a minute! Seeing this picture has given me quite a turn. Who is Virginia Lacey? Why, she's Kitty Lacey's mother, of course!"

"Do you know where Kitty Lacey is now?" Florence pursued.

"I'm not sure, dear," Rose said, now studying the letters in front of her. "I went to see my parents in India every holiday, so I didn't know the Lacey's well, and then lost touch with them. Ah, now here's a word. Q-U-I-E-T!" she declared, using one of the 'T' letters from Allison's word. "Your turn now, Florence. Or should I be calling you 'Fleur'?"

"It's OK. You can call me whichever you prefer. Lance started calling me Fleur, so people who know me through him call me that, but it's up to you. Especially as you originally knew me as Florence."

"Well, Fleur it is. As I was saying, it's your turn."

Florence stared at her tiles, but couldn't concentrate. The fact that Rose had identified the woman-by-the-wardrobe; the fact that this confirmed that she did exist and had lived in Lance's house, was too exciting and mystifying. All previous worries about her having inadvertently embarrassed and humiliated Lance by implying that he was even less capable of mobility than was the case, were dissipated.

"Do come on, dear! I don't remember you being such a slow player."

"Sorry! I'll be ready in a minute. Are the Throgmorton's still living at Wolvercote Hall?"

"Oh no, dear. That was a beautiful house. I remember it well. But it was pulled down many years ago to build holiday cottages. Yes, so the area did change a little, but only marginally. 'Lakeside Estates;' that's the name of those holiday cottages. You might have seen them from the road. I don't know what happened to the Throgmortons. Probably all dispersed."

"Ah, here's my word! I-N-E-P-T!" Florence said, using the 'E' from 'kittens'. "But Rose, I think you said Mrs. Lacey had a son, too. What was his name?"

"My dear, you *are* interested in local history, aren't you! Allison, it's your turn."

"Yes, I'm helping Lance to find out a little about the house he's living in. Who lived there before. That sort of thing. It's quite fascinating."

"Let me think. What was his name? Gregory? No, that's not right. George? No. Oh, I remember! Gordon! Yes, that's right; Gordon Lacey!"

"Gordon! Do you know what happened to him?"

"No!" Allison said.

"What?" Rose and Florence both asked together.

"N-O! And O-N! See, if I put my 'O' down here, I make both words!"

"Very clever, Allison," Rose said. "No dear," she added, turning back to Florence. "I can't say that I know anything about Gordon Lacey. I'm surprised that I even remembered his name! But I'll tell you who could supply you with all this information much better than me – Mrs. Landsdowne, that's who. She's lived here all her life, and is bound to know a thing or two."

Shortly after that the party reassembled, and the Scrabble board was folded and put away even though the game was incomplete.

"How many rounds have you had?" Lance asked.

"We didn't quite finish our first game," Rose replied. "We were chatting so much."

Lance, looking surprised, glanced at Florence, but she did not notice as she was in the process of slipping out to talk to Mrs. Landsdowne, who was tidying up the dining room and laying the tables for breakfast.

"Mrs. Landsdowne?"

"Yes, dear?"

"Would you mind if I ask you a question. Do you know of a Kitty or Gordon Lacey?"

Mrs. Landsdowne put down the serviette she was folding, and this time Florence could tell that she looked greatly surprised.

"Why yes, dear. I certainly do know Group Captain Lacey. But he's not from these parts now. He moved to Kendall. Might I inquire as to why you want to know?"

"I believe he used to live in the house that Lance now lives in, so I think he'd be interested in meeting him. Do you have any idea how we could contact him?"

"Not having a problem with the plumbing, is he?"

"Oh no; it's nothing like that. The house is wonderful! It's just that he'd like to find out about the people from the past who lived in his house."

"Well, come with me and I'll fetch my address book."

They walked out of the dining room and to the reception desk. As they walked, Mrs. Landsdowne added, "The Lacey's lived in Dr. Ramsey's house a great many years ago. Must've been many others since then – I don't recall all their names – and then surprisingly that lovely house stood empty for a number of years before Dr. Ramsey moved in and the house saw life in itself again."

"You must have liked the Lacey's a lot to remember them so well."

"Well," said Mrs. Landsdowne, suddenly surprisingly coy and bashful. "Gordon and I were sweethearts. He was my first sweetheart, in fact. But then, you see, he was much older than I, so it didn't work out. Besides, then I met Mr. Landsdowne, and the rest is history!" By this time, she had found her fat little address book, and pulling on her glasses from the chain around her neck, and licking her thumb to turn over the pages, she said, "Ah – here we are, dear. Group Captain Gordon Lacey. 119 King Albert Road, Kendall. And if you do see him, remember me to him, won't you."

"Thank you, Mrs. Landsdowne! If we do see him, I'll certainly give him your regards."

Shortly after that it was time to leave. Florence went to fetch the car, and then she helped Lance down the steps and into it. He did not want anyone else to help him on the steps, though he had plenty of offers from Mrs. Landsdowne, and Allison (under orders from Rose). "No, thanks," he said. "Fleur is my left leg." And then, as they started to drive off, he said to her, "You don't fail to amaze me! Here was Rose, determined not to say a polite word to you, and making me fear that you were having a dreadful time. Yet she ends up not even being able to complete a game of her beloved Scrabble in well over three quarters of an hour, because you were 'chatting' so much! You see how charming you are!"

She laughed. "Lance, I learned a great number of things! I can't wait to tell you!"

"And I can't wait to hear!" he laughed. And then in an entirely different tone, he exclaimed, "Oh damn!"

"What is it?"

"I forgot to take Mother's financial folder. Would you mind turning back, my sweet, and fetching it for me?"

"Certainly!" Florence said, secretly hating turning the car around in these narrow country roads, that twisted so much and were walled in by high hedges.

"Thanks. You see, I have power-of-attorney over Mother's financial affairs, but for some reason Juliet has been holding on to the folder with all the papers. I'm sorry to ask you to run errands for me, especially as it was silly of me to forget to take it."

Florence ran back into the guesthouse, and almost completely bumped into Rose.

"Back so soon?" she laughed.

"Yes! I have to pick up some papers from Juliet to give to Lance. Do you know where she is?"

"I think she's gone up to her room. One flight up, first door on the left. But wait, dear. Before you go I have something I'd like to tell you. You see, my dear, I owe you an apology."

"Apology? For what?"

"I had completely misjudged you. And I'll be the first to admit it. You see, when you left your husband, Howard, so soon after marrying him, I thought you were flippant and frankly immoral. But now I see how you nourish dear Dr. Ramsey in every way."

"Well, thank you, Rose. And there's no need to apologize. Really."

"Oh, but there is. I had made all the wrong assumptions about you. When I looked at Dr. Ramsey today, by which I mean when I got past the shock of seeing him sitting in a wheelchair and really looked at him, at his face, I realized that I've never seen him look so happy. And remember, I've been seeing him for ever so many summers here at Landsdowne's. At first I simply couldn't understand it. How could he be happy after what happened to him? And then it became clear. It's all because of you!"

"Well, thank you."

"What intrigues me, though, dear, is how this happened. I pride myself on keeping a sharp eye out for everything that is going on. But when you stayed here two years ago, I did not have the slightest hint that you and Dr. Ramsey were close friends, or even that you knew each other at all. As I remember it, the one occasion when you might have spent time together, with him driving you to Derwentwater to take the boat ride that I had recommended, you had chosen instead to walk alone deep into the countryside. That was the time when you became frightfully lost, remember, and I was so worried about you. So tell me, how *did* it come about that you and he-?"

"Rose, I'll tell you another time, if you don't mind. Lance is waiting in the car, and I want to make sure I catch Juliet before she goes to sleep."

"Of course, dear! And I do hope you come back and visit us here again soon."

"Oh yes; I'm sure we will. And thanks for giving me so much information earlier about the Lacey's. I'm sure Lance will be so interested to hear everything."

# EIGHTEEN

*LATER THAT NIGHT, FLORENCE* was about to start telling Lance what she'd found out from Rose and Mrs. Landsdowne, but then she suddenly stopped herself, saying, "But wait! Do you want us to talk about this and look at those photos, or should we drop it?"

"Well, it seems that you've discovered something very exciting, judging by the way you look. So please let me know what you've found out."

"Great! Then let's start with the photos." She went to her bag, and brought back the envelope in which they were contained. They were all black and white.

Pulling them out and looking at the one on top, Lance gasped. "It's her! The woman-by-the-wardrobe! And what's more this seems really similar to the photo of her that we saw in the grandfather clock!"

"Yes! I showed this particular picture to Rose, as it turns out she used to live in this area when she was a child. She immediately recognized her — she recognized her, Lance! — and she said she used to live *here* in this house! She said her name was Virginia Lacey."

"Incredible!" Lance said, turning pink and then pale. "So she really did exist, Fleur! And we've seen her! Proof at last! Oh, and look, Fleur! In this photo I think she's standing in my bedroom! I recognize the casement window and carving around it. There are no other windows like this in the house. This must have been when my bedroom was used as the dining room! Oh, this is amazing, Fleur!"

"Yes!" she agreed, so glad that he was now looking at these photos, too, and sharing in their extraordinary information.

"Let's see the next one!" Lance said. It was a picture of Virginia Lacey, in the kitchen, giving her dog some food. And the dog completely resembled Eloise, the one they had seen that night, only here the dog looked friendly and calm.

"Not only is the dog the same," Lance commented, "but the kitchen is recognizable, despite now having new cupboards and appliances!"

The following photo was of the whole family seated at the dining room table, Mr. Lacey carving a joint of what seemed to be lamb.

"They're the son and daughter, Lance! Rose remembered that the son was called Gordon and the daughter, Kitty."

"Kitty? That's what we kept hearing Virginia Lacey - as we should now call her - saying three nights ago. Amazing! But now, I wonder what this is?"

"It's hard for me to see what this picture is, too, Lance. But I think it's that when I followed Virginia Lacey, she stopped briefly to speak with someone. I think this shows who she spoke with."

"Looks like it might be a vicar. See his white collar?"

Then Lance turned to a photo of two lovers, holding both of each other's hands and looking intently into each other's faces. "Did you see these people when you followed Virginia Lacey?" he asked.

"Yes, that's Kitty. She looks different from how she looked at the dining room table. Somehow wilder and more passionate. But I'm sure it's her. And she's with someone who I only saw for an instant. He saw the dog coming – Eloise had broken free from her leash by then, and I went running after her – and he said, 'Good grief!' and then he was gone."

"Oh. What's next?"

"Lance, I must warn you. The next couple of pictures are quite upsetting."

"My God!" he exclaimed, looking at the next photo. "You saw this? Did you actually see this?"

Florence nodded.

"But this is awful. That dog is all over her! It's baring its teeth. See what an ugly snarl it has, with its top lip curled up? You said that dog seemed vicious."

Florence nodded again, incapable of speaking.

"I think the dog's bitten her leg, Fleur! See how it looks as though it's bleeding badly. Look at that dark, ugly stain. Oh God, it reminds me of your picture of me on September 11th!" He passed his hand over his face and swallowed hard. Florence reached down and instinctively rubbed his leg.

He turned to the next picture. It showed Kitty, now sunk to the ground, the dog ripping the flesh of her neck. Lance dropped the photo, turned to Florence, flung his arms about her, and held on very tightly.

"My love, you witnessed this? This is what you saw? No wonder you were in a state of shock. It must be terribly traumatic for you to even look at these pictures again."

Florence closed her eyes and then reopened them.

"Keep looking. Let's get through them," she said. "Actually most of the rest don't make much sense."

"Did you show all these photos to Rose?"

"No; just the one of Virginia Lacey."

"That's good. But wait! Before we look at any more, I've just realized something. But when I think about it, I think I've known this for ages. Just like becoming aware suddenly of a noise, which had really been going on in the background all the time, like the hum my fridge makes. It's this persistent, nagging feeling that I seem to have always had at the back of my mind."

"What? What is it?"

"I think I was meant to have met Kitty at 6.00 the next evening."

"What do you mean, Lance? How could you meet Kitty? And the 'next evening' after what?"

"The evening after I'd first met her. I was going to run an errand for

·

her; take something for her and deliver it to someone, so she wouldn't have to go herself."

"*Had* you met Kitty before? You hadn't told me."

"I don't know, Fleur. I don't know. It just seems like a vague memory."

"I'm confused, Lance."

"So am I. I don't know what I'm talking about. Sorry; maybe it's the strain. Let's carry on looking at more of those photos."

"Are you sure you're OK?"

He smiled beautifully, and Florence, though still perplexed and concerned, was always comforted and stimulated by that bright, intelligent smile of his. So she handed him the next photo, which was of Virginia Lacey on the steps of the local church, the vicar holding her hand with an expression of great benevolence. There was a picture of Virginia Lacey walking seemingly purposefully yet reluctantly forward, holding Eloise's lead, and her husband at her side. And there was a surprising photo, seemingly out of context with the rest, of a small baby in an old-fashioned cot, looking up at the camera and appearing to be cooing and gurgling, the way contented babies do.

"I wonder if that was Kitty as a baby," Lance suggested. "We know your camera has no regard for true chronology."

"Maybe," Florence replied, feeling weaker than she'd anticipated from looking again at the photos.

"But what happened to Kitty after the dog attacked her? Was she rescued?" he asked, pushing the pile of photos away.

Florence paused. She strongly suspected that Kitty was beyond rescue. But she found herself unable to say this to Lance, who owed his life to the fact that he had been rescued. It was too precarious. So she said, "Yes, I'm pretty sure she was rescued." And it became her truth now too. Something to which she could add increasing layers of conviction. "I didn't see the whole situation unfold, as I flashed the camera, and after that saw nothing, and returned to you. But I'm pretty sure that in the instance in which I took the photo, her mother arrived, and we know how commanding she was of that dog. Besides, I believe that the young man we saw in the earlier photo was leaving to fetch help."

"But what if she wasn't rescued?" he said desperately. "What if *I* could

362

have prevented her from being in any danger, by running that errand for her so she wouldn't have had to go out herself? I should have been there! I could have stopped this! Whether she was rescued or not, she was certainly agonizingly hurt, because of me. Because I must have let her down and didn't meet her as I said I would at 6.00!"

"Lance, I don't know what you mean. This was something absolutely beyond your sphere of influence."

"It's not only Kitty! It's you, too, who I should've protected!" he said wildly. "Now I know the root of why I'd been so upset. Don't you see, if I'd stopped Kitty from going out, you yourself wouldn't have been in terrible danger by following Virginia Lacey and that awful dog. I'd let Kitty down, and I was atrocious to you, not only by pushing you forward in my place, but also because I didn't preempt the situation from happening in the first place!"

"No, Lance! No. Even if you did tell Kitty somehow that you'd meet her the following evening at 6.00, we have no way of knowing if that following evening was when Kitty was attacked by the dog. In any case, I think we should take a break from all of this now. It's getting late."

"No! I'd like to finish now we've started. I'd like to know what else you've discovered."

"But you said yourself you're feeling the strain of all this. And you're being so hard on yourself."

Lance sighed, pulled off his glasses and rubbed his eyes.

"Let's come to bed, and carry on talking there," Florence suggested. And this was a good suggestion, because once in the bedroom, the atmosphere changed, and Lance was smiling brightly again.

"It's funny how we've been thinking Virginia Lacey's surname was Throgmorton," he remarked. "I wonder who the Throgmorton's are."

"Actually, Rose told me!" she replied, relieved that Lance seemed to be more himself again. "She said the Throgmorton's were friends of the Lacey's. They used to live in a big house called Wolvercote Hall, which has since been torn down. It's where the Lakeside Estates holiday cottages now stand."

"That Rose! She knows everything! And you're spectacular at finding good sources of information. It certainly helps that you're a researcher and reporter! So when you uncovered that letter in the grandfather clock, we mistakenly thought the family living in this house were the recipients of the letter, rather than that they were the ones intending to post it!"

"It seems so. But what a strange place to keep a letter if one intends posting it!"

"Yes, unless the sender intended it to be sent in secret."

"True. And we perhaps have a lead to unravel this a bit more. Rose told me that our very own Mrs. Landsdowne knew Gordon Lacey, the son. That's why I went to speak to her just before we left, and it turns out they used to be, in her words, 'sweethearts'! Actually, from the look on her face, it seems she still has some fondness for him. I asked her where he lives now, and she said Kendall. Is that very far away?"

"No, not far as the crow flies, or if we take the motorway. But it's a bit of a long, slow drive over mountain roads. Did she give you his exact address?"

"Oh my God, Lance! I just realized something!"

"What?"

"Mrs. Landsdowne said his address is *119* King Albert's Road! Don't you see!"

"See what?"

"*119!* It was the number in that recurring nightmare you used to have. You know, the one in which you had lunch reservations for the absurd time of 1.19! Remember! You were in that empty Hotel, in which the chamber maids kept making beds even though there were no other guests!"

"God, you're right!" Lance exclaimed, his eyes shining brightly. "And at the time we thought that the digits 119 represented the date of the attack on the World Trade Center, as it was on the 11th of September!"

"Yes, that's still true. But now there's this other thing, too. It feels beyond coincidence. Quite possibly you'd crossed into a different time dimension and you've already contacted Gordon Lacey, so it was an experience you'd had, that you could then dream about. At least, in terms of the number of his house."

"Fleur, this is incredible!" Lance leaned over and kissed Florence with excitement.

"Yes! And it's a bit frightening, too, don't you think? Are you sure you want us to contact him?"

"Absolutely! Look, we have some amazing photos. And now this about 119! What's more, we have Rose's confirmation about the identity of this woman in my bedroom -Virginia Lacey. So yes, let's definitely meet her son, Gordon, if he agrees to see us, and investigate whether what he tells us confirms or denies, or indeed elaborates upon or explains, what's shown in these photos."

The next day they phoned Gordon Lacey, who, if he felt at all surprised, certainly did not sound it, and invited them to visit the following morning. Meanwhile, that day, Lance said he wanted to go swimming, and asked Florence to come with him.

"I'll give Mei-Feng the day off," he said. "She usually takes me to the pool, but it looks like she's made some new friendly contacts at work, so maybe she'd like to see them instead."

"Does she usually swim with you, too?"

"Absolutely not! But I'd like you to, Fleur."

"But I haven't got my swimming costume with me."

"Well then, we'll buy you one!"

Later that day, with an ugly pink swimming costume with large orange flowers (it was all the village shop had) rolled in a towel and tucked under her arm, Florence escorted Lance to the pool. She changed quickly and waited at the poolside for him to come out of the men's locker room. Soon he emerged in his swimming trunks, moving awkwardly towards her with the help of his crutches. Some swimmers who had not yet got into the water, stopped and stared at him, and a cluster of children already in the pool, pointed and laughed.

"Fucking bastards!" Florence muttered. "I'd like to splash their moronic faces with armfuls of water!"

"They're only kids, Fleur. Let it go," he said, smiling and waving at the children, and to her surprise, one of the children smiled and waved back at him, which made Lance grin even more broadly. But this incident made her realize how much she'd grown used to the way Lance's left leg looked, and how now she saw it as strangers did; peculiarly thin, crooked, and with a large shiny pink area devoid of hair.

Near the edge of the pool she took the crutches from him, and helped him to sit down on the ground with his feet dangling into the water. She went to place the crutches by the wall, away from the pool so they would not get wet. When she turned around again to face the pool, Lance was no longer sitting at the edge. She had a moment of absolute panic, and then she realized he was already in the water and had started to swim.

She hurried over to the pool, and looking down at the blue, rippling waters, was amazed. In the pool there was no indication whatsoever of any impairment to Lance's body. He was strong and swift, nimble and graceful, and hardly splashed at all. He reached the other end, pushed off, and swam back to her. As he got close to where she was standing, he glided through the water, before putting his hand on the edge. He reached for her toes, and looking up at her, water streaming from his face, he smiled his beautiful smile.

"Come in and join me, Fleur!" he said.

"You're a marvelous swimmer!" she said admiringly, lowering herself down the steps and feeling the cold water inching up her body.

"I've always loved swimming!" he said. "Now especially, as the buoyancy helps so much. I think I should have a watery home! Come on; let's swim together!"

She swam along at his side, but her breaststroke was no match to his crawl, and soon he was far ahead. He turned and laughed, waiting for her to catch up. They swam together for a long time, maybe more than twenty minutes, through the intensely blue, sparkling water. When it was time for them both to get out, Lance, in sad contrast to his agility in the water, once again moved awkwardly and clumsily, and even more so now so as to avoid slipping on the wet floor. And when later dressed and with the leg brace fastened in place, he said, "This is an incredible contraption. It's reminiscent of an insect's exoskeleton, but it does provide me with much needed support."

"That's all that matters," she replied, and they kissed warmly, smelling the still lingering chlorine in each other's hair.

--------

The house at 119 King Albert's Road was narrow, with a green front door and a shiny brass knocker. Group Captain Lacey opened it as soon as they'd knocked. He was a tall, upright man with a pink face, strands of white, silky hair, and very blue but watery eyes. He showed them into a small living room that was jammed with overstuffed floral armchairs, and trophies and medals. Lance, who seemed to have benefited from the exercise of swimming, managed quite well again with the crutches and leg brace, which was just as well as there would not have been enough room for his wheel chair in that cramped room.

Group Captain Lacey immediately started talking to them proudly of his experience in the Royal Air Force, especially during the War, and telling them the story behind each medal that he had been awarded. Then, looking directly at Lance, he exclaimed,

"It looks like you sustained some war wounds yourself, young man."

"Yes, in a manner of speaking, sir. I was on the battleground of a war that had not yet been declared," Lance said obliquely.

"Lance was at the World Trade Center in New York last September 11th," Florence elaborated.

"Is that so? Rotten piece of luck. I knew as soon as you arrived that you were lame through combat and not disease. I've seen your expression in the eyes of plenty of wounded soldiers I've come across in my day. Still, I bet you're glad you're around to tell the story. Plenty of people did not survive. Well, I don't need to tell you that! Inside one of the Towers, were you?"

"Yes, sir. In the North Tower. At about the fortieth floor."

"Had a job there, did you?"

"No, actually I was working further uptown, at New York University. I was at the World Trade Center that morning for a meeting."

"Rotten luck!" Group Captain Lacey repeated. "And who would have guessed? The aeroplane is a thing of beauty. Been flying myself for years. Just goes to show you how anything, if it gets in the wrong hands, can become an instrument of evil."

He sat there shaking his head. Finally he clapped his hands together and asked if either of them wanted tea. He brought in a tray with three china cups rattling in their saucers, and a plate of packaged digestive biscuits. Then he sat down again with a wheeze.

"So, it was Betty Landsdowne as gave you my name, was it?"

"Yes, sir."

"And how would you be knowing her?"

"I've been staying in her guest house for many years. I take my mother there each summer. And Fleur had a holiday there two summers ago, which is how she and I met."

"A good lady, is Betty. A very good lady. Not afraid of a bit of hard work," he barked.

"She sends you her best regards," Florence said.

"What's that? Oh yes. Yes. Very nice indeed."

"Actually I wanted to talk to you about my house," Lance ventured. "I recently moved to the Lake District. Close to Landsdowne's, in fact. And, as we told you on the phone, it seems that my house is the one you lived in as a child."

"Yes? So you inhabit Fern View? And how is the place? Discovered the secret passageway yet, have you?" he chuckled.

"No? Where is that?"

"Well now, Kitty – that was my sister – Kitty and I used to go down the secret passageway leading to a space in the basement, all the time! The 'grotto,' we used to call it. It was Father who told us about it. He used to keep his fishing tackle down there. Made up all sorts of games down there, Kitty and I. It'd keep us entertained for hours. That made Mother happy. She'd complain otherwise that we were under her feet."

Group Captain Lacey took out a pipe, and lit it with a series of little puffs.

"Your sister...Kitty...Is she still alive?" Lance asked.

"No, poor dear. She died many years ago."

"I'm sorry."

"Yes. That was the turning point in my life, the night she died. I joined the RAF shortly after that."

"It sounds as though you had been very close," Florence said.

"Well, of course we'd fight like all brothers and sisters. But we were close, too. Yes. Shared secrets, that sort of thing. As we grew older, we'd go down to the grotto to talk about things we didn't want Mother and Father to know. Of course they'd find out in the end, as parents have a knack of doing. Some things you just can't keep secret," he chuckled at some private memory of his own.

"That's true. Secrets sometimes are blurted out."

"Not only that," Group Captain Lacey said, serious now. "Sometimes secrets have other ways of showing themselves." He puffed slowly on his pipe, the smoke partly obscuring his face. "High spirited and strong willed was Kitty. It seems that Connie was like that, too, but she was taken away too quickly to be able to tell."

"Who was Connie?"

"Why, Connie was Kitty's baby. Kitty was with child. That was one of our secrets down there in the grotto. She was always slim and managed to hide it well. And she dressed so cleverly. In fact, strange as it sounds, she hid it right up to the night of her delivery. Amazing thing, that! Mother wanted to get rid of the baby straight away, but Dr. McCauley and Father convinced her to let Kitty keep it."

"Who was the baby's father?"

"Ilyich."

"Was he a Russian?"

"Goodness me, no! Ilyich Throgmorton was no Russian!" Florence and Lance exchanged glances. "Mr. and Mrs. Throgmorton, the parents, were quite, shall we say, eccentric, and for some reason they loved Russian names. In fact, they called all their children by Russian names. Ilyich was the oldest, and heir to the estate, which by then – by the time Kitty gave birth – he'd inherited. And he had a brother Ivanoff, and another one, Igor. And three sisters; Sonia, Anna and Natasha. See! I remember it well, though it's been many years since I even thought about them."

"But if your mother agreed to let Kitty keep the baby, why was she given away? Did your mother change her mind?" Florence asked.

"No, she was given away when Kitty died. Mother went mad that night, and was never her true self again."

"Do you want to talk about how Kitty died?" Lance asked softly.

Group Captain Lacey carefully put his pipe in the ashtray, and for a while held his bent head in his hands, so that his pink, freckled scalp showed through the silver strands of hair. He was no longer the commanding, stiff, erect ranking officer of the RAF, but a lonely and vulnerable old man recalling the days of his youth, and possibly contemplating what had gone wrong with the promise of continued happiness.

"I'm sorry. We didn't mean to upset you. You don't need to tell us if you don't want to," Florence hastened to add, feeling terribly nervous at the memory of seeing the dog attack Kitty, and also wanting to prevent Lance from hearing about it, if indeed it did cause her death.

The Group Captain lifted his head, looking slowly at each of them.

"I'm an old man, and let's face it, I haven't got much longer in this world. I might as well speak of it now. I never did discuss it with anyone, so it'll be a relief to talk about it now. I don't know you and very possibly that's why I can tell you. That, and also you seem like nice people."

He reached slowly for his pipe, and took another puff. His blue eyes looked even more watery than before. "My mother had a dog. Eloise, it was called." Florence and Lance again glanced at each other, and then Lance reached over and held her hand tightly. "It was a nasty thing, and we all knew it. Only Mother would never admit it. For some reason, she loved that dog, even though it growled and snapped at people's ankles and was generally unpleasant.

"Well, even after her baby was born, Kitty continued to make frequent visits to see Ilyich. Mother couldn't stand him by then, as he'd refused to marry my sister, so she forbade Kitty to see him. But Kitty slunk out at night to see him, being the headstrong young woman she was. And Mother knew about that, all right, which enraged her. True, Ilyich helped financially with the baby, but he wouldn't marry Kitty, and Mother thought it was because he considered Kitty wasn't good enough for him. Came from a different class, you see. My thoughts on the matter were that he was a cowardly man and didn't want news of his baby out of wedlock to become public knowledge. But he still loved Kitty, or so Kitty claimed, and she was head-over-heels in love with him, so they continued meeting surreptitiously."

Group Captain Lacey ran a hand over his forehead. He then picked up his pipe, examined it, took a puff and then put it back in the ashtray before continuing. "Yes, as I said, these secret meetings infuriated Mother.

She still hadn't adjusted to the baby, and was very distraught, and knew where Kitty was going well enough when she ran off in the early evening so many times. And Kitty would often stay out later than was sensible, given not only Mother's temper, but also how remote and isolated the area was, and probably still is. But it didn't stop Kitty, even though I tried to reason with her too, and she was more likely to listen to me than to Mother. Mother would often take the dog, Eloise – 'Hell Louise' we used to call her as she was a fiendishly unfriendly animal - and go down the lanes looking for her."

Florence was hoping he would not go on. She was now feeling a mounting nausea, but she could think of no way of stopping this old man from recounting tales from his past.

"One night it was particularly late," Group Captain Lacey said. "It had already grown dark and still Kitty had not returned. So Mother and Eloise set out to bring her home, but her dead body was brought back to the house instead. The dog had somehow got free, caught up with Kitty, and mauled her to death. That dog was a pit bull, and I'm told that's how they behave when aggravated. There was nothing that could be done. By the time Mother reached Kitty it was already too late."

Lance let go of Florence's hand, inhaled deeply, and hung his head mournfully.

"And it turned out that that appalling coward, Ilyich," Group Captain Lacey continued, "had seen the dog coming and had bolted to save his own skin, rather than stopping to help and protect my sister. So in my mind it was he who killed her. Killed her by not saving her. It's small comfort that soon after she died, his grand house caught fire, and was almost completely destroyed. He was forced to move away, and good riddance!" Group Captain Lacy said, clapping his hands.

"As for Mother," he said after a moment, "if she had been distraught before about Kitty having a baby, and continuing to see Ilyich who refused to marry her, now she was over the edge. Father made her put the dog to sleep, which was the last straw for her. Plenty was the time when she'd stand in the dining room at twilight, in the gathering dark, refusing to switch on any lights, and she'd then take her imagined dog, plus the flashlight she always took with her as it was so dark outside, and switching it on would go out into the lanes, calling for Kitty.

"I put up with this only for so long; then I left and joined the RAF. Some time after that Father put Mother in a Home, put our house up for sale, and he moved closer to the coast. He liked to fish, you see."

Florence glanced over at Lance, who was still looking down at his lap. So, this *had* happened then! It had been as she had initially suspected. But then a nagging feeling occurred to her that there was something else still not accounted for, and she asked, "What happened to the baby? Where did she go?"

"She was given away to a family called Marsh, over in Sheffield. We none of us had any contact with her after that. She's probably grown up not knowing anything about her awful beginnings. Possibly not even knowing she'd been adopted."

"How old was she when she was adopted?"

"Seven months. I know that for a fact. The day she was handed over was my birthday. It's a birthday I'll never forget. And each year after that, on each birthday, I always say a little prayer for Connie, and one for Kitty too. And would you know, my next birthday's coming up soon. And I'll be seventy-nine!"

"Ah, we'll have to remember that!" Florence said, attempting to sound cheery. But when the atmosphere in the room remained sad, with the Group Captain's eyes abundantly watery and Lance still looking down at the ground, she added, "What a tragic series of events your family went through. I hope you feel a little better having talked about it."

"Well, that's life, isn't it! We none of us have it too easy, do we! Look what happened to you, young man, over in New York City," he said to Lance, who looked up momentarily to acknowledge the remark. "But I believe I do feel better getting this off my chest. I've held it in for years. Why, Connie must be a middle aged lady by now!"

"That's true. Now Group Captain Lacey, I was wondering if you might be interested in just one more thing," Florence said, taking from her handbag the envelope of photos addressed to Mr. Throgmorton that had been in the grandfather clock. "We found these photos in Lance's house, and believe they might be of your family."

He reached over and took the envelope hungrily. He looked through the photos quickly at first, and then more wistfully. Finally he said with a laugh that ended in a wheeze, "That's us alright! That's Kitty, bless her soul. See how pretty she was. And look at me! What a shame I didn't keep those boyish good looks! And yes, Father did enjoy his fishing, as I said before. Sometimes he'd take me down to the lake with him when I was a lad."

About his mother he said nothing at all. He kept turning the photos over and over.

"They're yours. You can keep them," Florence said.

"Why, thank you, miss!" he said. Then he caught sight of the name on the envelope. "Mr. Throgmorton, indeed! I'm glad they never got into his hands. But look, that's Kitty's writing on the envelope. Takes me back. I remember it so well."

"Also, I don't know if you saw, but inside the envelope is part of a poem, copied down in what looks like the same handwriting," Lance said, speaking again at last, his voice sounding a bit rubbery after having been sadly silent for quite some time.

"So there is! Always the romantic, she was! Used to love poetry. Never meant a thing to me, though."

He carefully inserted everything back in the envelope, tucked it into his jacket pocket, which he patted contentedly, and stood up. This was their cue to leave. But first Lance asked, "Group Captain Lacey, would you mind telling us where that secret passage is in my house."

"Well now, I can't do that, can I! If I did, it wouldn't be secret anymore. And Kitty and I swore to each other not to show it to anyone else ever."

"Oh," said Lance, looking disappointed.

"But there now, seeing that I like you, I will tell you this much. It's close to where we had the grandfather clock. Oh, but listen to me, now! That grandfather clock is probably long gone."

"Oh no, it's still there! Maybe not in the same position, but it's certainly there. Thank you, Group Captain!" Lance said, reaching for his crutches and standing up.

"It's my pleasure! Thank you for visiting me, and giving me a trip back to my youth. Remember me to Betty Landsdowne, now won't you. And don't be strangers, either of you. You know where to find me."

He showed them along the narrow passage to the front door.

"Come and visit us some time. Maybe you'd like to see your old house again."

"Well, thank you kindly. At my age I don't generally get out that much, but we'll see." Then, clapping Lance firmly on the shoulder, he barked, "Look after that leg of yours, won't you, old chap!" and closed the door, once again very much the Group Captain.

# NINETEEN

*FLORENCE AND LANCE DID NOT* waste much time looking for the secret passage. Once back in the house, even though evening was fast upon them, they stood in the hall, tapping panels on the wall, seeing if they would slide open, just as in old films.

"Perhaps it's behind the grandfather clock," Florence said, "And we're certainly not going to move that! Perhaps after all, he's a bit batty, or having a little joke on us."

"I doubt it," Lance replied, lowering himself on the wooden bench. "Look at everything else he told us. It's certainly confirmed-"

Just then Mei-Feng came down the stairs, and if she was at all surprised to see Florence on her knees now exploring for loose floorboards, she did not show it. Instead she went straight to the hall cupboard, took out a light jacket, and placing her hand on Lance's arm, announced that she was going to visit a friend and would not be back for dinner. She gave his arm a little squeeze, but to Florence she gave scarcely a nod.

"I don't think she's very happy about my extended stay," Florence said. "I think for her it's bad enough that I come on weekends, but now-"

"Wait a minute!" Lance said, growing excited. "I think Mei-Feng might have inadvertently provided us with a clue. The hall cupboard! Look in there, Fleur! We've tried everywhere else!"

Florence went to the cupboard and opened the door. It was dense with coats and jackets. She tried to push them aside, but they were tightly packed, so she started to remove them and placed them on the bench alongside where Lance was sitting. Returning to the cupboard, she said, "It's totally dark in here. Have you got a flashlight?"

"Virginia Lacey had that!"

Not really seeing what she was doing, she pushed against the back wall of the cupboard, and it gave way! She screamed and fell forward. At the back of the cupboard was a swing door, stiff now with age and swollen wood, but nevertheless it had swung open, leading to an even denser darkness behind, and a smell of frigid musty air.

At the sound of her scream, Lance had scrambled to his feet and come to the cupboard. "Fleur? Are you alright?"

"Lance! We found it! You were right!"

"Good God!"

"It's pitch dark in here. We really do need a flashlight."

"There's one in the kitchen drawer. And while you're about it, could you please bring some candles and matches. We might need them in the 'grotto'."

"Alright!" Florence said, emerging from the hall cupboard. But then she hesitated. "Lance, since we don't know the condition of this passageway or grotto, it might be best if you wait here and I'll go down first to explore and then come back and let you know what it's like."

"No way! Remember the promise to each other that from now on we'd definitely do all explorations together!"

"True. But Lance, this could be dangerous. It's totally dark in there, and even with a flashlight, there could be slippery or uneven ground that we might not see. It would be terrible if you fell and re-injured yourself."

"Fleur. Our promise. Either we go together or not at all!"

"OK, maybe not at all, then."

"Well, in that case, I might just go and explore it when you're back in London."

"No, Lance! No! Promise me you won't do that!"

"Of course I won't, Fleur," he said smiling. "Because our promise was that we would do these explorations together. So please go and fetch the flashlight and candles now."

She returned a few moments later with the flashlight, a box of matches, and only one candle plus a candlestick, which is all she could find.

"Let's hold onto each other along the secret passageway," Florence suggested.

"Good idea. I'll only take one of my crutches, then."

Florence pushed the door at the back of the hall cupboard and shone the flashlight around before stepping sideways into the total darkness.

"You know, we need those helmets with lights on them, that miners wear," he said.

"You're right!"

They were inching along the passageway. Florence felt frightened, not only of the dark, the unknown possibilities that might lie ahead, and the claustrophobia, but also about Lance, and whether it was sensible that he was attempting this. She alternately shone the beam of light at the floor of the passageway, to check for its smoothness and ease of walking, and at the dark walls and low ceiling. But despite her efforts, they almost literally bumped into what seemed to be the end of the passageway.

"Well, it looks as though that's it!" Florence said, relieved and disappointed at the same time.

"Maybe their grotto no longer exists. Maybe when they added the extension to the house, they dug up the grotto to lay the new foundations."

"You could be right. Well, that's a shame," she replied, now feeling that she'd like more adventure in this dark, musty place.

They were just about to turn back when another point of light – from where it was not certain – did a jagged dance along the dark stone walls, and then stopped on what appeared to be a doorknob. Florence immediately thrust her own flashlight into Lance's hand, and stretching forward her free arm, opened out her fingers, and sure enough, did touch cold metal.

"Another door!" she whispered.

"Does it open?"

She rotated the knob, but nothing happened.

"I might need to push hard against this," she said.

"All right," Lance replied. "I'll stand over here against the wall."

Florence pushed with both hands, but the door remained jammed. She leaned her shoulder against it, pushing now with the force of her whole body. At first the door still seemed reluctant to budge, but then it sprang open with a creak. They both exclaimed, and in their excitement, forgot to wonder about the source of that light beam that had directed them to the doorknob.

Clasping onto each other, they moved through the doorway, and then, from the light from the flashlight that Florence held, saw immediately in front of them was a flight of steps that seemed to descend steeply. Lance was still very unsteady on stairs, but she thought better of asking him if he wanted to turn back, as he was so curious and excited. Fortunately the steps had a banister, and so gripping on to that with one hand, and his other arm encircling Florence's back, he started to go down.

The steps seemed made of stone, and were damp and slippery in places. Florence suddenly experienced a terrible sense of vertigo, and was terrified that she would fall forward. What with one of her arms around Lance, the other hand holding both the flashlight and Lance's crutch, and her pocket bulging with the candle and candlestick, she experienced a complete loss of equilibrium. And if she tumbled, she knew she would take Lance with her. They might both be seriously injured, unable to move, and no one – absolutely no one, could rescue them as no one knew where they were, and no one would ever find them. Perhaps the mound of coats on the hall bench might offer a clue, but probably not quickly enough. She wished she had at least taken her mobile phone, though perhaps it would not have reception so deep underground.

But they continued to descend steadily, and as they did so, the sound of running water, faint before, now grew louder. The air felt even more frigid and damp.

"It seems that there must be an underground stream," Lance said, his voice echoing slightly. "Perhaps it feeds into the stream at the bottom of the garden."

Finally they reached the bottom of the stairs, and there before them, illuminated by Florence's flashlight, was a much larger opening.

"The grotto, Fleur! We found it! God, this is exciting! To think this exists under my house!" Lance exclaimed. "Shine the flashlight around a bit and let's see what's here. Actually, shine it to the left over there because that's where the sofa is and I'd like to sit down."

Florence shone the flashlight to the left, and sure enough there was a sofa.

"How did you know this sofa was here, Lance?" she asked incredulously.

"I just knew it was. I don't know how. Actually this grotto looks very familiar. That little desk and hurricane lamp; yes, I've seen them before."

"But how could that be possible? You hadn't known this place existed until Group Captain Lacey told us about it. And you didn't have a clue as to where the secret passage was and how to get down here."

"I don't know, my sweet. I just have a feeling I've been here before. Why don't you light the candle, and then come and sit next to me on the sofa?"

Florence lit the candle, and then sat down. The sofa itself was large and puffy, similar in style to that in Gordon Lacey's living room, and was beige with a trailing pattern of maroon velvet vines and maroon tassels. Above the sofa hung a picture of some flying fish.

"Come here!" he said to Florence, opening up his arms to her. In the candlelight his smile and the sparkle of his eyes appeared even more exquisite. She moved closer beside him, and the pent-up passion of the last week, due to their careful abstinence allowing time for her Howard-inflicted bruises and scratches to heal, in addition to their excitement at discovering this secret area, gave way to full expression. Lance unstrapped his leg brace and let it clatter to the floor, and they, despite the cold, rapidly removed just a sufficient amount of each other's clothes and made love in a fiery glow. When it was over, they dressed quickly and Florence pulled a thick blanket that had been folded and draped over one corner of the sofa, over them both to keep themselves warm. It was rough and prickly, and smelled old and dusty, but to them it was perfect.

Florence, leaning contentedly against Lance's shoulder, was suddenly startled by his urgent whisper, "Look!" which caused them both to sit bolt upright. She did look, though at first she saw nothing. Then, turning her head, she saw a white point of light beaming directly at them.

"What is that?" she asked, her heart beating quickly, and feeling a momentarily disconcerting disorientation.

"I'm not sure."

But the next moment it became clear to them, as the beam of light moved to the desk, and they could see that it emanated from a flashlight held by an older woman with large, flat cheeks and crinkly grey hair.

"Lance, there's a woman over there!"

"Yes, I know there is! I wonder if she's a ghost!"

The beam of light swung abruptly round again and pointed at them directly.

"Who are you!" she hissed. "I must be going mad! What are you two doing in my house?"

"Oh God! She can see us, just as we can see her!" Florence whispered.

"Madam, we're sorry if we're--" Lance began in a loud, cordial voice.

"Never mind. Never mind. First things first." She directed her flashlight towards the desk again, and was now greedily opening drawers and rifling through papers, all the while muttering, "Must stop the girl. Now, where did she put it?" Then there was a soft rustle of footsteps on the stairs, and a sudden, "Mother, don't!" A young woman with attractively billowing dark hair, and who was holding a hurricane lamp, hastened over to her mother's side.

"Kitty! There you are! You're a disobedient, good-for-nothing girl!"

"Why, Mother? Why?"

"Don't you try and look innocent with me! It might work with your father, but not with me!"

"Why are you going through my things, Mother?"

"Because he's been writing to you again, hasn't he! Come on now; at least have the decency to own up."

"Who's been writing?"

"You know very well to whom I'm referring. Well, don't deny it! He did write to you, didn't he! Ilyich! He wrote to you again. I know. Gordon told me!"

"Gordon? But he promised he'd never speak a word of this!"

"Aha! So it *is* true! I managed to trick you very nicely there, didn't I, my little miss! Now, where did you hide it?"

380

The older woman started to look through the bundles of letters again, even though her daughter, Kitty, tried hard to stop her.

"Those are my private letters, Mother! Please leave them alone."

"Ah! I found it! This is it. Why, it's dated July 10th, just a few days ago." She pulled the paper from the envelope.

"Stop! Please stop!"

"*'Darling Kitty'*," she read, in a mock passionate male voice. "*Just to think of you makes my heart thump harder in my chest.*"

"Stop it, Mother! Stop!" Kitty screamed.

"Oh, but I can't stop now. How very charmingly he writes. Let's read on. Where was I? Oh yes, '*...thumps harder in my chest. My mind soaks up every thought of your fair face, your fragrance, your fortitude.*' Now, what a clever writer he is. And so flattering," she said, in a scathingly sweet voice. Then abruptly she flung the pages on the floor, and rotating them under the heel of her shoe, said with vehemence, "He's nothing but a hypocrite and a fool! And you are a fool to be blinded by this ridiculous drivel. He'll never amount to anything!"

"No, Mother! You're wrong!"

"I am very seldom wrong, as a matter of fact. And in this I certainly know about that of which I speak. I forbid – do you understand? – forbid you to see him ever again. And I forbid you to correspond. In fact, sit down now, and write him the last letter you will ever write. Go on! Sit down! I will dictate it to you!"

Sobbing loudly, Kitty perched on the tiny stool and took out writing paper and a fountain pen. Her tears splashed on the paper.

"'We must part for ever!'" the older woman cried in a stormy voice. "Go on – write that down! And then, 'Kindly do not try to see me or write to me.' Write it, I say!"

Florence clutched on to Lance. "But this is awful," she whispered.

Lance nodded, not taking his eyes off Kitty as she sat bent over the appalling letter she was forced to write.

"Mother, I can't write this."

"Write it, I tell you! And be quick about it! There's just one line left. 'I find I can not love you.'"

"No!" Kitty screamed, kicking back the stool and standing up. "I will never write that! Not if you twist my arm behind my back, or lock me in my room for two days without food. I have agreed to write the rest, but will never, ever sign my name to such a statement that I do not love Ilyich!"

"You must!"

"You're forcing me to lie, Mother. And you taught us well never to do that – though I might add that it's not a rule you always apply to yourself."

"How dare you! Very well. You can leave off the part about not loving him. Just sign your name and give it to me, for the message is clear enough as it stands. I will go with it to the Post Office straight away!"

Kitty stood and angrily thrust the letter into her mother's hands. Her mother immediately sealed it into an envelope, and stuffing it into her pocket, turned and went up the stairs. Kitty bent down to pick up Ilyich's letter that her mother had trampled on the floor, tried to smooth out the creases between her fingers, and then lightly brushing the letter against her lips, put it in a pocket of her blouse, closest to her heart. Then she flung herself onto the stool by the writing table, and sobbed.

Lance sprang up and ran over to her. Florence was first amazed that he was going up to speak with her, but then realized that the larger issue was Lance's agility at being able to run like that. She scratched her head, feeling the short spikiness of her hair. But suddenly everything felt quite natural. Of course! Why shouldn't Lance run? He seemed like a very energetic man. She was on her holiday at Landsdowne's Guest House and had met him there, and he'd just taken her to see a house deep in the countryside, which was called Fern View, which fascinated him since he knew no one ever moved in despite many recent renovations.

They'd been peering through the windows, and then, only minutes earlier they'd found a door unlocked at the back of the house. Lance had walked boldly inside, but she'd entered slowly and on tiptoe. She'd whispered to him about her even greater concern about trespassing than she'd felt outside looking in.

"Don't worry, Florence," he'd said, smiling his brilliant smile at her. "This house is quite empty! And finding that unlocked door and being able to explore inside is such a great opportunity! All the doors have always been locked before. You must be my lucky charm! Perhaps we'll find the clue as to why so many people are about to move here, and have even invested so much money in renovating it, and then don't move in at the last minute!"

She'd been captivated by his smilingly luminous eyes, infected again by his boyish sense of adventure, and reassured by his conviction that the house was unlived in. He'd strode through the empty house, his footfalls echoing in the empty rooms, and she'd become daring and brave, so together they'd explored the downstairs, confirming the layout of the rooms as they'd interpreted them from looking through the windows.

And then he'd noticed that the hall cupboard door was hanging open, and the cupboard itself was empty of any coats, validating that the house was indeed uninhabited. Through the open door, Florence had caught sight of another door at the back of the cupboard, which had pleased Lance immensely. He'd opened it, and together they'd excitedly found the steps and had groped their way down to the grotto.

She looked now at Lance as he knelt down to speak with this young woman who was apparently called Kitty, and his face looked just as it had done a few nights ago when he was sitting in the pool of light under the green shaded lamp in the lounge at Landsdowne's and they'd been discussing the meaning of Time.

"Who are you? What are you doing down here?" Kitty asked Lance through her tears.

"Please don't be afraid. I'm a friend. I just want to help you as you seem so distressed," Lance replied.

"Oh yes; I think I remember you. You are a friend of Gordon's, aren't you?" Kitty said sniffing, and rubbing the side of her nose.

"Yes, I just saw Gordon the other day."

"But it's very bad of him to tell people how to come down here," Kitty said with a little burst of vehemence. "We swore to each other that this is our secret place. I am really cross with him about this. It's bad enough that Mother came down here." And with the memory of that, Kitty started to sob again.

"Please don't be sad," Lance said. "Gordon kept his promise and didn't tell me how to find the grotto. I found it myself. And maybe luckily so, since it seems that you could do with some help. Please try not to cry, and tell me what's the matter."

Lance had such a comforting way about him, and Kitty could not resist it.

"Oh, all right! I will tell you. What does it matter now, anyway? Mother has forbidden me to see Ilyich, which I absolutely won't do! Besides, I have something for him, but I don't know how to give it to him, since she made me write a letter to him saying we must never meet again, and now she's on her way to the Post Office to post it."

"What is it that you have for him? Perhaps I could help and take it to him for you."

Kitty rubbed her eyes impatiently, and looked at Lance.

"It's a ring," she said. "A very special ring, as it holds a little gold box on top, which can be opened up as it has a tiny hinge and a very little lid."

"That sounds beautiful. If you trust me, you could give it to me now, and I will take it to Ilyich. Just tell me where to find him. It would be no problem."

Florence sat quietly on the sofa, amazed that Lance was offering to do this thing. She nearly spoke, but saw how entranced Lance was with this conversation, how much he empathized with suffering and how much he liked to help people.

"I will tell you where you can find him. It's complicated as we have to meet in secret, so we generally find each other on a small footpath just off a particular country lane. And I can describe how to get there from here. It's not far. But I can't give you the ring yet, as I have something I first want to put inside the tiny gold box."

"Oh?"

"Yes," said Kitty. "I want to put a lock of our baby's hair inside the ring box. Some say it is unlucky to cut a baby's hair before the baby reaches one year of age, but I think that is all bosh! Anyway, she's almost one. She just turned seven months last Saturday. My poor Ilyich cannot even see his daughter, Connie, most of the time, so at least a little lock of her hair might go some way towards helping him feeling connected to her."

"That sounds like a lovely idea. Just tell me when you're likely to have the ring ready and when you would want to meet again, and I could go instead of you."

"Well, it seems that we don't have a moment to spare! I think my

Mother will have missed the post for today, luckily, so the letter will be picked up tomorrow, and that means it will be delivered in two days' time. So meet me tomorrow, at 6.00! Meet me down here in the grotto again, since you seem to know the way. Don't ever tell me your name. I don't want to somehow end up telling Gordon. This has to be our secret. And I will think of you as my guardian angel."

"I will, Kitty! I will see you down here again tomorrow. At 6.00 o'clock sharp."

"Good! And after I've given you the ring, be prepared to go out to find Ilyich just before it begins to get dark at about 9.30. He will be expecting me then. Give him the ring, and explain to him what happened. Actually, better than that, I will write a letter telling him how my guardian angel came to deliver this little ring from me to him. This way Mother can't say I disobeyed her. I didn't go to see him. Just make sure you go before dusk, so you can find each other. That is the time he will be waiting for me."

"I will."

"I can't thank you enough!" Kitty said, and then turning away from Lance she murmured, "Now perhaps Ilyich will want to marry me, so that the three of us can be united at last."

Kitty stood up dreamily, walked over to the stairs, and mounted them in a floating fashion. Florence and Lance wanted to follow. But Florence again experienced that odd disorientation and had to first steady herself. Also, since Lance needed to spend time strapping his leg brace back on, their focus shifted to the arduous process for him of mounting all those stairs. They eventually emerged from the coat cupboard into the hall, and Florence made her way to the wooden bench. She shoved the coats that she'd previously removed from the cupboard to one side, and sat down heavily, picking a large dust ball out of her hair that had swung forward over her shoulder.

"That was amazing!" she laughed.

He joined her on the bench, panting slightly, yet smiling all the same. "What are you referring to; finding the secret passageway and grotto, or our love-making on the sofa down there?"

"Well, both really!" she replied. And with a kiss, she jumped up and added, "And now, if you'll excuse me, I think I'll have a shower. I think I just walked through a thousand spiders' webs, to say nothing of the fifty years or more of dust."

A little later, feeling clean and refreshed, Florence rejoined Lance, who'd also bathed, in the living room.

"Do you know, my sweet," she started tentatively, "in the shower just now, where I often have my best thoughts, I had a feeling you *did* make a promise to Kitty to meet her the next evening at 6.00. It feels like a memory from so long ago, though. Funny that it's only just come back to me now. Two nights ago when you talked about this, I didn't have a clue what you meant."

"But that's terrific! Oh Fleur, I'm so happy that you remember this now, too! So if we both remember this, then it *must* have happened! And it's something I must do! Now I feel that I might still have a chance to save her, by running that errand for her."

"You mean, taking the ring with the lock of her baby's hair, to Ilyich, because her mother forbade her to see him again?"

"Yes, exactly! That's what I remember, too! Oh Fleur, this *did* happen! I *did* make that promise to Kitty! So I'll meet her in the grotto tomorrow at 6.00! I feel fairly certain that this must have been the *rendez-vous* she had in mind, since it was her secret place. Do you remember she called me her guardian angel?" he finished proudly.

Florence nodded, and then said, "But Lance, I don't want you to be hurt. Actually, please don't go! Don't risk endangering yourself this way. That dog was vicious!"

"Don't worry, my sweet. I won't be hurt. Or at least not fatally, as after all we know I'm alive after Kitty."

"But Lance, I don't want you to be hurt again! You've already been injured so badly! And I fear it wouldn't alter anything, anyway. She'd still be killed. Because she was killed. I witnessed the events leading up to that. My camera told the rest. And Group Captain Lacey confirmed it."

"But perhaps I can change that, Fleur! Perhaps I can spare this woman's life."

"No, Lance. We can't alter history. We can't stop the dog's attack from happening, any more than I could prevent you from being hurt at the

World Trade Center, as you had once explained to me. In both cases, what we saw was factual. One event was going to occur, the other has occurred. Both were unalterable."

"Oh yes; the World Trade Center," he whispered, turning inwards on himself. "I wonder if they've finished clearing all the rubble yet. They were taking it out on trucks and then barges, to a dump on Staten Island. Do you know what that dump is called? 'Fresh Kill'! Did you know that? What an amazingly appropriate name!"

Florence did not know what to say. She held his hand, which, in contrast to how warm and tingly it had been when they'd made love in the grotto, was now cold and inert.

"'Fresh Kill,' Fleur. A mass burial site, because contained amongst the rubble of the buildings were people. Crushed people. People who'd been hacked to pieces, or else incinerated. I could have been there, too, Fleur. Or at least pieces of me could have been."

"Lance, you're frightening me."

"Am I? I'm sorry. I frighten myself sometimes."

She put both arms around him, but he seemed to shake them off.

"Down in that grotto," Lance said, still stuck in his horrific thoughts, "once you blew out the candles, if we'd also turned off the flashlight, we would've been able to see what it's like in complete darkness. You can imagine how frightening that is. Like being trapped between the walls of a collapsed building. Or like walking, as Kitty had done, to meet her lover after nightfall, on a remote footpath off a country lane. Only to find that a savage dog is about to attack her. And what does her lover do? He turns away and flees!" Lance's eyebrows arched in a strange manner.

"Don't you see, Fleur!" he continued, sounding agonized. "Group Captain Lacey was right! It was tantamount to killing her. Ilyich should have put his own body between Kitty and the dog! He should have pulled a branch off from a tree and beaten off the animal! He should have done whatever it took to save her!"

Florence nodded, squeezing his hand.

"Fleur, when I first returned from America," he said, still sounding highly distressed, "and I told you about how Lovey Barker, up until then a total stranger, had found an ambulance for me, you and I had a fascinating discussion about whether it was our ethical duty to help others who we did not know, when extreme peril faced all of us, or whether we owed it to ourselves and our loved ones to save our own skin. In my case, Fleur, Lovey Barker, without apparently stopping to ponder this ethical debate, stopped in his own flight to help me. To enable me not to be one of those three thousand who lie in pieces in the Fresh Kill Landfill. But in Kitty's case, it wasn't a stranger. Ilyich Throgmorton was her lover! He accepted her love and impregnated her. They had a baby together. And then he left her defenseless against a dog which mauled her to death! That, too, is an atrocity!"

"You're absolutely right!" Florence said gently. "He should have tried to rescue her. It's tragic that she died."

"Yes, so I must prevent her death! I must be there meeting Ilyich instead of her!"

"But Lance, then she will probably die some other way or at some other time. Don't you see!"

"No, Fleur! I don't see! I can't accept this as an inevitability. I must try to save her. Because can't you see what her death did? She was like a link in a chain that comprised her family. Once she was killed and the link dropped from the chain, the whole family structure unraveled: Kitty's baby was given away, never remembering her mother, Virginia Lacey went mad, Gordon Lacey left home to join the RAF, the dog was put to sleep, and the father sold this lovely house and moved away. Kitty could have been alive today, slightly older than Group Captain Lacey. She could have been sitting in a high winged armchair, by a fireplace, with a china teacup and saucer on her knees, patriotically watching the Queen's speech every Christmas. Instead she's been dead for years. Dead, Fleur! It's so senseless! We're social beings, us humans, and if we don't help each other, what else is there?"

"Lance," she said to him, "Lance, you feel this way because you're exceptionally good and kind. Your values are so correct. I love you so much because of this. And I completely agree. There's no doubt about it that one should help a loved one in a dangerous situation. There's more debate, though, as to whether or not to help a stranger, though thank God Lovey Barker helped you! Thank God for that! And don't forget how you, too, have already performed a wonderfully heroic deed when you helped the pregnant woman, who was a complete stranger, earlier that morning of September 11th. She was able to escape from the World Trade Center because of you! You've already done so much. I am just not sure how it would be possible for you to help Kitty."

"But I must try! That bastard Throgmorton didn't help her, even though she'd given birth to his baby, and it was only seven months old when she died." Lance took off his glasses, and rubbed his eyes on his sleeve. "Connie, they called her. Huh! There was nothing constant for her in her life!"

"Perhaps she did manage to have a happy life, despite it all. Let's certainly hope so."

The following day Juliet telephoned Lance to say that their mother said she was seeing dancing dots in front of her eyes, (though it was later found to be because of faulty wiring in her bedroom at Landsdowne's, which caused the lights to flicker), and determined that she needed to see her doctor in Cockermouth at once, and that she needed both Juliet and Lance to accompany her. They were made to wait for ages in the waiting room, no doubt because the doctor's office had fitted her in at the last moment, so by the time Lance reached home and rushed as much as he was capable, down the steps and into the grotto, it was well after 6.00 pm, and all traces of Kitty were completely gone.

# TWENTY

*WHEN FLORENCE RETURNED TO LONDON,* after her ten days spent with Lance, she was amazed by the number of messages on her answering machine. Besides a message from her parents, there were several from her lawyer, the most recent of which said that the unfortunate incident with Howard might well precipitate a lot of complications, and she should be in touch at once. Elizabeth Carlisle had called three times; once to congratulate her on her most recently submitted story about the London Underground, and twice more to ask her about doing two more stories. These sounded urgent, and the message was already four days old. There was also a message from Anna, who said, "They're now predicting that this baby might come early, Florence. They advise that I try to prevent that as much as I can as there is still well over a month until the due date, so I'm confined to bed and told strictly to stay there. It's very tedious. Please come and visit!"

"Yes!" Florence told her, phoning her back immediately, hoping it was not too late at night to call. "I was at Lance's all week, and only just returned and heard your message. How are you feeling? I'll come tomorrow evening, and I'll bring something along for dinner!"

There was one message left on her machine that she had not yet listened to.

"Flo, it's Howard." Oh no, she gasped to herself, tempted to delete that message before listening to the remainder of it. "I'm phoning as I'd like us to talk about what happened," the message continued. *Ah*, she thought, *maybe he has some decency and will want to apologize.* "But you honestly can't say it was all my fault. You haven't stopped being a temptress, have you! I mean, when you showed interest in seeing my new flat, what could I do? Would it have been better not to allow you in? In hindsight it seems that the answer is 'yes', but I hadn't known it then. How could I be inhospitable to the woman who is still legally my wife? We obviously still have feelings for each other. When you put your hand on my knee, how could I help but respond? And then yes, things got a bit out of hand, but as I said, we still have feelings for each other. So, all in all, I think we both owe each other an apology. Phone me back, and let's get this over with. And the sooner, the better! Bye."

Florence was furious! What a cunning, devious man! She had expressed interest in seeing his new flat purely from an overwhelming desire to retrieve her photos, and she never, ever put her hand on his knee, or was seductive in any way. The mere thought was repulsive. Still, she realized, it was her word against his.

She wanted to call Lance; he had, after all, offered to take a more active role in her divorce, but this was too sordid. Also, what if it started to plant doubts in his mind as to whether she was in part to blame for what had happened? And now she did in fact start to blame herself. While staying with Lance, and feeling the warmth of his proximity and protection, she felt she'd been assaulted by Howard. Now, alone and exhausted, she questioned whether there had been anything in her behavior that had led Howard to ultimately do what he had done.

Even though tired from her long drive, she had a troubled sleep. Her word against his word. Howard would win. He was more powerful and aggressive than she was. And he was a man. She must see her lawyer. And

Anna, of course, too. But what about all her work that needed to be caught up on? When would she have time for that?

Early the next morning, she called Elizabeth Carlisle, but she had not yet arrived in the office. Then she called her lawyer and made an appointment. Luckily, since it was considered an emergency, she could be fitted in at 11.00. She then called her parents and had a quick but pleasant talk, and tried Elizabeth again, who was now in a meeting. Worries started to flood her mind. What if Elizabeth, having not heard back from her quickly, had given the assignments to someone else? Why hadn't she thought to tell Elizabeth that she would be away for a week and a half?

Feeling stressed, she went out to the gourmet take-out shop, and picked up a nice selection of food for her dinner with Anna and David. She returned to her flat, and while putting the food away in the fridge, she tried Elizabeth one more time, actually hoping that she would still be unavailable, as she had to leave shortly for her lawyer's appointment. But Elizabeth was there, and was talkative, too. She heartily congratulated Florence again on her latest story, and still wanted her to do the other two stories, which she discussed in slow, elaborate detail. And, she said, they each had quite a tight deadline.

By the time the conversation ended, Florence only had fifteen minutes before her meeting with the lawyer, and she usually allowed herself at least half an hour to get there. She'd have to take a taxi, and hope that there would not be too much traffic. Lance was certainly right about the difference between chronological and kairological time, and she definitely preferred the latter that they had enjoyed together in the countryside. Now Time seemed hostile and unfriendly, as everything needed to be done at once.

She was just about to leave when the phone rang. She picked it up hurriedly, with an angry sounding, "Hello!" It was Lance.

"Lance, I'm so sorry! I can't talk now! I've a meeting with my lawyer starting in ten minutes, and I'm so late leaving here. I'm going to have to run like mad, and I really hate running and being in such a rush."

"OK, Fleur. I'm glad you're taking care of that. Phone me later, my love, and tell me how it went."

"Yes, I'll do that. Bye!"

She put the phone down and ran out of her flat, down the stairs, and on to the street. She'd have to go to the main road to find a taxi, so she ran along her street, almost knocking aside a young mother dawdling by, with a pushchair and lots of shopping. Once on the main road, streams of cars flowed by, but not a single taxi. And when at last she spied one further up the street, coming towards her, she saw that it was occupied. She ran to another corner, hopeful that more taxis might pass that way. There was a man on the corner also trying to flag down a taxi, and when a taxi did eventually slow down in front of them, she asked if she could share a ride with him. He looked surprised, asked where she was going, and then nodded and said, "Hop in."

He tried making conversation with her as they crawled along, because yes – the traffic was extremely heavy. It might have been faster to take the tube after all. But she was too preoccupied to speak to the man. She worried about having been abrupt with Lance on the phone – he had sounded so warm and pleased to speak with her, and she had cut him off. And then, in a sickening panic, she realized how inappropriate it had been of her to moan to him about having to run, when probably one of his deepest wishes was to be able to run again. How could she have been so stupid and insensitive? Also she realized that since she had left her flat in such a hurry, she had forgotten to take the taped phone message from Howard that she had intended playing to her lawyer. Damn! Well, too late now.

She stared fiercely out of the window at all the cars in their way, like so many immense obstacles in a race, and she looked at every red traffic light with intense hatred.

"That won't make us get there any faster, miss," said the other passenger. "Might as well sit back and relax. That's what I always say."

She acknowledged him with a brief flicker of her eyes, but her lips remained pursed.

"It'll kill you in the end, all that tension. 'Snot worth it, in my opinion."

"Driver!" she said, tapping on the glass behind the driver's head. "Please let me out here. It'll be faster to walk!"

She fumbled in her purse for the money, overpaid him but it was quicker that way, and giving a brief nod to the other passenger, opened the door and rushed down the street to the lawyer's building.

When she opened the door to Leeman, Riley, Twigger, and Partners, Solicitor's Office, she was twenty-five minutes late and the waiting room was full of people. She apologized to the receptionist, and was told Mrs. Twigger was with another client and was running late herself. After all that!

When Florence eventually found herself in Mrs. Twigger's office, sitting across the wide, glass topped, paper-strewn desk from her, Mrs. Twigger reassured her that the end was in sight. Clearly Howard had been stalling, and she suspected that maybe it was because he had changed his mind and wanted to stay married – lots of divorce cases turned out that way, she told her in a tired drawl - but this attempted rape changed all that. At this point, Florence told her about his phone message, and how he'd inferred that she was to blame for seducing him. Mrs. Twigger seemed unimpressed. "Blame the victim," she said, pulling off her glasses. "A common tactic!"

"But it's his word against my word."

"Look dearie," (Florence hated being called that.) "We see this every day. He's a typical sociopath, is your husband. Besides, you have the doctor's report, and this taped phone message, so bring them both along to my office as soon as you can. Leave them with May, the receptionist. And my advice to you – don't talk to Howard at all. If he phones you again, tell him politely and briefly that all conversations will go through your lawyers. And above all, do not agree to see him again. Remember, you are adversaries! As soon as you furnish me with the items we mentioned, I'll send a letter to Mr. Davis, giving evidence of his client's behavior, and I will also suggest the date of August 14th for the four of us to meet in my office, so as to reach a final settlement. Does that sound good?"

"Yes, very! I can't wait for this to be over."

"Very well! Good day, Miss Hamilton!"

Florence took the tube home. She had to wait for ages for it to come, but that no longer seemed to matter. Once home, with a mug of hot jasmine tea in her hand, she went to the computer and logged on to the Internet. She was going to start some initial research for her new stories. There was an informative reference site she had used in her last story, so this seemed a good place to start, even if it meant travailing through a labyrinth of links until she could find what she wanted. She could not quite remember the web address of this site, so she scrolled through, looking at all the Internet sites she had most recently visited. It was then that she came across the T.S. Eliot site, with the poem, "Burnt Norton," that Kitty had excerpted and enclosed, along with some family photos, in an envelope addressed to Ilyich Throgmorton. Now that Florence had seen Kitty, however strange that might be, she looked again at the poem. Why had Kitty chosen it, and why those lines in particular?

*"Time present and time past*
*Are both perhaps present in time future*
*And time future contained in time past.*
*If all time is eternally present*
*All time is unredeemable"*

Did Kitty know, despite their love for each other, that they would never marry? Did she know she would soon die? And why did she send her lover photographs not only of herself, but also of her family? Was she trying to build acceptance and trust on both sides?

She was shaken from her thoughts by glancing at the clock. She was due at Anna's house in a few hours, and Elizabeth had requested an outline from her for the first story by the end of the day! So she clicked away from Eliot's poem, and into the reference site she had initially intended reading. She worked intensely, unaware of the afternoon slipping by. Almost immediately, it seemed, it was time for her to go to Anna. She hurriedly looked through the notes she had just made, drew up an outline which was sketchy at best – no time for the perfection she normally aimed for - and attached it to an e-mail to Elizabeth, with a note saying it was provisional and would almost certainly need revising, although there were some very interesting avenues that she wanted to pursue.

Anna did not live too far away, so Florence decided to walk. The bags of food were heavy, and her shoulder felt weighted down, as she hurried along the damp streets, in which a soft drizzle had started.

David opened the door, looking relieved to see her. Taking the bags from her, he said, "Anna will be so pleased to see you! Why don't you go straight up and see her now!"

"I'd love to. But first do you want some help heating things up?"

"No, don't worry, thanks. I'll take care of that. Anna's needs are far greater than mine!"

So smiling and giving David's cheek a little kiss, Florence mounted the stairs to Anna's bedroom. Anna, who had a small frame and slight build, looked uncomfortably bloated, as she lay with her head and shoulders half propped up on a mound of pillows.

"Florence!" she exclaimed delightedly. "I'm so glad you've come! I couldn't wait to see you!"

They hugged and talked excitedly about Anna's condition, the due date, and the names they were considering for the baby.

"If it's a boy, we're thinking of Adam or Sam. But if it's a girl, I really like Nina or Mimi – you know, Mimi short for Miriam. But David has recently come up with the name Dawn. And middle names, of course, will be after our grandparents on each side."

"What lovely names, all of them! Do you think it will be a boy or girl? Any hunches?"

"A few months ago I thought it would be a boy. I even dreamed that it would be! Now I'm not sure. At this point, all I care about is a healthy baby."

"Yes, of course. Well, I think it will be a girl! I've thought that all along. Remember how I told you that?"

"Yes, I do. Oh, but I can't wait for this stage to be over. I can't sleep well at night, and I'm so uncomfortable, as well as being horribly bored and impatient while David's out during the day. I have plenty to read, but I've read all the baby books twice, and anything else just doesn't hold my attention. Oh Florence, I'm so glad you're here! Did I tell you that already?"

"I'm just sorry I wasn't here as soon as you were told about needing bed-rest. But now I'm back, I'll come all the time, I promise!"

"Thanks! Please do that! And how was your stay with Lance? I tell you, Florence; I don't know how he does it. I presumably only have about a month of enforced immobility, and I can't stand it! But for him, it's his lifetime!"

"Well, not completely. He's recently been attempting to walk. He has to put a brace on his leg and use crutches, and he's a bit slow and wobbly, but he's doing it! One time, though, he unfortunately overdid it, and then it hurt him too much to walk for a couple of days after that," Florence added, thinking of the night they followed Virginia Lacey outside, but even to her dear friend Anna she could not give voice to this incident. "But in general he's walking a little more each day and is steadier, so he's making remarkable progress, especially since some stupid doctor told him he'd never walk again."

"Florence, that's wonderful! What courage and determination he must have!"

"Yes, yes; he does! Do you remember how, after the attacks on the World Trade Center, you advised me to pray for courage, strength and hope. Well, it certainly helped me, so I told him this during one of his bleakest times, and it looks as if – oh Anna, it's all thanks to you!"

"Hardly! But I'd love to meet him. Do you think I ever will?"

"Yes! I want you to officiate at our wedding, Anna! So what that he's not Jewish! You could still officiate, couldn't you?"

"What? You're getting married! Oh, Florence!"

"Well, we haven't talked about it yet. Not really. But it's what I want so much, Anna! I truly love this man."

"I can see. Tell me what he's like, Florence. I know you've told me before, but tell me again."

Florence giggled and squeezed Anna's hand. "Well, for one thing, he's very kind and gentle. And very affectionate. And he's so loyal too, which I could see straight away, as soon as I met him, from the way he is with his aged mother. Oh, and he's tremendously intelligent. We can talk about anything. He's really inspirational!"

"Has he changed because of what he's been through?"

"Well, he's still intermittently traumatized. But somehow he's even more magnificent!"

Suddenly Florence gasped, and her expression changed from the previous dreamy one, to one of extreme agitation. "Oh Anna, I just remembered I said such an insensitive remark to him this morning on the phone!"

"What?"

"I moaned about having to run all the way to King's Road so that I could catch a taxi, as I was late for my lawyer's appointment."

"What was insensitive about that?"

"How could I moan about running, when his own inability to run is one of the things that he misses so badly?"

"Oh Florence, while it is certainly true that we should all thank God every day for being able-bodied, and we should never take anything for granted, I shouldn't think for a minute that Lance thought your remark insensitive. He was probably more concerned about you feeling so stressed."

"That's true. He becomes very concerned when he knows I'm stressed."

"See! He and I think similarly! I already like him! But tell me; how is it going with your lawyer? When is your divorce going to be over?"

"Anna, there's one more thing I haven't told you. The reason I went to see my lawyer today was because Howard tried to rape me. That's why Lance invited me to stay for an extended time."

"Rape you? Oh no! How horrible! And it must have brought back the trauma of what happened with Renard, too. Do you feel like telling me about it?"

Florence told her the story, and Anna was appalled. David's step on the stair abruptly ended the conversation, though Anna quickly told Florence, "Lance is a good man! It was kind of him to invite you for a longer stay, and he was quite right to insist that you speak to your lawyer about this. Maybe now she'll step things up a notch, and stop Howard from dragging his feet."

"Speak to the lawyer about what, Florence? Are you OK?" David asked, entering the room carrying several steaming dishes on a deep blue tray.

"Yes, I'm fine now, thanks," Florence replied, wondering if she needed to elaborate. But Anna saved her by exclaiming, "Florence, what wonderful food you brought along! Chicken in a creamy sauce! Roast potatoes! Oh, and is that steamed spinach with mushrooms and pine nuts? Ooh, all my favourites! Thank you! It all looks so delicious! And nutritious, too! Where did you get such a lovely spread?"

The conversation once more swung to issues concerning the baby, a topic that held as much excited delight for Anna as talking about Lance had for Florence. They had a wonderful evening together, and Florence promised to return again on Wednesday.

"So glad we'll see you again in a few days," David said as he was showing her out. "But don't bring food again. There's no need for that. Just come yourself. I honestly haven't seen Anna look so happy for ages!"

"I'm delighted to see both of you!" she replied. "But I'd like to bring some dinner again. It's simple and such fun!"

It was only when she returned home that she realized she had not phoned Lance back, and now it was too late to phone. She felt dreadful, but sat at the computer and sent him an e-mail:

> *Lance, dearest one! Give me kairological time! Today I have been rattled and robbed of any feeling of calm since there was so much to do, and all of it in need of being done at once. Actually, I did have a high spot, too, though, and that's when I visited Anna, who's unfortunately been ordered bed-rest for the last stage of her pregnancy. I talked to her about you. It made me so happy to talk about you. It almost felt that you were with me! I stayed late at Anna's, and now back home I realize it's too late to phone you. I don't want to spend too long writing this in case you are still awake and at your computer. I want you to receive this now, to know that I love you, and am filled with passion thinking about you. Fleur*

Florence was woken the next morning at 6.10 by the ringing of the phone. It was her mother. Yes, they had recently gone a long way in mending their relationship, but to phone this early really wouldn't do!

"What can this mean, Flo? You've not returned the wedding present Uncle Lou and Aunt Jess gave you! I just happened to see them at Jake and Sue's Golden Wedding Anniversary, and we sat at the same table as them, and at first Lou wouldn't speak to me. Then he finally said why. 'Your daughter likes hanging on to material possessions, it seems,' he said. I was at a loss to know what he was talking about. Oh Florence, I know it was a difficult time, and you might not have got round to returning everything at once, but-"

"Ma!" Florence interrupted. "I haven't kept a single thing! Howard kept everything, and when I told him we should return the lot, he refused. It's him, not me!"

"That's not the story I heard. You know Lou knows Max, who used to play golf with Howard's grandfather. Well, he said that Howard said you took everything for yourself!"

"But that's not true! It's simply not true. I'd never do that. You know I wouldn't!"

Exasperated, Florence kicked off the duvet and climbed out of bed.

"But he said-"

"Look; you've been over here. Did you see any wedding presents? No! Of course not! So why do you believe Howard and not me? Besides, you raised me to be honest and fair. You know I'd never do a thing like that!"

"Very well, dear. I believe you. I'm glad we got that sorted out. Now I can go back to sleep, and you should, too. It's very early in the morning."

"Yes, it is."

"Sorry to have woken you, Flo. It's just that I lay awake all night worrying. But now we've got to the bottom of that! Go back to sleep, sweetie. Come over for dinner on Thursday. We hardly see you!"

"OK. Thanks, Ma."

When Florence finished talking, she could not go back to sleep. Why was Howard spreading malicious rumors about her? Who else had he lied to, while simultaneously gloating over his horde of fine china, sparkling crystal, and polished cutlery?

She decided to go to the computer and start work on her stories for Elizabeth. It was advantageous that she was up so early; it would make up for the previous day when she had spent so little time on her writing. And by 11.00 that morning she had accomplished so much, that she felt positively glowing. She planned to continue writing until lunchtime, and after lunch, she would take the doctor's report and the tape to the lawyer's office, and then resume work. At this rate, by the end of the day, she would have made significant inroads into her first story.

When the phone rang she was so immersed in her writing that she felt very absent and removed from whoever was calling her.

"Florence!" Elizabeth's voice brought her quickly back, but there was a sharpness in her tone that she couldn't understand.

"Hello, Elizabeth! I'm so glad you phoned. I'm making some really nice discoveries-"

"Florence, can you come into my office immediately to see me? There's something I urgently need to discuss with you."

"What? You mean right now?"

"Yes."

"OK. I'll come straight away. Is everything all right?"

"We'll talk about it when you're here. I'll expect you in half an hour."

Florence wondered what this could be about. Perhaps Elizabeth did not like the outline she had submitted the previous evening. But why did she sound so clipped? And why did she need to see her face-to-face? Since having started working as a freelancer, they had usually discussed her writing on the phone or by e-mail. It must be that Elizabeth hated her outline; after all, she had been too hurried, and so had not done her best work. Why, even last night as she was going to sleep, Florence had thought of moving whole sections around.

So, when Florence pushed open the glass door to Elizabeth's office, and saw her frowning face, she was nervous and a little taken aback.

"Sit down, Florence," Elizabeth ordered, as she simultaneously came around to the other side of the desk and stood over her. "I have something of major importance to discuss with you. Now, you know I have consistently liked your work, and was even starting to make moves internally to rehire you in a full-time capacity. That is what makes what has just come to light even more shocking."

"What? What happened?"

"I can describe it as none other than a breach. I'd put so much trust in you, Florence. Why ever did you do it?"

"Do what? I don't understand."

"I had been really impressed with your London Underground story.

401

I thought it was fantastic. I couldn't praise it enough. You captured every nuance, right down to the near hypnotized expressions on the riders' faces. It was almost as if you had a camera with you; you painted your pictures with words so exquisitely. I'd praised you elaborately and what I thought was deservedly, to everyone I knew. That's why I gave you two stories this time. But I'm glad this, this disgusting piece of information has surfaced now – as you've only just begun the stories and I can take them back and give them to someone else more trustworthy."

Florence, who had been obediently seated in her chair while Elizabeth stood over her, now also stood.

"Elizabeth, I don't understand at all what is going on. Can you please explain all of this to me?"

"All right! I'm coming to that!" Elizabeth spat. "I received a phone call yesterday, late afternoon. I'd been in a meeting, but a message was left on my machine. It was from a long-time reader of our magazine – a very incensed reader – who said that you had made up all your data, and that none of it could be substantiated. Made it up, Florence! That's the worst, most unethical thing a reporter can do! It's up there with plagiarism. I'm enraged! Think what it can do to the good name of our magazine! Inventing data to make a good story!"

"Elizabeth, that's absolutely not true! I would never do that!"

"This man might press charges. I don't know. But it's despicable! It's outrageous! I should have let you go when I first intended to last September, rather than keeping you as a freelancer out of the goodness of my heart! I'm, I'm…words fail me!"

"Please, Elizabeth! Why do you believe this accusation? Surely you know my work well enough to-"

"What I know well enough is that you go all the way to the Lake District every weekend, and recently for even longer, though of course that is not my business as you are a freelancer now. But what I suspect is that you probably only have half a mind, if that, on your work, as all you think about is going away. Now that this reader pointed this out, it all seems very plausible to me. So, as of right now, please stop any further work on those two stories. I'm going to hand them over to Tracey. I'll contact you again when we've cleared this matter up and looked into it further."

"Can I at least hear that message on your machine? Please let me hear what this 'long-time reader' said."

"Very well." Elizabeth bent over her answering machine and played a message, which she then skipped over, then another and another. Eventually she found the right one. Florence listened, fascinated and horrified. A man angrily hurtled accusations, just as Elizabeth had described.

"I don't know what to do. This is simply nonsense! On what grounds does he make these charges? He doesn't say that, does he! Just that he *heard* that I fabricated this information. He doesn't say how he knows that. But I promise you, Elizabeth, I swear that I rode on the tube every day for six weeks, interviewing passengers, as well as speaking with transportation planners. And the fact that I go to the Lake District has nothing to do with my work. While I am here working, I am enormously and completely scrupulous, and always work with integrity."

"As I said," Elizabeth replied, "We'll conduct an investigation. But until such time as we reach conclusive findings, consider yourself as ceasing to submit stories to this magazine! Good day, Florence!"

Florence walked to the door. She was shaking. A sudden inspiration made her swivel around.

"Elizabeth," she said. "What was the phone number of that caller? You have caller ID. Can you at least please tell me that?"

"Why? So you can call him yourself?"

"Not necessarily. But so that I can also conduct an investigation, or at least help you with yours."

"All right. Fair enough." Elizabeth went to her phone and looked back at the record of callers from the previous day. "Ah, this is it. 5.18. That's the time he phoned. Yes, the number is right here. It's 272-1550."

Florence lent back against the wall. "272-1550? That's Howard's work number!" Then, raising her voice, she screamed, "That's Howard's work number, Elizabeth! He's trying to ruin me! He tried to rape me a few weeks ago! He's been spreading false rumors about me not returning wedding presents when he's kept them himself! And now this!"

Hot, angry tears sprang to her eyes, but she refused to cry. Through her misty vision, she saw Elizabeth look shocked and then concerned.

"Sit down," she offered.

"No, I will not sit down!" Florence wailed. "I can't tolerate this! And yes! I recognize that man's voice now! It sounds like Steve, who works with Howard! Howard must have put him up to this."

Elizabeth wavered, pulled open a drawer and then reconsidered and shut it again.

"Why do you believe Howard over me? You listened to him last September, which was ludicrous. And now he's scheming again, and you're prepared to believe him!"

"Florence, I'm at a loss. Truly I am. Would you like some tea? Let's try to please calm down and speak about this rationally. If you're right in that-"

"I *am* right! That's Howard's work number. Why don't you phone him now and see for yourself?"

"All right! I will! Not that I don't trust you. In fact I have always trusted you very much, which has made this incident even more difficult for me to fathom. I hadn't told you this, Florence, but I was married once, and I know how nasty men can be in divorce proceedings."

"Nasty? I call this intolerable, devious, vindictive, bordering on criminal!"

"Yes, look – I'll just go ahead and phone and then…Incidentally, what's his surname?"

"Feldman."

"Thanks."

She dialed the number.

"Hello, Howard Feldman, please. Thank you." Elizabeth looked pointedly at Florence, acknowledging that this was indeed his number. "Hello, Howard! Elizabeth Carlisle speaking. How are you? That's great. No, nothing important. I'm calling as I wondered whether you could provide me with Florence Hamilton's phone number. I seem to have misplaced it, and there are several very important stories that need to be written, and she's just the one to do them!" Elizabeth sparkled at Florence, who was now sitting, propping her head with her arms which were firmly planted on the armrest of the chair. "Thank you. Wait! Are you sure that's the number? It doesn't sound right to me. I seem to remember a 3 and a

1 in it. Oh yes, well I'm sure that's so. Well," she said brightly. "So sorry to bother you at work, but good talking to you again!"

She replaced the phone carefully and looked at Florence. "You've got your hands quite full with this one, haven't you! He sounded so shocked when I told him I had work for you – though of course he could admit nothing about calling you a liar and a cheat – and then he even gave me the wrong phone number! When I said it didn't sound right, he apologized saying he hasn't spoken with you since you moved, hasn't seen you for ages, and might no longer be remembering it."

"The bastard!"

"Yes! Well, first," said Elizabeth, "I owe you a *big* apology. I've been tense recently, as sales on the magazine are down, so I've been getting criticized by Veronica. So I pounced on yesterday's phone call, and used you as a scapegoat. I'm terribly sorry."

"That's OK, Elizabeth."

"I hope you will continue working for us. Under the circumstances, I wouldn't blame you for walking away, but I hope you don't. In truth, I've always admired your work, as I've told you. And I like you as a colleague, and as a person, too. Of course, if you need time to think about it, I completely understand."

"No, it's fine. I want to keep submitting my stories to you."

"That's good. And I'm going to look into rehiring you in a full-time capacity, since you should never have lost that position in the first place. I'll do my best to convince Veronica. But the least said internally about this unpleasant incident, the better, if you don't mind."

"Yes, I understand."

"But as for you, my dear; you need to look out for yourself better. My advice is to see your lawyer immediately, and fully bring him up to date. Poor thing! From what you've told me, you've really been through a lot!"

"Actually, my lawyer is a woman. But thank you, Elizabeth, for being prepared to listen to me and believe in my work. If you don't mind, I think I'd better go and try and make that appointment with her now."

"Why don't you phone from here, and not waste any time? You can use the phone in Millie's office as she's not in today. That way you'll have complete privacy. And Florence, if you need an extension on those two stories, I think that can be arranged."

Later that day Florence was back in her flat, and trying to reach her lawyer for the fourth time. She had even delivered the tape and the doctor's report, but was told the lawyer was busy with another client and would phone her back. She had not phoned back. In fact, she continued to not phone back all week. "She's with a client in crisis, and Mrs. Twigger has to attend to that," the receptionist told her so many times, that eventually Florence asked, "What about *my* crisis? When will she attend to that?"

Florence spent most of the week researching information for her new story. She also had another wonderful evening with Anna, and a cordial visit with her parents, but she was glad when, late Friday morning, she set off to see Lance.

# TWENTY-ONE

*"I CALLED IN AN ELECTRICIAN* and had lighting installed in the secret passageway, stairs and grotto," Lance told Florence on Saturday morning.

"Did you?"

"You seem disappointed."

"No; not so much disappointed as surprised, really." She was also relieved, now she came to think of it, that Lance, who might still be tempted to return to the grotto in the hopes of finding Kitty, would not have to descend such a dark staircase.

"And in fact, I did go down to the grotto with Mei-Feng after the lights were installed," he admitted. "Actually, illuminating the 'secret' passageway, stairs and grotto makes it all feel not nearly as secret and remote as we'd thought. The passageway is not nearly as long, nor the stairs so steep. And the grotto is nothing other than a cellar room."

"It's a shame, in a way, to demystify it. But ultimately it's much more practical."

"Indeed! Now I've gained some extra space, and I intend to use it for storing papers, and I thought it would be nice to store some bottles of wine down there, too."

"Oh. A wine cellar! How lovely that would be!"

"Needless to say, when I went down there with Mei-Feng, there was no sign of Kitty or Virginia Lacey."

Florence shook her head. "It's incredible how you and I both have a dim memory of you having spoken with Kitty down in the grotto when you offered to take that ring to Ilyich. And of course, there was the other occasion, when we followed Virginia Lacey outside, after you'd seen her so frequently in your room by the wardrobe. And the possibility of you having met Gordon Lacey before, because of dreaming '119,' which is his address. It's amazing how the Laceys' Time and our Time have merged on these occasions."

"It's true, Fleur. And what about us, too? You and me. I think we have compelling evidence that *we must have known each other before we met for the first time* at Landsdowne's, if you see what I mean. It's just as T.S. Eliot said, later in that quartet: that everything exists; that, in his words, *All is always now.*'"

"That's impressive! How do you remember that?"

"I particularly liked it. It sums up so concisely Eliot's belief that the Present, Past and Future all coexist. Somehow you and I are privileged to be *receptive* to that coexistence of Times. That's unspeakably exciting!"

"I agree! And maybe Kitty and Virginia Lacey were receptive to that coexistence of Times, too, so that they could see and be responsive to us."

"Or maybe it's because they were so anguished and unfulfilled; their time being cut off before they accomplished what they were hoping and looking for. Kitty, especially."

"How sad. Though possibly very true."

"Yes. But T.S. Eliot must have been receptive to it, since he wrote about it in his poetry. We don't actually know the factors that make us receptive or not to the coexistence of other Times. Presumably everyone everywhere could exist in the Past, the Present and the Future, if what we understand about Time to be true, but most people aren't aware or receptive to this fact."

"Or they don't remember it. Just as it took me a while to remember about your conversation with Kitty. But maybe most people don't remember anything at all about incidents in the Future or from the distant Past, as they're blinkered by the existing paradigm about Time marching forward towards the future. Perhaps without this paradigm, they'd find life too confusing."

"Yes. Well, hopefully we'll soon be able to understand what makes you and I, and at least some other people, receptive to the coexistence of other Times."

"Yes, Lance! At this rate, I think we will!"

"But there is something else, Fleur, that I think will interest you. I asked Mei-Feng to clear out the desk down there so as to make room for my papers, and she brought up bundles and bundles of letters, as well as the hurricane lamp which we saw when we explored down there last weekend. I haven't yet looked at those letters, Fleur, as I thought we could look at them together. Actually," he added excitedly, "they're all addressed to Kitty, and judging from the envelope, some are from Throgmorton, and others are from a Harriet Marsh."

"Harriet Marsh! Why, that's the name of the family-"

"Exactly! They're possibly the ones who adopted Kitty's baby! You see those bags over there? All the letters are inside. Could you please bring them over?"

Florence did, and taking out the first bundle of letters, untied the string. But an uncomfortable feeling swept over her.

"I don't know, Lance. I feel this is wrong, somehow. As if we're eavesdropping or spying."

"But Fleur, that's what historical research is all about, really. Anyway, we've already witnessed so much. Doesn't it only seem natural to look into what we saw?"

"Yes, I suppose you're right. I remember I had felt this way about looking at that letter in the grandfather clock, but now am glad we'd seen it."

They started with letters to Kitty from Harriet, who wrote in a graceful, sloping script, with a flourish on the tails of the 'y' and 'g'. The letters were arranged chronologically, and the earlier ones were sent from a local address. These they read first. They talked about their schoolgirl pranks and adventures. Harriet always signed her letters 'Hatty'. There were not many of these early letters, but one especially caught their attention.

*Just think!* (it said.) *You like Ilyich and I like Igor. Wouldn't it be fun if someday we have a double wedding! Imagine the invitation! 'We request the pleasure of your company to the weddings of Miss Katherine Lacey to Mr. Ilyich Throgmorton, and Miss Harriet Marsh to Mr. Igor Throgmorton. Reception at Wolvercote Hall following the ceremony.' Oh, it would be such fun! We'd be sisters-in-law, Kitty! Kitty and Hatty! We'd be even more inseparable than we are now! And there'd be a garden party at the Hall, and we'd wear long, white dresses, and hats trimmed with an abundance of flowers.*

And another letter said, *I think Ilyich has the nicest eyes. You ARE lucky! But then, Igor is taller, and that is such a virtue in a man.*

But then the letters grew more somber.
"Lance, listen to this one," Florence said, starting to read it out loud.

*Kitty, Papa said we will move before the year is out. I don't want to go, and heaven-help-us, neither does Mother. But Papa said there's a lot more business down in Sheffield way, and he wants to get involved with making knives and blades. I think that's horrid, and told him so, but he sent me to my room for my impertinence. I've been trying and trying to think up a plan to make us stay. Promise me you'll help. Together we might come up with something perfect. What do you think about me jumping out of my bedroom window, and injuring my back? I'd be confined to my bed, and they wouldn't dare move me away. It would be so romantic!*

There was a long pause before the next letter, which arrived the following January.

410

*Well, here we are in Sheffield. It's not quite as bad as all that, and I do have my own room which I was allowed to decorate in any way I chose. I've made it pink, with little billowy curtains at the window, and it does have a very sunny aspect - when the sun shines, that is. Oh, but Kitty, I do miss you, and all our romps along the lanes and by the lake. I'll never find another best friend to replace you, and even though we are now many miles apart, we must write very often, and see each other whenever we can.*

Despite the promise of more frequent correspondence, the next letter in the pile was not written until March.

*Kitty, dearest; it's so dreary here. I hate to complain, but I've been feeling quite melancholy. The sky is constantly grey and sooty, and I'm frequently not allowed outdoors. And when Mother does consent to me going out, she insists that I tie a scarf over my nose and mouth. I've been dreadfully lonely. But one thing I've started doing is writing little stories. I imagine I'm back with you, and we have such adventures! I've called us (the two girls in the story) Maud and Mavis — you're Mavis — oh, and they do have fun! Hopefully you and I will have real fun again, soon. Do you still like Ilyich? I haven't heard a thing from Igor, even though I wrote him fourteen letters. Mother said he's silly and pretentious, and at first I was cross, but now I think she's right. I think I'm getting over the crush I had on him.*

Several letters followed over the next few years. One spoke of how much Hatty loved celebrating her twentieth birthday with Kitty, and another one, in a brief two lines, read, *I love your romantic sonnet. Do keep writing them, and let me see them!* But mostly the letters seemed a little sad and despondent. Then a letter came which was bubbly and vivacious

.

411

*My dearest Kitty! Life is wonderful, for both of us, it seems. I'm so happy to read of your deep love for Ilyich. You're very lucky to have each other. And it's been so long now, that you know it must be real. As for me, I've met the sweetest man. He's called Bertie Whistler. He's as merry as the day is long, and we have such a jolly time together. He takes me to the pictures, and afterwards we always go to my favourite Corner House restaurant, and he has mutton chops and pie, and I generally have the same, even though it is so fattening! Oh, and guess what, Kitty! My stories of the adventures of Maud and Mavis got published! Yes, in a little local magazine. It's not much, as it only has a small readership, but it's marvelously exciting nonetheless. Bertie took me to a special show at the Palladium to celebrate. Promise me, Kitty, that you will try to publish your poetry. After all, you've written a lot of poems by now. Your loving friend and partner in prose/poetry; Hatty*

It was way past lunchtime when they came across a letter indicating that all was not boding well for Kitty, as Hatty wrote;

*Dearest Kitty! Life isn't always easy. But things have a habit of working out. My advice to you is to ignore your mother (don't let her see this letter!) and go and see Ilyich anyway. You love each other and have done for years. Why should she want to destroy that? Think of it this way; he's the source of inspiration for you in all your poetry, isn't he! And all I know is that if my mother tried to stop me from seeing Bertie – which she wouldn't as she likes him so well – but if she did, I'd want to see him even more, so I'd do it anyway, behind her back, any way at all to see him. And so must you with Ilyich. You tell me you and Ilyich have promised each other your undying love, and that is so sweet! And you have so much in common with each other, what with your mutual love of poetry, and how you say he educates you about so many contemporary poets. I do like the sound of that poet called T.S. Eliot. Why, I swear I never would have heard of any of these poets if it wasn't from you through him. But remember, relationships, like fires, need to be kindled, so you MUST see him. You'll find a way, I know. You've always been rebellious and resourceful. That's why you're my best friend. I'm full of love and admiration for you. Hatty.*

Florence and Lance had looked at each other at the mention of T.S. Eliot, and then had resumed reading. Turning to the next letter, they read:

*Oh Kitty! Pregnant! My mind is agog with so many things. What will you do? How do you feel? Do your parents know? What do they say? Kitty, look after yourself, for my sake. Write back immediately! Hatty.*

This last letter was followed by,

*My dearest Kitty. You are so lucky to have Gordon. He is such a good, straight-forward fellow. Come to think of it, why didn't I develop a crush on him before we moved here? Why did I waste my time on Igor? Oh, I know. Gordon is too young. But he's showing such maturity now, vowing not to break your secret, and offering you help in every way. What a good brother, and a gentleman no less! But when will you tell your mother? You say it doesn't show now, but are you eating enough? You must eat for two now. Perhaps it would be better to come out with it, and tell Mrs. Lacey, just so that you can eat a lot! That's what I would do. But there again, I don't have your mother. I am glad the morning sickness has passed. Be well. H.*

A short, hastily scribbled note followed.

*Aaaaaah, Kitty; the description of the birth sounds torturous. How does the human race survive? You might well have put me off having children for ever! And then on top of it, to have to deal with your mother's hysteria. I don't know how you have so much fortitude. But most of all, CONGRATULATIONS, dearest heart! You did it! You have a baby! I'll arrange for a visit very soon. Can't wait to see you and meet little Connie!*

"Lance, let's stop now," Florence said, as she was feeling such extraordinary emotions of anticipation and dread.

"Let's go on for just a little bit longer," he replied. "If I'm not mistaken, we are almost at the end of Hatty's pile."

"I'm not sure I can stand much more of this."

"How many are left?"

She peered into the bag. "Just two. But Lance, it's so horrible given what we know about what happened to Kitty."

Lance smiled at Florence so kindly. "I know, my sweet. But we can't leave it now. That would be worse. I'll read the rest out loud, if you prefer. You've been reading a lot."

He looked at her enquiringly, and she nodded. Pulling out three sheets of paper from the next envelope, he read,

*Connie's an adorable baby, Kitty. She's got Ilyich's fascinating eyes, which, in combination with your coloring and your mouth, is captivating. I bet heads turn every time you take her out in the pram. You are lucky! Now I want a baby so badly. Thanks, Kitty, for asking me to be her godmother. I'll always have a special relationship with her. Keep on borrowing Gordon's impressive new camera and take lots of photos of her, and send them to me!*

*I visited Ilyich after seeing you, as I told you I would. Even though he's not with you all the time, he's a proud father. I can tell. And he loves you so much, Kitty! How can he hold back from marrying*

*you all because of that silly promise? No one would know, and what's more, no one would care in the slightest-*

"Promise?" Florence asked, to which Lance shrugged, and said eagerly, "Let's continue reading."

*-in the slightest. He told me he expresses himself best through poetry. But I don't care, and told him so. 'Don't hide behind that silly poetry any longer, Ilyich,' I said, 'But express yourself directly and go and tell Kitty that you want to be married!' Oh Kitty, please excuse me for acting so boldly. But really, you are each pining away for the other, and it all seems so ridiculous. Please know that I said what I did to Ilyich out of my great love, friendship, and admiration for you. Hatty*

There was just one more. One final letter from Hatty. Hesitantly, Florence picked it up and handed it to Lance, who looked at her, carefully unfolded the envelope, and taking out the letter, began to read in a slow, hushed voice.

*Of course I will, Kitty! I will certainly do that for you! Yes indeed; send all your letters to Ilyich to me, and I will gladly and promptly send them on to him. And I promise I won't read a single word! Your mother hasn't stopped you writing to me, has she, so she'll never know.*

*But forgive me for saying what weighs so heavily on my mind: these snatched and secret meetings you have with Ilyich, out in the lanes and in the dark, worry me tremendously. Yes, I completely understand that now he is engaged to be married to Bethany, you can no longer see him at the Hall. But even so, you have every right to see him in a civilized manner and in a proper setting that befits a person such as yourself. After all, you are the mother of his child!*

*Why he never married you, and instead, in a few short weeks, proposed to Bethany, a virtual stranger to him, is beyond my comprehension. It is unforgivable, especially since his heart is only for you. As a result of his most irrational conduct, he hurts not only you and himself, but is also being unfair to the innocent woman he will now claim as his wife.*

*You take great risks having these clandestine meetings with him. It seems to me that it would be less risky to write to him directly, than to meet with him in the manner in which you are doing this. Kitty, I worry about you so much! It is not my place to say this, but as you are so dear to me I will — If Ilyich can not see you in a proper manner, I say forget him! Do not see him again! Meet with him one last time to tell him this, and if he can not agree to meet you in a decent manner, be rid of him! Dearest Kitty, don't be angry with me, I implore you. I do this only for your own sake. Hatty*

After this letter, neither Florence nor Lance felt like eating lunch, or even speaking about Hatty's letters quite yet. Besides, Lance needed to attend to some matters in his online class — essays were due and he needed to mark them — and Florence, feeling she needed to clear her head, went outside into the back garden. The sky was overcast and it was a cool day, so she pulled the zip of her jacket all the way up to her neck. She walked to the bottom of the garden, and saw in the corner, where the drystone wall ended, some stone steps leading up to a path into the trees. She mounted the steps and followed the path up a hill, realizing that she was walking directly above the river that flowed into Lance's garden. Both the river and the path wound round several curves, and then the path descended to where the river broadened into a small ribbon lake below. The surface of the lake looked like a black mirror, reflecting deeply the trees that bordered it. A light drizzle started to fall, and the black surface of the water was dotted with tiny silver circles that shimmered and then vanished, as each raindrop touched the lake's surface and became absorbed.

She leaned against a tree trunk. The rain grew heavier, and she continued intensely watching the surface of the lake, with the increasing dots of silver lighting up the water and then disappearing. She liked the feeling of the rain washing over her. It seemed to be a cleansing of all the disturbing things that had occurred. She had a strong impulse to take off her clothes and dance around naked under the falling raindrops.

Instead she eventually retraced her steps back to the house. When she reached it, she saw Lance standing by the open kitchen door, jacket and leg brace on, crutches positioned under each arm, looking extremely anxious.

"Fleur! Thank God you're back! I was just about to come out and try and find you."

"Why? What happened?"

"You've been gone for quite some time. And it's pouring. I've been trying to call you on your mobile phone, but it just rang and rang."

"I'm sorry! I left my phone in my bag somewhere here in the house," she said, stepping into the kitchen and wiping her feet on the mat.

"Quick! Come inside and dry off. I was fearful that you were lost out there, just as you'd been two summers ago at Landsdowne's."

"Oh, Lance," she said, kissing him. "I'm sorry to have worried you. I wasn't lost. In fact, I discovered a lovely small ribbon lake, and found it refreshing to watch the rain splosh into it. I hadn't realized I'd been gone for a long time."

"Long enough for me to mark three essays, and by the third the low grade I assigned was more reflective of my mood than the merit of the paper. Poor chap! I'll have to give it a second reading. Here, Fleur; take this towel. Sit by the oven. It's warm as I turned it on to heat up our lunch."

"Thank you!"

"Fleur, forgive me for asking, but is something wrong? You don't quite seem your usual bouncy self. Is it Howard? Is he continuing to trouble you?"

So it was then that she told him about her week; about Howard's treachery and Elizabeth Carlisle's accusations and threats of taking away her freelance connection, and how her lawyer would not see her again. She told him everything, apart from how Howard had said she tried to seduce him. Lance listened carefully. Then, with the lightest of touches, he swept from her eyes a few hairs that had tumbled into her face, before folding his arms around her in a warm embrace. He held her for some time, burying his face into her neck, and giving her little kisses.

"Why didn't you mention this before? Oh Fleur, I'm sorry. Sorry you had to go through this. But also sorry that I was so excited about the discovery of those letters that it precluded my sensitivity to anything else. But this divorce is increasingly hard on you, and it should have been the first thing I asked about. Forgive me. Again!"

"Lance, it's fine. There's nothing to apologize about. Reading the letters, though admittedly hard emotionally, is fascinating."

"Yes, I agree. But Howard is turning out to be quite a dangerous man. He's now slandering you. How dare he!" Lance pulled away while still grasping Florence's upper arms. "But Fleur," he added, "I'm proud of how you spoke up for yourself with Elizabeth Carlisle. You did really well there!"

"Thanks. What it amounts to is that I take pride in my work, and – excuse me for saying this – but I believe it is of quite a high standard."

"Don't worry. You can certainly say that to me. You're not being immodest. I've read your work, and find it remarkably good. And furthermore, I have the privilege of knowing first-hand about your intelligence and integrity, as well as your phenomenal research skills!"

"Thank you. But this divorce is an entirely different matter. Not only was I unaware of the lengths Howard would go to, but I also thought I could feed any information to my lawyer, and let her resolve it all. After all, she's the paid expert! And paid handsomely, I might add. But I'm wrong."

"Yes. Is this difficulty of communicating with your lawyer a new thing? I don't remember you having complained of it before."

"No; now I come to think of it, although the issues seemed less urgent before, I always have had to wait a long time between appointments. In fact, precisely because the issues were less urgent, I didn't notice the long waits, and didn't care. I naively thought things were simple and they'd be resolved quickly."

"But this could be another reason why this divorce is taking so long.

Howard is slowing things down and adding complications, but also your own lawyer isn't treating your case with sufficient urgency or constancy."

"You're right."

"Well, you must insist on seeing her, Fleur. Next week you must do all it takes. And refuse to accept that she's always seeing to someone else's crisis. But I wonder if more is happening than we know. After all, she did give you a provisional settlement date of August 14th, didn't she?"

"But she's given me four settlement dates before that, all of them broken."

"I didn't know that. Well then, you must see her next week, Fleur. I'll call her for you if you think that would help. Sometimes a man's voice… Besides, if she tries to put me off, I'll tell her a thing or two!"

"Thank you, Lance. You're kind. But I'll keep trying. I'll do as you suggest, and refuse to be put off any longer."

"Good! And if you do decide you'd like me to call, let me know."

"I will. Thanks."

"Do you want some lunch now? I've heated up some soup. And I just had a thought! Let's go for a drive after we've eaten!"

"But it's pouring, Lance. And I know you don't feel so good in the rain. No, let's stay here and read through Throgmorton's letters. We might discover what Hatty meant when she talked about his promise. And Lance, I'm sorry for distracting us away from the letters by talking about the divorce, though I must say I feel better having spoken to you about it."

"Fleur, the rain isn't bothering my leg at all this time. Besides, it isn't always about me. You've been having a rotten time, and you deserve some attention now."

But in the end they neither went for a drive, nor read though Throgmorton's letters. Instead they retreated to the bedroom. Now warm and tingly, Florence said, "This is where I most want to be." Then, running her fingers through her hair, she said, "Oh Lance, I wanted to ask you; it's my mother's sixtieth birthday next weekend, and she's having a party for family and close friends. Would you like to come along? It would be wonderful to finally introduce you to everyone, and for them to meet you!"

"Thanks, Fleur! I wish I could. But I think the travel arrangements might be a bit too daunting."

She looked at his honest, fresh, engaging face, and said softly, "I know. What a shame. It'll be the first time we'll be apart for a weekend since you returned from America."

"I know." He leant over and kissed her. "Will Howard's parents be there?"

"Thank God, no. That was something I was so afraid of. Apparently they're in Japan. Oh Lance, I will miss you!"

"I'll miss you, too. But it's only an extra week. And so, let's make the most of this weekend!"

Later that afternoon they decided to investigate whether they could find Harriet Marsh in the phone book.

"For all we know, she might have married that man she wrote about, and be Harriet Whistler now," Florence said.

"True. Or she could have married someone else entirely. Also there's no reason to assume she stayed in Sheffield. But let's see what we come up with."

"If we look under Marsh, there are dozens of them," Florence replied, running her finger down the list in the phone book. "Even if we narrow it down to first initial 'H', there are still quite a few."

"And Whistler? I don't imagine there are as many of them."

"No, not so many," she answered, flicking to the end of the book.

"Let's try to make some phone calls," Lance suggested. "We don't know what we'll come up with, but let's give it a go. Would you like to do the talking, Fleur? You've got such a lovely voice."

They made many calls, but came up with nothing.

"Maybe Mrs. Landsdowne knows."

"Good idea! Why don't we pop over there and see? Besides, I should look in on Mother. Make sure the light isn't flickering in her room anymore."

"What? Are you suggesting we go right now?"

"Why not? And then maybe we could have dinner out. There are lots of lovely places around here. We could drive around until we find a place we like."

They spent a relatively short time at Landsdowne's. Rose and Allison were out, and while Lance spoke to his mother and Juliet, Florence sidled up to Mrs. Landsdowne, who was seated at the reception desk reading the local paper.

"Mrs. Landsdowne, I wanted to tell you that we saw Group Captain Lacey, and he sends you his best regards."

"Did he? So you saw Gordon!" Mrs. Landsdowne blushed girlishly, and took off her glasses, letting them hang on the chain around her neck. "What else did he say?"

"He wanted to know how you are, and he said he'd be happy to pay you a visit."

"Gracious me! What did you tell him? And how does the old boy look these days?"

"He looks very well. And he was very kind and hospitable to us. Thanks so much for putting us in touch with him."

"That's alright, love. Find out what you needed to know, did you?"

"Well yes, all apart from one thing. You know how it is; the more you find out, the more you realise you still need to know. Well, he mentioned someone called Harriet Marsh, who he said was a close friend of his sister's. You wouldn't happen to know how we might be able to find her, would you?"

"Harriet Marsh? Now let me see. It doesn't ring a bell. Oh yes, yes! Now I do recall Hatty! But she left years ago when she was still a young lass."

"Do you know where she went, or what happened to her?"

"No, dear; I don't. I can't rightly recall. I'm thinking her family moved to Newcastle, but it's been donkeys' years, so don't quote me on that!"

"Newcastle? I was under the impression that it might have been Sheffield. Oh well, this seems to be quite complicated."

"Sheffield? Well, you might be right. Sorry I couldn't be of more help, dear. Of course, Rose might know. I'll ask her for you when she comes in."

"Thank you!"

"It's my pleasure, dear. No trouble at all. And I must say it's nice to see you and Dr. Ramsey. He popped in a few times during the week last week with his Asian helper, and we were all so pleased to see him managing very well without the wheelchair! And just look how happy his mother and sister are to see him again today!"

Florence turned and looked through the archway into the lounge. Juliet had her head turned away stiffly, and was looking out of the window, but Mrs. Ramsey had such a look of rapture talking to her son. Lance, who was sitting in a firm high-backed chair, which was easier for him to get in and out of, caught Florence's glance, lent forward and kissed his mother on the forehead, said something to Juliet, and then rose and came towards the reception area. Juliet rose, too, and walking more briskly than he, reached Florence first.

"How are you, Fleur? Nice of you to come along. I'm returning home tomorrow, as an urgent case has come to my attention, and needs to be dealt with in a speedy manner. So it's lucky you came here today, as I was about to phone Lance to tell him about my hasty return home. Now, since I will be leaving so soon, won't you stay a little longer and have a cup of tea?"

"No thanks, Juliet," Lance, who had caught up with them, now said. "Fleur is unable to come up next weekend, so there are quite a few things we have to do now."

"Oh, so you'll be all alone with your little Asian girl! Well then, perhaps you can visit Mother a lot. She'll love that!"

They moved out onto the porch, so as to avoid some newcomers who were arriving and checking in at the reception area.

"Actually, Mei-Feng will no longer work on weekends," Lance told her.

"Really?" Juliet and Florence said together.

"Yes; she needs some time off, too, and there's generally little for her to do on weekends."

"Apart from next weekend!" Juliet retorted. "Oh well, I suppose there's nothing for it, but for you to come back home with me tomorrow!"

"No thanks; I'll be OK."

"I guarantee you'll be phoning next Saturday asking me to come and get you after all. And let me tell you now; that will be a major pain in the neck, having to drive half way across the bloody country again. So let's cut that out now. Come back to our house with me tomorrow, Lance!"

"It's no longer 'our' house, Juliet. My home is here now."

"Oh yes, and very sensible that is! For a crippled man to live alone, in one of the most isolated parts of England! Yes, I know; you have a girlfriend, but she lives hundreds of miles away in London, and sometimes – completely understandably – does not visit. And let's not forget the Asian helper, but you go and give her time off just when you need her the most! Where's the sense in that? Face it, Lance; you can hardly walk! How, pray tell, are you going to manage on your own?"

"Juliet, why do you demean your brother so much?" Florence burst out. "Why do you label him, and tell him what he can't do? Lance is the innocent victim of an unspeakably horrific event, and it's not only because of good fortune, but also because of his fortitude, that he survived when thousands perished. He's remarkably resilient and capable!"

"My goodness!" Juliet exclaimed. "I'm not saying that it isn't remarkable that he's alive. But face it; for all his so called fortitude, you can hardly deny that he's got very limited mobility."

"Yes, and until a few months ago, he had no mobility at all! Why don't you focus on how far he's come?"

Lance moved quietly over to a seat on the porch, and sat down, poking the white rubber tip of one of his crutches in the gap between the floorboards.

"I'm no less impressed than you are as to Lance's achievements. But what I'm talking about is the immediate present. Let's be practical, for God's sake! I think it highly unlikely that by next weekend he will have burned his crutches, thrown that appalling leg brace out the window, and be back to jogging a mile around Central Park, or wherever the hell it was he jogged! You want, not unreasonably, to think of my brother as whole again, and not disabled - and I want that, too - when this simply is not the case!"

"Juliet, I agree that we need to be realistic, and for all three of us to think up a plan for next weekend. But nothing can be achieved by insulting and belittling Lance, and giving him orders as to what to do, rather than letting him participate in the decision that affects him the most."

"Well!" Juliet said, turning away. "Thank you for your lesson in etiquette! And Lance," she added. "Do let me know if *you* decide to come home tomorrow, but give me plenty of notice!"

She bent down and gave him a peck on the cheek, and then walked haughtily back towards the lounge.

"Cheers, Juliet!" Lance said. He sighed and stood up, and then saying, "Let's go!" to Florence, made his way to the steps.

"I'm sorry if I spoke out of turn," Florence said to him as she helped him to descend. Strong gusts of wind were blowing into their faces, bringing lashings of rain. He stopped on the second step down and faced her, his cheeks gleaming with moisture and his glasses splashed with tiny beads of raindrops.

"Sorry? You were spectacular! First Elizabeth Carlisle, and now my sister! You're not afraid to speak your mind, and that's great!"

"Well, I seem to be changing. I used either to feel obliged to be demure and polite, or else I'd not think of an appropriate response until after the situation was over. But now I've found that when I am sufficiently incensed, the words just erupt from me."

"It seems that Juliet is very impressed with you! Hardly anyone stands up to her, so I think she enjoyed that very much!"

"Enjoyed? She looked awfully cross."

"No, it was an act. I saw the way she looked at you just before she returned to the lounge. And Fleur, if you talk like that to your lawyer, or to Howard should he contact you again, your divorce will be finalized within the week!"

She laughed. They reached the car, and Lance said he wanted to drive.

"Seriously though," she said to him as he reversed the car and turned it around. "I had no idea you intended not having Mei-Feng work for you on the weekends."

"Yes, I told her that we would start this next weekend. I suppose it's my impeccably bad timing again. But I came to the conclusion, as I was explaining to Juliet, that there's not much for her to do when you are here, and I sense a certain tension between the two of you, in any case."

"I'm sorry if you feel there's any tension between her and me, but don't do this on my account. I don't mind her being there." Which, of course, wasn't quite true.

"It's not only that. She's now made some friends online through her job, so it'll be nice for her to meet up with them."

"But perhaps, since you haven't yet started these weekends off, you can ask her to wait until the following weekend instead."

"No, I can't do that. She's already made some plans."

"Well then, Lance; I won't go to my mother's party."

"No Fleur; don't be silly! You must attend your mother's sixtieth birthday party. I won't hear of you missing it on my account. That's exactly why I hadn't told you about Mei-Feng having the weekends off when you first mentioned the party, as I thought you might say something like that. But don't worry about me. I'll be fine. I've got tons to do. I can use it to catch up with my online classes. And I'll go to Landsdowne's for dinner each night. Even though Juliet's leaving early, my mother is staying for another week as originally planned, and apparently Rose and Allison have offered to keep an eye on her. She'll be thrilled to see me visiting so often."

They drove along quietly for a few minutes.

"And then," Lance said, "The weekend after next I have some old friends visiting – Simon and Crispin – and I'm really looking forward to you meeting each other."

Just then they reached a T-junction, and Lance turned the car to the left.

"Shouldn't we have turned right?" Florence asked.

"No, why?"

"Isn't that the way back to your house?"

"It is. But I thought we'd have a drive and find somewhere nice for dinner."

"Oh, I thought we were going to look through Throgmorton's letters now."

"No; what made you think that?"

"Because you told Juliet we had so much to do, so I assumed that's what you were referring to."

"Fleur, my sweet, sweet love. Always keep that childlike innocence. No; I said what I did because, since you and I won't be seeing each other for almost two weeks after this, I want to spend every remaining minute of this weekend alone with you!"

She put her hand on his thigh, and squeezed affectionately.

"Lance," she said at last. "Why does your sister talk that way to you?"

"Oh, she doesn't mean any harm. It's just her manner. Basically she's concerned for my welfare and has my best interests at heart, but doesn't always have the gentlest way of expressing it. She's impatient, certainly, but never malicious."

"Oh, because-"

"Did you get any information from Mrs. Landsdowne about Harriet Marsh?" Lance interrupted her.

"Not a thing."

They drove along in silence.

"She seems to think she moved to Newcastle."

"Oh."

More silence.

"She said she'll ask Rose when she returns," she added.

"All right," Lance said wearily, as if having undergone an internal struggle and now was resigned with the outcome. "I'm going to tell you something, Fleur, that I've never spoken about with anyone." He looked intently at the narrow road ahead, manoeuvering the car around each hedge-lined bend with dexterity, but there was a little pulsating of his lower eyelid. "You know, of course, that Juliet is quite a bit older than I."

"Yes."

"Well, I must have been about six years old, and she was nearing twenty. My father was still living with us then. And well, one day, I went into the sunroom to fetch part of my train set, and they were in there."

"Who?"

"My father and sister. His trousers and underpants were down, and Juliet was only wearing a bra. At first they didn't see me, and I had no idea what was going on. I was about to talk to them, but something prevented me from speaking."

"Oh, Lance!"

He was quiet, silently guiding the car forwards. His eyelid continued to pulsate, and he brushed it quickly before putting his hand back on the wheel. The only sound was the rhythmic swish of the windscreen wipers. Clarity. Drenched windscreen. Clarity. Drenched windscreen. Clarity. Drenched windscreen.

"As I stood there," he said at last, "My father pulled her towards him, and they sank to the floor with him on top. I was terrified and screamed. I didn't know what he was doing to her. I thought he might be hurting her.

426

And then, all was ghastly. They struggled up from the floor. My mother came running in shouting. My father slapped her. She fell to the ground. Juliet grabbed her clothes and darted out of the room. No one took any notice of me, even though I unwittingly was the informant, and even though I seem to remember that I continued to scream.

"My father moved away soon after that, and I haven't seen him since. Juliet claims that I can't possibly remember my father as I was too young, and she's right. I don't. But I remember that incident."

He tapped his foot on the brakes as a small animal ran out in front of the car. He blinked hard and then continued.

"Juliet and I have never spoken about this. But after that day, my mother basically became as a child. She visibly and emotionally shrunk and withered, and was no longer robust. I wanted so badly to make her happy, to make up for what I had done. I wanted so much to see her smile again and hear her laugh. But if she did, it was only a temporary thing, and she'd sink back into this helpless, childlike, stunned stupor.

"And so I didn't really have a mother anymore, and neither did I any longer have a father. So Juliet took on the parental role. She loved bossing me around. Whether she had been bossy before, or became like that through what she perceived of as a necessity, hardly matters. But bossy she was. And still is. Her behavior has become habitual, and she still wants to protect me, even though I'm thirty seven."

They continued to drive. The rain had abated, and there were growing chinks of light between the clouds. The sun had started to set, illuminating sheets of clouds in beautiful alternating shades of pink and purple.

"There!" he said, glancing over quickly to Florence. "That's our family secret. Perhaps every family has one. I don't know. But I've told you ours. Do you hate us now?"

"Hate? Oh Lance, how could I possibly hate you? What a horrible thing to have happened to you at such an early age."

"Not just to me. To my whole family, as I spilled the beans. "

"Yes, but you are blaming yourself for what happened, when it absolutely wasn't your fault. You were not deliberately an informant. You said you wanted to 'make up for what you had done,' when you hadn't done anything bad, and certainly not intentionally. You stumbled across something bewildering, and you were afraid your sister was getting hurt. You reacted perfectly naturally."

"Maybe. But it was because I screamed that my mother came in, and that he pushed her to the ground, and that he left us, and she-"

"Lance, don't do this to yourself. You were so young then, and what you saw was clearly shocking and wrong. And you don't know what else might have been going on. Do you happen to know, in fact, if this was the only time your father and Juliet-?"

"I don't know."

"Do you think Juliet willingly made love with your father?"

"I suspect not. But I don't know that either."

"You can't speak about this incident to each other?"

"Absolutely not! It would be preposterous!"

"I'm glad you told me about this, Lance," she said to his profile, as he continued to look steadily at the road ahead, the flickering of his lower eyelid having stopped, but Florence noticed that there were red blotches about his neck and over parts of his cheeks. It had clearly been no easy matter for him to tell her this, but it certainly filled in the gaps of Juliet's story; explained why mother, brother and sister continued to live together for so many years; explained why, when Lance had been invited by NYU to stay on for extra time that he thought perhaps he should decline because of his mother, and why he was, at all times, so attentive to her; possibly even explained why Juliet could not be happily married. But he couldn't continue to live in the shadow of this event. It had occurred thirty years ago! "And I'm glad you went to America, Lance," she said, realizing for the first time the absolute necessity of this trip for him. "I'm sorry I had initially been unhappy at the thought, and nearly stopped you from going. I hadn't known."

"What?" he asked, turning to her again.

"It was good that you went to America; that you made an independent move."

"What made you bring that up?" He frowned, and unexpectedly pulled the car over onto the grassy verge and stopped. "Yes, I see what you're saying. It was indeed very good to be there. To be free. But sometimes, even though I know it's irrational, I think I shouldn't have left home, and this," he said, slapping his lame left leg, "is my punishment."

"No, Lance, no! Please don't hurt yourself further," she said, grabbing his hand. "Of course the attack on the World Trade Center was not a punishment to you for any wrongdoing. If it was, then one could conjecture that the more than three thousand people who died or were wounded there that day, were being punished too, and that makes no sense. You seem to be looking at it in a Biblical sense, as if it was analogous to the story of Noah's Ark, but that is ridiculous. You're letting yourself be influenced by that customer in the teashop who said something similar, but she was a perfect stranger!"

"No, Fleur. I'm not influenced by her. I'd been thinking this for a long time."

"But you were innocent – all of you innocent victims!"

"Perhaps."

"You were! And hopefully, with time, you'll be able to dwell again on all the fun and excitement you had had when you were in New York."

"True. And I do think about that too, sometimes." He bit his lip, and gazed through the windscreen. She thought he was going to start up the car again. But instead, he said, "And now, after all I've told you, do you see why I can't go back with Juliet tomorrow, to what she insists on calling 'our house'?"

"Yes, Lance; I do see."

He looked at her a little fearfully, as though he needed reassurance that after the tumbling out of wounds so deeply embedded in his past, that she could still accept him. And she, sensing his need, and still hugging her own sordid secret of Renard closely to her, reached over towards him and gently nuzzled up to him, as much as the gear stick and handbrake would allow.

"Because," he said, rubbing his hand up and down her arm, "had I gone back home to live with Juliet after leaving New York, I'd most likely be completely bedridden by now."

"Oh Lance, stop it!" she said, shuddering. "Actually, it might have been the opposite. Her behavior might have sufficiently irritated you, and empowered you to walk again."

"Possibly. But I doubt it. After I was injured, it might have seemed that I'd need Juliet more than ever. And, had I gone home, she would have fussed around me, doing everything and being well-intentioned of course, yet she'd have been complaining non-stop, and making sarcastic comments. I was sure of this. I'd been forewarned, you see, by the way she was when she visited me at St. Vincent's, and then again when she stayed with me in my flat on Cornelia Street. Please don't get me wrong; I'm exceptionally grateful for her visits – she was so kind and generous with her time and attentions – but I noticed more about her character then than I'd been previously aware of."

Florence nodded, silently thinking about her own impression of Juliet's forceful nature, but she felt it more diplomatic to keep this to herself.

"So it occurred to me," Lance went on to say, "that it was essential that I come back to England to my own place. And the more I thought about this, the more excited I became. Otherwise it would be like returning to England as a failure, an object of pity. But if I could start afresh in my own house, that would be right. I just had to think about where. And gradually I settled on the idea of the Lake District - an area I've always found charming, and one that would also put me closer to Mother. So I contacted an Estate Agent in the region, and she showed me on the Internet, pictures of different houses that were for sale. It's wonderful what technology can do these days. And then one day she e-mailed me a link to some photos of what has now become my house. I recognized it immediately as the house that had always intrigued me and felt strangely connected to. And I knew this was the one! I could hardly believe my luck that it was on the market, although I shouldn't have been surprised, really, as it stood empty more often than not, as we both know. So I made an offer straight away, and it was accepted. Just like that! No long-winded negotiations back and forth. It was all extraordinarily simple."

"And Juliet? How did she react?" She knew they'd talked about this before, but now everything seemed different.

"She was incredulous. Thought I was mad. Accused me of being wildly impractical. But, in truth, maybe she was glad, too."

Yes, thought Florence, remembering Juliet's conversation with her over dinner at the Stanhope Hotel in New York, in which she'd said that she'd really resent having to look after two invalids. But instead Florence said, "And your mother must be so happy to have you close by."

"Oh yes."

"But is she terribly upset to see you injured?"

"No; she's become very feeble-minded, Fleur, and has lost all track of time. The attack on the World Trade Center essentially did more damage to her than it did to me. The excruciating worry of it was the last straw in an already declining mind. After a few days of not being able to get through to me – and mind you, they never knew, as you had done, that I was even meant to be at the World Trade Center that day – they heard the news from NYU and Mother dispatched Juliet to come over to New York right away. But the sustained anxiety was the final trigger for her. She was so relieved to know that I did not die, but still her mind had been affected. So, since she has now lost all sense of time, she continues to think that I simply have a broken leg."

"Well, it's lucky that she thinks this way, as it saves her from further distress. And she's clearly so happy whenever she sees you."

"Thank you."

"I'm so pleased, for your sake, that you moved into your house. It's so good for you. And also it's good for us – for you and me."

"Yes, that's true," Lance said, turning off the car engine at last. "Of course, when making the decision to move to the Lake District, I couldn't predict how you'd react to me when you saw that I hadn't made a complete recovery. And, very fortunately, I had complete amnesia about you having married Howard. Had I thought of that, I think that might have done me in. It was agonizing enough worrying that you might reject me, seeing what a revolting mess I've become. But Fleur," he said, taking her hand, "You're superb to me."

"Thank you."

"It's so funny to think that Rose claims that she's the one who 'discovered' you. She said you cheered up Landsdowne's as soon as you arrived."

Florence laughed.

"She can't even begin to imagine the extent to which you cheered things up," he continued, laughing now. "Actually, Fleur, out of interest, something I've wondered about for some time…how was it that you decided to come to such an out-of-the-way place as Landsdowne's for that holiday? How did you even know about it?"

"Well, in fact it was completely random! I made a hasty decision to go away for a few days, and decided the Lake District would be nice. Once I'd narrowed it down to an area, I made a quick Internet search at work, and Landsdowne's just popped up and looked right."

"Well, I'm so glad it did! Just think; we might never have met if you hadn't made that trip, or if you'd chosen to go somewhere else."

"Yes; it's amazing. I don't even want to think about what would have happened if I hadn't come to Landsdowne's!"

"And to think; there I was, prepared to settle down to another summer of sedate, genteel old ladies, rowdy groups of Austrian tourists, and the preparation of my paper, when you appeared! I had to polish my Scrabble skills as an excuse to talk to you immediately!"

"And then, at the end of that first Scrabble game, you surreptitiously handed me the most minutely folded piece of paper asking me to meet you later by the window seat!"

"I was so glad you came!"

"You didn't doubt that I would come, did you?"

"How could I tell? I didn't know you then. But even so, I could sense, the moment I saw that you needed help with your camera, that there was something extraordinary about you!"

"Maybe it was something extraordinary about my camera!"

"That only became apparent later. But I knew straight away that there was something inspirational about you."

"Actually, Lance, I could feel there was something phenomenal about you, too. But I thought, at first, that you were married."

"Married?"

"Yes, remember? When we went to the Post Office to send off your paper, the woman there handed you a letter from a Ms. Ramsey, who she referred to as 'the missus' so I concluded that it was your wife. I was so relieved to discover that it wasn't!"

"Oh yes; I'd forgotten that! My sweet love; those were exciting times, weren't they, when we were first getting to know each other."

"And our relationship is every bit as exciting now," she replied frankly.

"Bless you for that!" he said simply, turning on the car's ignition, while humming a little tune, which made Florence deduce that he felt much lighter now he'd told her his 'family secret.' He headed very deliberately, as it turned out, to a very special restaurant indeed.

--------

The next morning, after breakfast, Lance declared, "Well, I think we've come to the end of the line with regards to our research of 'local history', as you call it."

"Why do you say that?"

"Well, for one thing, neither of us has seen Virginia Lacey again, and no sign of Kitty, either. And furthermore, as we were beginning to discover yesterday, searching for the then Harriet Marsh is like looking for a needle in a haystack."

"Lance, even if we do stop looking further, I think we need to become fully cognizant of how absolutely incredible our discoveries have been. We speculated that it was possible to travel along different and parallel Time axes, or that Time is circular, and now we feel pretty sure that either or both have been confirmed! We've witnessed things that historical evidence and conversation with others, have shown to be true. It's totally remarkable. We've become so embroiled in our discoveries that I think we've lost track of how remarkable this is!"

"That's true. You're right."

"But Lance, let's not stop there. I want to understand why we were privileged to be aware of Kitty and Virginia Lacey's Time; why it coexisted with our Time. I want to understand the meaning of this. I want, and imagine that you might too, to fully grasp why you had always felt connected with this house. There's still Throgmorton's letters. Let's not leave them unread."

"Actually, I see no point in reading them, Fleur. He was demonstrated to be a despicable character, and even if we read the letters, I can't imagine either of us wanting to try to track him down."

"But Lance, you can never tell. We've come so far. Let's read them!

433

There are not so many of them. And besides, it might shed some light on that promise that Hatty wrote about. Let's go back to bed and read them there!"

It was an attractive idea. It was raining once again, and the wind was screaming around the house. Lance, who did not use the leg brace or crutches in the house, but instead hopped or hobbled, holding on to Florence or to the back of furniture, was first in bed. He looked so lovely, lying there looking up at her, that when she slid into bed beside him, they at first cuddled up to each other, so it was way past mid-morning by the time they turned their attention to Ilyich's letters.

The first few letters were full of poems – *"How do I love thee? Let me count the ways…"* and then his own impassioned thoughts following from there. He even scrawled some of his own attempts at love poems, but Florence and Lance agreed that they were not particularly good. And he wrote at length about a great contemporary poet he had just discovered; T.S. Eliot.

"That confirms what Hatty wrote," Florence said.

"And also explains why Kitty might have wanted to reciprocate with that excerpt from Eliot that you discovered in the grandfather clock."

"Yes, but why did she choose that one? Was there any significance to it?"

"I don't know."

"Look Lance! Listen to this letter! I think this provides the answer to what was meant by the promise!" And then she read:

*My dearest Kitty: for you and you alone, my heart longs. But I need to reiterate what I had told you when last we met. I made a promise – what a disgusting thing a promise is to bind one so – but nevertheless I promised my father, on his deathbed, that I would marry the woman he had lined up for me. Miss Bethany Farthing. It was his dying wish, Kitty, and for all the love in the world, I am too superstitious; nay, too honor-bound, to shun it. What hell is this, to marry one whom I detest, and to always yearn for you. But you and I will meet, my darling. I'll make sure that we see more of each other than I will see my dreaded wife. This I swear to you. We will meet in secret. It will be our secret, Kitty, and I know your charming, romantic mind always liked secrets. I'll marry Bethany as my Father ordered, but my heart and thoughts will always belong solely to you. This much my Father can not take away from me. And now I kiss this letter before sealing it, so that when you open it, you will feel my kiss and know of my love for you, which will endure for ever and ever. Your Ilyich.*

"Well," said Lance, when he'd finished reading it. "He certainly does sound sincere in his love for Kitty. And now we've discovered what that promise was, it does justify his behavior to some extent. Perhaps, seen in this new light, he's not so despicable a character after all."

"I don't agree," Florence replied. "Yes, it might *explain* his behavior, but it doesn't *justify* it. I don't believe any parents have the right to inflict their wishes on their child when it comes to marriage, or to tell them how to lead their own life. I'm a prime example of that. I only went out with Howard to obey my parents' wishes. But parents have to realize that their children, once grown, must make their own decisions, as it is they who have to live with the consequences of that decision."

"Is that so?" Lance said, raising an eyebrow and looking up at her.

"What? That I only went out with Howard – and indeed married him – as that was what my parents wanted me to do? Yes, I'm afraid that was the case. But," Florence added, hurrying on to distract Lance from the topic of Howard, "Back to Ilyich and his father-"

"Well, as I see it, it was Ilyich's father's fault then, and not any wrongdoing of Ilyich himself. He was only doing his duty to his parents, which is, according to the German philosopher Kant, a very ethical way to behave. And I might add that you showed the same obedience to your parents by marrying Howard."

"Please let's keep Howard out of it for now. Sorry I brought him up. But I do think Ilyich should have been strong enough to protest – and so should I have been, too – but in Ilyich's case even more so since he already had a child with Kitty. I'm sure the question of his marriage must have been an ongoing conversation, and not one that originated on his father's deathbed."

"But whether it was, or not, don't you think Ilyich was completely right, and honor-bound, as he said, to obey his father's dying wish? Do you really believe that just because his father would no longer be around to see the outcome, that Ilyich could do as he wished?"

"I think the situation should have been averted. Look how irresponsibly he behaved! He must have made his wife terribly unhappy – it was totally unfair to start a marriage that way – and it was an awful way to treat Kitty! Perhaps she did not die because of the dog, but because of a broken heart! Maybe when the dog attacked, she had no will to live, and no urge to save herself."

"You might be right. Let's read on."

Several letters followed. Ilyich wrote once of having seen their baby – "what a *bonnie wee lass!*" – and how well he approved of Kitty's choice of Connie for a name. But several letters after this one were full of apologies for not seeing Kitty more frequently; he had not anticipated how married life would keep him so busy. Furthermore, now that he was master of the house, there were frequently business matters demanding his attention. In truth, he also said, he had not anticipated how hard it would be, given the secret nature of their visits, and the long, cold nights, to see much of Connie.

> *I wager,* (he wrote), *that by springtime, or early summer, when the air is once more soft and warm, and the days stretch out pleasantly with the sun, that you can bring our baby out, and I'll delight in seeing her again. She'll be so grown by then.*

"Ah, so he is seeing less of Kitty," Florence said. "I wonder if he was becoming increasingly attracted to his wife, or if it really was hard to get away. And now there's only one letter left in the bundle, so maybe we'll never know."

She took the letter from the envelope, and exclaimed that it was quite dirty and crumpled, as though it had become caught under someone's foot.

She started to read from it: "*'Darling Kitty: just to think of you makes my heart thump in my chest.'* Lance!" she exclaimed in great excitement. "Doesn't that sound familiar? I seem to remember Virginia Lacey sarcastically reading that out to Kitty in the grotto, just before you went up to Kitty and offered to take her ring to Ilyich!"

"I don't remember! Is it? Let's see what else it says," he said, taking the letter from her: "*'My mind soaks up every thought of your fair face, your fragrance, your fortitude.'* Yes, yes! That definitely sounds familiar! I was struck by the alliteration."

"More proof, Lance! More proof of how we connected with their time!"

"Yes, Fleur! It is. It's incredible."

Sitting up higher in bed, they read the remainder of the letter, which continued in the same vein of passion and remorse at not being able to see each other more easily.

"Well, Lance: that's all of them,"

"No, Fleur; there's one more. It wasn't tied up with the rest. Mei-Feng said she found it after she had brought everything else upstairs, when she had started putting my papers away."

He handed it to Florence, and they both saw that it had never been opened. She gave it back to Lance, who slit open the envelope and unfolded the letter.

*My Kitty; always, always, always my Kitty,* (he read.) *Thank you for the unusual ring with a lock of our Connie's hair inside.*

"Oh my God, Fleur!" Lance said, breaking off from his reading. "Proof of my conversation with Kitty!" And then looking back down at the letter he continued reading:

*... What a clever gift. I will wear it whenever we are together. I wish we could be together always, and I think we shall. I have a plan. I was going to speak of it to you, but then I heard your mother's dog, and had to depart rapidly for fear of being discovered, and*

437

*getting you into terrible trouble with her. Please meet me tomorrow evening, in the usual place. Meet me at 6.30. I will speak to you of my plan then, and tell you how it will be possible for us to always be happily together. I wait in joyous expectation. Your loving Ilyich.*

"Oh Lance," Florence said, lying back down and pulling up the duvet all the way to her chin. "Kitty never read this, as she was dead by then. He wrote it that night, the night she died. How awful; he wrote this not knowing she'd been killed. This is so sad."

He let the letter flutter to the floor and snuggled up close to Florence.

"What's more," he said, "it seems he's not such a traitor after all, by running when he heard the dog. It seems he ran off just before the dog reached them, not knowing it was off the leash and ferocious."

"True. But I wonder if he really had a specific plan in mind for them to always be together, and indeed, if he did, what it was."

"At best we could try to find out if he stayed married to Bethany, but even that won't answer our real questions. But Fleur, now having found out this new information, I definitely don't think he's so much to blame as I had before. It seems reasonable why he left when he heard the dog barking, as certainly for them to be seen together would only have plunged Kitty into deep trouble for disobedience and deceit."

"True. But they were naïve if either of them thought Virginia Lacey didn't know of their meetings. Why else would Kitty have gone out on so many evenings? We saw Virginia Lacey's agitation, her taking of the flashlight and the dog, and her venturing outside to look for her daughter. The whole thing between Kitty and Ilyich was fated from the start."

Lance listened thoughtfully. Then he scooped up the remaining letters, rolled over and put them on the floor, removed his glasses, and rolling back, took Florence in his arms.

"Yes," he sighed. "We certainly now have even more proof of how we intersected with their time! And we also inevitably have more questions. But for now, Fleur, it's getting late and you'll soon have to depart. It's going to be almost two weeks until we're next together, so let's freeze time at exactly this point!"

--------

But it was not two weeks until Florence and Lance next met, but rather was three weeks. The morning after her return to London, the first thing Florence did was to phone Anna and arrange to see her the following evening. Then she busied herself with her work, even though she knew that she must phone her lawyer. She kept putting off that phone call, and then realized that it was past 5.00 pm and there was no answer.

The following morning she phoned the lawyer straight away, but was told that the next available appointment was two Fridays' time, in the afternoon. Florence generally left for the Lake District early on Friday mornings, so she asked for another time, but the next opening was ten days after that! It was hopeless. So she took the Friday appointment and immediately phoned Lance.

"Of course it's my fault for not phoning sooner, but these gatekeepers with their tight schedules make me furious!" she moaned.

"You made the right decision," he assured her. "It's a shame there was no other opening, but you need to see her as soon as she's free, as you absolutely need this divorce behind you."

"True. These divorce proceedings are taking months and months, and Howard and I were only married a few weeks!"

"Yes, so see her that Friday, and then, if you're not too tired and if it's not yet rush hour, come straight here after that. Or take the train. But if it's too late, you could always come up early the next morning."

"But Lance; it will already be so long before we see each other. To delay by another day…No! I'll come that Friday, however late it is."

"I don't want you to tire yourself too much, Fleur. At least, though, you won't have to cook and we'll be treated to incredible food that weekend, because Simon and Crispin are coming then, too."

"Who?"

"Simon and Crispin. Remember I told you? They're great friends who I met at university. Well, anyway, Crispin is a chef, and works in a lovely little bistro in Soho. And he said when he comes here, he wants to cook for us all weekend!"

"How nice!"

"Yes! For one thing, it'll give you a break. And I think you'll love the dishes he makes. But meanwhile, Fleur, keep phoning your lawyer's office to see if they have any cancellations."

The week passed by quickly, as Florence was so busy with researching and writing her new stories. The highlight of the week was having dinner with Anna and David again. And soon it was Saturday, and the day of her mother's sixtieth birthday party.

As soon as she walked into the living room of her parents' house, she sensed something was wrong. And then she saw the source of her awkwardness. Sitting luxuriantly in an armchair by the window was Howard's mother! Florence immediately skidded around and went to find her own mother.

"I thought you told me Howard's parents were in Japan!"

"Don't I get a 'Happy Birthday' first?"

"Sorry, Mum. Happy Birthday! Oh, and here's your present. But seriously; I thought you told me they weren't coming."

"It seems they returned sooner than originally planned," her father said, walking up to them and planting a wine glass in her hand. "Poor Flo! Drink up, my pet! You're going to need it."

"Now don't be stupid, dear. Florence doesn't need to make herself tipsy simply because the Feldman's are here. Just say hello, Florence, to be polite, and then you can ignore them for the rest of the evening. There's enough other people here tonight for you to get lost in the crowd. And it's true what your Father said; I didn't have a clue they were coming, but, well, here they are!"

"But, Mum-"

"Oh, what a lovely necklace you bought me! Thanks so much, Florence dear! I'm going to wear it right now! Can you please help me with the clasp?"

--------

"That bloody woman," Florence told Lance on her mobile phone late that same night, from her old bedroom in her parents' house. "Howard's mother. She did come to my mother's party after all. They apparently returned from Japan earlier than expected. I bet she did it deliberately, so as to harass me."

"My poor love. What did she do?"

"It's more what she said. I'd been trying to avoid her, but she noisily called me over in front of lots of people, after having said loudly to the person next to her 'Do excuse me dear, but that's my daughter-in-law over there!' which of course made everyone feel very embarrassed. I tried to be gracious, and went over to say a hurried hello, and she sort of seduced me into the library."

"What!"

"Well, she started talking about a Tolstoy short story that she'd read, and so I thought she was being interesting at last. It was actually a story of his that I didn't know, and that's when she said she was sure my parents had it in their library, so why didn't we go and have a look, because I really must read it!"

"But Fleur, she was behaving exactly as Howard had done when he tricked you into going into his flat. Don't tell me you fell for it again!"

"I'm afraid I did. And then, once in the library, she clearly had no intention of looking for the book, even though I started combing the shelves. Instead she shut the door and started pleading with me to return to Howard, saying how he pined for me, and what a good man he was. At first I ignored her and kept looking for the book, but then she got hold of my shoulders, and spun me around, and asked if I'd listened to a word she'd said. I replied, as calmly as I could, that it was impossible for me to go back to him, and then she started yelling about how much money she'd wasted on me and how they had contributed so lavishly to the wedding, when all I did was run off a few days later like a complete ingrate. I wish I'd cynically asked her how long she thought I should have stayed with Howard for her to get her money's worth."

"Was their financial contribution to the wedding asked for, or in any way needed?"

"Actually, it was not. Howard and I paid for most of it, and my parents were prepared to take care of the rest. It was only later on that Howard's parents said they wanted to contribute, too, so they paid for the flowers."

"Well, there you are. So it was their choice. It was something they wanted to do. They can't blame you for what later transpired."

"No, but I wish I'd said something like that then. Instead I became completely tongue-tied. And stupidly I kept apologizing. I said I was sorry that she'd been so generous and it hadn't worked out."

"And what about saying that her son was a sociopath? Did you say that? Did you say that the reason it hadn't worked out was more to do with him than with you? Didn't you mention how he threatened you; how he tried to rape you; how he hurt you; how he slandered you? Didn't you say that the healthiest decision you ever made was to leave her son? Didn't you say all that?" Lance's voice was uncharacteristically rising with each question.

"No."

"Whatever happened to that feisty Fleur who wasn't afraid to speak her mind to Elizabeth Carlisle so as to keep her job and her reputation? Whatever happened to the Fleur who stood up to Juliet when she feared she was maligning me? Whatever made you *apologize* to Howard's mother? That only made it look as though you were the guilty party!"

"It's true. I don't know. I regressed."

"Why did you even go into the library in the first place?" Lance continued, his voice still loud and greatly agitated. "You needn't have done that! She couldn't make you! Yes, I can see that it must have been a shock that she was at the party, and it caught you off-guard, but Fleur, Fleur... Why don't you protect yourself more?"

"I don't know, Lance. I thought once I decided to divorce Howard, it would be the end of the story. I had no idea."

"Stories never end, Fleur. You know that. As long as there is life, there are still new possibilities."

"True, though I never foresaw this one."

"Excuse me if I sound disrespectful to your parents, but it strikes me as very insensitive of them to invite Howard's parents to the party, even if they were banking on them being away. But that being so, it didn't mean you had to talk to them. Having to be always polite is nonsense in this situation! Howard's mother is proving to be treacherous, what with her starting rumors that you greedily kept all the wedding presents, and now these hysterical threats tonight. Look, if you can't protect yourself and speak to Howard and his parents assertively, it's better if you don't speak to them at all. A quick nod and a 'good evening' to his mother was all that was needed."

Florence said nothing, and started almost unknowingly to tear a piece of paper on which she'd jotted down some thoughts for her next story, into long, thin, parallel shreds.

"I don't know if there's a delicate way of asking this, Fleur," Lance continued in a softer voice, "but is there any way in which you would actually like to return to Howard? Is this why you're unable to shake him or his mother off? Perhaps you have some feelings still for him."

"Oh God, Lance, no! No!!" Florence screamed. "No, no, no!" And then she added, "It's a silly thing, but I'm still afraid of him. And his mother. I've not been able to break that habit yet."

Lance was quiet for a minute. Then he said gently, "I'm sorry that I asked you that, Fleur. And I'm really sorry too, that this is so hard for you, and you're still afraid of him. I understand why you are. God knows you have every reason to be! And so in that case, keep completely out of his way! Keep a wide birth! Don't be a masochist! You having contact with him or his mother is equivalent to a moth constantly being attracted to a flame, until it gets sucked in and burned up."

"Yes, I know," Florence whispered, aware that she was trembling slightly.

"My sweet Fleur," Lance persisted, "please understand that I became worked up about this because I want you to try not to be afraid of them, or at least not to show it, because when you're afraid you give them power over you, and you lay yourself open to being hurt. And you keep getting hurt. I don't want this to keep happening to you. You're too good a person for that, and you don't deserve malevolent treatment from anyone."

And then, even more quietly, he added, "Fleur, you're all I've got that means anything to me, and God knows I'm not much of a companion to you. I haven't been with you when you've seen Howard or his mother, to stamp out any assault before it happens. The most I can offer you are my insights and advice *after the facts*, and I know that's not much, but I hope you'll take them all the same."

After the phone call was over, Florence perched on the edge of the bed she had slept in as a child, which now appeared hopelessly narrow and on a slant, and cried noisily, hollowly and uncontrollably. She half wanted and expected her father to come in and comfort her, as he used to do if she was upset when she was a child, but no one came. She cried for Lance, who she missed so much and felt so alone without. She cried for herself, for her hurt that he had pointed out to her; and for him, for his wounds that so restricted and curtailed his activities. And most of all, she cried in fury at her own weakness in not standing up to Howard's mother, which, as if not bad enough in itself, was far, far worse as she had hurt Lance by causing him to doubt her wholehearted love for him. She had inadvertently given the impression of still being desirous of Howard, and she cried almost hysterically at the vulnerability that that put her in. "I won't share you with Howard," Lance had once told her. What if he doubted her intentions now to the point of wanting to split up from her as he had done the previous time over the misunderstanding caused by the e-mail that had gone astray? How could she stand it if they were no longer together? She cried until she was depleted of tears, and exhausted she flopped down against her pillows, lying on her side and cradling her knees.

She was startled by the ring of her mobile phone, especially since it was now almost 2.30 am, and thinking it would be Lance again, she picked it up hungrily. But it was not Lance. It was David.

"Florence!" he said with much joy and excitement. "Anna gave birth an hour ago!"

"David! That's marvelous! What wonderful news. Mazel Tov!" she said, forcibly shaking herself into this different reality. "And the same birthday as my Mother! What did you have? A boy or a girl?"

"A seven pound, three ounce baby boy!"

"So it was a boy after all! Anna'd started thinking it would be a girl. What will you call him?"

"Sam! We both agreed to call him Sam. He even looks like a Sam."

"Lovely name! Who does he look like?"

"He's got Anna's eyes. Other than that, it's hard to tell. He's just one hour and four minutes old, so he's still a bit squished. You know how newborns look."

"How's Anna feeling?"

"She's feeling great! Ecstatic! But also very sleepy. Her labor started yesterday, during Shabbat dinner. So it's taken ages. All that time for the baby to come out – a very long, slow entrance into the world - after months of us worrying that the baby would come out too early!"

"Yes! Thank God the baby came just about when he was due."

"That's right! Just nine days before the due date. But that's nothing. That's not considered premature at all. He's already quite chubby! What a clever boy he is, waiting for the right time to be born! And luckily for Anna, even though the labor was long, it did seem very manageable."

"I'm so pleased for all of you!"

"Thanks. Wait! Anna said something. Oh, she wants to talk to you. Here she is."

"Florence?" Anna said in a small, weak, deeply satisfied voice.

"Anna! Oh, Anna, Mazel Tov! What wonderful news! And Sam, what a gorgeous name! I knew it'd be a boy!" Florence said, now feeling better and completely caught up in the excitement.

"Yes, you did, didn't you! Oh Florence, he's so sweet! And I've already nursed him. It's easier than I thought it would be. At least, I haven't a clue if he got any milk, but I assume so, as he was satisfied afterwards, gave a little burp, and fell asleep."

"That's so lovely! I can't wait to see you and meet him!"

"Yes, Florence. It feels like such a miracle to give life. As a rabbi-in-training, I've done countless baby namings, and they've all been moving, but I never fully realized, until now, until giving birth myself, what an enormous miracle it is."

"Oh, Anna, how tremendous! Can I come and see you tomorrow?"

"Oh, I just remembered; aren't you at your parents' house?"

"Yes."

"And aren't they expecting you to stay all weekend?"

"It's fine, Anna. They'll understand that I want to see you." Besides, she was still so upset that they'd betrayed her by inviting Howard's parents. Lance was right; that was completely inappropriate and insensitive of them. "I'll leave straight after breakfast!"

"Thank you, Florence! How good it will be to see you! I just hope I won't be too sleepy. Oh, and don't believe everything David said about the labor being so manageable. It was frightful! Searing pain, which almost felt continuous, as the contractions were so close together. And now I feel battered and bruised all over. But it's worth it, Florence. It's worth every ounce of pain. What a beautiful baby!"

It sounded as though Anna was on the point of drifting off to sleep, when suddenly she said, in an excited voice, "And Florence, the Briss will be a week from tomorrow. Well, given the time now, it'll be a week from today! Sunday of next weekend. I'd ask you to hold the baby when the Moil comes, but I think it has to be a man, and in any case, I don't think you'd actually want to see it being done. I know I don't. The thought of taking a knife to his sweet, tiny body appalls me. So I'm going to have my brother, Josh, hold Sam, and instead I'm going to need you to hold me!"

Sunday! Seeing Lance! Her weekend with him. She wasn't seeing him this weekend, and next weekend was already bitten into on the front end by her lawyer's appointment, and would now have Sunday taken up, too. Impossible to miss the Briss. But Lance. Oh, Lance. She started to miss him again, acutely, like a physical pain.

"Yes, yes; I'll support you at the Briss, Anna, in any way I can. And meanwhile I'll see you tomorrow! Can't wait!"

"I can't wait to see you, Florence. I love you!"

"I love you, too, Anna, and I'm so happy for you!"

--------

The following Thursday, after several dismal days in which her work proved insufficient distraction to missing Lance, Florence went shopping to find a present for Sam. She'd had a slight cold all week, so Anna had asked that she waited until she was over it before seeing the baby again. She did not want to buy clothes or Fisher Price toys, as surely Anna and David would be receiving so many of those, so instead she thought a really good book – one that could endure and be read and reread many times – would be a nicer alternative.

She entered her favorite bookshop, and walked over to the unfamiliar shelves of children's books. So many to choose from, and she had no idea how to make a selection. She tried to think back to cherished books from her own childhood, but running her finger over the spines of the books, there were none that she recognized. And then she remembered; she had always loved *The Secret Garden*, by Burnett, and indeed it was there on the shelf. Thinking of that book reminded her of *Tom's Midnight Garden*, that wonderful book of the magic of time, with its folds, pleats and distortions, that she now vaguely remembered having spoken about with Lance when they had their very first discussion of Time on the window seat at Landsdowne's Guest House. How she'd love to reread it again, together with Lance. She thought hard about who the author was, and then it came to her that it was Philippa Pearce. Here were the books with authors' last names beginning with 'L'. A lot of them. And then the 'M's'; possibly even more.

And then she saw it! She stopped completely in her tracks. *The Adventures of Maud and Mavis*, by Harriet Marsh-Whistler. She felt cold and her arms were covered with goosebumps, and just as suddenly her face felt very hot. She took the book down from the shelf and opened up the back cover. There, staring out benignly, was a black and white photo of an old woman, and underneath, the caption which read:

> *Harriet Marsh-Whistler spent her childhood roving over the rugged terrain of the Lake District, England, which constitutes the backdrop of* The Adventures of Maud and Mavis, *before moving to Sheffield as a young adult. Her early novels, set in the Lake District, are for children. Many of her novels of her middle period are written for adults, and set in industrialized, urban areas, including such works as* The Gem and I, Unwin Unbecoming, *and* Irresolute. *Her more recent works are again written for children, and again are set in the wilds of the Lake District. These include* To the Waters Deep, *and* A Boat Ahoy! *However,* The Adventures of Maud and Mavis *remains a best loved adventure story and a heart-warming children's classic. Marsh-Whistler now lives in London.*

*"Marsh-Whistler now lives in London."* So she *did* marry Bertie Whistler. So she *did* publish her story of Maud and Mavis to a wide audience, and it was well received. *"Marsh-Whistler now lives in London."* She checked the date of the publication, as perhaps this was old information. No; the book was on its seventh reprint, and this, the most recent, was dated 2000, just two years ago. She checked the name of the publisher, as perhaps this way she could obtain information as to how she could contact Hatty.

So, with *The Adventures of Maud and Mavis* tucked under her arm, Florence went to find *Tom's Midnight Garden*, which she managed to do without too much difficulty. Then, having decided upon a beautifully illustrated copy of *The Water Babies* for Sam, she went to the counter to pay.

"Do you think publishers might release information as to how to contact an author?" she asked the woman at the till.

"Oh rather! Many do that! That way the author can receive fan mail. Oh, so you're getting *The Water Babies*! I love that book."

The next morning Florence worked very hard, and was pleased with her progress on one of her stories. But despite this satisfaction, she felt a shadow of sadness about not now driving to the Lake District. Instead later that day she'd be making a local trip to her lawyer. However, she was well prepared for the meeting, having documented her pressing concerns and feeling alert and ready for immediate action.

The phone rang.

"Flo?" It was Howard.

"Howard, I'm afraid I can't speak to you. If you need to tell me something, please do it through your lawyer."

"But Flo, listen-"

"Sorry. 'Bye." And she put the phone down.

It rang again immediately. She didn't answer. She heard the answering machine pick up, and then Howard's voice saying, "My mother told me she saw you last weekend, and that you're looking very pretty, and I thought-"

She disconnected the answering machine and tried to return to her work, but couldn't concentrate. After a while, she decided to leave early for her lawyer's appointment. Maybe she would be seen sooner that way. She took reading material along, just in case she was kept waiting.

When it was time for her appointment, she looked up expectantly from the article she was reading, but there was no sign of her being called. She returned to the article, and twenty minutes later, feeling rather annoyed, went to ask the receptionist when she might see Mrs. Twigger.

"Very soon, dear. You're next," the receptionist told her.

She sat back down and continued reading, willfully curbing her annoyance by telling herself that the wait did not matter. It was not as if she had to hurry from the lawyer's office to drive to Lance, and she'd brought something to read, so she was using her time productively.

But now it was forty minutes past her appointment time, and over an hour since she had been sitting there. She again went to the receptionist's desk.

"It shouldn't be much longer now," the receptionist said sweetly. "There was quite a backlog from this morning, but she's moving right along!"

*"Moving right along!" What sort of ridiculous expression was that?*

"Because you know that it's now three quarters of an hour past my scheduled appointment time, and-"

"I know, dear. I'll call you as soon as she's ready."

There was nothing for it, but to sit down again. And being called "dear" by someone younger than she was! How humiliating! She tried to force herself to continue reading, but to no avail. She was by now so aggravated, that she hoped she'd still be able to think clearly when she finally was permitted in to her lawyer's offices. Why did Mrs. Twigger presume that her time was more valuable than her own? She stuffed the article into her bag, and randomly picked up a magazine lying on the low table in front of her. It was an old one; clearly they were not very good at time-keeping in this office. She started flicking through pages, and suddenly found herself staring at a photograph of the World Trade Center towers on fire. She read the piece with morbid fascination, re-experiencing the acute anguish she had felt then of not knowing if Lance was alive; being unable to contact him; the agony, powerlessness, and despair of waiting for news; the sham of her wedding. Even if she lived another seventy years, she felt sure she'd never experience anything so horrific. She did not realize, until the receptionist tapped her on the shoulder, that her cheeks were moist.

"Ms. Hamilton? Ms. Hamilton, are you OK? I've been calling your name, but I don't think you heard me"

Florence looked up, stunned. "Yes, yes; I'm fine." She quickly jabbed at her cheeks, noticing at the same time that the receptionist looked thinner and more wiry than she did when tucked away behind her desk.

"I'm awfully sorry, dear," the receptionist cooed. "But Mrs. Twigger is unable to see you this afternoon after all. She's been called away on urgent business."

"But this is ludicrous! I've been waiting here for an hour and a half! And I had to wait days to even get this appointment! And change plans for something I very much had wanted to do! Does she know I'm here?"

"Yes, she does. And there's others after you. She's terribly sorry. But as a special favor to you, she can fit you in on Tuesday, at midday. Would you like to take that appointment?"

"I'd like to see her now! Just for a minute or two!" She wanted to tell Mrs. Twigger to her face about the way she ran her business. No point getting cross with the receptionist.

"Oh no, dear. She's already left, I'm afraid. So do you want that Tuesday slot?"

"I don't know. I'm not sure I can-"

"Well, if not then, I can give you another one on Friday, a week from today"

"No. No. I'll take the Tuesday appointment. But she won't change that one around, will she?"

"Oh no, 'course not. Thanks so much. Have a loverly weekend."

Florence fled from there to the nearest park, and sitting on a bench and taking out her mobile phone, her fingers kept tripping over the numbers as she attempted to phone Lance.

"Thank God you escaped from the World Trade Center!" she said wildly. "Thank God you're safe!"

"Fleur, what is it? Why are you talking about this now?"

"There was an old magazine in the lawyer's waiting room," she sobbed. "With photos and personal accounts of the World Trade Center attack, and I couldn't stop reading it, and I kept remembering-" But she couldn't continue as she was crying too much.

"Fleur, Fleur, my sweet love. It's OK. It's OK. Don't read those articles if they upset you. There's nothing to worry about now. I'm here, and I'm fine."

"Thank God! But those days of waiting. Not knowing if you were alive. Not being able to reach you. Not knowing anything. Oh, Lance!"

"Fleur, you're very overwrought. I wish we were together now. But we will be soon. Oh, I do wish I could comfort you better than this."

"Yes, you are. You are comforting me. I'm feeling a little better now."

"That's good, my love. How did it go with your lawyer?"

"She didn't see me. I waited for an hour and a half in the stuffy, overheated waiting room. That's why I read that magazine. Then she was called away."

"No wonder you're feeling so bad. This is atrocious!"

"Yes! Had I known the thing would be cancelled, I could have come up to see you yesterday, and stayed until tomorrow, so as to be back in time for the Briss. Instead I don't see you for a second weekend in a row!"

"Sweet Fleur; I miss you, too. I miss you so much. But, my love, something has to be done about this divorce of yours. You need closure, and you need it now. I'm not sure what I'm going to do, but I'm going to make sure it happens!"

--------

Florence expected to be spending a horrible Saturday. But as things turned out, the day after the futile and depressing wait in the lawyer's waiting room turned out not to be horrible at all. In fact, it was exceptionally fine. That morning, Florence started composing a letter to Harriet Marsh-Whistler's publisher, but then had a sudden idea to look her up in the London phone book. And sure enough, there was only one listing for Marsh-Whistler, on a street not far from Marble Arch, so Florence decided to phone and give it a try.

The phone was answered quickly by a crisp voice saying, "Arnold?"

451

"No; sorry, I'm not Arnold. My name is Florence Hamilton, and I wondered if I could please speak with Mrs. Marsh-Whistler?"

"This is she. What did you say your name is?"

"Ah, good day, Mrs. Marsh-Whistler! My name is Florence Hamilton. You don't know me, but I wonder if we could speak for a few minutes. You see, a friend of mine lives in the Lake District, in the house that used to be owned by the Lacey family, and-"

"Lacey, did you say!"

"Yes, and we found out that you used to be great friends with Kitty Lacey, and-"

"What's your name again?"

"Florence Hamilton. But my friend, who lives in the Lacey's old house, is called Lance Ramsey. And he and I have become interested in the local history-"

"How did you get my name?"

"Actually, I bought your book, *The Adventures of Maud and Mavis*, and it said in the back cover that you live in London, so I looked you up in the phone book. By the way, I love your book. It's a lovely story." She had started reading it the previous evening, and it perfectly matched her impressions of Kitty and Hatty, and also she could so clearly visualize the countryside around Lance's house as the backdrop to the story.

"Thank you, my dear. Where are you now? Are you phoning from the Lake District?"

"No, I live in London. Actually, I'm not too far away from you, as it happens."

"Well, dear, this is fascinating! I was expecting Arnold to see me this afternoon for tea, but it looks as if he's not going to be coming. He never does. He only comes when I'm *not* expecting him! So why don't you come, instead, especially if you haven't got far to come? You sound like a nice girl, and you've certainly whet my appetite with news about the Lacey house."

"Thank you! I'd love to come and visit you!"

A little over an hour later, Harriet Marsh-Whistler was showing Florence copies of all the books she had written. They were lined up chronologically on a polished mahogany shelf, near the bow window overlooking Marble Arch itself. The flat was heated to a very high temperature, and had a vague smell of disinfectant. Harriet was sprightly and nimble, and had a maid, Sally, who seemed almost as old as she was, who brought in the tea things on a glittery silver tray.

"Oh yes; I'm still writing!" Harriet Marsh-Whistler answered to a question Florence had put to her. "If Astrid Lindgren can do it, so can I!"

"Astrid Lindgren?"

"Yes, you no doubt have heard of her. She's a very famous Swedish children's author, who wrote *Pippi Longstocking*, and such."

"Oh yes, I remember. Is she still writing?"

"Rather! And she's in her nineties. As for me, these days I find I live very much in my mind. I especially dwell there on my childhood days up in the Lake District, so when you phoned, I could hardly believe it! Of course, there's nowhere like the Lake District. Just the way the light and the lakes change with the weather and seasons, is magic in itself. So my newest stories take place again up there, as every children's book must contain some magic, don't you agree?"

She chuckled, and Florence thought she could detect, through her refined London accent, some subtle hints of a Northern intonation.

"Oh yes, that's certainly true," Florence agreed.

"But now, tell me more about you, and what you'd like to know."

"Well, as I said, my friend Lance lives in the Lacey's old house, and we've been speaking to people in the area. Do you know Mrs. Landsdowne, for example?"

"Oh yes – dear me! That takes me back! Betty Perth was just a little child when I knew her, but I heard she married Mr. Landsdowne. How is she?"

"Very well! She and her husband run a guest house. A very lovely place. It's where Lance and I met. Anyway, she told us about Group Captain Lacey."

"Who?"

"Gordon Lacey. Kitty's brother."

"Oh yes, I'd forgotten he'd gone off to the air force. So, he's a Group Captain now, is he! Highly impressive."

"Yes. Well, we visited him, and he-"

"How is Gordon? I used to have quite a soft spot for him. Especially after poor Kitty died. Do you know, had she lived, I'm convinced she'd have become a renowned poetess by now. Oh, but I don't suppose you know she'd died."

"Actually, we did find out about it. She was killed by the family dog, wasn't she?"

"Yes, poor Kitty. Actually, I'd hardly call that brute the family dog. It was owned by her mother, Virginia Lacey. Everyone else hated it." Harriet paused and cleared her throat. "But I've immortalized Kitty, you know," she said, regaining her composure. "My stories of Maud and Mavis are about our friendship."

"Yes, I know," Florence blurted out before thinking.

"How do you know that?" Harriet asked sharply. But then she dreamily continued, "Yes, there's great comfort in story-telling. A great comfort. Kitty is alive for me. Always will be. My new story is about her, too. Sometimes, these days, I no longer remember if I'm writing about adventures we actually had, or if I'm making the whole thing up. But it scarcely matters." She sipped some tea. Then, just as suddenly, she said, "Would you like me to show you some photos of my family?"

"Yes, please. I'd love to see them."

Harriet reached for a photo of a large group of people, standing in rows, all solidly facing the camera. "Here we are then, dear," she said, tilting the photo towards Florence.

"What a nice picture! Are they all your children?"

"Yes, I have five children, fourteen grandchildren, and two great grandchildren, with another one on the way, but this photo was taken before the great grandkids were born. Look, over here is Jimmy, and then Connie, and those three are Margaret, Robert, and Sybil. Those five are my children. And the front row is all the grandchildren. Too many to name. In fact, it's hard to keep track of all of them sometimes!"

"Five children! You and your husband must have been kept very busy!"

"Oh yes. Well Bertie – that's my husband – is no longer alive. He died four years ago, bless his soul. He was a good man, very good."

"I'm sorry. Is that his photo?"

"Yes, that's him," Harriet said, stroking the dull, scrolled metal frame surrounding a photo of a man with a great shock of white hair.

"He's a nice looking man."

"Yes, that he was. And a good husband and good father. They're hard to find, these days. Here, dear," she said, setting the photo down on the table, "have a piece of ginger."

Florence took a piece of oddly shaped ginger dusted with icing sugar, and popped it into her mouth, where it burned not unpleasantly.

"How did you meet your husband?" she asked.

"Bertie and I met when my family and I moved to Sheffield. I was just a girl. But Bertie and I had such fun together."

"Were you very young when you married?"

"Oh no, dear. Bertie waited quite a long time for me."

"He waited for you to grow up?"

"No, it wasn't like that. I wasn't *that* young. But he waited until I was ready, and by that time I had two children."

"Two?"

"My dear Florence! That is your name, isn't it? You surprise me. Most people would have been amazed to hear that I had *one* child before marrying, but you seem surprised that I had two of them!"

"Ah yes. Let me explain. We heard from Group Captain Lacey about how you adopted Connie after Kitty died. I just hadn't known that you had another child."

"What are you; a detective? You're very alert!" Harriet said, giving a tinkling little laugh.

"No, not a detective. Though I am a reporter. I write stories for - magazine. But don't worry; our conversation here is strictly private, and the only person I will tell is Lance."

"Who? Who will you tell?"

"Lance. My friend who lives in the Lacey house."

"All right, dear. That's very nice. You must be good at your work. And you have a way about you, that makes me feel comfortable talking to you about things. So, you're a writer like me!"

"Yes! And it seems we both love what we do. But please tell me, if you don't mind, about Connie, and your other child."

"I will tell you, dear, because I like you. But this is one story I won't write about. But before I do tell it to you, I just want to mention that

Astrid Lindgren also had two children before she married. That's another similarity between us. Oh well, be that as it may. Yes, so there I was, in my early twenties, when I heard news from Gordon that Kitty had been killed. I was naturally stunned, and then devastated, and went round to see the Lacey's immediately. And that's when I was asked if I would adopt Connie. She was a sweet little thing, without father or mother. So how could I refuse?

"But let me explain. I don't know if you're aware of this already, but Kitty was never married. The father of the child was a man who Kitty had adored almost all her life, it seems, but he married another woman, and so kept the illegitimate child a secret. This meant, of course, that after Kitty died, he could not raise the child, as it would cause any manner of scandal. His name was Ilyich Throgmorton, and he lived with his wife, Bethany, in a magnificent stately home, that had been in the family for generations. Let me see; yes, it was called Wolvercote Hall. It wasn't too far from the Lacey's house."

Harriet paused, then took some ginger before passing the plate to Florence.

"So, after my visit to the Lacey's," she said, blinking as she swallowed a mouthful of ginger, "it was then my dreadful duty to go to see Ilyich, to tell him the news about Kitty. My dear, I can honestly say that I have never seen a grown man so deranged. He staggered around like a drunkard, cursing and hitting his head with his hand repeatedly. It seemed that he knew that the dog had attacked her – he had apparently been there when the dog rushed towards them – but he had no idea that the dog had actually killed her, as he had clearly abandoned her; the simpering good-for-nothing that he was!"

Harriet started to cough, and it looked as though she might choke. Alarmed, Florence rose to pat her on the back, but Harriet put up a hand to stop her, and then with a final cough, managed to control herself.

"Ilyich seemed almost delirious," Harriet said, her eyes watering, though whether it had been caused by the coughing fit or her sad memories, Florence could not be sure. "He kept muttering something about how Kitty had just given him a little ring containing some of Connie's hair, and a letter saying her guardian angel was delivering it for her, but how this made no sense as she had given it to him herself, just before the dog attacked."

Florence gasped! So it *had* happened! They really had visited Kitty in her time of immense agitation! Not that she had doubted it, of course, but still the confirmation from Harriet was extraordinary. Harriet seemed to notice Florence's reaction, but probably putting it down to the drama of the story itself, she continued, more eagerly now, by saying, "Ilyich was sobbing so loudly as he told me this that I had to remind him to control himself, for fear his young wife would hear his mad rantings and find out about his affair with Kitty. But then he accused me of not believing him, and I clearly remember that however garbled his words were, he verified them by pulling out of his pocket the most curious ring. It had a raised gold box on it, which opened, and from it he showed me a little curl of Connie's hair. He also tossed to me the last letter that Kitty had ever written, which said something about a guardian angel, and he thought that this was a sign that she knew she was about to die. When he showed this to me, he was quite beside himself and virtually uncontrollable. Only after much time did he manage to pull himself together, but I knew his pain was great, as he truly loved Kitty."

"This is an incredible story," Florence said, "but please don't feel that you have to tell it all to me if it's upsetting you."

"No dear; that's all right. I never did manage, though, to understand what this was all about – that ring and Kitty's letter about her angel – and we novelists love to take intriguing events and make up a story about them - but as I said, this was one event that I could not possibly write about. It brings me to goosebumps all up and down my arms even to think about it. But perhaps that angel was comforting to Kitty, and with that thought I comfort myself."

Harriet paused to take a sip of tea, which must have grown quite cold. But clearly she had a lot more she wanted to tell Florence, as she then said, "I spent quite a lot of time at Wolvercote Hall over the next few weeks, lamenting the cruelty of Kitty's fate. His wife, Bethany, knew something was troubling him, but she was none too swift so his secret was safe. But one day, when I was at the Hall, his brother Igor visited. Now Igor was someone I had had an adolescent crush on before I moved to Sheffield.

Kitty and I had thought, as teenagers, that it was such fun that we should love two brothers, only her love was real, and mine was more an infatuation. However, when I saw Igor that time, and I was so sad and he was so sweet to me in my great sorrow, I mistakenly thought I felt attracted to him all over again. I was in such a raw state emotionally, as you'll understand. So I permitted him to be a little amorous to me, and, well – I won't go into the details, of course, but that's how Jimmy made his entrance into the world."

Harriet took out a little lace handkerchief and coyly blotted her lips. Then she sighed loudly, and looking at Florence a little bashfully, she said, "That love affair with Igor did not last, of course. There was something about those Throgmorton's; they were all about having illicit affairs, and nothing about commitment, unless, of course, you were from the upper echelons. So I eventually returned to Sheffield, with little Connie, who had just started to toddle around, and newly pregnant with Jimmy. And Bertie – as I said, he was a good man – had waited for me, always sure I'd come back. The fact that I'd returned with a child, and another one on the way, made no difference to him. He said we'd marry straight away, so that everyone would think Jimmy was his child, and he told me he'd help bring up both those babies as though they were his own. And he was as good as his word. Of course, we went on to have another three children together, but my Bertie, he never differentiated between any of those five little dears, and loved them all the same.

"As for the Throgmorton's, the last I heard was that there was a great fire at the Hall, and that beautiful house was left in ruins. And I did hear rumored that Ilyich did the one heroic act of his life – in every other way he was a remarkable coward – he returned into the burning building to snatch his son and bring him to safety. I think the whole family moved away from the area after that, but I didn't know, nor did I care."

Harriet resolutely bit into another piece of ginger, and seemed unaware that a glistening drip of saliva hovered at the corner of her mouth. It made its hesitant way in a meandering rivulet, between the creases and folds of her wrinkled chin.

"What a series of events," Florence retorted, forcing herself to recover from the enormity of this information about the curious ring, and Connie's hair, and the letter. She did not want to give anything away to

Harriet's sharp observation. "Thanks for telling me, especially as the parts about Kitty must have been so painful for you. You seem like an incredible person. Connie was lucky to have you."

"Well, she couldn't stay with the Lacey's. That much was certain. And I was her godmother – Kitty had asked that of me when Connie was born. Virginia Lacey, always a strict mother – and more so with Kitty than with Gordon (although some feel it's different with girls, though I must say, I never did) – now, where was I? Oh yes, Virginia Lacey went completely to pieces after Kitty was killed. Some even say she went quite mad, though I, having spent so long in their house after Kitty's death, think instead she had a tormented soul. She would go out into the lanes each night, with that awful dog of hers, searching for Kitty. As you can imagine, it would be pitch black outside, as it is in remote country areas far from any towns, but that wouldn't stop her. In fact, it was impossible to stop her. She'd take only her flashlight and her dog, and she'd go rambling about, searching, searching.

"But the authorities came and said the dog had to be put to sleep, since it was so dangerous, and neighbors were afraid of it. So, after the dog was gone, Virginia started wandering around outside even more, whether looking for Kitty or the dog, I don't know. So they had to put her in a Home. I visited her there once, but not again. And I stayed on with the Lacey's a bit longer, until Gordon left home – yes, as you reminded me, he enlisted in the RAF – and poor Mr. Lacey was left all alone. He realized he didn't need such a big house all to himself, so he put it up for sale, and moved out, even before there was a buyer.

"So, you see I had no option but to take Connie, otherwise she'd become a warden of the state. But I wanted to adopt her anyway. She was my direct link with Kitty. And I'll tell you something else, dear. I'm glad I had Jimmy since his father was Connie's father's brother, which made me think that those two wee babies were even more related. Also I was glad to have done something as naughtily socially unacceptable as Kitty had done. We were always sisters-in-arms!

"Ah, this all takes me back!" Harriet said, leaning back in her chair, and eating the remainder of the piece of ginger, which had grown sticky between her fingers. "It's lucky that Arnold did not come, as it's given me such a lovely chance to talk to you."

"Thanks! I'm having a wonderful afternoon. Is Arnold a friend of yours?"

"Gracious no, no! At my age, there are very few friends left. No, Arnold is my oldest grandson. In fact, he's Connie's son."

"Oh. Does he live near here?"

"Yes, he does. He lives near Euston. He's a good man; he's a designer, you know, in one of the Soho galleries. He often pops in to see me at times I don't expect him, and seldom at times I do!"

"Does Connie live close, too?"

"Connie! Oh no. She's up in the Lake District, and what's so funny, though she doesn't know it, is that she's really quite close to the house in which she was born! Mind you, she must never know about that; about how she was adopted, I mean. She of course wouldn't remember, so she thinks she spent her entire childhood in the city of Sheffield, until we moved to London, when she must have been in her mid-teens."

"She doesn't know she was adopted? You never told her?"

"Oh no, dear. As I said, we brought Connie up as our own. What's past is past."

Florence shuffled uneasily in her chair. "Do you think some time, when I'm visiting Lance, we could go and see Connie?"

"Why, yes, dear! She'd like some company. Northerners are very friendly, you know; more so than Londoners. Only you must never tell her about her natural parents. You must promise me that!"

"Of course we'd never tell her! Absolutely not! It would be devastating to find out a thing like that at her age! And from a stranger!"

"Yes, so you see her. And tell her you're a friend of mine. I hope you *are* a friend of mine, and that you'll continue coming to see me. You tell her you were in the area seeing your friend Lance. Is that his name? Nice name, that. Perhaps I'll use it in my next book. Yes, tell her you were close by, so stopped in to say hello."

"Thanks! I'll do that. And I've definitely made a great new friend this afternoon. I would most certainly like to continue visiting you! This has been an unexpectedly delightful afternoon!"

"For me, too, dear. For me, too. My children will most likely tell me off for opening my house up to a stranger, but I had a good feeling about you, and I'm glad I did. Look, I have some extra copies of *A Boat Ahoy!* It's all about a funny morning Kitty and I spent once long ago. We must have been about ten. We were- Well no, I won't spoil the story. Read it yourself, and you'll see!"

"Thank you so much. Could you please autograph this?"

"Certainly, my dear." Harriet fumbled in a drawer, and produced at length a fountain pen. Then, in turquoise ink she scrawled, *'To my sister-writer, and dear friend, Florence. With love from Harriet.'*

"Oh, and while I have the pen I'll write down Connie's address and phone number. I'll tell her to expect you. Now dear, just one more thing before you go; I'd love to see some of the stories you write."

"Yes! Next time I see you I'll bring some along. I'd be very happy for you to look at them."

"And dear; take some ginger pieces with you!"

"Thanks. But I couldn't possibly. You've already given me so much this afternoon."

And she had.

When Florence returned home, the first thing she did was check her e-mail. There was a message from Lance asking her to phone him, as he said he'd been trying to phone, but she was not answering her mobile phone, and he was unable to leave a message on the answering machine of her house phone.

"Lance!" she said excitedly into the phone, "Oh, I've so much to tell you! Sorry about disconnecting the answering machine, but Howard kept-"

"He's not bothering you again, is he?"

"Don't worry about that. Lance, listen! I just spent a marvelous afternoon with Harriet Marsh-Whistler!"

"You spent the afternoon with her! But it was only the day before yesterday that you found her book! Did the publisher respond to you that fast?"

"No; actually I found her phone number in the phone book, and phoned and she invited me over."

"Fleur, you're fabulous! What was she like? What did she tell you?"

"Oh Lance, she's quite wonderful. She told me so much, including the fact, by the way, that Connie lives quite near you!" Then she went on to tell him everything else she'd learned.

"And there's one more truly, truly remarkable thing Harriet told me," Florence added. "It's true! We *had* converged on to Kitty's time axis! Oh Lance; I can hardly believe this. But Harriet said that when she went to tell Ilyich about Kitty's death, and he was so grief stricken, he showed her a ring with a little box on top, which contained a lock of Connie's hair. And he also showed her the letter that Kitty had written, which said her guardian angel was going to deliver it to him from her. You! You were that angel! I remember she called you that."

"Yes, she called me her 'guardian angel'."

Florence imagined that when Lance said this, he would bow his head into his hands, and be racked with sadness and guilt because of not having arrived in time to take the ring from Kitty and therefore being unable to deliver it as he had promised. But instead he surprised her by saying, "My God, Fleur! So that is evidence that we did indeed join Kitty and Virginia in their time! Can you believe it? Remember how after a bit, we wondered whether we had made the whole thing up. God, this is incredible!"

"Yes, isn't it!"

"I can't get over this! Our theories and thoughts about Time seem to be gaining evidence. Hah, this is remarkable! We must give this further thought. I can't wait to see you, so that we can talk more about this! And consider this; if the Past, Present and Future truly intersect, then it is of course entirely possible that someone from a different time axis is observing, or even interacting with us!"

"Wow! This makes me feel that all semblance of order breaks down! It's even more evidence that the supposed linear and orderly movement of time is artificial, and only a way to cope and try to understand things."

"Exactly! Let's definitely keep exploring this next weekend when you're here. And let's also go and visit Connie, now that you've found out that she is close by. I can hardly believe this! You really made exciting discoveries, my sweet, amazing one! And meanwhile, I have some exciting news to tell you, too!"

"What is it?

"Simon will take on your case! He'll handle your divorce proceedings. I might not have mentioned that Simon is a lawyer, as I've been so busy e-mailing you about all the wonderful meals that Crispin has been cooking ever since they arrived. We're eating magnificently. I wish you were here to taste everything. I wish you were here in any case. But back to Simon; yes, he's a lawyer. Even though he specializes in legal rights of homosexuals, I told him about the problems you've been having with your divorce, and he felt outraged, and wants to help you out. He's sure the whole thing can be speedily wrapped up."

"Lance, thank you!"

"And he has an office in London, on the Bayswater Road. Look, he's here now. I'll put him on, so he can speak to you."

Florence talked to Simon for quite a while. She was struck by what an educated and kind voice he had, coaxing her to fill in the details as to how her divorce proceedings were being handled. He suggested that she request that Mrs. Twigger's office should transfer her file to him, and that she should meet with him the following Thursday morning.

Already uplifted from her afternoon with Harriet Marsh-Whistler, Florence was now even more jubilant. And that good mood stayed with her throughout the Briss the next day, in which she again saw Sam, her cold now completely better, and cuddled him a lot, inhaling his warm, milky smell, and marveling at his tiny pink fingers which spontaneously wrapped themselves around her thumb. The atmosphere in Anna and David's living room was so full of love, that even the indignity of the Moil's removal of the foreskin did little to spoil the general mood. A momentary squall from Sam, a contented sucking on cotton wool soaked in red Kosher wine, and then his cozy embrace by Anna who nursed him in a quiet corner of the room until he was sleeping soundly, was what it amounted to.

The week sped by, with Florence engrossed in her research, and seeing Anna, David and Sam, and then it was time to visit Simon. A friendly male secretary guided her to his office door as soon as she arrived, so she bypassed the waiting room completely.

"Hello, Fleur! Come in, come in! Good to meet you at last!" Simon said warmly. He was a good-looking man with blond, wavy hair, and large, light-frame glasses surrounding green eyes. He was dressed immaculately.

"Might I call you Fleur, actually?" he asked. "I see in your file your name is Florence."

"Oh yes; please do. Anyone who knows me through Lance calls me that."

"Great! Fleur, it is! Do sit down."

He himself sprawled in a huge chair behind his desk, crossing his legs and interlacing his fingers.

"It's so kind of you to take on my case," Florence said.

"Think nothing of it. I'm delighted to do so. But first, before we begin, let's get to know each other a little, since we didn't get a chance to meet last weekend. This is off the clock, you understand. Lance was so sorry you weren't there. I could tell he missed you terribly. He spoke about you all the time!"

"Did he? Yes, I wish I'd been able to be there, too. It sounds as though you had a wonderful time."

"We did. What a gorgeous house he lives in! And in such a breathtaking area, too. We took him for a drive, as we thought it would be good for him to get out a bit." Florence felt like saying that Lance was perfectly capable of getting out, and driving himself around, but did not want to interrupt. "He's doing remarkably well, all things considered," Simon continued. "Honestly, after hearing he was in the World Trade Center when it was attacked, Crispin and I thought he'd never make it. Crispin was inconsolable, and I can't say I was any better." He stopped and looked at her kindly. "It must have been terrible for you."

"It was at first when I couldn't contact him and didn't know if he was alive. That was agonizing. But he's pulled through remarkably well," she said, trying to strike an optimistic note.

"Yes, he has. He improves each time we see him. Let me see now; yes, I think this was our third or fourth visit. We've never managed to get away on the weekend before, as it's Crispin's busiest time at the bistro, so we've seen Lance midweek before this time. But last weekend was different as Crispin got some time off, so up we went."

"It made Lance so happy to see you both."

464

"Poor chap. I'll never forget the day we met him at Manchester airport when he returned from America. We were expecting to pick him out easily from the crowd coming through the gate, as he's pretty tall, isn't he? And then there he was, being pushed along in a wheelchair by an airline attendant, a travel bag dangling from the handles, and an Asian woman at his side, who we later learned was Mei-Feng, carrying more hand luggage. I simply couldn't believe it."

Florence, remembering her own shock at seeing Lance in a wheelchair, nodded empathetically.

"When he'd e-mailed us to tell us about buying his house, way back in early November, we immediately wrote back saying we'd help him with the move. We expected it to be a good fun, boisterous thing to do – you know, we thought we'd crack open a few bottles of bubbly to celebrate, that kind of thing - as we never doubted that he'd have made a full recovery by then. But nearer the time of his return, he e-mailed to say that it wasn't necessary for Crispin and I to help after all, as he'd hired a firm of movers, as there'd be much too much to do. But we replied saying we wouldn't hear of such a thing, and he could keep his movers if he wanted, but we intended to be there, too. He accepted graciously, though never wrote a word about his condition. I believe he was too shy to tell us to expect to see him that way. He is quite shy, you know."

"Yes, he can be," Florence murmured.

"So there we were, meeting him at the airport in January, and then we drove up to his house. And once in his house, the poor man had to just sit there - and I'm sure he was feeling very embarrassed and also humiliated, though he was hiding it well - and asked us politely to put his things in particular places. In some instances he requested that some of his belongings be put into upstairs rooms we thought he'd never be able to reach. It was more than sad. Christ, he expected to be confined to a wheelchair for the rest of his life! He'd completely given up."

Simon took a tissue from the box on his desk and dabbed underneath his glasses at his eyes. He then twirled a deep blue paper weight on his desk, and added, "After we'd had some dinner, which Crispin had made and brought up with us, and still drank the champagne that we'd been intending to enjoy all along, Lance loosened up a bit and became more

465

candid with us. He confessed to now thinking that the house was a terrible mistake; that even though apparently he'd wanted that house for years and was so glad to see it on the market just when he was ready to buy, he said he'd have been more sensible to move into a bungalow or a flat. In fact he said that this was certainly the most expensive and probably the most impractical thing he had ever done; this getting what he'd wanted but not what he now needed. And we could hardly dispute that, now could we!"

Florence, hearing Simon's story, and on top of it all never having known that Lance had had misgivings about moving to his house, felt her own eyes brimming, and Simon passed her a tissue which she did not use, but which she bundled into her hand, subconsciously tearing little holes into it, and making snake shapes with other ends of it. Then smiling, Simon added in a louder, more confident voice,

"But he said it was you, Fleur. You who literally got him on his feet again. Now, how did he put it? Oh yes, he said, 'Fleur gave me not only the motivation, but also her special form of kindness which was devoid of pity, or of being too smothering.' Something like that."

"It's hard not to be overwhelmed by pity, isn't it, even though we must never show that to Lance," Florence replied. "But anyway," she added, visibly brightening, "thank you for telling me that he said that. And incidentally, I think he deserves all the credit for not giving up."

"I'm so glad he met you, Fleur. Actually, he related to us about how the two of you met in that Guest House he goes to every year with his mum. That place that's usually filled with old fuddy-duddies. And he told us, too, about your clandestine meetings, so that none of the other guests had a clue you knew each other! It sounds delightfully naughty and deliciously romantic to me!"

"Yes, it certainly was fun!" Florence said, laughing now.

"And I'll have you know that any friend of Lance's is a friend of mine. He's an exceptionally noble, good man. We've known each other for years. Ever since university, actually."

"Yes, he is an exceptionally noble man," she echoed.

"And he's very concerned about you, Fleur. He said it's an outrage how Howard has been treating you, and how your lawyer has largely ignored you. He wished he could do more to help you."

"But he has! He's been so solicitous of me. And now he's introduced me to you!"

"Well, that's certainly true. Right! So let's get down to business. Now, I've looked through your file and…"

An hour and a half later, Florence emerged from Simon's office feeling very optimistic and assured of his competence. He had said things had obviously become quite complicated, but nothing was insurmountable or beyond repair, and he thought it was not unrealistic to expect that everything could be settled before the end of the summer. When she mentioned how Howard had developed a habit of launching surprise delay tactics, he assured her it was nothing he had not seen before – even warring couples of the same gender treated each other that way – and he knew how to overcome those situations.

--------

That Saturday Florence and Lance were on their way to see Connie. They had phoned her the previous evening, and Connie, already having heard about them and knowing to expect their visit from her mother, said she was all prepared to see them.

"I wonder what she'll be like," Florence said excitedly to Lance. "If she has Kitty's beauty and Hatty's flamboyance, she'll really be quite something!"

But they were both extremely disappointed. In contrast to their expectations, Connie was as limp and bedraggled as faded wet socks in need of darning, left on the washing line during heavy rain. Her thin, colorless hair hung in lank strands to her shoulders; her pale face lacked expression; and when she spoke it sounded as though she was reading out lists, so lacking in animation was her voice. She served watery tea in plastic beakers, accompanied by a few broken digestive biscuits, the type without chocolate on them. And whether she was describing a favorite television program, (usually an American one), a preferred café, or a new dress, she'd say, in her glum monotones, "It's to die for!" "Yes, the telly's on all day. I do love the program, *Everyone Loves Raymond*. It's to die for!" "Oh, that new café by the traffic lights, Rowan's, I think it's called. It's to die for!"

It seemed hopeless. However much Florence or Lance tried to steer the conversation away from such banalities and to family matters such as bringing in her mother Harriet, or her son Arnold, Connie's dull eyes would wander over to the television, which had been left on, and she'd grow distracted by what she saw. Finally, though, quite by chance, she said something of exciting potential.

"My Lord! Look at that advert for cars! They advertise them all the time. It's as if we can afford to have more than one car! Whoever heard of such a thing? Only in America they have four cars per family, according to my daughter what lives there, but not here, I'm sure!"

"You have a daughter in America?" Florence asked.

"Yes, that's right. But what do you need so many cars for, that's what I say. Take our Mini, now; it handles all the bends very well, thank you very much. And is good on the hills. One day me husband Gerald, now he was driving along, and he-"

"Where does she live in America?" Lance asked.

"What? Oh, me daughter. She lives in Bensonhurst, Brooklyn," Connie said, lighting a cigarette.

"So she's in New York! I was in New York last year!"

Connie had no natural curiosity. She inhaled deeply on her cigarette.

"Yes. Jennie's been there five years now, she has. Jennie, that's me daughter. Got a nice flat – now, what do they call them over there? Oh yes, apartment. We visited her there once, must have been three years ago. She showed us the view of the New York skyscrapers. They're to die for! What a sight!"

"Why did she go to America?" Lance asked.

"Well now, she had this waitressing job down the local pub five minutes away. You must have passed it on your way here; the King's Arms. Not yet even twenty, she was then. Anyhows, she met Blake there. He's from New York and was here on his holidays. It all happened very quickly. Next thing I know, she's going back there with him. He seems like a nice boy, but what do I know? We met him a few times at the pub, and then three years ago we went out there for the wedding. She wanted her wedding over there, see, rather than here. All la-dee-dah, she's getting."

"Does she come home often to visit?"

"Not as often as we'd like. Can't afford it. We're planning to go over there soon – not that we can afford it neither – to meet our new grandchild. It's our second grandchild, actually. Me son, Arnold and his wife, Amanda, they had a baby girl two summers ago. She's to die for! Such a sweetie pie! And so now Arnold says he'll be flying out there so the cousins can meet, and he's telling me to go and see Jennie's baby, too. Jennie's baby will be having her first birthday by Christmas. Me old man, Gerald, said we might be able to afford to go for Christmas this year."

After that lengthy conversation, Connie stubbed out her cigarette, nibbled on a digestive biscuit, and her eyes again sought out the television. Florence and Lance prepared to leave, but at the front door Lance said, "Would it be OK with you if I phone your daughter? I have quite a few friends in New York and speak to them often, so it would be nice to say hello to her as well. Who knows? Maybe she'll even know some of the same people I know."

"All right. I can't see as it would do any harm. This is her number. Got it in my head, I have." She recited a string of numbers, and Florence wrote them down.

As they were driving back to Lance's house, Florence remarked, "I wonder how Gordon Lacey would feel knowing his niece lived so close to him."

"Perhaps it's just as well we can never tell him" Lance replied. "Better to preserve those memories of that chubby, appealing baby."

--------

There then followed several weeks of relative calm. Simon seemed to be making good progress on the divorce proceedings; little baby Sam was growing and changing every time Florence saw him; Hatty (as she preferred to think of her) was delighted when she next visited to show her some of her articles; and at work she was busy and productive, and Elizabeth Carlisle kept plying her with more stories. Also, a magazine that she had contacted a long time ago suddenly asked her for a piece, too. And then there were the weekends with Lance, back to their usual rhythm after the long interruption.

One day, after having followed the river at the bottom of Lance's garden in the hope of reaching the small lake that Florence had once discovered, they paused as the path was rough and overgrown. They heard geese noisily calling to each other, and looking up, saw the V formation of the approaching birds, silhouetted against the bright sky. Then, as they flew past them, angling into the sunlight, they noticed how their soft underbellies glowed white gold.

Back in the house a little later, the phone rang, and it was Marissa calling from New York. She and Lance chatted merrily for quite a while, and Florence heard him tell her how much he enjoyed teaching online. Marissa, Lance informed her later, had answered that since location did not matter, he might consider teaching for New School University, which was in Greenwich Village, close to NYU. She knew some people who worked there, and would look into it for him.

"Do you like teaching online as much as you do in the traditional classroom?" Florence asked him when he'd finished speaking with Marissa.

"Yes, in some ways I do. Ironically it seems that the students and I get to know each other even better online than if we were face-to-face."

"Why do you think that is?"

"I used to think it was because of the relative anonymity of the computer screen. But now I believe that it's more than that. I think it relates to the use of Time, Fleur. Time again having an impact! Its asynchronicity allows everyone to contribute without interruption, which encourages them to be reflective, and to join in with the discussion when they are at their best and feeling inspired."

"Kairological time, then?"

"Precisely! I sense that the students are aware of these benefits, too. I've actually received some nice e-mails from some of them."

"Have you? Can I see them?"

Lance flicked open his laptop, logged into his e-mail, and started scrolling through. He found quite a collection of student e-mail from a few weeks ago when the course had ended. Florence read one after another. All so complimentary. "I loved this class. I didn't want it to end." "I feel as though I just finished a favourite book. But unlike a book, which I can pick up and read again, this class is over. Disappeared! I'm so sad. I want more!" "I'll definitely look for more courses taught by you!" "How do you do it, Dr. Ramsey? You respond to us all so thoughtfully, you challenge us to think outside the box, you include each and every one of us in your gracious comments, and you help us to see deeper and explore more profoundly than we've ever gone before."

There were more comments such as these. Florence read them all. They mirrored what she had seen at NYU, of Lance's students flocking around him after class, loving him, wanting more, capturing his passion for the topic. She went up to him, where he was seated on the sofa quietly reading, and buried her head in the warmth of his neck.

"These are incredible, Lance! You are so humble and modest. Your students adore you, and I quite see why!"

He smiled. "Thank you. It's an interesting idea Marissa had for me to teach online at the New School. I remember it well, and you probably do, too. We must have walked past it millions of times. Remember? It's on 12th Street near Sixth Avenue."

"Oh yes, I remember it! So you'd like to teach online for them?"

"I think so. I could add it to my classes at East Anglia. But you know, Fleur, just hearing from people in New York, and talking about places over there, gives me such an incredible feeling."

"Good or bad?"

"Good. Definitely good. I loved it there, and I'm beginning to think about it as it was, before the World Trade Center attack. Fleur, I know! I just had an idea!" he said, sitting up straighter, and looking very alert. "Let's phone Jennie! Connie's daughter. I feel like doing it now while I'm in the New York mood. Also, I think it'll give us a sense of completion, because if we talk to her, we'll have talked to each generation of the Lacey's."

"Yes, I'll get her number."

Lance punched in the number, and the phone was answered straight away.

"Hello. My name is Lance Ramsey. My friend, Fleur, and I recently met your mother. What? Oh good; so you were expecting we'd phone you! Actually, Fleur is here too, so would you mind if I put this on speaker-phone? Good! Thank you."

"Sure!" a very American sounding voice said to the room. "How are you guys? I wondered when you'd call!"

"Did you?" Lance said. "Sorry if we kept you waiting!"

"No, I mean it's so cool. Like, my granny told me about you. And you live near Mum, right, Lance? And you, Fleur, live near granny! That's so neat!"

"Hello Jennie! This is Fleur. How are you? You sound so American! I couldn't tell that you're English!"

"Yeah, well, I've been living here in the States for quite a few years now, so I guess I kinda picked it up."

"You must love it over there."

"Yeah. I like it. Great food. Great people. Of course, it's a little different now I've had the baby."

"Yes, you're a mum now! Congratulations!"

"Thanks! Yeah, Carrie was born last Boxing Day. Though they don't call it that over here, but *you* know what I mean!"

"She must be at a very sweet stage. A friend of mine recently had a baby, too. It must be lovely being home with her, and seeing all her new accomplishments."

"Well, to tell you the honest truth, I'm going stir-crazy. I mean, she's real cute and all, but if my job hadn't relocated to a totally far-away place, I'd be back at work by now."

"Who did you work for?" Lance asked, breaking again into the conversation.

"Morgan Stanley. I did data entry. It was kind of a drag, but I met some real nice gals there. I miss 'em."

"Morgan Stanley? Did you used to work at the World Trade Center?"

"Yeah, that's right. But they've moved to Jersey now, so it's a pain in the butt to commute from Brooklyn-"

"I hope you don't mind me asking, but were you working for them at the time of the attack on the World Trade Center last September?"

"Yeah. Matter of fact I was."

"Were you in one of the towers? Or in one of the surrounding lower buildings of the World Trade Center?"

"I was in World Trade Center Number 2. That was one of the towers. It was real scary."

"I was there then, too."

"You were? Who did you work for then?"

"Actually, I worked at NYU, but I had an appointment to see a colleague at the World Trade Center that morning. I was in the same tower as you."

"Wow. So you got out OK, obviously."

"Yes, I did."

"Great! Me too."

"We were lucky. So many killed, and some of those who escaped were injured, some for life. I don't need to tell you that."

"I honestly didn't think-" she paused. "Like, I didn't think I'd get outta there alive. And there was my baby to think of too, 'cos I was like almost six months pregnant. I can't remember all that happened, but I do recall that I didn't want to take the elevator, as I thought I'd be trapped in it, and I couldn't decide what to do. And then this man came up to me from nowhere, like I think he was English, and I guess he helped me down all those flights of stairs. The stairs were real crowded, and smoky too, and when I couldn't stop coughing, he gave me his handkerchief and told me to hold it over my nose and mouth. Jesus, that man, he didn't let go of me until we were outside the building."

Lance went very pale, and Florence felt goosebumps crawling up her arms.

"Yeah, and when I got out onto the street, I followed the crowd uptown, and then we swarmed over the Brooklyn Bridge. Everyone had white powder over their faces. They looked kinda funny. I guess I did, too! But I got talking to a girl who sold flowers at the World Trade Center - or used to - and talking to her made me less scared. That, plus once we got to Brooklyn, people were real nice. Man, they came outta their houses and were offering us water. One person even gave me her shoes, 'cos mine had those ridiculous heels which are not designed for all that walking, and I guess she could tell I was stumbling along."

"Did you – was he – I mean, did that man-?" Lance started spluttering.

"Wait! I can't hear you! Carrie's started fussing. Can you hear her? I think she needs a clean diaper and her bottle. Gimme your number, and I'll call you guys back!"

Florence told her Lance's number, and then, glancing over to where he sat on the sofa, she saw his upper body soundlessly crumple, and he slumped forward over his legs, grabbing on to them so tightly that his knuckles were white. Dropping the phone and inadvertently leaving it dangling off the hook, she ran to him, and placing a hand on him, felt that his body was completely rigid.

"Lance!" she cried, kneeling down beside him. "Lance, what is it?"

"My legs!" he said, his head still down on his knees. "They hurt! So much! They're on fire! Aaah! Shards of glass and vicious splinters of metal are piercing through to my bones. Oh Christ, I can't take this pain! I can't!"

It flashed through Florence's mind that they should never have walked so far alongside the river earlier that day, but this seemed different. Not like an ache from over-exertion.

"Lance, come to bed," she suggested, trying hard not to show the fear that she felt. "It'll help you to lie down comfortably."

He lifted his head, and she saw on his face a wild expression, a terrible grimace that spoke of untold terror and insurmountable pain.

"Can't you smell it? That foul stench of skin being scorched? Of flesh turning into cooked meat? You can smell that, can't you? And I'm bleeding horrendously; my leg's bleeding somewhere further down. I can feel the blood spurting from it."

"No, Lance, no!" she said in horror.

"I tell you it's true! Have a look for yourself! Go on, look!"

Very, very gently, and much afraid, Florence unstrapped his leg brace, which he had not yet removed from when they'd walked by the river, and then pulled up both of his trouser legs. Both legs looked as they had done that morning, apart from some red lines from where the brace was tightly fastened. But there were certainly no new injuries.

"Your legs look fine, Lance," she tried to reassure him. "But do come to bed, as I'm sure it'll help to lie down."

"No! I can't move! I'll never move again!" he cried.

"Oh Lance, it's terrible that you're in such pain."

"I don't think I can last much longer."

"What!"

"It's hopeless. I can't keep on struggling against this level of pain. I don't mind if I die!"

"Lance, don't give up now!" Florence pleaded, holding both his hands tightly in hers. "You're a survivor! You've been through so much, and you've made it! You can't die now. Please, Lance, please!"

"It's sad to die so far from home. To be buried away from loved ones."

And then she thought she understood. "No, Lance," she said soothingly. "You're not far from home. You're in your own house! The house you've loved and felt drawn to for such a long time. You're home now, and I'm here with you."

"God, this pain's unbearable!"

"I'd better call your doctor!" Florence said, feeling complete despair.

"No!" he shouted. "No doctors! I don't want to go to hospital! Lying there for weeks! No; don't call the doctor!"

"Oh Lance, I won't if you don't want me to. But what can we do?"

Without even a common household pain reliever, she was at a loss. Besides, it might be no match for what Lance was experiencing. She wondered where Mei-Feng had kept those herbal remedies that had helped soothe the aches he'd experienced after they had followed Virginia Lacey outside into the damp night, but she had no idea. Then she remembered how once, when she was a child, her father had given her mother some brandy as she'd had an excruciating toothache, and she had felt better after that. Lance had recently said something about buying a bottle of brandy. There was nothing for it; she must take charge of the situation. The brandy was certainly worth a try.

"Lance, lie down here on the sofa, and I'm going to fetch you something to make you feel better," she said authoritatively.

Carefully she helped him lie back and she lifted each of his legs on to the sofa. His legs felt surprisingly heavy, even the emaciated one. He lay in a foetal position, still gripping his knees, his face a ghastly white and beaded with sweat. She placed a blanket gently over him, and tucked it in around him.

"There. Does that feel a bit better?" she asked.

"No, it's still agonizing."

"I'll be back in a moment," she said, kissing him lightly on his forehead, tasting the cold saltiness of his sweat. "You'll be better soon."

She rushed to the hall cupboard, and to what they still called the "secret passageway." Switching on the light, she ran along it, down the stairs, and to the grotto. She had no idea how he organized his bottles, but prayed that she'd find the brandy quickly, which thankfully she did. She rapidly brought it upstairs to the kitchen. It was dusty and cold to the touch. Was she mad? Brandy? Whatever it was that was happening, could brandy really help? And what if Lance was already dead before she returned to him? She prayed ardently that he wouldn't die. He couldn't die. She prayed that he'd be better. *"Courage, strength and hope. Courage, strength and hope."*

The astounding thing was the suddenness of it all; the contrast between life-proceeding-as-normal, with riverside walks, and exciting conversations, and displays of affection, and geese noisily chatting to each other as they took off skywards into the sun; and this – this abrupt halt, this reversal of all that was good, all that was secure. Life was like that. And when you thought about it, there were many more ways in which things could go wrong rather than right. Looked at this way, it was amazing, in fact, that anything ever went right at all.

With fingers nervously fumbling, and despising herself for her slow clumsiness, she opened the bottle and poured out a generous tumbler. Returning to Lance in the living room, she found he hadn't moved. He was still in the fetal position, but his glasses were on the floor, and his jaws were clamped down firmly on the corner of a pillow, his eyes shut tightly.

"Lance," she said softly, rubbing his hair. "Try some of this. I brought you some brandy."

He opened his eyes and let the pillow drop from his mouth. She saw the teeth marks and wet stain on the pillow's fabric. Cradling his head, she helped him to slightly sit up and take a sip of brandy, then another sip, and then another. Then he turned his head away.

"Did that help?" she asked.

"Maybe soon." He tried to shift his legs, and cried out in pain.

"Have some more brandy."

"I think I need to elevate my legs. Have them in traction."

"I'll go and get some more pillows."

"No!" he shouted. "Don't go again!" Then, more softly he added, "It seems you were gone so long when you went to fetch the brandy. Please don't leave me now."

"All right, I won't," she said, trying to make sense of the contradictory signals, and feeling so strongly that she should phone for a doctor, but not wanting to suggest it again for fear of upsetting him yet more. Then she had a thought.

"I know, Lance. I'll sit here on the sofa with you, and you can put your legs up across my lap."

He was willing to give it a try. It was hard for her to sit down and rearrange his legs, as they were still rigid and completely inert, as well as being terribly painful to him. Also, he did not want to stop gripping them, but she told him the yoga techniques of relaxation and deep breathing that she recalled, and eventually she could peel his fingers away from the vice-like grasp he had of his legs, and he flopped back on the sofa. She immediately covered him and herself with the blanket, and gently put her own hands under the blanket on his legs, so as to radiate extra warmth and healing to them.

They stayed together in that position for a long time. She gently rubbed his legs, hoping that the energy from her hands would soothe him. From time to time she gave him more brandy. She told him stories, one after another; some from her childhood, some about articles she'd written before she met him, some just fantasies that she pulled from her mind. She spoke softly and continuously, all the time holding or rubbing his legs, attempting to heal them from whatever frightful occurrence had afflicted them.

And all the time he listened silently, sometimes watching her with hollow expressionless eyes, sometimes with his eyes closed, though even then she knew he was not asleep. She was becoming desperately thirsty and uncomfortable, and also uncontrollably sleepy. Eventually she couldn't help herself. She nodded off.

Towards one o'clock in the morning he mumbled something that aroused her attention, but she did not catch what he said. She sleepily asked him to repeat it.

"It's what I've been asking for and wanting more than anything else. Why didn't I react with jubilation?"

More alert now, she asked, "What are you referring to, Lance?"

"Ever since it happened, Fleur, I've been asking for a sign; for something, anything, that the pregnant woman had escaped safely. And now Jennie! Her story! Why can't I rejoice in that?"

"I've been thinking about that," Florence said slowly, "and I think hearing what she said was like a catalyst, bringing it all back to you. All the horror. All the fear. All the pain. You were understandably in a terrible state. Almost delirious. You even said at one point that it was terrible to die so far from home."

"Did I say that?"

"Yes. I think you were completely reliving the experience. Your body remembered how it had felt, and your mind reacted to it, probably for the first time, as when it occurred last September you were too drugged for your mind to react to what had happened to your body. But what's important is how you feel now. Do you feel better now, Lance?"

"I do feel better, Fleur!" he said. "I think the pain has left almost completely. It's more like shakily being on the edge of a terrible memory, and feeling vulnerable that it might return. But I don't think it will."

"Thank God for that!" she said fervently.

He pulled himself up into a seated position, and swung his legs off her lap. Then he leant towards her and put his arm around her. "Thank *you*, Fleur. You've helped to chase away those demons. I'm sorry if I frightened you, my sweet love."

"In a way, painful and horrific as this was, maybe it was a type of cleansing. You've suppressed the memory of that pain all this time. It was locked inside you, like flowing water under a layer of ice in a frozen lake. Then, when Jennie told us what happened to her, it was like taking a chisel to the ice and the water poured through. The pain's been released now, Lance. It's over. What terrible torture you suffered, but it's over."

"Yes, it's over now." He sighed, shook his head, and shut his eyes. "I had no idea what a burden I'd carried inside me for almost a year. I feel somehow so much freer and lighter now."

"I'm so glad."

"Jennie? Did Jennie phone back?"

"No, not yet. But I'm sure she will. Or else we can phone her again tomorrow, if you think you'd be able to talk to her."

They walked together to the bedroom. He was weak, walking tentatively, as though he was not sure he could do it, and leaned heavily on her. She helped him into bed and then went to the kitchen to prepare two steaming mugs of hot chocolate. She thought it would be nice to add whipped cream to each mug. As she stood there listening to the whirring of the whisk as it slapped the cream around the bowl, she could hear in its repetitive whine, "Die. Die. Die. Die. Die." "No!" she thought, and tried hard to hear some other sound, a different word. But it always went back to the same refrain. "Die. Die. Die." She couldn't wait for the cream to thicken, and as soon as it was barely so, she stopped whisking, and added a generous blob of it to each mug.

When she took the hot chocolate into the bedroom, Lance, who was sitting up in bed, greeted her with his beautiful smile, that made his face radiant and his eyes shine, and then she knew that he wouldn't die; that what she had heard in the electric whir of the whisk was only a mark of how shaken she'd been by what had just happened, rather than some ghastly premonition. She set the mugs down and climbed into bed beside him, and they both drank the warm, sweet, creamy liquid.

"I'm ravenous!" he said when he had finished, and that was understandable since they had missed dinner. So she returned to the kitchen and made the best simple, soothing food she knew; several rounds of hot buttered toast with orange marmalade, which she brought back to bed, and they fed the toasted triangles to each other, licking their fingers from the melted butter and tangy marmalade, and ignoring the crumbs on the sheets.

"Actually," Florence began slowly, "I've just thought of another explanation for what just happened. I think it might have been caused by overlapping axes of Time, which for some reason seems to be what particularly happens in this house."

"Yes, that could be true!" Lance replied, immediately understanding her thread. "The Past affecting the Present, and the Future affecting the Past. T.S. Eliot certainly seemed to have got it right in his poem, though

God knows what he experienced for him to be able to know this. It might even explain, Fleur, why we saw that glowing light in what's now this bedroom's window, the summer you were at Landsdowne's. Even though that was *before* the World Trade Center attack, and indeed even before I went to America, a confluence of so many overlapping axes of Time, in which 'normal' sequence and chronology no longer determined the order of things, could be a really plausible explanation! Of course we didn't understand that the glowing light seemed to be from Virginia Lacey's flashlight until much later, but it was there all the same."

"Yes! And even before the night when we saw that light, you'd been attracted to this house, and felt a connection with it, although you couldn't fathom why that was."

"Precisely! That's why I brought you here that day when you'd come to Landsdowne's on your holidays! And then, when we came, and looked through the windows, we could see how everything was newly modernized and it looked as though people were about to move in. But no one did!"

"That's when we guessed that the place was haunted! And we thought our hunch was confirmed when we returned that night and saw that light glowing through the window. That's why I was surprised that you moved here!"

"Fleur, when I saw that it was on the market again, I was thrilled, and thought it imperative that I take the opportunity immediately of purchasing it, before anyone else did. Now, having lived here for almost nine months, I think it's all becoming clear as to why I felt connected with this house."

"Yes, it is. We've discovered a much more interesting explanation than ghosts. For some reason - and this we don't yet understand – for some reason, actions at different time periods are apparent here. It's as you said so nicely; there's 'a confluence of overlapping Time axes' in this house. Though we haven't seen Virginia Lacey with her flashlight, or Kitty again for that matter, for quite some time."

"Maybe that's because we don't need them anymore. Maybe it's because we've put the pieces of the puzzle together, and it has led to the conclusion that Jennie – Kitty's granddaughter and Virginia Lacey's great granddaughter - was the woman I escorted out of the World Trade Center, and she thankfully reached home safely, and even more than that, she delivered a healthy baby! And Fleur," Lance continued, smiling broadly, "we must go to New York and see Jennie! And we could meet up with Marissa and others from NYU, and maybe even talk to the department chair at the New School. We have so many reasons to go to New York!"

"Yes; let's do it! It sounds like a really exciting idea! We could even walk across the Brooklyn Bridge!"

"You remembered!"

"Yes."

"Jennie sounds so lively and friendly, doesn't she! Not a bit like her mother!"

"She seems to have Hatty's vivaciousness, it's true."

"Yes, and maybe she has Kitty's beauty. I can't be sure because when I met her at the World Trade Center – doesn't that sound funny! – but when I met her the building was already in partial darkness and we were all scared."

He raised himself up on one elbow, his eyes ablaze. "Just think, Fleur! What an amazing coincidence that it was Jennie who I escorted to safety out of the World Trade Center! It's incredible!"

"It's fantastic, Lance. There was no possible way that you could ever have saved Kitty, but you saved her granddaughter, Jennie!"

"It's true!" he said. And laughingly he threw off the duvet. "It's totally amazing! Yes, indeed; I feel better now! Better, in fact, than I've ever felt. I feel as though I could spring out of bed and dance around the room! Come, Fleur; will you dance with me!"

"Certainly!"

And then they were spinning around the room, laughing and singing. Lance seemed to have summoned superhuman strength; the type one gets when one is highly excited and feels one can lift mountains, as he was moving and twirling as if he had never been injured at all. But just as suddenly he sank on to the bed, pulling Florence on top of him.

"That was wonderful!" she said.

"Yes," he said, panting a little. He smiled at her, and pulling her completely towards him, hugged her tightly.

"I can't get over that it was Jennie who I escorted out of the World Trade Center. It's such an amazing coincidence!"

"It's as if two Time axes inexplicably overlapped."

"Exactly! And actually more than two. Look how many time periods we've witnessed. Virginia Lacey taking her flashlight and searching for Kitty, and then you saw Kitty being mauled; and then skipping back to an earlier time when Virginia Lacey forbade Kitty to have further communication with Ilyich Throgmorton, and I spoke with Kitty and she asked me to take that ring to him, calling me her 'guardian angel.' And possibly, as you once said, I had met Gordon Lacey before we knowingly met him together, and that's how I knew his address. And maybe even this evening, if your theory is right that the unbearable pain I felt was because I went back to that Time axis when the World Trade Center was attacked. What intrigues me, Fleur, is why here? Why, in this house, do Times bend and convene? Why do seemingly parallel Time axes merge towards each other? Why have we seen the Past and the Present coexist?"

"I can't explain it, Lance, but I'm so glad you live here, and that we've witnessed so much."

"We're really on to something, Fleur! And I think we will find an explanation, you and I. In fact I'm sure of it!"

The later it grew, the livelier Lance became, so it was, by about 3.45 am, when the early dawn started breaking, and a joyful chorus of birds started to sing outside the window, that Florence, shivering with exhaustion, though with more that she still wanted to say, reluctantly fell asleep.

The next afternoon, as Florence was preparing to drive back to London, Jennie rang. It was only when Florence had woken at about noon and made her way to the kitchen to make coffee, that she discovered that she'd left the phone off the hook the day before, and quickly replaced it, so that when Jennie phoned, she apologized if it had been hard for her to get through.

"Hey, no problem!" Jennie said loudly over the speaker-phone. "Actually, I thought you guys would be mad with me, 'cos, like, I was the one who was guilty here, as I didn't call 'till just now. You see, the folk from upstairs dropped in for a visit right after you'd called yesterday, and Blake suggested we all go grab some burgers, and then we all chilled for a while, so by then it was too late, what with the five-hour time difference and all. And then today it was non-stop with Carrie. But here I am now! I didn't want you guys to think I'd forgotten you!"

"Good to hear from you, Jennie!" Lance said warmly. "It sounds like you're having fun in New York."

"Yeah! It's the 'city that never sleeps,' and neither do I, especially now Carrie's around."

"It's a really exciting city, isn't it!" Florence said. "I loved it when I visited."

"And speaking of visits," Lance said, "We're thinking we might visit New York City again soon, in which case it would be terrific to see you."

"Cool! When do you guys think you'll come?"

"We're not sure yet. We're just tossing ideas around at the moment. But we'll let you know when we've thought this through a little more."

"Sure!"

"Jennie, I hate to bring up what was undoubtedly a very traumatic episode for you, but I wanted to ask you about that English man who you said helped you to get out of the World Trade Center," Lance said.

"Did I say he was English? Yeah. He might have been English. Or maybe he was Australian. Possibly New Zealand. I can't be sure."

Lance and Florence exchanged quizzical glances.

"Well, what did he look like?" Lance asked. "Can you describe him for us?"

"You see," Florence put in helpfully, "we just wonder if it was someone we know."

"Gee!" Jennie said. "That would be totally awesome." She paused a moment, and both Lance and Florence held their breath. "Yeah, I remember now. He was real tall. Real tall and protective!"

Lance sat straighter in his seat, smiling with excitement.

"And," Jennie continued, "he had long blond hair in a ponytail, and a moustache and beard. Yeah, like a reddish color moustache and beard."

Lance's smile faded.

"Do you remember anything else?" Florence pursued.

"Well yeah, now you got me thinking about him, I remember he was kinda like a hippie. You know what I mean? Flowered shirt. Beads round his neck. And sandals."

Lance scooped up his crutches, hoisted himself up from the sofa, and with his head bent down, he slowly left the room.

"He was real nice," Jennie continued to chirp. "Oh yeah, and now I remember one more thing. It's funny how it all starts to come back to you. Yeah, he cursed quite a bit, and said something like – excuse my French – 'What a fucking thing to happen to a tourist on his holiday!'"

"Yes, that couldn't have been a good time for a holiday," Florence said bleakly, following Lance's slowly retreating figure with her eyes.

"Does that sound like the person you know?" Jennie asked.

"Well, no; I don't think it does after all," Florence replied.

# TWENTY-TWO

*ONE SUNNY LATE SUMMER AFTERNOON,* Florence, now a 'free' woman, sat composing a thank you letter to Simon. He had really handled the divorce with brilliant dexterity, had anticipated Howard at every move, and had quashed any attempts he still tried to make to ambush the progress.

As Florence was sealing the envelope, the phone rang.

"Hello?" she said.

"Fleur! It's Lance."

"Lance! Hello! How are you?"

"Look out of your front window, Fleur."

"What? Why?"

"Go on and look out of your front window, Fleur. Go on."

Thinking perhaps he might be commenting on a weather report he'd heard which would be affecting London, she went to the window. And there down below, on the other side of the street, was Lance! Lance, leaning against his parked car, speaking into his mobile phone! She pushed the window up, stuck her head out, and shrieked down, "Lance!" She nearly dropped the phone. He beamed up at her, and waved with his free hand.

"I can't believe you're really here!" she cried. "Wait! I'll be down in a second!"

She flew down the stairs. She hated having to retreat inside her building. Not seeing him, breaking the eye contact, made her wonder if he was really here. And did he come alone? Or had Mei-Feng driven him? Would he be able to manage all the stairs up to her flat? Why had he come now? Could he really be here?

She emerged into the sunshine, out of breath. And there, indeed, was Lance, a rucksack on his back, and still leaning against his car, smiling his beautiful smile. What's more, his car was empty, and no Mei-Feng in sight. She ran to him, and they hugged tightly.

"Lance! Oh Lance! I can't believe this! Oh, I'm so glad to see you. You have come to stay, haven't you? You will stay, won't you?"

"Yes, yes, Fleur. Yes, my love; I've come to stay, if you'll have me on this surprise visit."

"I couldn't ask for a better surprise! I can't get over the fact that you're here! Let's come inside!"

They walked together across the street, and up the steps to her front door. There were three flights of stairs to climb to her flat. Lance held onto the banister with one hand, and had his other arm wrapped around Florence, who held his crutches in her free hand. They made slow progress. A door banged open and just as quickly shut, as they were nearing the top of the first flight, and Liv Ericsson, a Swedish woman of almost spectacular beauty, came running down the stairs rattling a set of keys in her hand, and almost collided with them. She made her excuses, and went past, greeting Florence as she did so. Lance hardly glanced at her, whereas most people could not help but stare at her near perfection.

"How are you doing?" Florence asked, as they started to climb the last steep flight of stairs.

"It's a bit like climbing a mountain, but it'll get easier every time I do it."

"I wish I didn't live on the very top floor."

"Nonsense! It's the best place to be. I'm glad you're at the top!"

They finally made it to Florence's flat.

"It's charming here, Fleur," he said, his eyes sweeping the living room. "I've never seen where you've lived before in all this time. But it reflects you beautifully."

"Thanks. I'll show you the rest later. For now, why don't you sit down and I'll get you a glass of cranberry juice."

"Thank you," he said, gratefully sinking down on the sofa and mopping his forehead of sweat.

"How are you feeling?" she called from the kitchen.

"Marvelous! It's marvelous to be here!"

She handed him the drink and snuggled up next to him. "I'm so pleased you're here. I still can't believe it! What an incredible surprise! So, what decided you on coming here now?"

He unwound his arm from her, and his face took on a serious expression. "Well, as you know, we're coming up to the first anniversary of September 11th, and a few days after that it will be a year since your wedding. I think neither of us should be alone at this time."

"I'm so pleased you said that. I'd been secretly dreading this week."

"No secret dreads, Fleur. Remember how we once promised to tell each other everything. Well, there again, of course I'm guilty, too," he laughed, "as I hadn't told you I'd be visiting you. It was, actually, a completely spontaneous decision, but I didn't mention it both because I did want to surprise you, and also I suspect because I was not entirely sure I could do it."

"But you did do it! Was it very strenuous?"

"Much less than I'd anticipated."

"That's terrific. Look, you rest for a bit, as it was such a long drive, and I'll start preparing the dinner."

After they'd eaten, Florence started to worry about how Lance would be able to cope with having a shower in her bathroom, since his bathroom had rails.

"Lance, I've just had a great idea!" she said playfully.

"What's that?" he asked, smiling.

"Well, I've always wanted us to take a shower together. That idea has always appealed to me. Would you like-?"

"Fleur, I've always wanted to do that, too."

They peeled off each other's clothes, and walked together to the bathroom. She helped him into the shower. The water ran soothingly warm, and they lovingly caressed each other's bodies with soap. She squatted down to wash his feet, and as she was soaping up the foot of his left leg, he started to laugh.

"Ooh, that tickles!" he exclaimed.

She squinted up at him through the jets of cascading water, and she saw him towering over her, all frothy with lather and merriment. Laughingly she continued to wash his foot, although it was already very clean.

"Fleur, do you realize what this means?" Lance suddenly said loudly, over the sound of the running water. "The feeling's coming back! After a year, I have feeling in my foot again!"

She popped up to a standing position, and with the sparkling water continuing to splash down on them, they hugged ardently.

"Oh Lance, that's incredible! It's completely wonderful!"

"Yes! I was told this couldn't happen; that the nerve damage was too extensive. But it has happened! Touch my foot again, Fleur! Let's make sure I didn't imagine it."

Sure enough, he could feel Florence's touch again.

"Lance, this is marvelous! Soon you'll be walking without the leg brace and crutches!"

"I wouldn't go that far," Lance replied. "Not yet, anyway. It's quite literally one step at a time."

They climbed out of the shower, patted each other dry, and went to bed. And it seemed to Florence that she had never loved Lance as much as she did now.

The first anniversary of September 11th was a somber one, with Florence and Lance watching on television how New York City had designed two parallel beams of light illuminating the empty air where once the Twin Towers stood. There was also repeated footage of the towers burning against a clear, blue sky, and chaotic street scenes of people running, with a dense white cloud of smoke catching up to them. Florence could hardly watch, but Lance, leaning forward and gripping on to one of his crutches, was immersed.

Having got through that dreadful day, the following day Florence wanted to introduce Lance to Anna, so they called her, and were invited over there for lunch.

"I'm so glad to finally meet you," Lance said to Anna, once they were seated in her living room. "I've been wanting to thank you for a long time."

"Thank me? Whatever for?"

"Well, of course for all the love and help you showed Fleur, especially when Howard was so abusive, and I was in America. But, for my part, I also want to thank you for three words. Three words that you told Fleur, and she told them to me. 'Courage, strength, and hope.'"

"Oh."

"Yes, those three words gave me focus, and took away the negativity that was crowding into my mind. So thank you, Anna."

Anna's face was full of compassion. "I'm delighted it helped," she said softly.

"It still is helping, Anna," Lance said. "Every time I think how smashed my leg was, and how though much better it is still deformed, those words comfort me."

"Lance, on Rosh Hashanah and Yom Kippur we sound the *shofar*. And the first sound the *shofar* makes is *tekiya*, which means 'whole'. After that the *shofa* makes a triple sound, inferring a breakage into three parts, and then it makes a series of quick short blasts signifying a total smash. But it always ends with the *tekiya* call again, meaning wholeness has returned. The same will be true for you, Lance, I am sure."

"That's lovely, Anna. Thank you. I will remember that."

"And I think those three words – courage, strength and hope – of which you are so fond, might also have led you to tap into the bravery and amazing self-determination that was already innate within you. In other words, you have always been courageous, strong and full of hope, but until faced with a challenge of such horrendous proportions, you were not yet aware of this. Hell glared at you that day, but you've maintained your composure and your dignity."

Lance smiled sadly. "If that's indeed the case, it's only because of Fleur. She has always provided me with inspiration and a reason to keep going."

"'Fleur;' what a pretty name! How sweet it sounds! Yes, indeed; she is a wonderful person. But look, let's not embarrass her. Poor Florence; I see you're turning quite pink! I'm going to fetch Sam!" Anna said. "I think he's had enough sleep for now. If I let him sleep too long, then he won't sleep much tonight."

Anna hurried up the spiral stairs at the end of the room, and was back quickly with a warm, pink baby Sam. Lance was very playful with him, making him squeal happily and kick his legs in excitement. And while he was playing, Lance also answered Anna's questions about his research, his teaching, and what it was like living in the Lake District, as well as asking her questions of his own about motherhood, and what it was like at Rabbinical School, and some questions about the values and philosophy of the Jewish faith.

After a while, Anna had to go into the kitchen to do the finishing touches to the soup, and asked Florence to come and help her.

"Lance, would you keep an eye on Sam while Florence and I are getting the food ready? It will just be a few minutes," she said.

"Of course! I'd be only too glad to extend my playtime with my pal, Sam."

As soon as they were in the kitchen, and Anna was busying herself with the pot of creamy corn soup, she whispered, "Florence, what an incredible man! Sam has really taken to him, and babies are intuitively good judges of character. But really, he seems so kind and gentle, and also he's clearly amazingly intelligent and fascinating, yet he seems so humble and unassuming."

"I'm so glad you like him, Anna!"

"And it's very evident that he adores you. And I've never seen you look so radiantly happy! You two look really good together."

With Anna's enthusiastic words echoing through Florence's mind, after lunch they dropped in to see Hatty. The familiar smell of Dettol greeted them as they neared her front door. She was overjoyed by Florence's surprise visit, and bustled them into the living room, giving Sally, her assistant, orders for tea. Very soon the silver tray holding the little china teacups was brought in, rattling merrily, along with the inevitable plate of sugared ginger pieces.

"So," said Hatty, turning to Lance, "you're the one now living in the Lacey's old house. Fancy that! How do you like it?"

"I like it very much indeed. I'd noticed it a long time before I moved in. I'd wanted to live there for many years."

"Did you? Well, how nice that you are living there now! That house is coming back to me, now I come to think of it. Kitty's room was upstairs under the roof, with the sloping ceiling and the little dormer window. Oh yes, we spent a lot of time up there; that is, when we weren't outside!"

"Oh, she had that room, did she? That's the guest room now," Florence said, thinking of her first night staying up there for a few hours before coldness and fear made her retreat downstairs to find Lance.

"Yes, and Gordon had the larger room next to it, facing the side. And of course Mr. and Mrs. Lacey had the master bedroom. Such a lovely, spacious room, I remember. We peeped in there once or twice! I suppose that's your bedroom now."

"Actually, no. Our bedroom's downstairs in what I believe used to be the dining room."

"Oh, so you have that beautiful room, do you? I remember its wooden beams on the ceiling and its casement window. Well yes, I expect it would've been awkward for you to take the master bedroom. So many stairs up to it! Florence never told me you're a partial paraplegic. And Connie never said a word about you being crippled, either, but there again, she never pays much attention to anything. But poor you; it's a terrible thing to be a polio victim. Dreadful disease. You're lucky to have apparently had a mild case. Plenty's the one I knew who had to take the iron lung."

Florence was shocked and embarrassed, remembering Lance having once told her that now his identity would be defined by his disability, rather than by his personality. But Lance said with apparent though possibly enforced calm, "I never had polio, Harriet. I was in New York a year ago, and had the misfortune to be at the World Trade Center when it was attacked. My leg was crushed by falling debris."

"Lord, have mercy!" she exclaimed. She cupped her tiny face in her gnarled, liver spotted hands, slowly shook her head from side to side while tutting several times, and gazed at him steadily with navy blue eyes which matched the color of the veins on her hands. "You poor dear," she said at last. "What a barbaric day! I've lived a long time, through many wars, and never saw anything like that. Why, only yesterday was the first anniversary, and they reran all that awful footage on the television. Did you see that?"

"Yes."

"I did, too. The world won't be the same after that incident, you mark my words! It was a terrible time for so many of us. I don't know if you heard, but my granddaughter, Jennie, was there, too. Jennifer is Connie's daughter. Well, a year ago I had the television on, but wasn't really watching it, *you know*, and then suddenly they broadcast *that* news, and it got my attention at once. I knew Jennie worked in that building! I was so proud of her for having such a good job, in the tallest skyscraper in New York, mind you! So I immediately phoned her, but couldn't get through. Neither could Connie, who was also trying to phone her. But then what a relief when we finally did speak! Oh yes, I remember that conversation as if it happened this morning. It's one I'll never forget.

"'Jennie,' I say. 'How are you, darling?'

"'I'm alright, Nana,' she says. She calls me Nana. The only one of my grandchildren to call me that, and I must say I love that name.

"'But Jennie,' I say. 'Weren't you at work today? I heard the building you were in was hit by a plane and collapsed!'

"'Did you hear about that, Nana?' she says, calm as anything. But then I hear a slight catch in her voice. 'Oh Nana,' she says, starting to sob. 'Nana, it was so frightening. I didn't know whether you and Mum heard about it. I don't even know what happened. There was a sort of thump, and the lights went out, and people were pouring out of their offices, and no one knew what was happening. And there were messages over the loudspeaker, but I didn't know what to do, Nana,' she sobs. 'I didn't.'

"'That's alright, child,' I tell her. 'Calm yourself. You're home now. Everything's going to be alright.' It's what I used to tell her mother when she was a child, if she was ever distressed about something. 'Listen,' I say, 'maybe Mum is trying to phone you now. We'll speak later when you're feeling better.'

"'No, Nana,' she pleads. That child always was very close to me. It's a sort of special relationship we have. She even puts me in mind of Kitty, at times. 'No, don't go now' she says. 'Let's talk longer. I want to tell you more about it. I had to walk nearly all the way home, Nana,' she says, sounding suddenly quite proud of herself. 'I walked all the way into Brooklyn, across the Brooklyn Bridge, you know. There were tons of people walking, too. We were sort of all escaping together. And I kept walking even when I was in Brooklyn, but at last I caught a bus on Flatbush Avenue.'

"Well, seeing as you lived in New York, Lance, you must know where these places are. For me, I've been to New York a few times on book tours, and of course I'm familiar with the Brooklyn Bridge, but I don't know places in Brooklyn. Do you?"

"I don't know Brooklyn very well either," Lance replied, concealing his agitation well, or so Florence thought, that he desired Hatty to speak about Jennie's actual escape from the World Trade Center as soon as possible. "But it certainly sounds as though Jennie walked a very long way that day. She must have been tired."

"Yes, that's what I said to her. 'Jennie,' I say, 'are you very tired, my doll, from all that walking?'

"'Not so much from the walking, Nana,' she says, 'but because first I walked down more than forty flights of stairs to get out of the building.'"

Florence clasped Lance's hand, and for a moment was terrified that he would lapse again into that dreadful state he'd been in after they first spoke with Jennie. His expression was hard to read, but he was rigidly staring at Harriet, scarcely acknowledging her hand encasing his.

"'No!' I say," Harriet continued, unaware of the terrible tension her tale was creating. "'That many? Wasn't there a lift you could use, child?'

"'Nana', she answers. 'The lift was so jammed with people. And I was frightened that it might get stuck between floors. And the air in the building started smelling smoky. I didn't know what to do. I didn't know which way to turn. And then it was like my guardian angel came.'"

'Guardian angel!' That expression again. Could it be that Lance was conceived of as guardian angel to both Kitty and also to her granddaughter, Jennie, only in the latter case, could it really have been true after all?

"'What do you mean, child?' I ask, by now sitting on the edge of my seat," Hatty continued.

"'Well, Nana; this kind man came along, and he put his arm around me, and told me not to be scared. He said he would help me. He promised me we'd be out of the building very soon.'

"'Who was this man?' I ask.

"'No one I knew before. He said he was a doctor. Actually he sounded English.'

"Isn't that something!" Hatty said, looking at Florence and Lance, rather than gazing into the corner of the room as she had been while telling her story. "We English people certainly know how to stick together. We can find and help each other in any place, however remote from our own shores."

She picked up the sugar tongs, and spent considerable time trying to pluck a cube of sugar from the bowl to put in her tea. Meanwhile Florence looked at Lance expectantly, but to her surprise he merely shrugged. Maybe he was still smarting from Hatty's statement that she was surprised not to have been told that he was, in her words, a "partial paraplegic". Or maybe he could not get excited again about Jennie's escape from the World Trade Center, in the fear of once more having his hopes and assumptions dashed.

Hatty stirred her tea a long time, took a sip, and breathed out a satisfied sigh. Then, smoothing her skirt over her knees, she resumed her story.

"This doctor," she said, "helped her down all those flights of stairs, despite people pushing and more people joining on every floor. 'Jennie,' I say. 'He sounds like a marvelous man to have been so kind to you. If he's a doctor,' I say, 'why don't you switch to him as the doctor monitoring your pregnancy and helping deliver your baby?'

"'Nana, I'm not sure he's that kind of doctor. In America, they're all specialized in different areas. He might be a children's doctor, or a heart doctor, or a brain surgeon; I don't know!' she says.

"'But if he's English, it doesn't matter,' I tell her. 'He'll be good in all areas. And besides, he's already saved your life once! And your little baby's life, too. What is the doctor's name?' I ask.

Here Lance sat up and looked particularly attentive.

"'I can't quite remember, Nana,'" Hatty quoted Jennie as saying, and Lance's expression immediately became deflated. But Harriet had more to say: "'He wrote out his name for me on a piece of paper,' Jennie told me. 'I still have the paper,' she said, 'so I know he was real, and I didn't just imagine him. But Nana,' she says, sounding silly, 'when I came home, I stripped off all my clothes and put them in the washing machine, to wash out that white powder that was on everything. And while my clothes were washing I showered, and then had a long soak in the bath as my legs were aching so much. And when I was clean and dry, I went to transfer my clothes from the washer to the dryer, and that's when I realized that I'd left the doctor's note in the pocket of the skirt I'd been wearing. So I pulled it out of the wet skirt, but most of the ink was smudged, so I couldn't read it. I just saw Dr. 'La' and a street starting with 'Co'. I don't know; maybe it's Columbus Avenue, though I thought he said his office was in Greenwich Village, and Columbus Avenue does not go down there. I think he said he's called Dr. Lambskin. That's right! I remember now, Nana! Dr. Lambskin's his name!'

"'Well, Jennie,' I say, as I've always taken a very moral stand, and trained my family to do the same, 'even if you don't switch to him as your doctor, which I think you should, I want you to find this Dr. Lambskin in Greenwich Village, and write him a note of thanks. I'm going to send you $150, and as soon as you get it, put it with the note and send it to him.'"

Despite himself, despite earlier resistance, Lance was pulled into Hatty's story.

"Did she do it?" he asked. "Did she find this Dr. Lambskin?"

"Why no! Of course she didn't. Now, I don't want to give the impression that she kept the money for herself, but I suspect that might have been what happened. She's just a child, you see. Not exactly flighty, but impetuous. She'd had a very frightening day, but it was over, and she got busy with other things. Besides, her baby was soon on the way. But more than that, I think it's that sense of invincibility that so many youths have today."

Lance clasped his hands together, hung his head, and stared at a patch of sunlight on the floor close to his chair.

"Did she tell you whether she had tried to look for him?" Florence asked so softly that she had to repeat the question since Hatty could not hear it the first time.

"To tell you the truth, dear," Hatty replied, "I suspect she reverted to thinking this kind man was her guardian angel. The paper was smudged, and her memory impaired by great fright. There was little a child like her could do. But I'll tell you this, Florence, dear," she said, leaning forward and patting Florence on the knee, "every night in my prayers, I include a little prayer of thanks to kind Dr. Lambskin, Jennie's 'guardian angel'."

--------

The next morning Lance suggested to Florence that they have dinner at Crispin's bistro. "It might be hard at this stage to make a reservation, but let's try anyway. Would you like that?"

"Yes, that sounds lovely. Would Simon be there, too?"

"He's pretty likely to be there on a Friday. But I'll phone and ask him, if you'd like to see him."

So Lance made some phone calls, and booked a table for 7.45, with Simon planning to join them for dessert. As the weather remained unusually warm and sunny – a veritable Indian summer – Florence and Lance decided to go for a walk along the River Thames in the late afternoon.

"I think I'll take my camera," she said. "I have some unused film in it."

"Are you sure you want to bring it along? It's rather heavy. And besides that, who knows what pictures will actually come out!"

"True. But I want to see if I can get some photos of you here in London."

So, slinging the camera over her shoulder, they set out. They took the tube to the Embankment, and from there started strolling along the river, arms encircling each other, with the crutch in Lance's other arm poking out the paces he would traverse.

"Pretty different from the river at the bottom of your garden, isn't it!" Florence joked.

By this time they were crossing Waterloo Bridge, and Lance was eagerly remarking about how you could see St. Paul's Cathedral in one direction, and Big Ben and the Houses of Parliament in the other. She took his photo as he was saying that this surely must be the best view of London.

They crossed to the South Bank, and just outside the National Film Theatre they sat down on a bench facing the river.

"Lance," Florence said quickly, taking hold of his hand. "Lance, I'd like us to marry. I really would. I love you, Lance, and I want you to be my husband." She darted him a sideways glance, her eyes wide open, terrified about asking the question and dreading what his answer may be.

Lance gave a little laugh of surprise.

"What brought this up, Fleur? Is our visit to Anna yesterday affecting you?"

"It might be. But it's also because we promised to tell each other everything on our minds. Not to hold back. And this is something I've been holding back on discussing for a long time."

He dropped his hand out of hers, and gazed at the grey waters of the Thames churning sluggishly past.

"Why?" she asked at last. "Don't you want us to marry?" She felt suddenly very afraid.

"I don't know. As you know from what I've told you, my family's not much good at marriage."

"But that was them – your mother and father, and sister. This is us. It's not the same."

"I recognize it's not the same, Fleur. Don't ever doubt my love for you. In fact, I call you Fleur advisedly, because you are the flower that grows closest to my heart. And I knew that early on in our relationship. My doubts about marriage are not at all meant to imply that I want to avoid commitment. I love you sincerely and deeply and completely."

"Then what is it? Why can't you get past what happened to your family?"

Lance did not answer. Then she said, "Oh, I know! Your impeccable manners and kindness towards me are preventing you from saying this, but your hesitation is because of my own failure in marriage."

"No, Fleur! That's absolutely nothing to do with it!"

"Because if that is the case," she hurried on, "please know that that was a reflection of my relationship with Howard, and not an inability on my part to take marriage seriously!"

"It's alright, Fleur. I'm aware of that," Lance said.

"Because," Florence continued, still ignoring him, "I never wanted to marry Howard! I was a fool. We only married as I was doing what my parents wanted me to do. I never loved him! But I still was the obedient daughter."

"Fleur, stop doing this to yourself. You don't need to tell me this. You're only upsetting yourself, and I know this already."

"But Lance, there's one thing you don't know. And it's horrible. Quite horrible. You once told me your family secret, and I wasn't brave enough then to tell you mine! And when I tell you, you might want no more to do with me."

She was crying now. Lance was very concerned.

"My sweet; nothing you could tell me would ever alter my feelings for you. But you don't need to tell me anything if you don't want to."

"I must tell you. I should have told you before. But I'm not the pure woman that you think I am. I've had an abortion, Lance. Yes. An abortion."

Lance took her hand and stroked it, but his face was troubled. "Do you want to talk about it?" he asked.

"About five years ago I met someone called Renard through a friend from university. Well, we went out a handful of times, and then one evening he brought me to his home, and then he raped me. I was stunned. And I refused to ever see him again. But I found out that I was pregnant."

"God, how awful that he raped you! So, not just Howard, then – at least in his attempts."

"No, exactly."

"Hmmm. Well then, that certainly explains why you would've wanted an abortion," Lance said.

"The thing was, I never wanted my parents to know, as they would've been devastated. They are completely against sex before marriage! And they're horrified by abortion, and they would've never understood the circumstances. And I thought they never need know, until I met Howard, and I couldn't believe it, but he knew about Renard through some relatives of his ex-wife, and one of the first things he asked me when we'd just met was how was my baby. I stupidly blurted out to him that I'd had an abortion. It was the most ridiculous thing I could have ever done, seeing as his parents are such close friends of my parents. So Lance - and here is the even stupidest thing of all - I thought if I kept trying to please Howard, and doing everything he wanted, including marrying him, then he'd never tell his parents or mine about the abortion. So that's why I married him!" Her expression as she looked at Lance was of complete vulnerability and hopelessness.

"Oh, you poor sweet love," he said, putting his arm around her. "You went through a terrible time, and by doing what you did, you automatically invited Howard to have power over you, which, given his malevolent personality, is exactly the sort of thing he'd want. But Fleur, you didn't have to keep this a secret from me, as if you've been ashamed of your behavior. From what you tell me, you've nothing to be ashamed about, as instead you were a victim of a multitude of sins belonging not to you, but to Renard and Howard."

"So you're not disgusted with me?" she whispered, chewing a corner of her fingernail.

"Disgusted? Oh my love, of course not! Why would I be? It's terribly frightening that you were raped, and even more awful that you seemed to have nearly had a replay of it with Howard a few months ago."

"Yes, it was! But why did this happen twice to me? Am I so revolting a slut, or seductress as all that?"

"No!" Lance said emphatically. "No. Be kinder to yourself, Fleur. Stop giving yourself such degrading labels as being an impure woman, or a seductress, or a slut. If you really want to know the reason for your vulnerability, I think it's because of what I've told you before. You're naïve and trusting and innocent, and you don't pick up on the warnings that most people notice, as you want to always think the best of everyone. So, mixing with bad company is a dangerous place for you. But tell me, when you found you were pregnant five years ago, did you have to face that awful choice about whether or not to have an abortion all alone? And were you all alone for the procedure?"

"No, Anna was marvelous. She talked to me about every angle of the situation, and that really helped me. And she was the one to pick me up after it was over, and let me stay with her."

"She's a wonderful friend! I really like her."

"Yes, she is. Oh thank you, Lance, for understanding and not blaming me."

"I wish you would've told me this before, rather than being scared to tell me about it. Not for my sake, but for yours. So that explains why you married Howard!"

"Well, yes; but there was one more reason, as well," she continued almost inaudibly, winding some of her hair around and around her finger and tugging it roughly.

"What was that you said? One more reason? What was it, Fleur?"

"I thought you weren't interested in me."

"What!" Lance said so loudly, that some pigeons pecking at crumbs nearby took to the sky with a noisy flutter and beating of wings. "What are you talking about, Fleur? I never heard this before!"

"Lance, I had never wanted to tell you that I doubted your commitment as it reflects so poorly *on me*. My paranoia at that time points to all my demonic neuroses. Yes, I know…More degrading labels. But they're true."

"When was this, Fleur? I can only apologize if I ever gave you reason to believe-"

"It was after I stayed with you in New York spring of last year. I'd had such an incredible time with you. And then, the day I was leaving, you received that invitation to stay on another three years at NYU. You said you needed time to think about it, and would e-mail me your decision by the next day. That I'd be the first to hear. But that e-mail never arrived, and-"

"Christ!" Lance exclaimed. "Christ!" he said again, stamping his good leg heavily on the ground.

"It was my fault, Lance!" Florence said. "I didn't know you so well then. Well, I did, but I didn't. When two days passed and still I hadn't heard, and then I had to go to Paris with Howard, I started to think that maybe the time we'd spent together was only precious to me and had no value or significance to you. I couldn't believe that to be true, but not hearing from you made me doubt everything…And I didn't want to write to you, as I thought it would not be right to influence your decision about whether or not to stay on at NYU."

"Oh Fleur."

"Yes, and then I thought about how when you'd talked to me about whether to accept the NYU invitation or not, you mentioned that perhaps you should return to England because of your mother, but you said nothing about me-"

"That's only because-"

"I understand that now. And also I didn't know about the situation with your mother then, and your noble responsibilities towards her. But also Lance, and I'm ashamed to admit this, but Lance, I also wondered whether you were attracted to Marissa-"

By now Florence felt that she had unstopped all caution, and that rather than bringing Lance closer to her, which is what she wanted so much, she must undoubtedly be pushing him far away. Again she tugged at her hair, and a few strands came out in her hand.

"Marissa? She's a lesbian!"

"I know! But I didn't know that then. And I could see how close you were-"

"Even if she wasn't a lesbian, it's you I thought about constantly when I was in America. You who I wished were with me all the time, sharing in all my new experiences. And then you actually came, and it felt too good to be true, which unfortunately was exactly how it worked out to be. Fleur, listen," he said, leaning forward and looking at her, and gently removing her hand from her hair. "We were both of us victims of circumstance. I *did* give you reason to doubt my feelings for you – I realize that now - as I didn't tell you how I felt about you. I felt constrained to do so because of Howard. But when you came to stay, I couldn't keep up the restraint. I felt we were so mutually happy together. And then I knew the moment you left and went through the gate at Newark Airport that I was going to decline NYU's invitation. I *had* to be with you. I couldn't face another long departure from you. So I wrote the e-mail to you telling you this as soon as I returned home, intending for it to be waiting for you when you arrived back in England. God! Who would have thought that one e-mail, gone astray in cyberspace, could wreak such havoc on three people's lives!"

"Yes! I had been obsessively checking my e-mail ever since my return from being with you. And then, once Howard and I were in Paris, I was convinced that I'd never hear from you again. I even dreamed that you had decided to stay on in New York. One day Howard and I were walking in the Bois de Bologne, and he asked me to marry him, and a voice from outside myself said 'yes,' completely surprising me, and making me almost faint. I wanted to undo it straight away, but couldn't. So then I convinced myself that I could get used to him. That I'd pretend. That I'd basically make do. I told myself that most marriages were probably like that. Making do. But when we returned to London, and I saw your e-mail asking how I felt about your decision, and your concern about not hearing from me, and-"

She couldn't go on.

"Oh Fleur." He hung his head in his hands and sniffed. Then gradually he looked up, and out over the river. "The night I received that e-mail from you, the one saying you'd decided to marry Howard, I was on my way out to a concert at the Frick. It was appropriately sinister, turbulent music. Or maybe that was just my interpretation of it. And after it was over, I crossed into Central Park, and started heading uptown. I had no real destination. It was dark, yet I kept walking. And I knew that eventually I was so far North that the areas that bordered the Park were no longer particularly safe. But I didn't care. I would've welcomed being mugged. When I was little, if I fell and hurt my knee, Juliet would always say, 'Why don't you hurt the other knee? Then the first won't hurt so much!' So that's what I wanted. I wanted to hurt the other knee."

"Lance, I'm so sorry I hurt you. What a fool I was!"

"And I'm sorry that I stopped corresponding with you. It's funny that we're apologizing to each other now about these things that happened so long ago. But the important thing for us to remember is how incredible it was that we both contacted each other again *at the same time*, after several months had elapsed. That was amazing!"

"Yes," said Florence, brightening. "We couldn't stop being connected."

"Sometimes I wonder what would've happened if we hadn't reconnected. I think perhaps I wouldn't have survived the attack on the World Trade Center."

"No, Lance! Don't talk like that!"

"But I honestly don't think I would, Fleur," Lance said, his brow pinched. He sighed deeply and then went on to say, "One of the things I will always remember is vaguely awakening one day in that hospital bed after the attack – I don't know how long I'd already been there - and seeing your lovely, fresh face looking down at me with an expression of such concern. And I was so pleased that you were there, and I wanted to tell you that and also tell you not to be so concerned; that I was fine. But I couldn't speak. I kept being sucked down into an oblivious state, and felt too heavy to surface. Fleur, it had felt imperative to me that I struggle to the surface, to talk to you, and tell you not to be concerned. And one time I did manage to resurface and feel reasonably clear headed, but the room was empty and you were not there. I thought, in a moment of panic, that you had left me; that you couldn't stand to look at the man I'd now become."

"No, never, Lance!"

"I didn't know, Fleur. All I knew was the relief when next I saw you. Then there were other times when I saw you in my room looking at me again in the same worried way, and I wanted to speak, but there was that heaviness again pulling me down. And I struggled and struggled. I struggled to emerge because of you, Fleur."

Florence leaned sideways on the bench, encircling him with her arms, her head in his neck, and when she looked up at his face, tears were welling up in her eyes.

"And finally I made it, and was able to stay sufficiently alert, and talk to you. And others, too. But I wanted you alone. That's why I asked you to come back that last night you were there. I was so scared you might not want to come. But you did, and that was glorious. Do you remember that nurse who was so surprised to see you there so late at night?" he chuckled.

"Oh yes, she was very kind, actually. And I agree that we did have a glorious time together. I was so pleased you'd phoned to ask me to come then," Florence replied, smiling at the memory.

"Me too. But then the next day you left and returned to London, and I, as you now know, had forgotten all about Howard. But as the days and weeks went by I couldn't tell you about my true feelings for you, because I was so obsessed with what a repulsive mess I was in physically. I was so used to, as I'm sure you are too, recovering completely and getting back to normal after being unwell or hurt. In fact, I always took that for granted and never called it into question. But on this occasion I saw that this was as good as it would get, and that I'd have to completely redefine what would now constitute normalcy for me. So, in recognition of my altered state, I thought it would be understandable if you would want no more to do with me."

"No, Lance; never! I could never stop loving you!" Florence said, practically shouting. And then more softly she added, "Look; we've been through so much, and are so happy together now, and that's why I'd like to marry you, Lance. I want a real marriage this time; one that's brimming with love."

"But Fleur, we must be realistic that things have changed. We missed our opportunity of marrying when you had come for your spring visit to New York. Now, that would have been the time for us to have got engaged!"

"I don't think we've necessarily missed any opportunity."

"But Fleur, look at you! You're young and vivacious, and full of so much energy!"

"So what? I'm hardly much younger than you! Only a few years."

"Yes, but you're sweet natured and attractive, and highly intelligent. Plenty of men would want you in a second!"

"But I don't want any other man. I only want you!"

"But Fleur, I'm damaged goods."

"Why are you talking like this? Look at the progress you're making! You just drove all the way down to see me! And look at the walks we're able to now have! We never imagined this was possible. Only a relatively few months ago you couldn't get out of the wheelchair! And now look what you can do! Look how far you can walk! And besides, the feeling's returning to the part of your leg that's been numb for so long, so who knows what you might be able to do next! Every day you make more progress."

"I don't know, Fleur, but each tiny, incremental mark of progress ironically, after the initial elation, depresses me as it shows how far I still have to go. And age is not on my side. Oh, I know I'm not old now. But as I get older, my joints will stiffen further, and-"

"When you get *much* older, perhaps. But that's a long way off. Now you're in the prime of life. When we all get much older, we will all be dead!" she retorted, sitting up very erect. "Let's make the most of what we have now. I absolutely and completely love you and want so much to be married to you, and your injured leg doesn't make me feel that we've lost the opportunity of marrying. Isn't that even more of an indication of secure acceptance than if we'd married that spring, and then possibly you and others might have wondered whether I only stayed with you after the attacks on the World Trade Center through obligation – which, of course, would never have been true, but you might have thought it anyway?"

"Perhaps, Fleur. I'm not sure."

"Besides, many would say I'm 'damaged goods' too! A divorce at the age of twenty eight!"

"Let them say what they want! The important thing is that I don't ever want to be a burden to you."

"Lance!" Florence exclaimed, feeling suddenly and inexplicably hurt and angry. "Have I ever, *ever*, in my behavior towards you, indicated that I thought you were a burden? Have I? Answer me that!"

"Fleur, I'm sorry. I meant only to express my concern for you and for all that you take on. I didn't mean to offend you."

"Good Lord! What's happened to me? I'm so sorry for my reaction." She felt that her impetuous remark had caused irreparable damage, and once again her hand went to her hair and she started twirling and tugging at it.

But Lance calmly went on to say, "Relax, Fleur. It's OK. It's very understandable that you questioned this. You walk a fine balance, and you do so admirably." He lightly patted down the hair she'd been touching. "When I'm with you," he continued, "I feel so completely myself, and most of the time even forget that I'm disabled. It's only with other people that I feel self-conscious, to a greater or lesser extent, of my handicap. But then, even with you, I have some bad days. That's undeniable. And those days – no, really all the time, but especially on those bad days – I must be a terrible burden."

"No, Lance; I don't like you to not feel good, but that certainly isn't burdensome for me. I just want you to feel better."

He kissed her, smiling gratefully. "But Fleur," he continued, "I just remembered such an odd dream that I had last night. Kitty and Hatty, as I imagine them to have looked as teenagers, were scrambling up the slopes above the shoreline of a lake. And there were patches of snow on the ground between the trees. Yet they were running, laughing, feeling the wind in their faces. And when I looked more closely, it wasn't Kitty

505

and Hatty on those slopes, but us! You and me! You are I were running and chasing and laughing and slipping and laughing some more. And when I awoke, I realized that that freedom, that privilege, to be able to run effortlessly up the hills, was something I had previously taken for granted. And I'd never recognized, until this feeling on awakening of achingly grey boredom and restraint, quite what a freedom and privilege it had been until it had been taken away."

"Oh Lance," Florence said softly, "I'm so sorry about your response to that lovely dream." And then more emphatically, she said, "I'd prefer to think of it as a prophetic dream! We *will* go climbing up the slopes above the lake! Maybe not at first when snow is on the ground, but we will do it together, Lance!"

"Your words are very welcome and very empowering, my love. But we need also to be realistic. So Fleur, let's face it; it's hardly fair of me to inflict my restricted freedoms on you. That's what I mean by a burden. We simply can't ignore or deny that it exists."

"Lance, whatever I give to you, you repay me to a vastly larger extent. It's as Elizabeth Barrett Browning said, 'The more I give to thee, the more I have, for both are infinite.' I know I sound like Kitty now, quoting poetry to her lover, but I can find no better way to express myself. You are a constant source of joy and inspiration to me."

"Thank you," he whispered. "Thank you," he repeated, rubbing his thighs.

"It's getting chilly," Florence said after a while. "We should go. We can always talk more about this later."

"No, Fleur; this is important. Let's continue to talk now. Here; if you're cold, let's cuddle a while."

Some minutes elapsed, and then Lance said quietly, "I'm sorry I can't give you the answer you're hoping for, Fleur. It's not you I'm rejecting; it's the institution. I can't help it, my sweet, but I'm afraid of marriage. I'm afraid that it ruins relationships; that it tends towards the banal, towards mindless mediocrity and endless annoyances over such trivialities as to whose turn it is to take out the rubbish. You said so yourself; most marriages are about 'making do'. The days, the years slipping by. Ticking them off. Endless ennui, at best; cheating and deceit at worst. I don't want us to ever sink to that. It's exactly as D.H. Lawrence said; that 'it's better to desire than to possess.' This way the flame of longing remains ignited. In fact, I long for you during the week in such an acute way that it borders on pain. And then, when we see each other, it's so marvelous. I can't even express how exhilarating it is. When we have to part again, Juliet (Shakespeare's Juliet, not my sister – heaven forbid!) had it right that 'parting is such sweet sorrow.' It's such an exquisite pain. That's how I feel about us. And look, Fleur; one more thing. Now I've proven to myself that I can do it. I can also drive down to see you. You've been exceptionally kind to me. You've done all the driving all these months. But now we know that I can do it, too, we can share the driving, and sometimes we can be together in the Lake District, and other times in London."

"But we could be married, and keep our living arrangements, at least for now, and continue visiting each other as we're doing."

"Fleur, I don't know. It's too much to take in. I'll have to think about it."

"Haven't you ever thought about this before?"

"Not really. I love us the way we are."

Florence was silent, gazing out over the river. Eventually she said, tapping the camera case with cold fingertips, "And there are the photos from this camera, too."

"What do you mean, Fleur?"

"The photos, Lance. We've managed to explain all of them, understand them all, except for one or two."

"Yes? What are you getting at?"

"Lance, we've been convinced that this camera somehow – and we don't know how – has recorded events from different time periods. And we've verified them all. All except those few I was referring to."

"Fleur, we haven't talked about our theories of Time for a while. Not since Jennie described that hippy who rescued her, and then I wondered whether it was all a house of cards, all these theories of ours. We keep getting so close to a complete understanding, and then something prevents us, as if we're heading towards some sort of paradox. It's like the story of the barber who shaves all who don't shave themselves. But then, who shaves the barber?"

"Yes, I see what you mean. And that's intriguing about the barber! But surely we can't give up all our beliefs now," Florence pleaded.

"Don't worry, my love," Lance said, anxious not to upset her. "I don't want to stop believing that we've really understood something profound. Amazingly, incredibly profound. But when Jennie spoke, it did seem that much of what we'd felt we'd understood came toppling down."

"Lance, we can't put too much store by what Jennie told us. She might well be an unreliable witness, basing what she said on false memories. They might have seemed real to her as she spoke, but look – she suffered a terrible shock and trauma, and what's more, it was dark and noisy in the building, and this happened a year ago. And let's not forget that she's also had a baby in the meantime, which has kept her pretty occupied. As far as I'm concerned, I put more stock in what Hatty told us yesterday!"

"Don't misunderstand me, Fleur, but Hatty is an eighty-something year old woman, who wasn't there, and whose life work has been spent as a professional story-teller," Lance said with one eyebrow skeptically raised.

"But Lance, it isn't as if she was deliberately telling us what she thought we wanted to hear. She doesn't know that you had helped to rescue a pregnant woman from the World Trade Center, and she doesn't know that your title is 'Dr.', or that you lived in Greenwich Village on a street starting with the letters 'Co'. And she did tell us that she spoke to Jennie immediately after the attack, and said she remembers the conversation as if it had happened earlier that day!"

Lance made a noise a little like "Hmmph".

"Didn't you think it was significant that she said that Jennie told her that the man who helped her was a doctor? What, incidentally, did you call yourself to the pregnant woman you escorted?"

"I hardly remember now, Fleur. It was, as you said, so long ago." He looked down at his interlaced fingers, which hung in the space between his parted thighs. "Wait!" he suddenly exclaimed, brightening and looking up. "I *did* call myself Dr. Ramsey! I did so deliberately to make her – or whoever the pregnant woman was - think I was a medical doctor, as the poor thing was so scared, and I thought this would give her the confidence to come with me."

"Hah! Well, there you are, then!"

"Yes, but Dr. Lambskin? Isn't that the name Hatty remembered?"

"Lance, this might seem like a stretch to you, but do you think it might be possible that 'Dr. Lambskin' could be an abbreviated, mutated, half forgotten form of Dr. Lance Ramsey? She was scared, as you said, and incredibly distracted by her terror. And then there was the note with the name – you said you had written down your name for the pregnant woman you were with, didn't you! – only Jennie's note had been through the washing machine and most of it was subsequently indecipherable. But she could still read 'Dr. La-' on a street that began with 'Co'. I'm convinced. I really am. Dr. Lance Ramsey, at 535 Cornelia Street!"

"Fleur, I've considered this, too. But I'm more skeptical than you. Why did Jennie describe her rescuer as a hippy?"

"A hippy and a doctor? Hardly a usual combination!" Florence laughed. "Well, perhaps the only proof we'll have is if we visit New York. That's assuming you will accurately remember her, too, especially since ultimately you went through even more trauma than she did. But Lance, I do believe that Jennie is the one you helped to leave the World Trade Center. I believe that that's why you felt such a strong bond with your house, years before you moved in there. As I understand it, the past with Virginia Lacey and her flashlight, was linking you to a future that had not yet taken place!"

"Fleur, I love you! You're so impassioned!" Lance replied, his right leg jogging up and down. "And what you say, though maybe incredible to others, makes sense to us, as you and I have shared all these 'visions,' for want of a better word, that have taken place in my house."

"Lance, I just thought of something!" Florence said, jumping up from the bench and clapping her hands. "I've just thought of a way of linking T.S. Eliot's idea of fusing the Past, Present, and Future, with Kairological Time!"

"How, Fleur?" Lance asked, gazing at Florence with his luminous, intelligent eyes.

"Well," she said, perching herself on the very edge of the seat, "you know you said that Kairological Time is related more to our subjective needs than a steady, onward progression of ticks of a clock. So, don't you see, Lance! If indeed the Past, Present and Future coexist, then even though when we first saw that strange light shining from the house (which you never dreamed of moving to then), that this is so significant! We're constrained if we only think conventionally; if we say you had not yet gone to New York; you had not yet been a victim of the September 11th attacks; you had not yet purchased your house. Because, if the Past, Present, and Future converge, then these events all exist! And somewhere in your subconscious mind, or maybe because you travelled on a different Time axis, you were receptive to these Future events and you had a *need* to know, to understand, to make sense of a horrific event in which you had helped a pregnant woman to safely escape from a collapsing skyscraper. So it was *Kairological* Time, brought about by your imperative (yet subconscious) need, that enabled you – and me – to see Virginia Lacey's flashlight - though we didn't understand then that this was the source of that strange light we'd seen from what's become your bedroom window, and neither did we know the story behind it. But we know now, Lance. We've filled in the picture of all the generations, leading right up to Jennie. So I think that points to the fact – or to put it more strongly – *proves* that you were indeed her rescuer!"

"This is truly elegant, Fleur! And I'm feeling sufficiently excited to be less than an inch away from being convinced. In fact, it's very plausible and the logic quite exquisite," Lance said, beaming at her, his right leg still jogging animatedly.

"Well, Lance; if you do believe about the Past, Present, and Future being indistinguishable, and that on 'special occasions,' through Kairological Time, we can detect future events since they already exist, then can't we also argue that this is exactly what these photos from my camera are showing us?"

"Indeed, Fleur! Actually, I've just changed my interpretation about your camera!"

"What? Just now?"

"Yes, just this very moment!" he laughed. "As I once told you, I used to think your camera did the incredible things it does because of the way light is folded because of its mirror lens. And you yourself had once conjectured that perhaps your camera shifted onto a different Time axis, which I thought sounded reasonable and was perhaps caused by that very folding of the light beam so that it intersected with light from a different Time axis and swapped the events. After all, remember that light is an indication of Time, as in what you'd once quoted from *Genesis* about God saying 'Let there be Light!' and that's how it all began. But what's always troubled me is why, as far as we know, wouldn't everyone else's single lens reflex Nikon camera from the 1960's, with its internal design of the mirror lens, behave as yours does if this is the explanation? Well, now I see it differently! Now I've just realized that in fact your camera is an extension of you!"

"Of me?"

"Yes, you. We're quite similar, you and I, in that we both function naturally in Kairological Time. And you, just like me, have a strong desire, a *need* to know, about what will happen and how events tie together. We're the same, Fleur! So your camera, through your own projection of Kairological Time, records a confluence of the Past, Present and Future, and selects what is relevant from the pool!" Then pausing to wipe his brow, Lance added, "I can't actually believe I said that! It's true that I'm a Social Scientist, and we don't believe in totally rational behavior, but this is probably the most irrational statement I've ever made!"

Florence laughed. "Well, even if it is irrational, I like it! And it's true that my photos have accurately swung from the past with me playing with my cousin while he was attempting to make a motorized boat travel through the waters of Whitestone Pond in Hampstead, to what was, when we first saw it, my future wedding with Howard, in which my face conveyed utter depression and dismay. And there were others which also showed events that hadn't yet happened, such as you winning an award – I'm so terribly sorry I lost that photo, but I think we both remember it and think it matched what happened when Dr. Erikkson shook your hand on stage. And there were more, such as you boarding a plane, and then the truly frightful ones of the emergency scenes in New York, and also of your house with a ramp up to the front door. They were all events and scenes that we later witnessed, weren't they, Lance!"

"Yes, Fleur; that was undeniably the case. And let's not forget my favorite of you sitting and reading a book in the living room of my house well before I moved in there!"

"Ah yes, that too! And yet there are a few pictures, Lance, that still remain unexplained. As I'd once shown you, there were other photos of me dressed as a bride – *in a different dress from the one I wore when I married Howard* – looking radiantly happy. I like to think, Lance, that they show my marriage to you."

"Fleur, listen," he said, and then stopped. He kicked his right leg back and forth under the bench, and then spent what seemed like a long time rotating and inspecting his crutch. "Fleur," he finally continued, "this is a conversation that I had been dreading. But I see we have to have it now. You might have assumed, when you first showed me those particular bridal photos one weekend soon after my return from New York, that I ignored them through lack of interest. You might well have assumed that I'd since forgotten all about them. But neither assumption could be further from the truth. Those photos immediately terrified me, and have obsessed me ever since. In fact, I don't exaggerate when I tell you that those pictures of you as the stunning bride scare me more than the photos of the scene of me on a stretcher at the World Trade Center…Fleur, you're looking astonished!" he said, brushing his hand against her cheek. "And well you might. I suppose you thought you understood me, and now you have every right to call that into question. But don't you see, if indeed I object to the institution of marriage, that means you are marrying *someone else*, and I can't bear that thought. I truly can't, Fleur!"

"But Lance, I don't ever want to marry anyone else! I won't do it! I only want you. I don't ever want to lose you! Oh Lance, I had no idea that those pictures had that effect on you." She hugged him tightly, and they embraced for a long time.

"You're trembling, Lance."

"It's OK."

"But really, are you feeling all right?"

"Perhaps they're wrong, Fleur! Perhaps what those photos show is wrong! After all, most things are rarely 100% correct."

"But no; my camera can't be wrong! Nothing has been wrong so far!"

"But things can go wrong with assumptions, just as we might be wrong in assuming that Jennie-"

"No! Lance, please stop this, this loss of confidence!"

He looked as though he were about to object. Then he stopped, and in a quieter tone said, "Oh Fleur, I'm so sorry to have shrouded this anticipated happiness of yours in uncertainty. Because I realize that these pictures of you as a new bride had made you feel superbly joyful, and gave you something to hang on to. What a fool I am! I should never have cast doubt on the accuracy of the pictures from your camera!" He shook his head. "Please forgive me. These things sound different when spoken out loud. Forget all this! Look, let's move to that bench over there. It's more in sunshine than this one."

Not touching each other, they walked to the other bench a short distance away. It was hard for Lance to walk with only one crutch – he'd left the other one in Florence's flat on the implicit assumption that when they were out together they walked with arms around each other - but now he neither sought help nor affection, and she offered neither in return. In fact it wasn't until she was almost at the sunny bench that she even realized she hadn't offered him support, as she had been so preoccupied by what he had said. She felt cruel and hard not to have helped him. She sat down first, and felt almost sick to see him walking jerkily towards her, the tip of his tongue slightly protruding from his lips in concentration, and stabbing the ground with his crutch and leaning heavily on it.

*"If he steps on the pinkish paving stone over there, the one near the bench, then we will marry, and if he doesn't, then the photos were wrong!"* she thought illogically. But just as he was slowly heading that way, she felt something gently nudge the back of her neck, and looking round she saw a balloon bobbing up and down close to her, with its string apparently tangled on the wooden planks of the bench. A small girl came running up, pulling on it emphatically, followed by her mother who apologized to Florence, told the girl to be careful or she'd pop the balloon, and then proceeded to set the balloon free. By the time Florence turned back around and looked at Lance he had passed the pink paving stone without her knowing if he had stepped on it or not.

He sat carefully down, leaving a slightly larger space between them than was usual. In her mind she still saw him walking unsteadily towards the bench, seemingly with more difficulty than was usual. Surely when they walked together, he was not as jerky as this, although it was true that when he was tired or upset, it did seem to affect his ability to walk, and he really did need support on both sides for balance. *"Yes, he does have limited freedoms!"* she thought. And that thought filled her with renewed tenderness for him. *"But I will make it up for him! I will compensate for all that I can! And the only reason he'd wanted those photos to be wrong was because he doesn't want me to marry anyone else! There's no other reason for him suggesting that. Well, I won't marry again unless it's to him! I couldn't ever leave him!"* She edged towards him and lightly put her hand on his thigh, and felt he was still trembling. "Lance," she ventured, "since I did look like such a happy bride in that photo, do you think it at all possible that one day you might change your mind about marriage and we will marry after all?"

"My love, you looked so sweet when you said that; just like a little girl!" he said chuckling, and they fell into each other's arms, relieved to be reunited after the tension of the last several minutes. "And there is just one thing I know," he said into her hair. "I know that our souls are inextricably linked."

He released her and held onto both of her hands with his hands that were icy cold. But he was no longer trembling. They kissed lovingly and hugged again.

"No, Angus! Naughty doggie!"

They looked up and saw a sprightly older woman in a tweed jacket, with an inquisitive terrier, which was sniffing Lance's crutch and looking as though it was just about to pee on it.

"No, Angus! That's not a tree. I am frightfully sorry. Come here, Angus! More walkies! Come on! Again, my dears, my apologies. Angus is not usually like that," she said, jerking the leash and pulling the little dog away.

"That's alright," Lance said to her, smiling.

"Well, we both noticed you, Angus and me. I was only just saying to him – I talk to him all the time, of course – that I had never seen two people as in love as you are. You must be on your honeymoon! Oh well, enjoy it, dears. We must be getting on. Come on, Angus! Good day!"

Once the woman strode away with the terrier trotting at her ankles, Florence and Lance looked at each other and both laughed, each interpreting the situation as an omen in their own manner.

"Well, she certainly got it right," Lance said. "Our love is exquisite, and it will always be there, whether or not we get a license to publicly declare this to be so."

"Yes; our love is magnificent."

"So we should neither of us worry about this anymore. All things, even weddings, have to happen at the right time. Fleur, do you remember what the message says on the face of the grandfather clock? Do you remember it?"

"No; I remember it was a quotation from Wittgenstein, but I've forgotten exactly what it said. Why?"

"Because, Fleur, ever since you pointed it out to me, I've looked closely at the face of the clock every time I go by it, and I've committed its message to memory. *'Only a man who lives not in time but in the present is happy.'* That's what it says. So Fleur, can we follow its advice? It makes sense to me. I certainly don't want to be selfish about this, but I feel so happy in the present with you. I don't want to clutter up that happiness with plans; I don't want to strangle it with anticipations which end up exceeding the event. I strongly believe that things will happen at the right time, and maybe even in the right place. Who knows, we might move to America and I might feel different about marriage there. I really don't know."

She nodded. He rubbed his hands together, and then added, "So Fleur, I think what I'm getting at is that we can't force something to occur just because we've seen a photo of you as a gorgeous bride. In other words, just because we think we saw a glimpse into the future, we should not now deliberately try to create it. Does that make sense?"

"Yes, but I'd like to think that this is *meant* to be our future," Florence persisted, looking earnest. "After all, aren't there other photos in support of these? For example, there's a picture of two people standing on the doorstep of your house, waving. It's impossible to see exactly what they look like, as the photo was taken into the sun, but couldn't it be possible that those people are us? You and me! And another picture of a sweet little girl playing in your garden! Now I know we could say that this could be any child, but Lance, I want to think that this could be *our* daughter. I saw you play with Anna's baby, Sammy. I wasn't a bit surprised to see how kind and lovely you are with babies. Oh Lance, I would so much love for us to have a baby!"

Lance chuckled again, and his hand, now nestled still in Florence's, was warming up. "Yes, Fleur; it would indeed be wonderful for us to have a child. Maybe more than one. But that is not precluded if we don't marry. Attitudes are vastly different from when Kitty and Ilyich gave birth to Connie. There's no longer ostracizing of a 'bastard' born out of wedlock. The conventional expectation of the nuclear family of married parents, 2.5 children, a dog, a cat and a goldfish is on its way out. Families are taking on many different shapes these days. So in other words, I'm certainly not rejecting the idea of us having a baby; in fact I'd love it."

*"Yes, attitudes in general are changing about having babies when the couple isn't married,"* Florence thought, *"only not in my parents' minds."* But then it was as if she felt the binding of her parents' views unraveling from around her, and she was shaking them off, no longer relevant, as she felt such joy in what Lance had just said. So she snuggled up against him, glowing with pleasure, and said, "I'm so glad!"

He was delighted to see that his words made Florence so happy, and they sat cuddling for a while.

"But Fleur, one thing that I want to point out about the intriguing puzzle of the photos," he now said, looking at her with the excitement of a new thought, "and this is really more on a theoretical level, but given that we both assume that these photos are *correctly* recording the future - and yes, my love, I do see it this way again and thank you for putting me right on this – even so, we cannot be certain as to how to *interpret* them. After all, when you first saw the photo of the emergency scene in New York, you didn't know at that time that it was the September 11 attacks at the World Trade Center. Actually you didn't know where it was, other than supposing that it was somewhere in New York. And when you first saw a photo of the ramp built outside my house leading to the front door, you not unreasonably assumed that the house was occupied by an elderly couple. In fact you showed considerable kindness just now by not mentioning that the photo of one of the people on the front doorstep of my house had a walking stick, which had you thinking when you first saw it, that this provided further evidence that the house was definitely lived in by older people, but now you discretely think it might be me with that walking stick. Do you see what I'm saying, Fleur? We might be privileged to see a future slice of Time, but we might not accurately understand the context. That's what I meant about how we can't force these things to happen. We can neither prevent nor implement change of a future event. And think, you're the one who just said that the Past, the Present and the Future all exist already!"

"By that logic, Lance – and I know this was what I'd said, but I no longer like the way it feels – it means that everything is predetermined. That we have no free will; no freedom of choice. But that's absurd and entirely passive. We're always bumping up against paradoxes, as you just said. It's as if we're saying, 'this statement – really any statement – is a lie.' It takes us around in infinite circles. It's equivalent to saying, 'This statement is unprovable.' Oh, I suddenly feel so muddled. Why can't we remember all we'd said about Time that night at Landsdowne's when we first met, and we thought we'd unlocked Time's secrets and understood it completely?"

"Don't worry, my sweet," Lance said. "I felt momentarily pessimistic before when I said we're always coming up against paradoxes. But really I'm much more optimistic than that! We understood it all once. We'll get there again. We're already making great strides."

"I know!" Florence suddenly exclaimed, visibly brightening. "If indeed the Past, Present and Future all exist, then instead of Time moving as we have always assumed, it is *us* who moves. We are the ones who move between already existing events. Do you see what I mean?"

"Yes, Fleur. That's plausible. But let's consider this further. Do you remember in those early days at Landsdowne's when we were playing Scrabble and ideas about Time kept occurring to us through the words we made?"

Florence nodded enthusiastically, smiling at the memory.

"And one word we made," Lance continued, "is that we defined Time as the *interval* between two events? But if these events already exist and we move between them, it still *takes Time* to do so, implying that there is a higher axis of Time. And even though this is coming at our ideas from a different angle, this might return to our thoughts of all those axes of Time, each one timing how long it takes for a point to move along the axis of the previous Time dimension. In other words, I don't believe that we can truly depart from the concept that Time flows."

"Lance, I'm not sure. I'm so confused. All I do know is that in the case of us getting married, we *can* make it happen if we both want it." She looked at him imploringly.

"Yes, Fleur; that's true if that's what the future holds for us, when the present becomes the future. I said that because I'm again thinking of Wittgenstein's quotation about being happy by living in the present. And it will happen if we both agree that getting married will add to what is already a pretty perfect relationship between us."

"But when will that time be, Lance? And will it, in fact, ever be?"

"Fleur, things happen as they will. As I said, I still believe that Time flows and that we can equate it with the flow of a river, as we'd said when we were by that beautiful waterfall in the Lake District. Remember how we said that the water on the lake looks constant, but in reality if we were to return the next day, it would be filled with new water, as water is always flowing. So the Present looks static, as if it is one point in time, but really there is great flow and movement within it.

"And actually, since we're here now in London, we can say it's just like the River Thames in front of us! It's as if we're on a boat floating along the river, in backward-facing seats, so that we can only see what's immediately around us, and what we've left behind. Occasionally, very occasionally – more through Kairological Time as an expression of acute need, as you said – there'll be a swing in the river, and we might catch a glimpse into what lies ahead, but we cannot change the direction of the river's flow or the orientation of our seats, and neither can we fully understand what this future event means until we experience it. In fact, not until it becomes our Present Time. It's as if the river is very pompous, and won't give up its secrets. We must just wait until we float past."

"Well, I wish it wasn't so pompous, then!"

"But Fleur, consider this; the river that lies ahead might be swift flowing, rushing through narrow gorges or plummeting down water falls – again, just as we saw in the Lake District that lovely afternoon - or it could be broad, meandering and slow flowing over an open plane. Whatever path the river takes, we cannot change it, and we don't know its topography until we float past. We can no more exert change to the path of that river than we can change the Future, because if we could change it, it would not be our Future. You'd once told me you were so upset with yourself for not telling me about the photos of the attacks on the World Trade Center when you first saw them, but as I told you then, you made the right decision, because even if I had been equipped with that information, I would have been powerless to do anything about it."

The sun was moving away from their bench and again they were in the coolness of the shade, but Lance kept on speaking, slowly and quietly, as if he were working this out as he said it. "So, looked at this way, I actually think it's a good thing not knowing what lies ahead in the river. You want to know about happy events like marriage, and I don't blame you, but the Future holds much more than that, and inevitably there will be some less desirous events, too, and I'm just as happy – in fact more so – not to know about them yet. Does that make sense?"

"Actually, Lance, it does. So we shouldn't deliberately try to know what lies ahead on this river. And in fact, in your case in terms of feeling connected with your house, it was a *subconscious* need to know, and not anything you deliberately tried to find out."

"That's right! It's exactly according to Kairological Time, as you pointed out, which ought to be genuine feelings that we don't try to determine. So, by your very own analogy with Kairological Time, I don't think we should deliberately try to discover our future, even if it already exists. Only time will tell."

"You mean only Kairological Time will tell! It already seems to have revealed so much," she remarked.

"Yes! Because you and I are receptive to it! But remember this, too, Fleur, that all I've been saying about floating on the river on backward facing seats is only a fraction of what happens. It's by no means the end of the story. Remember the water cycle! At some point the water on the river will flow out to sea and evaporate, or even evaporate before it reaches the sea, and we will be transported upwards on the water vapor. And the water will then merge in the sky with other water droplets and become too heavy to stay aloft, so will fall back to earth. Maybe the water will fall into a lake or river, though it's more likely to fall on the earth and seep underground and be part of the water table or perhaps join an underground stream. And then it will emerge as a spring forming a new little stream which will become a tributary, and join the river again. And so it goes on."

Lance looked exhausted after saying all this.

"And we will be carried along throughout the whole cycle?"

"Yes, every ripple of the way. Again and again and again."

"Perhaps when the water is underground it corresponds with when we die."

"Yes, that seems like a rather literal analogy, but why not? Most of all I think perhaps it explains why it's incomprehensible for many of us to accept that our time, our life, is finite. That it will stop. Because if it's all a cycle, it won't stop. There's life again after death. And even though the water cycle could take a huge amount of time, depending on where it's occurring - the climate, geology, topography and those sorts of factors of that local area - the analogy as applied to Time could be instantaneous, which is why, as T.S. Eliot said, 'All is always now.' Everything is here. Our Past. Our Present. Our Future."

"Well, I won't need this anymore!" Florence said, rising suddenly and rushing towards the river, her camera banging against her hips. And at the bank, she hurriedly pulled off her watch, and flung it into the muddy waters, where it was rapidly swallowed up.

She returned to the bench, where Lance had anxiously started to rise.

"Thank goodness, Fleur!" he said. "I thought you were going to throw your camera in the water instead!"

He placed the crutch under his arm, and he intertwined his other arm around Florence, and she wound her arm around him, and in their customary fashion they started to walk towards Crispin's bistro. As they walked, so tightly leaning against each other and feeling each other's warmth and solidarity, Florence felt the rhythmic swing of his crutch as it moved forward for another step and then another and another, and felt too the slight lurch of his left leg as it touched the ground, in contrast to the new sturdiness of his right leg. And she knew this would mirror the rhythm of their life together.

# EPILOGUE

*IT'S TUESDAY AFTERNOON,* and Florence and Lance are looking for a parking space in the station car park. The handicapped spaces are all taken, and so far there seems to be no other openings.

"You'd better get out here, Fleur, and purchase your ticket, otherwise you might miss the train," Lance advises. "I'll find a space, and join you on the platform."

"But what if it takes you a while to find a space, and the train has already left?"

"All the more reason for you to run now, my sweet. And let's say goodbye now, just in case we miss each other in the station."

"Yes, but in that case, don't stress yourself by trying to see me off on the platform. Perhaps we should just say goodbye here."

"No; if there's still time after I park the car, I'm coming up to kiss you on the train. I wouldn't dream of doing otherwise."

They hug tightly.

"Oh Lance; somehow it's even harder to part at the station than if I were to get into my car."

"I know, my sweet. And it's been an incredible week we've spent together."

"Yes, yes; it has been."

"But you must hurry now."

"I'm so glad you came down to London and surprised me with your unexpected visit. And then you driving me all the way here so we could extend our time together-" She kisses him longingly. "So marvelous," she says into his hair. They kiss again, and she hurriedly leaves the car.

Panting heavily from having rushed to buy her ticket and from running up the steps to the platform, and with her suitcase which felt inexplicably heavy, she climbs into the train bound for London. She hopes he will make it up on to the platform before the train leaves. All around her people are slowly heaving their luggage onto overhead racks, or standing in crowded clusters. She is anxious to push past them and find a seat by the window, so as to be able to look for Lance. Making a determined lunge at an empty seat, she claims it as her own, and sits down heavily. Then she stands, pulls down the window, pokes her head through the opening, and looks up and down the platform for him. The train is due to leave. He hasn't made it in time. Then she spots him, and loudly calls his name, flapping her arms wildly. He sees her and moves towards her. He stands below her window, leans on his crutches and waves up at her emphatically. They blow kisses to each other and shout out inaudible comments. The train whistle blows, doors click shut, and immediately and really rather rapidly, the train slides out of the station. She cranes her head out of the window. She can still see Lance, a tiny dot now, as he watches the receding train.

When she can see him no longer, she settles down on her seat with an enormous feeling of emptiness. A large man, who is seated beside her, reads his newspaper, and breathes heavily. He looks at her, and asks her to close the window. She does so reluctantly, unwilling to yet abandon the abundant fresh air and bright sunshine outside. The compartment air, in contrast, is stale, close and too warm. It contains the watery smell of a tea urn further down the carriage, and of salami sandwiches now being unwrapped by a foreign looking woman and boy with a bristly crew cut, sitting opposite her. Each time the man next to her cracks open his newspaper to a new page, his arms extend to an increasingly wide V-shape, and she feels herself pushed closer and closer to the window.

The train is now traveling through a wooded area, with lines of slim, straight trees, each sufficiently far apart from the next to allow shafts of sunlight to spill in between. The train gathers speed. The alternating flashes of bright sunshine and stripes of black shadow feel like an appalling and relentless strobe lighting event. Florence closes her eyes, yet still behind her eyelids she sees the alternating flashes of light and dark. She wills herself to sleep. Dark. Light. Dark. Not at all in time with the train as it rattles along.

When she opens her eyes, she thinks perhaps she slept after all, as things seem different. The fat man is no longer there, though his newspaper, neatly folded on the seat beside her, is testament to his former presence. The foreign woman across from her stares sullenly out of the window, and the child, with his head in her lap and mud-streaked legs curled up on the seat, appears to be sleeping soundly. Florence looks out of the window, too, but does not recognize the flat landscape that they are now passing through.

She randomly picks up the newspaper. It's *The Telegraph*; not her favorite paper by any means, but better than standing up to reach her library book, which is in her case overhead. She reads the cover story with marginal interest, though decides to turn to page 5 to see how it ends. While turning the page, she sees a small story near the bottom of the front page; "French Family in Cornwall Celebrate Bastille Day One Month Late!" But isn't Bastille Day on July 14th so one month after it would be August 14th? She looks up to the top of the page to check the date. Yes; the date stamp on the newspaper is August 14th, and not September 17th as she had thought. But then she notices something else; it says it's the year 2000!

Why was the man reading a paper from so long ago? And with such apparent interest? But all at once her heart starts beating rapidly and she feels befuddled. To steady herself she thinks of Lance, and what they were doing before driving to the train station. But she can't seem to think of it at all. Instead she sees him leaping up the stairs at Landsdowne's two at a time, with a shawl that he's taking to his mother, and how, just before the turn of the stairs he turns and looks down at her with his beautiful, radiant smile.

What's happening? When is this? What year is she in? People are sometimes lost in space, just as she had been when setting out alone for a walk from Landsdowne's, but are people ever lost in time, as she feels she is now? Could it be that she's on a train on the way home from that solo holiday to Landsdowne's Guest House that she randomly selected as a means to escape Howard for a bit? Could it be that it really is August 14th, 2000, and not more than two years later as she's assumed? Maybe all the rest has not yet happened – Lance's trip to New York, her marriage to Howard, the attacks on the World Trade Center, Lance's return in an injured state to his newly purchased house in the Lake District, their inspirational and amazing love, their talk about whether or not they could marry – maybe that's why it all seems so remote and dull with distance.

She breaks into a sweat. The foreign woman is looking at her darkly and curiously. She attempts a smile, and in a voice which sounds peculiar even to herself, she says, "It's lovely weather, isn't it!"

"Problem speak," the foreign woman replies.

"Where are you from?"

"Me and my son, we from Romania."

Florence casts around in her mind trying to think what language they speak there, and trying to remember some French, but unable to muster even two words together.

"Romania must be very nice. Do you like it in England?"

"Yes, yes; very good."

"Have you been to America?" *And have you seen the World Trade Center? Is it still standing, or has it been blown apart? Are the twin towers solidly there, sparkling in the sunshine, or is it a vast hole in the ground recently cleared of rubble? Oh tell me, tell me the answers to the questions I put to you!* But the foreign woman appears to be losing interest.

"No America. Just only England."

"Do you know the date today?" And then abandoning all caution, Florence asks, "What year is this? Can you tell me the year?"

The foreign woman looks on hopelessly. "Problem speak," she says again, and then addresses herself to the task of running her fingers through the nubbly hair of her sleeping son. In agitation, Florence stands up and takes her novel out of her case. But instead of it being the novel she expected to see - a work by Ian McEwan recently borrowed from her local library and from which only the other day she read a particularly moving passage to Lance - she sees it's *Globalization: A Question of Time*, by Lance Ramsey, with contributions by Florence Hamilton. Her heart knocks ruthlessly against her rib cage and her breath quickens, and she is covered in a new coating of sweat. She opens the book and sees it is published in 2006! She flicks to the next page and sees there a personal inscription from Lance to her. It reads, in his characteristic squarish writing in Royal blue ink:

*My sweetest love; we did it! Working on this book with you, Fleur, was my deepest pleasure. May this be just the first of many shared literary adventures between us. Always your abundantly loving Lance.*

Utter disorientation overwhelms her. She fingers the book, and then scans the index of chapter headings, the dense pages of text, the favorable reviews on the back cover. Back inside the book she sees his ample examples of the rapid spread of globalization. She sees the chapter exclusively on Time that they wrote together. She sees sentences of his that she remembers editing and reworking for greater reader accessibility. *She remembers!* And, like a distant ripple, a hazy mirage on the horizon, she remembers also presenting him with his own copy of the book, with her own loving inscription to him inside the front cover.

She reaches in her pocket for her handkerchief, but instead feels the edge of something small and hard and light. A piece of paper, folded and refolded into a tiny square in Lance's characteristic style. She pulls it open, wondering when he might have slipped this into her pocket, at the same time as feeling a deep gratitude towards him, as he could always help, even when he was not physically with her. Surely this note would provide the answers she needs now to stop her excruciating disorientation. She reads it hungrily.

*Fleur, didn't we have fun over these last several days together!*
*Being with you is profound and exceptional. I certainly have much*
*to ponder. You know what I mean. Yours throughout Time - Lance*

But when did he write this? And what is it that he is pondering? No, for once she does not know what he means. Is this in reference to one of their early talks about Time, while perched on the window-seat at Landsdowne's? Or is it their talk about how the convergence of Past, Present and Future could tie together the four generations of the Lacey family, the house which Lance was always drawn to, and the World Trade Center attack? Or is it about their stumbling, probing talk about marriage while sitting together on the bank of the River Thames? Or is it about something else entirely? She rereads his note, gently presses it against her lips and gives it a soft kiss, and then refolds it and slips it back into her pocket.

Clasping on to their book, *Globalization: A Question of Time*, she stands uncertainly, smiling wanly at the Romanian woman who is watching her, and pulls open the door of their compartment. She walks down the swaying corridor, trying to find her balance on this rocking train. She places the flat of her free hand on the wall as she walks along. She is now in the restaurant carriage. Her mobile phone is ringing. She becomes aware of it above the noise of the train. She wonders how long it has been ringing. Leaning against an empty grey table to steady herself, she reaches into her handbag and snatches out her phone. She puts it to her ear at once without looking at the screen, as she doesn't want to miss the call, but even as she does so, she knows the battery is flat as she hears the warning beeps.

"Hello?" she says.

The train's whistle shrieks. Almost inaudibly above the noise a man's voice says, "Fleur! I can't wait to see you again! I want to tell you-"

"Lance, is that you? The most extraordinary thing-"

But even over the clattering noise of the train she knows it's hopeless. Her words are echoing back to her, as if she's speaking into a solid block of wood. The battery is dead. Her words are not being conveyed down the phone line. Did the caller say 'Fleur'? Or 'Flo'? 'Fleur'? 'Flo'? Lance? Howard? The phone's display screen is black, and will not provide information about the phone number of that call.

Or was it David? David, who she will always think of as Anna's husband. Even though Anna died three years ago when she was fifty. Even though Florence and David are now nearing their first wedding anniversary. David who she will never love but will always be grateful for, just as he will never love her but will always be grateful for her. David will remain faithful in his love for Anna, just as she can never, ever abandon her love for Lance. David who, in his kindness, will have come to New York to assist her, and take full responsibility, when she will not have been able to make a single decision after the unutterable tragedy.

Lance will have accepted a position as Associate Professor at the London School of Economics some years ago, and will have taught there with his own unique blend of humility and great excitement about his subject, and will therefore have been greatly loved by his students, as was true in all the other universities in which he'll have taught. He and Florence will have moved together into a bright, spacious ground floor flat in Pimlico, and they'll have gone to the house in the Lake District during the summer, Easter and winter holidays, and often at weekends. They'll have sometimes seen, returning home at night, a glow of white light from their otherwise dark bedroom window downstairs, and very occasionally they'll have seen Virginia Lacey by the wardrobe. But they'll have never again seen her vicious pitbull, Eloise, neither will they have ever again seen Kitty.

They'll have sometimes seen Lance's mother, who will have a tenacious hold on life, as if making up in quantity what her life might have lacked in quality. And in the early years they'll have sometimes visited Landsdowne's and all its usual inhabitants, until the old order changed and things became different, and not even Rose and Allison went there anymore. And most often they'll have gone to the Lake District because they'll have continued to love being in the house itself. And their twins will have been conceived in this house; Karinna and Gregor, named in honor of the Lacey children, Kitty and Gordon, born in the same house years earlier (and not, in the case of Gregor, named after her old acquaintance, Gregor Ian Chant).

Florence will have continued her writing, both for the magazine –
Elizabeth Carlyle will have long ago retired and been replaced by Emily
Johns who will have heartily approved of her work from the start and
offered many promotions - and she will also have continued occasionally
to write academic pieces with Lance. She'll also have been in the midst
of writing a story with Hatty, who she'll have continued visiting, though
Lance will always have found an excuse not to see her, but Hatty will have
died choking on a piece of ginger before they'll have seen their writing
project through to fruition.

And she and Lance will have often traveled to New York; indeed Lance
will have taught many online classes for the New School from England, but
will not yet have taken up the oft repeated invitation from Nikhil, his former
TA who will have worked his way up the ranks to now be the Department
Chair, to return as a Visiting Scholar to NYU, though he'll have intended
to do so. And they will have met two or three times with Jennie who has
none of the stodgy dullness of Connie, but who to them seems more
reminiscent of Kitty. But neither Jennie nor Lance will have been able with
any certainty to say that they escaped *together* from the World Trade Center
on September 11th, 2001. They will have also frequently seen Marissa and
her partner, Kaitlin, and on a few occasions they'll have eaten in the diner
in which Lovey Barker, the man who'd heroically found an ambulance
for Lance on that fateful day of the 9/11 attacks, will now have become a
manager and who will have been continuing his studies with the goal of
ultimately earning a degree in Hospitality.

And then, one unseasonably hot day in late winter, Florence and
Lance will have been to the top of 1 World Trade Center, which will stand
close to the footprints of where the Twin Towers once stood. After taking
several photos with Florence's camera - which they will have randomly
decided to bring to New York even though it will have been unused for
many years as they had meanwhile switched, as had nearly everyone else,
to digital photography – they'll have plans to finally fulfill Lance's long
cherished wish to walk across the Brooklyn Bridge. They'll have arranged
to visit Marissa in a café on Montague Street in Brooklyn Heights. But
first, because of the heat, Florence will have suggested that they purchase
a lemon sorbet from a street vendor on the other side of Church Street.

And Lance, whose left leg will have continued to strengthen though he still will have a pronounced limp but who will have been able to get by with only the use of a walking stick, will have offered to get it while she stands in the shade. As he crosses back with the ices, smiling beautifully at her as he approaches, she'll have hastily pulled out her camera from her bag at her feet, removed the lens cap, and intended (and hoped, as with her camera you never knew) to capture this radiant view of him. Yet what she'll have seen through the viewfinder is a yellow cab which will have sped around the corner, and unable to stop in time, will have smacked mercilessly into him, tossing him into the air and causing him to land flat on his back with a hard thud. She'll have dropped the camera, cracking its lens, and rushed to him, not heeding any other traffic, as he lies immobile in the intersection, the only movement being from the melting black streams of the sorbet snaking out along the hot tarmac. She will sit in the street and cradle his head in her lap, and a passerby will offer a pale green, mushroom shaped umbrella which she will open and hold over his face to protect him from the sun. And she will wait for what will seem like an interminably long time for an ambulance, in this city which is always screeching with emergency sirens. And it is indeed too late, as Lance will die in the ambulance on the way to Bellevue Hospital. The date is February 29th, so maybe he will only be dead once every four years, and alive in the years in between, but even she will know this is hopeless. That all is hopeless. And David, their dear friend for so many years, will somehow hear the news, and will come immediately to New York, and will take charge of all the necessary arrangements.

"This woman's unwell!" she hears someone say, and feels unfamiliar hands helping her up from where she has slumped between the grey tables in the restaurant carriage of the rushing train. And slowly, unsteadily, she is helped to a seat and obediently drinks a glass of tepid water, unknowingly leaving *Globalization: A Question of Time* kicked under the table.

# ACKNOWLEDGMENTS

Writing this novel has been a long, complex, marvelous and exhilarating journey, and I am particularly grateful to Jeremy Bender for his excellent insights and suggestions after generously reading the manuscript, and to Jen Hsieh, for all her skills and profound help in formatting *And All is Always Now* in readiness for publication, and her terrific marketing suggestions. I would also like to sincerely give thanks to Charlie, Ruby, and Jonathan Bender, and Mia Meng, as well as to Nick Northrup, and Adam and Holden Bender, for their patience and enthusiasm, as well, of course, to Billy, Nigel, and JoJo Stansfield, and to Chris, Leon and Elliot Delay. And none of this could have been possible without the initial inspirations from Thelma and Charles Loodmer, and Nicky Stansfield, who, through their creativity and love of culture and the arts, provided a solid foundation for my writing.

I would also like to acknowledge T.S. Eliot for his inspirational and most fitting poetry from his poem, "Burnt Norton," from his *Four Quartets*, as well as Faber and Faber Limited, and Houghton Mifflin Harcourt Publishing Company for granting me permission to use T.S. Eliot's incredible words in my work. And I give thanks to Beethoven, for his Kreutzer and Spring Sonatas, as well as more recently (for me) his Late Quartets, which in conjunction with T.S. Eliot's *Four Quartets*, provided an absolutely perfect blend of brilliant revelation.

# About the Author

Tisha Bender was born and raised in London, and went to the University of Bristol. She then attended the London School of Economics for graduate school. Since coming to America, she has taught in a number of U.S. universities, including Cornell Off Campus College and The New School, and has been teaching in the Rutgers Writing Program since 2004. *P.U.N.C.H.* is her first published novel, and she is also the author of two editions of *Discussion-Based Online Teaching to Enhance Student Learning: Theory, Practice and Assessment.*

Just as Tisha cannot be without a novel to read, she cannot be without a novel of her own to write. She writes in the way some artists draw, by 'taking a line for a walk' and discovering where it takes her. What she aims for is the exceptionally immersive state, often helped by playing some of Beethoven's chamber music, where the story unfolds and the characters sometimes speak in ways which surprise her, and she has to write as fast as she can to capture it. And when she is in that state she finds she's much more observant of beautiful moments in nature, or the idiosyncrasies of people, much of which she might insert into her evolving story.

www.tishabender.com